# The Year of the Red Door

### A Fantasy
### by
### William Timothy Murray

*"Whosoever discovers the Name of the King,*

*so shall he become King."*

# The Year of the Red Door

## Volume 1

# The Bellringer

## William Timothy Murray

*"Whosoever shall discover the Name of the King,*

*so shall he become King."*

The Bellringer
Volume 1 of The Year of the Red Door

Second Edition

ISBN:  978-1-944320-35-5

For permissions, review copies, or other inquiries, write to:
Penflight Books
P.O. Box 857
125 Avery Street
Winterville, Georgia 30683-9998
USA
infodesk@penflightbooks.com

Be sure to visit:

www.TheYearOfTheRedDoor.com

pfbcsrev1/b

To Deirdre

# Table of Contents

# Preface

Welcome to *The Year of the Red Door*. For those of you who are curious, I invite you to visit the accompanying web site:

www.TheYearOfTheRedDoor.com

There you will find maps and other materials pertaining to the story and to the world in which the story takes place.

The road to publishing *The Year of the Red Door* has been an adventure, with the usual ups and downs and rough spots that any author may encounter. The bumps and jostles were considerably smoothed by the patient toil of my editors who were, I'm sure, often frustrated by a cantankerous and difficult client. Nonetheless, I have upon occasion made use of their advice, which was sometimes delivered via bold strokes, underlines, exclamation points, and a few rather cutting remarks handwritten across the pristine pages of my manuscripts. Therefore, any errors that you encounter are due entirely to my own negligence or else a puckish disregard of good advice.

For those of you who might be a bit put off by the scope and epic length of this story, I beg your indulgence and can only offer in my defense a paraphrase of Pascal (or Twain, depending on your preference):

I did not have time to write a short story,
so I wrote a long one instead.

*The Author*

# Maps

# A Note from the Cartographers

The geography and place names depicted on the following maps are generally accepted to be accurate as of the year of their preparation (869 Second Age). Distances are approximate, given the scales of the maps. However, these are only intended to give a general sense of the scale and relationship of the various regions and features. They are not intended for travel or navigation. Any mishap as a result from the use of these maps for such purposes of travel are the responsibility of the user, not the mapmakers.

For maps more suitable for travel within particular regions of the world, all interested parties are invited to inquire at our establishment.

*Brannon & Gray Cartographers*
*No. 16, Miller's Pond Lane*
*Duinnor City*

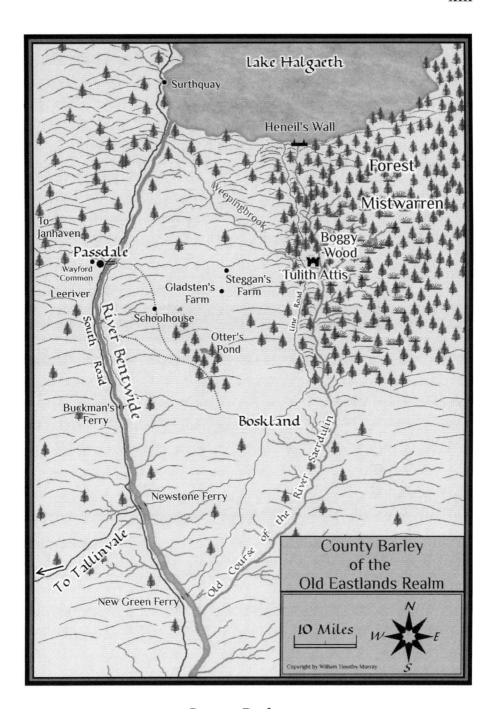

**County Barley**
Detailed maps can be found at:
www.TheYearOfTheRedDoor.com

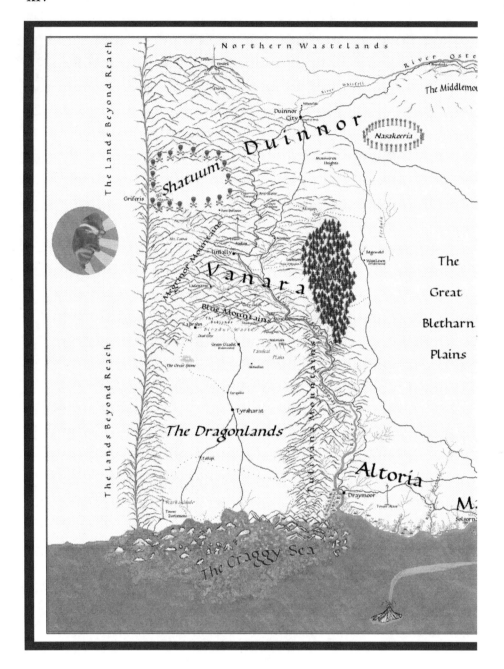

**The Western World**
Detailed maps can be found at:
www.TheYearOfTheRedDoor.com

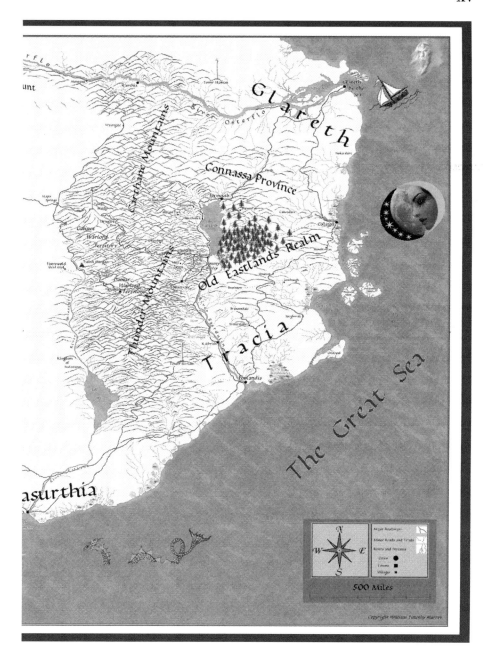

**The Eastern World**
Detailed maps can be found at:
www.TheYearOfTheRedDoor.com

**Duinnor & Shatuum**
Detailed maps can be found at:
www.TheYearOfTheRedDoor.com

**Middlemount & Nasakeeria**
Detailed maps can be found at:
www.TheYearOfTheRedDoor.com

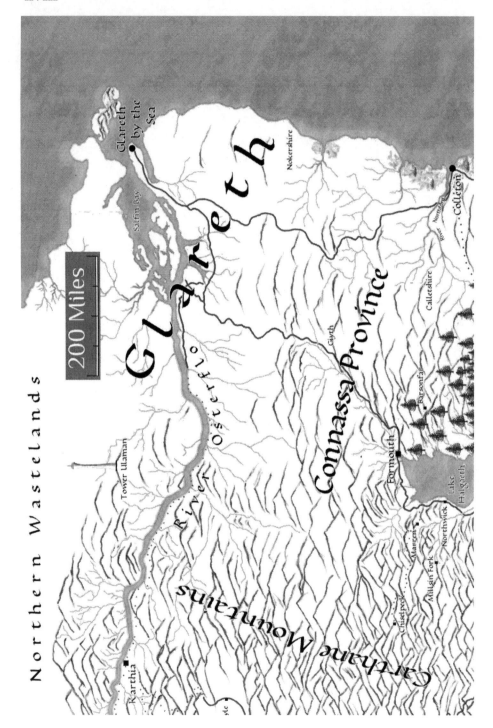

**Glareth**
Detailed maps can be found at:
www.TheYearOfTheRedDoor.com

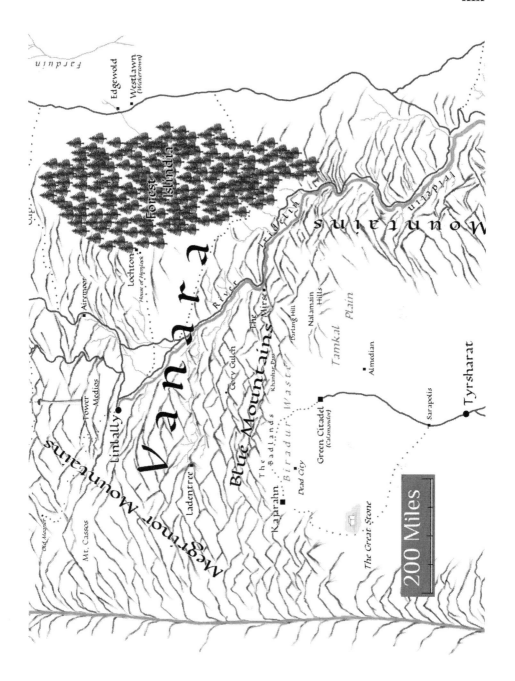

**Vanara**
Detailed maps can be found at:
www.TheYearOfTheRedDoor.com

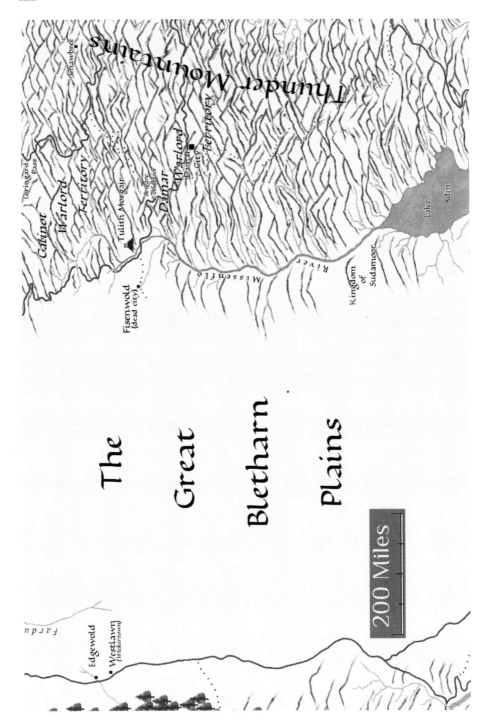

**The Great Plains of Bletharn**
Detailed maps can be found at:
www.TheYearOfTheRedDoor.com

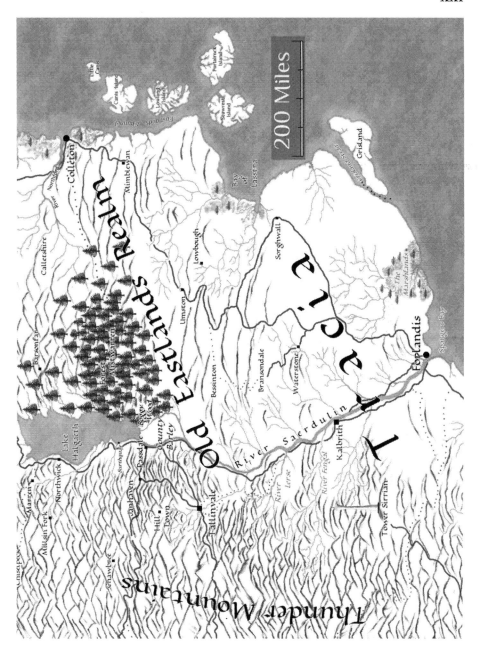

**Tracia & the Old Eastlands Realm**
Detailed maps can be found at:
www.TheYearOfTheRedDoor.com

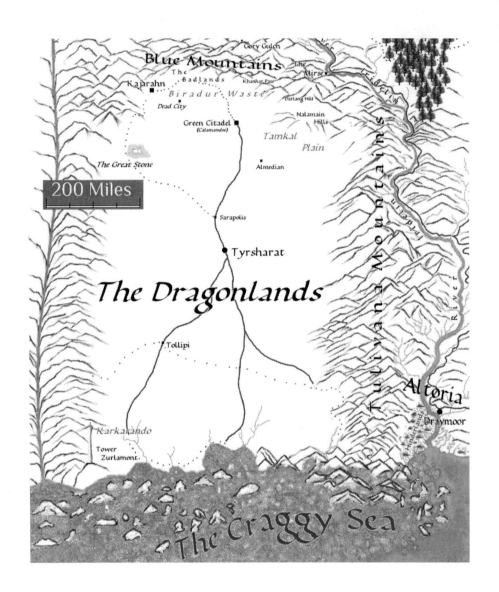

**The Dragonlands**
Detailed maps can be found at:
www.TheYearOfTheRedDoor.com

**Altoria & Masurthia**
Detailed maps can be found at:
www.TheYearOfTheRedDoor.com

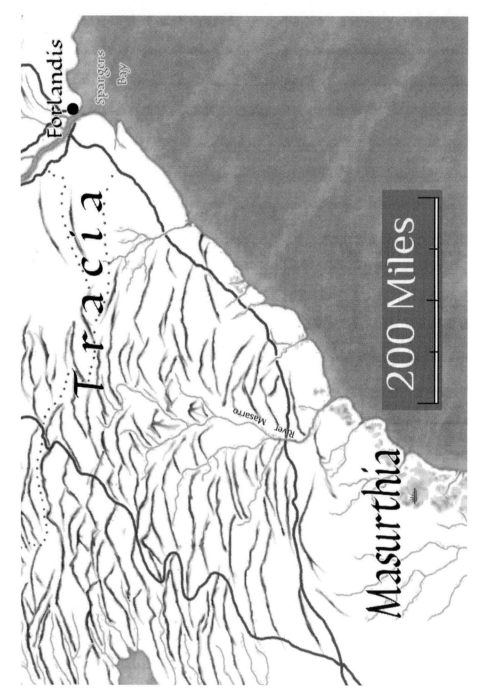

**The Frontier between Tracia and Masurthia**
Detailed maps can be found at:
www.TheYearOfTheRedDoor.com

# The Bellringer

*"Whosoever discovers the Name of the King,*

*so shall he become King."*

# Prologue

## Steggan's Fortunes

"I come from your brother. This is his daughter, called Shevalia. He charges you with the care of her until she is sent for. Meanwhile, she is to be known as one of your house, with your name. When she is sent for, she and this box must come together. Your brother holds you responsible for her safekeeping during this time of strife, and he bids you take these deeds for land in County Barley in the Eastlands Realm. With coin also that your brother supplies, quit this place and go hither to the north and take up your abode. That land is fertile and at peace. Your wife and this child will be safe from the turmoil that plagues us here, and you may make a fine living on the property given to you. Do you agree to accept this charge?"

Steggan Pradkin looked at the lordly messenger with suspicion, then at the box, old, made of polished wood, hardly bigger than a large book.

"I ain't seen me brother in ten years er more," he said, throwing a quick glance at the tiny girl standing aside and behind the seated messenger. She couldn't be more than three or four years old. "An' we're only stepbrothers, at that. In all these years has he done a thing for me? Why does he think I'm willin' to do this? An' why don't he come an' ask himself?"

"He cannot come or else he would. You do not have a name in these lands as he does, and you will not be known in the Eastlands. It is for the sake of his daughter that he does this. In exchange for your faithful service to this request, you will be amply rewarded, far wealthier than otherwise, and freed from being a tenant. When the girl and the box are sent for, you will again be rewarded. The land in County Barley has acreage enough for crops and cattle, good wells, a fair house, and a good barn. With the coin, too, you may buy all the other things needed for a successful farm. If you remain a tenant on this estate, your future will not be secure. Indeed, all here will fare poorly when the new governor of this province makes his laws, for the master of these lands is not friendly with those who have recently come to power here in Tracia. It will not be long before there is a new master of this estate, one who will not be so kind or lenient to his tenants."

"Hm. An' what's in the box, eh?"

"That is not of your concern. But the box and the girl must both be kept safe. If anything amiss becomes of either the girl or the box, you will rue the day you were born. When she is sent for, she and the box must come together. That is the way of it. Without her, the box is worthless. With care to business, and with the skill of your labors, you should have no want of money after but a few years."

"Well! A sweet bargain, for sure, it seems."

"I believe it is very generous," nodded the messenger.

"Hear that, woman? We can get out of this hovel an' in our own place!"

Steggan's young wife stood across the room, one hand propping up an elbow casually so that her other could more easily hide her swollen lip. She nodded, without removing her hand from her face, and said, "Oh, aye! Quite an opportunity, it seems."

The messenger glanced at her, quickly observing again her black eye and the cut on her cheek, and he was clearly uncomfortable with this interview.

"There is a stipulation," he said.

"Ah!" Steggan frowned and nodded, leaning back in his chair and putting his hands on the table. "I knew there'd be somethin'. Well, what is it, then?"

"Once every so often, perhaps every year, perhaps more often, you will have a visitor who will come to look at the girl and the box. He will have a key to the box and the means to see if the box has been tampered with. He will look at the girl to see if she is healthy or ill. He may also question your neighbors concerning you and the girl. If he finds anything amiss, if the box has been tampered with, or if the girl is mistreated in any way, a warrant will be submitted for your arrest."

"What? For what?"

"For theft of property. A price will be placed on you and your name given over to bounty hunters and reported to all the sheriffs of the land."

Steggan remained motionless, staring at the stranger. Behind him, his wife stifled a gasp as her eyes widened.

"The girl and the box are important. Neither would be given over to you in this way unless the need for care was great."

After a long moment, Steggan stirred.

"How much coin, then?"

The messenger reached for his saddlebag and removed three purses, letting each thud on the table.

"A stone of Duinnor silver, and a half stone of Glareth gold coin."

Steggan's face lit up as his wife audibly gulped.

"Enough to set you up nicely in your new home and to keep the three of you for a fair while," the messenger concluded flatly. "But you must make haste. If you accept this bargain, you must do so this night. If you do not accept, other arrangements will be made."

• • •

The girl, the box, the money, and the wife were soon all loaded into a cart, along with their sparse belongings, and after Steggan informed his overseer of their departure and settled his meager debts to the estate, he took them all northward. Within a month they found the place in County Barley, in the old Eastlands Realm, and they established themselves on the farm. They all toiled, even the little girl, but Steggan toiled the least, preferring the jug and the dream to the plow or scythe, and he sought more from the fruit of his schemes than from that of the land. Sometimes he seemed grateful for the change in his fortunes, but at other times he was resentful, saying that his brother ought to have done more, if he was so powerful and wealthy. Often was the night he held forth with jug in hand, his wife cringing while the little girl made herself scarce behind a chest or under a cot. And more often than not, the day after market would find Steggan at the tavern in nearby Passdale, then stumbling the long way home with little or nothing in his pockets to show for the produce sold that day, only to take more coins from the old purse and returning again the same evening to the tavern.

In spite of Steggan's behavior, and perhaps to the credit of the previous tenants, the farm did well enough for the first few years, and its fields and gardens provided food for the table with surplus to sell at the marketplace, which was enough to somewhat offset the growing expense of Steggan's drink. As foretold, during the third summer, a visitor did come to call, arriving during a time of day when Steggan was repairing a harness and his wife was hanging out the day's wash while the little girl pulled weeds from the kitchen garden. The visitor rode up on a fine horse, dressed in travel cloaks dusty with his journey, and, as Steggan put down his tools and approached, the traveler unbuttoned his overcloak and looked over the place.

"Are you Steggan?"

"Aye."

"Then I come to confirm the health of the girl and the safety of the box entrusted to your care," the rider said, dismounting. He pulled off his cloak, tossed it over the saddle, and hitched his horse.

"Do ye come from me brother, then?"

"I am his agent, duly charged."

"Well, come along an' I'll show ye the box."

Steggan led the man inside. Standing on a chair, he pulled the box down from a high shelf and placed it on the table.

"It is somewhat scuffed up," the visitor observed suspiciously, turning the box to examine every side. "There are scratches around the brasswork."

"I ain't opened it," said Steggan. "The scuffin's from movin' it 'round from time to time."

"I can see it has not been opened," said the visitor, taking out a key from a chain around his neck. "Please stand back."

"Ain't I gotta right to see what's in it?"

"You do not. Your right is only to benefit from keeping it and the girl safe."

Unwilling to press the subject with the stern man, Steggan stepped back, saying, "Well, that I've done, as ye'll see."

Steggan watched as the man turned the key and lifted the lid so that it blocked Steggan's view of the contents. The man's face remained expressionless as he gazed into the box and reached in to touch its contents. After a moment, he abruptly closed the lid and locked it, returning the key to hang about his neck beneath his blouse.

"Very well. And the girl?"

"This way, right this way."

Back outside, Steggan led the visitor past his wife, who looked on with concern.

"Ye best be startin' supper, hadn't ye," he grunted at her.

"As soon as I get these hung," she replied, making a show of hurrying. "Will he be stayin'?"

Steggan was more than mildly relieved when the visitor said, "No, thank you, madam. I'll be on my way after I see the girl."

"Oh, very well then," said Steggan, gesturing toward the garden. "Very well. Aye! Sheila! Girl! Get over here!"

"Why do you call her that?" asked the visitor.

"Well, it's a nickname," answered Steggan. "These ain't fancy parts an' she ain't got need of a fancy name, eh? Get on out here, girl!"

"I'm comin'! I'm comin'!"

There was a movement among the rows of beanstalks as a bundle of weeds appeared with two tiny arms stretched around, two naked feet underneath, and the very top of a head of light brown hair barely visible behind.

"Yes, Uncle?"

"Drop them weeds an' come here!"

The girl dropped her armful and stomped on them to approach. Wearing a simple blouse over pants, both made of sackcloth, she was barefooted with filthy feet and legs. In fact, she appeared to have not bathed in weeks, so mud- and soot-stained was every inch of her body. Her short-cropped hair was tousled and several twigs dangled from it. In spite of her appearance, she smartly stepped up to the two men and looked up at them, turning from face to face with her hands akimbo as if it was she who had summoned them.

"Dressed in a boyish manner," the visitor stated.

"Well, more fittin' when she's out of doors. An' she loves doin' things out of doors. Regular tomboy, she is."

"Hm. Has she any shoes?"

"Why, of course. Why ain't ye wearin' yer shoes, girl?"

"I don't like 'em!"

"Get 'em on, an' let us see 'em!"

She disappeared into the beans and quickly reappeared holding in each hand a tattered mass of something more akin to sandals, so many gaps there were in the leather.

"See, there they are," Steggan said to the visitor. "Well, put 'em on, girl!"

The little girl dropped to the ground, sitting, and struggled to put the shoes on her feet.

"Why is her hair cropped so short?"

"Oh, well, that's on account of she got it all tangled in with pine pitch last week, an' it was all we could do to save what she's got left."

"Hm. And does she ever bathe?"

"She certainly does," Steggan nodded defensively. "Most ever' fortnight, if me wife can catch her."

The visitor frowned as he watched the girl struggle to tie her shoes. After a moment, he gave an almost imperceptible sigh, and with a little shake of his head, he turned.

"Very well. I've seen enough. I must go."

Steggan watched the visitor ride off, then turned to the house and bellowed, "Get back to yer weedin'!"

The girl frowned and just before disappearing into the stalks, she kicked her shoes off.

"Did he say when he'd be back?" the wife asked as Steggan slumped through the door.

"No."

He pulled a cup and a jug from a shelf, kicked a chair over to the table, and sat down heavily, uncorking the jug and pouring its pungent liquid into the cup. Before him on the table was the box, and he hardly took his eyes from it for the rest of the night.

• • •

Two years later, the incremental increase of drink and brooding was taking its toll on Steggan, his temper, his increasing indifference to work, and the labors needed by the farm. So, too, it had its dark way with his wife, his niece, and those of the county who had at first been willing to be good friends and neighbors. When the visitor came again, Steggan had the temerity to insist on more money.

"You have been paid and rewarded in advance," the visitor told him. "The agreement stands, promises made. And they shall be carried out."

"Surely me brother will send for his child soon," argued Steggan. "Am I to take care of her, feed an' clothe her, for the rest of her life, then?"

"If need be."

"Then why don't he come himself? Aw, but I reckon he's too high an' mighty, eh?"

"His agents are faithful to him, sir. And I hope you are, too. I bid you good day!"

• • •

Matters only grew worse. Within the month of the second visit by his brother's agent, Steggan's wife had abandoned him and the girl, running off with a traveling tinkerman who passed through the parts. And, to Steggan's increased aggravation, the little girl was becoming ever more willful and disobedient. Steggan's fortune was soon depleted by drink so that he, by the necessity of his tavern debts, began to work somewhat harder than before, and to drive the girl harder, too, insomuch as his sorry state and her impishness would allow. The years crept by. And though the mysterious agent never returned, and neither was the girl sent for, Steggan nonetheless felt as though he was being watched. This feeling only increased his sullen and spiteful disposition, and he took to mumbling and glancing over his hunched shoulders. The farms and neighbors all around prospered in relative happiness and peace while Steggan's land steadily declined in fruitfulness. And while his neighbors enjoyed and celebrated each passing season, sharing with each other good company and kind spirits, Steggan and his young charge grew ever more aloof of them and ever more miserable.

# Part I

# Chapter 1

# The Surprise Visit

### Day 1
### 244 Days Remaining

When is the beginning of any story? Is it at the start of its telling? Or is it long before, in the eons of events, small and great, that lead to a tale's remembrance? It may be that any story is merely a journey where the teller guides the listener into a gentle boat and pushes out onto a river already long in course. And during that excursion, the listener may also feel the currents, and experience the bends and shoals formed by the force of history. Afterwards, when the teller of the tale has departed, and the passengers of his boat are safely ashore, they may then gaze farther downstream toward those days that come when the tale they just heard is forgotten and any remembrance of the past is washed away.

The time of this story began with signs and strange omens that appeared throughout the lands of the earth, and in the seas, and overhead in the skies. A new star appeared, briefly and brilliantly in the eye of the constellation Behemoth, and it lit the ice-covered lands of the north where it shone with the light of a half moon. It vanished after only a week, leaving no trace of itself.

At the beginning of this story, far to the southwest, and deep within the bowels of the earth, a dragon stirred from its long slumber. Turning over in its bitter sleep, it spat angry fire and smoke, shaking the ground far above his lair as he sent his molten bile through ancient cracks in the earth to the surface, spewing into the air, forming a new mountain with its ash, laying waste fair towns and villages, and smothering the grasslands with soot. For a year the dragon tossed and turned in its angry slumber, its hot venom flowing forth fitfully before all was again quiet and the new mountain shook no more, cloaking itself with gray vapors under which its shoulders became green with the next springtime.

That following summer was long in the old Eastlands Realm, not so hot, but pleasant with ample rain throughout so that by Midsummer's Eve the first crop of corn was already well tall and the woods were full of blackberries in green profusion. The mead of the region was deemed the best in many years and the wine that was vintnered that year in great quantities by the Eastlanders was for a long time sought after and well-savored as of special quality and rare lightness.

In faraway Masurthia, the coastal islands and capes were battered by typhoons. Every seaside tree and house within twenty leagues of the Bay of Famatir was swept away by the year's end, causing the peoples of that realm terrible hardship and sorrow.

Meanwhile, in the Thunder Mountains and throughout the foothills of the forest surrounding them, all of the trolls disappeared without trace. That was not a bad thing, some held, for they were a cruel and clumsy race and now the forest roads were suddenly clear of them. But, since their passing was so uncanny, some wondered what worse thing might now lurk in their place with the secret power to rid the land of trolls. Witches, maybe, or galafronks, even. Rumors began to filter out of the Thunder Mountains concerning bandits and marauders who had taken up in those mountains. However, such talk may have been much overstated by fireside and bedside, especially in the Eastlands where the elders liked for the youngsters to know their place.

Then, in the dry, hot deserts of the southwest, the Dragon People stirred. Ever at war with their neighbors to the north, they ordered their armies once again, formed their ranks, and gathered for a new conflict. Within their lands, they cruelly put down any who opposed them, and whosoever was not killed or could not escape became their slaves and thralls. So Belsalza, Emperor of the Dragon People, rid his court and his lands of any opposition and secured his domain as his forebears had done in ancient days. Soon his armies were on the march. There were some who continued to oppose Belsalza, even within his own lands, and they did so valiantly for many years, forming secret leagues and dangerous alliances.

Amongst the sailors and fisher-folk of Glareth on the east coast of the world, there spread word of new and wondrous sea creatures in far off waters. They were like fish, it was told, with butterfly wings that danced upon the waves about their ships and boats. Along with many of their watery kind, these lovely creatures dove and swam and danced upon the waters, calling to the seamen in a strange language like the chiming of soft bells, singing melancholy songs and songs filled with the music of delight. Upon their return, a deep enchantment came upon many of the seafarers, and they longed to go back to the strange and beautiful wave-dancers and to hear once again the watersongs. Of those seafarers whose hearts were filled with such yearning, and who did return to those waters, very few were ever seen again.

Far into the northern and western lands of the earth, and high up in the highest tower that overlooked Duinnor Realm, the secluded King of the Seven Realms learned of these strange and wondrous and foreboding things. As his agents came from far and wide to bring rumor and tidings, the King's astrologers made their observations known to him, his counselors gave their considered opinions, and his wise men brought their books and scrolls to show him what may have been written of old about such things. The King mulled over all that he heard and all that was shown him. He sent forth more of his agents to do his will, some to watch, some to listen, and some to lay in wait for any who might usurp his power.

Others watched, too. Some with their eyes, others by casting their stones and their bones, and a few by listening to their hearts and the murmurings of the earth and the stars. Thus, while the King was filled with dread and worry, though he never breathed his fears aloud, these others, scattered throughout the world, saw reason for hope in the subtle shift that was taking place in the cosmos, upon the earth, and within the seas.

As the years passed, some things changed only slightly with little commotion made or notice taken. The scattered ruins of the First and Second Ages gathered more dust and covered themselves a little more with vines and forest. A few more scrolls were lost to the tireless work of moth and mildew, their words never again to be seen. Fewer people cared to learn the Ancient Speech or to tell the stories of the beginnings of things or how Men came to these shores. A few more shadows crept into places once full with light, a few more paths disappeared forever under root and brush, and once-great highways grew thin, like rivers in a long drought, until only the thread of them remained. The neglect of people was matched by the attention of nature, and so many honored barrows of old became merely tree-covered hills. And there were fewer still of those who were here first, who remembered through their long years the joy of a young world not yet troubled by strife or sadness, a time when their hearts were not yet hardened by the melancholy passage of steady Sir Time whose tread is too light to be heard, and whose path can never be retraced.

Yet all these strange tidings and signs and slow change, seen and unseen, meant little to the peoples of the old Eastlands Realm, and their years were full of peace and bounty. They quietly flourished amongst the confusing happenings of the world, paying little heed to rumors and tales from across the mountains or over the plains. The years passed, one after another, with little difference from one to the next. Disputes were few and petty, families grew, and many grew wealthy, if peace, bountiful harvests, fat babies, warm hearths in the winter, and cool rains in the summer are any measure of wealth. The springs and summers as well as the autumns and winters all had their toils and joys, their beauties and their bounties, and generally each season passed into the next not too quickly, nor too late.

And so that is how things were on a morning of the last summer of the Second Age, though few knew it would be the last. So early in the morning it was that the night's coolness still hung in the misty air as Mr.

Robigor Ribbon opened his shop doors and pulled back the curtains on the display closets. It was a sundries store, packed with everything from dried herbs dangling from the ceiling to bolts of cloth on tables. There were clay jars full of buttons and others full of beans, racks of pots and pans, shelves of candles and lamps, kegs of oil, crates of tea, blocks of soap, and bags of seed. There were racks of hats, vials of ointments, a shelf of pipes and tobaccos, bottles of ink, a vase of quills, a corner of tools and ready-made nails, a barrel of pickled cucumbers. And there was even a small case of modest jewelry—mostly brooches and bracelets and necklaces (although there were a few nice rings)—and it had a lid with a looking-glass on the underside that, when lifted up to reveal the contents of the case, provided a way for the buyers to admire themselves. It was just a little shop, and it was so packed and stuffed that it was a tight squeeze to pass between the tables and shelves, but it had years of cozy wear on its strong wooden floors. This floor, and the cellar below, had served as Mr. Ribbon's place of business for many years, ever since he left his grandfather's farm out in the county countryside. Already an astute trader of grain and produce, it was that year that he made his first arrangements with the blacksmith to sell ready-to-use tools and farm implements on commission and had soon after made trades and deals and bargains with craftsmen and traders far and wide. On a summer day twenty years earlier, he purchased the building here in the small town of Passdale, and that very same week he asked Mirabella Tallin to marry him. A year later, they were wed, and the upstairs floor became their new home, though in terrible need of repair. By the following summer, it was also the home of their son, who was now growing into a fine young man. Mr. Ribbon was pleased at how his wife had made such a cheerful and cozy home for them upstairs, and he was justly proud of his shop and of the important role it continued to play in the life of Passdale and the surrounding County Barley.

Mr. Ribbon could hear the clatter of pots upstairs as Mrs. Ribbon put away the breakfast wares, and, as he settled onto a stool at his desk, he heard a slight creak on the stair behind him.

"Ye best tread lighter to sneak up on yer ol' man," he said, putting on his spectacles and opening a ledger book.

"I was not sneaking. I was walking natural," retorted a boy who came up from behind and shoulder-bumped his father (something he would not dare do if Mr. Ribbon had a quill in his hand, for young Robby knew the business lay on every stroke of his father's pen). Mr. Ribbon looked at the young version of himself, smiling back. The boy, having just turned twenty-one, had his father's broad shoulders and, although Ribbons might never be tall folk, Robby was still growing out of his teenage scrawniness and showing all the signs of the Ribbon stockiness to come. They also shared the same black hair (though one was curled with some silver threads), the same chocolate eyes, full nose, and, as of recently, the same height.

"Ye'll be taller than me, if ye keep havin' these growin' spurts, an' if yer mum keeps feedin' ye so!" he uttered aloud before he could stop himself.

Robby laughed awkwardly at the sudden sentimental outburst. "I already am! By a couple of inches, at least! Stand up!"

"I'll stand up to hand ye this!" the father replied, getting up and reaching toward the wall where the cleaning tools waited. Before Robby could protest, he was given a broom.

"Why don't ye take care of the front this mornin' whilst I look at what needs doin' today."

"Yes, sir."

"Thank ye. An', son?"

Expecting additional tasks, Robby looked back at his father.

"Yes, sir?"

"Ye did a good job with the books, yesterday. I went over 'em last night an' ever'thing was perfick. Yer numbers whar right, an' yer stock estimates whar good, too. An' I agree that we oughta forego any more pelts. They're in the way an' ain't nobody int'rested in 'em. Good job. Good job, indeed."

"Thanks, Daddy. I want you to be able to count on me to help."

"I know I can, son. I know I can. Ye make Mirabella an' meself most proud of ye."

Mr. Ribbon turned back to his ledger as Robby walked out onto the store's porch. Across the dirt road that ran in front of the store was a low stone wall bordering the Bentwide River, flowing away to Robby's right and thence southward. Across the river, the far banks rose up gently into fields of grain. Just as he stepped out of the store, the sun broke the mists over the distant ridge and bathed the morning in its golden light, setting the mists that rose over the river aglow as they burned quickly away. To the northeast, he could see the track of the river, marked by dense poplars along its banks, bend away toward the tall bridge that spanned the water, its stone towers just visible through the thick foliage. He closed his eyes, yawning wide and stretching his arms out, one holding the broom. With his eyes still closed, he listened. Already, Clingdon's anvil was ringing from the other side of Passdale, behind Robby, and he could barely hear the creak of Greardon's waterwheel, turning the stones of his mill just down the road to his left.

He turned that way to begin his sweeping, heaving another yawn as he opened his eyes, and saw for the first time a fine-looking, rusty-brown horse in saddle tied at the end of the porch, its head bowed out of sight to munch the grass below. A wave of surprise and bewilderment washed over him as he took a step toward the animal, but nothing like what he felt in the next moment as he tripped and tumbled over some mass at his feet. He hit the floor with a thud, and, rolling over, found himself gaping into the face of a strange man who had apparently been asleep with his back against the store wall and his legs sprawled across the porch. He had many weeks of travel-beard on his sun-darkened face, and brilliant green eyes that now opened below the brim of his hood and fixed Robby. The brown and olive cloak to which the hood was attached wrapped around the stranger like a blanket, mud-spattered and dust-covered.

"You should watch where you are going," he said to the boy plainly.

"You should watch where you sleep," Robby shot back, more than a little flustered and getting to his feet. "Who are you? And what business have you loitering on our porch?"

The horse lifted his head and looked on curiously as he munched. Robby, picking up his broom, noticed several things at once as the stranger got to his feet and stretched. He was tall—the top of Robby's head came up to this man's shoulder at best. His hood fell back from his head, revealing shoulder-length, light brown hair, the bangs on his forehead broken by a white streak of hair joined underneath to his right eyebrow by the line of an old scar. He kept his cloak, which fell down nearly to his ankles, pulled around him, but Robby saw that hanging from a shoulder belt was a dark leather travel case, embossed with a strange emblem, and Robby saw also the plain signs of a sword hilt jutting out from under the cloak.

"Well?" he prodded.

"Well." The stranger finished stretching and dropped his arms to his sides, looking at Robby with a smile and with what seemed to Robby a familiar squint. "If this place is still Ribbon's, and if Robigor Ribbon is still the proprietor, then I have business here."

"I am Robigor Ribbon." Robby felt a little petulant after having been unceremoniously tumbled to the floor. It was true; he did carry his father's first and last name.

"If that is so, then you have shrunk and grown young, and a bit more irksome than when we last saw each other, and yet your memory has grown old and forgetful." The stranger crossed his arms and tilted his head, eyeing Robby with a cocked brow. Robby felt his cheeks redden with embarrassment, as one might when caught in a lie, even though he had not actually lied. "And, yet," the tall man went on, "I do believe we have met, on several occasions, in fact. And though you carry the name I ask for, I think there is another who does, too. And if the other is your father, then he would want to see me since I have ridden hard and long to see him. If not," he shrugged, "I will deal with you."

Robby was not sure what "deal with you" meant, and he felt his face turn from pink to crimson, just as he realized that all along he had been somewhat frightened of this man, though the fellow had done nothing to warrant the reaction. "Inside," was all he could squeak out. "My father is inside."

The stranger suddenly chuckled and grinned, "Surely you don't recognize me, but we fought many a war together on the sand hill and in blacksmith Clingdon's old barn when you and I both were nigh ten or twelve years younger and you were only up to my waist."

Robby felt a strange sensation come over him as memories unfolded in his head.

"Ullinseed?" he whispered to himself, then, with more confidence, "Ullinseed! Can it be you?"

"That is what you used to call me."

Robby's mouth dropped open, remembering the bright young man that had stayed with them for a season when he was ten or so years old. He recalled trailing after him from here to there throughout the countryside on some business beyond his young comprehension. And he remembered wrestling with him on the kitchen floor over a piece of sweet cake, laughing until they cried. He remembered lying on the floor in front of the fireplace while Ullinseed and his father sat in their chairs smoking their pipes long into the night, while his mother knitted. They talked about all manner of strange and wonderful things and faraway places and tales full of mysteries and adventures and other serious things, too. Each night, they talked and talked until Robby could no longer keep his eyes open but still tried to listen until their voices became murmurs mixed with the crackle of the dying embers. He vaguely remembered being carried to bed, sometimes by his father and sometimes by Ullinseed.

Robby woke suddenly from his near-dream, staring blankly at Ullinseed's outstretched hand. Robby grinned, too, and took the hand.

"I usually do watch where I sleep," said the traveler, putting an arm around Robby and leading him inside, "and this lapse on my part will not soon be repeated on your porch!"

"I'm sorry for the way I acted," Robby said seriously, "but we've had a certain number of strangers about, lately."

"I probably would not have acted so calmly myself," Ullinseed laughed, "so don't be sorry. These are times to be careful in. You challenged me, and rightly so. Just as I hope you would do any stranger. Look at this," he waved his hand around as they entered. "Business appears to be just as prosperous, and perhaps more so!"

Mr. Ribbon heard the commotion and the voices outside and was working his way from the back stockroom to the front when, turning a corner, they came into view. Mr. Ribbon froze, broke into a smile, and stretched out his arms. Robby watched the two men embrace, patting each other on the backs heartily and shaking hands.

"It's good to see you again, Robigor!"

"It's been too long, Ullin. Three years? Four?"

"About that, I think, since I last passed through, but much longer since I last saw Ribby," he said putting a hand on Robby's shoulder. "And now he's a man! Hard to believe."

"Yep, I reckon ye did miss him the last few times ye came through, with him at his letters an' all. Come. Come on in. Mira! Mirabella!" As Mr. Ribbon called upstairs, he pulled at the arm of the welcomed guest who gently resisted the tug.

"I cannot stay long," he was saying as Mrs. Ribbon appeared. A little taller than her husband, thin and with skin like milk, her crimson hair pulled up, she was still tying the side laces of her bodice. When she saw the stranger, she halted, staring at the visitor. Suddenly her entire countenance transformed as her face lit with recognition and joy so that her green eyes welled with tears, and she rushed to him.

"Ullin!" she cried out in happiness. "Oh, Ullin, blessed stars above!" To Robby's shock and some dismay, Ullinseed picked his mother up and twirled her about like a lass, barely missing a rack of jars, the both of them laughing with delight.

"Do you remember Robby?" she asked when her feet were back on the floor. Holding out her hand to her son, she pulled him to her, putting her arm around his shoulder proudly.

"Oh, yes, I remember him quite well, though he is a man now. But I think he does not well remember me."

"Yes, I do," Robby stammered, trying to smile. "At least I think I do."

"Robby," his mother put a hand on both of his shoulders and looked straight into his eyes. "This is Ullin Saheed. He is your cousin, my brother's son."

"Oh, yes," Robby said, shaking hands again with him. Robby had forgotten that he had a cousin and that he once had an uncle, too. While Robby tried to remember what had happened to his uncle, and why his cousin looked so much older than his mother, his parents were trying to bustle Ullin Saheed around.

"What do you mean you can't stay long?" Mirabella was demanding. "At least for a few days."

"I'm sorry. Not even for a night. My business will not wait. It brings me here, but then I must be off. I must push through Forest Mistwarren, thence to Colleton, and from there by boat to Glareth by the Sea. I hope to return this way. Even then I will not tarry long. I must reach Loringard before the snows cover the pass and block my way back to Duinnor."

"I suppose you go to see your mother in Glareth?" she asked.

"I hope to see her, yes. But it is business that takes me there, not pleasure."

"What could be so urgent that you cannot stay but for a—"

"Mira!" Mr. Ribbon broke in gently, then looked at Ullin. "Yer business, urgent er no, is yer own affair. Can ye not stay at least to rest for a little while? An' maybe get a decent meal?"

"As it happens, since my business brought me here to see you, I've allowed time. First, however, I need to see to my mount. He has carried me faithfully and fast and with little reward or rest for sixty-odd days."

"Of course. Robby! See to Ullin's horse, won't ye, son? Get him liveried over at Torman's. An' hurry on back, as we might be needin' ye."

"Wait," Ullin said as Robby turned to go. "Would you mind first removing the saddle and bags, and lay them up on the porch. That and a tarpaulin over the saddle might keep away questions at least for the short while I am here. There are too many people around that would ply me with handshakes and questions and hold me from my course."

"Surely, surely. Robby, see it done just as he says an' get on back as soon as ye may."

"Yes, sir, but if secrecy is needed, who shall I say the horse belongs to?"

"Tell Torman it belongs to the Post Rider, which is true enough since that is what I am these days. Thank you, Ribby." Ullin said.

"I am called Robby, now, as I'm grown up and no longer a child."

"And you may call me Ullin Saheed, since your skills of speech are much improved, too. Or just Ullin, as do most."

Robby smiled and nodded. "I'll be back as quick as I can."

Ullin's horse was eyeing Mrs. Ribbon's herb planters, just out of the reach of his tether, when Robby came outside. Soon the cinches and straps were loosened, and Robby was pulling off the saddle. He could not help but notice the strange embossing on the saddlebags and buckles, some foreign lettering he supposed, something like the script of the Westlands in some of his mother's books. As he removed a bedroll and bundle that hung on the back of the saddle, he saw protruding from it the hilt of yet another sword, longer and finer than the one worn by Ullin. He put it carefully down in a pile to take inside and quickly had the saddle off and up onto the porch. After taking the other things inside and tucking them away in a corner, he covered the saddle as requested. He quickly took up the reins to lead the handsome horse away, but the beast was reluctant to leave the thick grass.

"Come, there," Robby said soothingly, "you'll have your belly full soon enough. And a nice grooming, too."

The horse glanced at the store, then allowed himself to be led away.

• • •

"Special Post, eh?" Mr. Ribbon asked as he and Mirabella led Ullin upstairs.

"Yes, for nigh onto a year I've carried that commission, too, for special dispatches."

"Where is the usual man, Bob Starhart?" Mirabella asked. "It's been well over a fortnight since he has come through."

"An' how did ye come to be commissioned as a Post Rider, anyhow? D'ye still carry the King's sword?"

"Yes, I am still a Kingsman as well. How I came to be also riding Post is a long story, and the short of it I will tell you later. Of Bob Starhart I cannot say, and I'm very concerned. I was to deliver to him several dispatches to be taken to other parts and was to receive from him the Post for Barley since I was to come this way, anyway. But when I reached Janhaven, where the Post Station is, they had not seen Starhart for three or four weeks. That was yesterday. His wife was much concerned, too; she was at the Post Station when I arrived. And, by the time I left there, she had convinced the Post Riders there to send out another search party for him southwards along his last route. My understanding is that they've already scoured the countryside for him, and this was to be their last attempt to find him. I would have accompanied them, but my business cannot wait."

"Oh, that don't sound good at all," Mr. Ribbon said. "I certainly hope he ain't met up with them bandits that's rumored to be about them hills 'round thar."

"I was told that a number of unsavory characters have been passing through and loitering about Janhaven," Ullin nodded. "As you can imagine, everyone over there is quite worried."

"Here, let me have your cloak to clean. There is bathing water and soap over here," Mirabella directed Ullin. "Clean up a little and come to the kitchen. Our questions can wait until after you've eaten and had a bit of rest."

• • •

Robby hurried to the livery stable up the road about a furlong, and was glad that he did not run into anyone along the way. He had a strange feeling that he was caught up in some mystery and was a little perturbed by it, too. At the very least, he did not want to answer any awkward questions about the horse and was grateful that only the stable hand was at the livery. After leaving instructions to give the horse the best—water, oats, a check of the shoes, and a rubdown—and telling the attendant to put it on the store's account, Robby started back home. He almost broke into a run but checked himself to a very fast walk. He was irked by the notion that Ullin, having arrived out of the blue and full of mystery, was probably explaining everything at this very moment, so that by the time he got back home all would be told, and he would stay in the dark. He took the steps by twos onto the porch and into the store and the stairs likewise, panting as he got to the top floor. His mother was busy in the kitchen, and in another room his father was looking over some papers, some rolled up and held by leather cords, others folded and sealed. He heard pouring water from the washroom, and, walking to the open door, he saw Ullin rinsing his face in the washroom. His cloak, sword, and travel bags were out of sight. He was wearing a dark green jerkin over a black blouse from which, as he bent over the basin to dash more water onto his face, a silver locket dangled. The legs of his breeches were tucked into high, brown boots, almost up to his knees, that were laced tight. Robby saw the right boot had a sheath made into the side of it out of which a dagger hilt protruded.

"You certainly are well armed," Robby said, leaning against the doorway, trying to breathe easy and act nonchalant. Ullin turned, wiping his wet arms with the towel.

"Better than some," he said. "Not as well as others."

"I noticed you had a long sword in your bedroll, a shorter one, and your boot has a dagger."

"The dagger and the long sword are my own. The other shorter one is standard issue to Post Riders."

"I never saw Bob Starhart carry one."

Ullin hung up the towel and shrugged, putting the locket back under his blouse.

"Mr. Starhart is not a Kingsman," he stated.

"Do you have much call to use any of them?" Robby went on.

"Sometimes. When necessary."

"Where did you learn to use them?"

"Far from here, in the King's Service," Ullin replied, rolling his sleeves back down and moving toward the door. "Now, what about you, though? You look well. The last time I came through, I was told that you had just finished your letters with the local schoolmaster. I thought you were to go to Glareth to continue your studies there."

"Yes, that was the plan." Robby shrugged and went on. "But one thing and another has put me behind. For one, I had to take care of the shop for about a year while my father traveled back and forth to Colleton on trade business. By the time that was all settled, I had missed two terms. Then, on top of that, I decided to wait for a friend of mine to finish his letters so that we could go to Glareth together and take the entrance examinations together. Only he's taking longer to get his papers from the schoolmaster than I hoped."

"I see. Then you must be pretty impatient to get on with things."

"I don't know. I suppose, in a way. But I don't mind waiting a bit longer, as it turns out. He's a good friend. And when he does get his papers, it'll be good to have a friend to go with me. And I'm still reading with Mr. Broadweed, the schoolmaster, to keep my skills up. He has lots of books that he lends to me. That is, when I'm not helping with the shop."

"And what of your friends? Do you see them much? Or has your work in the store prevented that?"

"Yes, I've been busy. And Billy, the friend I mentioned, the fellow I hope to go to Glareth with, is kept busy at his family's estate, too. That is, when he's not at school. His place is Boskland, if you know of it. And my other good friend, Ibin, has taken up metalwork there, too, sort of. So I don't get out and about much these days, except for running errands and such."

"Yes, I know of the Bosklanders. A hearty old clan, by the tales of it. And I seem to remember," Ullin said, as Robby guided him down the hall, "a bratty little girl who threw dirt clods at us. For almost a whole day she followed us across County Barley taunting us. Remember how you'd tag along with me on my mapping surveys? Anyway, she certainly was a wild little girl. Do you know who I mean?"

"Oh, yes," Robby felt his heart thump and hurried Ullin to the kitchen.

"Whatever became of her?"

"I'm not quite sure," Robby said awkwardly, feeling his face redden. "I wish I knew. I haven't seen her around lately."

Ullin looked at him with more insight in his concerned expression than was comfortable for Robby.

"Hm. That's too bad. I hope she is getting along all right," he said. Before he could say more, Mirabella took over.

"Here. Sit. I've got some leftover breakfast pie, baked just this morning, and I have put with it some slices of ham. There's a plate for starters. Here's some hot coffee. A jug of cold apple juice. And here is a bowl of strawberries. There's more of everything, so eat to your fill."

"This is quite enough, and more." Ullin sat and looked around the table where no other plates were set. "But what of you?"

"Oh, we have already had our breakfast," she replied. "I'll see what I can do about that filthy cloak," she said as she left the room.

Robby felt a hand on his shoulder and saw his father motioning him aside.

"Son," he said. "I need ye to do a few things."

"Yes, sir?"

Mr. Ribbon took out a scrap of paper and handed it to Robby.

"I need ye to watch the store whilst Ullin's here. An' I need ye to put these things together for him. The best stuff, top drawer. An' pack the pouches full an' tight solid, an' all. Only in the amounts I've written, an' no more."

"I understand."

"Lemme know as soon as yer finished an' ready for me to check it."

Robby looked at the list then back into the kitchen at Ullin.

"Off ye go, son. An' don't ye let on that anybody's here 'cept us Ribbonses, lessin ye must."

"Yes, sir."

Once more, Robby felt he was being put out of the way, so to speak, of the information he dearly wanted. As he began looking for the things on the list, his curiosity grew more intense. It was as if it had been building up for years and years, with no way out. Anyway you looked at it, he should have been away from Passdale years ago, getting his schooling at Glareth and then traveling about on trading business. As it was, at twenty-one, he would be older than most of the applicants at the Glareth Academy, and would be older, still, when he graduated. The delays were vexing, but he knew they could not be helped. The store, their livelihood, must come first, and his father's travels had been necessary. As impatient as Robby was, he understood how things were, and made the best of things. But there was so much he did not know about the world, especially that which lay beyond Passdale and Barley, and he was anxious to get on with learning about other places. Now, with Ullin's sudden appearance, he was face to face with a potential fulfillment of his curiosity, but instead he was thwarted at every turn from satisfying it. He could almost hear his father's voice telling him that he was too young to understand that to satisfy one's curiosity, one must often let other longings remain unsatisfied, that the path to one is sometimes the path away from another.

At the moment, Robby's path was clearly in the bins and drawers, shelves and jars of the shop he had always known. Over the years, since he was eight or nine, whenever helping his father stock, he had mentally noted where things were from, or else he had asked his father. After a while, he understood that more than half of all the things in the shop came from places he had never been; indeed, the world of Passdale and County Barley was very small. As a lad, he wrote down the names of those places, even making copies of the ledger books. But, in his copies, instead of amounts and values, he put place names, and, if he knew or could find out, the distances and direction from Passdale to those places. Once, he took his list to schoolmaster Broadweed, hoping he could show them to Robby on a map.

"Well, I have a few old maps here," the scholar told him. "But don't you know that your father has better maps than any man within thirty leagues of here? And for a man who's rarely been more than that distance from Passdale, he probably knows more than anyone in these parts about, well, about other parts. And your mother knows even more."

That was indeed a surprise to Robby. Certainly the boy had seen the maps and charts, but he somehow did not realize they were real. Later, when Robby asked his father about them, and when Robby showed his list, his father was amazed at the boy.

"Well! I never did see a list like this un here!" he said, scratching his head. He looked at Robby, and laughed. "I reckon it's time yer ol' man gave ye some lessins, eh?" And night after night, they had pored over the maps, with father telling son all he knew about every place on the maps, which was not all that much aside from where things were made and a few stories he had picked up. Even then, there were many things in the shop from places not on the maps, and Mr. Ribbon was hard pressed to figure out where on the maps to point. So Robby copied the maps in his own young hand, and made notes right on the maps, such as:

> Bransondale—good pottery
> Millsin Fork—flint
> Tilderry—linen
> Dirkshire—cheese, soft white

Barsonfar—cheese, hard yellow
Tallinvale—glass, clear and blue-green

From those youthful days to now, it never occurred to Robby to ask his father where he got those maps. Perhaps more irksome at the moment, Robby had not yet seen even a fraction of the places he had charted. Now, as he pulled down a blanket and put it on the table, he said, "Lowbough," which was where it was woven. He reached for a vial of ointment, "Umston," and a block of oilwood, "Chawbree," and turned to prepare a couple of pouches of tobacco. "Bessinton," he said as he picked up the pouches, and "Farbarley," as he opened the keg.

A short time later, Mirabella came downstairs and saw him standing before a table, list in hand, going over the things he had laid out there. He pointed at each item, looking at the list, saying, "Bessinton, Passdale, Hazleton," and so on while his mother watched silently from the stairway. She let him continue until he had checked everything on the list. When he put the paper down, she approached.

"It appears you have gathered bits from the whole of the Eastlands and beyond," she smiled. Robby looked at her and then around the room.

"I suppose," he said. "But most of Eastlands' bits will stay here."

"Including yourself?"

"What do you mean?"

"I know restlessness when I see it," she said mildly. "And I know how disappointed you are that you have not already gone to Glareth and out into the world."

"I try not to let it show," Robby said.

"It doesn't show all that much," she answered. "You are remarkably patient for someone your age, and for someone who has been kept from the things he desires. Billy's mother tells me that he is progressing with his studies fairly well, and I have no doubt that you'll be at the Academy in Glareth in time for the spring exams."

Robby just looked at her, shaking his head, and was about to say something when she nodded and touched his hand.

"Your father needs you," she said. "Go ahead. I'll finish this."

Upstairs, Robby found Ullin and his father at the kitchen table. Mr. Ribbon was leaning back in his chair watching Ullin finish a bit of ham.

"Ah, Robby," Ullin said, picking up his napkin and wiping his mouth and beckoning him closer with his other hand.

"Son, have a sit," Mr. Ribbon said. "Ullin wants to ask ye somethin'."

Robby noted a seriousness in his father's tone, a kind of business tone he got sometimes, and he knew something was afoot.

"You know your way around these parts?" Ullin asked.

"Pretty well," Robby sat down, noticing a small parcel under Ullin's left elbow on the table beside his plate. "I mean, yes."

"Do you know the place called Tulith Attis?" Ullin asked. "The old abandoned fortress?"

Robby's pulse quickened at the name.

"That's its name in the Ancient Speech," Mr. Ribbon said before Robby could respond. "In Barley, we call it Haven Hill."

"Oh. Yes, of course. That's the ancient name of the hill that Tulith Attis stands upon," Ullin nodded. "Well, Robby, you know the place then?"

"Yes. I mean, I know of the place," he said. "I've seen it from a distance."

That was true, and Robby hoped it would suffice, for it was also true that he had seen it up close.

"Ye have, have ye?" his father asked.

"Why, yes, sir. A few years ago, Billy and I took horses from his place and rode along the Line Road, and we could see it from the road."

Robby hoped that he would not be pressed on the matter, for he did not want to tell the whole truth of the disastrous outing. It could have easily been worse, but for a lucky bit of soft ground that saved Robby from broken bones when his spooked horse threw him. As it was, he and Billy spent the best part of the day trying to round up the errant mount. After that misadventure, he made a vow to himself that he would never go anywhere near the old fortress again. Divulging the details now, after all this time, would only disappoint his trusting father.

"Hrumph!" was all Mr. Ribbon said in reply, but he probably would have said more if company had not been present.

"So you could find your way there?" Ullin asked, wondering why Mr. Ribbon seemed irritated at the boy. "To Haven Hill?"

"Well, at least as far as the North Line is easy enough, especially from here. And there's a path that leads off from there toward the place, if I recall."

"Well, good, then." Ullin picked up the packet, wrapped in leather and bound with a small lead seal. "This is for a man who lives out that way. His cottage is on the ridge on the side of the Hill, not far from the fortress. His name is Ashlord."

"Oh, I know him!" Robby said. Something was up, and he was quickly becoming involved in it, which was much to his liking. He checked himself and went on casually, "I meant to say, I know who he is. I've only had a few words with him. He comes in two or three times a season, for herbs mostly, some oil, or salt, and various little things. Strange man, if you pardon my saying so. Strange looking, tall, long black hair and beard. Dresses funny, too, not like most Barley folk. Never says much, but is polite enough. And he always pays with silver flats. Do you want me to show you the way out there?"

Ullin and Mr. Ribbon looked at each other and then back at Robby.

"No, I believe I could find my way without much trouble, but my business takes me elsewhere sooner than I would wish and in a somewhat different direction," Ullin explained. "I was delayed in getting this far. If I am to make my destination on time, I cannot go to Tulith Attis. I know it is just a short way off my path, but my appointment in Colleton cannot wait. Even a few hours may make all the difference."

Robby looked at him in disappointment. It would have been great fun to be Ullin's guide for a day.

"Ullin wants us to make the deliv'ry for him, son," Mr. Ribbon put in. Robby's heart lifted, again. "But I must stay at the store, an' the deliv'ry won't wait, so we're askin' ye if ye can take charge of this."

Robby looked back and forth, then broke into a grin.

"Sure! Why not? I mean," he suddenly faltered, remembering they were talking about Haven Hill. "I mean...do you mean me? By myself?"

"I wouldn't ask ye to go whar thar's any danger, er anythin'. Ye know that. It's just that it's a long way out an' back."

"And it cannot wait," Ullin added. "You must go today."

"Thar ain't a horse to be had at the stables, what with them all bein' used by Greardon this week. So it'll be on foot for ye," Mr. Ribbon continued. "Which means ye'll not be back afore dark, even if ye left right away."

Robby's mind raced over everything he knew about Haven Hill, the legends told about it, tales of ghosts and other frightful creatures that disturbed the place, and the great battle that had occurred there ages ago. And some kind of curse that lay upon its summit, at least according to Billy Bosk's mother. But he could not remember any details, only that there were legends about it, and that Billy's mum did say that it was a cursed place. That had been part of the attraction of the place, why he and Billy ventured out there that day. Now, recalling how his horse had thrown him for no apparent reason, he tried to look calm, but he found himself swallowing hard and clearing his throat to speak. He noticed his mother standing in the doorway, listening and looking on, her forehead wrinkled with concern. When her eyes met Robby's, she gave him an odd, almost searching look, but she said nothing.

"Well," Robby said at last, turning back to Ullin, "I'd best be on my way, then."

"Are ye sure, son?"

Ullin glanced back and forth from Mr. Ribbon to Robby.

"I have asked too much," he said. "There is a look upon both your faces that tells me there is more to what I ask than I know."

"No, no! Not at all," Robby shook his head. "I want to go. And the moon is full tonight so the way home will be well lit. I'll make the delivery to Ashlord and be on my way back well before dark. I shouldn't be out very late if I leave soon."

Robby looked at his father.

"I'd go with ye, except I got word the Nor'wick wagon's comin' today, an' I must be here an' check the shipment," Mr. Ribbon said. "An' it'd take too long to go by way of Boskland to pick up yer friend Billy to accompany ye."

For a moment, Robby almost thought—and almost wished—his father would either say no or else arrange to come along. But there was something hopeful in his father's expression. In spite of his reservations, Robby nodded confidently.

Mr. Ribbon returned the nod, smiling, then turned to Ullin. "Robby will take care of it. Just as ye wish, Ullin Saheed."

• • •

Ullin's horse was brought around within the half-hour, and, during that time, Robby changed clothes, put on his walking boots, laced them tight, and prepared a shoulder bag of things: a small brass folding candle-lamp with a glass lens, a spare candle, flint and steel, and his order book and pencil.

"You never know," he thought. "Ashlord might want to place an order to pick up the next time he comes to town."

He put everything into his bag beside the special parcel he was to deliver, and stuffed a lightweight, hooded cloak in, too. Robby hurried out into the hall, looking for Ullin, wanting to ask a thousand questions, but there was simply no time. Anyway, Ullin was saddling his horse and preparing his bags, and Mr. Ribbon insisted that Robby look over a map of County Barley with him.

"This is whar yer goin'," Mr. Ribbon said to Robby, putting his finger on a blot near the edge of the map. "It is only a league or so from the north line here. An' if ye go this way, along the east-west path ye'll come to Oldgate soon enough. Ye'll first pass through some farmland, on along past Steggan's old place, an' on over the Weepingbrook, a shallow stream right along here. Keep on an' not far is Oldgate. Can't miss it. That's whar ye'll run into the Line Road, runnin' north an' south, right here, see? Goin' on through the gate will put ye on the old east road, just a path, now. Mr. Bosk told me awhile back that he think's thar's been plenty of comin' an' goin' since the path stays clear from troddin' through summer grass an' winter snow, though they ain't seen nobody. Probably that Ashlord feller walkin' it. Anyhow, ye should have no trouble stayin' to it. See, it goes fairly straight on to Haven Hill, on across the barren fields whar a town was, long time ago. The path keeps goin', right between two old barrow-mounds. It turns just this side of the Hill an' winds back 'round the northern side an' on 'round it. Here's the thing, son: I don't know exactly whar Ashlord lives, but I think it is on the low side of the hill, which is the furthest south an' east. Along the way must be another path or trail leadin' off to his place.

"Now, listen," he gave his son a firm look, "I want to tell ye to go no further than Haven Bridge. If ye pass by the hill an' ye get to an old stone bridge, ye've gone too far. Promise me this: If ye reach the bridge an' ye see no sign of that Ashlord feller, or his place, turn straight back. On the way back have another look, but don't dawdle. The road ends at the bridge, an' it's too easy to get lost on the other side, in what's called the

Boggy Wood. Them woods is a bad place, tangled an' full of twists, turns, an' all manner of beasts. A hunnerd men with axes couldn't hack thar way through it in a year, I'd say, an' more likely to get lost, anyhow. Will ye turn back at the bridge?"

"Yes."

"An' if ye don't see no other way that might lead off to Ashlord's, ye'll come straight back, deliv'ry er no deliv'ry, the way ye came."

"Yes."

"Good." Mr. Ribbon rolled up the map and offered it to Robby. "Do ye want to take this along?"

"No. I think I'll be fine without it. Besides, unless we have a carrying tube for it, I'd have to fold it up. I know it's too valuable for that."

"Not as valuable as ye are."

"Maybe, but I don't think I'll need the map," Robby reiterated. "And it's one less thing to carry."

"Well, alright, then," his father nodded. "Just one er two more quick things, an' once again listen close to me."

"Yes, sir?"

"We've all heard them stories told 'bout Haven Hill," he said. Robby nodded. "Now, some of them stories ain't nuthin', but some of the other, well, some stories are true, in some manner. Leastwise, I believe them to be."

"Which ones are true?"

"A great battle was fought thar, hunnerds of years ago. I've seen the books that it's written in, ye've pro'bly seen 'em, too, an yer mum can tell ye more, since her people run back all the way to them times. Billy's folk do, too, an' Billy's namesake died thar, so they say."

As he spoke, Mr. Ribbon went over to the other side of the room and pulled a small chest from under a table and brushed aside some old and dusty ledger books.

"I know them stories to be true, son, 'bout the battle, I mean. Even though a lot of the what's an' why's been long forgotten by most folks 'round these parts. But take a look at this."

He rummaged in the chest and pulled out a small bundle of cloth. Untying the bundle, Mr. Ribbon removed some old corroded bits of metal, the largest piece about the size and shape of a terribly banged up bowl.

"What's that?"

"Hold up yer hand like a fist."

Robby followed the instructions and held up his fist, as if he was showing off his biceps. Mr. Ribbon took the heavy bowl-like piece and carefully put it on top of Robby's fist, upside down, it seemed.

"An' hold this other piece right here, like so," Mr. Ribbon said, putting another small piece in Robby's other hand so that it jutted down from the inverted rim. "Hold it right thar." Mr. Ribbon took two more pieces, rather flat and held them one to each side of the bowl.

"What do ye see?"

Robby turned his head back and forth, still holding the little piece as he was shown. Suddenly he saw it.

"A helmet! It looks like an old helmet! That's the nose guard, and those are side pieces. Or what's left of them."

"That is exactly right!"

The two of them stood there, each holding their pieces so that Robby could continue to look at the assembly.

"I found this out at Haven Hill when I was a lad," Mr. Ribbon took the pieces and put them on the table. "An' I found this, too."

He pulled out another small wad of soft cloth and unfolded it in his hand to reveal a small round object, no more than four acorns wide, like a small brooch. It was gold and enameled with green and blue, and studded with a white gem encircled by seven tiny rubies. On one end was part of a metal loop where once a chain had passed.

"An', behold," Mr. Ribbon put his thumbnail against one edge and it opened. Inside, tied in a tiny intricate knot, was a lock of golden hair. Oddly, the room became cool as Robby felt some deep sadness flow through him. He felt as though he was falling into the locket, swirling through time, to a distant age and a faraway day when this locket was tenderly assembled and held close, perhaps in a moment of loneliness, or perhaps fear.

"Oh, Daddy!" Robby whispered in astonishment, tearing his eyes from it to look at Mr. Ribbon as he rubbed the goose bumps from his arms. "You found this on Haven Hill?"

"Very nearby, when I was not much younger than yerself, whilst helpin' to clear some rocky land out on the other side of Bosk Manor," Mr. Ribbon said, gently closing it up and folding it back into the cloth. "I'm told soldiers still wear lockets such as this, to remind them of home an' sweethearts."

Robby nodded, remembering the locket he saw dangling from Ullin's neck. Mr. Ribbon put everything away, and pushed the chest under the table. "I've often thought I should've left 'em as I found 'em, an' I thought one day to put 'em back."

"Why?"

"I dunno, son," Mr. Ribbon shrugged. "I get this funny feelin' sometimes, when I think on it, that they were meant to be found, somehow, an' somethin' done with 'em. Somethin' proper-like. But maybe not by me. I dunno who. It upsets yer mother that I've got these things. But she's no clearer than me on what to do with 'em."

He waved his hand in the air as if fanning away smoke. "Never mind all that, though. I showed ye these things to let ye know, as ye have a right to, that somethin' happened out thar, long time ago. Hunnerds of years ago, as some puts it. So while ye can leave off believin' monster stories an' the like, just ye know that sometimes thar might be some speck of true out of what people grow thar tales, like seed that with a lotta waterin' an' sun years after years come up to be a great tree, spreadin' more seeds an' more, 'til the one thing seen ain't no more like what started out than a pebble to a mountain, yet mountains be made of pebbles, if ye catch me meanin'. So when I tells ye to be careful out yonder, it ain't for the likes of ghosts an' other such silly whatnots, but more for the likes of men an' beasts, an' for watchin' yer step. An' be respectful of that ground out thar, since so many are said to have died thar."

"Yes, sir. I will," Robby said. "But when I get back I think I'll have a lot more questions."

Mr. Ribbon laughed. "An' I reckon it's about time ye did!"

When father and son came downstairs, Ullin was giving Mirabella a last hug. She kissed him on the cheek, and he turned to lift the bundle prepared for him from the table. She turned to Robby.

"Take these, too," she said. She put bread, sausage, and cheese, along with a small knife on a piece of cloth alongside a water flask and was beginning to roll it up within the cloth when Mr. Ribbon spoke.

"Hang on, dearie," he said, picking up the knife. "Lemme get Robby a better one."

He turned to a case behind him and tried to open the lid.

"Bother! Jammed again?" he grunted, prying at it with his fingers. "Robby, could ye see if ye can open this dang thing?"

Robby nodded and felt along the lid to see where it was hung, but it came open easily. Mr. Ribbon shook his head.

"Don't know why I always have trouble with it, but ye never do!" he said. He took out a large knife in a sheath of embossed leather and handed it to Robby. "This here's more fit for a trip! Stick that in yer belt. Do ye have yer lamp?"

"Yes, sir. And a spare candle with my flint and steel."

"Good," Mr. Ribbon nodded. "But take this, too." He fished around on a shelf and picked up a small tin box. Inside was a glass vial containing a few firesticks. Inside the lid of the box was a strike-plate. After checking the contents carefully he handed the tin to Robby.

"Are you sure? I've got my flint."

"Yes," Mr. Ribbon said. "No sense in wastin' time an' fumblin' 'round in the dark tryin' to start a far when alls ye need is to light up a candle. Just be careful with'em an' go sparingly if ye needs 'em. If ye keeps to the main road tonight, the moon'll most likely give ye enough light."

Robby nodded and placed the precious item in a little pocket inside his shoulder bag. He stuffed the food bundle and water flask into the bag and slipped the knife under his belt.

"All set," he said.

"You have the parcel?" Ullin asked.

Robby reached into his bag and produced it.

"Good. I'll accompany you as far as the other side of the bridge."

Then he gave Mr. Ribbon a hug and a handshake while Robby hugged his mother, saying, "I'll see you tonight."

Robby shook his father's hand as they walked out of the store, and Mr. Ribbon patted him on the back.

"You both be careful!" Mirabella ordered as Ullin strapped his bundle behind the saddle and took the reins, leading his horse alongside Robby.

"I hope to see you about two months hence, maybe less!" Ullin called back.

Mr. and Mrs. Ribbon watched them move off down the road.

"I wonder how things will go when Robby gets to Ashlord's," Mirabella said.

"I reckon we'll find out," her husband shrugged. "I'd be upset, if it was me. But we kept our word, as we promised. Hopefully, it'll all work out."

When Robby and Ullin passed out of sight, they turned back into the store. Mr. Ribbon sat at his desk while Mirabella tidied the shelves. Some minutes later, Mr. Ribbon looked up from his ledger.

"Dagummit!" he said. Mirabella looked over from the closet.

"What is it?"

"I should've asked Robby to take an order book." Catching his wife's sidelong look, he shrugged. "Well, ye never knows, but Ashlord might wanna put in an order for somethin'! Ye know, for the next time he's in town."

"Oh, honey!"

• • •

Ullin and Robby walked down the road alongside the river wall, bearing north toward the bridge. The sun was full up, nearing midmorning, and the day's heat was growing. All of the shops and houses along this part of Passdale faced the road and river, and here and there along the wall stood massive poplars, their leaves shooshing in the unsteady breeze with a rain-like patter. The market stands were already up, and a few were busy. People were coming and going at the potter's place and already there was a short line at the barber's next door. The waterwheel at the mill steadily creaked and groaned a short distance away. As they crossed a small stone bridge where a stream flowed into the river, the mill came into view, nestled up against the hill where the stream jumped down from rock to ledge on the hill behind and then onto the long sluice that spilled over the wheel. A few farmers passed, coming from various parts of Barley, their carts laden with melons and squash, corn and sweet peppers.

They walked silently for a while, Robby wanting to ask so much, but he was unable to decide which question to ask first. Just as he had worked his nerve up to ask about Ullin's commission, a large dog broke from a nearby house and ran up, barking at Ullin's horse.

Ullin made a sudden feint at the dog and said some words Robby could not understand. The dog sprang backwards on its haunches, then turned and trotted off. The horse, meanwhile, seemed not in the least perturbed.

"What is your horse's name?" Robby asked, completely forgetting his intended line of questions.

"Anerath," Ullin said. "That means Water Prancer in the Common Tongue."

"Anerath," Robby repeated. "He's a fine-looking horse."

"A fine friend, he is, too." Ullin smiled reaching to pat Anerath's shoulder.

"Is Anerath's name from the Ancient Speech?"

"Aye, one of those still used in the Westlands. Vanara, mostly, but also around Duinnor."

"Do you speak the Ancient Speech?"

"Surely, when needs," he looked at Robby. "It is my own native tongue, though few in these parts outside of Tallinvale still use it."

"I guess I don't know what you mean, Ullin," Robby said. "I thought you were from around here."

"Yes and no. My father was born in Vanara, the land of our grandmother, in the west. That is where your mother was born, too. Our grandfather brought his family back into the Eastlands to his ancestral lands many years ago, and I was born in Tallinvale, southwest of here. When I was young, my own father left to serve Duinnor. So, in my time, I left, too, to serve the King as he did. That is our way, for the law says the eldest male of every Named House must serve the King of Duinnor until released."

Robby shook his head. "So you are my mother's brother's son. My cousin. She talks very little about her family. But then, I have not asked as much as I probably should have, either. Sometimes I think my parents are complete strangers, so little do I seem to know about them. And what I learn is so often by accident or else in bits and pieces. I never seem to get the whole story."

Ullin laughed.

"So it always is!" he said. "I, too, have thought that of my parents. But I suppose all parents are thought of in that way by their children. And, yet, perhaps we know more than we can say about our parents, even while our parents say less than they know."

"Maybe," Robby thought about that for a moment. The road followed a bend in the river where the bridge came into sight. It was a suspension bridge, of sorts, with two tall stone pillars at each end between which ran a wood-decked roadway. Over the pillars ran huge cables of rope anchored along the sides of each approach and fanning out downward in the middle of the bridge to support the trusses that held up the deck. The pillars stood nearly four stories tall, allowing the bridge they supported to be high enough over the river so that boats could pass underneath. The water was fairly shallow, only a fathom at most, but it ran swiftly along these narrows, and there were a few old gray rocks that jutted up from the river bottom to break the surface, their mossy tops a soft perch for the turtles basking there.

Robby knew the story of the New Passbarley Bridge, as was its proper name. Not many years ago, the bridge was no more than legend, for only the great stone pillars survived from the ancient days when the river wall was constructed. There was once a city here along the river, it was said, the wall built both to protect the city against flood as well as a structure to build wharves from. In those days, the river was higher and deeper, and legend had it that boats came up from the sea as far as here, where they loaded and unloaded trade goods. That was long ago, and whoever did those things had long since left, and the old town fell into ruin. But after five centuries, people began to increase in these parts again, and some of the present houses, like his own, were built on old foundations. When Robby's father started his business in Passdale as a young man from the county, he tried to have goods from farms across the river brought over by ferry, but the ferryman's price made business profitless. He was not the only one being gouged by the ferrymen up and down the Bentwide, so he ran for mayor of Passdale and won. In that position, Mr. Ribbon worked feverishly with key folk from Barley and Passdale to get the old bridge rebuilt, raising funds, organizing labor, and even directing some of the construction work. When it opened at last, it put the ferryman out of business, but it created a flourishing trade between Barley and Passdale, uniting the two sides of the county that the river divided. It was in no small part due to that feat that Mr. Ribbon held the respect of people far and wide. The people of Passdale, as a way of gratitude, granted him the title "Mayor Barleyman" for he was the first outsider ever to be mayor, and the Barley folk named him honorary "Sheriff of Twobanks." It was much due to Robigor Ribbon that the goodwill that now existed between Passdale and Barley came to be, but, as his modest father liked to say, "Friendship is easy when it puts somethin' in yer purse." It had been years since Mr. Ribbon had given up the post of mayor, but he was still often fondly referred to by his former title. And it was true that Ribbon's efforts paid handsomely, not only for his own business interests, but for most folks around. "Amazin'," Mr. Ribbon was also fond of saying, "what a little bridge here an' thar will do!"

"So, Ullin, do you know the King?" Robby asked. "I mean, have you ever met him?"

"No, I have never seen the King, and those few that have say the vision of him is one of beauty and fright. When he goes forth from the High Tower, which he seldom does these days, all bow their heads or avert their eyes from him lest their dreams be filled with disturbances and their sleep filled with a terrible restlessness. They say woe unto he who fixes a steady gaze upon him, for madness will surely follow."

"I've only ever heard of him as 'the King.' But what is he called? What is his name?"

"He is known by different names to different peoples. Some call him Culfinor, meaning Lonely One. In Altoria he is known as Halassir, which is to say Vision King." Ullin stopped for a moment to adjust Anerath's straps and cinches and to check again the tightness of the belts holding the saddlebags. "The wild Northmen call him in their tongue 'snowstorm,' because their legends have it that he first appeared out of a great blizzard in the days before the stars of Behemoth shone and while mists still lay upon the world." Ullin gave Anerath a good pat and the three moved on.

"But no one knows his right name, nor whence he truly came, and it is said that whoever learns the name of the King will slay him and take his place as our sovereign, whether for better or worse. It has been that way for five kings before. Our present ruler is the Sixth Unknown King to sit on the throne of Duinnor."

"Oh!" Robby raised his eyebrows at the mystery of it all. By now they were on the bridge approach and the roadway changed from hard-packed dirt to flat stones leading to the bridge. "Mr. Broadweed, our schoolmaster, taught us that the King has ruled for more than five hundred years."

"Aye, he has reigned longer than any before him. This is the year five hundred and thirty-eight of his rule over the Seven Realms."

"And you work for him? For the King?" Robby asked. "He sent you here?"

"The King has many servants and counselors and lords who do his bidding. I am a Kingsman, a soldier of Duinnor, but I am also in service to Prince Toliss of Duinnor, who oversees the King's Post. It is through him that I received the Post Commission. I am what is called a Special Rider, since I do not ride only one route back and forth, over and over, as most Post Riders do. Instead, I go wide and far, delivering special dispatches and important letters, often to or from important persons. This journey is but another errand."

"Important persons? Like Ashlord?"

"Yes. And others."

Robby tapped his shoulder bag, and asked, "Are these from the King?"

Ullin smiled. "No. Not this time. But all letters and dispatches carried by Kingsmen Post Riders are to be treated as though they are to or from the King himself. With urgency and with care."

By now they were just before the bridge entrance gate, and they waited for a farmer riding his oxcart to pass through. The bridge tender in his box halfway across craned his neck out this way and the other, looking for traffic. Deeming it clear, he pulled on a certain rope which by a system of pulleys, levers, and counterweights lowered a "Do Not Cross" sign on the far side entrance and lifted a "Cross Over" sign above Ullin and Robby. They mounted the ramp and up onto the bridge-way, which was just wide enough for one cart, or three horses side by side. Robby walked on in front with Ullin behind. As the stone ramp gave way to the wooden deck of the bridge, Anerath's hooves clopped warmly behind the pair. When they neared the middle, they could see for miles into the croplands of Barley, ahead and back just over the low hills of Passdale to the pastures and woods and higher hills beyond. The sun glistened on the flowing water below and a breeze picked up and stiffened. Ullin nodded to the southeast.

"Looks like we'll be having some weather soon."

Robby squinted his eyes against the sunlight. Just barely above the horizon was a dark line from north to south.

"G'mornin', Master Ribbon," the bridge tender called out from his box as they passed by.

"Good morning, Mr. Arbuckle," Robby waved.

"How's yer mum an' pop?"

"Fine, thanks."

"Off to Barley?"

"An errand," Robby said.

"Surely. An' yer friend's got him a mighty fine lookin' horse, he has."

"The finest that ever crossed this bridge, I'll warrant!" Ullin shot back.

"Eh? That be a Westerman if I ever heard one. Might that be Miss Mirabella's brother?"

"You mistake me for my father, Mr. Nosey," Ullin teased. "An' the last time you did that, you nearly died of faint."

"Oh, yeah," Arbuckle scratched the back of his head. "Ye pop's been de—, er, I mean, he ain't no more with us, er, beg yer honor's pardon."

Ullin laughed as they moved out of earshot of the muddled geezer.

"He's a funny old kook. Must be a hundred by now," Robby said.

"More like two, if you ask me," Ullin chuckled.

"What was he going on about? What was that about your father not being around?"

"My father has been dead for many years."

"Oh," Robby blushed, feeling completely stupid. "I think I was supposed to know that. I just forgot. I am sorry."

"You know," Ullin said, glancing at Robby, "sometimes I forget, too. Even though I promised I never would."

They remained silent the rest of the way off the bridge. Robby was beginning to feel a little overwhelmed by all of the new things he had heard today. And the day was still in its morning.

"If all goes well, I'll pass back through here in about two months," Ullin suddenly said. "I hope I'll see you then. I regret missing you the last few times I came through. But each time you were at your letters, or else it was so late at night I didn't want Mira to wake you."

Ullin stopped and Robby realized they were at the crossroads where they must part. Robby's way ran straight away east from the bridge. Ullin's road ran north and east.

"Wouldn't it be easier for you to take the north road back on the other side of the river?" Robby asked.

"I would have to pass the long way around Lake Halgaeth, and I haven't the time. I must go along the lake's south shore and cross over Heneil's Wall, then northeast through Forest Mistwarren."

Robby understood that he was making for the coast and would bear steadily north and east until at his journey's end.

"They say the forest is dangerous," Robby suggested.

"I have been through it many times. It holds no more danger than Barley does," Ullin said, "and less than I have come through from the West."

He checked the saddle and straps one last time and then said to Robby, "Take care along with you to Tulith Attis. And give my regrets to Ashlord when you make your delivery."

"I will," Robby replied gripping Ullin's hand. "And you take care, too."

"Always."

Ullin nodded and shook Robby's hand. He mounted Anerath and reined him around. The horse, patient and docile until now, suddenly seemed eager, his hooves clicking urgently to bear his rider away.

"Then, farewell!"

Horse with rider sprang away.

"Farewell," Robby cried out after them, but Anerath and Ullin were passing away faster than Robby could have imagined possible. Only then did Robby wonder at the extreme urgency of Ullin's errand. Suddenly, he dug into his bag and pulled out the parcel. Panic briefly gripped him, and he felt he was part of the urgency, though he could not explain why he felt that way. But he did not want to let Ullin down. Relieved that he had not already lost the parcel, he put it at the bottom of the shoulder bag and tightly tied down the flap. He pulled the strap over his head and across his shoulder and headed off.

## Chapter 2

## A Simple Errand

Robby wondered at what sort of mission would require a Kingsman such as his cousin to ride Post. Surely the letters that Ullin carried were of far more importance than ordinary correspondence, so important that he could not trust them to strangers. As he walked up the hill away from the bridge, he imagined that perhaps great events stirred in the world and that he now participated in them, at least in some small way. His modest knowledge of the world hampered his speculation, but he thought that, surely, there were momentous things happening outside of Passdale and County Barley. Although the packet was small, the burden of it tugged oddly at his heart. It gave him a sense of importance, if for no other reason than to free Ullin to carry out the rest of his mysterious mission. Already he looked forward to seeing Ullin again, and perhaps learning more. But two months would be a long time to wait.

He passed by the houses of Barley, waving at some of the folk as he went, and then walked briskly on into the croplands as the road led away from the River Bentwide and gently sloped up a ridge of low hills. His way of steady marching was his habit, instilled by his father's training on many errands for the shop, and he had every confidence that his pace matched the importance of his delivery task. The breeze became gusty, and in the lulls the sun's heat felt good. Fields of second corn stood ripening, and a few farmers were out reaping early corn. As Robby advanced, the corn gave way to rows of beans and peppers, and, far off where the ridge ahead sloped down toward the river, Robby could plainly see the Saliley family's vineyards. Slowly upward he trudged until he reached the ridgeline, and there he stopped for a moment to adjust his shoulder strap and look around.

Behind him lay the shallow valley of the Peninflo, as the Bentwide was properly called. The bridge was plainly in sight as well as the poplars that lined the riverside road. The houses and shops of Passdale looked homely and friendly, and Robby could barely see the waterwheel turning. Behind them were patches of pastures and woodland rising up higher than he now stood. Off to the north, the Bentwide hooked back eastward, and in the distant west and northwest he could make out a light blue line of mountains, hazy and almost blending with the sky. Looking the other way, downstream past Passdale, the river bent away southward and was lost to view where it settled back into its southeastward course, running down its long journey to the sea. Robby turned, faced into the wind, and saw in the southeast a black line of clouds slowly catching up with the sun. As he remembered Ullin saying that the weather was changing, he caught the unmistakable aroma of rain on the breeze. Determined to hurry on, he looked northward where the land was flatter, fields of barley giving way here and there to small streams thinly lined with trees before rising again in the distance. With a last glance southeastward and another tug on his shoulder strap, he set off down the hill.

On this side of the ridge the soil was drier but no less rich, and he saw many farmers and field laborers going about their business with more haste than was characteristic of them. Perhaps they, too, quickened their pace before the coming rain. Lesser roads and tracks led off left and right with fair frequency, and the folk he met seldom greeted him, though he was familiar to most of them. Though Robby nodded in his friendly manner, many simply eyed him curiously, wondering, perhaps, who he was out to collect from. Robby smiled, anyway, held his head up, and marched on, reminding himself that they were good people, and some were distant relatives, even. If need be, they would surely not deny him shelter if the storm broke on his way back.

He kept on at a good pace, turning mile into league, still pondering the business he carried in his bag and wondering what kind of man the recipient, Ashlord, would be. He remembered the gentleman's visits to the store, helping him find some spices one time, and selling a bit of oil to him on another occasion. He was a tall, lean fellow, penetrating dark eyes, dark skin, and long black hair and beard to match. He had worn a long, dark-blue cloak and carried an artfully twisted, walking stick.

Robby's thoughts suddenly changed when he came to a fork in the road where another path carried off southward. He paused, looking at an old abandoned farmhouse in the distance through the trees, remembering the last time he had been this way. That was well over a month ago while on an errand with his father, and it was not a pleasant outing. Finding a dead man, hanging from the rafters, can never be pleasant. A flash of memory—a gnawed and mangled body in the reeking and fly-infested gloom of the house, swinging from the rafter by the chain that wrapped his neck—gave Robby a shudder. He shook his head, not wanting to think about it right now, or ever again, and he resumed his purposeful stride eastward with renewed vigor.

By now it was nearly noon, and Robby was grateful for the spots of shade he passed through since there were fewer trees along this stretch. The road itself narrowed and grew rougher and grassier as it was used less and less the farther he went. It dipped down here and there where little brooks trickled across, and then the path rose back up across low rises, curving away to the left and then to the right, but ever keeping a eastward heading.

The farther he went the fewer people he saw, and the fields were less tended, some with saplings growing up in them. The road, now only a wide path, showed few signs of maintenance. In many places, tall grass grew thick and straight, unbent by traffic, and blackberry bushes edged inward, their thorns sometimes snagging Robby as he passed through. In other places, the encroaching brambles were so high that he could not see right or left for more than a few feet.

This was not the same way to the Line Road that he and his friends Billy and Ibin had come. That day, they started out going north from Billy's home in Boskland, near the south end of the county. Today's walk was farther than he had ever been along this way, farther even than he and his father had come when they walked out on business. The closeness of the weeds and brush, the clinging blackberry limbs, and his limited field of view made him uneasy. Yet the birds still sang, the thrashers with their songs and the redbirds chipping about, and the sun still beamed warmly, so he marched on. After another hour, the thickets cleared somewhat and the path rose upward on a gentle grade. Entering a grassy hillside meadow, he was strangely reassured by the sight of several cows munching nearby. They raised their heads and chewed steadily as they eyed Robby. Still moving upward, the path followed along a low ridge, and the land slowly opened up.

He topped the hill, just as the sun passed noon, and another ridge appeared a little more than a furlong ahead, covered in oak and pine. The path led Robby downward through an unused pasture where it met and crossed a small willow-lined stream at the base of the far ridge. The path bent away south to a plank bridge, after which it rose sharply up the wooded ridge. The bridge was barely wide enough for the narrowest of carts, and, Robby noted, far too rickety to trust with much weight. He stopped and gazed over the thin handrail at the shallow water gurgling over rocks and around roots.

"This looks like a good place for some lunch," he said aloud as he sat down on the bridge. He let his legs dangle over the side, the soles of his shoes just touching the water, and he put his shoulder bag beside him. The breeze had abated somewhat, and the drooping branches of the willow trees wafted gently while they whispered to one another. The stream gurgled quietly below as Robby drank from his water flask and opened the bundle of food his mother had prepared for him. Taking a bite of bread, he unwrapped the sausage and took out his knife to cut a slice of it to put with a piece of cheese. He was trying to remember the name of this place; his father had pointed it out to him on the map. He seemed to remember that it was an odd one, but for the life of him he could not recall it. Looking around, he thought maybe some feature would remind him of the name. On the east bank was a line of large gray stones, many covered with thick moss, jutting out of the base of the ridge. On across the bridge, the path bent northward, rising steeply uphill and disappearing into the trees. Behind him, on the upstream side, the stream was pretty much the same, a few more of the odd stones huddled together, several leaning over the water that swirled around their feet. Robby still could not remember the name of the stream.

As he cut another piece of sausage and raised it to his mouth, he realized that all sound had ceased, and he sat still, listening. The breeze died, the willows drooped stiffly, and even the stream stopped gurgling. No birds could be heard, and, looking up, he could see no movement of them in the trees. Slipping his knife back into the sheath beside his pack, he stood up to have a better look around, but as he did so, the breeze resumed, several wrens tittered past, and the stream raised its murmuring with the willows. All was as it was before, but the silence had been so uncanny that Robby wondered if he had merely imagined it.

Shrugging it off, he sat back down and took another swallow of water. He figured he had better drink his fill here and replenish his flask; no telling how far until the next stream. After quaffing the last Passdale drops, he stretched out on his stomach to reach down and put the flask into the stream. Holding the spout under the clear water, the flask bubbled as it filled, the stopper on its chain swirling about. Gently raising it, he reached down with his other hand to catch the stopper and put it on, and he could see his reflection in the pool. Just as he had the stopper on, something caught his eye. There on the water was his reflection rippling in the current, but another one had joined his, a vague dark shape leaning over him. The hair on his neck stood on end.

"Whoa!" he let out a yell and rolled over on his back, recoiling from whoever it was. His fear turned to relief and bewilderment; no one was there.

"Hello? What's this?" he said, sitting up and looking around. "Am I such a child that I am imagining things?"

He took a deep breath, and shook his head. "Oh, well, still time for another bite or two."

Laughing at himself, he drew his knife and cut another slice of sausage. He ate it with a swig of the fresh cool water, and it was then that he noticed that the breeze had stopped again. Again, the willows hung stiff, the birds disappeared, and the stream's noise ebbed. Putting the last morsel in his mouth and packing his leftovers away, he thought he heard a different sort of sound. He put his knife down and picked up the water flask, packing it away as he listened. It seemed that the odd sound was coming from upstream. Standing up, and slinging the pack over his shoulder, he peered in that direction but could see no sign of activity, though the sound, an odd hum, seemed very nearby. The gray rocks that leaned over the water seemed sullen, and for the first time he noticed that no moss grew on them while all others, the flatter, lower stones, were covered with the stuff. Wondering why, he stared at the large stones, also wondering what kept them from falling over, and as he did so, he thought he saw some shape in them that he had not noticed before. It was as if they were old, life size statues, time- and weather-worn, of a small group of people kneeling before the stream. As the idea took hold, he discerned more features and saw that some of them held their arms out over the water while others had their hands over their faces. More and more details seem to emerge as he stared, the strange sound increased, and his entire body broke out in goose flesh as he realized they were the wails and moans of weeping, as if coming from inside the stones themselves. He tried to dismiss the entire vision, to force what he saw back into rocks and what he heard back into the movement of the wind, but his effort was in vain. He felt heavy and growing heavier, the bridge underneath his feet groaned and creaked, and his arms and legs felt cold and stiff and thick. Suddenly fear shot through him like a kind of madness, and he broke his feet loose from their anchors and fled, slowly at first, with great lumbering steps that pounded across the bridge, sending up splinters and cracking the timbers. As he left the bridge and stomped up the far bank, he seemed able to move more lightly, as if a great weight was lifted from him. He kept going, quickly moving uphill, then the uncanny sensations completely evaporated, the breeze blew again, and the air was filled with the sound of leaves shushing and birds singing. He stopped and looked back to the bridge just a few yards away but saw nothing unusual or alarming in the least. The stones were just stones, and the stream was just a stream.

Again, he laughed nervously and shook his head.

"What on earth has come over you!" he chided. With a paradoxical lightness of heart, he trudged on up the way through the woods as the path ascended the ridge. He walked on, not seeing the brown-clad figure scurry out from the heather on the far side of the stream and dart onto the bridge, pausing only momentarily to pick up something, before scrambling on across and disappearing off the path and into the trees.

As Robby continued upward, he almost forgot about his destination, being so confused and bewildered. He kept going over in his head the sensations that had overcome him, the heaviness and the growing paralysis, and he now realized what a profound sadness he had felt just a few moments ago. He could find nothing in his youthful experience with which to compare it, nothing so strange and uncanny, except perhaps something that happened when he was a very little boy and sick with fever. His memory of it was somewhat nonsensical, but he did remember clearly the worried looks of his parents. And he especially remembered two strangers who came and went. Both were gentlewomen, and together they came, finely attired, one in a black and red gown with red rubies and a similar cloak, and the other lady dressed in silver-white and emeralds. Like sisters, they were, so closely they resembled each other. Each in turn leaned over him and looked deep into his face and spoke to him softly. They spoke to each other in the same tone and in a language like the chiming of glass in the wind. Together they questioned him, and he answered them each in the same tongue and with his own voice. He thought they were the most beautiful things he could ever see, yet he feared them deeply, and he feared the decision they grappled with, though he knew nothing of the substance of their debate. After a long while, they came to him together and laid their hands on him and sang a delicate little song that was for him alone to hear, and he feared them no more. It was only then that he perceived his parents nearby, his mother's head on his father's shoulder, his arm around her, both looking on. The two strangers turned to them and spoke more words that he could not make out. As his parents bowed, the two ladies faded away and the room became dim with only the flickering candlelight. His mother came to him and smiled and wiped his brow while his father knelt by his bed and took his hand, great pools forming in his eyes. Robby remembered sleeping a deep, peaceful sleep and the memory faded. Soon he had recovered from the illness and was his own playful and laughing self, tottering about gaily. The words spoken he soon forgot, the faces of the strangers faded and grew vague, and now all that remained was this bit of memory and the melody of that song, which he now found himself humming as he walked up the path. Once, many years later, he had asked his parents about it. His father looked up silently from his book. His mother stopped her sewing.

"Sh-h," she said. "Do not ask, and speak not of it to any person. Only give thanks for your recovery, for you were gravely ill and your father and I had little hope for your life. The two strangers, as you call them, were from far away, and but for them you surely would have died that night."

"Now," she said reaching out and giving him a hug, "do not trouble yourself any more about it."

But Robby did think about it. Maybe not all the time, but often enough. Perhaps it was that memory that sparked in his early days an interest in other lands. Now, as he trudged along, he realized that he was finally fulfilling, in a very small way, his longing to see new places. As he topped the ridge and started downward, he thought that, in spite of his father's admonition, there might indeed be more dangers than man or beast. He threw a glance back the way he had come, but the stream and the bridge were long lost from view. The fear he remembered when the ladies were at his bedside was a different sort than had gripped him on the bridge. The ladies were good, he concluded, turning away to resume his way. What he felt at the bridge was terror. This only made Robby feel more childlike, for there was nothing at all to be afraid of, he was certain.

As he descended, the way became rocky and the undergrowth grew sparse. The trees thinned, and there was open country ahead. When he emerged from the wooded ridge, he could see, stretching from right to left as far as his eyes could reach, a low rock wall that marked the North Line, with the Line Road running just to this side of the wall. Directly ahead, just over a furlong, was Oldgate, its two stone pillars marking a gap in the wall. The strip of land between the ridge and the Line was grassy and flat but lumpy with rocks, their gray-green backs jutting up here and there like mossy turtles. The breeze stiffened as he came into the openness of the strip, and Robby saw that the clouds covered the whole of the south and eastern skies and would soon be overhead. When he came to the intersection of the Line Road running along beside the wall, and stood before Oldgate, he saw horse tracks. They went along the road that ran south from here toward Boskland on the other side of Barley. They were probably tracks left by one of Billy Bosk's kin riding line patrol as was their traditional duty in this country, ever since the year that the Eastlands Realm was forfeited to Glareth. Since then, it was left to each of the old counties to make for their own defense. The Line Ride was not much more than a token effort since there was never any need for defense in the peaceful Eastlands. But the Boskmen took their duty seriously, as their House was one of the ancient ones of the realm. Robby could see where the rider had paused, a shuffle of hoof prints, before continuing on northward. Robby looked south somewhat furtively, down the road that led to Boskland, wishing his friends were with him now.

Turning back to his own way, Robby could plainly see, framed between the stone posts of Oldgate, the sullen outline of a distant hill on the horizon about two leagues away. The road appeared to run straight for it, through a brown and rocky plain where only a few trees struggled. He took a deep breath and strode onward, and he could now see that the pillars of Oldgate, standing some three times his own height, had strange symbols carved into them. The curved runes and letters of some ancient language, he thought, for he could read none of them.

"Good that I cannot," he thought as he passed hurriedly between them. "For I might not like what they say."

The road rose and fell and was less straight than it first appeared, but it was more or less flat and fairly direct, and it held toward the Hill. The breeze increased, hissing along the stunted grass, more brown than green, and in the southeast Robby saw flashes of lightning in the clouds, which froze him in his tracks. He did not like lightning, no one did, but he had always been fascinated by it. The power of those bolts to set fire to trees and houses, accompanied by their terrible cracking booms, was fearsome, to say nothing of the danger of being struck dead by one. More than one Barley farmer had been killed by them, and distant flashes were enough to send most people scurrying indoors or to their cellars, while those caught too far from shelter most usually responded by covering their eyes and falling to the ground. As a child, he was warned to stay away from the window during such storms, yet, on several occasions, Robby had slipped out of bed to kneel beside his window to watch the jagged fingers claw across the night sky. His friend Billy loved to tell gruesome stories about how one of their field workers was blown to bits by a bolt, with parts of his body, so Billy claimed, landing all over the place, and his clothes floating down from the sky, burning as they fell. Billy's mother, who was a wise country woman, once said that lightning was attracted to liars and cheats, wagging her finger at her son as a warning. Although Robby had serious doubts about the tale, and about what Billy's mother had said, he later realized that Billy never told yarns when there were dark clouds in the sky.

But once, while camping with Billy and Ibin, the three of them stood out in a night storm to watch it pass, braving the terrible noise and ground-shaking booms until, shivering with wet and fright, they could bear the storm no longer and retreated into their tent. There they huddled together, their eyes closed to the blinding flashes that penetrated their flimsy, wind-buffeted canvas, and pushed their hands hard against their ears to thwart the hammers of thunder. It was all very foolish, they knew, and they made a pact not to tell anyone, not only because they feared their parents would ban any future outings, but also because it was commonly considered bad luck to look upon lightning.

"What should I do?" he asked aloud as a jagged finger flashed across the southeastern clouds. He looked back the way he had come. Oldgate was still in sight, less than a mile back, and the green line of trees rising behind it. The low roll of thunder reached him, and he made up his mind.

"Ashlord's house has to be closer than any shelter I'd find by turning back," he thought as he looked around the strange landscape around him. The land was patchy with quick-moving shadows as the clouds blew in, covering and uncovering the sun. Stunted brush and grass rattled and hissed in the breeze, and just a few feet away was the crumbled remains of an old stone column, broken and mossy. Momentarily distracted, he realized as he continued to look around that many of the rocks jutting up through weed-choked mounds were likely the ruins of the town that was once here.

Shaking himself, he resumed with quickened step toward Tulith Attis just as the line dark clouds touched the sun. Soon Oldgate was out of sight and the way turned broadly northward; Robby saw that it turned again to the east up ahead where it ran between two high and long grassy barrows.

There was something eerie about how the mounds rose up, smooth and green with grass, rising out of the stunted and rocky fields all around. They were nearly rectangular in shape, their sides sloped with unnatural steepness for a height of ten or fifteen yards, running parallel for nearly a hundred yards with only some twenty yards between them. And there were seven standing stones arranged in a semicircular fashion where the way passed between the two mounds. Here the path widened, paved with huge flat stones so tightly joined that very little grass grew between them. As he continued along, Robby looked from side to side cautiously, feeling as if he were walking down a long, open hallway. These barrows were the burial places, it was said, of those who had died here in days almost forgotten, in the great battle his father had spoken of. And it was right here where his horse had suddenly panicked that day, some three years ago, bucking and twisting so that Robby flew from the saddle. Fortunately, Robby had landed against the grassy slope and not on one of the paving stones.

Robby paused, halfway through the barrows, hesitant and once more filled with a bewildering dread. He realized that, for all his pride and bravado, he had been afraid of coming out here ever since he agreed to do so. Perhaps that was why he let things get to him back at the stream, why he had convinced himself, even momentarily, that he saw and heard such strange things near the bridge, giving in to the fear that he sought to hide from Ullin and his father. And he was disappointed that he could be so spooked and nervous.

The air swirled around the mounds and came up behind him, interrupting his thoughts and nudging him along. He walked on, hearing only his own footfalls softly echoing from the grassy sides of the barrows. In spite of his resolution to put childish fears aside, the quietness of the place and the cool green of the mounds on either side of him, peaceful and brooding, had their way. He longed to climb one of them, to have a look around, to come up for air, so to speak. But he dared not. He had no desire to linger. And there, straight ahead, framed by the walls of the barrows, was Haven Hill, rising steep and stark, topped with the ancient battlements of Tulith Attis. All this only renewed Robby's pensiveness, as if his surroundings crowded and pressed around him. It was a feeling of closeness like when one's collar was buttoned too tight.

He hurried on and was soon away from the barrows, now giving his attention to the Hill, its abrupt slope jutting up on one side and tapering away out of sight farther south. High atop the hill, Robby could make out huge stones, covered in ivy and brush, and he wondered what power could have overthrown such a defense. The sun suddenly and completely disappeared into dark clouds. The wind blew steadily with sudden, powerful gusts, and Robby hunched against the buffeting, pressing forward along the path. Before he realized it, he was at the base of Haven Hill, directly beneath the summit of Tulith Attis, and the battlements high atop the sheer side of the hill loomed over him. Here the path forked, one way leading south, the other way north, each along the base of the hilltop fortress.

This he did not expect, nor did he remember seeing any sign of another road on the maps. Now he wished he had brought one along, after all. Both roads looked equally disused and both disappeared a short distance away to his right and to his left as they passed around the hill before him. No sign of house or trail of chimney smoke or footprints or bent weeds showed him which way to go, which way would lead to Ashlord's place. He remembered from the map that the main road led around the north side of Haven Hill and ended at a bridge.

"Well," he thought, "that shouldn't be too far off, and, since I shan't go any farther than that, I might as well try that way first. If I find nothing, I'll turn back and try the other way."

Turning his back on the south way, Robby started off northward as the first big drops of rain began clicking on the weeds and stones. He quickly pulled his cloak from his shoulder pack and threw it on, keeping the pack beneath it. The cloak would help some if it rained little, but was too light to be of much use in a downpour. "Better than nothing, though," he said aloud as he fastened it on.

The road hugged the base of the hill that rose steeply to Robby's right as he passed around it. From his point of view, the battlements high above leaned over him, ready to tumble down at any moment, it seemed, and in several places the ivy and brush had not yet taken hold of the walls and parapets, and he could see the gaps made into them for archers and other defenders to do their work. Robby passed other enormous stone blocks, vine-covered and cracked, alongside or even in the middle of the pathway, as if they had come loose and fallen, or had been cast down from the ramparts above, half buried where they crashed. On this side of the hill the way wound downward, still keeping to the foot of the fortress, but soon he could no longer see the top for the trees that grew there, great oaks and mighty poplars with sprawling limbs. The rain began in earnest, and the wind bent the trees, tearing off leaves and scattering them in the air around him. He pulled on his hood and strained to see any path that might lead off to some house, but as he kept on he could see no sign of one. He was now entering the rim of a dim forest, it was nearly as dark as night, and everywhere branches tossed this way and that noisily. Lightning flashed above him and instantly cracked sharply through the air. He briefly halted, gritting his teeth, but then continued on, the rain turning cold and hard, adding its noise to all the rest. Several times the heavy gush of raindrops fooled him into thinking someone was behind him, and he whirled around to see who it was, but no one was ever there. He reached for his dagger, his only weapon, but found that it was gone: he had left it, he realized, on the bridge at Weepingbrook, the stream's name no longer escaping him. He would just have to pick it up on the way back home.

He threw off his hood so as to peer around more easily, and trudged on, rain streaming down his face, the roadway now muddy and filled with water running down from the fortress slopes in little streams every few yards. The darkness of the storm deepened, and he could see that the road straightened ahead, and he saw some vague lines which, as the road once again leveled, became the outline of an old stone bridge.

"Oh, good grief! Ashlord must live around on the other side."

Robby turned to go back, then stopped, looking at the bridge.

"I don't know when I'll be along this way again, so I might as well take a look," he shrugged and proceeded onto the bridge.

It was a carefully laid structure, larger and longer than he had first thought. As he approached, he saw that the stone curbs that lined each side were above his waist, and the width of the bridge was twice that of the road itself. He could not see to the other side where it entered the gloom of the Boggy Wood. As he cautiously stepped onto the bridge, he felt it must have been built on tall stone arches, such as he had seen in some of Mr. Broadweed's picture books, for the bridge was the most massively built structure Robby had ever seen, with the exception of the looming fortress itself. Keeping to one side, he moved around brush and limbs that littered its surface. Several times, he stopped to lean over the side to have a look below. The bridge seemed to stretch over a deep ravine, wider than the river Bentwide and so deep he could not see the bottom in the darkness of the storm. He kept moving, and kept trying to see over the side; but even with the flashing light, he could not make out what was below, seeing only the tops of trees, no river or stream. Passing what he thought was halfway, he continued on carefully toward the other side to see where the bridge ended, thinking at first that part of it perhaps had fallen away. But as he neared, he saw that the far wood had encroached onto the end of the bridge. There, a large tree had fallen onto the bridge, and through its rotting branches grew an immense tangle of vines covered with black thorns that glistened ominously in the rain. Robby stared at the natural barrier, trying to look beyond it into the forest itself.

Making out nothing through the thorny brambles that covered that end of the bridge, he shrugged again and turned around to go back the way he had come. As he neared the middle of the bridge, something moved into the roadway ahead and Robby stopped, blinking rain from his eyes in an effort to make it out. Whatever it was, it was low to the ground, crouching, and Robby instinctively tensed, balling his fists. Perhaps it was only some leafy branch, blown down by the storm, and he edged nearer. Another form appeared to one side and behind the first one. In spite of the storm's noise, he heard a sound, a low guttural noise that sent the hair up on the back of his neck. Lightning flashed and cracked, and he could see them briefly and clearly, another loping into view during the brilliant moment.

"Wolves!" he breathed, backing away quickly. This was what his father had warned about, and now, without his knife, he was defenseless. In vain, Robby looked for a stick or branch but saw a loose stone, the size of his fist, and picked it up as he continued to back away. The wolves seemed reluctant to enter the bridge and did so slowly, snarling as they came, their heads down below their hunched shoulders, miserable and hungry-looking in the cold rain. Robby saw two more join in at their rear.

"Begone!" Robby called out suddenly, waving his arms. It did not work. On came the animals, and Robby continued backing up until he could feel the thorns clawing at him from behind, moving in the wind and slashing at his cloak like hundreds of thin arms tipped with talons. Now the lead wolf was within ten yards, and Robby had nowhere to go. Lightning flashed again, and Robby saw a small opening in the vines, low down, that appeared to run under a great branch of the fallen tree. Turning around, he saw that one of the wolves had jumped up onto the stone curb to his left and was quickly approaching. Just as the beast was readying to leap at him, Robby threw the stone with all his might and turned to scramble under the vines. The rock hit the wolf squarely in the head, sending him sideways in pain, and, losing its footing, it fell yelping off the bridge, its cry cut short by the beast's impact far below. The other wolves moved in as Robby crawled under the trunk, the thorns he pushed through clawing and digging into his cloak, holding him back. Pulling hard, he heard the fabric rip and more yelping as thorns whipped back and into the eyes of one of the wolves and pierced the ear of another as they hurled themselves snarling and biting at Robby's feet. This sent them into a frenzy of snapping and biting at each other, starting an incredible fight among themselves. Robby continued to scramble away as fast as he could manage, jerking and pulling through the thorns, heedless of the cuts and gashes they inflicted, trying to shield his face and eyes from the barbs. Suddenly he was free of the vines and stumbled into some clear ground on the other side of the bridge. He got to his feet and charged on through the thick brush until, between the rain and the darkness and his own panic, he could no longer tell where he was, much less which way he should go.

# Chapter 3

# The Fortress

He did not know how far from the bridge he had gone, or if any of the wolves had managed to follow him, but it was not long before his panic gave way to growing alarm at his situation. He sat down on a log to rest and to think. He was on the wrong side of the bridge, in a wood he was warned against. It was raining cold buckets. He was cut, and watery blood ran down his arms and legs. It was dark in the wood under the clouds and would soon be even darker as night fell. Even if he could find his way back to the bridge, there was no telling if the wolves still prowled there. And if he got past them, it was a long walk back around Tulith Attis to the fork in the road. From there who could say how far to Ashlord's house? Robby was beginning to doubt whether Ashlord even lived out here. Who in their right mind would?

"Ashlord better have some good reason for being so hard to find," he said, standing up. "Well, there's nothing for it but to go back." He looked around and found a large, thick stick and swung it against a tree trunk several times. It didn't break.

"This will do, I guess. What I wouldn't give for one of Ullin's swords, or even my little knife!"

The way back toward the bridge was just as hard as the way from it, and he had to skirt several large thorny vines that he did not remember passing previously. Knocking his way through thick bushes with his makeshift cudgel, he felt as if the wood did not want him to return to the bridge. He had the silly but eerie sensation of being watched, and he did not like the way the trees waved their limbs about so freely. After an hour of struggling along, he suddenly found himself at the edge of a steep drop-off. Robby realized that he had gotten off track and was uncertain which way to turn to find the bridge. He could see no more than a few yards through the brambles in either direction. Chancing a fall, he edged down the slope a few feet to try for a better look, and he soon spotted the bridge to his right, much farther away than he imagined it could be. A sharp flash of lightning revealed how massive it was, spanning across three tall arches, below which grew tall oaks that did not even reach the lowest arch. He also saw the unmistakable shapes of several wolves moving about the bridge.

"Well, that's pretty hopeless," he said. Looking across the ravine and upward, he could make out through the trees the ramparts of the fortress and thought he saw, lower down, some remnants of a wall. It was then he realized that this part of Haven Hill was man-made, an ancient fortress, since ruined by the wear of uncounted years and nearly covered over by time.

He weighed his options. Hanging about in the woods as night fell was not something he wanted to do. If he could get across this ravine, and move up the other side undetected by the wolves, he might be able to climb that lower wall. Up there might be a way around and back to the other side. He doubted the wolves would be able to climb as well as he, anyway.

He started down the ravine. By now it was late afternoon, and, even if the sun had been out, Robby would have been in deep shadows. As it was, with rain pouring from black clouds, the light was so dim, and the flashes of lightning so sudden and garish, that Robby strained to see, with moments of brilliantly clear sight followed by brief blindness before his eyes readjusted to the gloom. Several times he missed his footing and slid downwards, once even slipping over the side of a steep overhang only to spill down through the top of a tree, snapping off branches as he fell, and landing against the hard roots. Before he could grab hold of anything, he slipped farther down a muddy slope, tumbling several yards before coming to a sudden stop sideways against a mossy rock. He knew that he most certainly could not climb back the way he had come, so he continued on downward, hoping the way up the other side would be easier. While negotiating a mossy outcrop where rainwater poured downward in hundreds of little waterfalls, he lost both his grip and his footing once more and slid with the slushing water into a bone-chilling and muddy stream at the very bottom of the ravine. The cold flow pushed hard, knocking him off his balance each time he tried to stand.

The stream was nearly twenty feet wide and no telling how deep, but the current wedged him up against a log that nearly spanned all the way across. Gripping the slippery surface of the log, he inched out into the flow until his feet no longer touched bottom. Breathing hard with cold and fear, he knew he had to keep going. Pulling off his shoulder bag, he put it on top of the log to keep it as dry as possible and slowly made his way across, pushing the bag ahead a little and then, by gripping dead branches, moving forward himself. The water threatened to pull him under, and the log lurched and shifted constantly, but more branches still attached to the log underwater provided some footings here and there. After a long, slow time of it, with many pauses to consider his next hand-hold, he was within five feet of the steep far side. First, he flung his bag onto the bank where it landed safely in some brambles, and he then lunged forward. After swallowing much mud, he pulled himself out and up the bank by grasping at every root and rock he could lay his hands on. Thoroughly soaked, he dragged himself onto a slippery outcrop, turning over onto his back, dizzy and cold, his breath like clouds as he panted.

The light continued to dim, and the storm roared through the trees, drowning out the sound of the stream. He thought he could see a ledge farther up, but he could not be sure with all of the water streaming off it and down onto him. Toward the bridge, this side of the ravine sharpened its slope until, just before the spanning arches, it was a sheer rock face. Yet the ledge seem to go in that direction, so he carefully began climbing, picking up his bag as he went, moving sideways away from the bridge since that seemed the easiest way up. Stopping often to catch his breath and to study his way, he inched upward, slipping time and time again, checking his fall by clawing at root and rock.

It was now raining torrents, everywhere water poured into the ravine, and Robby had to keep his eyes shut tight and his head down to shield against the gritty debris that gushed over him. Nearly at the end of his strength, he finally gained the ledge and crawled over it. He then tried to squeeze under the stump of an old, blasted tree where he thought to find some shelter. After his exertions, he was now hot and somewhat thankful for the cool rain. Only moments later, he was shivering, and he realized he had to keep moving, or perhaps never move again. He made himself get up, and he began going along the ledge toward the bridge.

He had not gone far when the ledge widened out and leveled somewhat so that he could walk along it without holding onto anything. Several times he had to negotiate around or over fallen rocks and trees, but he now made steady progress. The ledge turned abruptly to the left around an outcrop and into a gash in the sheer rock face. Looking down, he could see the stream only a short distance below, swelling over a waterfall. Looking up, he could only see flat rock where not even moss or ivy had taken hold, disappearing into the gloom above. Gripping what he hoped was a sturdy root, he leaned around the slippery corner, and, much to his surprise, saw a series of flat stones set into the rock like steps, leading down a few yards then back up to an open area almost level with his head. It seemed like the out-jutting of some greater ledge, perhaps, but Robby could see little from his position and started toward it, clinging to roots until he was sure of his footing on the first step. Easily making the other steps from there, he walked upward, passing blocks of stone that rimmed the wall with large, thick, rusty iron rings set into them, as if to hold ropes or chains, though none could be seen. As he wondered at their purpose, the steps took him to the top of a large balcony or landing, of sorts, paved with flat stones. They were coated with thin moss, and through the cracks small oak saplings struggled to root from their acorns. Trying to make out the purpose of this structure, Robby explored it carefully, seeing no way off except the way he had come.

It was about forty yards, squarish, with three of its sides formed by sheer walls rising upward out of sight. The back wall of the place, directly below the battlements high above, was covered with dead trees and limbs that had fallen from overhead, and were covered with ivy and brush. The opposite side, facing the ravine, dropped straight down and was as sheer and slick as the upward walls. He supposed he would have to backtrack along the ledge the way he had come until he could find a spot to climb down, there to make his way upstream to find a better place to climb out. Robby moved to the back of the landing, looking for some place out of the driving rain. Lightning flashed, briefly revealing the outline of something against the wall. Looking carefully, he could barely make out some broad stone steps leading into the huge pile of brush that had built up against the wall over many years. When the lightning flashed again, he saw a stone archway set into the wall behind the brambly mess.

"Aha!" he cried. "A cave or some little porch set into this wall would do nicely right about now!" He quickly pulled away some of the limbs and branches. "Especially if it is not presently occupied," he added, glad that the vines he blindly tore away were not thorny.

It was not a cave, but was some other kind of opening about twice his own height and almost as wide. When the lightning flashed, he could see only a few feet into it, but he made out the distinct lines of broad steps leading upward into even deeper darkness. Cautiously, he picked his way through the remaining debris, and for the first time in hours was out of the rain.

He plunged onto the interior steps and sprawled out, exhausted. After a moment, he began taking stock of things. It seemed warmer in here, not as dank as one might have imagined such a place, but he hardly had a mind to think on it. Soon it would be dark in earnest, and this seemed as good a place as any to wait out the rain. But the storm only seemed to increase its fury, and the crashing thunder rang inside the tunnel like kettle drums as the wind tore into the place, sending sheets of rain and leaves along with a few branches flying inside, driving Robby up a few more steps. Robby thought of his parents, and he regretted not turning back at the first sign of rain. If he had done so, he would nearly be home by now. He was angry at himself at how sick with worry they must be, and he was sorely tempted to leave at that very moment, and he stood up as if to do so. Suddenly, something came to him, like a voice, almost. "Be safe," he could hear his father say. The thought calmed Robby, and he resolved not to compound the poor decision he had made earlier with another one now.

So, he sat back down. His stomach growled, and he fished around in his bag for some victuals, and his hand passed over his lamp. He pulled it out and examined it in the nearly continuous flashing light. Folding it together, he saw that the glass was still intact, which was something of a miracle given the beating his shoulder bag and all its contents had taken. The parcel was still there, too, and the rest of his meager gear. The bread was a soggy mess, and the cheese a bit mushy, but he was happy to eat, and soon it was all gone. Feeling a bit warmer than before and better for the food, he decided it was time to explore this hole, and he got out the little tin of firesticks that his father had given him.

"I'd feel better for sure if I still had that knife, too," he said to himself as he opened the tin. Robby proceeded carefully. The vial was sealed with wax over a cork and held six small splinters of oilwood; the tip of each had been dipped into an alchemy paste and allowed to dry. The dried paste formed a hard tip that would, when struck just right, bubble and boil and emit a sulfurous odor. If luck was with you, the tip of the splinter would catch on fire. One had to be very careful with them, he knew. Not only could they seriously burn you, they were also unreliable, especially in the wind or when wet, and they were very expensive—this little tin was the price of a good pair of boots. Mr. Ribbon called them more of a novelty than anything else, but held that even impractical things sometimes had their uses. By now Robby's hands were fairly dry, but it was still windy in the hole, and moist, so he moved up a few more steps with his lamp and the tin of firesticks and crouched over them. He undid the cork on the vial, trying not to let the water still dripping from his head touch them, removed one splinter, and carefully recorked the vial. He opened the small lamp's door and tightened the candle and put it down on a stair step. Finally, he held the tin containing the firesticks so that the bottom of the lid was exposed, and he deftly scratched the firestick against it. A glint of red light appeared on the splinter and brightened as it boiled, sending tiny streams of smoking, red drops of fire crackling out from it. It faded. Just as Robby's heart sank, the wooden tip burst into bright flame with a *piff!* Elated, Robby quickly lit the candle and blew out the splinter. Making sure it was out by squeezing it between his fingers, he put the piece of wood back into the tin and slipped the tin back into his bag. He picked up his lamp, closed its door, and held it up to direct the light around him.

The room he was in was only a landing at the opening of a stairway passage, its walls and arched ceiling laid in smooth granite. As he reached out to touch the wall, he noticed for the first time the many cuts and scratches on his arms and hands that, washed by the rain, now bled profusely. Looking himself over, he realized he was covered with gashes and cuts, and his clothes were a ragged mess, blotted all over with red. He was in pain, for the many wounds stung, his muscles throbbed, and his bones ached. Yet he considered himself lucky to have escaped the wolves and to have found a place like this to wait out the storm. Wiping some of the blood from his arms and hands, he continued to examine his surroundings.

The staircase, broad enough for four men abreast, curved gently upward and out of sight around a bend and into the darkness above. Everywhere was grime and spider webs, and in the corner a startled chipmunk chirped and disappeared into a tiny crevice. Robby could see by the wear on the stone that the steps had once been well used. Here and there water trickled down the side of the walls near the opening, but farther in and upward they were dry, and no water ran down the stairs from above. He closed and secured the flap on his shoulder bag and slowly ascended the stairs, silently counting his steps, thinking to gain some clue to how high the stairs went. He soon realized the calculation would be beyond him, and, anyway, what did it matter? There was no air movement, and he was sure the way must be blocked up ahead. The rusty remains of iron braziers were set into the wall at regular intervals, and, as he climbed, the moist grime was gradually replaced by dry dust. By now, the crash of the storm was somewhat distant and hollow-sounding from below. After a little more climbing, the stairs ended onto a landing, and he stood before a large door of worm-eaten oak nearly a hand in thickness, studded and shod with once-strong iron, now rusted and flaking away with age. He pushed on it, and, to his surprise, it cracked and groaned and opened about a foot before its rusted hinges gave and the door sagged and jammed on the floor as a brief, cool feather of air touched his face. Squeezing through the opening, he discovered a large room, and as he swung his light around, he caught his breath and flinched at the shape of a man standing near the wall. Although there was nothing to fear from the statue, his heart still pounded as he continued to peer around.

It was a large round chamber, and his feeble light did not reach to the other side or to the ceiling. By working his lamp up and down, he saw the shape of the room and many colors. Immediately beside the doorway sat several large wide-mouthed ceramic jars, sealed with stone stoppers and putty. Behind them in an iron rack were old wooden torches, their wicks long rotted away and the shafts so brittle that when Robby touched one, it fell into dust. Realizing what they were for, Robby put down his lamp and broke open the nearest jar. Just as he thought, the pungent aroma of stale, pitchy oil wafted out as soon as he opened it. An idea came to him, and, taking hold of the oak door, he pulled away many splinters as long as his arm. Ripping some strips of cloth from his already ragged cloak, he bound the sticks together tightly and plunged the end of the bundle into the jar. He lifted the makeshift torch out and let it drip before carefully lighting it with his lamp. The brand blazed to life with bright, orange-yellow light. As Robby gently swung the torch around, he gasped again and took a step backward.

The round walls were covered in murals, six in all, three on two sides of the great room and each of them separated by the column base of one of the six crossing arches that ran up and joined far overhead on the white-tiled ceiling. The arches were painted in gold, and into the columns were carved life-sized figures of men and women, some mighty warriors in mail, some with crowns or circlets of gold upon their heads, and some holding scepters, all standing erect and tall but with their heads bowed upon their chests, as if resting or in prayer. In the center of the room was a marble banister bordering a round dais. There, suspended from the center of the joined arches by a chain of ornately worked iron, each ring as large as Robby's hands, hung a vast bell, nearly a third as wide as the room itself, cast in black iron, set with silver runes, and adorned with green enameled ivy from which bloomed golden flowers. Robby bent to pass under the banister and ran his hand along the cool rim of the bell, wiping away some of the dust that lay upon it. Its bottom rim hung at his knees, and the top dome of it was far over his head as he passed around it looking at the strange designs, much like those upon the pillars of Oldgate. Striking it with his fist, it made not a sound nor did it move, but Robby thought he heard a noise circle the room like a soft and sudden inhalation of air, and the flame from his torch flickered in an unfelt breeze. He looked around, startled at the whisper, and the hair on the back of his neck tingled. The thin cobwebs that draped the room stirred ever-so-slightly, giving the figures an illusion of movement and raising gooseflesh on Robby's arms. A distant rumble reminded him of the storm outside and the wind that must be howling up the staircase tunnel.

Robby turned his attention to the rest of the strange room, determined to explore and understand as much as he could. The murals depicted many different kinds of scenes: One was of a fearsome battle, with antler-helmeted combatants and silver-helmed archers amid a great slaughter of men and beasts and other strange and frightful creatures who walked upright, but they were not men. Another mural showed a great fleet of ships plying the blue-green seas under billowy white sails, landing upon a green-hilled shore. One mural revealed a blue-towered city of green and gold set against dark forested mountains, and another portrayed woodland gardens thick with blossoms of every color and description awash with springs of flowing water in slanted beams of sunlight piercing a green forest canopy. He passed from one mural to the next, studying the faces of those depicted and the device upon their shields, sails, and banners—a pale-blue star entwined with green ivy with gold flowers on a field of white. And around each mural, above and below, were more lines of the ancient writing, their curved shapes meticulously carved into the stone. On the far side of the room from where Robby had entered was a wider and higher doorway, and the figures on either side were of a finely robed man and woman, he with a golden, ivy-encrusted helmet, and she with a silver circlet. Each held up one hand, as in a gesture asking someone to wait. The man gripped a sword, its tip resting at his feet, and the woman held a scepter. Like all of the other statues in the room, their heads were bowed. He stopped underneath the lady, put his hand on the pedestal, and leaned in to see her face. Robby was surprised at the detail in the carving that showed the eyelashes of her closed eyes. He thought her face familiar, though he could not say why. Beneath her ivied crown flowed coal-black hair that curved down around her bowed head and draped over her shoulders and across her back. Her face was pale, yet so delicately painted that he could see a faint blush upon her cheeks, as if embarrassed by his gaze. Seemingly, not a speck of paint had ever flecked away, her lips still as rosy-red as when the statue was made, and the more he looked, the more he thought he saw a slight smile upon them. And for the second time in a single day, he remembered the strangers, the gentlewomen that came to him when he was sick as a child, and he thought he saw their faces somehow reflected in that of this eerie statue. A little melody, melancholy and delicate, now came back to him as he remembered the mysterious song they had sung to him, sweet and low, as they bent over his fevered body, touching their hands upon his brow.

Between the two statues opened a high arched door to another room, smaller and rectangular, but of equal height. Robby's torch revealed that its walls were unadorned, except by the same white tile that covered the ceiling of the bell room. Its chief feature was a great portal, fitted with a massive iron door guarded on either side by fierce-looking stone warriors, each standing from the floor nearly to the ceiling, one brandishing a sword held with both hands high to one side, the other wielding in like manner a great war hammer. Unpainted they were, and coarsely carved, their eyes as blank as their expressionless faces. Between the two, the iron door stood, solid with no bands or rivets, smooth and without hinge, lock, or handle, a solid wall of metal completely sealing the portal, with not even a crack between it and the stone into which it was set. Robby stared up at it and then at the two towering guards that straddled it, and saw over the door, carved on the lintel, an inscription in the same familiar but indecipherable writing as upon Oldgate. He remembered his order book. Placing the torch into a brazier on the wall, he took out the small, leather-bound pad of paper and copied the inscription as best as he could. He might someday learn this script, he thought, or perhaps come back here and decipher it along with the other runes he had seen. As he copied, the light from his torch grew dimmer, and he hurriedly finished the job, then returned to the oil jars.

As he worked to make another torch, he could faintly hear the noise of the storm thudding through the staircase nearby. Thinking he had best check on his exit, he gathered his things and started down. The air became decidedly cold as he descended, and when he came to the bottom, the gusty wind through the door nearly blew out his now-feeble torch.

"I'd better have a look around," he said, thrusting the torch into a safe nook. Satisfied that it would not immediately blow out, he pulled his hood over his head and ducked through the brush covering the doorway and out onto the landing. It was still raining, but the noise of the stream was as loud as the storm. He walked to the edge and saw in the lightning flashes that it had swollen considerably by at least three or four feet. Clearly, it would be impossible to ford the swift and violent currents now crashing through the ravine, fed from all sides by countless rivulets.

"Well," he sighed, "there's no getting back that way."

Turning toward the bridge, he looked again for some way to it, but the wall was as sheer and smooth as before, with no step or handhold anywhere that he could see. It occurred to him that perhaps the way he had come, the ledge walkway, led to another pass or path that went farther upward against the side of Haven Hill, a way that he had perhaps missed earlier. After all, he reasoned, he had not been looking very carefully before, being in something of a panic. He resolved to go that way as soon as there was light. Meanwhile he could sleep dry and relatively warm on the inside of the hill. There was no more food left, but surely enough water.

After being inside, it actually felt good to Robby to stand outside in the open, even in the driving rain, and so he was reluctant to go back in. To him this place was fearful, though strangely fascinating, and almost peaceful.

"But it has the peace of a graveyard," he blurted out, glancing back at the light flickering behind the branches and vines from the obscured doorway. He turned and looked at the stream again, and realized that his eyes had adjusted to the dark, and he could make out the gushing water even without the lightning flashes, as if some strange glow filled the sky above and filtered downward with the rain through the trees overhead. It seemed that the water was even closer to him than before. Shaking himself, he gasped at the realization that the water was indeed rising very quickly, and, unless he was mistaken, it had nearly doubled in height just since only a little while ago. Every stream and brook, swollen into a flood, was draining into the ravine, it seemed. And, in addition to the roar of thunder and the racing water, he heard the crashing of trees as they were swept into the flood.

"Not good!" he said. "Not good at all!"

He sprang back into the tunnel, grabbed his bag, leaving the torch behind, got back out onto the landing, and started down the steps to the walkway along the ledge. If he could find another way around, and up, he might save himself. Otherwise, he faced being trapped in the interior of the fortress if the waters continued to rise. And he knew full well from living beside one that rivers always crested after the heaviest rains had passed. He bounded down the few steps and up onto the ledge and rounded the corner, slipping as he turned, nearly flinging his shoulder bag away as he regained footing, and, at the same time, surprising a scraggly wolf.

"Whoa!" Robby cried, scrambling back. The wolf growled and snapped at him, retreating a few feet as several more crowded up behind, all snarling. Robby raced up the steps, onto the landing, and into the tunnel, snatching up the dying torch. The wolves were already scratching at the limbs, and one had his head halfway in when Robby thrust the torch into his face so hard that it nearly extinguished in the wet fur. The wolf yelped and backed out, but others scrambled to get past him and into the entrance. Robby flew up the staircase, now guarding the end of the torch with one hand like a candle, so afraid he was that it would go out. At last, huffing and panting, he made it to the upper landing and into the bell room.

"Trapped!" he cried, unable to close the door. "Trapped!"

He set to work, and quickly pulled more of the timber from the door until he had a large, thick stick. He hesitated for a moment, hefting it in his hand. No, he decided, it was too rotten to use as a weapon, so he worked feverishly to rip more fabric from his cloak while the other torch slowly faded. He could hear the noise of the animals on the staircase as he finished tying off the makeshift wick and thrust it into the pot. He gently picked up the dying ember, and, pulling the new torch out of the oil pot, he touched it to the old one. The new torch exploded into flames, dripping with fire as Robby moved through the door. Out on the staircase, he could hear them coming and thought the best plan was to take the offensive, to drive them out and clear a path through them to the ledge. Soon, he feared, the water would seal them all inside together.

Robby could not know the extent of the wolf pack, which was in fact several rival packs driven together by the rising floodwaters and now converging on the same place for lack of anywhere else to go. As Robby strode down the stairs, he thought he had only four or five to confront. However, more than sixty of the beasts were clawing and biting at each other to make the landing, some falling off the ledge or pushed off by other wolves. Many of them were swept away by the rushing waters before they could make the landing or else their numbers would have been many times greater. So it was that the rising waters threatened all alike as Robby descended the stairs. As he rounded the last bend, he was assaulted by a cacophony of howls and whines and barks and snarls as the beasts pushed themselves into the tunnel and up the stairs. Robby's sudden reappearance startled them and caused those nearest to him to rush back into the doorway, setting off another vicious fight with those behind still trying to enter. Robby instantly realized the situation and fled back upstairs, knowing he had no chance of pushing through such a deadly mob.

He reached the landing and entered the bell room, and he immediately he tried again to shove the great door closed, but it was hopelessly mangled and far too massive for him to budge. He turned inward, suddenly feeling threatened on every side: the carved figures surrounding the room now menaced the place, their forms stern and forbidding in the blazing light. He considered trying to climb the bell, but there were no handholds.

He grabbed one of the full jars of oil and heaved it up into his arms. Carefully holding the torch away from it, he lifted the other open jar by its rim and made his way back through the door. By now the wolves were coming up the stairs, and he could hear their noisy approach and smell the foul reek of their coats. Dropping the torch, he continued down a few more steps and poured the oil from the open jar, letting the stuff run down the staircase. He let the jar roll away, bouncing a few times before it shattered. He could hear the scratching and sliding of claws from around the curve as the wolves met the slippery oil. He lifted the other jar with both hands over his head and let it fly as far as he could. It struck the stairs and showered oil and gooey pitch downward, setting off a new round of yelps. Picking up the torch, he nervously lit the oil. Flames ran down the stairs, lighting up the passage in a garish light and filling the air with black smoke. As the fire reached the bend and exploded downward, the howls became frenzied and hysterical. Running back up the stairs, Robby turned, and, in disbelief, saw several flaming wolves following him.

The stench of burning fur mixed with choking smoke assailed his lungs. And now it was hopeless, indeed, for the way was blocked by both flames and enraged wolves, and Robby was on the verge of desperate tears as he fled through the room and to the other side, looking for another way out that he had missed before. But there was none, and he found himself before the great iron door. By now smoke was filling the bell room, and several smoldering wolves entered the far door. And though Robby could not see from where he was, at the very instant the beasts stepped into the main room from the stairway, all of the carved figures lifted their heads, and their eyes opened with a blaze of golden light. Coughing and gagging on the smoke, Robby backed into the iron door between the great warriors, oblivious to their glowing eyes. He stared at the approaching wolves, and the others that were joining in, thinking the eerie and growing light in the room was from the fire, fixated by the foam-dripping fangs of his attackers. He turned and pounded at the iron door with his fists.

"Open!" he cried. Robby flinched away as the door lurched with a shrill grinding of metal against metal. It then slid straight down out of the way and disappeared through a crack in the floor, landing somewhere below with an earth-shaking thud that brought down dust and chips from the ceiling. Bits of stone flaked from the cheeks and bare arms of the two warriors, and Robby stumbled forward in a nightmare state of panic. He did not notice holes in the ceiling where steady streams of sand now came pouring out, nor had a mind to care if he had noticed. But the opening of the iron door set in motion the release of sand from three chambers above, each housing an iron ball the size of a pumpkin. As the sand leaked out, each ball descended in slow turn, one before the other, sinking downward onto rails that would set them rolling along stone-laid tracks within hidden conduits above.

Meanwhile, Robby stumbled along the passageway before him, dark doorways opening to his left and right, but he kept on straight. Behind him, the noise of a terrible fight broke out, and he thought he heard the sound of ringing steel and pounding iron amid the screams of the wolves, and it distantly occurred to him that the beasts must have tipped over some of the statues in their frenzy. Suddenly, he came upon another door, this one of stone with the remnants of a lock as big as his hand. He slapped the lockplate, and it instantly burst asunder, the door toppling away from him and shattering into heaps of rubble. Cold wind and rain burst in from the gloom beyond as Robby scrambled out and onto a steep mossy staircase. His torch sputtered in the wind and died, lightning flashed overhead, and as he climbed the last few steps, he found himself to be on the very crest of Tulith Attis, surrounded by the ancient walls of the fortress.

The storm roared with terrible cracks of continuous lightning and thunder. After a moment, disoriented by the rain and noise and brilliant flashes, Robby saw a wide, round ground, a bailey surrounded by high, vine-covered walls. Turning in every direction, trying to see a way out of the fortress, he spotted the decrepit gateway at the far side and ran toward it, dodging holes and scrambling over rubble, shielding his eyes against the hard rain and the blinding lightning. He saw as he went many ivy-shrouded stone columns, just over his height and shoulder wide, standing in groups all around the yard, and some atop the parapets, but he had no time to wonder at their purpose. Halfway across, the lightning flashed again, and he could clearly see the gate ahead, and, just as plainly, a throng of wolves moving through it into the fortress. Sliding to a halt, he saw a stairway leading up the side of the east wall, and he ran to it and up, slipping a time or two on the mossy stones, until he reached the top of the great wall of the fortress. Peering over the side, he looked for a way off the summit. But all he could see in the flashes of light was a raging river where once the ravine had been. He ran across the wall to the other side, then along the southern face, scrambling around crumbled portions and climbing over piles of rubble. When he had gotten all the way around to the opposite side of the fortress, he looked westward, toward Barley, but could make out no details in the flatlands beyond the base of the hill and could barely even see to the barrows below. The only way off the ramparts was back down the way he had come or else over the side down the sheer walls. He made up his mind to do that, if he had to. He could still hear the noise from within the bell room, and he could not understand how the wolves could be so delayed from following him. In a panic, he continued to run along the wall, dodging around the odd columns that he met, but he could find no place where he thought he could scale down the outside face of the walls. At one point, when he looked over, he realized he must be over the gate, for when the lightning flashed, he saw what he thought to be hundreds of wolves crowding through the wall and disappearing below. Edging over to the inner side, he looked down and saw them emerging into the fortress, running here and there as if looking for him. Scrambling back, he ran along the ramparts, crouching against the torrential rain, searching for another way down and away from the wolves.

Deep within the fortress, one of the great iron balls settled onto the inclined track that had been crafted for it and began to roll. Like thunder rising from the ground, its course rumbled through the interior of the hill. Robby heard the queer sound and froze. The iron ball burst through the ceiling of the bell room and struck the bell with such a roar that Robby stumbled, instinctively clutching his ears. The fortress shook violently as the din reverberated, the ivy fell from the stone columns, and loose blocks crumbled from the parapets and tumbled down. As the sound faded, the second iron ball began its course and rumbled along its track toward the great bell. During this, the wolves were howling deliriously at the air, running around senselessly, biting stone, vine, and their own flesh alike in their madness. Robby staggered to his feet. The second ball struck the bell with the same force as the first. The clang ripped through the stormy country, and Robby reeled sideways to stay on his feet, screaming with pain, but he could not hear himself over the toll. Losing his balance, he stumbled and slipped off the edge of the wall. Thrashing wildly for some vine to hold, he fell forty feet, landing squarely on top of a wolf with a sickening crunch, killing the beast instantly, and knocking the breath out of himself. Gasping for air, he crawled to his feet, and in madness akin to that of the wolves, he ran, yelling as he went, to the center of the fortress, kicking or beating away with his fists the foul-smelling animals that threw themselves at him, biting at his legs and arms and leaping against his back as he fled. Once more there came a rumble of iron and the crash of the great bell, and once again the ground shook and even the rain seem to flee away. Robby and all of the wolves were completely knocked off their feet, stunned into senselessness as the boom ripped eastward through the Boggy Wood. It galloped away westward over the far mountains and the plains beyond, it thundered and rolled north and south, and it blasted the very rain from the air.

In the stunned silence following the deafening toll, still air descended thick with fog, disturbed only by the return of a distant echo. Overhead, the storm-clouds thinned, and high Lady Moon cast her full pale light on the blue-gray mists that floated all around. Robby staggered to his shaking knees in shock and bewilderment, his head spinning. The dreadful ringing in his ears was made all the louder by the stark hush that settled like a mantle on the old fortress, as tangible as the thickening fog. Around him, the wolves lay scattered, some struggling to gain their feet, others mewling, and a few already up and coming at him, swaying drunkenly from side to side, their heads down, bloody foam dripping from their snouts. Robby heard a slight snap, like the breaking of a dry twig, and then a crack, and another one, sharper, more distinct, from another direction. More snaps, like the breaking of brittle crackers, or the clattering of small pebbles falling upon stone, coming from all around the fortress. He got to his feet, fell down to one knee, got up again, and fell again on all fours, weak and terrorized. Looking around, he saw no source of the odd sound in the strange light, but he was dizzy, and he staggered onto his side, his head spinning, looking for an escape. A new movement caught his eye.

What he saw was more than he could bear. The columns that stood all around were shedding chips of stone, cracking and crumbling away to reveal vague shapes of some other material beneath. The shapes grew more distinct. To Robby's shock, a face appeared on the one nearest to him, then a shoulder and part of an arm. Robby whimpered, backing away from the emerging form. The wolves began barking and snarling at the columns, all of which were hatching strange beings. Robby then saw what looked to be polished steel, scarlet robes, and glittering mail, as from each column a soldier emerged dressed in gleaming armor, bearing in one hand a straight, bright sword and in the other a shield. Upon their heads were helmets of black, threaded with green vines and golden flowers, like the bell in the bell room, and the device upon their red, burnished shields was the same ivy-shrouded star he had seen on the sails of the ships in the mural. Their faces were fair and pale and their eyes silvery-green like the maple leaf in spring. They looked sternly at one another as if awakened from only a moment's nap, and gazed hard all around, filling Robby with a new terror, though he was half-entranced by their appearance.

At that moment, the wolves were filled with fury. They charged the strange warriors, screaming with their dog-like voices—words almost, their barks and howls like horrid curses—flinging themselves through the air with their front paws outstretched, baring their claws. Yet the soldiers strode into them resolutely and hewed into the beasts with their swords. Screaming with terror, Robby crawled on his back, unable to get to his legs or to turn away from the hideous onslaught. Steel sang through bone and hissed through flesh. All around, Robby saw the wolves regroup and attack the ghostly fighters again and again. One of the soldiers who wore a circlet of gold rather than a helmet was beset by six of the creatures. With his blood-dripping shield he confidently faced and made a slaughter of the beasts, neatly lopping off the head of one and hewing another entirely in half. Robby marveled fearfully at this man, and yet he wanted to run to him for protection, and perhaps even to serve him, but too many wolves were between the two. In a language unknown to Robby, the great warrior cried out.

"No mercy! Death to all intruders of Tulith Attis!"

And all around from his comrades came the answer in defiant voices, "Death to all!! Death to all!"

Finally, Robby got to his feet and was turning to run when a great wolf came sailing through the air, swinging his claws at him. Before he could react, an arrow pierced the beast's neck, and it was already dead when it collided with Robby, knocking him back down. Yelling with revulsion and fear, he shoved the carcass off his chest and was getting to his feet again when another wolf fell dead before him, this time with an arrow through its eye. Suddenly, he found himself encircled by soldiers, the remaining wolves scattering away into the blades of their rallying comrades. Standing before them, his heart racing and his head spinning, he felt sure of his doom, for their faces were fell, and no mercy showed in their green eyes. Hearing a call, the soldiers stepped back from him, and Robby saw the one with the golden circlet on his brow coming quickly, his sword dripping, and his face full of rage. He strode resolutely through his men and raised his sword against the hapless boy as he came. His strength all but gone, confused and in despair, Robby fell to his knees, his arms drooping at his sides in paralyzed terror and resignation. An arrow hissed over Robby's head and struck the captain square in his forehead, but the missile shattered into a hundred splinters as if it had struck solid stone instead of flesh. All of the other soldiers again drew their swords and stepped forward to their captain's defense, though none was needed. Another arrow struck him in the neck and glanced away into the darkness. The warrior stopped a few yards away from Robby, distracted, though hardly scratched by the arrows, and sought past Robby for their source. Robby stirred, and, looking over his shoulder, he saw two more figures trotting up from the gloom of the gate. One was tall and rail-thin, with straight black hair flowing down to his chest and a black beard to match. He wore the robes of a foreigner and bore in his left hand a sword, still in its scabbard, as though hastily grabbed and not yet buckled on. Robby immediately recognized him as Ashlord. The other figure was shorter and dressed in a brown cloak and hood, with the leggings and boots of a hunter and was presently bending his bow with another arrow from the quiver on his back as the pair speedily approached.

"Put your useless arrows away," Ashlord told his companion.

As the soldiers continued to converge on Robby and their captain, Ashlord lifted his right hand high, and in a strange dialect he shouted, "Halt! Stay thy hand! He is but an innocent boy and is no ally to these vanquished beasts."

The captain of the guard lowered his sword and frowned at Ashlord.

"Who saith?" he demanded. "What authority hast thee over my duty?"

Ashlord and his companion continued to approach until they stood to either side of the stricken boy. Robby looked up weakly, but Ashlord did not remove his gaze from the captain.

"I am Collandoth, called Ashlord, watcher of this place," Ashlord said, his voice like distant thunder, low and powerful, demanding the attention of all. "Hear my words!"

Waving his hand at their surroundings, he continued, more softly, "Lookest thou. See this place. Dost thou perceive any Dragonkind? See thou any enemy? Look thou at yon battlements? See thou the tree and brush that hast sprung up where once thy sentries stood? See how yon vine dost root into cracks that only Time's own tread may open? See yon gates, once mighty and strong, which art now but rust and corrupted bars, fallen from their weather-corrupted pintles. These are not the heavy works of a day, nor even a year, but of the long light wear of Time's tread. Indeed, five hundred times, and more, hast the stars of summer strode these skies since the day thy stony sleep began. Five hundred years and longer thou hast awaited the summons of the Great Bell. But, alas, when the enemy came, it was never rung, never wast thou called, the battle fought and lost without thee. It is over! Those days art long passed away."

The captain looked around, his followers doing likewise, as Ashlord spoke, seeing as if for the first time their surroundings.

"But how can this be? Only yesterday, forsooth it seems, we were put to slumber, by incantation's spell, within the stone. Only yesterday. The battle? Lost? What of our comrades? What of Lord Heneil and his fair wife? What of our kindred? What sayest thou of our children?"

"Gone," answered Ashlord. "Slain."

"No. Sayest not that, Collandoth!" the captain begged, shaking his head in terrible anguish while a groan went up from the host as if they had been struck with a blow. "Yet, nightmares hast shewn to me the terrible thing thou sayest. Into stone we were cast, and into sleep's slumber to tarry our signal. Yet our eyes did see, but darkly as in a dream, what seemed the quick and terrible change around us. Only yesterday, to sleep we fell," he repeated, "and the dream but a single long night's vision?"

He looked around at his comrades, and at the ruins surrounding them, forlorn in the pale light.

"It is too much to believe, yet," he looked back at Ashlord, "we must by the truth of our hearts know it to be so. The battle lost? All slain?"

"Yes."

The captain nodded.

"Then it was all for naught," he said as he turned away, walking toward the shattered gates. His sword fell to his side, and he let it drag, saying as he went, "All for naught. For naught."

Robby watched the captain walk away into the mist, his comrades following him, and as rain began to fall, the captain and all his soldiers faded from sight, the mists vanished, and black clouds raced to block Lady Moon's view of the scene. Lightning flashed and the rain poured, mixed with hail, and the wind swept across the hill. Ashlord turned suddenly to Robby, leaning down and clutching his shoulder.

"Are you alone?" he shouted over the noise of the resuming storm, speaking in the Common Tongue. "Is anyone else with you?"

"Wolves," Robby stammered, his head spinning again, and he pointed feebly at the dark. "Soldiers," he said, pointing the other way.

"I told you he came alone," spoke Ashlord's companion, who rushed to kneel at Robby's side to steady him. Robby tried to turn toward him, but Ashlord put his face close to Robby and shook him. Robby, dazed, stared back at Ashlord blankly.

"This is important!" he persisted. "Did you meet anyone? Did anyone help you?"

"No," Robby said weakly. "Nobody."

Robby felt his face go hot, but his whole body shivered with cold. Ashlord's face dimmed, and everything turned sideways as Robby slumped over.

"Oh, oh!" he heard Ashlord's companion say as if from a great distance.

Then all was silent.

## Chapter 4

## A Fair and Fatal Glimpse

Months before Ullin departed from the west, while winter still blocked the high passes of the Carthane Mountains, another messenger rode out from Duinnor. His horse trudged through snow and ice bearing him along the mountains southward and westward, about as far west as one could go before entering the shadowed realm of Shatuum. After a long journey of some weeks, he came to a small village called Averstone. The people there greeted him suspiciously and were even more unhappy when he asked how far it was to his destination. They told him it was only a league or two away, and since there was more than an hour of light left in the day, he decided to press on. The trail from Averstone passed through twisting defiles filled with slippery ice so that he often had to dismount and lead his horse, slowly climbing and descending. He had hardly gone a league before dusk settled over the wilderness, and he considered turning back. But as he came over a ridge, he saw, perhaps another league away, the dim outline of the lake that marked his destination. Relieved, he rode down from the pass, taking care to let his mount pick the way. By the time he reached the bottom of the ridge, the sky had lost any glimmer of sunset, and a moonless night was settling heavy and cold onto the mountains.

The lake was as still and unmoving as glass beneath the winter stars, crowded on every side by the steep shoulders of silent black mountains. The messenger shivered, and so did his horse. Rising up from the center of the lake was a towered castle, and so well did its dimly lit windows blend with the reflected stars on the water's surface that the horseman did not at first see it, though he knew it was there. Rounding a bend, and seeing two low-burning lamps at the shoreline, he continued more cautiously, his horse's steps echoing dully from the looming slopes. The ferryman rose from his stool and picked up a long staff to lean on, waiting for the stranger to dismount and approach. When the old man judged the distance was close enough, he swung the staff hard at the messenger who caught it in his gloved hand before it struck his head. Although it was a hardy swing, and the messenger was surprised at the gesture, he immediately saw that there was no malice to it and, somewhat confused, he let go his grip on the staff.

"Then ye have sight," said the ferryman, leaning again on his staff.

"How else may a person find their way here?"

"An' what brings ye here?"

"I have dispatches for Lady Esildre."

"I'll take 'em an' see to it she receives 'em."

"I must deliver them in person."

"She don't take kindly to visitors."

"That can't be helped."

The ferryman hesitated, then turned and rummaged through a box near his stool.

"Then ye must wear this hood, an' keep it on 'til yer once again on this shore."

"No. I am to deliver a message to none but Esildre, and I will not be duped into passing it to any other person."

"I cannot refuse ye," said the ferryman, shrugging and stuffing the hood into his vest. "But I take more over than ever come back."

"I have been warned already not to look upon her face and not to let her eyes meet mine. If my master thought it not in my power to obey his instruction, he would have sent another."

"Very well. Tie up yer horse at yonder post an' come aboard."

He was soon on the barge, and the ferryman began pulling his lines, sliding the boat across the black surface with soft creaks and gurgles as they moved. The passenger watched the undulating wake distort the star-speckled water, and then looked ahead at the castle growing taller as they approached. He saw the peculiar way in which the ferryman handled the ropes, getting his grip and pulling as he walked a few steps toward the stern, then letting his thumb and forefinger circle around the rope as he returned to the prow, repeating each pull.

"You are blind," observed the passenger.

"Aye, since the war. It was a Dragonkind fireball what took me sight an' mangled me face, making me unfit to look upon."

"You do not have much call to pull across the lake, I imagine."

"No, not much. Besides servants of the lady, yer the first in nearly a year. From Duinnor, I reckon? By yer manner of speech."

"Yes."

"A Kingsman?"

"I am."

"Then it's a long way ye come."

"Four weeks and some days."

"Hm. The last feller I pulled across was from Glareth."

"Oh?"

"Aye. Only one way. Never came back. If he ain't still with her, then the fishes got thar food, for I'm the only ferryman on this lake. Year 'round, the water's too cold for swimming."

The messenger shrugged, a gesture lost on the ferryman.

"Are ye one of the Elifaen folk, Kingsman?"

"No, not I."

"Well, good. At least yer torment'll end, sooner er later. As will mine."

"You're as glum as the night."

"This ain't no joyful place, sir."

By the time the barge gently bumped against the landing, someone was standing there with a candle. It was a servant of the house, a fair maid with the same distant look that told the messenger that she, too, was without sight.

"Not too late," said the ferryman, once again holding out the hood.

"No. I go without it."

"Sir," said the maid, "my mistress knows of your coming and awaits you."

He followed her up the stairs and into a damp hallway, lit only by his guide's candle.

"Are all her servants without sight?"

"Yes, it is for our protection. None are immune to her curse, neither man nor woman."

"I see."

"I am sorry that you do."

They came to another flight of stairs as a long whimpering moan floated through the passage sending chills down the visitor's spine. Sensing his discomfort, the maid hesitated.

"A guest," she said, "who came some many years ago and will not leave. Or cannot."

Eventually, after trudging through long wide halls, darkened passages, and up numerous flights of stairs, going higher and higher into the forlorn place, the maid opened a door and they entered a large well-lit room. It seemed out of place, even gay, with brightly colored pillows and drapes, warm blazing hearths on either side, silver-stemmed candelabras, bowls of fruits and flasks of wine, and vases of flowers all around.

"Please make yourself comfortable. Partake of food and drink as you may desire," he was instructed. "Lady Esildre will be with you shortly."

"Thank you."

Left alone, he took off his cloak and gloves and put them and his shoulder bag on a table and went to warm himself by the nearest fireplace. He thought he heard the faint strums of a harp—from an adjoining room, perhaps—barely audible over the pop and hiss of the fire. For many moments he listened, until his hands were no longer numb with cold. Going to the ornate sideboard, he took a goblet and poured wine, drank it quickly, and was pouring another when the strumming stopped. Only the crackle of the fireplaces remained as he looked around the room at the fine tapestries, the likes he had never seen before. Touching one of the flowers floating in a bowl of icy water, he wondered how they could be so fresh in the dead of winter. Wondering at that marvel, he turned the latch on the window, and, letting cold air in, he looked out at the night, surmising that he was in the highest tower of the place. Finishing off the goblet, he closed the window and turned back for more. A gauze-covered figure stood in the middle of the room, and the sight of the apparition sent his hand to his sword.

"Raynor sent you, did he not?"

The messenger stepped forward cautiously, and he saw that it was a woman's figure beneath the gauze.

"Pardon me, Lady," the messenger bowed. "You startled me. Yes, Raynor sent me to seek you out and to bring to you some messages."

"Are you not very young to be traveling alone this long way from Duinnor?"

"I am five and twenty, in the reckoning of Men. And I have served against the Dragonkind for three years."

"Yes. I see. You are most capable, I am sure. Raynor would not have sent you otherwise. But it is a great danger to you. Surely you know of the curse upon this place? Upon me?"

"I have been told. Yet, I do not know that I believe it."

"Oh?"

"Before I am to deliver the message," he stated, "I am to be sure of you."

"And I must be sure of you. Do you not find my figure attractive?"

"I most assuredly do. And if you would be so kind as to turn around and reveal your back to me, I will have the first of my proofs of you."

"That is most impertinent!"

"Even so, I'll have a look at you!"

The messenger jerked away the gauze and the lady's hands went instinctively to her eyes.

"Do not look upon my eyes!" she cried.

"I look upon the rest of you!" he returned, spinning her around roughly.

"How dare you!"

He looked at her bare back, at the two scars each running from shoulder to hip.

"As I thought!" he cried, pulling the gauze from around her head and face so that he could look at her. "You are not Esildre! You are the maidservant who showed me in!"

The poor girl, now trembling with fear, tried her best to recover, clutching the insignificant cloth against her chest with both fists, looking with blank eyes straight ahead.

"Indeed she is."

The messenger turned and just across the room stood Lady Esildre, covered with a dark blue robe from head to foot, the hood draped over her face so that only her nose and mouth could be seen.

"You may go, my dear," she said to the servant who hurried away. Turning to the messenger, she said, "Few know the pattern of my Scathing."

She turned away and lowered her robe so that he could see her bare back and how the two scars turned inward just above her waist and then back outward to just above her hips, an unusual pattern, known only to one Elifaen House.

"I have been instructed in their pattern, and was ordered to touch them," he said, "to be sure they are not put on by some trickery of paint."

She had her doubts, wondering why Raynor would order such a thing. But she conceded.

"Then you may do so."

He did, putting his hands on her skin, feeling the run of her scars, and the curve of her body. He detected only a slight tremble. Her light brown hair hung straight down her back, and, as he pushed it away to examine the full length of her marks of Scathing, he felt a stirring within himself.

"Your hands are warm," she said. "Is that all that you require as proof of my identity?"

"That is all, my lady, and I apologize for the impertinence," he said, bowing and stepping away. She turned back to him, her robes still hanging down from around her arms. "But I am required to test you."

"And I must test you, too," she said, her voice trembling. "No man has touched me for a long time."

"That is not my purpose here, only it was required of me. I have important messages from Duinnor."

He struggled to keep his eyes downward, allowing himself only to look upon her legs.

"I am not an ogre," she said.

He ventured a glimpse, no more, and turned away. Only a glance, but, as if from steel and flint, it sent a spark into tender, alighting an ember that rapidly grew.

"Do you wish to have the messages I have brought?"

"I wish for much," she smiled, pulling her robe up, satisfied that he was true, and relieved to avoid torment.

"This is the first: I am to say this to you: ' The star of the west sinketh away, and that of the east rises.' "

"Is that all?"

"Yes, Lady. It is the key to a water cipher." He produced a small wooden box from his shoulder bag on the table and held it to her. "Here are the cipher potions."

He opened the box and showed her the three small vials within, one of red crystal, one of green, and the other of blue.

"First the red, then the green. I am to abide until after the ciphers have been revealed to you. There is a third vial, here," he held up a small blue vial. "I do not know its purpose."

"Very well."

As he held out the box to her, he made as if to drop it. Instantly, she responded to catch the delicate vials, but he grasped it away. Without thinking, she shot a look of surprise at him. So quickly had he changed his mind! So easily had he connived to make her look fully at him! And so readily did she fall for the old trick!

But it was too late for either to resist. His eyes sunk into hers, and hers drilled into his. Tears came as she felt his loneliness, the longing for his faraway love, and the terrible pain of separation upon one so young. More pain came when she realized that his absent lover was dead, and that, in some manner, he was to blame. For his part, he cried out with pain and madness, the darkness of her past swallowing him, burning out of his chest and loins as her insatiable desires entered him and took hold of his will. Then she transformed. Indeed, Esildre was no longer there at all. Instead, impossibly, his own true love stood before him, urging him, as if from the grave, in a way she had never done in life. Yet—so overwhelmed by longing was he, and pleased at her presence—no urging was needed.

"You have always resisted me before," he said, drawing her to the couch. "But I will give myself to thee and comfort thee."

"I must give myself to thee!" his lost lover replied.

• • •

Afterwards, Esildre lay alone on the floor, gazing across the room at the window through which the young man had flung himself. She wept bitterly, reaching out to the blowing drapes as if to clutch at him, to hold him back from it. Wailing, she beat her fists upon the floor, scratching herself with her clawing nails, her face and her chest—wounds that bled profusely but quickly healed and left no blemish—cursing herself and her existence, pleading to Beras for release, cursing Secundur to free her soul. The noise of her agony drew forth attendants from their chambers, and they gathered outside her door, weeping, too, at what they knew had happened, yet none dared to enter until bidden to do so. Elsewhere, deep within the castle, came another voice, the voice of a man imprisoned in her anguished domain. It was a voice full of jealousy and madness, and he laughed at her, believing she surely would now return to him and relieve his terrible desires—the insatiable desires that she had kindled. But the truth of his own madness, telling through his nervous and fading mirth that descended into weeping, was that she never again would lay her eyes upon him.

• • •

Around noon the next day, as new falling snow blew through the window and settled on the bare skin of her back and shoulders and onto the floor all around her, she stirred and saw the little box of vials upon the table beside the young man's bag. Rising, she pulled on her robe and sat for another day upon a chair, looking across the room at the potions, one red, one green, the other blue, glistening in their crystal vials.

Three days later, she still sat. Her servants, gathering their bravery, had entered to tend the fire, to close the window, and to ask of her needs. But she did not reply to them. She continued to sit and stare at the vials, as if in a trance, her face expressionless.

Many times had Raynor sent letters to her, but never before in cipher. And never before had he sent a man to deliver them directly to her. Why this time? Why were they not delivered to the ferryman? She turned to stare at a writing desk on the far side of the room, near the other fireplace, and looked for a long time at the pile of letters near her inkwell and quills. A blank sheet lay there, too. She never answered any of his letters. She was always tempted, for he had been a good friend to her and to her brother, and his missives were kind and ever full of concern for her. He never scolded her, never questioned her reasons for not answering, and never mentioned her depraved existence at the gloomy castle. And, unlike nearly everyone else she had once cared for, he was never mortified by her debauched history with her former captor. Raynor knew Secundur's power, and the power of the curse upon her.

She had not seen Raynor since some years after her escape. Not since her self-imposed exile. She did not like remembering those years of new-found freedom, or any of the years that went before. A hundred years since her escape? No, closer to three hundred. For another week, she sat, contemplating the mystic, her old tutor.

But why use a cipher now? Her thoughts abruptly came back to the messenger. And why, oh why did the young man insist on delivering them in person?

At last, stirring from her chair, she called for her servant and ordered a fresh washbasin be brought to her with full pitchers of water. She bathed away the dried blood from her now-invisible wounds, her tears mingling with the rosy water that ran onto the cold stone floor.

Later, she ordered the basin taken away, and for several new basins to be brought, along with another pitcher of water. When that was done, she bade her servants go away, and she bolted the door after them, turning to the vials.

First the red vial. She knew the process, and untied the packet of letters. The first letter, sealed with red wax, she opened and unfolded. It was a single sheet and appeared to be blank. She placed it into a basin and poured water over it, then she added the clear contents of the red vial and swirled the liquid into the water. Almost instantly, writing appeared, in cipher. Mentally using the quote as a key, she read Raynor's instructions, written with a mix of numbers and runes:

> Just as the first, do then the next, with dark and equal wine.
> Go quick to dry before the flame, my words then to divine.

Taking the second letter, and breaking the green wax seal, she placed its two sheets into a new basin, and over it she poured first a goblet of water then a goblet of dark red wine before adding the contents of the green vial. She knew not to let it soak but for the slightest moment, or else the paper would dissolve, and she carefully lifted out the sheets and held them close to the fire. They cracked and stiffened quickly, as she watched the small lines of writing appear, nearly covering the entire front and back of each sheet. Going to her chair, she sat and read.

Esildre,

Forgive the secret manner of this letter. My apologies, too, for having it delivered as it was by the messenger. His name is (or was, as I assume he has by now succumbed to you), Nermon Denegan. He was arrested last month for the rape and murder of a young lady of Glareth whom he had been courting. The crime took place here, in Duinnor, and against the protests of Glareth he was tried here for his acts. But since he was favored by those close in service to the King, he was not convicted as he should have been. However, I was party to the proceedings and saw plainly, as did others, that he was guilty, even though he was acquitted.

Freed, the man's behavior continued the same as before. Yet, his commanders and comrades could no longer abide his conduct, but nor could they expel him from the ranks. I was approached for advice, and since I was preparing this letter to you, I suggested that he be assigned to me as a special courier.

He knew your reputation, for tales of you are regrettably commonplace, and so he was quick to agree. I gave him strict instructions to leave these missives with your ferryman, and to tell him the key to the cipher. Of course, I suspected that he would not obey, and I had reason to think that he made a bargain with some other person, highly placed, to relay the contents of this note back to Duinnor. Even with the cipher key, he could not know how to use it, so to obtain the knowledge he was paid for, he would first have to let you have them. Trusting in his character, I knew that if he obeyed my instructions, and thus survived to return to Duinnor, then he must be innocent of my suspicions, and probably of the crime of which he was accused. Otherwise, I was confident that you would serve as the ultimate hand of justice.

Since I predict that using you in this manner will anger you, I do apologize again. Although we have never spoken of it, I can only assume that you suffer greatly at each such encounter. But, where in years past madness may have gripped you, and you may have indulged it, I feel that you have come to understand somewhat Secundur's curse upon you. If you feel nothing but anger at me, and no pain at the messenger's demise, I am wrong. But if you feel any remorse, even knowing that justice was served, then I am correct. If you have such feelings, then your healing is surely at hand, though the curse upon you remains. Forgive me this test of you, and read on.

Esildre stood abruptly and paced back and forth across the room, clutching the letter fiercely, her face red with insult at Raynor's abuse of her. As she slowed her pace and stared across the room at the window, she more carefully considered his words and searched her heart.

"Could it be true?" she wondered silently.

When she first came here, all were invited, and many, many came. But they were the dregs of society, rejects from every realm. Men and women alike attended the fantastic celebrations she threw, full of drinking and music and debauchery. The worse ones, criminals who had no place else to run, hardened soldiers ready to forget what their eyes had seen or their hands had done, pox-riddled lords and ladies—all of them were easily seduced and driven into madness. Some went away, never the same, useless and babbling. Some met their end in the cold waters of her lake, or by their own blades. A few, refusing to depart, had to be chained. One or two, who turned their induced insanity against her servants, she slew. Between visits, she swore she would entertain never again, so wracked with black depression they left her. She gouged out her eyes. But they grew back. And once, in the throes of despair, she attempted to gouge out her heart with a dagger, but was prevented by one of her astute and quick-witted maidservants who was near at hand and who pressed herself against Esildre's chest and put her arms around her.

"Please, no! For our sake, stay your hand! Where would we go, my lady?" the blind girl pleaded. "No one but you would take a sightless servant. The men would become beggars and starve. And the girls would be preyed upon, defenseless. Oh, I beg you, do no harm to yourself!"

Esildre never understood how the blind girl knew to block her dagger-thrust. They fell into tears together, falling to their knees in their embrace. And Esildre made her a promise to keep them and provide for them as long as she lived.

That was when Esildre finally began to see. At least she had some purpose left to her. She would keep to herself, and see no more visitors. It was just as well, for fear of her had spread, and after but a few years no one else dared come. And no one was bidden. She kept her castle dark, and made it foreboding in appearance. Hiring mercenaries on occasion, she turned away settlers, and made travelers unwelcome along the roads that skirted her lands. Alone with her servants, she began to believe that she might find peace.

Then, decades later, a party of innocent travelers came, having lost their way in the mountains. Realizing where they were, they feared to accept the shelter she, through her servants, offered them. But a winter storm raged, and the passes filled with ice and snow, so they reluctantly accepted. For a week the storm pounded the mountains, freezing her lake, and covering her castle with ice. For three weeks after the skies cleared, the wind blasted the land, and nothing melted. All during this time, she succeeded in avoiding her several hapless guests. They dined together, and she alone. She permitted them books from her library, and wine from her cellars. But she kept her maidservants away from them. Indeed, when the first warm sun came out to slicken the ice with meltwater, they prepared to depart, anxious to continue their journey. That night they celebrated, sending their thanks to Esildre and begging the honor of her company before taking their leave. She kindly refused. When they had drunk their nightly portion of wine, and her servant refused more to them, they beat him until he relented the key to the wine cellar. Later, they forced her chamber door. She killed two before the others had her pinned. But they met the same fate, in turn, as all the others had. None of them ever left her castle alive.

Yes. She regretted it. She sat back down with Raynor's letter in her lap. She could have prevented that night. Were they all bad men? Was it her presence that made them so? Was it her eyes?

She glanced at the window, considering again Raynor's words. Yes, deserving or not, she regretted the fate of the man who had just died. She regretted them all. And she had been filled with regret all along, all throughout her sordid time at this castle, though for so many lost years her regret was masked by the depravity of Secundur's shadowing curse. But, at this moment, reading again Raynor's words, she knew that even though her curse remained, the madness of it was gone. If she carefully guarded herself, all would be safe.

Smiling, and shaking her head at Raynor's insight, faraway though he was, she continued to read, noticing for the first time that one edge of the sheet had telltale signs of having been nibbled. This made her smile even more, and she anticipated good news concerning the small creature who did it.

> Be that as it may, I have important news for you. First, there are many signs that point to the end of the current reign. I do not merely mean the continued weakening of resolve, or of the favoritism of our courts in making just sentences. There are signs in the sky, and in the stirrings of Men, and farther west, in that shadowed land that, alas, you know too well. I hope we may speak of these things.

Of immediate concern to you, however, is that I have recently learned the true fate of your brother, Navis. It has been many years since his disappearance, and until now it was assumed that he was lost in Shatuum, and his mission to find you, and his life, ended there. I'm afraid he never made it that far. Let me tell you how I know.

As I have written you before, my dear companion, Beauchamp, the Familiar who has been my friend, was parted from me many, many years ago, and I gave up hope of ever seeing him again. I have ever after regretted sending him on the errand that parted us! But, miracles abide! He returned to me just two months ago, filling me with joy! And he is at this very moment nibbling the page I write upon to send his own greetings to you.

Naturally, he has had much to share, having been gone for nearly three centuries, and I am still learning from him somewhat of his adventures, which took him as far south as the Green Citadel, where he was trapped for most of his time away. But he escaped and, with some help, made it out of the desert lands and all the way back to me. I cannot share all with you, but by way of him, I learned the terrible news of your brother's disappearance. In fact, Navis was murdered by the very men who were sent as his escort. It took place many leagues west of here, on the border of Shatuum.

I know this news is disturbing to you, and I am sorry to give it. I remind you, as I have in letters past, that I tried my utmost to dissuade Navis from his mission to find you. Perhaps I felt it was ill-fated. But it would be truer to say that I cared deeply for him, and his ambition to find you filled me with fear. That was long ago, and I am deeply saddened by this new knowledge of his fate.

It was related to me that members of your brother's party set upon him at night. Having committed their vile act, then one other of the party murdered all the rest, too, presumably so that none could speak of the atrocity. He could not know that humble eyes saw all from the edge of their camp. Beauchamp was shortly thereafter captured, and, as it happened, was taken away far southward as part of a menagerie of animals for exhibit, eventually arriving within the Green Citadel of the Dragonlands. It has been this long before he could escape and find his way back to me to relate his fantastic experiences.

Beauchamp could not know or say the person's name who murdered your brother, but as soon as he revealed that portion of his adventure, I began to make discreet inquiries. Thus I have endeavored for the past month to learn the person's name, and to learn how he came to commit the act. I will tell you this much, but must refrain from telling you more until we may meet: The person is Elifaen. I do not know his House, but I think he was born sometime in the early years of this Age. His history is sketchy at best. But I discovered that he came into the service of one of the highest of this land. He served as the guide to Navis and his party, and he alone returned, saying they had all entered Shatuum, releasing him from their service. I have sought to find this person, whose name now appears on many leases of Vanara and properties in Duinnor. My intention was to confront him, or at least to make his whereabouts known to you. But he is no longer in Duinnor. I have learned that he was seen traveling from here with a small armed party late last year. And I have reason to believe he has some business in the old Eastlands Realm or perhaps in Glareth. Whether that is actually true, or whether he is still in the east, I cannot say. I intend to send word to a trusted colleague of mine, by the name of Collandoth, who now resides in those parts, to be alert for him, to be wary of him, and to send word of any news he may have of the person. However, it will be months before my letter will reach him, and longer, still, before I may hear from him.

I can say no more, for I am watched closely, and all my dealings are scrutinized. I beg you to come to me secretly, in disguise as a pilgrim to the Temple. I know that you will be reluctant to do so, but only in person may I share the name of your brother's killer. I will dispatch a trusted guide who owes me a favor, named Tyrin, to await a pilgrim at the village Averstone, close by to your lands. Though somewhat a rogue, he is a brave and honorable man from Glareth Realm, capable of protecting you. He will arrive around Midsummer's with coin enough to keep him. He knows only that he is to remain at the inn until he is sent for by your servant, or until I summon him back to Duinnor, even though he may be weeks or months in the waiting. He will be rewarded again, once he delivers his charge safely to the Temple. I implore you to send for him to be your guide. Why you shall need him will be revealed in due time.

Should you decide to come, and ONLY if you intend to come, read the final missive, using the potion in the blue vial. It will aid you greatly with your needed disguise, and thus help you have an uneventful journey. Tyrin will leave you at the Temple, and he will inform me once you are within. I will come to you there.

ONLY if you are determined to come to me: Float the missive in a bowl of clear water, and pour the full contents of the blue vial over the missive all at once. You must put your face very close to the water to understand!

Your anxious friend,

Raynor

Esildre unfolded the last edge and a small circle of parchment fell onto her lap. Picking it up, she noted that it smelled oddly like citrus. Standing, she put it beside the blue vial, and paced once again.

"I may as well have murdered Navis myself!" she cried out. When she had finally escaped the clutches of Secundur, and learned of the disappearance of her brother from relatives in Vanara, she immediately traveled back to look for him in Shatuum, Secundur's shadowy realm. But once at the border with that land, her heart faltered. She knew if she re-entered the place, the lord of that land would have her again. It was then, at that moment of her faltering, that the madness of her curse overcame her. What could she do? No one, until she herself did it, ever escaped from there! How could she go back? There, at the edge of Shatuum, Secundur's curse landed its first blow upon her.

Now, this! That, all the while, Navis had never even made it that far. That he was murdered!

"Perhaps he could have found me!" she cried, new tears pouring from her eyes. "Oh, my brother! Perhaps you could have broken my bonds and freed me after all! Why did I ever go there? Oh, I am so sorry! Forgive me!"

To the Elifaen, time does not pass as it does for mortals. Already it was many days since the messenger came, and now many more days and nights passed in her grief. She wandered the halls of her castle, aimless, like a ghost, speaking to no one. Finding herself at the high windy ramparts of the place, she stood, nearly motionless, staring away at the mountains by day and at the stars by night. For a month and longer, she grappled with herself. Winter gave over to spring, and still she debated. The icy white of the mountainsides slowly gave way to green, and the daytime air grew warm while the night-time insects learned to buzz. Midsummer's Day came and went, the ramparts grew hot in the full sun of the long days, the nights no longer held any threat of chill, and still she sparred with the shadows of her heart, agonized over her shame, and debated her decision. Was she to be feckless? She dreaded leaving her sanctuary, drab and grim though it was, and contriving to avoid the gaze of others. She hated the prospect of talk that would spread through Duinnor should she be seen there. How could she go? But how could she refuse?

It was at dawn on the thirteenth day of Seventhmonth that she returned at last to her chamber, and she sat in her chair and stared again at the blue vial, undisturbed where she had left it, and the little circle of parchment nearby. Slowly, she had become resigned to her duty. She would go to Duinnor and meet with Raynor. She would learn the name, and all else that could be learned, and then she would track down her brother's murderer.

Raynor was right. She must travel in disguise or else her curse would tempt any who saw her. A pilgrim, yes, that would work. But what could the third missive say to help her with that? And why should she need a guide? Or protection?

"Does Raynor forget that I am a veteran of great battles? Or that I know the way to Duinnor like the back of my hand?"

No, she decided, Raynor had good reasons, whatever they were.

She went to the basin, poured water into it, and then floated the wafer of parchment on it. Kneeling over it, wondering again what words could possibly help her disguise, she poured the contents of the blue vial over the wafer. Small letters immediately began to form as the wafer sank, and the citrus odor became stronger.

"Look very closely," the writing said, and, in even smaller writing, "Wash your face only with Temple water. Look closely!"

She leaned closer, to be sure of the words, her nose almost touching the water as it grew cloudy. Suddenly the basin erupted with smoke and a bright orange flash, and scalding water burned into her eyes and face. Screaming, she fell back, but instantly the pain was gone. Feeling her face, she touched hard scales, and, opening her eyes, she saw nothing but the faintest blur from the brightly burning hearth.

"Raynor!" she cried, her anger rekindled. Aggravated and once again offended, she crawled back to the basin to wash away the scales. As she dipped her hands and bent her head to splash, she hesitated. Her anger suddenly vanished, replaced by a modicum of reproof as she realized that this ruse was probably the safest thing. If her eyes were scaled over, the curse must be rendered ineffective.

"How did he know?" she wondered. But how do any of the Melnari know what they do? Raynor may be old, but he was certainly not without perception.

Within the hour, Esildre began putting her arrangements in order. She ordered all of the servants, except three, to their quarters, and then summoned the ferryman to send him to Averstone. He knew the way, sight or no sight, and would ask for the Glareth man. He would say that a pilgrim bound for the Temple of Beras had gotten lost and had stumbled upon Esildre's castle. The Glareth man was to come and fetch the pitiful creature to Duinnor as quickly as possible.

• • •

And so it was done, and within only a few hours Esildre stepped off her barge, dressed in the plainest traveling robes, using a walking stick for guidance. The Glareth man was there, and he rushed to take her elbow and to guide her up the uneven path from the shore to an awaiting horse. He introduced himself as he did so, saying nothing about the terrible scars and scales that covered her face and eyes.

"Ah, there you go!" he said, once Esildre was in the saddle. "I'll keep ahold of the reins, but you should hang onto this saddle rope, just to keep steady. Let me adjust those stirrups. I seem to have them a bit too long."

"Thank you," she said in the Common Speech, since that was what he spoke.

"Not at all," he replied. After a few minutes, he had her stirrups adjusted. "Do you want me to tie your bag onto the saddle?"

"No, thank you. I'll keep it over my shoulder."

"As you wish."

Tyrin mounted, tying the reins of her horse onto his saddle.

"I don't know much about pilgrims, or such," he said, "so you must forgive my ignorance of your ways. And, though I've been in Duinnor for a while, I've only been up to the Temple once. Just to see the sights, so to speak. Oh, and what's your name?"

"My name?"

"Yes, your name. Old Raynor said you'd tell me yourself. And he didn't say I'd be escorting a lady, either."

"Oh, pardon me for not saying." Esildre mentally scrambled for an answer. "You may call me Shevalia." It was an old family name, rarely used. And she immediately regretted it, wishing she had thought it through and chosen a more common name.

"Shevalia," Tyrin repeated. "Pretty. Well, Miss Shevalia, let us be on our way. A long way to go!"

"Yes. Let's."

"So, anyway, as I was saying, I ain't had much call to know pilgrims, though I'm something of one, you might say, goin' from place to place. I'm from Glareth, originally. You?"

"Vanara."

"Ah! Should've known. My line of work, when I can find it, is along the lines of swordplay, if you know what I mean."

"You're a mercenary."

"Well, if you put it bluntly. I suppose I am. Or have been, anyway. Me and my mates—they're still in Duinnor—we figured we'd come out this way, westward, to see what kind of trouble we could get into. But there ain't a lot. Between the Kingsmen, Duinnor Regulars, and you Vanaran folk, there just ain't much call for our services north of the Dragonlands. And we prefer cooler places. No call in biting off more than we can chew with Dragonfolk. So, anyway, we sort of like Duinnor, though work is scarce. I mean, we don't mind too much. We'd rather carouse than fight any day of the week, when coin's ready and honor's kept. A trade's a trade, that's all. And, I suppose we're a might picky about the jobs we do agree to take. Once, down around Tracia, oh that was years ago, now, yeah, we sure cut our teeth down there. And that ain't all we cut, neither! Oh, I hope you don't mind this kind of talk. I ain't the pious sort, but I don't mean to offend."

"Not at all," Esildre said with a smile. "Your way of speaking is refreshing."

"And you've got the tone of fine breeding in your manner," he said. "If you pardon me saying so. So, anyhow, one of my mates heard about some trouble down southward, out near the plains, I think. So we might pull up and head down there now that it's warmer."

On and on he went, for hours without stop, as talkative as a spring wren. Just as he would for days. And for weeks.

• • •

Even though their pace was easy, they made very good progress, with Tyrin expertly guiding Esildre along the rough paths through the mountain forest. Their good progress was due in part to Esildre's habit of encouraging Tyrin to travel some while longer each day than he wished before making camp for the night. And also owing to her custom of waking him well before dawn to be on their way again. She desired and asked for no rest, except when Tyrin said the horses needed it. In fact, he was so impressed by her toughness and endurance that he made comment upon it on more than one occasion. Which inevitably led him off into some tangential line of discussion, during which he, of course, did most of the talking. She deflected some of his questions, about the length of her pilgrimage, about the practices of pilgrims, about her family, about her upbringing, and about how she managed to get so far from Vanara before meeting up with him. Each question had its own traps, so she often said, "I'd rather not say," or else she would turn her answer into a question, which inevitably took Tyrin a very long while to answer, turning explanation into tale, as it were.

One day, he asked whether she had been blind all her life.

"No. I was injured by scalding water when I was younger."

"Oh, my goodness. I'm very sorry. That's just terrible! I imagine, but may be too bold in my saying so, that it may not be as bad for those who have never had sight. Don't know what they're missing, so to speak."

"I don't know about that," she replied thoughtfully, thinking of some of her servants. "I at least know the color of the sky. The beauty of a waterfall, and the hues of each season and their different moods. Those memories are still with me, and it is pleasant to remember them."

She did not understand the feelings welling up within her, why her throat tightened and she had difficulty swallowing. Suddenly, thinking of those left behind in her castle, some sightless from birth, others from illness or injury, her eyes watered. She employed the blind for her own reasons, and until her maidservant pointed it out to her, she never realized the haven she had made for them. Her past arrogance now stung her, and their suffering under her earlier treatment clamped her heart with regret. Remembering Raynor's directive not to wash her face, and fearing that tears would undo her disguise, she stiffened and suppressed her feelings.

Thought led to thought during this unusual length of silence from Tyrin, and she found herself wondering what natural, unaccursed attractions men and women may truly have for one another. Before the war, she had been as a child in a woman's body. Then she became a warrior, hardened to suffering, though her body never changed or declined, and she knew from the courting of so many that they thought her fair and attractive. But the war in the east changed her within. When she and her comrades, moving steadily from Duinnor into the Eastlands, came through the terrible battlefields, strewn with thousands of the fallen, and when she saw there the suffering of brief, mortal Men and their heroic sacrifice, she nearly broke.

Tulith Attis changed all that. When she saw the slaughter there, like none she had ever witnessed, the walls stained with blood, the hacked remains of men, women, and even children, that was when her own hatred kindled true and hot. She and her comrades mercilessly swept across the Eastlands, transforming mere retribution into brutal insanity, unable to stop their bloodlust even when the last Dragonkind invader had been killed. Crazed and without reason, they then turned on each other, Man against Elifaen, and each against their own kind. Only the Queen, Serith Ellyn, was able to put a stop to it.

Though she obeyed her Queen, and laid aside her arms, Esildre found that she cared no more about any thing. The last of her grace was gone, her beauty meaningless, and her soul as empty as the eyes of the dead.

Then came her father, with his entreaty to go to Secundur. And she did.

"Only now?" she mused silently as she followed along behind the equally silent Tyrin. "Only now do I feel my true heart trying to beat again? Only now? After all the centuries of captivity, and after all the years since my terrible freedom? Can Raynor be right? Am I truly changing? Or is this yet another snare laid by Secundur's curse upon me? I am as a child, again, starting over. What can I know of the world that may be good and true? How do natural people treat each other? What sight do they have, that I never had?"

"Is my face terribly disfigured?" she asked aloud, impulsively, and with immediate regret. "Speaking as a man," she added, wondering why she was acting so girlish.

"Well," Tyrin considered, slowing to ride alongside of her, "I wouldn't say so, exactly."

She chuckled at his tone of voice.

"No, no," he stammered. "Here's the thing, and I'd sooner go blind myself than give you any offense, but the face don't count for much, does it, now? I mean to say, no. Aw, heck! I mean, yes, even though you've got awful scars and such, they can't hide the beauty of your face, in spite of all, for any who'd care to look. And most certainly not the beauty of your smile."

Esildre felt a rush of heat in her cheeks. She was confused by the sensation until she realized that, underneath her scales, she was blushing.

"Oh, my!" she whispered. Tyrin heard her, and smiled.

"It's the gods' own truth," he continued. "Oh, pardon me for saying that! But here's another thing, and you may as well know it now, for it's sure to come up if we ever run into any other ladies along the way. That is, I'm the most handsome fellow you could ever ride along with. It's the truth! I'm tall, well-built (but not stocky), and I'm strong and quick. I have a pleasing face, and I possess the most charming smile that ever graced a mortal man. You can ask anyone at all! On top of that, I like to keep clean, wear good clothes, and drink fine wine. And I've got good manners, to boot!"

"So you are a mercenary and a rake, too!"

"I beg your pardon!"

Esildre fell into unrestrained laughter.

"Never in life, good lady!" he laughed with her. "Oops! We're comin' up on a sharp, narrow turn. Let me lead on."

For the first time since beginning their journey, they rode along in complete silence for an entire hour. During this time, Tyrin dismounted and tied his reins to Esildre's saddle, then took the reins of her horse and led the way carefully around fallen logs that partially blocked the path, and downward into a wood.

"Bend down a bit," he instructed at one point. "There's a low hanging limb. That's good, we've passed it, now."

Esildre inhaled deeply, smelling the fresh pine scents, and turned her head to listen to a waterfall shushing somewhere in the distance. As they continued on and its sound faded behind them, she found herself wishing, incongruously, that this journey would never end. Listening to Tyrin speak soft encouraging words to her horse as he led her along, she wondered why, in spite of all, she felt so...*happy*.

• • •

And so, on the same day that Robby set out on his errand to Tulith Attis, the pair arrived in Duinnor, having an entirely uneventful journey. But Tyrin seemed to grow short of words. They continued to chat during this last day of their journey, but he was less jovial, it seemed to her, and far less anxious to reach their destination as he had been but a few days before. They reached the Temple just as the sun was setting, where they had to dismount to climb the long stairs upward. He silently took Esildre's hand, not her elbow, and, throwing her bag over his shoulder, he guided her carefully up the hundreds of steps of the long ascent. Once they reached the broad portico, Tyrin hesitated, glancing away at the city some miles off, and at the western sky, still brightly aglow with sunset.

"I have the coin, here, to give to the monk," he said. "But I find that I have little desire to say goodbye to you."

"You have been a kind man," she said, reaching out for him. He took her hand again. "And I hope you will not forget me. I shall never forget you."

"Oh, how could I ever forget you?" he said with distress that was not in character with his usual tone. Though she could not see, she sensed his eyes upon her. "And if you should ever again require the services of a mercenary, or a rake, why, I'm your man. And I ever shall be!"

She felt his lips on her scarred cheeks, one cheek then the other, and she closed her eyes beneath their scales. She felt the coin pressed into her hand, and his hands wrapped hers, gently pressing her fingers around the coin.

"Here. Take this."

She heard his receding footsteps, the bang of the door knocker, and then heard Tyrin going down the stairs and away.

When the great doors were pulled open, and she handed the monk her coin, she hesitated. The monk gently took her arm to lead her in. Though blind, she instinctively glanced over her shoulder as she entered.

Tyrin had only gone a short distance down the stairs. He saw her turn her head toward him just as she entered the sanctuary. Then the doors closed behind her. Finally turning away, he trudged slowly downward.

"Well. I must tell Raynor she has arrived. He, at least, will be happy."

• • •

Esildre was guided into the Temple and through the halls to a small chamber that had been prepared for her. As they went along, she wondered what had just happened, and she touched her cheek where Tyrin had kissed her. She smiled, but behind her scales, her eyes watered, and deep within, in a place she did not know she had, she felt an ever-so-slight flutter. They came to what would be her room, and the monk guided her within.

"If you wish," said the monk, "one of the females of my order would be happy to help you wash. Raynor of Duinnor, who has anticipated your arrival, has instructed us to allay your fears while you are in this place. The shadows of Shatuum cannot touch you here, nor touch any who are within these walls, and none who serve the master of Shatuum may enter into this sanctuary."

"Thank you," she bowed. "But if you would only provide the things needed for washing, I would prefer to bathe myself."

"Certainly," the monk replied. "You are free to walk our halls, and to share in our humble meals. You may join in our meditations and our prayers, if you would care to do so. Just outside your room and down the hall will be an attendant, who will provide someone to guide you, should you desire it."

"Thank you."

The monk bowed, and stepped aside as an acolyte entered bearing a tray of washing things. Placing the tray on a table, she then led Esildre to it, and helped her feel with her hands those things upon it.

"I would be glad to help you."

"No. Thank you. I will manage just fine."

"Very well. We will leave you."

Esildre heard the door close, pulled back her hood, and immediately began washing. In only a few moments, the false scars of her face were washed away, and the scales that blinded her were dissolved. Her eyes stung at first, and the lamp that burned dimly nearby now seemed far too bright. But these sensations soon passed, and her vision was fully restored but a short while later. She sat on her cot, looking at the tiny unadorned cell. On the floor was a small, triangular meditation gong, no larger than her hand, hanging along with a small mallet from a wooden stand. Nearby was an incense burner, several sticks of incense, and a small blue rug for kneeling or sitting. There was a tiny table, hardly large enough for the basin and pitcher, but there was nothing else, not even a stool for sitting, not even a window. For a long while, she sat, thinking about Tyrin.

• • •

Time does not pass for the Elifaen as it does for mortals. A season may pass as an afternoon, and a century may be as only a few months, yet a moment may be as a year. Indeed, this was almost their undoing when they first lost their wings and were made to walk the earth with their feet. Hunger was new to them, and many starved, wasting to nothing before realizing that the ripe fruits would not wait for them, or before understanding the need for haste. They learned that survival in life was as it was in battle, that life may hang in a blink of time. But when they were not pressed by cold, or hunger, or danger, they might contemplate a stream for days, or consider the next stroke of their paintbrush well past the drying of the paint in the pot, or pluck the same harp string over and over, eyes closed, listening to each difference of tone made by every possible kind of stroke.

So it was with Esildre as she sat, engrossed in her thoughts, turning over her questions again and again in progressive variation. Hours passed, and she ceased wondering when Raynor would come, ceased even in the recounting of her troubles. Inexplicably, her musings wandered again and again back to Tyrin, and she felt again a certain glow, a lingering reflection of what she had felt in his presence. It was an unfamiliar sensation, warm and pleasant and mysterious, and she was baffled by it.

Outside of her mind, the moments slipped silently by. The peace and quiet of the Temple gave her only the noise of her own breathing to hear and the sound of her own memories until she hardly thought at all, until her internal dialogue ceased altogether and a peaceful calm overcame her.

Then, suddenly, the great gong of the temple banged, and so did the little gong in her cell, now gyrating wildly by its cords. Leaping up, she heard the echo of hundreds of chimes and bells and gongs all throughout the temple. Flinging open the door, she ran into the hallway, amid a rush of confused monks going in every direction.

"What is happening?" she cried. "Why do the bells ring?"

"We do not know! We do not know!"

Filled with a powerful sense of danger, she ran down the hall, following the monks to the main sanctuary. A second great wave of ringing and banging resounded, the huge sanctuary gong swinging without cause in its ornate frame, its violent decrescendo unnaturally sustained. The monks cried out in dismay, many prostrating themselves to chant their prayers, others going to light incense though it was not time for the lighting of it. Confused, Esildre did not know what to do, but the strange feeling that help was needed, that danger was imminent, somewhere far to the east, swept over her. It did not matter that she had no weapon, and no means but her hands to fight with, the need to engage the enemy was urgent. Momentarily frozen with panic, she felt a rush of air as the huge doors of the temple were pulled open, and she ran outside along with many others to the portico just as the third deafening knell rolled across the land. At the portico, Esildre saw that the Five Stars of Duinnor hung as steady as ever high over the night-time city in the distance below. But she could see lamplights glowing to life as they were lit behind thousands of windows, and she could hear the distant chorus of thousands of bells and gongs, cymbals and chimes of every note and tone, from the city, the temple, from house and hovel, and places near and far, all ringing of their own accord.

The sound slowly died away, echoing from far hills, yet her heart still pounded as she stared out at the suddenly awakened city. After a few moments of eerie silence, the military trumpets of the city began to blare out their summons. War drums began to throb, ordering soldiers to take up their weapons and their posts. All along the walls and watchtowers of the great city, torches were lit and furnaces stoked. The city gates were pushed shut, soldiers crowded the parapets, and archers strung their bows, all in preparation of an impending doom.

# Chapter 5

# A Stormy Recovery

Day 5
239 Days Remaining

Four days later, Robby rolled over onto his side and painfully propped himself up on an elbow amid unfamiliar surroundings. He could hear rain and see the nearby window's panes, foggy and awash with water. It was daytime. He saw his shoulder bag hanging on the wall, alongside his torn cloak. His other clothes were clean and folded on a shelf nearby. A curtain was drawn around the alcove where he lay in a cot, and he smelled something like a stew cooking nearby.

He began to remember. His journey to Tulith Attis. The flight from the wolves. The mysterious bell room and the ghostly soldiers—all was like a dream to him, but for the evidence of his bandaged and sore body. What followed in his memory was even less clear. He seemed to remember being carried for a long while, up and down, in darkness split by lightning, and being deliriously cold and feverish. Ashlord's face, hovering very close to his own as his hand felt his brow. Looks of deep concern.

There was another face, too, appearing and disappearing beside Ashlord's, a face formed by Robby's own delirious dreams. He remembered, with chagrin, giving himself over to the madness of delirium, shaking so uncontrollably with fever that he could not speak. And he vaguely recalled being bathed, and even fed, by both Ashlord and the other one. Of how they smiled so kindly at him, covering him with blankets as he tried to complain about his pain, saying words of comfort while he had nightmares about wolves and soldiers and ghostly spirits turning him into stone, alternately shaking with fever and suffocating from intense heat while the noise of a terrible storm passed all around. He remembered struggling to get out of bed and to be off home, and Ashlord catching him as he fainted.

More memories whirled. Someone coming to him to offer comfort, that impossible face of his mad desire, the face of a girl, a young woman, a person he dearly missed. How she shared her warmth with him under blankets as he shivered with the chills of delirium and fever. Later, she was there again, clad in a hooded, brown cloak, standing over him, reassuring him that she would not be gone very long. He did not believe her because, even though he felt her lips touch his brow, he knew she was not actually there at all. He was overcome by madness and grief as tears streamed from his blurry eyes, soaking the pillow on both sides of his head as he watched her recede from view.

He remembered comings and goings and stirrings all about him as he slipped in and out of dark dreams. There was one in particular that recurred, a feeling more than a dream, of someone trying to get his attention, an indistinct shape, just out of his vision. No matter how he tried, desperate yet afraid to see who it was, he could not bring the figure into focus. Like the person he longed for, this one, too, kept slipping away. Another fever-induced delusion, this strange dream? It seemed so real, though. So very real.

Now, floating into what he was certain was wakefulness, he turned painfully onto his back and saw perched directly over the foot of his cot, on the thick oaken rafters above, a small owl, no more than the size of his hand. At first he felt the odd aura of dreamtime surround his perception. Robby blinked the feeling away. Strangely, next to the owl sat a small furry creature the same size as the owl with large eyes and little round ears. Like a squirrel it was, but smaller than most and light brown, and Robby first took it to be a chipmunk, but for its large eyes and fine coat. Both creatures watched him intently. The small furry thing sat up on its hind legs, and let out a sharp chirp. It crouched, then hurled itself downward, and as it did so, it spread out all four legs, making its body wide and flat as it swooped past Robby and landed on the bedpost behind him. It scurried down the post toward Robby, now sitting upright in surprise. The owl flew off over the curtain while the flying squirrel boldly hopped onto Robby's pillow and immediately burrowed itself underneath only to reappear on the other side a moment later. Robby put out his hand and the little thing hopped into it, purring for a moment before springing onto his shoulder. Just then, the curtain was gently pulled back, and Ashlord stuck his head under the line that held it up, his long, black hair hanging over his shoulders and his penetrating, black eyes glinting with a look of satisfaction.

"So you are awake," he said, smiling. "And you have met one of my household."

"Yes," Robby said, looking at the thing that was now jumping back onto the bedpost. "What is it?"

"He is a flying squirrel," Ashlord replied holding out his hand into which the nimble thing hopped. Robby noticed the head of the little owl peeking out from under Ashlord's long hair. It flapped his wings to get the hair off and hopped sideways out to the edge of Ashlord's shoulder. "And this, as I'm sure you know, is an owl."

"Is it a baby owl?"

"Oh, no," Ashlord chuckled. The owl stared at Robby coldly and slowly blinked at the question. "She is quite grown up. And she is older than I am. Her name is Certina. This little furry one we call Flitter," he said, putting the creature down on the bed. "Run along."

They watched Flitter hop gracefully off the bed and skitter under the curtain. Ashlord sat down on the cot and put his hand to Robby's brow and nodded.

"Your fever has broken," he said. "And most of your wounds are now on the mending side. At least there will be no more festering, I think."

"Where am I?" Robby asked.

"You are in my cottage at the southeast end of Attis ridge. You have been here four nights. Most in these parts call me Ashlord."

"My parents!" Robby gasped, starting from the bed. "They'll be worried sick! I have to go! Oh, my gosh!"

Pain shot through Robby's body, and he winced as Ashlord put out his hands to him.

"You are in no condition to go anywhere," he said gently. "And besides, the storm persists and all of the roads are impassable. I will get word to your folks as soon as I can, if I can, and I'll see that you get home as soon as possible."

"But I can't just lie here!" Robby insisted in spite of the pain.

"Well, in that case why don't you get dressed and sup with me?" Ashlord stood up. "But be careful with yourself. You've taken a mighty beating and have some nasty wounds. You lost a lot of blood before we found you and more still until we could properly clean and bandage you. On top of all that, you've been feverishly sick with what is called Wolftooth, if you know of it. Some call it Slobberfang. So easy does it! There are your clothes, what is left of them. If you feel the need to get up, then please join me when you are ready."

Ashlord retreated and closed the curtains while Robby struggled out of bed. He quickly realized how weak he was. Every movement pained him, and he became dizzy more than once as he dressed and put on his boots. His clothes had been mended and cleaned of most of the mud and blood. His cloak was clean, too, though in hopeless tatters.

When he pulled the curtain aside, he emerged into a large room. The walls were of stone, covered with all sorts of shelves and hooks supporting herbs, books, clothes, and a few weapons. Gourds and bottles hung from the rafters along with many potted plants and some nets full of vegetables. On one side of the room were two long tables strewn with scrolls, stacks of books and manuscripts, papers and bottles of ink. There were maps on the walls, too, as well as other charts—of the stars, Robby thought—and many lamps stood on the tables or hung low from the ceiling. Nearby was a fireplace, now burning lowly, and a few straight-backed chairs. On the other side of the room was a larger fireplace, for cooking, and more tables and cupboards and wooden closets. Ashlord was bent over a pot, ladling steaming portions into bowls. These he carried to a table, broke bread onto some plates, and set them out along with spoons.

"Ah, good. Sit here," he said when he saw Robby. He pulled out a chair at the table near the cooking hearth and motioned to him. Robby realized he was famished, and as he ate the hearty stew, it quickly did its good work on him. Ashlord sat across from him, eating more slowly, and keeping an eye on the boy. Certina and Flitter sat together on a rafter and watched.

"What brings you out from Passdale?" Ashlord asked at last.

"To see you," Robby nodded, his mouth still half full. "Pardon me," he said after he had swallowed. "I came to see you."

"Oh?"

"Well, not exactly to see you. More like to bring something to you. A parcel," Robby wiped his mouth and got up. Soon he had returned with his delivery. "This is why I came. I was asked to bring it to you by the King's Post Rider." He handed over the parcel and Ashlord looked at it curiously, almost nervously, as he turned it over in his hands, examining it carefully.

"It hasn't been opened," Robby said earnestly. "Not since I've had it, unless, since I've been here...."

"Oh no," Ashlord said. "No one has gone into your things."

"Well," Robby went on, "anyway, that is why I came. The rider said it was urgent, yet he had another errand equally urgent and could not go in two directions at once. I don't think I'm explaining this very well."

"Well enough," Ashlord said, "if Ullin Saheed Tallin was the rider."

"Yes, he was! How did you know?"

"He alone delivers dispatches with this seal in the Eastlands." Ashlord held up the parcel showing the lead seal and the lettering molded into it. "And I believe you and I have met before?"

"Oh, yes, forgive me. I am Robby Ribbon, son of Robigor Ribbon. We run the sundries store in Passdale and that is where we have seen each other before. Ullin Saheed is my mother's brother's son."

"Your mother's brother?" Ashlord raised his eyebrows. "Your mother is Mirabella Tallin?"

"Yes. Do you know her?"

Ashlord looked away, absently staring at the fireplace.

"Ullin's cousin. That may explain some things," he said to himself. "Excuse me, do I what?"

"Do you know my mother?"

"Oh, no. I mean, sort of. I saw her once. More than once. Many, many years ago. I knew Ullin's father quite well, though, and somewhat well your mother's other brother and her father, your grandfather. I knew Ullin had an aunt. But I did not know that she was married and had a child."

"Oh?" Robby was starting to think this was really something. Perhaps, after years of mystery he might at last learn more about his family.

"Yes, but that was long ago." Ashlord's voice trailed off and his eyes wandered back to the fireplace. "I thought she still lived in Tallinvale. I certainly did not know she was married. Or had a child."

Suddenly the door burst open and the brown-clad figure came in, bent over against the blowing rain. He closed the door and stamped the wet off, removed his quiver of arrows and hung them up beside his bow on the wall next to the door. Still facing the door, he pulled back his hood and shook out his wet hair. It was long and brown, and Robby realized as the cloak came off and the figure turned around that it was a girl. And not just any girl.

"Sheila Pradkin!" Robby exclaimed, standing up in complete surprise. "What on earth are you doing here?"

He remembered the night on Tulith Attis, the arrows that flew. And he again had dim memories of the brown-clad figure next to his bed and the girl, unclad, in his bed. He felt the blood run to his face, and he knew he was blushing, which embarrassed him even more.

"I might ask the same of you," she retorted.

"Sheila told me she was acquainted with you," Ashlord put in. "Come in. I was expecting you, so I put out some food for you."

"Good!" she said, and unceremoniously sat down and began eating. Robby slowly took his chair and quietly resumed eating, too. Ashlord look back and forth at the two, as if waiting for more from them, and hearing from their silence more than he needed to know.

"Well," he shrugged at last. "So we all have some explaining to do. But first, Sheila, how do things look in the countryside?"

"The roads are all still flooded," she said with her mouth full. "Pardon me. No sign of letting up. Lots of deer coming up the hill, as well as every other manner of beast."

"Just as I thought," Ashlord said. "More for you?"

Robby shook his head.

"No, thank you. That was just what I needed. Very good stew," Robby added, looking at Sheila.

"I am the cook around here," said Ashlord clearing his plate. "Sheila's talents lie elsewhere."

"Oh," Robby said. He could hardly take his eyes from her. They had known each other since childhood. She was something of a legend around Passdale and Barley. The Wild Girl, some called her, because she did not go to learn letters with the other children, but was ever seen in the fields and woods hunting or fishing or sometimes working the crops with the Barleymen. She also looked different from the other girls Robby knew. Most of the Passdale and Barley girls tended to be either on the round or straight sides, thin or thick, one might say. However, Sheila was Robby's height, maybe just a little taller, and was neither thin nor thick, except in those places where it was becoming to be so. Tomboyish though she may be, there was nothing boyish about her appearance, other than her manner of dressing. Before two years ago, they had barely spoken.

After a chance meeting, they quickly became friends, of a sort, though they tried to keep their relationship a secret from others. They traded lessons. She taught him to fish, and he gave her lessons in reading and writing and even some numbers. They each learned, though Robby was slower to catch fish than Sheila was to understand letters and words. And they grew ever closer, striving to guard their secret at Sheila's continuing insistence, even though it became more and more difficult, and, for Robby, more uncomfortable to do so. Naturally, their friendship grew into something much more significant. Their time together was filled with joy and young passion, and at every parting, they longed for and watched for another chance to be together.

More recent events sprang to Robby's mind as he ate and tried to think what he should now say. A month and a half ago, during the Midsummer's Day celebrations, Robby had overheard several Passdale boys saying unpleasant things about Sheila, and a fight resulted from his challenge to them on the subject. He got thoroughly beaten up and was only spared further humiliation when his friends Billy and Ibin happened along. Afterwards, when he told them what it was all about, he swore them to secrecy, not wishing for Sheila to know that he defended her so inadequately. Sheila found out anyway, and she came to see him at the shop, two days later, acting awkward and yet, it seemed, somehow vulnerable to Robby.

"I didn't ask ye to defend me," she had said.

"I did not defend you very well," Robby laughed, fingering a cut on his forehead, "Billy and Ibin did a better job than I did, even though they didn't even know what it was all about."

"Still," she said, touching his brow tenderly, "I never had a friend like ye. To stand up for me. I ain't very proper, an' I don't know gentle ways."

"Sh-h," Robby said taking her hands. "I am only a shop clerk, and that is probably all I will ever be. But I will always love you."

Suddenly she threw her arms around him and burst into tears.

"Oh, Robby," she stammered. "It ain't right!"

Then, hearing someone coming down the stairs, she tore herself loose and fled out the door. Robby started after her, but heard his father's voice calling.

He had not seen Sheila once since, and none of his friends knew where she had gone.

• • •

"She has been here these past many weeks," Ashlord said, as if he had read Robby's thoughts. "My pupil. And during that time she has learned much, I would say. More, even, than most would at old Broadweed's school for as many years." There was an air of pride that touched Ashlord's words, but Sheila remained silent and kept her eyes on her plate as she finished her food. "Of course, someone had already gotten her off to a good start."

Ashlord smiled at Robby, took the parcel of letters, and moved off to the opposite side of the room. There, he stoked the fire, picked up a few things, and moved some books from a chair. Robby watched him as he took an ember from the fire to light his long-stemmed pipe. He then sat down in front of the hearth, letting the parcel rest in his lap as he puffed and thoughtfully stared into the flames. Robby turned to Sheila.

"Are the roads truly blocked?" he asked at last in a low voice. She picked up her plate and put it away.

"Yes, from the foot of Tulith Attis to as far as the eye can see, floodwaters cover the land," she said.

"So I'm stuck here."

"As we all are."

"And I have been here all this time. All this time since you found me?"

"Yes. You lost a lot of blood and had wolf poison in you." She poured a tankard of ale from a small keg. "Here. This will help relieve your anxieties."

Robby noticed the very different way she spoke, now. It was more careful than before, and her Barley accent and drawl less distinct, and the words she used, like "relieve" and "anxieties" seemed odd coming from her lips.

"Has it been just the three of us, then? While I was sick?"

"Yes, but for two nights when Ashlord was away."

"Where did he go?"

"I do not know. His ways are his own."

"So you took care of me?"

Sheila looked at him, and he thought he saw a slight blush pass her cheeks.

"You were very cold, and I did not know what else to do."

"Well," Robby said, pretending he did not remember, "whatever it was you did must have worked as I am feeling much recovered. And I will always be thankful to you. And Ashlord."

"It was he who saved you," she said filling another tankard. She walked to the other side of the room and held it out to Ashlord. He shook himself from his thoughts and took it, nodding. He took a sip and then looked over at Robby.

"Come over here, you two," he said. "I think we have much to discuss."

Sheila and Robby brought chairs over and the three of them sat in a semicircle around the fire. Outside, the wind still blew and the rain pelted the windows.

"Might I ask how you came to be within the old fortress of Tulith Attis?" Ashlord queried.

Robby related the whole story starting from when Ullin showed up on the porch of their store in Passdale. He talked about the strange experience at Weepingbrook bridge, about the wolves, and how he discovered the bell room with its great bell, and how, when the wolves reappeared, he escaped through the iron door. Lastly, Robby told about the ghostly soldiers, or, rather, what he thought he had seen, for he was unsure of himself.

"Were they real? Truly?" he asked.

"Oh, yes," Ashlord said.

"But who, or what, were they?" Robby asked. "And I recall you saying something to them."

"Hmm. In good time," Ashlord said, taking a puff on his pipe and letting out a cloud of scented smoke. "Much of what you have told me I already surmised, and it is an amazing tale. And your adventure has touched events that run deeper and farther than you can imagine."

Robby saw that the parcel was still unopened on Ashlord's lap, and he looked over at Sheila, who had been silent the whole while, occasionally stirring from her seat to tend the fire.

"What do you mean?" Robby asked.

"Let us keep the story in order," Ashlord said at last, "by having Sheila tell her part. She is more than my pupil. She has become my agent, so to speak, and my helper. You see, I have been expecting this parcel, which contains some various letters to me, and I have been worried at the lateness of them. So, on the morning that you set out from Passdale, I asked Sheila to go there to make inquiries about the post. Knowing that Ullin Saheed would be carrying these, I also knew that he would have other important errands. I suspected he might be pressed for time. So I thought to save him the trip to Tulith Attis by sending Sheila to meet him."

"But I arrived too late," Sheila picked up. "Ashlord instructed me to make my purpose known to no one until I saw Ullin Saheed. I thought to meet him on the road on this side of the bridge, and I was to share a secret password with him so that he would know I am Ashlord's servant and the parcel would be safely delivered by me. When I came near to the Passdale Bridge, I saw the two of you coming together. I recognized him from Ashlord's description. I saw him take the other road as you came on toward me. So I climbed a tree and hid while I considered what to do.

"It was not possible to overtake Ullin, and yet I could not make up my mind whether to return to Ashlord or else try to get some news from town about when Ullin might return. While I debated, you passed by my hiding place. I almost called out to you, but Ashlord instructed me not to tell anyone at all about my task. Well, I decided I should return to Ashlord, so I dropped out of the tree and picked up the road behind you.

"It was not long before I had you in sight. I was sorely tempted to catch up to you, but, again, I remembered that Ashlord said no one should know my purpose, and," she glanced at Ashlord, then down at the floor, shrugging, "and I didn't think I could keep it from you if you asked. So I followed. I admit I was in more of a hurry than you seemed to be. And several times I thought you had seen me."

"I never did!" Robby said. "But I wish that I had. Your company would have been welcome, and maybe would have saved us both a lot of trouble, as it turned out."

"That is true," Sheila replied, nodding, "but how was I to know? At any rate, I did follow, never letting you leave my sight. When you came to Weepingbrook I could not believe you tarried there. Have you not heard the stories?"

Robby shrugged and was about to say something when Sheila continued.

"You must have, but either you put no credence in them or else have no fear of such things. I was sorely tempted to cry out at you when I saw you leisurely eat your lunch there. And you actually drew your knife!"

"So? I needed to use it. What's wrong with that?" Robby looked back and forth from Ashlord, whose eyebrows raised as if waiting for Robby to answer himself, to Sheila who was looking at him with indignant surprise. "I don't understand."

"Sheila assumes that the lore that she has been taught is known to all," he said. "But Men have lost much, in memory and elsewhere, and few speak of such things as you have blundered into, Master Ribbon. Yet, your narrow escape, of which Sheila has told me, from the bridge at Weepingbrook is but one of many such wonders. You seem to have a knack for such blunders, and a gift for narrow escapes."

"I don't know what you are talking about," Robby said. "At Weepingbrook, I mean."

"You left this behind there," Ashlord reached over to the table and picked up the knife that Robby had left on the bridge.

"I picked it up after I saw you flee the bridge," Sheila added.

"I did not flee," Robby stammered. "Only, only—"

"Only you forgot your knife," Sheila retorted.

"Did you know this knife was made in Duinnor?" Ashlord asked, handing it to Robby. Robby looked at the blade and shook his head.

"No," he said seeing for the first time the small markings on the base of the blade. "It came in a case of trading goods awhile back."

"Well, more about it later," Ashlord said, waving his hand in dismissal of the current subject. "Let Sheila continue."

"There's not much more to say after that," she resumed. "It wasn't until you were nearly at Oldgate that I thought you might be going to Tulith Attis and carrying dispatches from Ullin. I couldn't be sure so I kept low and continued to follow. But the land between here and Oldgate is open, with little cover, and I had to linger a far ways behind you. When you took the North Road around Tulith Attis, instead of coming to the east, I was confused. I thought maybe you were lost or else you were on some other errand. Anyway, in the storm I lost sight of you several times as you neared the bridge. I could hardly believe my eyes when I saw you go across the bridge. Then I saw the wolves coming between us. By the time I got near enough to use my bow, you had disappeared. I killed three of the wolves, but there were more than I had arrows so I could not cross the bridge to follow you. Still, I called out to you, but the storm was so loud and the noise of the wolves, too, that I barely heard my own shout. I myself was chased by the wolves and managed to kill four more before reaching the safety of this house."

"She told me what had passed," Ashlord picked up, "and we immediately set out to find you. We searched as far as the bridge, but saw no sign of you, nor any signs of wolves, except the carcasses of those Sheila dispatched. Thinking that you might have come back this way, missing us in the dark, we were nearly back here when we heard the tolling of Tulith Hammer, for so the legends call the bell you discovered."

"Won't you please tell me what happened?" Robby pleaded. "Why did the bell ring? What was that room where it hung? And who where those soldiers, and what did they want with me?"

"There is much to explain, indeed," Ashlord said, rising from his chair. "And since the rain allows for little else this day," he said peering through a foggy window then turning back to Robby, "the telling of whys and wherefores is the least we can do. However, you come into the middle of a tale that has not yet been finished in its making. Indeed, wherever I choose to begin the tale would even be in itself starting after the beginning, since its very beginnings are lost to all memory."

Robby closed his eyes trying to follow the meaning of Ashlord's speech. After a moment, he stopped trying to untie the riddle of the odd man's words and opened his eyes. Ashlord was holding a metal box out to him, about two hands wide and about as deep. It was made of copper, and its hinged lid was shut with a clasp that had a lock made into it.

"Could you open that for me while I fetch something?" Ashlord asked. Robby took the box and looked at Sheila, who shrugged. While Robby looked at the box, Ashlord rummaged through some papers on a nearby table.

"What I wouldn't give for a thimble of True Ink!" he muttered.

"Pardon me?" Sheila asked.

"Nothing. Nothing. Just talking to myself."

Robby fingered the lock and tugged gently on the lid. There was a light click and the lid opened. The only thing inside was a small key, which Robby removed.

"Ah, thank you." Ashlord said taking the key and the box. "I've been trying to open that box for ages." He closed the lid and put the box on the table. "Just needed the right touch, I suppose," he added, looking at Robby with a mischievous glint in his eye as Certina landed on his shoulder.

Cocking his head to look at the creature, he nodded and offered the key to her. She promptly took it in her beak and flew off.

"Now, where were we?" he said, sitting back down. "Oh, yes! Well, an explanation. Hmm. Where to begin?"

Ashlord sat back in his chair and gazed at the ceiling for a long moment. Robby saw nothing very interesting up there.

"I suppose you have heard of Faerum?"

Robby perked up.

"The mythical land where the Faere Folk are supposed to have come from?"

"Ah, well, Faerum is not mythical, it is not a land, but many lands, and they did not come from there. Faerum once was where we now sit, and it covered all the lands of the world from the sea to even the unknown places beyond the Westlands. All kingdoms were once part of Faerum, a vast empire of forests and fields, mountains and rivers. Faerum was here before Men came into the world, and, it is said, will be restored when Men are a faded memory. It is told, in legend and in song, that once the Faere people were given unto the earth and the earth to them, and that they were made by Beras, lord of all the gods, to be immortal and without sickness or trouble. That they needed not any sustenance but sunlight and shade, moonbeam and starlight, water and wind. And so they rejoiced in the earth and lived happily and in peace with all the creatures of the earth and with rock and river and in every place of the world above or below or upon the ground and within the waters of the rivers and streams, the lakes and the seas. Many ages passed uncounted. Eventually, Dragons appeared and multiplied their offspring across the land, making waste the forests and the fields and befouling the waters and the air. They made slaves to serve them, and it was they, those slaves, who became the Dragon People. It was in those days, so the songs go, that some of the Faere Folk first took up arms and learned the craft of war. They lay spells and enchantments upon most of the lands yet unspoiled by the Dragon people. But there was a sundering among the great houses of Faerum, for many chose not to wage war and deemed it an evil thing, and they shunned those who did the fighting. Chief among these was Aperion, King of the Faere, and he took away the peaceful ones of the Faerekind, though some have lingered, it is said, in hidden places of the world. But those who remained to fight against the Dragon People accepted their curse, calling themselves the Elifaen, meaning the Fallen Children. Sometimes they are called elves in the Common Tongue. There arose from them great warriors and armies, and they contended with the Dragon People for dominion over the earth. For many ages there was war and waste, and much of what the Elifaen sought to preserve was destroyed or lost. Many of the Elifaen died in battle or were taken as thralls, and their numbers dwindled, for they have very few offspring. The long wars with the Dragonkind sapped the Elifaen of their vitality, poisoned their hearts with hatred and shame, and, understanding what they had lost, they slowly became a forlorn people.

"Then Men came to these shores in great ships likened unto floating cities, though where they came from has been lost to memory. Here they sought a home and a rest from an age of wandering upon the seas, and they built towns and farms, thinking the land free of inhabitants, for the watching Elifaen kept themselves hidden, at first. But the marauding Dragon People soon discovered Men and made war upon them, and the Faere Elifaen learned of the beleaguered newcomers and came to their aid. It was then that a great alliance was made between Elves and Men, and the Dragon People were defeated and driven from the lands. For many generations there was peace once again in the lands, and Men grew in numbers while the remains of the Faerekind, the Elifaen, continued to diminish. Many kingdoms of Men were established and many cities were built and much learning did the Elves and Men enjoy. But the spies and provocateurs of their enemy spread discord among the victorious and won over many who attacked the cities and lands of the Elifaen, slaughtering many. And so the Elifaen were falsely lured into war against Men and there was much chaos in the lands. But the Elifaen were no match for the fell warriors of the race of Men, and even as the armies of Men fought each other, the Elifaen ever suffered the worse brunt of all fighting. Until, many hundreds of years ago, the Dragonkind raised a mighty army, sweeping north and east across the world, laying waste the cities and lands of both races. So Elifaen and Men joined to face the armies of the Dragon People.

"It was here, at Tulith Attis, that one of the greatest battles of those days was fought. The battle that took place here is a tale of itself. Suffice it to say that Tulith Attis, the last refuge of free peoples of this region, fell at last to the enemy, though it fell by betrayal, not by might. Yet that betrayal availed the enemy naught, and served as a noose about their necks. The enemy was delayed here in their effort to take the fortress, so gallantly was it defended. That delay was their ultimate doom, for, but a few days later, there took place another great battle along the banks of the Saerdulin when the combined armies of Duinnor, Glareth, and Vanara caught and surrounded the Dragonkind. It was a fierce battle beside the river banks, and the invaders were utterly defeated. However, new seeds of discord were sewn amongst Elves and Men to grow and fester to this very day.

"After the battle was over and the burial mounds were raised, there was a terrible blight upon these lands for many years. In that age, before the battle, even, the river that flowed behind this fortress was changed in its course. It took a new path for many miles between what is now Passdale and Barley. Along that stretch, it is now called the Bentwide in the Common Tongue. Eventually, people once again came to live in these parts and scattered villages grew up. Yet ever has there been a wariness of

Tulith Attis, and few dare come this way. The eastward road, once a highway of trade and commerce, now lies abandoned and lost in the Forest Mistwarren, which surrounds the Boggy Wood. And it is said the Boggy Wood still carries the curse laid upon it by the Dragon People."

Ashlord sighed heavily and tapped out his pipe into the fire. Sheila sat quietly and Robby stared at the fire in thought. He already knew some of what Ashlord related, at least in broad strokes. Who didn't? Ashlord was obviously very learned about such things, much more so than Mr. Broadweed, the schoolmaster. Robby was unsure what all this had to do with his errand. He waited patiently for Ashlord to continue, but once more the man seemed lost in his own thoughts.

"So what was this place? I mean originally?" he ventured at last.

"A stronghold overlooking the bridge, originally," Ashlord said. "But in latter days it was a garrison town, and the abode of the Elifaen Prince Heneil and the House of Fairfir. It was he who built the circle room and made from it a way to the river. From here, boats could easily ply down the old river southward to the sea and many sailed up from there, for the river narrowed just between the landing and the bridge. It was Prince Heneil who reached an accord with the Men of this region and gathered the people together in haven against the approaching armies. And it was he who sealed the great iron door against the attackers.

"You see," Ashlord went on, "it was a trap laid to catch a traitor. For Heneil knew there was a plot brewing against him, but knew not who the agent was. He knew that one of the Elifaen, those who have Faere blood, could open that door, but any that did so would find themselves beset by the stone warriors in the Bell Room. It was they you heard behind you, slaughtering the wolves that chased you. And as another trap, he devised the great bell to toll, summoning his warriors from the field to the summit where the women and children took refuge, guarded by Heneil's most trusted men. In stone he set them, to stand guard needless of food or drink, hidden by a covering likened unto columns of stone. Their awakening signal was the tolling of the great iron bell, and their duty was to slay any intruder. But never were they called, and the families they were to guard had a gruesome fate. This much I can say: when you opened the door to escape the wolves, you rang the Great Bell, and you awoke much in this hill. And perhaps elsewhere, too. Narrowly did we arrive in time to save you."

"What did you say to him? The captain that came from the stone. I've never seen the likes of him or his fellows. Fearsome they were, yet—"

"Beautiful?" Ashlord finished. "Yes, handsome and fell. Elifaen of Heneil's household, from the Time Before Time, when the world was made."

"What did you say to the captain?"

"I challenged him to stay his hand, and I told him the battle was over."

"I think you said more than that," Robby stated.

"Well, yes. He did not believe me at first. You see, it was as if only a moment had passed since he and his men were spellbound. I explained to him that the battle had been lost at great cost and that the war was long over."

"What was it that he kept saying as he left?"

" 'All for nothing.' "

Robby fidgeted in his chair. Outside the rain battered and the wind continued to blow.

"So, where did he and his men go?"

Ashlord shrugged.

"None can say where the spirits of the past may go, nor when they may come again."

Robby sighed, not very satisfied with the answer. "All of this is hard to believe," he said, shaking his head. "There's something not right about all this."

"Don't be troubled by the tales of an old man. Many reasons may yet be found for your adventures," Ashlord said. "Maybe what you need is more rest, Master Ribbon. And perhaps I need more time to think things over."

Ashlord's eyes, black as coal, glittered in the firelight as he smiled kindly at Robby. Robby realized that though the food and ale had relaxed him, he was still very tired.

"I have to admit, I am still pretty sore," Robby said standing up.

"We will eat again after awhile, and maybe then you'll have more questions," Sheila said going to the door. "I'll get more firewood from the shed."

"And I would like to take a look at these letters that you went to so much trouble to deliver," said Ashlord. "I think you should lie down and rest awhile more."

Robby was suddenly overcome with sleepiness, and, nodding, he went back to the cot and started pulling off his boots. Barely did he have them off before his eyes were closed. Soon he was snoring softly, in the company of mild, peaceful dreams.

While Robby slept, Ashlord carefully opened the parcel from Ullin. Inside were three letters; he read each one carefully, then read all three again. As the rainy day moved into night, Ashlord remained in front of the fire, puffing on his pipe, the letters in his lap. Now and then, he gazed over at Robby asleep on the cot. The rain continued to fall for many hours, and after it was fully dark, it turned to a cold drizzle. Sheila built up the fires, as Ashlord stirred from his chair and consulted some maps. Certina ignored Flitter who was trying to show off his gliding skills by leaping from the rafters to the kitchen table and then scrambling back up the wall and into the rafters to start over again.

Robby tossed and turned for a while, then fell again into a deep slumber. Many hours later, he opened his eyes and saw Certina sitting on the rafter over his bed. She soared down and landed on his chest and stared at him with her big, amber eyes. Half-asleep, Robby imagined she was talking to him, but her voice was so low that he could not understand the words, or else they were of a language that he did not know. Robby closed his eyes again to listen more carefully, not daring to stir lest the owl fly away. There was something terribly odd about her, he was thinking, but also comforting. When he opened his eyes again, she was gone. He could hear the crack of the fireplace, and the flickering light danced in the rafters above the curtain that someone had pulled about his alcove. Ashlord and Sheila were talking softly, but Robby could not make out what they were saying. He listened more carefully and realized the two were speaking in whispers. He slipped quietly out of the bed to peek through a small gap in the curtains.

As Ashlord handed Sheila the small copper box, he pointed at it. She whispered back to Ashlord, turning the box over and over in her hands. She was clearly amazed at something, and when she glanced Robby's way, he ducked back from the curtains. A moment later, he peeked again. Sheila was excitedly telling something to Ashlord, who was nodding his head. Sitting back down on the bed, making it creak, Robby then drew the curtains, stretching and yawning.

"My!" he said in a jolly tone, "That was a good nap!"

"Ah, Master Ribbon," Ashlord greeted him. "How long have you been awake?"

"Oh, I just woke up."

"You did?" Ashlord stood. "Then I suppose you are hungry again."

"Well, sure, but," Robby started.

"But?"

"Well, it looked as though you two were discussing something," he probed, "and I don't want to interrupt. I've been such a bother already."

"No bother at all," Sheila said before Ashlord could respond, going to the kitchen area. "I'm a bit ready for some breakfast myself."

"Breakfast? What happened to supper?"

"I'm afraid you slept through supper," Ashlord said. "And all through the night and day, and now it is nigh upon dawn."

Robby was dumbfounded. He certainly did not feel like he had slept that long. Yet, however long, he *was* uncommonly rested.

"Oh, well," he said at last, shrugging. "I'm sorry if I've kept you from anything."

"No, no, nothing," Sheila said, taking down some eggs.

"Actually," Ashlord approached, "the rain seems to be tapering off, and my bones tell me the sky will be clearing before midday, though it will be cool. I'm of a mind to go for a walk up the hill to see the results of all this rain. Once you've eaten a bite or two, and have your boots on, perhaps you would feel up to going along? The walk may do you some good if we do not press too hard. And we may be able to see if the roads have cleared enough for passage."

Robby eagerly agreed to this and soon had on his boots and cloak. He took his cloak back off when he realized Ashlord was scrambling some of the eggs for breakfast. Sheila led him through a small door to a room where he could wash his face.

"We must talk," Robby said to her quietly and urgently.

"Not now, Robby," she said, handing him a towel. "But, yes. We'll talk."

When he emerged, the table was set. Robby ate quickly, not only because he was hungry but also because he was anxious to get home, and he looked forward to being on his way. He still had many questions about this place, too, and he hoped to get a few more answers before he left. He also hoped for a private word with Sheila, some explanation as to why she disappeared from Barley, and what she had been doing since she left.

She ate silently beside him, and Ashlord ate not at all, poring over scrolls and scratching his head all the while. At last, after the two had eaten their fill and cleaned the plates, Ashlord approached Robby.

"I'm afraid it will be a cool day," Ashlord said, "and your cloak is probably too light, and it is rather spent. I have a few things that might fit you that would be good enough until you get home."

So at Ashlord's insistence, Robby accepted a heavier shirt and vest as well as a coat to wear over them. Robby slipped his cloak on over them all, tattered though it was, but it had a hood and it was still drizzling out.

"I don't think you'll need your bag," Ashlord said as Robby reached for it. "But you may find this useful." He handed Robby a long, thick stick, almost up to Robby's shoulder. "Our way may be muddy or slippery and it may help you through the rough spots."

Soon they were outside, and Robby could discern in the gray light a yard of sorts, fenced in by a stone wall. Everywhere there were the remains of gardens hopelessly washed out and squashed down by the heavy rains. Ashlord led Robby through a gate and along a path. Sheila followed with her bow and quiver of arrows, and Robby remembered the arrows that had struck the stone ghost-captain on the hilltop. His memory was still vague and confused, but it began to dawn on him that she had many talents, hitting a target with an arrow while on the run not the least of them. He knew her to be an expert archer. After years of a confused relationship with her, and these past weeks of her absence, he longed to talk to her. Yet she seemed stern as he had never imagined her, and he wondered if it was his presence that made her this way or if some change had come about in her. Her boisterous laughter was nowhere to be heard; indeed, she had smiled very little since his arrival. And he had already noticed how her speech had changed. Her loss of the Barley twang and her more proper way of saying things was evidence, no doubt, of Ashlord's intense tutelage. Most striking, though, was the powerful air of sadness that seemed to surround and weigh down upon her.

The threesome continued along the path, winding up and down, but mostly upward, through the misty drizzle that blew about. As they made their way through a thin copse, Robby realized they must be halfway or more up the hill, but the air was so gray he could see little of what lay below them to either side of the ridge. The path broadened as they continued, and it was soon lined with paving stones. As the drizzle finally thinned, Robby saw they were headed toward a steep bank rising dark green ahead. As they neared, Robby realized it was part of the ancient walls that surrounded the upper fortress, now covered with ivy and brush. An opening in the wall, about ten yards wide, must have once been the main gate. Inside the dark tunnel-like passage that passed nearly thirty feet through the thickness of the wall, Robby perceived huge iron bars twisted and bent that must have once been part of a portcullis. As they emerged, Robby saw that few trees grew inside, but grass and moss was thick everywhere, with ivy running over many places. It was bigger inside than Robby remembered, and he reckoned you could fit almost half of the houses in Passdale within the grounds surrounded by the walls. Suddenly, Robby halted, looking around warily as a pang of fear shot through him.

"Where are the wolves?" he asked. "I mean, the dead ones."

"I came up here yesterday and cleaned up a bit," Ashlord said.

"You did? In the pouring rain? What did you—"

"I stripped down naked so that the rain would cleanse me as I worked. And I hauled the carcasses up there." Ashlord pointed up at the eastern wall. "I threw them down into the gully below. There were a few stragglers, too. They went the same way."

Ashlord led them the opposite way along the base of the western wall to a steep stone staircase. Seeing Robby's hesitation, he stopped. "I felt it a disgrace that they should litter these grounds with their stench. It's perfectly safe, now. I do assure you it is."

Robby came along, and they climbed the stairs onto the ramparts. He followed Ashlord hesitantly.

"I often come up here, you see," said Ashlord waving his arm. "To think. And to watch. And I've come to think of this place as, well, as my own, in a way."

"Watch for what?" Robby asked, looking around.

"Hmm, well, for whatever might be seen, naturally," Ashlord said.

"Or unnaturally," Sheila muttered from behind Robby.

The air brightened dramatically, and a cool breeze danced by from the northwest.

"Ah!" Ashlord said. "It looks to be clearing earlier than I thought."

He stopped and sat down on a large, square stone and pointed across toward the opposite side.

"Over there is where we found you the other night," he said. "And that must be where you emerged from underground."

Robby saw that where the opening had been was a large hole, filled with a jumble of rocks and mud. "Is the storm the cause of that?"

"I do not think so," Ashlord said. "It seems you set in motion a chain of events that was intended for less gentle persons than you."

"What do you mean?"

"When you described your adventures to us the other night, you failed to mention if you saw any writing, in particular over the iron door."

"Yes. Yes, I did," Robby nodded. "I even copied it down into my order book. I could show you if I had brought it along."

"No need," Ashlord stood, picking up his walking stick. "I believe it was something like this." He began scratching figures on the ground and Robby thought he recognized them.

"I believe those are the writings I saw," Robby nodded. "Do you know what they say?"

"Oh, yes. I do," Ashlord smiled. "But when they were carved and the bell room assembled, it was never imagined there would come a time when that writing would not be understood. The language is long lost and the present speech of the west is its closest relative. Had you been able to read the Ancient Speech, you may not be standing here now, for surely you would have not attempted to pass that way. Sheila can tell you what it says."

Sheila came closer and looked at the writing, then she carefully and slowly read each word aloud, as one not practiced in the art of reading.

"By the hand of Amandoel—Is it Amandoel?" she asked Ashlord.

"Yes, that is right. Amandoel," Ashlord nodded.

"By the hand of Amandoel," Sheila continued, "this door is sealed and barred, lest the bell of Attis toll and wake the stony guard."

Ashlord nodded and smiled at Sheila.

"When did you learn to read the Ancient Speech?" Robby asked, astonished at her ability.

"Ashlord taught me," she said, a bit embarrassed. "I'm still learning. I'm not very good at it."

"Your skill is remarkable, Sheila, for the short time you've had to learn. That reading was very good, indeed," Ashlord said. Looking at Robby, he continued. "Although there is much of the story that I am not sure of, I will tell you some of what I have come to know about this place. I have been to the Circle Room, and I have gazed upon the murals and studied the Iron Door. Not for many years, though. How I came to live here is a long tale, too, but it is bound up in the story of this place. Although the great battle took place before my time, the history of Tulith Attis and my own are intertwined, somewhat, just as now your life now is. Perhaps I am getting ahead of things, but much is happening in the world. The signs of change and omens of great struggles long put off have been building for many years and their fulfillment is nigh at hand. Your coming here has something to do with it, though I cannot yet tell what it may be. Although many have tried, including myself, it was you who awoke the guard of Tulith Attis, and have fulfilled part of the old prophecies, even though your manner of doing so nearly cost you your life."

"But you said the other night that only Faerekind could open the door," Robby interrupted. "But no one at all was with me."

"Yes," Ashlord nodded. "And that was a great mystery to me, for you certainly do not have the look of the Faere. I believe there is more to you than can be seen."

Robby looked at Ashlord, his dark eyes glinting as the first rays of sunlight in many days broke through the clouds. Robby realized what Ashlord was saying and looked at Sheila who was standing near the edge of the wall looking on with a rather stern expression.

"No!" Robby insisted. "My father is Robigor Ribbon, and his father was Hannis, son of Balfast. My mother is Mirabella, daughter of Danig Tallin."

"I know. I know," said Ashlord, shaking his head and holding up his hand. "It was all a great mystery to me, too. For how could a store clerk, the son of a store clerk, be one of the Elifaen? Yet, you possess one of the rarest gifts of the Faere, one that very few of that race has ever had, the ability to open sealed doors and release locks. You proved it when you opened the little box I gave you. For many years, I have purposely kept that box closed and locked, with the only key to it within, as a test. I suspected that one of the Faere people might someday return to Tulith Attis, and by the means of having them open that box they would be revealed to me. You see, my purpose here was to learn who betrayed the hill that day, and I believe it was one of the Elifaen, descendants of the Faerekind, not one of the race of Men as is commonly taught. It was he that I thought I was to watch for, to wait for, and to discover. But I was wrong. It was not the first time I have been mistaken, and will not be the last, I fear."

"I don't know what any of that has to do with me," Robby said.

"It has to do with you because you proved that the door could be opened," Ashlord explained, "and that it was not just a ploy. Heneil, called Amandoel by his people, built it, and he suspected that one of his own kind would betray them. He thought that the traitor would lead a force of the enemy through the tunnel passage to assault the fortress from within. So he placed the Iron Door there with its guards. Since the door was never opened, most have since thought that a Man, and not an Elf, was the traitor, because Men could not hope to open the door, but might manage to open the main gate, there, from within. The Iron Door in the bell room remained shut, and has for all these long years. After this place was betrayed, what else could people think but that it was a Man?"

"Why do you think it was not a Man who betrayed the fortress?" asked Sheila.

"Because only a few Men were here, perhaps less than two hundred. And all were killed, and, later, their bodies identified by kin. So the books say, and I believe it to be true," Ashlord said. "How those Men came to be here is a tale unto itself, and though it is worthy of the telling, that must be left for another time. They did not betray the fortress, and the armies of Men had not yet arrived, and would not do so until six days later. Someone who was trusted betrayed this hill, and he was not a mortal. Heneil thought the threat might come from his rear, by an attack up the river and by a party of Dragonkind led through the inner passage, through the Circle Room. Whoever the traitor was, he was probably already here and must have known of the trap of that room. He could have opened the door and come that way, but his identity would have been revealed. Better to cast blame elsewhere, after the foul deed was done."

"But I opened it!" Robby said.

"Yes, I know."

"There! Your story just doesn't make sense, then."

Ashlord tilted his head. "Did you know that your mother's mother was Elifaen, a descendant of the Faerekind? And that makes your mother Elifaen, too."

Robby's head began to spin. Never mind that it was unlucky to speak of the Faere Folk, according to common Passdale ways. Ashlord's suggestion was just plain preposterous.

"No. I mean," he stammered.

"Your grandmother on your mother's side died long before you were born," Ashlord said. "Do you happen to know how old your mother is? Or, tell me this, have you ever seen her bare back?"

"What? No!" Robby said indignantly. This line of talk was getting more uncouth by the moment, and Robby was beginning to feel a little offended. Calling someone Faere was not considered a compliment. Robby was about to respond by saying so when he stopped himself. He did not, in fact, know his mother's true age. Every birthday, she celebrated her twenty-ninth as a matter of jest, telling Robby that when he reached twenty-nine, she would tell him her true age. And, also, Robby did remember seeing his mother's back, when he was a small child and she would bathe with him. She had two long scars; they curved down her back from the top of each shoulder to below her waist.

"How did you know about those?" Robby asked quietly. He glanced at Sheila who was looking down at her feet.

"Every Elifaen bears those scars," Ashlord said. "For it is a curse to them, and a reminder always of their fallen state, that when they were cursed for taking up arms, they were stripped of their wings. From that day forward, however long they abide on the earth, never again will the

Elifaen fly. Heavy their bodies became, and, though lightly do they yet walk, no more do they commune in the air. And it became their lot to feel the heat of summer and the cold of winter, and to have thirst and hunger, which they had never known before, and they were suffered to endure all manner of the pains of mortal beings save sickness, old age, or natural death. And from that day, from the shame of their appearance, have the Elifaen covered themselves with clothing, for until then clothing was a thing of the Enemy, who needed protection from nature. All of their offspring who carry the blood of the Faere come to have those same scars."

Ashlord looked solemnly at Robby, who had shoved his hands into his pockets and was staring blankly back at him. "I didn't know the Faere could fly."

"None who have remained in this world can," Sheila said.

"Your mother, Mirabella Tallin, was born of an Elifaen mother and a Mortal Man," Ashlord said. "And so you have Elifaen blood, Master Ribbon."

"Is that why the door opened?" Robby asked reluctantly. There was more to be learned, he feared, than he wanted to know. "Is that why the bell rang?"

"I do not know," Ashlord said, "for I have never heard of the children of such unions having any of the gifts of their forebears until they are old in years. And only the Firstborn of the Faerekind, those from when the world was newly made, are said to have the gift of opening all things closed and locked. Yet I believe you to be Faere Blessed, and so are doubly touched by those folk. Indeed, I now know that two Elifaen sisters visited you when you were a child. Twins, they were, one with the aspect of red and black and one with the aspect of white and green. I believe they were summoned to come to you and to debate your life."

"To what?"

"The one in black came as a representative of what follows when death comes. The one in white came to represent what follows when life comes. They debated over you. Should Death take you? Or should Life retain you? It is an ancient practice for the descendants of the Faerekind to represent the gods to Mortals, and to judge when called upon by their kin. Your mother, being kin to both races, most certainly summoned them, and they came for her sake. They cured you of your illness, but something else happened, I know not what, and they chose to bestow their blessing upon you. Perhaps they gave you their blessing in order to save you from death, or perhaps it was for some other reason entirely."

"How did you know about that?"

"I told him," Sheila spoke up. Seeing the look on Robby's face, she continued, somewhat defensively. "Well, everyone talks about how queer your mother's family is. A mixed race family from the ancient western lands. And how she is estranged—is that the right word?—estranged from most of her kin. Anyway, Frizella Bosk told me that when you were little you got very sick and that Faere Folk came to see you. She said that she saw it with her own eyes, through a crack in the door, as she was there, too. Her own efforts to help you had failed, she said. And she told me how your mother somehow summoned, through prayer or something, these Faerekind ladies. She said she never told anybody and made me promise not to tell. It's just that, well, she thought I should know. And I thought Ashlord should know."

Sheila looked genuinely embarrassed, but Robby wasn't sure why. Robby, for his part, kept shaking his head, looking back and forth from Ashlord to Sheila.

"Ought to know? Why?" he asked at last. "Why should it be that my own mother wouldn't tell me? And why, if it was such a secret, would Billy Bosk's mum tell you? And if you promised, why did you tell him?" Robby jabbed a finger at Ashlord, still looking at Sheila.

"Frizella had her own reasons for telling me," Sheila replied, "and I only told Ashlord just last night because of what happened to you here."

"And the reason your parents did not tell you is easy enough to guess," Ashlord picked up. "The Elifaen still have many enemies, and they are yet mistrusted by Men. Their numbers are in decline, and those who live apart from their own kind and in the midst of Men expect little help or protection from them. Your parents wanted only to protect you from the prejudice of others, I'm sure, and perhaps from other things. They know they cannot keep this from you forever. Perhaps they hope to tell you when you turn twenty-nine; only they can say. But it is important that you keep your knowledge to yourself."

"Why?"

"Because any sudden reaction or slip of the tongue may alert the spies and agents of the enemy." Ashlord stood up just as Certina flew out of the sky and landed on his shoulder. "Who knows the danger to you, but why take unnecessary chances? Your secret is safe with Sheila and with me, but I'm afraid we were not the only ones who heard the Great Bell. Word may eventually reach the traitor of Tulith Attis that the Iron Door has been opened."

"Why should that matter? Surely he is dead by now, as are all else who might care."

Ashlord shook his head. Certina flapped her wings and twisted her head sideways. He put his hand on Robby's shoulder.

"You do have much to learn," he said kindly. "The Elifaen do not die, unless by violence, of melancholia, or, in some cases, of grief. Chances are, the traitor still lives. And who knows what power he may have gained by now? Certainly, the knowledge that the Door was set as a trap by Lord Heneil, will rekindle suspicions against all Elifaen. There are only a few who still remain from those days, and fewer still who were here, for nearly all were slaughtered in battle. The list of suspects grows shorter with this knowledge, and there are many, Faere and Men alike, who still yearn to settle that score."

Ashlord spoke these last words with frightening sincerity. Suddenly, he bent his head and Certina whirred softly in his ear. Ashlord nodded. Certina took off into the air and disappeared from sight.

"So Elifaen and Faerekind are one and the same people?" Robby asked.

"Not precisely, though the terms are sometimes used loosely. The original Faerekind who retained their wings have all but gone away from the earth. Those of their kind who have remained, who as a result were stripped of their wings for disobedience, are called Elifaen, the Fallen Ones or Fallen Children, as are their descendants. You have much to learn. So the only way to buy time," Ashlord continued as he walked toward the ramparts where Sheila stood, "is to tell no one about your adventure here. Let any who heard the Bell guess at its meaning. Meanwhile, I believe we have other things to worry about."

Robby followed Ashlord. All while they had talked, the sun grew brighter through the cloudy sky and the breeze grew stronger, melting the mists and blowing them away. Now, looking southward, Robby could see lakes of water from the base of the hill to the distant line of gray that marked the north ridge of Barley. He could barely make out the thin muddy strip that was the road, and it disappeared completely under standing water in many places.

"Can it be that we have company?" Ashlord said. "What do you make of that, Sheila?" He and Sheila were looking at the same distant point, but Robby could not see what drew their attention.

"A strange creature," Sheila said at last. "Two legs and four arms."

Robby squinted and at last saw some movement on the watery plain from the direction of Oldgate. The three gazed at the bizarre sight, none of them able to tell what it was, only that it was nearing, light glinting from the splashing water, moving roughly along where the roadway should be. Whatever it was, it did not seem to be making fast progress. Robby looked at Sheila who shrugged back at him. He was growing nervous, not desiring any more encounters with strange beings, but Ashlord smiled and pulled out his pipe from his pocket. Shaking his head and chuckling softly, he packed the bowl and lit it by holding an odd crystal over it which seemed to focus sunlight intensely on the tobacco. After drawing it to life, puffing out great clouds of scented smoke, he spoke.

"Do you not recognize them?"

At that moment, Robby and Sheila both understood what they were seeing. A very large man was wading and splashing toward them along the muddy road. He was carrying on his shoulders a much smaller man.

"Ibin and Billy!" Robby exclaimed, grinning. "It can be none else."

"It has to be," Sheila agreed. "But what are they doing out here?"

"Coming to find their lost friend would be my guess," Ashlord said.

While they looked on, Ibin trudged, waded, and splashed nearer. Perched on his shoulders, the much smaller Billy Bosk tried to keep his balance by clinging to Ibin's head or by waving his arms about wildly when Ibin stumbled a bit. They disappeared between the two barrows for a few moments, and, when they emerged, it was apparent they were having a very rough time of it, for they were covered with mud from head to toe. Billy, who would seem to have had a high and dry ride, was just as caked and soaking as Ibin. At last, they made it to the fork in the road, just beneath the wall.

"Stand back out of sight, please," Ashlord said to Sheila and Robby as he stepped up onto the wall. With staff in hand, Ashlord called down to the two newcomers.

"What business have you with Tulith Attis?" he cried out threateningly, the breeze tossing his long black hair about wildly and bending his black beard into a hook.

"Put me down," Billy said to Ibin. "Put me down on that rock thar!"

Ibin deposited Billy on a rock that protruded from the water, making him as tall as Ibin.

"Who're ye to ask?" Billy crossed his arms and cocked his head back.

"I am the keeper of this place, and you may soon be trespassing upon the King's ground."

"Ah, well, then, Mr. Keeper of Haven Hill," Billy retorted. "I advise ye to tell us whar we can find the house belongin' to Ashlord, for our business is thar."

"And if I do not?"

"We will find our way to him with er without yer directions, but the memory of me kith is long, an' insults not soon forgotten, ol' feller!"

"Ah, you threaten me! I tremble with fear! My knees quake with terror! I am squashed with remorse at my hasty words! I plea for mercy! Indeed, I surrender! The way to Ashlord's house is along the right-hand path from where you stand. Keep to the right turnings and forks for half a league and you cannot miss his dwelling. But be warned: Tread lightly on this ground and mark your footings well, for the way is slippery, and Ashlord does not generally care for unexpected visitors."

"Care er not, he'll have 'em," Billy replied. Turning to Ibin, he said, "Well, it's no more trudgin' through mud an' muck anyways."

"That'sfine, that's, that'sfinewithme, Billy," Ibin replied grinning. Billy knew that it would be equally fine with Ibin if they had a hundred leagues of mud-trudging, but nodded and smiled back at him. Turning back to the summit, Billy was just about to call to the man who had challenged them, but he was gone.

"Hullo!" he cried. "Hullo up thar, Mr. Keeper! Well, don't that beat all!"

Turning away from the wall, Ashlord hurried past Robby.

"Sheila, stay and see if they were followed while Robby and I return," he said. "Keep out of sight, though."

Sheila nodded and moved farther off along the wall where some saplings were taking hold. There she sat under their branches with her back against a stone, her brown cloak pulled about her, and her bow across her knees. As Robby and Ashlord descended the steps, Robby looked back and could barely make her out, even at this close distance. Quickly they passed through the gate and out along the ridge of the hill, making their way back to the cottage. Several times, they frightened packs of deer and flocks of birds, but just as the deer started or the birds flapped their wings to escape, Ashlord would mumble something, and they would immediately calm down. In that manner, the pair strode through herds of deer and flocks of all manner of birds in a strange silence, all the while the creatures' eyes fixed upon them as they went by.

"Why didn't you want Billy and Ibin to see me?" Robby finally ventured, uneasy at the huge buck staring at him from not six feet away as they passed.

"Only for fear that other eyes might be watching," Ashlord said matter-of-factly. "Your friends may be true and trustworthy, but if they had seen you there, so may have others watching from the open plain."

"My friends are the best that one can have. Who else do you mean? Who would be watching?"

Ashlord shrugged as he stepped over a stone in the path. "Who knows? Perhaps no one. But I have felt the eyes of others upon this place of late. And too much has happened in the last few days, too many threads leading up to your presence here, for me to take matters lightly." He suddenly turned and looked at Robby. "I'm not convinced that your coming here was a mere accident. If so, it is the kind of accident that may stir the hornets' nest. Let us make sure we do not get stung before we are ready to swat the hornets, shall we?"

Robby shook his head.

"Can't you talk straight?" he grumbled as he followed Ashlord on. "All this stuff is too much. Ancient armies. Traitors. Faere blessings and all. I only came to deliver some letters. What do all your plots and plans have to do with me? What are you so afraid of?"

Ashlord stopped again and turned to face Robby. The look on Ashlord's face was almost pained, yet there was a touch of pity in his eyes as he leaned on his staff and gazed at the youngster.

"What am I afraid of?" Ashlord repeated.

"Well," Robby suddenly felt a little peevish, "yeah."

"How can I tell you, who have had so little training in the ways of this world?" Ashlord said. "Try to imagine all of the dark dreams you have ever had, all of the black tales you have ever heard, and the terrible storms you have seen cross this land. Imagine them all rolled into one, joined together by a single dark hand, and unleashed upon all the inhabitants of the earth. That is what is happening, dear boy. It is to read the signs of the coming of those things that I keep watch on this place. It is possible to prepare for, maybe even to prevent in some part. Thrice has the power of darkness assailed the world. But those times were but a test. Thrice before were the creatures who filled the lands with terror driven away. Each time they returned more powerful than before. And there is one who nurtures them, learns from their defeats, and readies them for their next assault. Many there are who would see those days come again on the earth, and welcome them, even."

"Who? Who would want such things?"

"Some who would gain from it. Others with revenge in their hearts. Agents all, wittingly or unwittingly, of shadow."

"Why here? What is so important about this place? And why now?"

"This place is not important, at least the Enemy thinks it so unimportant as to let it pass his notice. At least until recently. His watch upon this place has been unsteady, distracted by the many other happenings of the world, and by his many intrigues. I have established myself here to prevent his serious notice of it until the time is come. And to delve into other matters. Why now? It is because the time has come. You have brought the time to bear by ringing the Bell and awakening the spirits." Ashlord said sternly. "Soon all the lands will hear of it. Though many will wonder what to make of it, the agents of the Enemy will know it is time to take action."

"What enemy? Who? And why? What difference have I made? It was all an accident, anyway."

"Are you an accident? No. You are the difference. Don't you understand? Someone has awakened the guardians of Tulith Attis. Only someone who has the power to open the Iron Door can do that. And that would only be a Faerekind, one of the Ancient Ones, a Firstborn. Have you not been listening? Your action will draw the enemy's attention this way, and you are the one he will now seek out. Heneil did not devise the Iron Door and the Great Bell thinking that a Man would be traitor of this place. Think of the effort it took to cast the Bell, to hang it, and to erect the means of ringing it. Think of the wealth and labor spent to do it, and the key, the Iron Door, with its own incantations to keep it locked. The threat of a mere mortal could never provoke such fear, nor prompt such effort. Heneil knew that if any could overthrow Tulith Attis, it would only be one of his own kind, an Elifaen, a Firstborn of the Faerekind. You have proven, by the ringing of the Bell, that Heneil's fears were not idle, that the legend of the enchanted Bell is true. All the world will now know. Men did not betray Tulith Attis. An Elifaen did. One who must have known about Heneil's trap and found another way to treachery. If the traitor is still in the world, who do you think he serves? What am I afraid of? There is too much to tell and not enough time to teach you!"

Ashlord turned and hurried off. Robby hesitated then trotted to catch up.

"What do you plan on doing?"

"Doing?"

"Yes," Robby grabbed his sleeve and stopped him again. "I mean. What should I do?"

Ashlord smiled and shook his head.

"Be patient with an old man, for one," he said. "Give him time to think, and trust that he will try his best to guide you. Let me assure you that you are not alone. I am not the only one with eyes upon the world. If the Enemy thinks his opponents are on the move, he is not far wrong. Though unspoken and unknown by most, there are a few of us who are readying ourselves for him. And He knows this."

"He who? Who is the enemy?" Robby asked. "The Dragon People? Their king?"

"Yes, and their king. But also others. And one, especially, who guides much evil doings, I fear, and who will soon strive to usurp their king, and all kings, for that matter," Ashlord said impatiently. "You do not know of the one I speak of. I will not yet say his name to you. As I said before, you have much to learn. But at the moment, we must hurry, or else my welcome to your friends will be undone."

Ashlord moved on again and Robby, as confused as ever, followed.

# Chapter 6

## Reunions and Revelations

Day 7
238 Days Remaining

"That's gotta be the place!" Billy gasped, bending to put his hands on his knees to catch his breath. Just behind him, big Ibin climbed the steep path, and at Billy's exclamation, he stopped to look, too. Farther up the hill was a low stone wall, and beyond that could be seen the top of a thatched roof with a smoking chimney.

"Lo, what a climb!" Billy complained. "If this here Ashlord's anything, he must be part goat to climb this."

"YeahIwishIwasagoatrightnow. Thisis, thisis, thisisverysteep, Billy," Ibin agreed.

Ibin was most interested in two things: eating and tagging along with Billy Bosk. It became apparent from Ibin's youngest days that he was different, slower than most, touched, as it were. He struggled in school for the first year or two, but Mr. Broadweed, the schoolmaster, pretty much gave up on him after that. Ibin learned his letters and was good at numbers, but in an odd, unpredictable sort of way. And while he had a gift for songs and for remembering every bit of poetry he ever heard, nearly everything else was beyond his comprehension. By the time he was nine, he simply came to school out of habit, for he seemed to learn nothing. Though his learning came to a halt, his frame got taller and broader as time passed. By the time he was a young teenager, he was already a foot taller than most other boys his age, and nearly twice their weight. He was tolerated by the other children, but especially well liked by the little ones who enjoyed his gentle nature and his strength. During play breaks, Ibin could often be found crawling all over with small children, several climbing him like a tree while he swung others who clung onto his oak-like arms, and all, including Ibin, screaming with laughter and delight. Although Ibin participated very little in the lessons, his eyes twinkled with enthusiastic attention to everything that was said, to all the readings-aloud of the other children, and to everything else that went on, sitting on the edge of his bench and leaning forward in rapt anticipation of whatever might happen next. After a few years, Mr. Broadweed thought Ibin's presence, towering at the back of the schoolroom, had a much needed calming influence on his own disposition. He would carry firewood and do other chores for the schoolmaster without tire and always behaved respectfully and with uncanny good manners, most unlike some of the other children. Especially unlike Billy Bosk, the terror of the school, and one of the chief reasons Mr. Broadweed needed Ibin's calming influence.

For Billy knew no limit to mischief, and practical jokes were his specialty. Turning wall maps and pictures upside down, putting snow down the backs of girls, coating the drawer handles of the schoolmaster's desk with syrup, composing fake love letters to Mr. Broadweed from the girls—whatever would be sure to cause a stir. Billy once even filled Mr. Broadweed's water pitcher with tadpoles. Yet, Broadweed did not think himself especially singled out, for Billy teased and taunted all equally and ceaselessly, and more than once Billy sported a black eye as a schoolyard reward for his antics. Yet all his rambunctious ways were with the greatest of mirth and never did he complain when he got as good as he gave, wearing his shiners with an exasperating pride. Twice Billy was expelled from the school when Mr. Broadweed could not take it any more. And twice Mr. and Mrs. Bosk pleaded with the schoolmaster to re-admit Billy, and both times Broadweed gave in. After all, the Bosk family was one of the oldest and most powerful in the region, and it would not be wise to cross them. Besides, Broadweed suspected that, in truth, they wanted Billy back in school because, for all their power and influence, they could not handle his mischief any better than anyone else. Just when Billy's behavior seemed to be leading to a third and—Mr. Broadweed hoped—final expulsion, a tremendous change came over the boy. No one ever knew what happened, but it occurred during the summer of Billy's fourteenth year and perplexed Mr. Broadweed so much that he made a special appointment to discuss it with Billy's parents. They, as it happened, were just as baffled as anyone. Whatever it was, his antics for the most part ceased, and he became a much more serious student, though of modest ability. Everyone was too relieved of the torment to be very concerned, though most thought it must have had something to do with Ibin, for it was from that time onward that Billy and Ibin became the oddest companions, fast friends, apparently, and nearly inseparable.

A less likely pair of comrades one could hardly imagine: Billy, short, thin, and nimble, quick-witted and quick-tempered, of a famous and respected family, paired with Ibin, a hulking tree of a man, slow-minded, as patient as a rock, with hardly any family to speak of aside from his two elderly parents. After a few months, it was no surprise at all to see them both together; indeed, most thought it strange, now, if ever one was seen without the other. When Ibin's parents grew poorly in health, Billy finagled employment, of sorts, for Ibin at his family's estate, and even managed to have Ibin stay in the manor house. Ibin became part of the family, and when his parents died, Mr. and Mrs. Bosk thought nothing of allowing him to stay on with them permanently, for already Ibin and Billy were to each other the brothers that neither otherwise had.

• • •

On they went, until at last they made the iron gate of Ashlord's yard. Still puffing for air, the two went straight up to the door and Billy was about to bang on it when it flew open. Surprised, Billy stumbled backward into Ibin, for there was a man, looking so much like the one they had seen earlier, standing in the doorway before them, smoking a pipe and glaring at them. Except this one wore a green robe whereas the first wore a blue one.

"You are trespassing. Go away!"

"Just a dang minnit!" Billy stood forth again. "We're on business."

"Then state your business before I have my servants seize you and send you ankles over elbows back down the hill much faster than the manner in which you came up it."

"Are ye Ashlord? Our business is with him an' none other."

"I am he, and what business would I have with two ruffians, pray tell?"

"Ruffians!" Billy was indignant. "Ye've no call to address us in that manner, whatever our business might be. I'll have ye know I'm Billy Bosk, of Boskland, an' at me whim an army of Bosklanders could swarm over yer little hut an' level it to the ground! Ruffians! With good intentions we come, long an' hard in the way of it, only to be treated so! Now hear our business!"

"I am listening," Ashlord replied calmly, leaning against the doorframe as he tamped his bowl with a twig.

"Well," Billy said, standing with his hands on his hips, "a courier set out from Passdale four days ago bearin' letters for ye. When he didn't return, we got worried, for he is our good friend. Our business is to find him. Have ye seen him?"

"If you mean Robigor Ribbon, the Younger," Ashlord replied, "I'll have you know he is a guest of the Hill, and he does not wish to be disturbed. Good day to you! Be off!"

"Now hang on right thar!" Billy said, sticking his foot in the door as Ashlord was closing it. "What kind of guest d'ye mean? If Robby's all right, we'd like to see ourselves, if ye don't mind. Robby! Robby are ye in thar?"

"Begone!" Ashlord said. As Billy tried to peer inside, Ashlord snapped his fingers in front of Billy's face with such a crack and flash of light that Billy stumbled backwards, stunned. Ashlord slammed the door.

"Why, I'll be!" Billy said, fuming. "That whar some low trick! Ibin?"

"Yeah, Billy?"

"Do ye mind openin' that door for me? I think it's good an' stuck."

Ibin pushed on it gently.

"Yeah, Billy, it'sgood, it'sgood, it'sstuckgoodandtight."

"Well, why don't ye get it unstuck for us?"

"Alright."

Ibin backed away a few steps and then charged the door like a bull, roaring somewhat like one, too, and Billy fell in right behind him. Just before they struck the door, it flung open, Ibin tripped and tumbled onto the floor of the interior, and Billy piled on top of him. To their bewilderment, Robby stood over them holding out a couple of tankards.

"Care for a cool ale?" he said, grinning broadly.

"What the blazes?" was all Billy could stammer out.

"Robby!" Ibin jumped up excitedly, dumping Billy backwards onto the floor.

Ashlord was sitting at the table, calmly puffing his pipe, barely able to contain his giggle. Upon seeing him, Billy was further embarrassed and angry.

"What kind of trick is all this?"

"Don't be mad at Mr. Ashlord," Robby cut in, shoving one of the tankards into Billy's hand and taking his other to lift him up onto his feet. "He was only looking after my interests, so to speak."

"I needed to be sure of your loyalty to your friend. Most others would have given up and gone away," Ashlord said with a glint in his eye.

"Hrumph! Could've just taken our word."

Ashlord shrugged. Turning to Robby, Billy went on.

"We've been worried sick about ye an', hey, what's that?" Billy looked closely at Robby's face and arms. "Ye look as though ye had a tussle with a panther!"

"Well, I had a rough time getting out here," Robby said. "No panthers, thank goodness, but I ran into some trouble with some wolves and such."

"Wolves!?" Ibin gasped. "Idon't, Idon't, Idon'tlikewolvesatall!"

"If it hadn't been for Ashlord, I wouldn't be here to greet you."

"So, why all the stuff at the door, then? An' what about that other feller back up at the Hill?"

"Oh that was me," Ashlord said, and as they looked his robes became the dark blue they were before.

"Huh? Ye mean to say ye made it all the way back here ahead of us?"

"You went the long way."

"Yeah, on account of yer directions," Billy glared. "Why didn't ye tell us right then an' thar that Robby was all right."

"Because I didn't know if you were alone, for one," Ashlord said. "And, for another, you never asked."

Billy looked askance at Robby. "What's he talkin' 'bout?"

Sheila came in, nodding to Ashlord. Billy was surprised beyond words.

"They are indeed alone, for now at least," she said putting up her bow. "But if I know his kin, there'll be a troop of Bosklanders out here before long."

"Sheila Pradkin!" Billy exclaimed, finally finding his tongue.

"HelloShe, HelloSheila!" Ibin said, grinning. "WecametoseeRobby."

"Aren't you thirsty?" Robby, still grinning, goaded Billy who had not yet taken a sip, though Ibin was near halfway finished with his tankard. He added, a little more seriously, "You don't know how good it is to see you two. To have two such good friends who would come all this way to look for me, well, I'm thankful for it!"

"But what happened to ye? Why didn't ye go back to Passdale when the rain came?"

"There is a lot of explaining to do," Ashlord said, standing up. "And time enough to do it in. But I wonder if you two would first like to clean up a bit, for the sake of my cottage, if not for your own?"

Indeed, Billy and Ibin, covered with mud and grime, had now made a mess across Ashlord's neat floor, and for the first time the newcomers looked at themselves and at each other.

"Here." Sheila handed each of them a blanket. "Go outside and take off your things. Wrap up in these and then go around back where there's water, soap and towels beside the well pump. Clean up, if you can, or you'll be scrubbing floors all night."

In short order, Robby and Sheila had the newcomers stripped and washed, and soon they were back inside with refilled tankards, wrapped in warm blankets at the kitchen table.

"No, you first," said Robby. "After all, you're the newest guest here. How did you know I was out here, anyway?"

Ashlord, who had laid out some cheese and bread, moved off to the other fireplace on the far side of the room and sat down in his chair with his pipe.

"Well," Billy said, taking a quick gulp of ale. "Mmmm! Late the mornin' ye left Passdale, Ibin an' me stopped by to see ye, to pick up a load of nails an' cloth an' such. Yer dad said ye'd gone out on some deliveries. Anyhow, we picked up our things an' went on, but not afore we ran into some folk an' got to talkin' an all, an' them folk said ye'd left with some stranger-type feller. A Kingsman is what Mr. Arbuckle, the bridge tender, said. If we warn't needin' to get back with our wagon, we'd been after ye right then, I can tell ye, just to find out more an' come along, don't ye know."

Billy took another gulp of ale and wiped his mouth with his blanket.

"So, anyways, we made it back to Boskland just when the sky fell out. Lo, what a rain! An' the more the night went on, the harder it fell. I was just gettin' a bit a shut-eye between thunders up in me bedroom when BOOM! the whole house shook an' the winders rattled. Nearly knocked me right out of of me bed. I thought it was just a close lightnin' bolt, but it didn't sound right. More like a great anvil got hit by some mountain-sized hammer, it did, with a eerie ringin' sound. Ibin was in his room across the hall from me, an' I heard him gettin' up out of bed when it happened all over. CLANG! That one got me up just as Ibin came bustin' in my door a-hollerin', 'The Dead Men er comin'! The Dead Men er comin'!' Course, I didn't know what Ibin was blitherin' 'bout. 'Oh, stop yer blubberin', will ye?' I told him, 'It's just wild storm, is all!' An' just then it happened again, BRA-A-A-ANG! an' knocked me down just as I was tryin' to put me slippers on. By this time, everbody was rushin' out into the hallways, an' the alarm went up all over Boskland. Ever' man an' boy come rushin' to the house. Pop was already outside lookin' off to the northward when I got out into the yard, an' already twenty men whar gathered 'round. Acted like he knew what the sound was, but he never said.

" 'Well,' says Pop, 'since we're all up, an' it's still pourin', might as well check the line.' Me ol' man starts hollerin' out for his men. 'Tobin!' he hollers, that's the field foreman, 'Tobin! Send runners to the fields to check the floodin' an' riders up to the groves. Eddard!' that's the head foreman 'Eddard! Put riders on all the lines!' It was a good thing too, 'cause soon reports whar comin' in from all sides 'bout the streams swellin' up an' threatenin' to spill over our fields, an' roads gettin' full of mud. It warn't long afore we're all out in the fields diggin' an' fillin' bags of dirt, tryin' to stave off the water."

Billy took another long gulp before continuing. "Come midmornin' next day, yer dad shows up at our place in the pourin' rain askin' after ye. What a storm! Our fields were floodin' for sure an' the creeks an' ditches spillin' out all over so as we had our hands purty full. Me mum came out to the fields with yer dad an' found us workin' thar, an' I knew as soon as I seen him that somethin' was bad, serious wrong. It's a wonder he made it at all out that far with all the roads flooded. Anyhow, that's when he told us whar he'd sent ye an' hoped to find ye with us. Said he tried to make out the way ye'd gone, but he couldn't find a crossin' at Weepingbrook, as it was all swollen an' the bridges were knocked away. I think he must've stopped at ever' single house in Barley he could get to 'til he finally made his way cross the county to Boskland. Oh, he was plumb wore out, cold an' wet an' all. But we got right at it, an' took six men an' horses an' set out on the Line Road toward Oldgate. We only got 'bout a mile off, though, when the sky truly fell. Woo! What a storm! Wasn't it, Ibin?"

"Yeah, it was a real, it was a real, it was a real bad storm," Ibin agreed. "Scary."

"A foot of water whar on the road, an' it was black as night. The thunder an' lightnin' scared us all, an' the horses none too calm, neither. We tried leadin' 'em by the reins, but when we got up to our waists in water, we had to turn back. Ibin an' me argued to keep goin', an' I think me ol' man would've kept on, too, but Mr. Ribbon said he didn't want to risk nobody else. He was determined to keep on by hisself, but me ol' man said if it whar too much for 'em all together to help each other, it whar too much for Mr. Ribbon all by hisself. 'Alls we can do is trust to Robby's good wits,' is what me pop told yers. 'An' make another try when the water goes down.' "

Billy took another long draft, finishing the tankard, and shoving it back.

"I'm sorry for all the trouble I've caused," Robby said.

"Aw, it ain't nuthin'," Billy replied, slapping Robby on the shoulder, causing him to wince. "An' 'specially when we got back, I'm afraid ye became the least of our worries. Nigh on a hunnerd people whar at our place by day's end, all flooded out of thar homes an' lookin' for shelter. Afore we knew it, we're puttin' folk up in the house, in the barns an' tackrooms, out in the armoury, down in the cellar, up in the attic, even in the old tower—anywhar with a roof an' floor above water. Ye never saw such a commotion an' clutter. Babies wailin' all over, folks cryin', carts an' wagons in all the yards. Sure had our hands full. Yer dad pitched right in, askin' everbody if they'd seen ye an' all as he unpacked carts an' moved bins an' bales to make room for families."

"Then, along 'bout midnight, came the blacksmith, ol' man Clingdon, from Passdale, come all the way out to Boskland to fetch yer dad back to Passdale. He told us the waterwheel at the mill broke loose an' killed the mayor."

"No!" Sheila gasped.

"Mayor Greardon?" Robby asked, stunned. "Killed?"

"That's right. Killed by the wheel cause he couldn't shut off the sluice, er somethin', an' the wheel tore right off, an' broke the shaft, an' somethin' fell on him whilst he was tryin' to stop it all. Anyhow, some part er other dragged him down into the water an' drowned him."

"Oh, his poor wife!" Sheila said.

"And a young son, too," Robby nodded.

"Yeah, it's bad," Billy continued. "An' thar whar other things goin' on in Passdale, too. The storm did a lot of damage, an' folks felt like Mr. Ribbon was the one man everbody trusted who could pull the town together. I don't know what all was goin' on. I wasn't thar, of course. Anyways, yer dad an' the blacksmith left right away, soon as Clingdon got something hot in him."

"So, next couple days, we stayed busy 'til the rains slacked up an' finally let off. Even my sister was put to work, stuck-up though she is, an' with her maid got all the big rooms set up for the older folk what came along. I kept pleadin' with me ol' man to send some men out for ye, but he wouldn't spare none. So, finally, this mornin', afore dawn, Ibin an' meself decided to come on just the two of us. We took a couple ponies an' a spare for ye as far as we could. At last, we couldn't get 'em to budge no further through the flooded-out road, so we turned 'em loose to go back home an' kept on without 'em. If it warn't for ol' Ibin, here, big an' heavy, we'd a washed right away. We didn't, though, an' got on through the flood. An' that's that. Here we are!"

"When do you think your kinsmen will come looking for you?" Robby asked. "If I know your dad at all, it won't be long."

"Oh I doubt we'll be missed at all afore sunset. An' Pop ain't likely to send out a party at night in this muck. So I guess, if we can stay the night, an' be on our way in the mornin', we'll probably run into 'em on the way back. That is, if Mr. Ashlord will let us stay the night."

"Oh, no worries there," Ashlord assured them. "You are most welcome to stay as long as you wish."

"Thank, thank, thankyouMr.Ashlord," Ibin said, picking up the flying squirrel from his shoulder and placing it beside the owl on his knee. The two creatures had not left Ibin alone since his arrival and seem truly delighted to play on him, Certina flying from head to shoulder to knee to arm and Flitter chasing after her, leaping as deftly as she flew. Ibin grinned the whole while.

Billy took a bite, and, throwing a look at Ashlord and Sheila, asked Robby, "Well, out with it, then. Y'gotta tell us what happened with them wolves. Did ye hear that weird sound out this way? The three bangs what woke us all up?"

Robby looked over at Ashlord questioningly. Ashlord answered his unspoken query with a nod, and Robby turned back to Billy.

"Yes. We did hear the sound," he sighed. "I'm afraid it was my doing."

Then Robby told Ibin and Billy the entire tale of his last few days, much interrupted by Billy with questions until Robby got to the part about the chamber where the bell was, and the strange statues. Billy then became quiet, listening intently without comment or question. His unusual seriousness indicated to Robby that the story was deeply disturbing to him. When he got to the part about the battle between the wolves and the soldiers, and when Ashlord and Sheila showed up, Robby faltered a little bit, but kept on until he told all he could remember. Billy remained quiet and thoughtful, and the room was silent except for the crackle of the fireplace and the soft puffing of Ashlord at his pipe. He looked at the youngsters around him, arrived at some conclusion about them, and nodded to himself as if he had made a decision. Standing up, he emptied his pipe into the fireplace and turned to the group.

"I think a little sunshine would do all of you much good," he said. "And I'm afraid I need some rest as I have had little lately. As I'm sure you have much more to talk about, I ask you to leave me for awhile. Sheila, perhaps the boys would be interested in the old southern keep? Why don't you take some food and show them that part of the Hill while I rest?"

Sheila was agreeable to this, and soon the three boys, with Billy and Ibin back in their mostly dry clothes, were being led up a path through a jumble of mossy boulders and rocks and onward through a green pasture-like field and then into some woods, moving south along the ridge in the opposite direction from the fortress. On this side of Haven Hill, the ridge was flat and broad, and in many places the group could see the remains of stone houses, overgrown with ivy, or rock walls surrounding small lots of green grass. They emerged into an open area, and before them stood a small fortification, or at least the remains of one, with heavy stones set without mortar curving around and disappearing into the trees to their right and left. Clambering up the walls, they found they could see for miles across Barley, the woodlands below fading in the far distance to rolling fields of cultivated lands, bluish-green in the moist, hazy air. The sun was warm and bright for the first time in days, and they sprawled out on the rocks to enjoy the light and heat. Ibin found the cheese and bread in one of the sacks Ashlord had handed them, and soon he was passing around the skin of water, too.

"That Ashlord's a queer sort of feller, if ye ask me," said Billy taking a bit of bread Ibin offered. "I mean, livin' in such a place as this."

"Odd," nodded Robby. "I'll grant you that. But, as I've come to learn, and be grateful for, he sure knows a lot about things."

"What sorta things, is what I wonder," Billy stated.

"Well, like the other night, I mean. He knew who those stone soldiers were. And he knows all the history of this place, it seems, and a lot of other history, too. Things we never were taught by old Broadweed. Like the great battle that took place here. I mean we all know about it, but Ashlord seems to know a lot about it. Almost like he was here when it happened, though he said it was before his time."

"Thatwas, thatwas, thatwasalongtimeago," said Ibin.

"Yeah, it was. I know it's crazy to think such a thing, but it's just that with all he told me about it, I have a feeling there's a lot more that he could've said but didn't," Robby said. "And then there's you, Sheila. What are you doing out here, anyway?"

"I told you," she said bluntly. "He's my teacher. I never went to Broadweed's school, as you well know. Yet, I'm not stupid. I've always been kind of wild, I suppose. Isn't that what folks in Barley and Passdale call me? The wild girl of the woods? I've heard them talk. And frankly, there's some truth in it. I never had a family like you three have had. Billy's mum is the only female friend I've ever had, and I think she took me under her wing out of pity's sake. Anyway, I decided that I needed to catch up, somehow, with my learning. You got me started, Robby, teaching me letters and somewhat of reading them. You were the first person to give me any credit for having any sense. So, well, to cut a long story short, one thing led to another, and I decided to come out here and talk to Ashlord about giving me some lessons."

"But how come ye just up an' disappeared?" Billy asked. "I mean thar ye whar, an' suddenly yer gone. Most peculiral. It's been months an' months!."

"No, it hasn't!" she replied.

Robby had his head down, remembering the visit by Sheila at the shop and realizing that he was probably one of the last people she had seen before leaving.

"Was that what you were trying to tell me when you came by the shop?" he asked softly. "That you were going away?"

"Sort of," Sheila said.

"An' Ashlord took ye in?" Billy asked.

"Well, he didn't want to, at first." Sheila took the skin and drank a swallow of water. Since it was getting hot, she took off her coat and vest, exposing her tanned arms and shoulders and revealing the light sleeveless blouse she wore over her breeches. "He thought it seemed improper for a young girl to stay with a man, a stranger, such as himself, and he was worried for my reputation, or so he said. I guess he found out I didn't have much of one, and I think he went to see Mrs. Bosk, and maybe some other folks, too. I don't know. But anyway, I showed up here, asked him to take me in as a student. I pestered him all day. He kept asking me why I came to him. I kept telling him. There were long spells when we said nothing, and I waited as he went about his studies or did chores. I offered to help with his work, and he would just chuckle. After a long while of silence, he'd suddenly ask me again, in some way or another, about my reasons. He never once got angry at me, he never said a harsh thing, and I got the feeling that he knew more from my words, or from just looking at me, than most would ever know about me. Suddenly, toward the late afternoon, while splitting some firewood, he stopped, put down the axe, and picked up his cloak and walking stick. He said he had to look into a few things, and he told me to make myself at home, to explore the fortress, if I wished, and to help myself to his books and food. He said that he would have an answer for me when he returned, and he just walked off.

"Late the next day, he came back and said he would agree to me staying with him, but only if I would promise to keep his confidence, to do as I was instructed, and to remain 'pure of heart and of body', as he put it, and, finally, he said I was to refrain, if I could, from letting anyone know that I was here. I agreed, and he set up a room for me, sort of. At least until Robby showed up. And, ever since, he's been teaching me letters and languages and other things besides. Stories. Things about the trees and the animals I never knew."

"You mean, I've been taking your bed?"

"Yes, you have."

"But where does Ashlord sleep?"

"I don't think he sleeps at all," Sheila said. "In all the time I've been out here, I have not once found him asleep. He's always up before I am and long after I fall asleep. Although sometimes he sits for hours and hours just staring, eyes wide open, sometimes mumbling to himself."

"Then what's all that back thar 'bout him needin' rest?" Billy chimed in.

"Oh, I don't doubt that he needs rest," Sheila said. "He's been pacing and mumbling and all distracted and agitated ever since Robby showed up. And he went all the way to Heneil's Wall two days ago and then straight back. I think something's going on that might be very important."

"Like what?" Billy asked. Not getting a reply, he looked from Sheila to Robby and back. "What's goin' on?"

Robby looked at Sheila, and she nodded.

"I think you may as well tell them everything," Sheila said. "After all, if you can't trust these two who came all this way to look for you, I doubt if there's any you can."

"Trust with what?" Billy was getting impatient.

"Ashlord thinks maybe somebody might come after me," Robby said. "And maybe other things, too."

"What? Why?"

Robby told Billy and Ibin about the little box Ashlord kept and about the traitor at the battle for Tulith Attis and that it was a Faerekind that laid the trap, but it was a Faerekind who was the traitor, too, and not a man as legend had it. Robby told them about being sick as a child and the two ladies that sang to him at his bedside. And, at last, he told them about the scars on his mother's back, that he, too, was of Elifaen blood, since those traits were passed from mother to child.

"Aw, we all know that already!" Billy said, waving his hand at Robby.

"You do? How?"

"Everbody knows about the Tallins," Billy said. "How they got granted lands by the King himself. How every Tallin generation sends one to serve the King. When Lord Tallin was a Kingsman in Vanara, he took a Faere wife, an' she follered him back east when they lost thar lands in the west."

"But I didn't know my grandmother was Elifaen!" Robby said. "I only met my grandfather once, or so I've been told. But I was a baby, and I don't remember it. My cousin Ullin Saheed is the only one of my mother's family that I know."

"Haven't you ever thought that strange?" Sheila asked.

"Yes, but, well, my dad told me that my mother's kin thought she married beneath her and so was estranged from her family. I just figured that my mother didn't want to talk about it."

"Well, right she don't!" Billy said. "Look here, Robby, ye know I'm yer friend an' any who'd say a bad thing 'bout ye whilst I'm around'll pay with a bloody nose, at least. So I'm the last who'd say anythin' against ye or to hurt ye. But yer mum's hidin', I think."

"From what?"

"From everybody in Barley an' Passdale!" Sheila said. "You hear how the Elifaen are talked about. Not long ago, they weren't even allowed to pass through, unless they knew somebody or else paid a toll. People don't care so much any more, but still—"

"Thing is, Robby," Billy interrupted, "they ain't trusted. Folk still talk of the war in these parts an' how men an' Faere Folk broke apart an' fought durin' them days. Folk made up all kind of tales 'bout Faeres an' bad luck, 'bout how they steal babies an' cattle, an' seduce ye with thar words an' stuff. I mean, I know all that's a bunch of crap, an' yer mum bein' married to yer dad an' the kind of man he is, well! At first people talked about the success with the shop an' how he came to be mayor for a while. An' that it was on account of yer mum's charms an' stuff, is what folk said. But now he's the most respected man around these parts, an' nobody thinks badly of yer family. An' yer mum's won over nearly ever'one around, the only real lady, me mum says, in all these parts. Still, I reckon yer folks're wary. They don't want thar boy ill-treated. Remember when I first met ye in Broadweed's school? Remember what a rascal I was? How I teased ye for bein' a wingless waif? Well, I didn't mean no harm by it, but those were mean things to say, an' I don't know how ye ever got past that to let me be yer friend later on. But name-callin' an' such as that I picked up from the other kids."

"People can be pigs," Sheila said suddenly.

"Right," nodded Billy. "So if yer mixed up in some Faerekind business, it figures it might bear on yer family."

"So what of it!" Robby got up abruptly and tossed away a rock he had been rubbing. "I mean, all I did was try to save my skin. I can't help it if those wolves chased me through that chamber! And now all this stuff! All the strange things about my family, the strange Faerekind ladies who sang to me, and, well, blessed me, I suppose. All this with the stone soldiers from all that time ago, ancient spells, and whatnot. Traitors and traps. It's all just a big accident!"

"Don't count on it," Sheila said.

"And Ashlord," Robby went on, "telling me about those old days as if I had something to do with them. Talking about my mother. The funny thing is, he seems to know more about me than I do. In a way. I mean, who is he, anyway?"

"He is a teacher, a scholar from the west, a Wise Man, as they say," Sheila said bluntly.

"That's not what I heard," said Billy. "I heard he was a conjurer-king."

"A what?" Sheila asked incredulously.

"A conjurer-king," Billy repeated. "A king what can call on the spirits of dead folk. What can lift heavy stones an' not lay a finger on 'em, an' can steal fire from the sky, an' speak to animals an' make 'em do his biddin'."

"Oh, posh!" Sheila exclaimed. "Conjurer-kings are just tales. He's just a scholar who knows a lot about things. He knows things that we would never understand if we tried all our lives. And he's old, too. Older than he looks."

"Well, anyways," Billy went on, not the least perturbed by Sheila's skepticism, "Bob Starhart, the post rider, says he's some kinda criminal, exiled from his home far off in the Westlands."

"Oh, please! How dare that stupid old clod say such a thing!" Sheila was indignant. "Ashlord is the kindest man I know. And even though he's a bit odd and no doubt has a troubled past, he's no criminal!"

"I don't think my cousin Ullin would have anything to do with criminals unless it was to take them on," Robby added. "But Ashlord does seem, well, sort of royal, if you know what I mean. I mean to say, he's different."

"And what kind of name is 'Ashlord,' anyway?" Billy quizzed. "Sounds made up to me."

"It isn't his true name," Sheila retorted. "It is just what people call him.. His true name is Collandoth, a name in the Ancient Tongue, I think."

*'Far off from home the king did roam*
*Away from kith and kin*
*The keys to his kingdom*
*And his oaken throne*
*A quest alone and tasks unknown*
*And whispers on the wind.*
*Through false blame another name*
*He needs must now put on*
*To root out treason*
*And by that reason*
*Take back his oaken throne.'*

Robby, Billy, and Sheila stared at Ibin as he softly sang, but when he noticed them gaping, he stopped and looked embarrassed.

"Another one of yer rhymin' songs, eh, Ibin?" Billy asked.

"Yeah. A, it'sa, it'sarhymingsong," Ibin said, nodding. "Iheardit, Iheard-itsomewhere."

"Ibin's full of such," Billy said, smiling proudly to Robby and Sheila. "Ain't ye?"

"Yeah, I, I, yeah, I, yeahIknowalotofthem," Ibin beamed excitedly.

"Where did you hear that one, Ibin?" Sheila asked.

"Oh, I heard, oh, I heardthatonefromtheFaeres," he said matter-of-factly. "They know, they know, theyknowalotofsongs. I like them a lot. Andtheyletme, andtheyletme, andtheyletmesingwiththemsometimes."

"The Faere?" Robby asked. Ibin nodded.

"Ibin always says that," Billy said. "Well, not always, but a lot of times. Sometimes ol' Ibin here disappears for days at a time, comin' back happier than ever before, hummin' tunes an' whistlin'."

"When's the last time you saw any Faere folk, Ibin?" Robby asked.

"OhIseethemalot," Ibin said. "Iguessthelasttime, Iguessthelasttimeit-wasawhileago, yeah, awhileago. Midsummer's, backaroundMidsummer's-Day. Yeah, I saw them, I saw them at the Firefeast."

"Ah," Sheila said. "A lot of folk were coming through then. Minstrels and the like."

"YeahIsawtheminstrels,too," Ibin said. "ButIlike, IliketheFaeresongs-better. Ilikethembetterbecause, because, Iliketheirsongsbetterbecausetheydon'tgoaway."

"They don't go away?" Robby said. "You mean you don't forget them?"

"No, I, noI, noImeantheFaeresdon'tgoaway."

Robby blinked, trying to make out what Ibin meant.

"Youdon'thavetowaittoseethemif, if, ifyouwanto."

"I have no idear what he means," said Billy. "Only that I know for a fact he didn't see no Faere folk at the Firefeast, 'cause I was with him the whole time."

"Yeah," Ibin said. "Billywasthere, too. Billywastherebuthewasasleep, hewas asleep, hewasasleepwhentheFaeresongsweresung."

"I don't know what he means, either," said Sheila. "But the Faerekind who are still in the world don't call themselves Faerekind any more. They're called the Elifaen. That means 'Fallen Ones.'"

"Well, whatever they're called, Ibin's right about one thing," Robby laughed. "Billy did pass out pretty early, if I recall rightly."

"Yeah, well, I might've," Billy said. "I might've been tuckered out from the fight with them Passdale gruffs."

"I guess so," Robby said, not daring to look over at Sheila.

"In fact," Billy plowed unwittingly ahead, "I think that was the last time I saw ye, Sheila. So have ye been out here ever since?"

"Mostly," Sheila said.

"Tell me about the roads, Billy," Robby asked. "I'd like to get back home."

"They ain't too good. Ibin an' me came from Boskland, o'course. An' that's probably the best way back for ye when we go. Yer dad said the bridge at Weepingbrook was gone, an' that it was all swollen. I imagine, though, that we'll be hearin' the horns of Boskland afore the end of the day tomorrow if we're not back by then. I don't think me ol' man'll rest when he finds out I'm not in the house tonight. I bet he'll be out with a party of men afore dawn, if not earlier."

They talked on for hours while the sun grew hot. Billy stripped off his shirt to sun his back and Ibin did the same, exposing his brawny shoulders next to Billy's wiry frame. Sheila took off her blouse, too, down to her halter, without a bit of shame. Robby hesitated for a moment, then gingerly took off his shirt, too.

"Man, yer pale as a ghost!" Billy chuckled. "Ye oughta get out more, me friend."

"Yeah," Robby nodded, "I know. But I've been pretty busy at the store, and there hasn't been much time for outdoors this summer."

Seeing the gashes and bruises that covered Robby's body, Billy put his lips together and blew a silent whistle, shaking his head at the evidence of what his friend had recently been through. The worst wounds were on Robby's arms and left side. Many had been bandaged, and the one on his side was showing a little blood. When Billy gave Sheila a look of concern, she nodded.

"Here," Sheila said, moving over to kneel next to Robby, "let me fix that. Lift your arms."

Billy resumed talking about the flood, the roads and the damage to the crops while Sheila worked. Robby could not help wincing a time or two and tried not to let his eyes wander as she leaned over him. Her hands were firm and warm and her golden brown skin glistened. Her breasts pressed against him as she reached her arms around him to pull the bandage. She smelled of anise and lemony-thyme mixed with sweat, and the aroma of her body took him back to the last night they had together several months ago. He recalled her body next to his just two or three nights ago while he was delirious with fever.

"There," she said. "That will do until we get back to the cottage and can change them properly."

"Iamsorryyouarehurt, Robby," Ibin said. "Ihope, Ihope, Ihopeyou'llbe-abletocomebackwithus."

"Oh, no worries about that!" Robby smiled. "My legs are good, and I'm ready to go whenever we can."

They chatted on for a little longer, Robby now uncomfortably distracted by Sheila, though she only sat and said very little. Whether it was how the breeze tugged at her light brown hair, the angle of the light on the curve of her waist, or the way she sat with her legs tucked beneath her, leaning on one arm while twirling a dandelion in her other hand—whatever it was, she looked a vision to Robby. He struggled to pay attention to Billy's prattle. The sun angled farther over to the west, a cool breeze gained strength and drove away the warmth from the rocks.

"O-o!" Billy shivered. "Whar did that come from?"

"Ashlord said it would turn cool today," Robby remembered aloud.

"It's probably time we got back, anyway," Sheila put forward, pulling on her blouse.

They all agreed and soon were dressed and on their way back to the cottage. To their pleasant surprise, Ashlord had a fine meal ready for them when they arrived. After they had eaten, he carefully checked and cleaned Robby's wounds, and he applied cooling salve and new bandages, too. Satisfied that Robby was mending, the entire group took chairs outside to watch the sunset and the stars come out. Ashlord seemed to know all about the stars, and he enjoyed sharing some of his knowledge, their names and the constellations, and why they were named as they were.

Pointing almost directly overhead, Robby asked, "Is that one called The Swan?"

"Yes, that is The Swan," he confirmed.

"Probably the only one I'll ever see," Robby chuckled. "My dad taught me just a little about the constellations."

"Ye wouldn't happen to have another one of them pipes that ye could spare?" Billy interrupted as Ashlord tamped some Westleaf down into his bowl.

Ibin's eyebrows rose with anticipation.

"Certainly do!" Ashlord rose and went into and back out of the cottage, bringing with him a pipe and a pouch.

"It's barely been used," he said, handing it to Billy.

"Oh, it's for Ibin," Billy said, handing them to his friend. "I knew he wouldn't ask."

"Thankyou, Mr. Ashlord," Ibin said, grinning and already filling the bowl. "Mineisinmysaddlebag. Iforgot, Iforgot, Iforgot, Iforgottoget-itoutwhenweleftBucky."

"Bucky's one of the ponies we had to leave behind halfway here," Billy explained. "An' he had some gear on him that Ibin brought along. I have no idear what all else Ibin had in that bag. I bet most of it was sausage an' cheese."

"Apples, Ihadapples, too," Ibin said. "ForBucky."

"Ah, right. Apples."

So Ibin and Ashlord puffed while the others fell silent as Lady Moon, growing shy behind her fan, gained her height. Every so often, Ibin would point up and ask, "What'sthat, what's, what'sthatone?" Ashlord would name the star and explain what he knew about it, saying something like "That is Mintar, one of the Wanderers. He'll be gone over the horizon by next full moon and will reappear in the spring." Or, "That is Carella, eye of the constellation called Brinathar, the Lion. He stands guard over Ererdid, over to the left, the Sleeping Queen. He goes before her, it is said, to make her way safe and her dreams peaceful."

"And that one?"

"That is the Great North Star, around which all the others wheel and turn."

Billy, wrapped in a blanket, nodded a time or two, snapping his head, trying to pay attention, but failing miserably.

"Well, I think you two boys must sleep on the floor tonight," Ashlord said, knocking the ashes out of his pipe. "I'll be sure there are enough blankets and a good fire."

"Sheila can have her cot back, too," Robby offered. "I think I'm well enough for the floor."

"No," Sheila said. "One more night in the back room won't hurt me and you're still sore, I'm sure. Besides, I'm already settled back there."

"If that's the way you want it," Robby acquiesced.

Ashlord stood up.

"Tomorrow morning," he said, "we set out for Passdale by way of Boskland. With luck we'll have Billy and Ibin home before noon and Robby home by dark. It'll be a long walk. The long way around, for you Robby, so get a good night's sleep. That goes for all of you."

He picked up his chair and took it back inside and the rest did the same. Soon Sheila had distributed plenty of blankets to Ibin and Billy, and an extra one to Robby. Robby undid his shirt, watching Ashlord put more wood on the fire and extra logs beside the fireplace, then he blew out the candles on the mantel as the boys settled down.

"Where do you sleep?" Robby asked softly as he passed by the alcove.

"I do not sleep," Ashlord smiled. "I'll wake you early. Good dreams."

"Good dreams."

As he pulled the curtain around the alcove, he caught a glimpse of Ashlord taking the bundle of letters to the meal table to have another look at them under the light of the lamp. The crickets seemed especially active, and their droning lulled Robby into a kind of half-sleep. Flitter and Certina watched Robby toss and turn for a while and then moved off to check on the others. But Robby never reached the delicious sleep he longed for. His dreams were full of all that had happened and of memories of being with Sheila at Midsummer. His emotions were full of perplexity and wonder and sudden fits of anxiety as he remembered the wolves and the stone soldiers. He recalled Sheila's face when he was sick and out of his head, her look of concern and her tenderness as she stroked his hair from his forehead and placed a wet cloth there. Now, struggling to sleep, he realized how terribly he had missed her.

And so the night went until at last he opened his eyes, giving up his effort to find sleep, and sat up on the cot.

"Better to just get up for awhile," he thought, "than to wrestle so!"

He wrapped a blanket around himself, stood, and peered into the main room. Ibin and Billy were fast asleep, each snoring lightly in front of the dying fire. The wooden floor was cool, and Robby tiptoed past the two and gently placed a couple of logs on the embers before retreating to the kitchen table. Ashlord was nowhere to be seen. The lamp was blown out, and the letters were gone. Looking toward the door that led to the back room, he thought about Sheila. Pulling out a chair, he turned it around to face the fireplace across the room, and sat down. Flitter was curled up into a tiny ball on Ibin's shoulder, and Certina sat still as a statue on a rafter overhead. One of the logs began burning, and long narrow tongues of flame flickered up, giving the room a shadow-dance aspect in the yellow light.

"Robby."

Robby fairly jumped, and turned to see Sheila emerging from the shadows at his side.

"Why aren't you sleeping?" she asked in a soft whisper. She, too, had a blanket wrapped around her, and she wore furry slippers. Robby shrugged and shook his head.

"Just a little restless, I suppose," he answered.

"How are you feeling?"

"Oh, I'm fine. A few little aches, here and there. Why aren't you asleep?"

"I'm sleepy," Sheila said, putting a chair beside his and sitting down. "But all I do is toss and turn."

"Me, too."

They sat and watched the fire across the room. The logs were beginning to crackle and the flames jumped deliriously, sending yellow-gold light flashing across the room in variations that matched its rhythm.

"I have missed you," Robby said at last.

"I have missed you, too."

"Why did you leave and come out here? I mean truly. Was it because of me?" Robby looked at Sheila.

"I don't know if I can explain it to you so that you'll understand," she said.

"Understand what?"

"Oh, Robby," she shook her head. "The world is bigger than we are! And there is so much happening in it beyond our Barley and our Passdale. And yet," she looked at him earnestly, "I would not have left for all the world if only I could have stayed. There just wasn't anywhere else I could go."

"I don't know what you mean."

"I'm not considered a respectable girl, Robby. You know that."

Robby shook his head.

"I would never be accepted in Passdale. You were the first person to give me any true attention for just me. You taught me to read, and about numbers. And you stood up for me at Midsummer's, and got pretty banged up because of me."

"That wasn't about you!" Robby retorted.

"Oh, Robby! I know it was because I heard what those boys said. I know what they think of me. I've heard it all before, and it is common knowledge how I am thought of both in Barley and in Passdale, and what I am called."

Robby felt himself blush in shame for the truth of her words. He knew full well that she was called awful things. But he was more ashamed of how he kept his relationship with her a secret. Guessing his thoughts, she asked, "Do you remember when I asked you not to tell anyone about our friendship?"

"Yes, I do."

"That was two years ago."

"A little more than two," Robby nodded.

"Yes. And you kept that promise, too."

"It hasn't been easy. And I am ashamed of making it because I value your friendship and am proud of it."

"But, you see, I was afraid, Robby," she said. "Afraid that if your parents found out, or if your other friends found out, well, that—"

"That they would come between us?"

Sheila nodded.

"So little do you know my parents or my friends!" Robby shot back at her. "Or me, for thinking I would let them stand between us."

Her eyes were now great flame-filled pools looking back at him. When the tears let go of her eyes and streamed down across her face like golden glittering jewels, he felt his heart crack. He reached out and touched her face with the back of his fingers.

"I am so sorry," he said, his own sight blurry. "I tried to find you."

"You did?"

"Yes. I went to the pond where we used to meet. And I went to other places, too. I went out to your house, your uncle's place, but that didn't work out so well."

Sheila stiffened. "I bet he was drunk, as usual," she said scornfully.

"No, Sheila," Robby said withdrawing his hand. "Don't you know?"

"Know what?"

"He's dead."

"Dead?"

"Yes, didn't you know?"

"No."

"Oh, my stars!" Robby dreaded telling her but knew he had to.

"What happened?"

"I hate that I am the one to tell you this news. My dad and I found him. I talked my dad into going with me by saying that I had to return a bracelet that you dropped at Midsummer's. Do you remember the bracelet with the silver charms?"

Sheila nodded.

"Well, I found it after the fight that I got into, right there in the grass. My hand somehow touched on it when I fell down. Well, alright. When I was knocked down. Anyway, you left in such a hurry from the store when you came by that I didn't have a chance to give it to you. But, as I was saying, I told my dad that it was yours and I wanted to return it to you. He wouldn't let me go out there by myself, the way your uncle was, and all. But I pestered him for days until he relented, so we hiked out to the place. The stench was awful in the yard, and my dad called and called into the house, and we heard the dogs barking inside. I was truly scared, but my dad pounded on the door, yelling your name and yelling your uncle's name, until he started trying to bang it open with his shoulder. I lent my own shoulder to it and the door gave right away and the dogs lit out of there like they were on fire. But we nearly fainted from the smell, and we could see him. He was hanging from the rafters by a chain around his neck, his feet chewed off by his own dogs that were locked up inside with him."

Robby saw no reason to tell her the extent of the gore in the place, or the fact that the body was torn and shredded by the dogs and hardly a thing below the waist was left.

"It was pretty awful," he went on, "and I hate to tell you these things. But if you don't hear it all from me, you'll sooner than later hear it from someone else. As soon as we were sure you weren't there, we left to fetch Sheriff Fivelpont."

"Uncle Steggan," Sheila said, wiping her face. "Dead!"

Robby noticed that her tears had quickly dried.

"I can't say as I'm sorry," she said. "Not one bit. But for him to hang himself! That just doesn't seem like him."

"That's what Fivelpont said," Robby went on. Robby also saw no point in relating all the other things the Sheriff had said about Sheila's uncle. He was of the opinion that Steggan was too mean and ornery and drunk to ever hang himself. "But he couldn't find any other explanation so he let it drop. I mean, the door was bolted on the inside. Still, a lot of questions were asked about you and your whereabouts, and while me and other folks were worried about you and what your uncle might have done to you, other folk were sort of thinking the opposite and wondering if you might have finally gotten even with him for treating you like he did. Everybody knows that he beat you."

"That figures," Sheila said. "I can't say it didn't cross my mind more than once. And I should have. But if I had had the courage to do it, I wouldn't have done it that way, I don't think."

"Well, as soon as I could, a few days later, I headed out to Boskland on the pretense of seeing Billy," Robby went on. "I knew that you and Mrs. Bosk were friends and that you'd go out there off and on to visit, so I thought that if you were in trouble maybe you'd go to her."

"You were right," Sheila nodded. "I did go there first. But I guess by the time you got there, I had already left to come out here."

Robby nodded and went on, "I asked her, and she said you'd gone to stay with a friend—she wouldn't tell me who or where—but only that you were safe and couldn't have had anything to do with your uncle's death. She told me that it was best to let you be and that I'd hear from you in good time. By then, Sheriff Fivelpont had already decided that you couldn't have done it, and were probably away hunting or such. He made arrangements for your uncle's body and had the place cleaned up and left a note for you in case you went back there. That's what my dad said anyway."

"I haven't been back there."

"I know. There's more," Robby said. "Nobody knew of any other next of kin, so your uncle's property was rightfully yours. Except, the thing is, he ran up a lot of debt. That responsibility would fall on you. But since you couldn't be found, a magistrate's council was called, and it was decided to give you a month to claim the property and to make settlements. If you didn't show up, then your uncle's place would be sold at auction. After debts were taken care of, the leftovers would belong to you. My dad was appointed to be the trustee of your share. The auction was held about two weeks ago."

"I don't know what to say," Sheila managed. "I don't care about any of his money. I'm just glad I don't have to see him any more!" She got up suddenly and dashed back to her room. Robby stood and took a few steps after her, but stopped. He could hear her sobbing, and although he wanted to comfort her, he did not think that he could, and he did not understand why she was so sad about a man that he knew she hated. It seemed to Robby that with her uncle dead, Sheila would be better off, and should be relieved. As he stood there, perplexed, he felt a breeze and turned to see Ashlord entering the front door. He nodded at Robby and leaned his stick against the wall as he closed the door.

"You cannot sleep," he said as he slung off a shoulder bag and hung it on a peg. "And you've been talking to Sheila."

"That's right," Robby replied a bit more defensively than he intended. "We talked."

Ashlord walked over to the fire, gently stepping over the sleeping figures lying before it, and warmed his hands for a moment before turning around to let his back warm. Robby sat down as Ashlord's shadow and his hidden gaze fell across him. Against the glare of the fire, Robby could not discern Ashlord's expression. After a moment, he came over and sat where Sheila had been, putting his hands on his knees and gazing, as Robby did, at the fire.

"I hope you told her about her uncle."

"Yes. I did."

"I have wanted her to know," Ashlord sighed. "But Mrs. Bosk insisted that I protect her from any news of Barley or Passdale until such a time as she could send a message to me. Mrs. Bosk told me about the uncle, you see. I was reluctant to take Sheila in. Her showing up here took me completely by surprise. So I went to Boskland. Sheila stayed here and was not privy to the conversation I had with Mrs. Bosk. As I said, Mrs. Bosk told me about Sheila's uncle and about Sheila. She was worried that Sheila would be blamed for her uncle's death, even though Sheila couldn't have done the deed."

Ashlord paused and looked hard at Robby.

"I can see that you do not know," Ashlord said to him, "that her uncle beat her nearly to death and raped her."

Robby's heart thudded as the words sank in, and his breath became shallow as he gaped at Ashlord.

"When she showed up here, she was still terribly hurt. Mrs. Bosk told me that she was nearly dead when she was found at their door. Sheila escaped her uncle and crawled halfway across Barley at night and in the rain to get to Boskland, to people who might help and protect her. I honestly don't know how she made it that far alive," he said, casting a look back at her door. "But she is a remarkable girl! And her resilience is exceptional."

Robby could feel himself pale as dark anger churned in his chest and hot tears stung his eyes.

"When?" he hoarsely demanded. "When did that happen?"

"It was a fortnight and two days after Midsummer's when she showed up here. She stayed two weeks at Boskland before that. I don't think

Frizella, that is, Mrs. Bosk told anyone about Sheila's presence there, not even Billy."

"She came to see me. Sheila did, that is. I think it must have been the day she left," Robby said. "At the store. I think she may have already had it in her head to go away somewhere, and I think she was trying to say goodbye."

"Perhaps so. And perhaps it was Steggan's discovery of her plan to leave that set him off, unleashing his violent rage against her," Ashlord said. "I learned that Mrs. Bosk tried to talk Sheila into coming out here on several occasions, so perhaps Sheila was already considering it. I have not asked Sheila about any of these things. Frizella Bosk is a wise woman in many ways, in spite of her rough edges. When I went to see her, she explained the situation to me, and she convinced me to take the girl in and to offer what protection and instruction that I could. I also agreed not to question Sheila about these things or to impart any news to her. She has always been free to come and go, if ever she wanted. But she stayed and quickly became one of the best pupils I have ever had. Still, she does not talk to me in the way that she might talk to you. She has mentioned you only twice, and then only in passing. Otherwise, she rarely speaks of Barley or Passdale. I have kept her busy, and I think she has recovered as much as one might in such a short time. Better than most would, I daresay. And I hope I have been a good teacher. Still, it has been hard on her to be without her friends."

Ashlord heaved a sigh.

"It is a sorry world that treats people so!" he proclaimed.

"At least her uncle had the decency to hang himself," Robby said.

"I agree. But from what I gather, I don't think Steggan was the sort of man to feel any guilt. Perhaps, one way or another, justice caught up with him."

Robby thought he heard a note of threat in Ashlord's voice. Ashlord knew more than he would say, Robby figured, and, although he was curious, he did not press Ashlord. Instead, Robby sat, clenching and unclenching his fists in anger and frustration, shaking his head. The two sat quietly for a few minutes until Ashlord softly slapped his knees and stood.

"You have a long walk ahead of you tomorrow," he said. "So I suggest that you get some rest."

"What about you?"

"I have already rested," Ashlord said. "And I will have more rest before morning. But, first, I must gather more starcup blossoms for my mixtures. You can only find them at night after heavy rains have fallen and when the skies are clearing. I have already filled one pouch, but need another." He picked up a shoulder bag and opened the door, taking up his stick.

"Sleep!" he commanded before stepping out and closing the door.

Ashlord's footsteps receded, and Robby sat a while longer, watching the fire, pondering what Ashlord had just told him, his drowsy eyes watery with anger and sadness. He stood, feeling again the urge to go to Sheila, but he went instead to his cot.

"Sleep!" he muttered, crawling under the blankets. Soon enough, sleep came. It was not fitful as before, and he dreamed about the store and trying to sweep away piles of sand that blew in through the door as customers came and went. The sand made the door hard to close, and kept blowing into his eyes, too, but Robby was glad to be home, and he did not mind the annoyance. Just before he managed to shove the door to, he saw a figure standing in the road, looking at the store. The person was wrapped from head to foot in dark robes, snapping and blowing in the gritty wind. Hearing his father call to him, he closed the door and happily turned his attention to the customers and their mundane needs.

# Chapter 7

# Sheila's Secret

Day 8
237 Days Remaining

The following morning before dawn, Ashlord roused his guests, who groggily ate breakfast then packed for the trip back. Each was given a small flask of water and a walking staff to help with any boggy places they might encounter. Robby had his shoulder bag and staff, and Sheila picked up her bow and quiver.

"Keep watch on my things, Flitter," Ashlord called to the squirrel as he closed the door. Certina was on his shoulder, but she flew off as he led everyone out of the yard and through the gate. He turned to the southward path.

"We don't foller the road west, back through Ol' Gate?" Billy asked.

"No," Ashlord replied. "The way you came from Boskland, which is normally the easiest way, is still too wet, I'm sure. We'll follow the ridgeline of the hill and then down through the pinewood before turning westward to the Line Road. We'll keep to higher ground as long as we can, and move faster and easier than going the other way."

"Right!"

So he led the group along the path and past the spot where they had sunned the afternoon before. They went down steep stairs set into the broad wall of the old keep as the hill dropped off rapidly into a series of lower ridges, and they followed these for a long while. To their left, the land descended sharply to a line of trees that marked the banks of the newly flowing river.

"What was the river called in the old days, Ashlord?" Billy called ahead.

"Billy," Robby shook his head, "you truly don't remember the name of the river that runs behind and around Boskland?"

"Um, Sardlin'?"

"Saerdulin," Ashlord answered. "Its right name is Saerdulin."

"Oh, yeah. Saerdulin," Billy grinned.

They could not yet see the river, but they could hear it roaring over long-dry falls and cutting afresh through channels choked with an age of growth. On the other side, as far as could be seen, lay the Boggy Wood, dark green and forbidding, with columns of fog lifting up here and there. To the west, on their right, the rain-soaked plain gave off its own mists, shrouding the fields of mud and rock with sheets of pale gray, obscuring any view of the Line Road or the Barley Ridge beyond.

The path was narrow and dry, and after going steadily up and down, it turned suddenly east toward the river, and they passed through thickets so that they could not see left or right or ahead for more than a few feet. After a short distance the path rose, steeply following ancient flagstones covered with grass and weeds, and, as the path continued to climb upwards, the flagstones turned into steps. The way switched back on itself, cutting up the side of a slope and over rocky outcrops. Abruptly, they found themselves standing in the open again, atop the ruins of a small battlement overlooking the river. Through an opening in the trees below they could plainly see where Saerdulin bent southwestward gushing brown with mud. As they watched the churning water, a huge oak lurched and then fell over into the torrent to be dragged away.

"Here the ancient course of the river could be watched and a signal fire lit," Ashlord said, pointing north where the walls of Tulith Attis were barely visible, shrouded in the morning mists. "There was once a road on the other side of the river that could also be watched from here, but it has long since vanished. In the old days, the river was calm and steady all the way up to the base of Tulith Attis, and boats could go from here all the way to the sea."

"This was only a stream just a few days ago!" Robby uttered. "I waded across it, sort of."

"If this is so flooded, I wonder what the River Bentwide must look like!" nodded Billy.

"What about Passdale?" Robby worried aloud.

"I think Passdale was spared the worst of it," Ashlord reassured him. "The River Saerdulin, meanwhile, has taken back its ancient course and will be a stream no longer."

Turning away, he continued down the other side of the rise and the others followed, descending into a sparse pine wood. The moist, straw-strewn path muffled their footsteps. It was still slippery in places, from all the rain, but soon leveled out and wound gently around the straight trunks. Everywhere birds tittered and called, and late-summer crickets brrrred. Several times they heard the thumping of deer dashing away, and once or twice a frightened rabbit scampered off at their approach. In some places the path they followed was muddy or strewn with recently fallen limbs, but these were minor obstacles that did not hinder them from proceeding at a good pace. In spite of his aches and pains, Robby kept up easily, anxious as he was to get home. He stayed close behind Ashlord, with Billy and Ibin just after him and Sheila at the rear of their line. Robby paid attention to Ashlord, saw how he quickly moved around the bends, and he noticed Ashlord's head constantly turning this way and that, to check on those who followed him, and to survey the surroundings. At times, it seemed to Robby that Ashlord was listening for something, and at other times he would fix his gaze upon some obscure point in the trees, yet he never tripped or stumbled. Even when he was not watching where he was going, he seemed to see his way around thorn branches or over tricky roots and slippery rocks. They traveled in silence for a long way through the pine woods until at last Robby spoke.

"You said the battle was lost and the fortress taken," Robby said. "What happened afterwards?"

"Ah, well," Ashlord sighed, stepping over a large branch that had fallen across the way, without looking at it at all. "A great deal, apparently, although the details are sketchy, and the many stories and legends tell things differently.

"According to the Annals of Duinnor, a great slaughter took place within the fortress and the blood of women and children spilled over the walls and was seen by the remnants of Heneil's forces who were engaged upon the plain. It is said that they were surrounded and could not get back to the fortress. One legend says that a single small group, led by Heneil's wife herself, fought their way out from the fortress and made it as far as the place where Weepingbrook now runs. There, so legend has it, they came upon the bodies of their husbands and fell into deep mourning, their tears forming the waters that have ever since run there. Some would not leave that place and were left wailing beside the bodies of their men. As the rest fled, those who remained swore horrible oaths upon any who crossed them, upon the land, and against all who occupy the earth. Some say their spirits, still brooding with malice against Duinnor, abide along those banks even unto this day. You see, the defenders of Tulith Attis knew that Duinnor was on the way. But, as you have guessed, they did not arrive in time, and those who defended the place thought themselves doubly betrayed. Your local tales have it that Weepingbrook stream is haunted, I know. And Sheila thinks you stirred those spirits against you with your Duinnor blade."

Robby glanced back at Sheila who merely nodded in return.

"But then there came an army of men from the northern coastlands of Glareth," Ashlord went on as he ducked under a branch, "and, with the forces of Vanara and Duinnor, arriving at last from the west, a great army converged upon Tulith Attis. Of course, they were too late. They immediately set out in pursuit of the retreating Dragonkind, meeting them in a great battle on down along the banks of the Saerdulin where the River Lerse flows into it. There, the Dragonkind were utterly defeated and destroyed. But the seeds of discord were planted, and word of the fall of Tulith Attis and the treachery that caused it spread wide and divided the Elifaen from Men. Mistrust and misunderstandings erupted into feuds within the armies. All of the lands of the Eastlands and Tracia, already laid waste by the Dragonkind, fell into chaos as discord descended into violence. Vanarans fought Glarethians, Men against Elifaen, such was their lust for blood and blame. Duinnor quickly withdrew its army to prevent their men from being drawn into the squabbles. Had it not been for Queen Serith Ellyn of Vanara and Prince Thalamir of Glareth, who managed to regain control over their armies, all the world may have been thrown into civil war and chaos. When at last the armies retreated back to their own lands, warlords sprang up, taking what lands they could control, vying with one another for power. The Elifaen withdrew to Vanara and Glareth. The power of Duinnor was shaken, and the Fifth Unknown King's reign was weakened for a time, until the coming of the present Sixth Nameless King who reasserted Duinnor's might and reunited the lands of Men and Elifaen under the Seven Realms."

"But what about Heneil?" Robby asked, skirting a mud puddle. "What happened to him? And his wife? Lyrium? Was that her name?"

"Yes, it was. No one knows," Ashlord said. "Heneil's forces were utterly defeated before help could arrive. Some say that a few escaped down the Bentwide in boats, and that Heneil was among them, while others say he was killed, along with his wife, at the summit of Tulith Attis. Of his wife, there are no tales that I know of. But neither Heneil nor his wife were seen again in Vanara or Duinnor or any place known in the world. Lost, too, were Heneil's brother, Pellen, and his wife, Myrium, who was Lyrium's sister. All were most likely killed when Tulith Attis was betrayed and stormed by the Dragonkind."

Ashlord looked over his shoulder at Robby close behind.

"You saw the statues in the bell room," he said. "Some tales say that the woman depicted there is Lyrium, standing opposite her husband, Heneil."

"Then she must have been very beautiful," Robby nodded. "If the statue only captured part of her loveliness."

"Yes, born of starlight and moonlight, it is said, during the Time Before Time. The love story of Heneil and Lyrium is still sung by Elifaen folk and Men alike. In their day, all knew of their love and their affection for each other, and many refuse to believe they could meet such a violent and horrible end. Many say they abide to this day in a peaceful land far away."

"Yesyesyes!" Ibin chirped up from behind, and then he sang these lines:

"Green are the fields that glow in sun,
Clear are the waters that playful run,
Bright are the stars that twinkle away,
In the land where Heneil and Lyrium stay."

"Thar he goes, again," Billy said to Sheila.
"Oh, leave him alone," she answered. "He has a nice voice."
Billy shrugged just as he stepped into a deep mire.
"Aw, yuck!"

Not two hours later, they were crossing through an opening in a low wall, and scrambling down an embankment to emerge onto the Line Road.

"Ah!" Billy cried out. "I know whar we're at! Only 'bout three leagues from home, Ibin!"

"Good!" Ibin said.

"Now listen to me for a moment." Ashlord called them to gather around him. "Much has happened to us all these past days. Robby here has been through more than he deserves, and I know you are his friends. So be careful of your tongues! I ask you to tell no one about what happened to Robby at Tulith Attis. Only that he was attacked by wolves and was driven off his course. Sheila and I found him and took him in."

"Robby?" Billy looked at Robby with concern. "What goes on?"

"Please do as Ashlord says," Robby replied. "I don't understand everything, but Ashlord seems to think that I might be in some kind of danger."

"Danger?" Billy quizzed. "Oh, yeah. What ye told us yesterday."

"Here is how it is," Ashlord explained. "Robby stumbled into something ancient and menacing. He may have awakened the attention of those who wish to keep their secrets. Not only he, but all of you are in danger of their plots. If they learn that Robby was the one that rang the Great Bell of Tulith Attis, his life may be in danger. I will endeavor to keep his identity safe in my own way."

"But what secrets?" Billy implored. "What secrets about who?"

"Now is not the time for you to learn all the history to do with these things. I will only tell you this: There is a brooding one, seeking to reassemble the might he once held and to enslave all to his will. It was he who stirred the Dragonfolk, it is said, though he cares not for them. And he who incited the Faerekind against the Dragonkind and caused the Faerekind to split their ranks, forming the Elifaen and those who have departed from the world. It was he, setting himself against the gods themselves, who fomented strife in later days between Elves and Men."

"You mean Secundur? The Prince of Shadow?" Sheila asked.

"Yes, but do not so easily throw his name into the air," Ashlord said sternly. "He has many servants, and the one who betrayed Tulith Attis during the battle that took place there may have been in his service, and he might still be a servant of the Shadow Lord. Say nothing of these events. Say nothing of the awakening of the stone guard. Let those that may have heard the Great Bell form their own beliefs. Meanwhile, learn as much as you can about the world. Let Sheila teach you some of what I have taught her. Do not take histories or legends lightly!"

"Are you not going on to Boskland with us?" Sheila asked.

"No, I must return to Tulith Attis for a time," he shook his head. "I ask you to go on with Robby to Passdale and there to see his father. I know he has some business with you."

"What business? I have no business with him. And, I—"

"Sheila!" Ashlord gently interrupted her. "Your uncle's affairs must be settled. And there are other reasons to go. I need you to do this. While learning may never cease, there comes a time when one must apply the learning and abilities that one has, limited though they may be. It is your time to do that." He put his arm around her and led her a few steps away from the other three.

"Those things I taught thee now come to pass," he said, speaking softly so that the others could not hear, and in the ancient dialect, slowly and clearly so that she would understand. "Young Robby has stumbled into them. He must have some role to play that only the Great Powers may know. Keep him safe until he reaches home. Encourage his continued learning. Look to thine own affairs, too. Above all, stay away from Tulith Attis unless I summon thee. Dost thou understand?"

Sheila nodded, then, fighting back tears, she shook her head. "No."

"My dear!" he said tenderly, putting his hands on both her shoulders and facing her. "Thou art the brightest pupil I have ever taught. When thou came unto me, I thought thou wouldst be a burden. But I was wrong! Thou hast helped me in so many ways. And there is nothing for thee to be ashamed of. Indeed, I bid thee walk proudly amongst those who once gave thee no kindness, who may have scorned thee, or who ill-treated thee. Be now confident in thine own self! Be brave amongst them. But do not disdain them. Remember our friendship in the lessons we hast shared. I will not abandon thee, but nor canst I be at once both here and there. I possess as much trust in thee as I would in mine own self to see Robby home. The Ribbons are trustworthy and upright. And, from that lady thou mayst well learn some things that a woman and a lady ought know, things that I cannot teach."

"How long will it be?"

"Perhaps many weeks, maybe fewer," Ashlord said. "I do not know."

"So be it," Sheila said. "I will do thy bidding, though I think of the Hill, now, as home."

"I am afraid it is no longer safe for thee," Ashlord said. "But so our work begins. Fare thee well!"

"Farewell, Collandoth!" Sheila stepped away, taking resolve from his words. Then Robby stepped forward.

"Won't you come with us to Passdale?" Robby pleaded. "My parents will want to thank you in person, and, anyway, I need your guidance. What will become of me? What of the Bell and the traitor of Tulith Attis?"

"Be alert to all things, but do not worry too much, yet," Ashlord reassured him, falling back into the Common Speech, putting his hand on Robby's shoulder. "I will strive to learn more, and then I will come to see you after a while. Meanwhile, keep these things to yourself as best as you can."

"I will," Robby said.

"Get yourself home safe. You have a long, soggy road ahead, yet! So be careful!"

Robby thanked Ashlord again and again shook his hand. Ashlord smiled, then turned away and quickly strode back into the wood the way they had come, soon lost to sight.

"Well!" Billy said. "He's gonna miss out on some fine victuals in Boskland, is all I can say!"

"I wish he was coming with us," Robby said. "I know my parents would like to thank him for all he's done."

"Come on, let's go," Sheila said, already moving off down the road.

• • •

They had not gone two miles when the road became soggy, then muddy, and then covered with a few inches of standing water as it panned flat through the woods. They sloshed through that for about a mile before the road became dry again along a gentle rise where they stopped and surveyed the way ahead. Before them the road sank below slow-moving water, emerging about forty yards farther on before curving up and out of sight around a bend.

"Looks like it's gone down a bit, Ibin," Billy said.

"Yeah, it'sgone, it'sgonedownalittle."

"This is whar we gave up our ponies," Billy explained. "It was up to thar bellies, an' they wouldn't budge after goin' halfway in."

"Doesn't look too deep, now," Robby suggested. "Nor too swift."

"Naw, probably only a foot at the very most, now," Billy agreed.

Just then, they heard the thunder of approaching hooves.

"Riders coming on the road!" Sheila exclaimed. "Let's move out of sight until we make out who they are."

"Bosklanders, most likely," Billy said, reluctantly following Sheila's instructions and moving off the road and ducking down behind thick brush. Sheila notched an arrow, keeping her bow low as they watched the bend. Suddenly, four horsemen appeared, cloaked in brown and black, wearing black iron helmets and with swords on their saddles, galloping hard into the water toward them. The blast of a horn drew their attention back to the bend where, a mere moment later, came twelve other horsemen, wearing the gold and green colors of Boskland. The four riders drew up sharply and stopped right in front of their hiding place, then three of them reined their horses around as the fourth continued on faster than ever. Robby could hear the ring of steel as they drew their swords and spurred their mounts back at their coming pursuers. In the middle of the stream the two groups met, geysers of water splashing up around the melee while sparks flew from steel meeting steel. The three made it all the way through the Bosklanders, felling two of Billy's kithmen, then wheeled around at the far side to come again, the Bosklanders pulling at their reins in confusion and dismay. Just as they met again, Sheila stood and let fly her arrow, striking the lead horseman in the neck. But the other two came on, and another Bosklander was unhorsed as they swept through. Sheila and Billy dashed out into the road as the two horsemen bore down on them at a gallop. Sheila gave one an arrow in the chest and then rolled out of the way as he passed, while Billy struck the other from his mount with his staff. Struggling to get back up, Billy struck him again on the side of his helmet, splintering his staff in two, then Ibin walked up, as calm as ever, and put his foot on the culprit's chest, pinning him down as the Bosklanders surrounded them. The man under Ibin's foot produced a dagger to strike Ibin's leg, but Billy kicked it away. The other horseman, whose mount had come to a halt several yards away, fell sideways out of his saddle onto the roadway and lay still.

"Billy Bosk!" cried one of the men in gold and green as he rode up. It was Billy's father, who dismounted to give his son a hug. He was barely taller than Robby, and built like a stockade, thick and strong, but with the same nose and red hair as his wiry son. "We whar comin' for ye, but got a bit distracted by these raiders. Son, are ye all right?"

"Yessir, Pop!" Billy nodded. "Nuthin' a little head bashin' don't cure!"

Billy grinned as Mr. Bosk looked down at their prisoner.

"Good work!" he said. "An' well, if yer archer ain't none other than Sheila Pradkin!"

"Yup," Billy said. "Fine shootin', don't ye think?"

"Young lady," Bosk said, "ye've more spunk in ye than half the men in Barley! I thanks ye for yer help!"

Mr. Bosk put his hands on his hips and looked at the whole group, now that Robby had emerged from the bushes.

"I should of known ye'd be together," he said shaking his head and smiling. "Master Ribbon! If ye can only know the trouble ye've put me. Me wife half out of her wits with worry first 'bout ye then 'bout Billy an' Ibin. An' yer own folks prob'ly done lost thar minds with fret!"

"I'm truly sorry, sir," Robby said, turning red at the scolding. "But at least for my part, it couldn't be helped."

One of Bosk's men came up and interrupted.

"Branard an' Terrent're fine," he said. "Just got the wind kicked out of 'em. Geever's been slashed fairly bad, but'll live if we get him back home an' to some care."

"One of 'em got away," another man said to Bosk.

"I know," he said, looking down the road. "Ringalf! Lessicks! The two of ye track that rider. Catch him if ye can. Kill him if ye must. Go no farther than the day will allow. I don't want ye out after dark."

Immediately the two were mounted and riding away hard in pursuit of the escapee.

"Oakson!"

"Yes, sir?"

"Ride back to Boskland with word to prepare for wounded. Tell the lady 'bout Billy an' the others here. An' send someone back with more mounts. Get ye somethin' to eat an' a fresh mount for yerself. I want ye to ride to Passdale an' let folks thar know 'bout things this way. Be sure an' see Mr. Ribbon an' tell him his son's comin' home!"

"Yes, sir!"

"Wait," Robby cried, fumbling in his shoulder bag. "Give my dad this, if you will. And this."

He hurriedly pulled his order book out and tore a page out of it and scribbled a note saying:

Father and Mother,
I am well, though tired and a little sore. I will be home before nightfall. Sheila Pradkin is coming with me. She and Ashlord have taken care of me these past days. Sheila will need a place to stay for a while in Passdale. Will you please make a place for her with us?
I hope you are well. I love you!

Robby

Oh yes, please treat the carrier of this note kindly, for he has had a long and rough day.

Robby folded and tucked it under the string that bound the packet from Ashlord and handed them to the rider.

"Thank you very much!" Robby said and watched the rider gallop off.

"Now," Mr. Bosk said, turning to the prisoner. "Let's see what we've caught."

Leaning over, Bosk made sure no weapons were still on the now-passive intruder. Robby saw that he wore a heavy black leather doublet, brown wrist braces and gloves, and heavy riding boots and a black cloak, muddy and torn. Bosk reached for the man's helmet and pulled it off. Upon seeing the face, they all stepped back aghast. Instead of a nose, he had two small holes above his lipless mouth, his skin was leathery gray, and his yellow eyes had vertical slits for pupils. He had no facial hair and only a thin mat of silver threads that dropped down over the ridges of his forehead.

"A Dragonkind!" one of the men gasped as everyone made ready their swords.

"An' he's got the sickness," said another, backing away a step.

"What's he doin' in these parts?"

The Dragonkind hissed an unintelligible curse at the group and slowly stood. He was thin as a rail yet taller than anyone present by a head, except Ibin. His eyes had a look of fiery contempt, and the worst of his glares he sent at Sheila who, though trembling at the sight of the creature, had a notched arrow pointed at his head.

"S-s-s-silly Northmen peepleses," he hissed. "I eats you gutses, I shall, yessss, I shall tear out you bowels and gnaw as you watches me eats you!"

"Quick! Bind his legs!" Sheila cried. "Get a rope on him!"

But before Sheila could make herself understood, the Dragonkind whirled on one leg and with the other kicked Mr. Bosk square in the chest, knocking him away. With a speed unimaginable, he dodged Sheila's arrow and the two swords that swung at him. He grabbed one man by the throat while slamming his other hand straight into the face of another man who fell stunned to the ground. Using the first man as a shield, blocking Sheila's attempts to find a target, he crashed through the others. Suddenly, Ibin ran past Sheila with arms outstretched and tackled both the hapless shield and the Dragonkind, twisting around and pulling the both of them down on top of himself. Sheila's arrow struck the Dragonkind's back but barely penetrated his thick doublet. He squirmed away from Ibin and sprang back up on his feet as Mr. Bosk hacked at him with a sword, nearly severing his right arm, but still he fought on, kicking one man in the head so hard his helmet flew off, while at the same time striking another in the chest with his good arm, in a strangely graceful, if fierce, movement. Another of Sheila's arrows found its mark in the Dragonkind's side, but it, too, had little effect, and in spite of his wounds, he kicked away another man, and scratched the face of a third with his claw-like fingers.

"Give him room!" Bosk cried out to his men who then backed away. Surrounded, the Dragonkind flew into a frenzy, one arm dangling useless at his side, yet the other suddenly wielding a sword that he had taken from someone. At no time did he cry out in pain, and though he staggered, he did not seem to care about his wounds. Suddenly the place grew quiet, save for the rasping heave of the creature's breath and the buzz of late summer locusts high in the trees. Gathering himself for one last bout, the creature lurched forward at Bosk but had gone no more than a step when a third arrow struck him through his right eye, and he fell dead.

"Great stars!" Billy uttered. "What is that thing?"

"He was once a Dragonkind feller," said one of the men.

"But he's had the desert sickness a long time, I'd say. By the looks of him," said another.

"Purty far gone, I'd say," said one of the older men.

For a few moments, everyone simply stood around and stared at the body in disbelief. Then Mr. Bosk's voice shook them all from their gaze.

"Look at the others!" he shouted as he made his way up the road toward the riderless horse.

Some of the men splashed into the water to drag one of the intruders onto the bank while others went with Bosk to look at the man that lay on the road. One or two of the Boskmen, wounded and in great pain, stood near the last of the three bodies or sat down on the ground. Sheila was already trying to tend to the worst of them and called out for Robby's help. Ibin stood up and watched, not knowing what to do, while Billy trailed along behind his father.

"How did you know we should tie his feet?" Robby asked Sheila as he helped her remove the leggings from a wounded man.

"Ashlord told me about a battle he was in, long ago. He mentioned how the Dragon People can fight with their feet, just as the Elifaen can do."

"I never—"

"This one's a man!" called out someone looking at the body they had dragged from the water.

"This one, too!" cried another after turning over the body in the road. Billy and his father looked at the dead man's face carefully.

"D'ye recognize him, son?"

"No, sir, I don't believe so."

"Me, neither. I reckon he's not from these parts," Bosk concluded. He went to examine the horse.

"Whoa, easy thar, boy. I'll not hurt ye," he coaxed the horse gently until he could take the reins. Looking the horse over, he saw it bore many spur scars and was bleeding on the flanks, while his legs were scratched and cut from rough riding. He looked over the saddle, paying attention to the leatherwork and the metal buckles, then pulled open the flap of a saddlebag, but found nothing but stale salt meat and moldy cheese. In the other pouch was only a whetstone and some heavy twine. The saddle was old and worn but had been recently repaired in one or two places. Pulling up the horse's flank coat, he looked over the brand.

"Here," he said, handing Billy the reins. "Bring him along."

He strode back to the bank to look over the other body. No one recognized this man, either, and his pockets contained nothing of worth or importance. One of the Boskmen came wading through the stream, leading the two other horses of the dead men.

"I think I recognize that horse!" Robby said.

"If I ain't mistaken," Bosk nodded as it was led toward them, "that's Bob Starhart's mount."

"Yes, sir, I believe it is," Robby nodded. "The only horse I've ever seen with a white mask."

Robby referred to an odd white mark that ran up the horse's snout and spread out around his eyes.

"Bandit, Bob calls him," Robby said, reaching out for the reins. "And look!"

Still on Bandit's back was the post rider's saddle, clearly embossed with the King's Post insignia. But, instead of the post bags, black leather saddlebags were tied on. Inside one pouch was flint and steel, some punk wrapped in parchment, and a whetstone. In the other pouch was more rotted food, a small tin flask with Bob Starhart's initials engraved on the side of it, and some odd bits of flat, square metal, about two fingers wide, thinner than a knife blade, each with a round hole through its center. On either side, strange shapes were stamped.

"What are these?" Robby asked.

"Coins," Bosk said. "Dragonkind coins. They ain't got no value in these parts, 'cept maybe for the copper. Keep 'em. Maybe yer dad can make somethin' with 'em."

"But, Pop, what's all this about?" asked Billy. "Who're these men?"

"I'll tell ye all 'bout it on the way back," Mr. Bosk said as he walked to where Sheila was tending the wounded.

"How's young Geever doin', Miss Sheila?" he asked, bending over the pale young man in her care.

"Pretty banged up besides a nasty gash on his ribs here," Sheila said putting the final wrapping on him. "Seems I've been doin' a lot of bandaging, lately."

"Huh?"

"Never mind," Sheila shook her head. "But we'd better get this fellow back. I don't trust that wound to stop bleeding until a proper poultice can be made for it. I'd rather not move him, but I think he'd be better off indoors where he can be properly looked after."

"Can he ride?"

"I can still ride," winced the young man. "I ain't so bad off as all that."

"Rubbish," Sheila scoffed. "But I suppose you'd better make a try of it."

"Ibin!" Mr. Bosk called. Ibin was still standing with a blank expression, but he now smiled and trotted over.

"Yessir?"

"Why don't ye help Sheila get this feller into a saddle. Be easy with him!"

"Yes, sir, Mr. Bosk."

While Ibin did as he was told, Bosk waved over a couple of his men, and, pointing at the woods gave them some orders. They left and came back shortly with three long poles cut from saplings and sharpened at the tips. One by one, Bosk held the dead men up by the hair and with one blow each, cut off their heads. He then mounted his grisly trophies on the poles and gave them to three of his men.

"Carry these afore us, an' put 'em over the gates of Boskland as a sign for any to see what may happen to them what come lootin' an' pillagin' in our lands," he ordered. "Have thar carcasses dragged behind to be burned. I'll not leave 'em to foul the road."

Soon they were all mounted, with Billy and Ibin sharing one of the larger captured horses, riding alongside Mr. Bosk. Sheila and Robby had a horse each to themselves, Robby on Bandit riding just behind Billy and Ibin. Up ahead went three riders carrying the poles, and at the rear of the group rode three more, dragging the bodies of the dead by rope tied about their feet. Robby thought that if he had not already been so tired and hurt, he would surely be sick at the sight. He could not bear to look at the severed heads before them, and he thought the gesture ghastly. But he did not protest and would not question the Master of Bosk Hall. He knew the Bosks to be tough and hearty folk, with a long tradition of protecting this part of Barley against thieves and intruders. Bosk Hall was the only place in Barley that kept arms, partly because the Bosk family was charged with enforcing the King's rule in these parts, and partly because they had always done so, probably even before there was a King. There was seldom any trouble in these lands and rarely did the Boskmen ever have need of their arms. Occasionally, a gang of thieves would come out of the Boggy Wood, or down from the mountains, but the last time there had been any serious trouble was long before Robby was born. Still, whenever there was any need of organizing a defense, people in Barley looked to Boskmen to see it done. That, and the fact that Bosk Hall was on high ground, was probably why the people on this side of the county sought out Boskland as a place to take refuge from the floods. Robby kept his gaze from straying too far ahead of his horse's ears, and he was thankful for the clopping hooves that muffled the sound of the bodies being dragged behind them.

"So, what's all this about?" Billy asked again.

"Early this mornin'," his father began, "we got word that looters whar seen over at ol' man Packlin's place. So I called the men to arms, an' we went out lookin' for 'em. Meanwhiles, they must've finished up at Packlin's place an' headed our way. We caught 'em down at Sam Goodwin's place, goin' through his house an' barn. Thar was a fight, apparently, an' I'm afraid Sam got run through by one of these bastards. Anyhow, by the time we got down thar, they was slicin' up one of Sam's pigs. They took off when we come over the hill. I broke the men up, some to see to Sam, an' some to go to Packlin's to look in on things out thar. The rest of us lit out in chase. The ground out thar's fairly high, but the roads're soggy, an' so they headed north 'cross the fields. Somehow they got 'round us by cuttin' east an' back toward Boskland. They didn't know the land, though, an' we made up for our mistakes by takin' a side lane. An' we nearly caught 'em as they rode onto Bosk Manor grounds. We would've caught 'em, too, but for the almighty commotions, what with all the people an' carts an' panickin' as they rode through, wavin' swords an' yellin' an' such. They rode right through, right out on to the Line Road, like they suddenly knew whar they was goin'. They got a good lead on us, but we narrowed it 'til they turned on us back at the stream."

Bosk turned in his saddle and nodded at Sheila.

"Lucky for us to run into ye, with yer friend an' her bow an' quiver!" he said. "Pro'bly saved a few of us."

"Sheila has a knack for showing up just when you need her," Robby said.

"Oh?"

"Yes, sir," Robby went on. "And she is not afraid of wolves, either."

"Wolves?"

"Robby had something of a run-in with a pack of 'em," Billy explained.

"Wolves? In Barley?" Bosk shook his head. "They must be comin' out of the Boggy Wood. Wolves! An' raiders! Not good!"

"Yes, sir," Robby went on. "I probably saw two hundred or more."

"Robby!" Sheila hissed. Robby suddenly realized that he might have to explain more of how he escaped the wolves, and he remembered Ashlord's admonishment to keep certain things quiet. "Well," he stammered. "Maybe not that many."

"Two or two hunnerd's too many either way!" Bosk declared. "An if I warn't so relieved to see ye alive, ye little brat," he shot at Billy, "I'd beat the tarnation out of ye. As it is, yer Mum nearly beat it out of me for lettin' ye out of me sight."

"Well, somebody had to look for Robby!" Billy fired back. "We couldn't just leave 'im, could we? I knew ye'd not spare the men right off."

"I'll not gainsay yer loyalty to yer friends. Not in front of 'em, anyways," Bosk said, nodding at Robby. "But thar's yer family to think of, too."

"Yes, sir, I know."

"An' draggin' Ibin along with ye!"

"Oh, I, Isnuckout, ohIsnuckoutanfollowedBilly!" Ibin said proudly. "I toldhimI'd, Itoldhim, ItoldhimI'dwakeyouupifhedidn't, ifhedidn't, I'dwake-youupifhedidn'tletmecomewithhim."

"I bet!"

"He did!" Billy protested.

"Oh, no! Wait!" Robby exclaimed, tugging on his reins and coming to a sudden halt. "What about Ashlord?"

"What about him?" Sheila asked as the rest came to a stop.

"That one that got away," Robby pointed back down the road. "The only way for him to go is east. He can't go west very far because of the flooded Weepingbrook and the bridge being out there. This Line Road goes north then turns west and must be flooded out at the Weepingbrook ford, too. And surely he won't come back this way. That only leaves east. Toward Tulith Attis. We should warn Ashlord!"

"How do ye perpose to do that?" Billy said. "We'd never reach thar in time."

"And why?" Sheila asked.

"Why?" asked Robby, gaping at her incredulously. "That fellow's liable to do anything!"

"Nobody can get close to Ashlord without him knowin' 'bout it well beforehand," Sheila calmly said. Mr. Bosk chuckled and Robby shot him a look of dismay.

"Now, now," he said to Robby. "It's only that it'd be better for that scoundrel if he avoids Haven Hill! Ashlord's the kinda feller that ain't likely to be taken unawares. The kind that's never seen lest he wants to be seen, if ye take me meanin'."

"I'm not sure that I do," answered Robby.

"Come along, now. We've got wounded," Bosk said reining his horse back around. "What I mean to say is, that Ashlord feller's pro'bly been in more fights, I reckon, than all us put together—leavin' out Billy, of course—an' he can take care of hisself."

"How do you mean?" Robby asked, prodding his mount up next to Mr. Bosk.

"Alls I mean is that he's done his share of soldierin', an' other kinds of fightin' asides that," Bosk said. "A queer kind of feller, maybe, but upright, I do believe. I wouldn't want to be the one to cross him the wrong way."

"Well, how come he lives out yonder all by hisself?" Billy asked from the other side of Mr. Bosk. "I mean, what's he do out thar?"

"Looks at the stars, for all I know," Bosk retorted. "Why don't ye ask Miss Sheila? She's been out thar with him, ain't she?"

"You knew all along where I was?" Sheila piped up from behind.

"Naw, not all along," Bosk said. "Frizella's got her secrets, for sure. Only some ain't so secret as she may think! But I'll not be the one to let 'em out of the bag, so to speak. No, no! Not if I want to keep me ears from gettin' boxed off!"

"Well, anyway," Billy broke in, "we already tried with Sheila. She's no good for askin' 'bout Ashlord."

"Well, ye just better ask him yerself the next time ye sees him, is all I'll say!"

"Whenever that may be!" said Robby. "I just hope he'll be all right. I owe him my life."

"I'm sure he'll be just fine," Bosk repeated.

"Less talk and more moving," Sheila scolded. "Or your man is going to bleed to death!"

They picked up the pace, cleared the woods, and soon were into the open country of Boskland proper. Everywhere the flood damage was apparent. The violence of the storm began to dawn on Robby as he saw knocked-down corn stalks, many uprooted fruit trees, and the widespread erosion caused by the washing storm. In several places the road was deep with mire, and a stone bridge had water streaming around both sides of it, so full and broad was the once-tiny brook that normally ran barely noticed underneath. Twice they had to leave the road and wade carefully through soggy fields because of uprooted trees that blocked the way. Billy pointed to a great oak, or the remnants of one, standing alone on a hill, its limbs burned to a crisp.

"I saw lightnin' hit that tree four nights ago," Billy said. "We was workin' the field over yonder, tryin' to build a dike. Most awesomest thing I ever saw. Plumb lit up with far an' burnin' limbs, all flyin' way up through the sky, an' bits an' pieces of it fallin' like rain, 'cept all smokin' an' such. Three of our men flat ran away at the sight of it, but not Ibin er me! Did we, Ibin?"

"No, we, wehad, wehadtoomuch, wehadtoomuchworktodo," Ibin said.

Robby noticed that Ibin kept his eyes down at the road, and he concluded that the gentle fellow was bothered by the severed heads, too.

As they rounded a bend, they could see someone riding to them with the spare mounts Mr. Bosk had requested. Behind them trailed a stocky little pony, all on its own, gingerly flinging its mane in anticipation.

"Bucky!" cried Ibin, joyfully squirming from his saddle, nearly knocking Billy off as he went. Ibin ran to meet the pony, who obligingly tossed his head and neighed in greeting and even gave a little dance-like step. Soon Ibin was on the pony's back, and together they turned toward Bosk Manor well ahead of the rest, Ibin's legs bowed so that he could get his toes into the stirrups that quite nearly dragged the ground as they went jauntily along.

"How that wee creature can bear the weight of him, I'll never guess!" Bosk shook his head in wonder. "But Bucky'll have nobody on his back 'cept Ibin, an' that's the truth of it! How else d'ye think he got his name?"

With Ibin happily leading the way, and soon nearly out of sight, and others of the group, including Billy and Sheila, receiving new mounts, the rest of the way passed more quickly. Robby, still on Bandit, asked what would become of Starhart's mount.

"Oh, I dunno," Bosk reflected. "I reckon we'd better try an' get him to the Post Station up at Janhaven. I dunno if ol' Bandit belongs to Starhart, or if he's a Post mount."

"I think he's a Post mount," Robby offered.

"Well, anyway, we'll see to it, regardless," Bosk said. "I only wish I knew what became of Bobby. What with these raiders about, more's the worry."

Robby nodded, recalling what Ullin said about post rider Starhart being missing. But he had not been present while his parents and Ullin speculated on Starhart's disappearance because he had to go take care of Ullin's horse.

"Well, I guess we know who crossed Mr. Starhart," he offered. "And I suppose the worst is what we should assume."

"Yep. I reckon so," Bosk nodded, glancing behind them to make a check on the group. "Yer dad tells me that yer cousin, Ullin, has gone an' took up post ridin'," Bosk said, as if reading Robby's thoughts. "An' yer dad also told how he sent ye up to the Hill, so as Ullin wouldn't need to go."

"Yes, sir."

"Well, that was mighty brave of ye," Bosk said. "Not many folks'll go out that way. Not with all them tales, of course, an' not since them murders, an' all."

"What murders?" Robby asked.

"Oh, get on!" Billy said. "Ye mean to say ye don't know 'bout all that?"

Robby shook his head.

"Well, ain't much to tell," Bosk said. "It whar years ago. Afore Ashlord took up out yonder. I was doin' the Thursday Line Ride. I always ride the Line Road on Thursdays, even today. Me ol' man an' a couple other fellers an' me all rode out together to ride the Line, then to duck down the west way over Weepingbrook to Passdale an' get a few things. Anyways, we come up on the Gate an' looks out toward the fortress an' sees all these buzzards circlin'. Well, naturally, me ol' man would have nuthin' but to go look-see, so we rides out yonder toward the Hill. Ye know them two barrows that the road cuts between?"

"Right before you get to the fortress? Yes, I do," Robby replied.

"Well, back then thar whar a gang of good-for-nuthin' Farbarley boys who liked nuthin' better than causin' trouble, waylayin' folks on the road, all sorts of mischief. Mostly petty stuff, but they whar mean. Anyhow, whar nine of 'em. They took it into thar heads to dig into them barrows an' to see what they'd find. They got 'bout four er five yards in the side of the north un, up on the far side."

Bosk went silent for a moment, and Robby looked over at Billy who was staring at his father in rapturous awe of the story. Robby guessed that Billy had probably heard it a hundred times before.

"Well," Billy said. "Tell Robby the rest of it!"

Bosk nodded, looking straight up the road as he went on.

"We found all nine of 'em. Throats cut, ever' single one. Not even one sign of a fight or nuthin'. Ever' last one just like the next. Four were brothers. The youngest only twelve years! Not a one over eighteen."

"What happened?" Robby asked.

"What d'ya mean?"

"I mean, who did it?"

"Some say the Faere spirits buried in them barrows did it. Others that it whar the ghosts of the Dragon Men what died thar," Mr. Bosk said. "But some hold it whar some other band of thieves what came on 'em."

"You mean to say nobody knows?"

"Yep, that's right. Oh, thar was one feller folks suspected of the deed. One what hung with them boys at the tavern a good bit in them days. But nuthin' came of it. An' anyways, that feller's dead now, too. Done in by uncanny foul play, like them others."

Mr. Bosk gave Robby a knowing glance, then dipped his head toward Sheila. At Robby's puzzled look, Mr. Bosk nodded.

"How 'bout that!" Billy said, nodding in a triumphant manner. "I'd forgotten all 'bout it, else I most likely would of stayed home."

"Right whar ye belong, ye little rapscallion!" Bosk barked at Billy. "If I warn't so glad yer alive, I'd make ye wish ye warn't for worryin' yer mum so!"

Robby's thoughts wandered through the recent events, and a wave of dizziness quickly shot through his head. He remembered the odd feeling he had when walking between the two mounds, and now, with all that had happened, he was in no mood to dismiss anything out of hand. It was the first time he had heard the story, and Mr. Bosk could mean no other than Steggan, Sheila's uncle. The dizzy spell passed, and he realized he had been shaking with fright, probably ever since Ashlord left them, and he felt a little feverish, too. One inadvertent look ahead, catching a glimpse of those piked heads, sent a wave of nausea through him that he barely controlled. His head felt little better than his stomach, as it was pounding with fret, bewilderment, and wonder over all the things that had happened since he left home a few days ago.

"What next?" he thought to himself. "Dragon People, wolves, a haunted fortress, and, now, murders!" He felt embroiled in some plot beyond his comprehension and surrounded with violence and threat on every side. The enigmatic Sheila and the more enigmatic Ashlord he somehow explicitly trusted, but Robby now had a wariness that made him nervous. "I've always been a fairly easygoing fellow," he mused silently as they negotiated another new spring across the roadway. "Maybe a little deception now and then, more faults of omission than lying, in order to stay out later at feast days than I should have, or sneaking out of my bedroom window to see Sheila. But I never neglected my schoolwork or chores, and I've never stolen anything or cheated. And any fights I got into were not of my making. Why on earth has all this happened to me?" He felt a certain pang of being manipulated, and he did not like the sensation. He could not help feeling somewhat herded along like a stupid cow, goaded, led, or prodded along a path beyond his understanding. The story of those murders only added to his sense of dread.

"How long has Ashlord been living out at Tulith Attis?" Robby asked.

"Oh, let me think. I believe he first took up out thar 'bout two or three years after the incident with them murders," Bosk said thoughtfully. "It whar after me ol' man died, 'cause Ashlord came to deliver some letters to him from Duinnor, an' I took 'em. One of the letters whar a writ from Duinnor to show that the Hill an' its boundaries whar to be in the care of Ashlord, an' that he was to be the sole authority of law on the Hill an' answerable only to the King, an' all that. Very official-like. I remember it whar the first time I used the Bosk seal, 'cause I had to send an acknowledgement back to Duinnor. I didn't have the seal, see, 'til me ol' man died. That was in 859. Ashlord left for a few years, then he come back 'bout five or six years ago, I believe. Maybe it's been longer than that."

They continued on, Billy and his father turning their talk to all of the storm damage as they passed field workers trying to salvage a crop of late corn, mostly mashed down by wind and rain. Soon they were passing under the arch of Boskland Manor where Bosk ordered that the severed heads were to be mounted on the arch pikes. He then ordered the bodies taken aside and burned as soon as dry wood could be stacked. The rest of them rode on, passing the now dismal inner gardens that Mrs. Bosk so tenderly kept. Ahead rose the sprawling three-story Bosk House with its red brick walls and its high gables. Mrs. Bosk rushed out as soon as they were within the yard, pulling the wounded down from their mounts and helping them indoors while other folk thronged out to see the remains of the intruders and to hear their laird's report.

"Come along Master Ribbon!" Mrs. Bosk called back to Robby as he dismounted. "I'll be having a look at ye."

"Oh, I'm fine," Robby answered back.

"Oh, I'm sure ye are. I'll be lookin' at ye all the same."

"Better do as she says," Mr. Bosk said. "We'll have ye home soon enough."

As soon as she had seen that those worse off were well-tended, Mrs. Bosk came to fetch Robby into her large kitchen, Sheila having told her about his recent wounds. The kitchen was where she did most of her business, even though she was the lady of the house and did not need to be there at all if she did not want to be. But she never let anyone forget that she once was a kitchen servant herself—as if anyone could forget that—and that nobody was too good for her kitchen, or not good enough. She sat Robby down in a chair beside a worktable and pulled up a chair in front of him. Before he could protest, and talking all the while so that he could not, she had his coat and shirt off and was unbinding his wounds while he held his arms high to allow it.

"So ye had a run-in with some wolves, eh? Well, they's nasty critters! An' ye can't be too careful with bites from the likes of them. So hold still whilst I take a look. Ow, that's gotta hurt somethin' terrible!"

"Oh, it's not too bad," Robby said, wincing as she undid the last of the bandaging.

"Well, somebody's done some good tendin' already, I see. Some festerin' was here, but well on the mend. Was it that Ashlord?"

"Yes, and Sheila."

"An' Sheila? Well, they did right, I see. A good poultice. Nice, clean. Yer gonna have some scars, can't be helped. Turn 'round an' lemme see yer side. That's good. Hm. Sit down while I get some clean bandages. I expect ye were purty surprised to see Sheila out yonder?"

"Yes, I was," Robby said. Mrs. Bosk brought over a pot of steaming water and put it on the table. She then pulled a bottle of murky liquid down from the shelf. "I didn't know what had happened to her. But I should have figured that if she was in trouble that she'd come to you."

Raenelle, Billy's older sister, then came charging into the kitchen.

"Mother," she exclaimed, appearing a bit exasperated, "Daddy and Sheila want to put Geever into the guest room. Oh! Hello, Robby."

"Hello, Raenelle."

"I'm sorry to burst in on you," she said, tossing her black hair over her shoulders. "Mother, we'll have to move Mr. Landers and his wife out."

"Go tell Sheila to put Geever into Billy's room, Raenelle. I'll be up an' see to him shortly."

"Yes, Mother."

"An' get out of that smock in into somethin' ye can work in, girl!"

"Yes, Mother."

Raenelle frowned and departed, still eyeing Robby and his wounds as she left.

"That girl's been far too prideful since she got back from school in Colleton," Frizella said as she turned back to her work. "Mr. Bosk wants her to be a proper lady, if at all possible. An' I reckon I do, too. Still, she pitched right in durin' the storm, like any good Bosk. Now. What was I sayin'?"

Frizella carefully poured some of the steaming water into a smaller bowl and put the pot back onto the stove.

"Oh, yes. I reckon I should've sent ye word," she sighed as she poured some of the tincture from the small bottle into the bowl of hot water and dipped a rag into it. "Hold still whilst I do a little cleanin'. This'll sting, some. Yes, I thought about it. I saw the two of ye together a few times. I saw the two of ye fishin' down at Otter's Pond one time. Another time when I was goin' down to Passdale, I seen ye sittin' under a tree in a field over on Day's farm. I think ye were readin' to Sheila out of a book."

"Oh," Robby said, somewhat embarrassed. "Well, we'd go there sometimes, and I'd try to help her with her reading some."

"I see," Mrs. Bosk nodded as she carefully wiped dried blood from Robby's side with the moist cloth. "An' she'd help ye with yer fishin'?"

"Something like that," he said meekly, realizing how ludicrous it sounded, even if it was mostly true.

"Well, I knowed ye liked her," she said. "An' I knowed she liked ye, too. But she came in a bit of trouble, an' I thought the best thing would be to keep her awhile. All quiet, like."

"I know what happened to her," Robby said. Mrs. Bosk stopped what she was doing and looked at him with her searching blue eyes, her lips pursed in consideration. "Ashlord told me what her uncle did to her."

"I see."

She looked at him a long time, then, although she spoke softly, her words thundered in his head.

"Then do ye know that when it happened, she was pregnant?"

Robby's heart stopped then flew into his throat and pounded away there. His face reddened and his mind raced. A hoarse, "No," came from his throat.

Mrs. Bosk nodded. "Fairly far along, too. I didn't think Ashlord'd tell ye that part. Ye know I'd never do anythin' to hurt ye. Yer mum an' me go way back, an' I think of ye as like one of me own. So I want ye to know this: That night she came here, after that vile uncle of hers did what he did. She was half dead, first from the beatin' he gave her, an' other unspeakable things, an' then from her crawlin' an' scratchin' halfway 'cross the county to get here."

"But why didn't she come to Passdale?" Robby shook his head. "Passdale is a lot closer to her uncle's place than here!"

"Oh, dear lad," she brushed a curl of Robby's hair from his brow. "She came here 'cause she didn't want ye to know. She didn't want ye to know what Steggan did. An' she was more than four months on, just startin' to show. She wanted to have the baby somewhar else. An' she didn't know what to do."

Mrs. Bosk stood and walked to the window, looking out to the side yard and the folks coming and going, the smoke rising some distance away from the pyre being lit.

"It was a fitful rain that night. Cold. Windy. I was the only one up, cleanin' late right here in the kitchen, when a powerful knock came on the back door yonder. Figured it must be the foreman comin' to fetch Mr. Bosk 'bout somethin' er other. But when I got at the door an' pulled it open, thar she was, slumped down on the porch. Thinkin' back, I don't know how on earth she made it in her condition. Like I said, nearly dead from the beatin' she took, an' from a mighty loss of blood, her clothes all torn up, soaked to the bone. I have no idear how she knocked so hard on the door, the way she was, seein' how she couldn't even stand. I thought someone must've helped her along, but thar warn't nobody else around."

"A terrible night!" she went on, turning back to Robby, her eyes glistening. "She pleaded with me not to let her lose the child. I tried, Robby. Tried all I knew. But the both of 'em couldn't be saved. A terrible night! She cried an' cried, an' I cried right along with her whilst I worked. She kept callin' yer name. Out of her head, like. Beggin' ye not to go away, not to leave her. Between tryin' to keep her calm an' tryin' to convince her ye warn't here an' never was, an' tryin' to do me work on her. Awful, awful night!"

She wiped her eyes and sat back down and picked up some bandages she had made.

"It was hard, an' if it warn't for the foxdire what grows in these parts, I don't know what I might've done."

"Foxdire?" Robby asked absently, his eyes on the floor and his thoughts in disarray.

"Aye, some calls it Grave's Breath, 'cause if it's pure it brings on a sleep no one may wake from. But just a little of the essence, mixed with a jigger of Fetch an' honey let Sheila sleep, an' it calmed her down enough for me to work on her. It had to be done, else thar'd be two graves on the hillside, 'stead of just a little secret one."

"So that was that," Frizella continued, binding Robby's wounds as she spoke. "I kept her in one of our old tenant houses down the lane where I could be with her quickly an' often. No one knew but just a few of us. I kept it from me husband, even. Raenelle wasn't yet back from Colleton, or else I'd have gotten her to help out some. But it's just as well my daughter was still away, I suppose. Sheila's a strong girl, an' she got strength back quicker than one might think possible. 'Bout a fortnight later, it was just after Raenelle came home from school, after a lot of private talkin' with Sheila, she left to go on out to Ashlord. That's where her mind was made up to go, anyways."

"Why?" Robby shook his head. "Why couldn't she have just told me? Or sent word? Or something?"

"Don't ye see? Who's Sheila Pradkin? To folk around here, she's the Wild Girl. Dirty. Uncontrollable temper. Poor. Crude. Unschooled. Left pretty much to shift for herself, she took up huntin' an' fishin' an' doin' men's things. Always been that way. An' along come the son of a big man of Passdale! The son of the most respected man an' lady in all of County Barley! A smart, good-lookin' boy. Different in most every way from all the rest. Why, even in the way ye talk yer different, more like yer mum's folk than us country people. An' a well-off family, too. Don't ye see how she was thinkin'? I know! Look at me! Now the wife of the Laird of Bosk! I know what people say. People talk how I trapped the poor rich sot! Forced him through some folk magic to love me!"

"That's all rubbish!"

"So it is, but alls I'm sayin' is that Sheila felt somethin' of them kind of things."

"But why to Ashlord's?"

"It was her idea, ye see, afore it all went wrong, to stay out thar with Ashlord 'til it came time to have the baby, at which time she'd come to me, or send for me. Ye see, she wanted to learn, Robby. To change." Mrs. Bosk smiled at him. "A desire for that much at least, ye gave her. Whether to impress ye, or for her own reasons, I can't say. But some of both, I think."

"She had already impressed me," Robby said. "Obviously."

"She never told me who the father was." Mrs. Bosk was still smiling, but with her head tilted, as she tried to explain. "She didn't need to. Me own way of seein' it is that she fought too hard to keep the child for it to be Steggan's. It wasn't as if she didn't want me to know. Just that thar was no point in sayin'. An' I didn't see the use in askin'. When she left, an' walked down that lane to go to Ashlord, I think she was the saddest creature I ever saw. She's been through enough, Robby Ribbon, so I asks ye to leave her be for a while. I know Ashlord's done wonders, but it's all been too short a while. Ain't nobody who's been through what she's endured don't need a little extra room, extra consideration, if ye know what I mean. Now. I wish we could talk more on it, but go ahead an' get dressed. I'll shortly fix ye somethin' to eat. It's already cooked an' just waitin' for a plate to be put on. While yer dressin', I'll fetch in the others, an' ye can all eat together."

A few moments later, a plate of steaming vegetables and stewed beef was set before Robby along with a glass of cold apple cider, and he began eating, though rather unenthusiastically and with a knotted stomach. Sheila and Ibin came in, but Billy was delayed in the hallway to receive from his mother a severe and protracted tongue-lashing, overheard by all in the house and most in the yard. When it died down, Billy entered the kitchen, red-faced and subdued, though smiling meekly.

"Well this is more like it!" he said, pulling up a chair next to Sheila and across from Robby. Sheila and Billy talked of the wounded while Ibin and Robby listened. Billy changed the subject to the men on the road.

"Who d'ya reckon they whar?" he asked. "Part of them bandits that folk say took up in the mountains, I bet. Some kind of scoutin' party, I bet."

"Well, they picked a lousy time to scout these parts," Sheila offered.

"Yer right," nodded Billy. "Folks've got enough to worry 'bout with the floodin' an all."

Robby could still feel the warm blush of red in his face from his conversation with Mrs. Bosk, and he could not have felt more awkward in Sheila's presence. He tried to avoid looking across the table at her even though, ironically, she was all he wanted to look at. He wondered what she thought of him. Maybe she knew he was not as tough as she was. She probably felt sorry for such a poor specimen of a man, having to be rescued, patched up, and guided home like a child. On the road, he took no part in the fray, hanging back like a coward. In reality, it was because he did not know what to do. Still, besides Ibin, he was the bulkiest of the four, and he now felt guilty at his earlier hesitation, and a little ashamed of it. The fact was, he knew himself to be an awful fighter who had never won any fight he had ever been in, whether for jest, wrestling with the wiry Billy, or in earnest, as when he stood against those Passdale boys. Now, with what Mrs. Bosk had told him, it all made a strange kind of sense to him. Sheila actually wanted nothing to do with him. Still, she was a good person, and Robby supposed she had felt obliged to thank him for standing up for her, for the fight he had gotten into over the bad things said about her. So to thank him, at least in her own awkward way, and to say goodbye, were the reasons for her coming to the store the next day. But mostly to say goodbye.

"I just don't understand," he blurted out. Sheila turned and saw him staring at her with a look of deep confusion on his face, contorted with the effort of fighting back tears of frustration and anger.

"What's the matter?" she asked.

"What don't ye understand?" Billy asked.

Even Ibin had stopped eating and was looking at him.

"Nothing," he said, trying to recover his gaffe. He shrugged. "I mean everything. I mean anything. I don't understand anything. Good grief! I can't even speak!"

"Look, Robby," Billy said, putting down his fork. "A lot's happened to ye. An' a lot's happenin' all over at the same time. Ain't none of us can understand these things, I'll warrant. 'Cept maybe that Ashlord feller. Maybe not even him. I know I talk a big talk. But that's all it is, just talk. Soon ye'll be home, an' ye'll get a chance to rest an' think things over. Yer the smartest feller I know. Ye'll figure some of it out, at least. An' if thar's anything we might do to help, count on us. Ain't that right?"

"Yeah, Robby," Ibin said. "We'llhelp, we'llhelpyou."

"Whatever it takes," Sheila said with an earnestness that tumbled all of Robby's thoughts into a heap.

"I appreciate that," Robby said to them. He wanted to scream out that it wasn't he who needed help, it wasn't he who was betrayed, assaulted, and forced into a self-imposed exile. He shot such an intense look of sorrow at Sheila that it made her swallow a sudden knot in her throat. He looked down at his plate. "I don't think I need help. Or, at least, not right now. If I do, I don't know what with, anyway."

Raenelle and her maid came in and went to the stove to fetch some pots of hot water. Raenelle was still dressed in her nice smock, although she now had her hair pulled up and behind her head. As her maid carefully lifted the pot, Raenelle looked over the group at the table.

"Hello, Sheila," she said stiffly.

"Hello, Raenelle," Sheila replied coolly. It was apparent, as always, that the two girls had little liking for one another, and Billy had implied on more than one occasion that it was not just because Sheila rubbed her the wrong way, so to speak, but also because Raenelle had a liking for Robby that made her jealous. Raenelle held the door for her maid and as they left, Frizella hurried back in along with several other servants.

"I hate to hurry ye along," she said. "But we've got to get some food goin' for the men who'll be soon comin' in, an' we'll need the kitchen. Billy, ye'll be needed. Ibin, too. So don't get it into yer heads to go into Passdale with Robby. Mr. Bosk is arrangin' a mount for ye, Robby. An' as soon as yer ready, I know ye'll be wantin' to get on home. Sheila, yer welcome to stay as long as ye like. An' we can use yer help, too, if ye've a mind."

"Thank you, Frizella," she said. "I'll be going with Robby, just the same. I've got to take care of some things, besides seeing Robby home."

Robby and Sheila made their goodbyes to Ibin and Billy, and Robby thanked Mrs. Bosk as the three walked to the side door together.

"Just make sure ye take care of yerself!" she told him with a gentle hug.

"I have not yet thanked you properly," Sheila said to her, lingering behind the others. "For taking care of me. For saving my life."

"Oh, honey!" Frizella gave Sheila a long, firm hug that, between them, spoke volumes of understanding and sympathy. She held Sheila out to look into her eyes. "I'm just so glad yer well again! Someday maybe we'll get a chance an' catch up with each other. But I think yer stay out at the Hill has done ye good."

"Yes, it has. In so many ways."

"That Ashlord's a wise man, an' I can tell he's made his mark on ye in a big way. Yer speech has even changed, it seems, an' ye look strong!"

"I am. And I think Ashlord taught me more in these past weeks than I have learned my whole life. I can read fairly well, now, and write some, too. Oh, I have so much to tell you!"

"Then come back an' see me as soon as ye can, d'ye hear me? But alright then, much to be done right now! Gimme another hug an' get on over to Passdale as safe as ye can!"

The stable foreman was waiting for them outside with two saddled horses. One of them was Bandit.

"Master Bosk ain't here to see ye off," the foreman said. "But he figured ye'd be able to take Bandit, an' maybe yer ol' man can see he gets back to the Post Station, if that's the way of it. 'Sides, ye'll take good care of him if I know the Ribbons at all. He's been rode hard, an' mistreated. But he's up to gettin' ye home. Here's a few gold pieces that Mr. Bosk wanted me to give ye for Bandit's livery."

"I can't take that," Robby said. "Not after all that's been done for me."

"Ain't my say so," said the foreman. "Ye'll take it, or else I'll hear 'bout it from the Master of Bosk Hall."

Robby took the coins, slung his shoulder bag onto the saddle hook, and climbed up as Sheila mounted a fine old mare nearby. The two rode out from Bosk Manor and under the gateway now decorated with the grim trophies just as the sun passed midday and imperceptibly began its downward slide. As they headed west toward the Bentwide, the wind picked up, and a cool breeze fanned across Barley. Sheila and Robby spoke very little for most of the way, and Robby kept the pace up, as anxious to get home as he was to avoid any uncomfortable conversation. Sheila, for the most part, rode several yards behind, but, after awhile, she nudged her mount up alongside Robby.

"You need to go a little easier on Bandit, I think," she said. "He's had a rough few days. And he's not the only one, unless Mrs. Bosk's bandaging is better than my own."

Robby managed to smile.

"You're right," he said. "I should be more careful on both accounts."

Robby slowed Bandit's pace, and then he and Sheila continued on more leisurely, side by side. They remained silent and traveled far, and, coming to the Bentwide Road about two hours after leaving Bosk Hall, they turned northward and followed the way along the riverbank.

"You know," Robby observed, "the river doesn't look as high as it should be. With the rains and flood, it should be fairly surging. It looks too low, considering."

Sheila nodded, looking down the bank at the gurgling water. It was muddy, but the old moss-covered rocks that lined the banks were dry, and there was little or no debris floating by as with the Saerdulin or most of the creeks they had passed.

"Pretty strange," she said at last.

They continued on, each silently pondering the mystery until, after another hour, they came within sight of the farthest outskirts of Passdale across the river, the water even lower than before.

"So Ashlord taught you a lot, I guess," Robby finally ventured.

"Not as much as there is to know," she said. "But for me he has been a miracle. You helped me with my letters, and he picked up where you and I left off with them. He has a strange way of teaching. For three weeks I did nothing but read. It was a struggle. Not only was I not a very good reader, in spite of your valiant efforts, but the books he had me read were so difficult. All about history, legend, and lore. When the books ran out, he had me copy sections and read them to him. He has a tablet that you can write on and then wipe away what was written and write more, using a kind of clay stylus. So over and over and over I read, wrote, read aloud, wiped away, wrote more. And we walked, too, and walked and walked. On some days he barely said a word, and on other days there was not a moment that he was not talking himself hoarse. Even when doing chores, cutting wood, doing wash, or cleaning the hearth, he'd talk and question me on what I had learned. He would speak in foreign tongues, and he also taught me some of the Ancient Tongue still used in the west. He sent me on errands, too. Once all the way to Janhaven by way of the back roads, with strict instructions not to be seen by anyone, even if it took a week. Just to deliver a letter! He taught me other things, too. Or at least tried to."

"Like what?"

"Well, about living, I guess you could say."

"How so?"

"Well, Ashlord is a very patient man," she tried to explain. "But he can be quite passionate about certain things. About the past. About how folks ought to act and how folks should treat each other. He's got a sense of honor, of right and wrong. He's not a rash person and takes everything into consideration. I've met only one other person like him."

"Oh?"

"Yes. You."

"Me?" Robby was shocked. "I don't think I'm like Ashlord at all! I don't know what you mean by that."

"You like to read," Sheila went on. "You're patient and kind. Not quick-tempered, and you try to do the right thing, even if no one's watching or making you do it."

Robby felt suddenly embarrassed by the flattery.

"Trying ain't always doin', as Billy might say," he said. "You think too much of me."

"I have often thought of you, Robby Ribbon."

Robby stopped his horse and looked at Sheila who halted close to him. He dismounted and took Bandit's reins in hand and led him closer to the bank. Sheila did the same and followed alongside. They walked slowly for a few yards, then Robby sighed and turned to Sheila.

"I know what happened," he said. "And I am very sorry. I don't know what to say, except I want you to know that I never meant to cause you any harm or any sadness."

Sheila looked searchingly into Robby's eyes, then reached up her hand and put it on his face.

"If I am sad," she said, "it is not because of you. And if any harm has come to me, it was not of your doing. You must believe me. I hold you blameless."

"But, Sheila. The child!"

Sheila frowned, realizing that it was something she had to discuss with Robby.

"I know that by the law of our people, I should have told you," she said. "But by that law we would be married."

"Would you not have me then?"

"I would not bind you," she said, taking his hand, "nor would I hold you to this land. Your yearnings are not for wife or family. You have always looked beyond our fields and rivers, longing to see the wide world. Yet, out of the good within you, you would stay to make me happy. But at what cost to your own heart? Would you have me live my life looking upon a husband who dreams to leave me but, honor-bound, will not? Who would shower every good thing upon my path while his own stretched out untrodden?"

"Oh, Sheila—"

"No! There are other girls, Robby, less uncouth than I, who would not be bothered overmuch by such things. Who would not mourn your staying, or be very sorry if you departed. Many a girl who would make a good wife to you and a good mother to your children. Worthy, and with fine dowries. There are some, I dare say, who might even love you."

"But none that I would love."

She looked at him as tears dripped from her eyes, but her gaze was steady, and she did not sob.

"Perhaps not. Time will have its way, as it does with all but the Faere folk."

"So what are we to do?" Robby asked, shaking with a terrible flutter in his chest.

"About what?"

"I mean, what am I to do?" he tried to explain. "I do love you. You say I would long to leave, even if we married. Why shouldn't we leave together? Why can't you share my dreams with me? Why can't we—"

"No, I say!" she shook her head, releasing his hand. "For you to be free, I must also be free," she said, though she did not believe it.

Robby felt the lump in his chest rise to his throat blocking his words. For some inexplicable reason, he battled not only with his confusion over Sheila but also over the sudden gush of emotions welling up inside of him, emotions seeking words.

"But my heart is bound to thee!" he suddenly blurted out in a language he had never heard with his ears. Sheila looked at him in astonishment at the sound. But, unconscious of the language he spoke, mindful only of the meaning he strove to impart, Robby went on.

"My fate is thine, whither I be with thee or far away. I have joined my life into thy life and my fortune and my future into thy fortune and thy future. Whether ye have me or another or none at all, in this world or in the next we will be together. Like the river that wanders from its course, runs dry, and comes back to its old tracks, our love, too, will someday return, for it is as much a part of us as the rivers are of the land."

Sheila understood every word, though she had never before heard that tongue, and behind his voice was a sound like the airy chiming of glass, like crystal leaves trembling in a breeze. Robby turned and led his horse onward, leaving her shaken and awed. His words still rang in her ears, the clarity of sound and meaning, and she felt she was making a terrible mistake. But she loved him more than she ever had, if that was possible. She had the sensation that she was standing in some awful dream, full of melancholy and mystery. Yet, somehow, his words confirmed in her heart that this young man was the only one in all the world that she could love, and with all the love she would ever have. In a trance of heartache, and through blurring eyes, she watched him mount his horse.

"I think we should be getting along," he said in ordinary words. He managed a sad smile. She nodded and climbed into the saddle and followed after him at a short distance, and her best efforts to suppress the sob rising from her breast only made her tears stream more fiercely for many minutes before she gained mastery over them.

And so they rode alongside the river Bentwide, its waters mysteriously diminished, and on toward the bridge. The sight of home across the river filled Robby with renewed eagerness to be there, but he could not see anyone about. What he did see disturbed him. Many of the massive poplars were uprooted and torn asunder. Several houses were missing parts of their roofs, and the marketplace was wrecked. Everywhere was debris, blown about in mad confusion. Here and there were canvas tarpaulins covering blown-out windows. As they neared the bridge, he saw the wreckage of the mill on the far side. The wheel, what was left of it, was on its side halfway down the riverbank, with boards and timber strewn all about it and tree branches, torn from their trunks, tangled all over it. A gaping hole was in the side of the mill where the wheel had once turned, and the roof had collapsed around a vanished wall. Without the guidance of the sluice, the stream that had powered the mill now ran wide and shallow across the road and trickled down the riverbank under the broken wheel.

Looking ahead, he saw a tall woman standing at this side of the bridge. Her red hair glowed in the afternoon light, and she pulled a cloak tight about her against the wind as she looked his way. At the sight of her, Robby kicked hard.

"Mother!" he cried. She waved, running toward him. When he reached her, he jumped from the saddle and gave her a hug and many kisses.

"Oh, Robby!" and she began to laugh as tears came to her eyes. "I thought I'd never see you again!"

"It seems like a long, long time!" he said, grinning.

"Your father will be so relieved. I don't think he has slept more than an hour since you left. And is that Sheila?"

"Yes."

Mirabella Ribbon let go of Robby, except for his hand, and greeted Sheila, who was just getting down from her saddle.

"It is good to see you, Sheila," Mrs. Ribbon said taking her hand without letting go of Robby. "It has been too long."

Sheila smiled awkwardly and nodded.

"And I understand that you have looked after Robby for us?"

"Well," Sheila's eyes darted at Robby for a moment with a little embarrassment. "Just some."

"I know Mr. Ribbon will be happy to see you, too."

"Oh?"

"Yes, but I'll let him tell you himself."

"Where is Daddy?"

"He's at the Common House. He's serving as a kind of temporary mayor."

"We heard about Mayor Greardon. Billy told us," Robby said.

"Yes, it's terrible! His wife and son are inconsolable."

"What's to become of them?" Sheila asked.

"We don't yet know. It looks as though some of their relatives will be taking over the mill, if they can get it repaired, and will provide for Mrs. Greardon and little Jay."

"So you got my note?" Robby asked as they turned toward the bridge.

"Yes, and the packet from Ashlord," she said. Turning to Sheila, "You will stay with us, I hope?"

"I haven't thought of where I might stay," Sheila said. "I can stay anywhere. There's no need to go to any trouble on my account, Mrs. Ribbon."

"Nonsense!" Mrs. Ribbon laughed. "In the first place, I'm Mira to you, or else 'Mirabella' if you want to be fancy about it. And in the second place, I've already begun preparing a room for you. Frankly, it will be nice to have some lady-company in the house. Two men are two too many sometimes!"

Sheila laughed at the idea of anyone referring to her as a lady, though she was sure Mrs. Ribbon meant it in all seriousness. Mrs. Ribbon, much like Mrs. Bosk, had a way of putting one at ease quickly. Fast friends, Mrs. Bosk and Mrs. Ribbon were in many ways entirely different. Mrs. Bosk was short, round, and plump, with all the usual mannerisms of Barley folk. Mrs. Ribbon was thin, tall, and, to say the least, elegant by any standard. Yet she was not above getting her hands dirty with work, and she never lorded her good looks or family name over anyone. Although Sheila had never talked much with Mrs. Ribbon, she had reason to believe that she was a good and fair person. Mrs. Bosk had assured Sheila on more than one occasion that the Ribbons of Passdale, all of them, man, wife, and son, could be counted on to do the right thing. As they continued on along the path to the bridge, Sheila had the distinct impression that Mrs. Ribbon knew far more about her affairs than she would ever let on. She seemed shrewd, in a kind sort of way, much like Ashlord, and the more she thought of it, the more alike Ashlord and Mirabella seemed.

The bridge had survived the storm with little damage, and, as they crossed, Robby commented on the low water level.

"Yes, a party of men have gone upriver to see if there is some blockage," his mother said. "Their fear is that the storm may have somehow blocked the river with a rockslide or such, and it might suddenly give way. The water did rise for the first day of the rains, but then slowly began to sink, just as the rains got heavier and heavier. It has continued to drop, doing just the opposite of what it should do after a rain."

"Ashlord told me I shouldn't worry about the Bentwide flooding," Robby said to her. "I wonder how he knew?"

He then told his mother about the River Saerdulin and how it had assumed its ancient course, just as the River Bentwide now seemed to be abandoning its way.

"I don't think those men are going to find anything to their liking," Robby concluded. "At least, not if they want the river to be as it was before."

## Chapter 8

## Robby's Ill-Kept Secret

After tying their horses behind the store, Robby and Sheila went inside and followed Mirabella upstairs to the kitchen. While they washed, she prepared a light supper and shared the news from around Passdale. Much had happened since Robby left. There was the rain, of course. Rain and more rain, then torrents with howling wind and twisters, all accompanied by the most fearsome lightning. In spite of the terrible fear of the wind and lightning, people worked frantically to shore up their houses. The River Bentwide swelled nearly to its topmost banks, and water was less than an arm's length from the river wall. On the day Robby's father left to look for him, the townsfolk began sandbagging the lowest banks and gaps in the river wall as the waters continued to rise. Yet, by the middle of the next day, the river began to subside, and slowly the water went down, even though all of the tributaries running into it were pouring more water than ever could be imagined. Little brooks had become gushing jets, and streams had become rivers unto themselves. Mud slid down the hills behind Passdale, and trees uprooted and toppled all over town. Especially heartbreaking was the loss of many of the beautiful poplars that grew along the river.

Then there was the accident at Greardon's Mill. The mill pond above Passdale broke from its dam and burst the sluice gates, pouring trees and boulders against the waterwheel, jamming it as brush piled up around it. Meanwhile, the water flowed around and undercut the stone supports. As the stones gave way and crumbled, the wheel broke and twisted against the wall of the mill, pulling out its axle and sending beams crashing down. As the wall collapsed, the wheel came free and careened downstream and nearly to the river before falling over and crashing on the riverbank. Mr. Greardon, who was inside the mill trying to free the wheel before it smashed the wooden gears, was knocked into the flood and pinned under the water by falling beams. Everyone heard the crash and came running, but Greardon was dead by the time he was pulled from the wreckage. While several other homes and buildings were damaged, some beyond repair, everyone else in Passdale escaped serious injury during the storm. The Mayor's loss was a serious blow to the town, just when his leadership was most needed, for he was a wise and energetic man. Some decided that Mr. Ribbon ought to be found to take his place until a proper election could be had, since none of the town's council members wanted the responsibility, and most of the town folk were relieved at that. So the blacksmith, Mr. Clingdon, one of the heartiest men around, went out to find Mr. Ribbon and to bring him back. At Mirabella's advice, Clingdon first went to Boskland, thinking it would be the safest place for both of the Ribbon men to find their way to, and hoping they would both be there.

"When the two came back without you," Mirabella said to Robby as she filled the teapot with hot water, "I nearly died of worry. Your father reassured me of your good sense to take shelter, but hardly had time to console me before he had to go off and meet with the council. They swore him in on the spot, and he got right to work, organizing work parties, reviewing the town's finances, our emergency stores, and planning for repairs and relief. From what little he was able to tell me, Passdale has fared better than other parts of Barley. Was there much damage out that way?"

Before she could be answered, the store's doorbell jangled violently as the door opened and slammed, immediately followed by loud footsteps coming up the stairs by twos. The kitchen door burst open, and there stood Robby's father, panting.

"Robby!" he cried, taking his son into his arms. "I came as soon as I heard ye whar back in town. I was down at the Common House."

Mr. Ribbon saw Robby wince at the pressure of the elder's grip.

"Yer hurt!" he said.

"Oh, just a little," Robby grinned. "I'm on the mend, though, thanks to the good care of Ashlord and to Sheila, here."

"I should've never sent ye out thar by yerself!"

"I'm fine. Everything is fine! I just had a little trouble, is all," Robby hesitated, "with a few wolves."

"Wolves!" Mirabella gasped.

"Wolves?" Mr. Ribbon cried.

"And the storm," Robby added.

"Wolves?" Mr. Ribbon repeated. "In Barley?"

"Yes, sir. I was attacked by a few, and if it had not been for Ashlord and Sheila showing up when they did, I'd be a goner. And they patched me up pretty well afterwards, too."

"Oh, my!" Mrs. Ribbon said, sliding into a chair.

"More than a few," Sheila said softly.

"Oh?" Mr. Ribbon picked up. "How many more."

"I killed many that night," she said bluntly. "Ashlord killed many more."

Mr. Ribbon settled into a chair, too.

"Tell me what happened."

"Well, Ullin and I parted after we crossed the bridge," Robby began. Between nibbles, he related the story, leaving out the fact that he had crossed the bridge and found his way into the interior of Tulith Attis.

Instead, he merely said that he sought shelter from the storm in the old fortress and was trapped there by the wolves. He told them about being attacked and being saved by Ashlord, leaving out the part about the Great Bell and the stone sentinels.

"By the time Ashlord and Sheila got me to their place, I was pretty exhausted," he concluded. His mother and father listened intently. Mr. Ribbon shook his head at the tale. Mirabella looked at Robby carefully, and then at Sheila as if to ask a question, but she remained silent.

"So, what with the storm and all," Robby continued, "I stayed on with them until Billy and Ibin showed up yesterday. Billy told me about you coming out to look for me, and how Mr. Bosk basically forced you to give up."

"How is that?" Mirabella asked, looking at her husband. Before Mr. Ribbon could answer, Robby recounted what Billy had said about the flood and the danger they faced if they kept on after Robby.

"If I'd a gone on," Mr. Ribbon shrugged to his wife, "Mr. Bosk an' the rest would've felt obliged to go on, too. I was willin' to take the risk by meself, but I didn't see how I could lead the rest on. What else could I do?"

"You did the right thing, dearest," Mirabella said, taking her husband's hand.

"Anyway," Robby continued, "we set out this morning, then ran into a little trouble on the Line Road."

As he told them about the four horsemen, and the Dragonkind man, his mother wore a grim expression, and his father stood from his chair and paced back and forth.

"Wolves an' Dragonkind in Barley!" Mr. Ribbon muttered when Robby finished his tale. "I suppose I should raise the alarm, but who is thar that'll come? Everone's scattered or so busy, tryin' to take care of thar homes an' such."

"I don't think there are any others," Sheila said. "Just the one that got away, and he's probably caught by now."

"Still! Lootin' an' killin'!" he looked at the three sitting at the table, then sighed and his shoulders slumped. "Dang it! I gotta go."

"Oh, Robigor!" his wife said, disappointed. "You've barely had time to eat!"

"Can't be helped, lovie," he shrugged, giving her a kiss. "Sheila, perhaps in the next day or two we can chat, an' I can thank ye proper-like for all ye done for Robby. I hope ye'll not mind stayin' with us. We'd be glad to have ye on as long as ye like."

"Thank you," Sheila said. "I hope it isn't a bother. I'll help out in any way that I can."

"No bother at all!" Mirabella said. "Though I might ask for a little help with some small things."

"Robby, I know yer tired, but as soon as ye can, I'd like ye to take over the store from yer mother," Mr. Ribbon said, giving his son a gentler hug than before, then moving to the door. "I'll most likely be purty occupied the next few days, but I'll manage to check in on ye as much as I can."

"Don't worry about anything here," Robby assured him. "I'll do my best."

After he departed, Mirabella took Sheila to show her the guest room. There were six rooms upstairs, three bedrooms clustered at the back of the house, with the door to the master bedroom at the end of the hall and the doors to Robby's room and the guest room opposite each other. There was the kitchen, at the other end of the hall, where they also took their meals, and the sitting room that served extra duty as both study and parlor. There were two washrooms, one for clothes and such, and the other for more personal use. Robby's father had the upstairs built to his own design, along with an ingenious system of terra cotta piping and handpumps that provided water for the wash basins from a well. It was a well-lit home, with ample oil lamps on the walls and hanging from the ceilings, and plenty of windows to let in sunlight. Sheila had never been upstairs before, and she was surprised at how cozy and warm it was, not at all like the grander but somewhat dark and drafty Bosk Manor. This place was more of comfort and grace than power and station. Everywhere was Mirabella's touch, from the tasteful curtains to the flowers in every room. Sheila stopped to look at the modest portraits along the hallway, as Mrs. Ribbon opened a closet and pulled out some fresh linens.

"We have not had a guest for a long time," she said. "But I try to keep the room dusted and the sheets changed out. I haven't been able to get to it this week, though, except to clear out some boxes earlier today when I received Robby's note. I hope you don't mind if I go ahead and change them now?"

"Oh, no, not at all." Sheila hoped she would not be asked to help, since she did not have much practice at domestic work. But she felt awkward just standing around while Mirabella stripped the bed, so she joined to help in spite of her nervousness.

"I'm afraid I'm a bit clumsy when it comes to things like this," she said, trying to tuck a corner. "I haven't had much practice, as you can see."

"I am good at it only from picking up after two men for years," Mirabella laughed. "When I was your age, I didn't know these things, either!" She did not explain that there were servants to do these chores when she was Sheila's age. And Sheila understood that Mrs. Ribbon came from a rich family, grander even than the Bosks.

"I've as often slept out of a bed as in one," Sheila went on, "as I imagine you know. I barely remember anything about my parents, and, well, I've pretty much had to take care of myself."

"I know," Mirabella nodded. "One does the best one can, and you could have done worse. Still, I believe you are somewhat changed since we last spoke. That was last year, I think, or even before. Your speech has changed. You have hardly a hint of Barley. And, look at you! I remember you as a vivacious girl. Daring! Full of fire and brashness! Now you seem more, well, you seem calmer?"

"If you mean less wild," Sheila said, somewhat taken aback by Mirabella's description of her, "I suppose I am. Ashlord has been laboring me hard with my manners and my speech. He has tried to teach me the proper ways of saying things and often he insisted that I read aloud to him. There were times when I hardly uttered a word without being corrected! Before, I could barely read. Robby got me started. Ashlord sort of picked up where Robby left off."

Mirabella stood back and watched Sheila finish the bed.

"Robby missed you," she said to her. "When you left, he looked for you all over Barley. Oh, at first he tried to hide what he was doing by inventing unnecessary errands to run. When he ran out of excuses, he asked to take leave of the store for entire days. I think one time he went as far south as New Green Ferry, thinking you had kin there."

"I should have at least written a note to him, I know," Sheila admitted. "I just needed to be away."

"Well, we are all relieved that you are well. Mrs. Bosk assured me you were, and I trusted her as I always have. She told me as much as she could without breaking confidence with you. That she had looked after you for awhile, but that you were under Ashlord's care. She asked that we not tell Robby. So we arranged for Robby to have more to do around the store and house than would allow him to take off. We never told him why, though. I thought that if he wanted me to know about you and him, he would tell me. Still, I tried to work it into conversation that I felt you were safe and all right, without letting on about my own inquiries."

"Mrs. Bosk is a good woman."

"The best in Barley," Mirabella agreed. "And Robby tells me you only just found out about the death of your uncle."

"Yes, that's right."

"Did you know that Mrs. Bosk insisted that Ashlord not tell you?"

"No."

"She wanted to protect you as much as she could. I believe she thought that if you knew about it you would return too soon."

"I probably would have."

"Well, it was a gruesome business, and the less you had to do with it the better, probably."

"Just so you know," Sheila said, "I'm relieved that he is dead. Even glad. Even if he was kin of mine."

"Just to be frank," Mirabella replied seriously, "you are not the only one who was relieved at his death. He was not a pleasant man, to say the least."

"I know."

"I don't know how you endured him all these years!"

"I didn't, for the most part. He's why I spent so much time hunting and fishing and sleeping out in the woods. I was always afraid of him. I stayed on there because, because I—"

"Because you had nowhere else to go," Mirabella stated flatly.

Sheila nodded.

"And that, my dear, is a shame on me and Mrs. Bosk and all of the good folk of Passdale and Barley! I am truly sorry for not being more concerned for you."

"How were you to know?" Sheila retorted. "I spoke to no one about it. Not even to Robby! And I did not expect any help from anyone."

"We have eyes," Mirabella shook her head. "And I, for one, at least should have asked more questions about that dreadful man."

"What is done is done," Sheila said. "There is no use in agonizing over the past, as Ashlord would say, if only we learn something from it. I would not have been a happy or gracious guest in any home that tried to take me in, anyway. But now, well, I will try very hard. And I hope that you will forgive my ignorance and look beyond my poverty."

"Oh, Sheila!" Mirabella declared, putting her arm around the girl. "You are not as ignorant as you think. And you are never poor if you carry your valuables here." She touched Sheila's chest lightly. "Come. I know you must be tired. Would you like to take a bath and clean up?"

"A bath?"

"Why, yes. A hot bath."

Sheila's eyes lit up at the prospect.

"Yes!" she nodded. "But, oh!"

"What is it?"

"I have nothing else to wear," she said. "And these buckskins are filthy!"

Mirabella laughed, pulling Sheila into the hall and toward the washroom.

"You forget!" she said. "I own the store!"

Then in a whispered, mischievous tone, she teased, "I only let the boys run it to keep them busy."

• • •

It was well after dark before Robby finished the store's books. While Sheila was luxuriating in a hot soapy bath, Robby was adding and subtracting, tallying accounts and reviewing the inventory books. There were a lot of purchases on credit to record for all of the things people needed to make repairs—nails, canvas, some lumber, oil, tools, and the like. He noticed that his mother had done most of the transactions at well below the standard prices. That was not a surprise to Robby; the Ribbons had a habit of bending prices downward when times were hard. He also noted that many of the new credits that she had given exceeded the normally allowed amounts. That did not surprise Robby, either. As he put away the books and blew out the desk lamp, he remembered something his father had said on more than one occasion, "The profit made on goodwill may exceed that attained from gold." Robby smiled at the sentiment now being put to practice.

He checked the strongbox and the doors and windows one last time and slowly climbed the stairs. He was tired and sore, and he had too much to think over. He knew he should clean up and take a bath, but he just wanted to crawl into bed and sleep. As he entered his own room, he could hear his mother talking to Sheila in the room across the hall, making sure she had everything she needed. He closed the door, sat down heavily on his bed, and looked around. All of the familiar things, from the curtains to the little writing table in the corner, looked somehow different. An odd feeling came over him that all his life, up to now, these things had been dull, not even real, and now they had somehow become real. He noticed how worn the wooden floor was, how the middle drawer of his chest of drawers was a little uneven, and how the water basin seemed a more vivid blue-green than before. They were all just the same as they ever were, yet nothing seemed the same, now. It was an odd sensation, almost like a mild intoxication. Maybe he was just tired. Maybe it was just the overwhelming events of late. Whatever it was, Robby felt himself changed from the person he was just a few days before, though he could not decide what was different.

"Perhaps nothing has changed after all," he muttered. "Except now I just know a little more. Though what good will knowing do?"

His words sounded hollow; the little knowledge he had illuminated nothing, like shining a light up into the night sky of his ignorance.

Standing up, he left his room and went to the sitting room down the hall and to the cabinet where the map rolls were kept. He pulled out several and looked at each carefully. They were all maps of the region, and most had all of the major features, rivers and roads, boundaries and place names, but some had a little more detail here and there than others. Shuffling through them, he was interested for the moment in the River Bentwide and its course north of Passdale. Most of the maps showed Lake Halgaeth from which the river flowed, but none so far showed what he thought he remembered seeing on one of them. At last he pulled out a map that he immediately knew was the right one. He unrolled it, revealing gold leaf lettering in one of the ancient cursive scripts all around the border of the map. The rest was done in distinct black ink, and, though it showed few roads and only a little of the region around Passdale, it did have more detail of northeast Barley than the others. Depicted were the inlets of Lake Halgaeth where various rivers and streams were. It showed the Saerdulin's old course running past Tulith Attis, as well, and even the Line Road. On the map, the east road extended past the old fortress and on through the Boggy Wood. From there, it traced a path eastward and there was a note on the edge of the map that said "To Colleton." What interested Robby in this map was the lightly inked line running behind Tulith Attis, and, printed along it, "Old Course of River Saerdulin." With his finger, he followed that line as it curved south and westward, growing faint until it joined the Bentwide some ten or so leagues south of Passdale. Reversing his way, he followed the line back north and eastward, passing Tulith Attis where the bridge was well marked, and continuing with his finger northward to Lake Halgaeth. There, where the line reached the boundary of the lake was a small thick mark, drawn across the first line. Beside it, in small script, were the words "Heneil's Wall." That was it, what he thought he had remembered.

"I bet it washed out," he said aloud.

"What would that be?" Mirabella said from the doorway. "I'm sorry, I didn't mean to startle you."

"I didn't mean to jump so!" Robby said with a chuckle. "I didn't hear you come in. This is what."

He showed her the map and saw a look of concern on her face when he pointed at the spot he had found.

" 'Te Lamath Heneileth.' That is what it was once called, 'Heneil's Wall,' " she said. "I saw it once when I was a child. I was traveling with my family, down from Glareth in the north, and we took boats to cross the lake. The water was black as coal and as still as glass, and I will never forget the fog, lifting in straight columns all around like a forest of ghostly tree trunks, and the only sound was that of the dipping of our oars. It was cold and I slept some, bundled down low in the boat beside my mother. But she woke me and pointed toward the crescent moon between the twin towers of the wall, like two horns rising against the moonlit sky, shrouded with mist and black in the shadows. The boatmen boats had steered us out of our way to see it, at my father's request. We went right alongside the wall, nearly close enough to touch its mossy stones. It seemed to have taken us a long time to pass it, and I was afraid, but more afraid to cry. I don't know why, but the memory of those dark towers with the moon between them sometimes haunts my dreams."

"Well," Robby said, breaking himself from a near-trance at her story. He heard so few of them from her, and he was now so terribly curious about anything she might tell him about herself, that he wished she would just keep on talking. But he lacked the nerve, just yet, to ask questions. If she did not want to tell him about her family and her past, he thought (as he always had), then she must have good reasons.

"I don't think anyone will be frightened by Heneil's Wall anymore."

"You think it is gone?"

"Yes, I do," Robby nodded. "I think it washed away in the storm."

"I do, too," she replied. "And I think you know more about it than you let on."

"How do you mean?"

"Well," she sighed, "I think Ashlord told you a great deal, and maybe he told you not to share some things. But I know that more happened at Tulith Attis than what you said earlier when your father was here."

Robby felt his face redden, but he remained silent.

She removed a piece of paper from her apron pocket. Robby recognized it as the note he had hastily written and given to the Bosklander who was ordered to ride to Passdale ahead of him.

"My note to you."

"Yes, your note," she said. "Or should we say, 'your notes?' For there is more writing here than perhaps you intended for me to see."

She held out the paper to Robby.

"What do you mean?" he said, taking it. There was his note, written plainly, but in a hurried hand, on one side of the paper. He turned it over and saw, to his own surprise, the inscription he had copied from over the Iron Door.

"Oh, this?" he stammered. "It's just some—"

"Before you weave yourself into more trouble," Mirabella interrupted him, holding up her finger, "perhaps I should tell you that I know those runes, and I know what they say. I should also tell you that I know where it was written, and that, although I have never seen the bell room, I know well the phrase you copied and have known of it since before I ever crossed Lake Halgaeth. Indeed, all of the children of my day were told of it."

Robby stood staring at his mother, caught out in his earlier omissions and not knowing what to say.

"Mother, I... It's just that..." Robby stammered, but could not figure out what to say. He saw the growing look of concern, and pain, on her face.

"I'm sorry," he said at last. "I did not tell you everything that happened." Robby plopped down into a chair and shook his head. "Ashlord asked me not to tell anyone. And I'm not sure you would believe me if I told you."

"I know you are in some kind of trouble, Robby," she said, taking a chair beside him. "Or else you would not have been asked to keep secrets from your parents."

"I'm not sure he meant for me not to tell you, Mother, but I don't know what I am to do. I'm not in any kind of trouble, exactly."

"Then you must be in danger," she concluded bluntly. "Or else you would not have been in the bell room of Tulith Attis in the first place. I do not want you to break your word with Ashlord, but I think your parents have a right to know if their child is in danger. We all heard the Great Bell, though most did not know what it was."

"Did you?"

"Yes. I felt it as much as heard it. As if something spoke to me inside, calling me to come with sword and fury. I sat up straight from the deepest sleep and nearly frightened your poor father to death with my wails. I've never had such a feeling! Robigor had to hold me back. At the time, I dismissed it as an awful motherly worry about you, and I wanted to rush out to Tulith Attis immediately, in spite of the storm. I felt as if something was out there, in the dark and rain, that needed to be attacked." She looked at Robby and said, "I have tried all my life to spare you from the burden that was laid upon my kind, and upon my family. My life with your father has been a blessing from the heavens, and I thought Passdale would shelter us from the intrigues of the past. When I heard the Bell's three tolls, I feared that doom was upon us, upon our family and our people."

"I don't understand," Robby said. "How can I? You have never told me much about yourself or your family. I never knew you were a Faere Child!"

"I am Elifaen."

"See? I don't even know the languages or the right names for things. And now I have stumbled into things that I never imagined could be possible. Ashlord thinks I am in danger from the Dark One, or at least from some servant or other of his. I don't even know who or what the Dark One is! Just scary stories, a few legends here and there, and that's about all. Yes, I rang the Bell, though I did not mean to do it, or even know that I had done it, I was in such terror! Ashlord told me later. He says I have a role to play in things. And, on top of all that, there was the Dragonkind on the road to Boskland. Everything has gotten so jumbled and complicated."

"I will make a pact with you," Mirabella said. "I will answer all of your questions, if I can, if you will strive to answer all of mine."

"I'm not sure if I know any answers. And what about Daddy?"

"We will tell each other what we think," she said. "First, tell me what happened. I will try to find a way to tell Robigor, if that is needed. Together we will work out what needs to be done. I know you are tired, but your father will be home soon, I hope, and it is better that I know before he gets here, in case there is anything that needs explaining to him."

"Very well," Robby said. "I'll start by telling you that in the storm I missed the path that leads off to Ashlord's place. Instead, I stayed on the way that goes around the north side of the fortress to the bridge, and, in spite of my promise to Daddy, I crossed it."

## Chapter 9

## Ullin at Colleton

On the night that he sent Robby to Tulith Attis, Ullin sat with his back against a tree trunk with his ground sheet pulled over him against the driving rain. Anerath, having no such shelter, stood nearby as watchful and as patient as ever, shaking his head from time to time to sling off the rain. Ullin's sleep was as fitful as the tossing branches overhead. He worried about sending Robby out on such a stormy night, and he hoped that Robby made it back home before the worst of the weather came. He fell into and out of sleep, shrugging off the wild sounds that forests make in storms, jerked alert again and again by the cracking thunder. He wished he could find good sleep, that he could settle into a pleasant dream. Around midnight, the hairs on his arms and on the back of his neck stood on end, and he immediately tossed off his covers and stood. The forest was pitch dark, but he could hear it coming from the southwest like a stampede. When the first peal of the Great Bell struck Forest Mistwarren, all of the trees in its path shuddered. It shot through the forest like an airless wind, and when the thunder reached Ullin and Anerath at its greatest pitch, the Kingsman cried out, putting his hands over his ears, and Anerath reared and spun. Heavy silence fell upon the wood, and Ullin cautiously removed his hands from his ears. Above, the sky lightened by the dimmest degree as Lady Moon sought an opening in the clouds to peer through.

The second peal came. Ullin cried out at the rising crescendo, and his knees buckled in fear. Anerath twirled around and around, bucking, but he did not run away. Again, the silence that came afterward was as dreadful as the passing echo. By now, Ullin was as confused and in terror as Anerath, and he drew his sword and dagger. Then came the third, mightiest toll of all, rolling over the forest with such force that it bent the trees and blasted their leaves of the last drips of rainwater. Ullin screamed, but he managed to stand, his weapons at the ready.

The quaking sky rolled away, and complete silence fell upon the forest. The rain ceased, not a drop fell from the branches, no creature stirred, even Ullin and Anerath stood shock-still, while Lady Moon at last parted the clouds and lit up the descending fog and rolling mist with her pale gaze. Ullin feared that he knew where the sound had come from, and he was gripped with panic. A dreadful feeling overcame him that he should ride back the way he had come, through darkness and terror, and hie to Tulith Attis. He sheathed his weapons, hastily rolled up his groundsheet, tied it onto his saddle, and put a foot into the stirrup. Then, just as he shifted his weight on the stirrup to mount, he remembered. It was an odd warning, spoken by Ashlord years ago, when Ullin had first escorted the mystic to Tulith Attis. Before parting company to go his own way, he asked:

"Collandoth, what exactly do you mean to watch for at this forlorn place?"

"What? Not what. Who. But if you ever have a sudden and uncanny urge to drop whatever it is that you are doing and come back here, do not do so."

"What do you mean? Do you not desire me to visit you if passing through?"

"I speak not of when you pass through," Ashlord had said. "I speak of when you are elsewhere, going about your duties, and may be suddenly and strangely overcome with a powerful sense that you should forego your duty and come here. I admonish you not to do so. You must keep on with our work, and the dispatches that you carry must get through."

Ullin took his foot from the stirrup. In spite of Ashlord's warning, he was still filled with doubt and uncertainty. He stood, holding Anerath's reins, wondering what to do. The rain suddenly fell like pebbles. A long thread of lightning shot overhead, its crack following closely, and the storm resumed with as much if not greater fury than before. Still uncertain about things, Ullin stood all night, gripping Anerath's reins, watching, waiting.

Hours later, when he could make out the outline of the trees surrounding him, he knew that morning had come. He took from his saddlebag a hard, sticky block and broke off a bit of it with his teeth. Putting it away, he chewed his breakfast as he led Anerath through the forest back to the path.

• • •

If it had not been for Anerath's sureness and speed, Ullin would have never made it to Colleton in time. As it was, the storm pounded Forest Mistwarren with such fury that horse and rider spent as much time off the trail as on it. It was a miserable passage with dark, wet days, wind beating through the trees, rain blowing sideways, and the path mud-mired and slippery. The nights were just as bad, and Ullin saw no point in spreading his bedroll, and no hope of a fire. Those nights he spent crouching against a tree trunk with his legs pulled up and his ground sheet pulled tight over his head as Anerath stood watch. Twice they came to washed-out bridges and had to find their way to fording places. And twice they were forced around gullies awash with runoff. After five days, the storm eased, and as the two reached the edge of Mistwarren and saw the gentle cultivated hills of Calletshire spreading out before them, both horse and rider were relieved that now they could make a better pace.

Over the next days they rode through the countryside, taking shelter in the barns or stables of friendly farmers who were too busy with storm recovery chores to care much about the stranger's business, but not too busy to accept his silver. Ullin's worries over the strange sound heard while in Forest Mistwarren did not abate, but they merely added to all his other concerns. And now, with fair weather and good roads, he was anxious to make up for time lost back in the Thunder Mountains. Anerath, sensing this, was more than happy to comply, clipping along so enthusiastically that Ullin felt obliged to restrain him somewhat. They could already smell the sea air, and Ullin saw no sense in pushing Anerath any more than was needed.

Nine days from Passdale, they came over a rise and saw Colleton no more than a league away, resting at the mouth of the Northford River. Beyond the city could be seen the hazy blue-gray sea. Hopeful that he had not missed his rendezvous, Ullin paused to scan the old city. It was not the town it once had been. Indeed, its decline began long ago, even before the days of old King Inrick who once ruled from there, back when the Eastlands Realm governed itself. Its once-busy port was now mostly used as a provisioning place for ships bound north and south, mostly those from Glareth. Trade ships loaded and unloaded very little cargo, any more, and even fewer passengers. The town's spires were decayed, and many of its houses and structures were in a terrible state, needing but receiving little repair, and quite a large portion of the old city was simply abandoned. Only those districts close to the docks and wharves still thrived, but it was not enough to keep the rest of the city as prosperous as it once had been.

Even so, it was a welcome sight to Ullin, who looked forward to a restful journey by boat to Glareth by the Sea. That is, if he had not already missed his appointment. And, if he had missed the boat, at least there were inns where he could find a good bed and good food before setting out northward overland. However, as he rode down from the bluff and along the road leading into the marshes that nearly surrounded the inland side of Colleton, he quickly saw that his hopes of bed or boat might be in vain. The wooden bridge that crossed the first of a series of tidal estuaries was quite nearly demolished. Coming to a halt, he slumped in his saddle, watching workman pulling away dangling bits of plank and board from the pilings of the bridge. Nearly the entire deck was gone, leaving only a narrow walkway consisting of planks laid end to end across the cross-members.

"Hello there!" Ullin called to the nearest workman. "Is there any chance of getting across today?"

"Not with yer horse," the workman called back. "But yer welcome to go on by foot."

"And the other bridges, the ones to the south?"

"Well, they're a far sight worse off than this one. An' thar ain't but us what ye see here to do the work of puttin' 'em back together."

Ullin knew better than to try to ride across the estuary. Even at low tide, Anerath would most likely become hopelessly stuck in mud before they went twenty yards. He jumped down and began pulling his gear off. Once he had his things rebundled and tied with a cord to sling over his shoulder, he removed Anerath's bridle.

"I'm very sorry to have to do this," he said as he tied the bridle onto a saddle ring, "but you'll need to find your own way back. I'm not sure you understand me, but try to make it back to Tulith Attis, to Collandoth if you can. Take the long, safe way around. I'd remove your saddle, too, but Collandoth might need it."

When he had the bridle tied off and out of the way, Ullin put his arm around Anerath's neck and gave him a pet.

"You've been a good friend. I wish I could be a better friend to you than I am, and take you to Colleton. But it's thirty miles to the next nearest road to the coast, and another fifteen up along the bluffs to the city. I can't risk missing the boat, if it hasn't already departed without me. And I don't even know if they would take you aboard. So it is perhaps better for us to part company here. I'm sorry. Be safe. Go. Go ahead. Farewell!"

Ullin watched Anerath trot off hesitantly, then turn to look back.

"I'll be fine," Ullin said, smiling. Anerath tossed his mane and hurried off westward. Pulling up his bundle and slinging it over his shoulder, Ullin turned and crossed the bridge. The walkway was so narrow that Ullin had to watch where he stepped, otherwise he would not have dared look down. If he fell, he would probably not be hurt, landing in the mud twenty feet below. It might as well have been two hundred feet down for all it mattered to Ullin, for he did not at all care for heights.

Soon he was off the wobbly planks and onto solid ground, and he hurried on, having to cross several more less damaged bridges until he made it to the edge of town. There, he came to a checkpoint manned by Colleton guards. Everyone had to line up to pass a table, where one of the guards sat with an open volume and a pot of ink. At last Ullin's turn came, and he spoke before he was asked.

"Kingsman, Special Post."

The man sitting squinted up at him, taking the papers Ullin held out.

"I see," he said examining Ullin's orders. "Your business in Colleton?"

"I come to take passage to Glareth."

"I see," the man said as he wrote Ullin's name and the purpose of Ullin's visit in the volume. He then handed back the orders without looking up as he continued to scribble. "Good journeys, Commander. Next!"

Ullin was allowed to pass, and he entered the decrepit western districts of the town, passing hurriedly along the cobblestone streets, pushing past slower pedestrians and dodging the occasional horseman or wagon. Many of the buildings and shops were empty, and shingles and loose splinters of wood lay everywhere, lingering evidence of the storms that had battered the place. He went through the center of town, passing the old castle where once the kings of the Eastlands Realm ruled. Although in terrible state of repair, it served as the city hall and as the headquarters of Glarethian administrators, whose duty it was to be regents over the Eastlands under Prince Danoss. From this point onward, the streets were busier, as carts laden with goods came and went from the docks and wharves ahead. A brisk sea breeze blew steadily, rustling the moss hanging from the old oaks and snapping the pennants that hung in front of shops and taverns. He could already see ships' masts over the roofs down the way, and he picked up his stride.

Soon he was walking along a stone-laid road beside the many docks, eyeing the ships and boats tied up, some flying colors of Glareth, and some from as far away as Altoria. Fearing that he was too late, he grew worried as he came to a small ship, a cutter, tied at the very last dock. He breathed a sigh of relief when he saw the ship's name, "Sea Arrow," across its stern, but was somewhat disappointed that it was so small, with no oar ports. At the gangplank were two Glarethian seamen standing watch.

"Are ye the Kingsman we await?" said one.

"I am, I think."

"Papers?"

Ullin handed them over.

"Ah, Commander Tallin. Ye were expected five days ago," the sailor said, having looked over the orders. He handed them back, saying, "We'd just about given up on ye, an' we're all prepared to leave at ebb tide, not being able to put off our departure any longer. Captain Sands ain't aboard, sir, but should be back in a few hours. If you wish ye can come aboard an' see to yer bunk and stow yer gear. Or, if ye like, there's a tavern down the way yonder, should ye care for a bite an' a pint."

"How long, then?"

"Five hours or so afore slack water, another hour after that afore we cast off."

"I see. Can you guess how long until we reach Glareth by the Sea?" he asked, eyeing the ship. Besides having no oarsmen, there was only a single very tall mast.

"Ah, no more than six days, I expect. Five's more likely, though. T'would be sooner but for the light winds this time of year."

"Only five or six days? With no oarsmen?"

"Aye, sir. None needed. She's a fast cutter, she is! One of the new breed of ships, ye might say, that Prince Carbane builds. Smallish, but none faster, neither by nor large. Easy crewed, by just the five of us, along with Captain Sands. Ye'll see."

"Hm," Ullin said, still skeptical. "Looks more like a lake boat."

"She's akin to them, sir, in a manner of sayin'."

"And where is the tavern you mentioned?"

"Just up the way there, to the next street, then on down and on yer right. Called 'Fisherman's Green.' Shall I take yer bundle on aboard, then?"

"Yes. Thank you. I'll keep my shoulder bag, though. Take care of that, will you?" Ullin requested, gesturing to the hilt of his longsword protruding from his bundle as he handed it over.

"We certainly will, sir."

Ullin pulled off his cloak, put the strap of the dispatch bag over his shoulder, then pulled his cloak back on.

"Just so ye know," one of the seamen said, "the place is crawlin' with Redvest people. Not all in uniform, neither. They don't cause much trouble, kind of keepin' an eye on us, I think. But we've had a few run-ins. An' I doubt they care much for Duinnor threads, if ye take me meanin'. Nor hilts."

"Thanks for the advice. I'll be careful," Ullin said, pulling his travel cloak around over his tunic and over the hilt of his Duinnor issue as he walked away.

"At the ebb!" one of the men called after him.

• • •

Ullin had little trouble finding Fisherman's Green. When he entered, it was bustling with customers, sailors and soldiers mostly, crowded at the bar and at the many tables and booths. A few men in red tunics and cloaks glanced Ullin's way as he stood looking for an unoccupied seat, but they turned back to their tankards as he made his way to the bar.

"A table and meal?" he inquired over the noise of talk and the wheezing of a concertina nearby. The barman did not hear him, but the man standing at the bar next to Ullin spoke.

"It will clear out soon," he said. "The tide's rising, so most'll need to make their ships soon, if they don't want to be stranded."

Ullin nodded, noting the man's accent, his penetrating blue eyes, and the Tracian cut of his clothing. Before he could reply, however, the man turned away and continued his conversation with his drinking mate.

"A table and a meal?"

This time the barkeep heard Ullin.

"No table 'til one comes up empty. Ye can eat here, or ye can wait. Won't be long, I expect, for one of them small booths over yonder, if that'll suit."

"Yes. A beer in the meantime, if you will."

Strongly desiring to take the weight off his legs, have a meal, and perhaps a nap, Ullin settled for the beer instead. Drinking, he turned to face the young girl whom the concertina player was now accompanying. As she sang, the noise subsided just a little, and a little more as many of the customers quaffed the last of their rum and beer and staggered for the door.

"I cannot wait," he heard the man nearby say to his companion. "So I trust you to give it to him."

"I understand. I'll do so as soon as he shows up. Don't think he'll be too happy, though."

"Can't be helped. I must go. Good luck!"

"Good journeys."

Ullin felt a tap on his shoulder. Turning back around, he saw the man smiling at him.

"I think the barkeep beckons you," he said.

"Oh. Thank you."

"Not at all," the man said, walking to the door.

"I've got a small booth yonder," the barkeep said to Ullin. "Usually reserved for four or more."

"I'll pay for five tankards, if that will do," Ullin said, offering the man a few coins. "I'll only have one, though. And a light meal."

"Fine. Good. Will fried cod and hushpuppies do?"

"Yes. I should say so."

"Then go on over, an' I'll have yer next tankard brung over to ye right off, with a plate."

Between the beer and the pile of food that Ullin ate, he soon felt better, but much in the way of needing sleep. Judging by the clock, he guessed he had a couple of hours. A placard beside the clock had a large arrow on it indicating that the tide was still coming in. He caught the attention of the serving girl, the same lass who had been singing earlier.

"Will you still be serving two hours hence?" Ullin asked.

"Aye. I work all night, don't I?"

"I might like to close my eyes for a bit," Ullin said, offering her a large silver coin. "If you see to it that I'm awake in two hours, you'll have another of those."

"I'd be happy to do so! Thank ye, sir!"

Ullin watched her slip the coin into her apron and move off to the next booth. He shifted his shoulder bag beneath his cloak around and behind him and slouched back upon it. Closing his eyes and leaning back, he pulled his travel cloak across his knees, and underneath, put his hand on the dagger hilt at his belt.

As much as he needed and desired sleep, it did not seem to come to Ullin as easily as it once had, particularly since the odd and uncanny experience in Forest Mistwarren. These days, when he did find sleep, it did not seem as restful as before, his dreams not as peaceful nor as sweet as they once had been. Little things perturbed him and kept slumber away, like the call of night birds that never bothered him before, the puff of wind through the trees, or the chatter of talk.

So, while the hubbub of the tavern went on around him, accompanied by the clank of pewter tankards and the scrape of chairs pushed and pulled, Ullin was continually aroused from his nap. Once, when he felt the shift of the backboard behind him, he fully woke, gripping his dagger more firmly and sitting up. But it was only the occupants of the next booth taking their seats. Glancing at the clock, he saw he had nearly a full hour longer to wait, so, frowning, he slumped back down and closed his eyes to try again. He did not sleep again right away, for the voices of the men behind him intruded too much on his efforts.

"Yes, a list of places to look over," one man was saying to another.

"You must be joking."

"You can take it up with Vidican when you rejoin him. He'll want your report, regardless."

"Yes. Yes. But, look here, all these little villages, too? And back to Mimblewan, Lowtree, and then on to Umston. All the way up to Passdale and every little village in between? I'll have to cross the Saerdulin twice, back and forth."

"I know. No one else can be spared. And you know the lay of the land."

"You know that I'm to remain here until my relief comes. That's not for another three weeks. All told, it will be at least two months, or more, to get all this sightseeing done."

"Then arrange things so that Passdale will be your last stop before turning back south. By then, you'll not have to go but a week's travel, at most, to meet up with Vidican."

"He'll be that far along?"

"He departs within the fortnight."

"Hm. So still the same plan?"

"Unless you bring him word to do otherwise, yes."

"And every place on this list?"

"Yes. Others have had a close look, last year. Just a glance is all that's needed, I'd say. You be the judge. I must go. I have my own business to attend. Good bye, Captain Pargolis."

"Good bye, Toradatis."

The conversation ended and Ullin leaned his head back against the wall, hoping for just a little more rest. He dozed, his head back, facing the ceiling and snoring lightly, all to the amusement of the serving girls who passed by. Customers continued to depart for their ships or their businesses, and the tavern became quieter as they did so. The man behind Ullin, the one called Pargolis, remained, swilling his steady refills, growing all the more discontented with his previous conversation.

Meanwhile, Ullin dreamed of a faraway land, a lonely and vast expanse. He stood alone, watching wind-driven dust pile into dunes. He slowly became anxious, conscious of being in the open, a conspicuous figure against the light-colored sand. Suddenly a hard bump behind him jarred him awake. The man behind him was now laughing. Ullin frowned, rubbing his neck and shifting on his bench to reposition his head for further sleep. Glancing at the clock, he saw that more than two hours had passed, and the tide indicator pointed down. The girl had failed to wake him.

Scrambling off his bench, he hurried to the door and was nearly at it, checking his anger at the serving girl, when he heard a squeal from behind him. With his hand on the latch, he turned to see the very same girl trying to twist away from Pargolis, her wrist caught in his grip as he groped his arm around her waist. Ullin looked at the door, sighed, then turned around and walked toward the struggling pair. Now the man was standing and bending over the girl as she freed herself and stumbled away in tears. As Pargolis staggered after her, he felt a hand on his shoulder. Turning, he caught Ullin's fist with his jaw, the blow knocking him backwards against a table then onto the floor.

"Go," Ullin said to the girl. "Tell the barkeep what happened, and don't come back."

"Thank you," she said, hurrying off. Ullin went back to the door and had it open when a dagger flew past his head and lodged into the doorframe. He swung around just as Pargolis plowed into him. Ullin threw up his hand at the dirk now swiping at him, catching the man's wrist against his own, and the two tumbled out into the street and right into a foursome coming into the tavern, knocking two of them down. Ullin swung his attacker away, and managed to get at his dagger and draw his sword before the man came back at him with his own weapons drawn. Seeing the Kingsman insignia on Ullin's tunic, Pargolis hesitated, then spat blood from his mouth.

"I should have guessed," he said, coming at Ullin. "Kingsmen never know when to mind their own business, nor when to keep their hands to themselves."

"You are one to speak," Ullin shot back, "having been so rude with your own."

It was then that Ullin realized that the men they had collided with were all Tracians, like Pargolis, and they, too, were picking themselves up, gathering around, and drawing weapons. Two of them were armed with light, fast rapiers while the rest had sabres. Ullin's standard-issue gladius was outmatched, regardless of his skill, and he glanced past them down the lane toward the docks. Now they were in his way.

"Pargolis," one of the men said, "who's this we're about to skewer?"

"Just another Duinnor bastard," Pargolis said as the men came on.

Ullin parried Pargolis's drunken sword-stroke with his long-bladed dagger and caught the swipe of the dirk on his sword pommel, knocking the short blade from Pargolis's hand. In counterstroke, Ullin then cracked his pommel on his attacker's chin.

"I'd love to stay and teach you better manners," Ullin said, "but I have a boat to catch!"

With that, Ullin charged, parrying and jabbing, wounding two before he was through them, running as fast as he could for the docks. Before he was ten feet away, a thrown sword caught him on the ankles and tripped him. Ullin went down hard, and they were upon him in an instant.

Rolling over, steel rang against the cobblestones beside his head, a thrust caught his cloak, while a boot kicked his ribs. Somehow, he managed to avoid their slashes, and, swinging his sword to clear the way, he got to his knees, slashing and lunging. One man went down when Ullin's dagger plunged through his thigh, but now the two he had previously wounded were at him along with Pargolis, swinging hard. Ullin threw his dagger, but Pargolis dodged and it flew instead into the eye of the man behind. Ullin got to his feet, slashed, and ran.

"You coward!" one of the men shouted. Ullin fled, desperate to get to the docks and to the Sea Arrow, realizing that if the ship had cast off he was running to a dead end. He made the corner and turned. A dagger clipped his elbow and another stuck in his calf. Ullin careened in pain, crashing against a pushcart. He grabbed it for support and reached down to jerk out the dagger. Whirling around, he ducked as a sabre chopped into the cart and got stuck. Ullin shot his sword into the man's chest, grabbed the sabre, and kicked the dead man into the other men coming up.

Now it was a fight. Ullin staggered, limping and ducking and weaving, parrying and slashing with sabre and gladius, moving backwards as he fought down the wharf toward the berth which, he saw, was now empty. Too busy for disappointment, he put his mind to the task at hand, dispatching another man. Pargolis somehow got close enough to punch Ullin in the side, but received in turn Ullin's kick to his groin. During this, Ullin saw, not twenty yards off the end of the dock, and moving slowly under tow by a boat of rowers, the Sea Arrow. Its sails were being hoisted, making for the open sea. Ullin threw another punch and ran in spite of his uncooperative wound. Holding both weapons in one hand, he pulled off his cloak as he ran. Suddenly turning, he threw it into the face of the man just behind him, then shot the sabre through his shoulder. He swung wildly at Pargolis with his gladius. The Tracian ducked the swipe but could not avoid Ullin's kick behind his knee. As Pargolis fell, Ullin blocked another sword thrust from his partner and kicked him in the chest, knocking him over Pargolis, still on his hands and knees. Ullin ran a little farther, sheathing his gladius, then, turning, he threw the sabre at his pursuers, who broke their stride to dodge the whirling steel.

"We've got him now," said Pargolis, coming on. "He's nearly at the end of the wharf."

But Ullin did not slow down or hesitate when he reached the end, diving over the side. Coming up, he swam for the receding ship, struggling against the weight of his shoulder bag, oblivious to the daggers and swords splashing around him. He could not hear the shouts of the sailors at the stern of the Sea Arrow who had seen the melee and now cheered Ullin on, nor the jeers and curses of those ashore. Ullin's clothes were too heavy, the shoulder bag like a millstone, his sword an anchor, and he was too exhausted to reach the ship. Somewhere above him, over his failing strokes and clumsy splashes, and through his water-filled ears came strident calls and shouted orders, the noise of sails beginning to snap as they caught air, and the rushing gurgle of a stern wave. Suddenly Ullin felt a shape, a rope in his fingers. He got his hands on it, but it slid through his grip until it came to the large knot at the trailing end. He was immediately pulled forward so violently that he nearly lost his hold, seawater shooting down his mouth and nose as he was dragged through the water. He came up for air, gasping and coughing, now almost skimming across the surface. Abruptly, he banged against the hull, spun around in the wake, and banged again, once more nearly losing his grip. He heard a splash, and then another, and felt hands pushing and shoving, tugging at his tunic and pulling his arms.

"Get that line around him afore we all drown!" someone bellowed in his ear as a rope was being shoved around and under his arms.

"We've got ye! We've got ye!"

"Haul away!"

A few moments later, hoisted up and over the side, Ullin was sprawled on his back, violently coughing out seawater while his two dripping rescuers got the ropes off their catch.

"Nicely done, men," Ullin heard someone calmly say. "Nicely done, indeed."

"Thank ye, Captain."

Blinking water from his eyes, Ullin looked up at the ship's captain standing over him with crossed arms.

"Commander Tallin, I presume?"

Ullin, still coughing, only managed to nod.

"You're late."

# Chapter 10

# A Soft Nudge

Day 22
223 Days Remaining

Five and a half days later, the Sea Arrow made port at Glareth by the Sea, delivering its passenger, Commander Ullin Saheed Tallin, and his important dispatches to the Ruling Prince of Glareth Realm. Ullin spent the rest of the day conferring with Ruling Prince Carbane concerning the news within those dispatches. The next day, Ullin traveled to a village not ten miles south where his mother lived in a cottage on the bluffs overlooking the sea. Though mother and son were happy to see each other, it was a sad visit, overall, for Ullin. His mother, Lady Sharyn, was in decline, confusing the years, sometimes asking after Ullin's father, whom Ullin barely remembered and was long dead. The next day, he bade a tender farewell to his mother and returned to Glareth by the Sea to attend to his business there. The morning after that, he departed in the company of Prince Danoss, Carbane's son, heading south on horseback to Formouth on the northern shores of Lake Halgaeth. It would be a long ride of some twenty days, during which time, the Kingsman and the young Glarethian prince would become well-acquainted.

While Ullin and Prince Danoss traveled in the eastern world, far, far away in the west, in Duinnor Realm, and just outside the city for which the realm was named, Raynor impatiently slogged up the long high stairs to the Temple. It was a warm day and clear, but he did not stop even once to look back over his shoulder at the city in the distance across the valley, nor had he slowed his determined stride one bit since the gates were at last thrown open at dawn. On the uncanny night, three weeks ago, when all of the bells of the land were set ringing, filling the land with alarm, the city gates were hurriedly closed, and all of the city's inhabitants were barred from leaving, regardless of the urgency of their business. Frustratingly, it was only a few hours after Tyrin arrived to inform Raynor that his charge had been safely delivered to the Temple, just as Raynor had instructed. Raynor paid the mercenary, and when asked, informed Tyrin that he would be going to see the lady first thing in the morning. And, no, there was no need for Tyrin to accompany him. Now, Raynor wished he had gone immediately to see Esildre, and for the past week and fortnight, he paced and fumed at his error. But when the announcement was made that the gates would be reopened to traffic, and all would return to normal, Raynor was amongst the first to pass through them, hurrying out across the valley toward the mountaintop Temple of Beras.

"No doubt she is as anxious to see me as I am her," he now commented to Beauchamp, who was peeking out of Raynor's shoulder bag with all the caution that an uncomfortable rabbit can express. "Yet," Raynor went on, "with all the commotion these past weeks, I wouldn't be surprised if she has given up on me and departed."

As he climbed the last few hundred steps, he saw her standing above, waiting for him on the temple portico. She was dressed in plain robes and sandals such as those that some of the monks wore, but no monk ever made them look as attractive as she did. When he was in easy speaking distance, he addressed her.

"It is good to see you again," he said.

"And you, at last."

"I know! I know! It has been a long three weeks, full of anxiety. But the gates were just opened this morning."

He finally made it to the uppermost landing, and bowed. She nodded, somewhat coolly.

"It is just the two of you," she commented.

"Yes. Beauchamp insisted on coming along. Were you expecting someone else?"

"No. I suppose not."

She wanted to ask after Tyrin. Instead, she steeled herself for the conversation that was about to take place.

"Hm. Well, I suppose we should get right to it, then. Perhaps we might avail ourselves of one of the gardens?"

She led on, though Raynor knew his way around the Temple grounds as well as any.

"I hope your stay here has been pleasant, at least," he said as they entered the great building and turned down the first of many passages and hallways.

"Yes. I must admit at first I was very anxious. The monks were, too. Night and day for seven nights and days they chanted and fasted and chanted. And there was much coming and going, since many people sought refuge here during the crisis. Once things calmed down, I did, too. And I have rather enjoyed the freedom granted to me, to roam without care, to be at my ease. To not be guarded in my manners or actions. I can't say that I've had a more peaceful fortnight in centuries. If ever."

"I was hoping as much for you. Though I should have come right away," Raynor confessed. "That is, as soon as I knew you were here. I thought you might like your night's rest, after such an arduous journey. It was my intention to set out from the city the very next morning. Little did I know what was about to happen!"

"What did happen? What made all of the bells ring like that? I certainly felt, at first, some looming catastrophe was upon the world."

"I would rather not guess," Raynor shrugged as they dodged a group of monks coming down the hall with large baskets of vegetables. "But surely only a powerful enchantment may do such a thing, the likes of which the world has not witnessed since before the First Age, at least."

They at last exited into a small garden at the southern side of the Temple, and found a secluded place amongst ancient fruit trees and thick roses bushes. Raynor put his shoulder bag down beside a bench so that Beauchamp could hop about and explore while he and Esildre had their discussion.

"I am truly glad to see you, dear Esildre." Raynor gestured to the bench and after she sat, so did he. "And I should add that, in spite of what you may believe, I never once gave up my hopes for you."

"Thank you, Raynor. It is good to see you, too. There is so much to talk about. Perhaps I should first tell you that my existence over the past long time has been, as you probably know, quite sordid and full of shame. I tried to change things, but could not change what I am."

"I know you think so. Yet, you did begin the change. Long ago when you forbade visitors to your estate. When you sought isolation rather than continued depravity and debauchery. Forgive me if I speak frankly. I do know all about those years before you stopped receiving guests at Elmwood Castle."

Esildre gazed at Raynor with appreciation.

"I do not mind forthright words from you," she said. "And I am not surprised at your knowledge of my acts. Yes, I did try to withdraw. But the Lord of Shadow still has his way with me, and his curse is as potent now as ever it was."

"I do not think so," Raynor smiled. "Not as potent, else you would never have fought against it. And surely that is what you were doing, fighting against it, when you closed your estate to outsiders and brought into your service only the blind. It was a beginning. And in all the years since, you continued to fight against the curse Secundur laid upon you. Elsewise, you would have thrown open your doors and sent forth your invitations as you once did."

"Perhaps. I was often tempted. Out of boredom. Out of loneliness."

"Yet you have not done so."

"No."

"And when you gave those hapless travelers refuge from the ravages of winter, lo those many years ago, it was they who committed crimes against you and your servants, not the other way around. That you slew them, one way or another, was understandable."

"How do you know about that?"

"Your servants may be blind," Raynor smiled again, "but they are not without wit or wile. Your ferryman delivers letters not just to you, but also to a certain old friend of mine who long ago took up residence in your hall, and who, among other things, tends to your wine cellar."

"Do you mean old Garson? A friend of yours?"

"Who do you think suggested that he seek employment with you? It was a shame he lost his sight, a terrible accident, and yet he was too proud to accept my charity and my support. Yes. He wanted to earn his way, as he has always done, and he did not wish to burden his family in Vanara. So I sent him your way."

"You old trickster! So you have been spying on me!"

"Not at all! Garson cares for you, as do all those in your household. It was he who wrote to me, asking what might be done for you, to alleviate your suffering. And thus began our correspondence. I only encouraged him to be faithful and patient."

"Oh. Oh, my goodness."

Esildre looked away in thought. She slowly shook her head, appreciating those she left behind as she never had before. The young maidservant who begged her not to end her life. The old ferryman who diligently and skillfully went back and forth across her lake on all manner of business. And Garson, the butler and chamberlain of her castle. Only since leaving her castle was she truly beginning to understand their loyalty to her, and her own affection for them.

"I suppose we should discuss matters more at hand," she said softly, not wishing to appear sentimental.

"Of course."

"The man who murdered my brother. What is his name?"

"Bailorg Delcorman is his name."

"And what do you know about him?"

"I have made inquiries. Discreetly and privately. Publicly, he is known to be a man of business. He owns the controlling liens on leases throughout Vanara, but hides them within the ledgers of a counting house here in Duinnor. He is Elifaen, though his partners who own the counting house are Men. My informant within their firm tells me that they do not know how he came by his fortune. Yet he finances their speculations, and arranges for them to handle leases and liens as he directs. Further inquiries among certain Elifaen in the city revealed that his ties with your father are very close, indeed. I have a friend in the Palace who tells me that he has been seen, off and on, for as long as anyone can remember, in the company of your father, Lord Banis, or in his chambers. Bailorg comes and goes from the Palace without question. And I discovered that, last year, Bailorg displayed a letter bearing your father's seal so that he and those in his company would be unhindered during their travels. Much the same as letters that court dignitaries and ambassadors carry abroad. Shortly afterwards, Bailorg traveled alone to Vanara. There he disappeared for a time, then he reappeared back here in Duinnor in the company of several mercenaries before departing for the east."

"Hm. And what connects him to my brother's murder?"

"Your father."

"What?"

"Your father hired Bailorg to kill Navis."

"That's ludicrous! Why?"

"Your father and the King now have an accord with Shatuum."

"What do you mean?"

"Your father auctioned you to Secundur in exchange for the use of his black eagles."

Esildre shook her head disbelievingly.

"When Navis set out after you, the King at first forbade it. I believe he did so out of charity for your brother, a great hero and well liked in Duinnor. It was your father who convinced the King to permit the expedition. And it was your father who provided Navis with his travel companions and his guide. Navis told me so himself before departing Duinnor. As I said in my letter to you, I was against it. It filled me with dread and worry. I myself prepared to go with him, but I was summoned to the Palace and placed under false arrest for a minor infraction of law. A week later, when the charges were dropped and I was released, Navis had departed. I am now convinced that my arrest was contrived to keep me from accompanying your brother. From preventing his murder."

"And so it was this Bailorg who was his guide? Who murdered Navis and his co-conspirators?"

"Yes. When Bailorg returned, he reported that all was well, and that Navis had entered Shatuum with his escorts. It is recorded in the annals and diaries of the King's Court that he made such reports before those in the Court who were friends to Navis and his fellow Kingsmen. It was at that time that Bailorg began securing liens against lands in Vanara, particularly in the regions under threat of attack from the Dragonkind. Before he departed with Navis, so it goes, Bailorg was nearly destitute. Upon his return, he was richly rewarded by your father for his service to your brother. In the years that followed, Bailorg came under scrutiny many times for a variety of suspicious acts. He was suspected in the murder of another Kingsman. And he was recently implicated in the attempted murder by poison of the wife of Lord Arata. She has been outspoken in her support of her husband's efforts to dissolve claims upon Vanaran lands. But in each of these instances, and others, Bailorg was exonerated by those in service to your father. I believe your father and Bailorg are each in the other's clutches, each using the other for their own ends, protected by mutual self-interest. Bailorg blackmails your father even after all these years since your brother's murder. And your father blackmails Bailorg likewise. Neither can denounce the other. I am only surprised that Bailorg has been permitted to live this long, though it is said he goes nowhere without protection. So that is why I asked you here. To help me gather evidence for the courts. So that you may present the claim, and to bring down Bailorg's master, your father!"

"How can I believe you? That my father was responsible for his own son's murder?" she countered.

"It was your father who coerced you to Secundur!" Raynor stated. "Think upon it! Remember how, when you returned from Tulith Attis, your father renewed his request that you go to Shatuum? And in your dark depression—for what you saw at Tulith Attis was surely horrible—you gave in to him. You must know that your father used you for his own gain! Surely, during all the years of your isolation you have pondered it over and over. You know your father to be responsible for your captivity by Secundur. And Navis did, too! And do you think Navis could be permitted to bring you back so soon after your departure to Secundur? Before your father's reward for giving you over was fully reaped?"

"Then why did he not permit Navis to enter Shatuum? Would not his death be assured at the hands of Secundur's legions?"

"Do you forget his prowess at arms? No warrior of the Elifaen has been so fierce or so mighty since Cupeldain. Was it not Navis who entered the Crevasse of Fire and smote Jatarak the Ogre? Was it not Navis who slaughtered an entire legion of the Dragonkind at the battle of Saerdulin? You were there. You, of all people, know best the skill and cunning with which your brother fought, the ease with which he dispatched his foes. Who could say that he might not win against Secundur and carry you away? That was my hope for him. And your father's fear! If Navis triumphed, the black eagles would be withdrawn, and Lord Banis's rising influence upon the King would vanish. That is how Lord Banis measures the value of power against paltry love!"

"Then I will go immediately to my father," Esildre declared, standing abruptly. "I shall confront him directly! I will know if he lies to me."

"No, no! My dear! You would not survive the interview, I am certain. He is too powerful, and must be confronted by fair courts. That is where you must bring your complaint against him."

"Then it is only through Bailorg that such conjectures can be proven!"

"Yes, but we must lay the groundwork for our case. Going for Bailorg first will only forewarn Lord Banis. We need allies. Let us go to Lord Arata. He is not sullied by corruption, and he is powerful. Surely, if he believes us, Lord Arata can convince others to join our cause, and evidence may then be gathered and presented to bring your father to justice."

"No. This is too much!" Esildre blurted out, losing her patience. "I cannot wait for any such insurrection. And before I join it, or believe your words, I must hear from Bailorg's own mouth that my father ordered him to murder Navis! Until then, I must assume someone else holds Bailorg's leash!"

Raynor shook his head. "To do so, you would have to capture the villain. And he is far away. Likely in Glareth, the old Eastlands, or Tracia. Let us send word to those places asking of his whereabouts. And, as we await the answers, let us patiently build our case in other ways."

"No. I'll go myself and find him."

"That would be folly. Word of your presence in Duinnor will soon leak out. You must remain here and protected. Do you think you would survive a fortnight of travel?"

"I must risk it," Esildre angrily replied. "Do you think I cannot take care of myself? After all these years?"

"Oh, Esildre! Long have you been away! Much has changed, and there are many who would march blindly to your father's commands. He did not hesitate to kill his own son. Do you think he would hesitate to stop you? Do not make me regret this, as I regret my failure to protect your brother."

By now Raynor had risen, too, and argued with obvious pain and consternation. As Esildre turned away to depart, she felt a soft nudge against her ankle. Looking down, she and Raynor's rabbit exchanged looks. Her shoulders slumped, and though she did not smile at Beauchamp, her frown vanished. Incongruously, she thought again of those in service to her household. As she watched Beauchamp hop away and stretch out on a cool flagstone, she wondered why they were so protective of her. Was it merely that she provided them with a place to live, with dignified, honest work? Were they only looking to their own interests? Or did they, after all, care about her? It was perhaps Raynor's distressed tone that sparked these thoughts. Or maybe it was Raynor's humble Familiar, devoid of malice, gentle and affectionate. In spite of Raynor's words, Beauchamp's nudge reassured her by giving his own opinion of her heart. It was as if he was telling her that she need not be angry, she need not be combative. But she could still be gentle and assertive, if she only remembered. She did remember. She remembered that once, long ago, before Secundur took her, she was moved to gentleness and pity toward those who were scorned. As it happened, she was herself later scorned, due, in part, to her loss of gentleness and her own contempt for pity. But, just now, that slight touch reminded her. Her anger at Raynor faded and vanished, and her eyes welled with emotion.

Raynor remained silent, watching her, wondering what moved her to change in posture and countenance so quickly. He knew, of course, that time does not move for the Elifaen as it moves for others. During those moments, he suspected, a long chain of thought slowly pulled her heart this way and swung her emotions that way.

Still gazing at Beauchamp, Esildre said, "You are a good friend, Raynor. But I am not convinced, and I do not think I shall be. I appreciate all that you have done on my behalf, and your continued affection for the memory of my brother. And I thank you for coming here to speak with me. My mind is made up." Now she looked at him earnestly. "Since the bells rang the night I arrived, my heart has stirred with a desire to go east. I cannot say why. It is a land filled with bad memories for me. But I long to look upon the sea once more. And I promised some in that land that I would see them again someday, if they are still there. Perhaps my longing to go is partly to do with those things. And partly, too, with your news. All these things direct me eastward. Please do not be angry. Or disappointed in me. I ask that you help me make my arrangements, in secret if discovery would put me in danger, so that I might travel. I must go. To find Bailorg and confront him in my own way."

"Folly," Raynor said. "Folly."

They searched each other's eyes for a long moment, then Raynor nodded.

"Yet, I anticipated as much. Like your brother, you are headstrong, in your own way."

Raynor sat back down and exhaled a long sigh through his nose.

"I shall await your return, as far as events may permit," he said. "Meanwhile, I have already, this morning before I departed the city, made arrangements for you. It happens that two of your great-nephews, the twins, each as inscrutable and silent as the other, are in Duinnor. I have made an effort to tutor them as I once did you, but they hardly respond to my lectures, and are by far the worst students I have ever had. But they are not bad boys, and they are experienced in combat owing to their adventures in the Dragonlands. That is why your nephew sent them here, so they might not so easily rekindle a war there."

"Kranneg and Tulleg, you mean?"

"The very same. I approached them with the notion of accompanying you on your journey, should you decide to go. To my amazement, they each constructed an entire sentence to express their enthusiasm. So I'll send them to you in the morning, along with buckmarls, provisions, and your old armor."

"My armor? I would not have imagined that you still had those things."

"You said you'd be back for them someday. And I have kept them safe and free of corrosion. Your sword and daggers, too. And also a trunk of clothes and whatnot that you left behind."

"A friend, indeed! And you knew all along I would insist on going."

"I'm afraid I hoped for otherwise," Raynor shrugged. "And I still say it is folly."

# Chapter 11

# The Faere Coins

Day 29
216 Days Remaining

Mirabella Ribbon had many secrets to keep, some old, ancient even, and some very new. If she kept any secrets well, she kept none so well as she did those of her son's. She prevented Mr. Ribbon from learning the true nature of Robby's misadventures by diversion rather than deception. By graceful interruptions she steered conversations with her husband toward different, less awkward topics. She thoughtfully listened to Mr. Ribbon's questions about Robby's story in the evenings as they prepared for bed or lay sleepless in the still of the night, never giving any definite opinions of her own or any answers, either. She knew he was close to knowing that much more had happened to Robby than the boy would tell him. At times she was almost certain, by the way her husband looked at her, that he knew she supported Robby's reticence to say more about his adventures. But Mr. Ribbon never pressed her, and he never became angry or impatient. His was the quiet sort of wonder, the "somehow it don't quite fit" kind of quandaries, and the "I must remember to ask Robby about" musings. He believed in giving Robby a wide path to make for himself, and he held his son in great respect.

"Why, when I was his age," he would say to Mirabella, "I warn't half so responsible. Couldn't care less for chores er mindin' rules er learnin' a trade. Compared to me, Robby's a reg'lar scholar, too. Knows more 'bout books an' letters than most any boy 'round here ever did, I reckon. We're mighty lucky to have him, an' I'm mightily proud of our son. 'Cept, I sometimes wish he was a little more talkative."

On he would chatter, roaming into something or other about Robby's trip to Haven Hill that seemed odd, or something concerning Robby and Sheila and what was going on between them, "'Sides the obvious, o'course."

Mirabella let him muse aloud, biding the time when he would know all.

"In good time," was all she might say. "In good time, all will show forth that needs to." And she hoped it was true.

• • •

The weeks went by, and they were busy ones. Mr. Ribbon was ever going here and there about town, at the Common House, or wherever his business as the interim mayor took him, while Robby remained at the store, and Mirabella, often with Sheila, went around Passdale helping friends and neighbors recover from the damage of the storm. Mirabella also found time to advise Robby privately on what he should do. Which was, in short, to do nothing out of the ordinary, and to this Robby applied himself with all-too-familiar experience. In exchange, she told him a little more about her family, how they had left their home in the west and moved to the Eastlands to live in Tallinvale, their old family estate. How it was tradition for the eldest son of each family to tie himself to Duinnor to become a Kingsman, a soldier of the King. And that she had two brothers who had done so, just as her father had before them. Her oldest brother, Dalvenpar, had been killed in battle away in the west. Her next older brother, Aram, also died in the same manner. Ullin Saheed was his son. When he was of age, Ullin went to Duinnor to become a Kingsman, too, like his father, his uncle, and his grandfather before him.

"Why do Tallin men serve the King of Duinnor?" Robby asked one day at noon meal.

"That is an old tradition," she answered. "All lands belong to the King, you see. Any who defy Duinnor soon suffer the consequences, one way or another. One way for Duinnor to see to it that far-flung houses remain loyal is to demand that every eldest male heir of the Named Houses serve the King."

"Like hostages?"

"Not quite," she said. "But it can amount to as much if loyalties are questioned."

Robby shook his head, saying, "Doesn't seem right, somehow."

"Right or wrong, that is how it is."

"Why isn't it like that here?"

"For one, we are far away from Duinnor. For another, the great houses of the East still swear fealty to Duinnor and keep with the tradition. Every man, if summoned, must serve the King, of course, in one of his many armies, or in some other capacity. But the eldest of the Named Houses are required to serve as Kingsmen. The House of Ribbon is not a Named House, so don't worry about being called away."

"And Bosk is not a Named House, either?"

"No, it is not, though an Honored House and a worthy one. Its pennant hangs in the Great Hall of Duinnor, as do all pennants of Named and Honored Houses."

"The Great Hall? Is that part of the King's Palace?"

"Oh, no. The King's Palace is elsewhere in Duinnor City. The Great Hall is but one of the buildings of government, wherein is the Hall of Banners. Other places with their own buildings include the Court of

Houses, the Hall of Warriors, the Hall of Ordinaries, and the Court of Lords."

"Duinnor must be a big place."

"The city alone is very large, indeed. The Realm is actually one of the smallest of the Seven."

"It must be something to see."

"It is, truly. But it is not the most beautiful city, in my thinking. There are many beautiful cities; Glareth by the Sea is one nearest to us. But the one I will always think of as the most beautiful is Linlally, called the City in the Sky, because it is nestled against the high mountains of Vanara. The White Palace of Linlally sits above the city, floating upon a mountain lake. It cannot be seen from the city below, so high it is. But, from a distance, one can see the great mountain Cassos in the west, looming over Linlally. Down its side flows cold streams which fill the lake where the White Palace is. And, out from the lake flow five splendid waterfalls, called the Falls of Tiandari, which cascade downward to another lake far below. From that lake flows the River Iridelin, stepping back and forth over falls and shoals through the city itself. It is, in my thinking very beautiful, indeed."

Mirabella paused, tilting her head as memories of Linlally flowed through her mind. Smiling, she said, "Sometimes, when Sir Sun plays his light just right upon the mists of Tiandari, and when seen from a far distance, the White Palace appears to float atop arches of rainbows."

• • •

Over these weeks, bit by bit, Robby gained knowledge of his mother's family, and of the world, too. When they spoke, they spoke frankly, but never when Mr. Ribbon was nearby, for mother and son kept their pact, and it had not yet become necessary to let on anything to the father that he had not already pieced together for himself. Robby also found that when his mother spoke to him, she did so with a kind of melancholy joy, and he gathered that she did not speak of these things to anyone else, even her husband, and he wondered why.

"There are names for such as us, though they are seldom used," she said to him one late afternoon when the two were putting away bolts of cloth. Sheila was upstairs attempting not to burn a soup, and Mr. Ribbon was off at the Common House. "Those born of Elifaen mother will be Elifaen, too, and are called Sylphaen. The Faere bloodline is passed from mother to child, you see. All others, such as Ullin, whose mother is not Elifaen, are called Sylphmar. That is the way of it. These are words from the Ancient Tongue, and mean, roughly 'part Faere,' or 'part Fallen,' sylph Elifaen, or 'part Mortal from the Sea,' sylph Mar. Here in the east, they are sometimes used as terms of disrespect or insult. But in the west they are used less harshly and may even be used in praise. You are Sylphaen. Ullin is Sylphmar. Someday, you will become Elifaen. Ullin will not."

"Ullin's mother lives in Glareth, doesn't she?"

"That is so. She left Tallinvale when Aram, Ullin's father, died. Ullin went with her, but he returned to Tallinvale the following year and stayed until he left to become a Kingsman."

A cry and a sharp curse from upstairs, followed by a crash of metal pots, signaled Sheila's loss of temper.

"Oops!" Robby stated as he suppressed a laugh. "That doesn't sound good."

"No." Mirabella smiled. "I think I'd better go up and see if I can save our supper!"

• • •

Meanwhile, Sheila had more or less become part of the family. She helped wherever needed without complaint, and she tried to learn what she could from Robby's mother. She seemed grateful enough for their hospitality, and seemed right at home in many ways. Yet, each time Robby saw her, he was a bit surprised, and pleased, at her presence. They seldom had a chance to talk privately, but the more she was around, the harder it was for Robby to take his gaze from her. And it seemed that she continued to change, almost before his eyes. She grew more confident around others, and, in his estimation, her beauty increased daily.

Mr. Ribbon had provided her with an allowance, "to keep ye 'til we have a chance to talk 'bout things," and with it she purchased clothes more fitting a young mistress, putting away her buckskin breeches and shirts for cotton and linen dresses and blouses and bodices. Her new clothes made her appear more feminine than she had ever before, a fact that Robby could not fail to notice. There were moments, while she and Mirabella laughed merrily together over some private joke, when Sheila was briefly like her old self. Robby observed, however, that as soon as the laughter faded away, a serious if not sad demeanor crept back over her. Once or twice, while Robby was working the store, he would suddenly see her staring at him from across the room with a look of such intensity that he would stop what he was doing to ask what was amiss. She would only shake her head, apologize, and say that it was nothing.

One evening after supper, when the store was closed and Robby's father had been summoned back to the Common House for a late meeting, Mirabella sat with Sheila in the parlor room upstairs and chatted away as she showed Sheila how to knit.

"My mother taught me how to do needle-lace, but it was Frizella Bosk who taught me, years ago, how to knit with yarn," Mirabella said as she handed across the needles. "Now you try."

Sheila bit her lip and tried to remember what Mirabella had just demonstrated. After a minute or two, with Mirabella intervening only once, she had the hang of it, though her hands felt clumsy and slow.

"You are doing fine. Just keep going with that for a bit."

"Frizella told me that she used to work for you and Mr. Ribbon," Sheila said, not looking up from her work.

"That is so. I knew Frizella from before I was married. I knew next to nothing about housekeeping when I married Robigor, much less anything about keeping a store. Frizella's father was an old friend of Robigor's grandfather, and somehow it fell into place that she was able to help me out. She got me started cooking, sewing, cleaning, and knitting. You know, she was pretty wild herself when she was a lass, but always a kindhearted person. She always had an eye for Mr. Bosk, and Mr. Bosk made it a point to come around wherever he thought Frizella might be. To see her, of course. I daresay he was smitten the first time he laid eyes on her. Oh, in those days they were the talk of the county! Somehow they just hit it off, and it was clear to any who had eyes. I owe her so much. Even after she and Mr. Bosk married, she came to stay several times to help me out. One year, when a terrible sickness swept through Barley, she came into Passdale just to help me, having heard that Robigor had taken ill. She looked after little Robby. That was so that I could I tend to the store and to Robigor who was out of his mind with fever for five days."

"Did you or Robby get sick, too?"

"Not then. But many other children did fall ill. Passdale lost over sixty people in just a fortnight. Barley suffered worse, and the Bosk family lost many of their kin. It was a terrible time."

Mirabella watched Sheila thoughtfully for a moment.

"Robby was very ill, a couple of years before, when he was around five years old. Frizella was here, then, too. I was out of my mind with worry, for nothing I did seemed to help. I sent word to Frizella, asking for her advice, and she came directly. But even she was baffled by the illness."

Sheila stopped and looked up at Mirabella who now smiled.

"Of course, he recovered," Mirabella said.

"Of course, since there he is."

Robby entered the room with a book under his arm.

"Do you mind if I join you ladies? I'd like to finish reading this book that I have on loan from Mr. Broadweed."

"Robby, why don't you sit here, where the light is good? I think I'll make a pot of tea."

Robby nodded and sat as Mirabella left the room.

"You've been very busy, lately," Sheila said as she continued knitting.

"Yes, with the store. So have you, I take it. I heard something about you helping Mrs. Greardon?"

"Oh, well, I've only been helping your mother. She's been doing most of the work. Mrs. Greardon is trying to take care of so much of her late husband's business so that she can support their little boy. She's not bearing up too well right now, and Mira is helping with the cleaning of the house. It turns out that the Greardon house nearly lost its roof, among all of their other misfortunes, and everything in the house got soaked in the storm. Mirabella and I have been trying to help her sort out what can't be saved, and cleaning and washing everything else. Some of her late husband's kin and a good number of Passdalers have been doing the same at the mill, trying to see if it can be saved at all."

"Can it?"

"I haven't heard. It seems to have something to do with the foundation, but I'm not sure what."

They chatted like this for a while until Mirabella returned with a tray and served them all a cup of aromatic tea. Robby sipped while he read, and the women discussed a few more points of knitting. After a while, all grew quiet, knitting needles clicked, pages rustled, and tea was slurped until Sheila began stifling yawns at such an embarrassing rate that she excused herself to bed, bidding the mother and son a good night. Robby watched her leave, and saw her throw a last glance and smile back at him just as she passed through the door. Mirabella saw him look after her, but said nothing and kept at her knitting. After a moment, Robby turned back to his book and continued reading about the Seven Realms. The book was a hand-copied manuscript, written as a school text, and it had little in it that was not already familiar to Robby: a dry review of the end of the First Age, with the coming of Men to the eastern shores, and the beginning of the kingdoms of Men leading up to the founding of the Seven Realms. There was, however, a portion pertaining to Vanara and the Elifaen that lived there, and how, more than any other place, Men and Elifaen established close ties of trust and loyalty to each other. This led Robby to think about marriages between the two races and to wonder about his own family. He looked up at his fair mother, bent over her task in the soft light, the open window on the far side of the room permitting a breath of cool air to slip in, which playfully tousled a strand of her red hair, causing it to fall across her face.

"Mother?"

"Yes, Robby?"

"May I ask about your scars?"

Mirabella looked over at Robby, her brows up and with surprise in her eyes.

"I was wondering," he asked delicately, "if you have always had them? From birth, I mean."

Mirabella put her knitting in her lap to give Robby all her attention.

"No," she said. "The scars came upon me when I was very young. Before my becoming a woman, even. That is sometimes the way for children born of my people. Of our people, I should say. Some of us are permitted a time without pain, a time of joy and peace within. Mine was truly a blessed childhood, and I had not a care in the world, in spite of all that went on around me. I think I was wiser, too, in those days of my youth, than I have ever been since."

"What do you mean?"

"It is hard to explain unless you have known it," she said wistfully. "I could hear better. The air through the leaves of summer was as a crowd of voices. In winter, when limbs are bare, a thin whisper. The water pouring from the brook over rocks and ledges. I can't explain. And I could see better. I could almost see things...*breathe*."

She shrugged and smiled, shaking her head.

"How did it happen? How did they form?" Robby asked awkwardly. "The scars, that is."

"For each person it is different, and may come at a different time for one than another. For some, it comes at a very early age, for others in later years, and, for a few, not until the final moments of their life. The emerging of the scars is called the Scathing, and it is accompanied by a kind of sickness, or, to be more truthful, a kind of madness. With me it came suddenly. I remember playing in a field, gathering wildflowers and weaving them into garlands. There was a lark that played along with me, and a little fawn, too. A shadow fell over us, as if covering the sun, and I grew dizzy. I felt a burning on my back, and, as I was later told by my brother, my screams brought my father running for me. I do not remember the next days very well, only that they were full of pain, delirium, and restlessness. This ended with a deep and utter sadness, and I tried to throw myself from my window, somehow having it in my mind that the rushing of air as I fell would somehow cure me. Or that, if I was a good girl, I could fly away into the sky. Of course, my family prevented me from fulfilling the nightmarish desire, and I recovered very slowly, if indeed it can be said that the Scathing is a thing to be recovered from. I was still suffering when my family left Vanara later that year and came east."

"Do you still suffer?"

"Not all the time. That is to say, the pain is more subtle as the years pass," she answered. "The physical aspect of it is tolerable, and sometimes I do not notice it at all. That comes and goes. The other part..."

Mirabella paused, searching for words. She looked at Robby and smiled weakly.

"The other part is not so much a pain as it is an odd blend of emotions, melancholia, anger, resentment, and remorse. Feelings that I have had since childhood, when the scars first formed."

"Remorse? What could you have done to have such feelings? As a child?"

"Children feel guilt and shame even when none is warranted. More bitterly, in some ways, than do grown-ups," she replied. "But what I speak of is the remorse of my people, remorse for my people, the things we have done, the price we have paid in what we have lost. Once we communed with all nature, living in harmony and in a delight of understanding. The Faerekind were here when the world was formed, Robby, and when the forests were young and the rivers first took their courses. Our people saw the mountains rise to mighty heights and took joy in the rains that smoothed them down. We rode the air with the birds and the butterflies and needed no sustenance but air and laughter, sunlight and moonlight. But our wings were stripped from us, and our form became heavy in the world, and we lost more than just the ability to fly. We were no longer able to commune with the earth or sky as we once had done. Although I was born long after that time, I still feel it, I still taste it as a part of my past, though I have no memory within me of that age. There is a story told of a prince among our kind, a mighty warrior and poet, who, when he realized the extent of our loss, wept for a hundred years until his eyes dried of tears, and then he took his own life. Indeed, suicide is common among our kind, so dark is our hearts."

Robby considered what she said and wondered at her. He knew no others of her kind, and had only met, very briefly and many years ago, a passing troupe of Elifaen during festival time. They seemed happy enough, with their gay songs, but now, as he recalled, even the happiest of their songs were wistful.

"Will I also go through the Scathing?" he asked.

"I do not know. I once thought you would. When you were a child, and very sick, I thought you were going through it then, but I was wrong. It may be that you will never know it. If the Scathing does come to you, you will have no warning, no sign of its coming. So you cannot prepare. You may as well not fret one way or the other about it. Only hope, if it does come, that you have good people about you."

Mirabella put her knitting into the little basket beside her chair.

"Now I would like to ask you something," she said with a wry smile, leaning over the arm of the chair toward Robby. "I know you and Sheila have had a special relationship. I just wonder, is it very special?"

Robby reddened just a little and closed his book.

"Yes, for my part anyway. She is as dear to me as any other person. More than any other, I think."

"But this arrangement we have here, her staying with us, does not suit you?"

"Oh, it suits me fine. Except, well, we haven't had much time to spend together."

"I know you've been very busy with the store. I'm sorry."

"No, I don't mind that. It's good, in a way, to be busy."

"But?"

"I don't think it matters that she and I have so little chance to be, well, to be alone. I don't think she wants it. Not right now."

"I think she wants it more than she lets on," Mirabella said, shifting her legs up underneath her so that she was bundled into the chair like a little girl. "I find it strange, though. It's obvious she cares a great deal about you. She looks for you, pretending not to. And when you are not around, she finds a way to ask after you. Oh, without seeming too concerned, mind you, but still she asks. When you are around, I see how she looks at you. And how you look at her, too. Only, I think she has a lot on her heart right now. She knows, I think, that she can confide in me, but she has not chosen to do so. Not yet. Maybe never."

"Mother, please don't press her too much," Robby asked earnestly. "You are right, there are other things on her mind, weighing upon her. Some have to do with me and some do not. I don't feel right about telling you about them, what I know of them, anyway. If she wants you to know, I think it is her place to speak, not mine. I hope you understand."

"Of course I do. You can rest assured I'll not pry. I'll keep an eye out for her, though, and, if it comes up, I'll do my best to respect her privacy, too. She isn't the only one in this house with reasons to keep a cautious tongue. Let's just see how things go."

• • •

Work at the store continued to be brisk. While Robigor, the elder, was busy as Acting Mayor, Robigor, the younger, ran the store as he was taught, under the watchful eye of his mother and with only the occasional supervision of his father in the evenings. The people of the Eastlands, resilient and hearty stock, quickly recovered from the floods and realized that the damage was not as severe as it could have been. Grateful for that, and for Mr. Ribbon's wise and careful management of civic affairs, and for his way of bringing folks together to agree upon ways to work together, the people received what they needed to rebuild, and to salvage their late harvests. While many of the fruit trees were ruined, and most of the late corn and melons washed away, much of the barley and wheat had already been harvested and beans, nuts, and grapes were aplenty. They knew they would not starve this winter and so they got on with their lives. Everywhere there were discussions about the four raiders, especially the Dragon Man and the one that got away—for he was never found by the Bosklanders—and the entire countryside remained watchful. Doors that were seldom closed were now being locked, people were keeping dogs, and few went anywhere unaccompanied. Rumors spread that the lone intruder was nearby, that he lurked behind every bush and tree, and that he only waited for a chance to thieve and plunder. There was talk about bandits who gathered in the Thunder Mountains, and some feared they would send forays against Barley. But there was no thieving and no plundering, unless one counted those few apples hoisted in the market, or that extra ale that went unpaid until the next day down at the tavern. Folks regained their stride, never too hurried nor too worried (as was their way), for there was too much work to do to waste effort fretting about some lost badman in the dark. With nothing more serious happening, and having survived the storm, there was something of a pleasant relief in the air as preparations for the Autumn Festival began.

Indeed, these preparations kept Mr. Ribbon especially busy as it fell to him to make most of the arrangements for the public event. And, as mayor, he had many other responsibilities besides. The most pressing was to have a survey of the roads and bridges completed as soon as possible. There was also the annual census to be prepared for the King's Treasure. Besides the Renewal Oaths to be taken during the festival, there were the required accounts about taxes and tariffs that were required by the governor (thankfully, there were few taxes in these parts and no tariffs at all, though the question did arise at a recent council meeting of whether some new tax was needed to pay for the repairs to the roads and bridges). As well, Mr. Ribbon had to deal with any petitions unanswered by Duinnor (no petitions, either, and Mr. Ribbon had never heard of one being made), and many other formalities that needed put to parchment and sent on to Formouth, where Prince Danoss sat as administrative governor of the Eastlands Realm. At the same time, the Bosks were pressing to raise a new county militia once more, to be placed, naturally enough, under the command of the Laird of Bosk Hall. One afternoon, after a meeting at the Common House, Mr. Bosk and Mr. Ribbon stepped onto the store porch together. As they entered the store, Robby heard Mr. Bosk trying to convince the mayor to sway the council.

"We don't yet know anythin' 'bout them looters," he was saying as they came through the door. "Might be more of 'em. Now ye wants a fine turnout at the Festival, don't ye? Well, folks ain't likely to leave thar homes if they be worried 'bout the likes of strangers an' robbers an' such."

"Ye won't get an argument from me 'bout that," Robigor was nodding. "But thar's a lot on ever'one's plates, right now. Most ain't finished makin' repairs, an' winter's fast comin'. Thar's few to spare for any militia till we have the roads in repair, an' thar's little money in the county treasury to cover the like."

"Affernoon, Master Ribbon," Bosk nodded to Robby and quickly turned back to his father. "Looky here, Robigor. I've got as much work to get done as any. I can raise fifty er sixty men, fast like, good Line Riders all, trained an' ready to make defense. But that ain't enough to take on the likes of what we seen last month if a bigger party of 'em come. Master Ribbon whar thar. He can warrant the fight them fellers put up. I don't dare send less than three patrollin' together, an' that ain't nearly what it takes to cover the county proper-like. I can raise another hunnerd or two hunnerd, maybe, but they'll need trainin' an' arms. That'll take time an' help. If some others from Passdale, Leeriver, an' the rest of Barley join in, we can have nigh five hunnerd. Once they're all trained an' armed, we can break into companies. Whilst some goes 'bout thar work, others'll be on patrol. If the alarm is raised, they can all come out."

"Son," Mr. Ribbon turned to Robby, "any word on the Janhaven wagon?"

"Yes, sir," Robby said from behind the desk where he was working on the books. "The new Post Rider came along earlier and said he passed the Janhaven wagon with Mr. Furaman himself driving, and Mrs. Starhart was riding with him, coming to ask you a few questions."

"When was that?"

"Oh, the rider came and went around noon," Robby said.

Before Mr. Ribbon could say anything more, Mr. Bosk continued.

"See? Bobby's still unaccounted for," he said, putting his hand on Mr. Ribbon's shoulder. "An' them folk up in the mountains, up to no good, er somethin' worse. I'm tellin' ye, we're gonna need that militia 'fore long!"

Robby knew that his father was of two minds about the militia, and, as mayor, he did not want to commit one way or the other just yet.

"I tell ye what I can do," Mr. Ribbon said at last. "I can ask for volunteers to enroll to be called on if needed. Some kind of pledge they'll give. To serve until some regular arrangement can be worked out. Maybe I can make out like they're for surveyin' the roads, er something. But I believe I can get the council to pay for a few arms. I'll work it so as I only get volunteers who'll be trustworthy. Meanwhile, I'll speak to our blacksmith here in town an' see 'bout some arms makin'. I can't promise anythin', mind ye."

"Now yer talkin' sense," Mr. Bosk grinned. "I ain't holdin' ye to anythin' as I knows ye'll try an' see what ye can do."

Mr. Bosk shook hands with Mr. Ribbon and strode to the door.

"Nearly forgot!" he said turning back and walking up to Robby to stand across the desk from him. "I meant to tell the both of ye: I sent a party out to Ashlord's, a week or so ago, just to look in on him, mostly at the proddin' of me wife, ye see. Anyhow, they didn't see sight nor sound of the feller, though his cottage door was open, so they peeked in. Nuthin' looked amiss, so they said. One of the men what knows Ashlord a little from seein' him abouts, said his stick an' his shoulder sack whar gone. No sign of trouble, no blood, nuthin' looked ransacked er anythin' like 'at. But the men got the jitters, I think. They left a note for Ashlord tellin' they'd been in the place, but assured me they didn't mess with anythin'. I'll be sendin' another party out yonder in a week or two, unless we hear from him. Anyhow, I meant to let ye an' Miss Sheila know we tried lookin'."

" 'Course, it don't mean nuthin'," Mr. Bosk went on smiling. "Ashlord's got his own kind of business, comin' an' goin', an' who's to say he ain't on some travels, er somethin'? Alrighty, then, I'll be off! Tell Miss Sheila me wife says hullo an' how d'ye do an' all. Oh, yeah. Billy'll be comin' along in a day er two with a wagon of goods for ye an' the market."

"Oh that'll be great!" Robby said. "Tell him I've been busy at the store, but I'm sure we can get together for awhile. That is, if he has time."

"Oh, if I knows me son, he'll make plenty of time for jabberin'!" Mr. Bosk laughed and departed.

Mr. Ribbon stood looking at the empty doorway with one hand on his hip and another scratching his chin in thought. Robby turned back to the books and had only dipped his pen when he heard wagon wheels approaching. The sound shook Mr. Ribbon from his meditation, and he walked to the door to look up the road.

"The Janhaven wagon," he called back in.

Robby left the desk to stand beside his father and watched the wagon lumber slowly toward them behind a team of six horses. This was the big shipment Mr. Ribbon had been waiting on for weeks, and it was sure to take all day to unload.

"Better go fetch yer mother," Mr. Ribbon said. "I'll warrant Mrs. Starhart's come 'bout her husband, an' me druthers would be to let Mirabella speak to her first."

Robby, his mother, and Sheila returned downstairs just as the wagon pulled up front. After greetings and introductions, Sheila and Mrs. Ribbon took Mrs. Starhart upstairs while the men began unloading the shipment.

It was a massive load of goods: kegs of oil from Wayregyle, bolts of fabric from as far away as Draymoor, and porcelain plates from Sorghwall. There were boxes of silver jewelry from the mountain town of Chiselpeck, and some glassware from Mimblewan near the coast. There were crates of tea and bags of salt, paper and parchment from Giyth, and a whole log of oilwood, to be split later for matches and firesticks. Robby worked hard, carefully unloading each keg, parcel, crate, box, or bundle, and checking each one and the contents against his order book along with his father and Mr. Furaman. Furaman was the owner of a large trading firm that operated from his stockade near Janhaven, a few miles west of Passdale at the foot of the Thunder Mountains. From there, Furaman gathered and traded goods from all parts, and Mr. Ribbon and Mr. Furaman had a long and mutually profitable arrangement. Since Mr. Ribbon was the primary distributor of Furaman's goods in and around Barley, and since Furaman could obtain just about anything anyone wanted, they supplied each other with orders. And Mr. Ribbon arranged matters so that whenever the Furaman wagon came with a shipment, it never left empty. Every two or three months, the wagon came and was unloaded, and then Mr. Ribbon and Furaman saw to it that it was filled up again with metal goods, tools mostly, well-made by the blacksmith, bags of flour from the mill, smoked hams from Boskland, and various other stocks held by Mr. Ribbon in the Ribbon's cellar and the storehouse nearby. In return for this service, Mr. Ribbon received a commission from the local producers as well as a discount on orders from Furaman. Nobody ever accused Robigor Ribbon of not having a head for business! Right now, however, the business was overwhelming his son, who had been at it for three hours straight. The wagon was unloaded, but everything still needed to be unpacked, sorted, shelved, stored, and the inventories reconciled.

It was usually at this point that the blacksmith arrived to help with the reloading, and to receive payment for his goods, along with a few other folks that had the same interest. True enough, as Robby surveyed the store, trying to figure out how to get to the desk with all the stuff in the way, he heard voices outside as his father greeted the arrivals, and they set to work around back. While they began the job of reloading Furaman's wagon, Robby unpacked and put away things, toting sacks and kegs down into the cellar, and stowing away bolts of cloth and yarn in the cedar closets. It wasn't long before all this was done and the wagon, too, was filled to capacity and tarpaulins were spread over the cargo and tied down. As Robby finished clearing a path to the accounting desk, his father came back in along with the others.

Furaman and Mr. Ribbon each took a seat at the desk, side by side, and got out their books and quills and opened the inkwell. The blacksmith and the others lined up and soon were receiving payment from Furaman, minus an agreeable commission for Mr. Ribbon, and sometimes settling up with the store. Some preferred that their payment be in store goods, and Mr. Ribbon and Mr. Furaman arranged that on the spot. There was rarely any grumbling or disagreement because the two businessmen handled everything above-board and kept to their agreements. On each visit, Mr. Furaman made it clear what he would pay for goods on his next visit, and how much he needed, and so on, having everything written carefully and signed. Finally, the last man was paid and departed (Mr. Ribbon always gave them a little extra for their work, too.), leaving the two businessmen to settle their accounts with each other. Once this was done, Furaman turned to Mr. Ribbon.

"Now. I'd like to broach something of a delicate subject with you, Robigor."

"Oh?"

"It's about Lally."

"Yes?"

"Well, er. I mean to say, Lally, being my sister and all, is right concerned after her husband, Bob, who's been missin' this long while."

"I well understand. We all are worried."

"Well, them Post Riders have all given up on Bob, an' them fellers ain't slackers. I mean to say, if there was any hope in findin' him, they'd have done it by now," he said. "Then I heard tell, his horse was recovered in these parts, being ridden by some robber."

"That is so."

"Well, Lally came along to speak with you about it."

"Why?" Mr. Ribbon asked. "She knows as much as meself."

"Well, alls I'm askin' is that you hear her out," Mr. Furaman said. "An' if there's anythin' I might do to help things along, I'll certainly do it."

"I'm not sure what ye mean."

"Maybe we can get Lally down here now an' have a word or two," Mr. Furaman said.

"Well, why don't we all go upstairs?" Mr. Ribbon said, getting up from his stool. "Robby, I think we oughta close up shop, for now, so ye can come up with us."

"I didn't mean for you to close the store," Mr. Furaman said.

"Oh, never mind that!" Mr. Ribbon replied. "Robby was thar when Bob's horse was found, so it might be good to have him in on our chat."

They all went upstairs where Mrs. Starhart had been entertained for more than three hours by Sheila and Mirabella. When the men entered the living room, Mrs. Starhart was examining a piece of lacework that Mirabella had made and was commenting on the delicate pattern.

"Yes," Mirabella agreed, "and very difficult to do, if I do say so. It is an old family pattern, taught to me by my mother and passed down from one generation to the next. Oh, here are the men."

Sheila rose from her chair, and Mirabella took the lace away.

"I suppose you'll want to speak with my husband, now," she said. "You've been so patient all this time."

"Oh, my, no!" Mrs. Starhart said. "I'll not take the men from their work! An' you've been so nice to me. I know I'm a bother, interruptin' your chores, an' all."

"No bother at all, my dear!" Mirabella smiled and bowed. "I am pleased to have you. Only I must run along to see Mrs. Painmoor, just down the way. I told her I'd come before the day was out to collect some jam and apple preserves she set up for me. I'm afraid it is late. Won't you please stay the night?"

"No, no. It is very kind of you to offer. But I'll not hold my brother's business a single moment longer than necessary."

"I'm afraid we do have a long ride back to Janhaven," Mr. Furaman put in. "An' we'll be stayin' at my cousin's house this night, a few leagues up the road."

"Well, I'll take my leave of you then," Mirabella nodded. "I do hope things work out. I'm sure Robigor will do whatever he can."

"Would you like for me to tag along and help you carry things?" Sheila asked Mirabella.

"No. I'll only be bringing back a few things, I think. But, thank you for offering."

"Thank you again," Mrs. Starhart said as she gave Mirabella a little hug. "Good bye!"

"Good bye."

"I'll see ye later tonight, dearie," Mr. Ribbon said as his wife kissed him on the cheek. He turned back to the others. "Now, Mrs. Starhart! I'm sorry to keep ye waitin' for so long."

"Not at all, Mr. Ribbon," she replied. "I only wanted to have a little chat with you, an' ask you a few things."

Robby brought in another couple of chairs for Furaman and for himself. When they had settled down, and Sheila had resumed her seat, Mr. Ribbon turned to Mrs. Starhart.

"Now. What can I do for ye?"

"Well," Mrs. Starhart said, looking at her brother, who nodded her on. "I understand you're the mayor, now."

"Yes. That is so. Only until the next election can be held."

"Well, you know about the disappearance of my husband, Bob?"

"Yes, Ullin Saheed told us about it," Mr. Ribbon said. "An' I understand from yer brother that no sign of him has yet been found."

"That is so," she replied. "Them fellers he works with have scoured the countryside for two months an' come up with nary a hint. It's like he just vanished into air. An' then there's the matter of his horse, turnin' up in Barley, 'cross the river, ridden by a robberman. I hear tell that one of them robbers was a Dragonkind man!"

"That's right. Robby an' Sheila both whar thar when he was killed."

"Yes. So Miss Sheila, here, was tellin' me a bit earlier. Pleased to make your acquaintance, young man."

Robby nodded and took her hand in greeting. "Ma'am."

"Well, it's like this," Mrs. Starhart went on. "On the mornin' I last saw Bob, a man comes to the house sayin' he's got a parcel of letters needin' delivery to Duinnor. Now my Bob's a stickler for rules, an' he tells the man that no parcels can be accepted for Duinnor except they be weighed an' paid in the proper manner at the Post Station at Janhaven. An' Bob tells him further that, the next Rider goin' northwest warn't due to leavin' for a month at least. Well, the man gets all insistent-like, sayin' he's come all the way from Barley an' got no time for goin' to the Post Station. So he shoves a pouch of gold at Bob an' everthin', tellin' Bob to pay out the delivery an' to keep the rest. Now, I pressed Bob right off to do as the man said. I didn't care for the looks of him, a rough sort, shabby, with the smell of drink about him. An', anyway, it was a fair bag of coin, too, he offered. But, no! Bob wouldn't hear of it! 'Gots to be weighed proper' says Bob, 'marked an' sealed right,' he says. Anyways, the man kept after him, an' I did too, though now I regret it so!"

Mrs. Starhart had worked herself up into a tearful shrill and was now barely able to speak, so choked with sorrow she was.

"Oh, my poor Bob! I know he's dead! Dead on account of that parcel!"

"Now, now, Lally," Mr. Furaman went over and knelt by his sister, trying to comfort her. "You've got no way of knowin' those things."

"Oh, yes," she sobbed. "After forty years with a man, you gets a way of knowin' when somethin' ain't right. But he took 'em. Bob took the pouch of coin an' the parcel an' gave the man his word them letters would be taken over to Janhaven Post Station an' sent off to Duinnor. Bob promised to take it that very mornin'."

"Who was this man?" Mr. Ribbon asked.

"I don't know. Never laid eyes on him afore or since," she replied, wiping her nose with a handkerchief. "Tall, red-faced, farmer-lookin' sort. Greasy brown hair. Blue eyes. Stern lookin'. Didn't see no horse or wagon."

"What did he seem like?" Robby asked. "I mean, did he seem like he might hurt you if Mr. Starhart didn't take the parcel?"

"No," she answered thoughtfully. "Not like that, though at first I thought he might. No, I decided he was more nervous-like. Like in a great hurry. Didn't get all that calm when Bob took the parcel. Left in a big hurry, thankin' Bob an' all, like was proper, but in a big hurry. Bob left on Bandit soon after, goin' the other way up to the Post Station in Janhaven. An' that's the last I saw him! I knew he'd be gone a week or so, an' I warn't worried none at first. But after two weeks, I knew something was terrible wrong. I'm afraid the Thunder Mountain Band must've took him. See, Bob was born an' bred in them parts an' nobody knows them hills an' ridges this side of the mountains like Bob. Sometimes, Bob'd make a ride for the post down the west side of the ridge, along the narrow south road from Janhaven, see? An' he knew some place along where he could cut through an' over to the Old South Road from Passdale an' take up his route down at Newstone Ferry. Often it was, the Post men say, when dear Bob'd return along the Passdale road. Anyways, whether a hidden pass, or some ol' troll tunnel, Bob knew a short way through an' never wasted time or horse-breath."

Mrs. Starhart caught herself getting off track and waved a hand around at herself, shaking her head.

"I know I'm not makin' a lot of sense. But I mean to say that Bob rode off a long while back, before Midsummer's. Then Bob's horse, Bandit, turned up all the way over in Boskland, across the river. An' I asks myself, how did Bandit get across that river? An' in the hands of them bandits. I thinks they must've took Bob an' his horse somewhere south of Janhaven. Them fellers didn't come this way an' cross the bridge here at Passdale, an' I'm sure Bob was done in by 'em afore they crossed the Bentwide. Bob got to the Post Station all right, accordin' to the captain there, an' he was right away sent on out to make deliveries down south county-way, they tell me. So that means that them fellers what took Bob's horse had to cross the Bentwide either at Buckman's Ferry, or farther down at Newstone Ferry. Any farther south an' they'd a never made across to Boskland."

"Well, they didn't cross at Buckman's," Robby's father said. "That was the first place the Bosklanders rode, an' it is still unused. Been that way nearly a year, now. They went on down to Newstone an' didn't find anythin' out of place thar. That's pro'bly where they crossed, one by one, so as not to rouse any suspicions. The ferryman told Bosk several strangers, five or six, came through one at a time over the course of two days, all with horses or ponies. One roused 'em up out of bed an' paid a pretty penny to cross in the pouring rain, the day before the storm let up. Bosk figures that must've been the Dragon Man, lettin' the dark an' rain cover his looks. Mr. Bosk told the folks down thar what happened, an' they are all lookin' out for yer husband, in case he was made to show 'em the way. That's been awhile ago. An' none of us here think they were part of them mountain bandits. That is, we've never had any trouble with 'em before, an' it ain't like them to be this far east, much less to cross over the river."

"Hm," Mrs. Starhart huffed, then sniffed, touching her nose with her handkerchief. "So that don't get us nowhere. I was just hopin' you might cast some light on it for me. I suppose we'll never know what truly happened to Bob. But as them Post Riders thought so highly of Bob, him havin' been one for so many years an' even trained a bunch of 'em, they come to see me purty often. An' their wives an' children, too, to give me company an' to share me grief. Well, it's been let on that there's been some unseemly kinds hangin' about nearby the Post Station these last weeks. They hangs about a tavern up the road a ways from there, where the Post Riders take refreshment an' all. Anyway's they ask questions, sort of, proddin' 'bout the Duinnor post, an' about how folks might pay for sendin' parcels about an' so forth. At first, so I've been told, no one thought much of 'em. An' since one question would come from one feller, an' a few days later a new feller would show up an' ask another, an' then after a spell, some other feller'd show up askin' more questions, well, some of Bob's mates started gettin' concerned. The thing was, nobody put much to it at first, but then one of the Post Riders made a comment about it to another, sayin' how the stranger who bought him a pint was fancy-dressed in blue. Another Post Rider made mention of a different stranger, fancy-dressed in green with a feathered hat. Then, one after another, they all put it together that them strangers were all part of one and the same band of bandits so-called the Thunder Mountain Band, what are all so fancy-clad in their attire, they say. Well, as my brother can tell ye, Janhaven got filled with worry that some kind of raid was comin'."

"That's right, Robigor," Mr. Furaman put in. "I started keepin' my stockade closed up, an' the Post Riders put guards around their station for all hours. The thinkin' was that maybe they'd be after the gold an' silver paid out for deliveries."

"An', what tops it all," Mrs. Starhart continued, excitedly, "was that a new feller showed up. Different than the rest. Fancy dressed, too, but all in a western kinda way, not like the coats an' hats them others wore, but more like the garb of some of them Duinnor folk or Glareth people that come through from time to time. Anyways, so Mr. Calman, one of the Post Riders, told me this feller says he wanted to get back some letters that he sent out, and wanted to add some more notes to the bundle. Well, Mr. Calman was most adamant that any letters given over to the Post can't be given back. Well, then the stranger got all hot and insistent. Mr. Calman said things got all tense and heated, but when some of the other Post Riders came along, the stranger changed his tone considerably. Then he asks if the Station had any old coins they might want to trade out for new ones. Said he represented a collector, some great lord wishin' to remain unknown, who had a hobby of collectin' old stuff. Anyway, so the stranger said, any coin, silver or gold, from the last age or before, would be traded for twice its weight in like metal, regardless of condition. But Mr. Calman told the man to be on his way, that he'd not look to the Station strongbox at all."

"Oh! That's most unusual!" said Mr. Ribbon with a quizzical look.

"Aye, everyone thought so. An' the man made rounds all over Janhaven, an' he did, indeed, buy a few old coins some folk had, an' he showed 'em off to others. When he made his way back to the Post Station, he fairly insisted that the clerk there look through the treasury there for old coins. Which the boy did, but as there warn't any, the man went away. When Mr. Calman came along an' heard all about it, he roundly scolded the poor lad for letting on how much treasury was there, sayin' to the lad that he might as well have announced to every bandit in the hills there was a hoard sittin' there waitin' for the takin'."

By now, Mr. Ribbon had a confused look. Like him, Robby and Sheila also had trouble following what Mrs. Starhart was leading up to. Sensing that she was being rather long in her talk, she waved her hand about in the air again.

"Well," she went on, "now why would a person want old coins? I think it was only a way to be sure that his letters were sent out. I think the first feller was to deliver them for the second feller, but the second feller got it into his head that the letters didn't get to the Station, but he had no way to check on it an' see."

"Why didn't the man deliver his letters himself?" Robby asked.

"Why does anyone get someone else to do their errands?" Mrs. Starhart answered firmly. "Well, when I put it all together that it was about them letters given over to Bob that day, I decided I'd better take a look at them coin the man left. See, Bob didn't take the purse with him. He said he'd figure on weighin' in the parcel an' payin' out from his own purse, telling me that them coins the man left was far too much, an' the feller would probably be back for the change. So I went on an' fetched out the purse the feller left, an' that's what I've come to show you. Sure enough, they're all old coins, indeed. Old like what that second feller was lookin' for. An' no wonder they was the beginning of such bad luck all 'round! Look!"

Reaching into her apron pocket, she withdrew a leather purse and from it took out a large coin. "Have you ever seen the likes of this?"

She held it up for all to see. It was red gold, as big as a large plum with a green emerald set in the middle of it. So brilliantly did it catch the lamplight and flash it back with yellow and green glints that everyone in the room caught their breath.

"Oh, my!" Sheila whispered, sitting up rigid. A wave of fearful excitement shot through her body as vague, intriguing memories sparked in her mind. Confused, but fascinated, she glanced around to see how Robby and Mr. Ribbon were reacting.

"What kind of coin is that?" Robby asked.

"If I ain't mistaken, that's a Faere coin," Mr. Ribbon said.

"Then I was right!" Mrs. Starhart said to Mr. Furaman. "Bad luck all 'round, for any what owns one!"

"Oh that's just an ol' tale," Mr. Ribbon said, holding out his hand. Mrs. Starhart gave the coin to him, and he turned it over and over, looking at the intricate designs cast into it.

"The stranger, curse him, left us with a whole bag of 'em!" She emptied the purse of coins onto the little end table, each coin as brilliant as the next, each with a different kind of jewel as fine as the emerald in luster and clarity. Mrs. Starhart went on. "I knowed right away this here purse was what all the fuss an' strange talk was about. I just knowed it! An' as soon as I saw 'em, nobody had to tell me they was trouble. Alls I want to do is get rid of 'em. I was gonna bury 'em in a barrow, follering the 'structions given me by an old hag what lives nearby. She said they're blood money coins, from the ancient times, an' nobody but folk with Faerekind blood may have any good of 'em. Well, I didn't know, but I went an' asked me brother, here. But he says not to do that, not to bury 'em, that is. He says, 'Bring 'em to Robigor Ribbon. Ask him what to do.' So there. Asides from askin' you 'bout Bob, I come to ask if we might make a trade. These are all of 'em. Seven altogether. Each one with a different kind of stone in the middle."

"Mrs. Starhart," Mr. Ribbon said, passing the coin to Robby to look at. "I don't know how much they're worth, but I reckon more than I have in the house an' store put together! They're at least thirty-weight in gold."

Sheila, on the edge of her chair, eagerly watched the coin turning over in Robby's hands.

"An' each jewel by itself, why, I reckon to be worth more than the gold of all of 'em," Mr. Ribbon was saying. "I'm sure yer brother, here, could trade 'em down at one of the coastal towns for more than I could offer ye."

Robby held the coin out for Sheila to take, and she did so, grinning and handling it delicately. It was heavy, and the gold and jewel glittered fiercely. And, strangely, it was warm to the touch, not like metal at all.

"My sister will not permit me to carry them, or even touch the bag what holds 'em," Mr. Furaman shrugged. "Not even to make a trade an' be rid of 'em."

"I think they ain't gonna be done with me or my kin until they's good an' gone from us!" Mrs. Starhart uttered. "I ain't wishin' no harm on you, but since you're already touched, pardon me sayin', by the Faere, havin' Miss Mirabella as your wife an' all, I reckon you're as safe from harm as anyone might be. An' your prosperity's the proof of that!"

Mr. Ribbon glanced over at Robby, who was looking back at him. The realization from Robby's calm expression that there was no cat to let out of the bag only served to confuse Mr. Ribbon all the more. He saw that Robby was obviously acquainted with the fact of Mirabella's race. Robby said nothing, only smiled and raised his eyebrows at his father's awkwardness.

"Oh, I hope I didn't say anything to make offense!" Mrs. Starhart said, seeing Mr. Ribbon's strange expression.

"No, no," he said weakly, a bit red in the face. "It's only, I hadn't thought of it that way, is all. Don't look at things in that manner. An' I suppose it's been years since I quit puttin' stock in what folk say 'bout the Elifaen Faerekind," he said, glancing over at Robby. "But I still don't know what to tell ye 'bout these coins."

"If you'll take the coins off my hands," she proposed, "I'll take the goin' rate in trade for the weight of 'em, in plain Realm gold or fair silver, if you got it. If not, perhaps a credit for the amount against goods from your store. That would be more than fair, I'd say. But I'd ask you to tell no one how you came by 'em."

Mr. Ribbon looked at Furaman, who shrugged, then back at the coin in Sheila's hands. She handed it back to Mr. Ribbon, and he turned it over and over, thinking.

"Well," he said at last, "I believe I might handle that, though our stock of coin ain't great at the moment. Let's go see."

Agreed, they all went downstairs where Mr. Ribbon carefully weighed the coins, then he balanced a weight of gold coins out for Mrs. Starhart, then a fourfold weight of silver. This satisfied Mrs. Starhart very much, and she and her brother soon departed, leaving Mr. Ribbon, Sheila, and Robby staring at the seven artifacts laid out on the desk before them.

"They must be ancient," Sheila said at last.

"Beyond imaginin'," Mr. Ribbon said.

"From the First Age, you think?" asked Robby.

"I have no idear," said Mr. Ribbon. "An' ain't that the mystery of it! I know a little about Faere coins, only from havin' seen a few, a long time ago. But they was small, silver-like, with a little bitty specks of jewels or pearls in 'em. Never seen nor imagined great big ones like these here."

"What are you going to do with them?" Robby asked.

"Just keep 'em, I guess," Mr. Ribbon said, shaking his head. "I mean, thar ain't no place 'round these parts to trade 'em. It'd be a shame to melt 'em down or pull out the stones. Mebbe next spring, when we head up to Glareth to get ye to school, we'll take these along."

"They are like jewelry," Sheila observed. "Not like coins at all. They are just so beautiful!"

"You're right," Robby agreed. "It's kinda hard not to stare at them. Like watching a fire."

"Like all Faere craft," Mr. Ribbon said.

Robby looked at him in wonder. He had not confronted his father on his secrecy about his mother, but had instead let his mother tell him about her family, and now he understood his father's reluctance. Mrs. Starhart's fear and mistrust of all things Elifaen was common in this region, and, as his mother had explained, fear can sometimes turn into darker emotions and cause even good people to act badly. She also explained that her kind was not blameless, either, but did not deserve the shunning that many Men gave them. Now Robby understood that his father's desire was to protect his family from as much of that prejudice as he could. And if Mr. Ribbon did so by hiding much, so be it.

"I suppose I have a lot to explain," he said awkwardly to Robby. "But I see that ye know more than what's been learned from me."

"Mr. Ribbon," Sheila put in gently, touching his arm, "Robby knows about Mirabella. He was bound to find out. Everybody around here knows, and eventually he would stumble into it. Only, it would have been better for Robby if you had told him all along. Now he doesn't know how to act around folk."

Mr. Ribbon sat down on the stool, and, taking off his spectacles, nodded at Sheila.

"Yer a good girl, Sheila," he said. "An' kind to speak up for Robby. An' of course, yer right. Son, when I whar a few years older than ye are now, I saw yer mother for the very first time. My heart was hers, an' I bound meself to make her heart mine. I was raised by folk who whar like Mrs. Starhart, all full up with bad talk an' bad blood with the likes of yer mother's kinfolk. Well, long story short, Mira's kin didn't care much for the likes of me, though they always treated me proper-like. But Mira decided she'd be me wife, an' her folks didn't like that a bit. So she had to leave 'em, see? An' she came here to live in Passdale with me as her husband. Oh, what scandal thar was over that on every side, an' at first folks 'round here treated her most unkindly. An' some folk even stopped tradin' with me, for a while. Well, folks might've changed some since then, havin' lived around her an' havin' gotten to know her these years since. But I guess I never did change. I guess I still mistrust folk, fearin' they might go back to the way they acted before they liked yer mother so much. An' I didn't want ye to suffer such from what they might say er do."

"Daddy," Robby said. "I don't blame you for anything. But, you see, things have happened, and I've asked questions that Mother had to answer. She told me all about why you were so guarded against me knowing. But now that I do know some things, and want to know more, I can't pretend that I don't."

"Son, I tell ye," Mr. Ribbon said, putting his arm around Robby and pulling him close, "ye have some magic about ye that must've come from Mira's side. Ye take after her in more ways than just yer way of talkin'. Ye got a kind of spirit about ye that must've come from her side. An' hers is a fine old family, too, I want ye to know, with much honor in thar stories an' many a grief, too. Thar ain't nuthin' to be ashamed of, 'cept havin' a fool for a father. In yer heart ye should be proud of yer ancestry, though the days of glory may have passed away. I only ask ye this: beware of folk what smile kindly at ye but look for somethin' to hold against ye. Be proud of yer heritage, but don't flaunt it about. Keep it to yerself if ever ye can. An' don't hold it against the likes of folk like me, who are ignorant an' ordinary, with no charm, an' no glorious past to brag about."

The door bell jangled as Mirabella entered the store, carrying a bundle wrapped in linen and carefully tied with green ribbon. When she saw the three behind the desk, and Mr. Ribbon with his arm around Robby, she stopped.

"What's this? I thought the store was closed. Have Mrs. Starhart and her brother left already?"

"Yes, dearie," Mr. Ribbon said, grinning. "An' with a little business completed. Look here."

Mirabella put her bundle on a nearby table and walked around the desk, squeezing past Sheila. When she saw the coins lined up across the desk, she put her hand to her chest. Confused and wide-eyed, she looked at her husband and back at the coins. Carefully, as if she might break it, she picked one up and held it.

"I haven't seen one of these since..." her whisper trailed away as a prickly sensation ran up and down her back.

"A might uncommon, eh?" her husband beamed.

Mirabella looked at him, astonished.

"How in the world did you come by them?" she asked, her voice cracking.

"Ah, well, Mrs. Starhart had 'em," Mr. Ribbon said. "Why don't ye let Sheila tell ye whilst Robby an' I finish up down here. Meanwhile, take 'em an' put 'em in the upstairs strongbox."

Mr. Ribbon watched the two women depart upstairs, each caringly holding a few of the coins.

"I don't remember Faere coins being so large," Mirabella was saying to Sheila as they climbed the stairs, "nor quite so fine!"

Sheila noticed that Mirabella's hands were shaking as she suddenly stopped, and her expression changed from one of wonder to that of shock, her mouth open. Although it was only a moment, as far as Sheila was concerned, it was an eternity to Mirabella. She stared at the two coins in her hands, and she felt as if she was falling into them, growing lightheaded and dizzy. The prickly feeling on her back changed to a burning sensation running down her scars and back up, as if they were on fire. The glint of gold and the flash of the red ruby and the blue sapphire mingled with impossible memories, splattered blood and the terror of falling through a clear sky from dizzying heights—memories she had not had since being Scathed as a child, when her scars first formed. As on the night the Great Bell tolled, her ears rang again, but now the sound was mingled with wails of anguish rather than the sound of a storm. Then, suddenly, there came into her heart a paradoxical wave of terrible hope, contrary to all she felt. For a brief instant her mind's eye saw a figure, holding out the coins. His features, all but the broad white wings spreading from his back, were entirely indiscernible in the awful light that emanated from him. Like lightning, he was. With a crack, the vision disappeared as swiftly as it came. Stunned, Mirabella shoved the coins at Sheila.

"What is it?" Sheila asked as Mirabella hurried back down stairs.

Robby and Mr. Ribbon looked up from the account books as she hurried past to a shelf of ceramic jars.

"Don't mind me," she said as she grabbed one of the jars, removed the lid, and dumped the many packets of firesticks out onto a table.

"Mira?" Mr. Ribbon asked.

"I'll clean that up later," she said, taking a folded kitchen towel from another shelf and hurrying back to the stairs.

"Sheila. Here, would you be a dear and wrap them up in this towel?" she said, putting the towel down onto the stair step.

"Of course."

"We don't want to damage them, do we?"

Mirabella put the jar down, too.

"Put them in this jar. Yes, they'll just fit. Let's get the lid on, Sheila."

As Sheila put the lid on and latched the bale, Mirabella tugged a chain from under her blouse and pulled it over her head. "Come," she said, shoving the key dangling from the chain at Sheila. "Take the jar to the study. You know the strongbox there, in the corner?"

Sheila lifted the heavy jar as Mirabella ushered her upstairs and gently pushed her into the study.

"Yes, but I—"

"Lock the jar of coins inside of it, if you don't mind. I suddenly feel the need for a bath. Go ahead. Give the key to Robigor, when it's done."

Somewhat flustered, Sheila watched Mirabella hurry on down the hall.

"Would you like for me to heat some water?" Sheila called after her. But Mirabella did not answer. Almost as soon as the washroom door was closed, Sheila heard the sound of the pump handle groaning furiously and water splashing into the tub.

• • •

Robby and his father worked away far into the night, putting the final touches on the books and shelves and making ready for the following day, which was sure to be busy since everyone knew that a shipment of goods had arrived. By the time they had finished and were climbing the stairs, Sheila was already in bed, and they could hear Mirabella down the hall emptying the bath water into the drain. Mr. Ribbon went to the pantry and removed a bottle of wine and two goblets and poured for himself and Robby. The two sat down and drank in silence for a few minutes before Robby spoke.

"Daddy," he said, "I haven't been honest with you about a few things."

Mr. Ribbon looked up expectantly, took a sip of wine, and nodded.

"Ye mean 'bout what ye know 'bout yer mother."

"No. Other things. And it bothers me that I haven't talked to you about them."

"Son, I am as proud of ye as a father can be of any son. I can't say as I've had good reason to keep things from ye, so I can't say as I've set a very good example. I'll have to understand that maybe thar's some kinds of things ye feel ye need to keep from me. I guess that's the way of it with fathers an' sons, sometimes. I only hope ye know I'd do anythin' for ye, right er wrong. If what ye need is listenin', er if bein' in the dark 'bout things is what ye need of me—either way, I'm here for ye. An' if ye ever find yerself in any trouble, I want to help ye if ever I can."

"I know," Robby nodded. "But I'm torn. I don't want you to be in the dark, but I don't want to break faith with others who have asked me to remain silent about some things."

"Well, if bein' silent is the good an' right thing to do, then do it ye must, son. Ye must be the judge of that, yerself."

"That's just it. I think for now it is the right thing. I just wanted you to know that I've got a lot on my mind these days. It's just that I wonder, I wonder if maybe you could talk to Mother sometime. She knows some of what troubles me. Maybe she can explain better than I can. Anyway, I don't want you to think less of me if ever you find I've held back from you."

"Aw, Robby! Come here, son!" Mr. Ribbon put his arm out and took his boy into a great hug. "I think more an' more of ye ever' single day. I trust ye. Alls I ask is that ye come to me if ever ye need me. No matter what, I'll stand for ye."

Robby stifled a yawn, and Mr. Ribbon nodded.

"Now, off to bed with ye! I'll put these away."

Robby nodded and said good-night. Mr. Ribbon watched him go, swallowed the last of his wine, then carefully rinsed the goblets and dried them. As he put them away, he heard Mirabella slip out of the washroom and into their bedroom. Going into the hall, he hesitated at their bedroom door, then stepped across to wash his hands. Having done so, he was about to turn down the room lamp when he saw protruding from behind the tub a pile of clothes and towels. It was not like Mira to leave things in such a state. Then he saw a dark red liquid speck on the floor at his feet. Bending over, he touched it and held his finger close to the lamp. Going over to the pile near the bathtub, he crouched with the lamp, reached awkwardly around the tub, and tugged away Mirabella's blouse. It was wet from having been rinsed. Previously white, the back of it was now bright pink. Putting the lamp down, he pulled out the rest of the wet clothing and towels and carefully wrapped them into several clean ones from a shelf nearby and took them, along with the lamp, across the hall and into the bedroom.

Mirabella was in bed, the side table lamp unlit. He shoved the bundle under the bed, turned down the lamp he held until only the merest light glowed and put it on the table. He quietly undressed and gently slipped under the covers beside his wife. She was lying on her side, facing away. He carefully spooned her and put his hand on her waist.

"Yer havin' another bout with yer scars, ain't ye?" he asked.

"Yes. I'm sorry."

"Don't be. It is I who am sorry, me love."

He knew there was nothing he could do for her, but he mourned, anyway, for her pain.

"Ever since that night. The night Robby went out yonder to Haven Hill."

"Yes."

"An' it's gettin' worse, ain't it?"

"Yes."

"Do ye know why?"

"No."

Mr. Ribbon heard the clear note of uncertainty in that single word. And another note, too, almost a whimper, one not of pain, but of fear. He settled his head onto his pillow, his hand still on Mirabella's waist. The two remained awake, their eyes open to the dark for a long while until sleep finally overtook them, carrying one into dreams and the other into nightmares.

# Entr'acte

## Entr'acte

## Lost

It was on a beautiful autumn day in the Year 798 of the Second Age that a family made its way through a thick and happy crowd: two small boys, their mother, and sitting atop the father's shoulders, a little girl of no more than six with flowing scarlet hair. The girl understood only that this was some great festive occasion, having something to do with the Queen. Regardless of the event, she was happy to be with her family, merrily riding her father's shoulders with her hands firmly around his brow so that from time to time he had to push them up from his eyes. Although she had seen them before, when they came to the edge of the small lake and she saw again the five tremendous waterfalls at the far side, she was thrilled. The falls poured down from a dizzying height into a loud hissing spray of mist shimmering with rainbows. Though several hundred yards away, the falls could still be heard over the hum and talk of the crowds who gathered at the water's edge. Suddenly the noise diminished, the falls thinned to mere wisps of white threads, then disappeared altogether. At this, the crowds hushed, too, in wonder and awe. From far above, horns blared out. All eyes turned to gaze upward at the top of the sheer cliff from where but a moment before the water had spewed forth. There, at the very top, was a wall running around the edge of the cliff where the trumpeters blew their ram's horns. At the center of this wall jutted out two bird-like wings of stone that held aloft a platform reaching out over the precipice. A tiny figure appeared on the platform.

"There she is, Danig!" cried the little girl's mother.

"Yes," said her father, bending so that he could see, his hands firmly gripping the ankles of his little girl. "Do you see her, Mira?"

"I think so. She is so tiny! I thought she would be taller."

Her father laughed and removed one hand for a moment. Then he held up a spyglass.

"Here. Remember how I showed you to use it!"

Mirabella took the spyglass and held it up quickly, turning the eyepiece and moving the glass up and down in small sweeps.

"Oh!"

There was the Queen of Vanara, in a long, feathered robe, her breastplate gleaming as brightly as her winged helmet against the blue sky. Mirabella's father tried to remain as still as possible so that his daughter had little problem keeping her eye on the Queen.

"Oh, father! She is so pretty!"

Another figure appeared next to the Queen, and she turned to him.

"Who's that?" asked one of the boys.

"That would be her brother, Prince Thurdun," said Mirabella's mother.

"He's a great warrior," said the other boy.

"I know that!"

Mirabella watched as the Queen took something from the Prince, and, holding it up over her head with both hands, she turned, stepping right up to the precipice to face the crowds below. The object she held seemed to be an arch of clear glass, and Mirabella could see what appeared to be tiny dots set within it. Suddenly the sun caught the objects and they flashed. Within each golden flash was an even brighter glint, blue, green, red, yellow, orange, purple, and white. The crowds around Mirabella erupted into cheers and applause.

"What does she hold up?" Mirabella asked loudly over the cheers, trying to keep the spyglass upon the Queen even though her father was being jostled by the press.

"Those are the Bloodcoins of the House of Fairlinden," answered her mother.

"Her grandfather received them from Aperion himself," said her father. "She shows them to her people only once every twenty-four years."

"It is a sign and a token of our heritage," said Mirabella's mother.

"Oh."

The trumpets continued to blare as the Queen turned, the ancient objects held high to her people, glinting like stars in the daytime. Indeed, someone nearby said loudly, "Duinnor may have its five stars, but we have our Seven!"

Mirabella wondered why the man said that, but was distracted when, suddenly, five jets of water burst from the wall below and to either side of the Queen's platform, shooting out and descending through rainbow-lit air.

"And see?" her father said. "The Falls of Tiandari show the colors of the stones!"

With the resumption of the water's cascade, the cheers grew even louder than before. As the Queen disappeared, Mirabella lowered the spyglass, still watching the high platform thoughtfully. Her father turned to go.

"Come down for a time, Mira," her father said as he lifted her over his head and lowered her to the ground. "It's time for our feast!"

She handed the spyglass back to him, and he took her hand, following his wife and two boys back toward their carriage.

"Father, will she ever give them back to Aperion?" Mirabella asked, looking up at him.

He looked back down at her, clearly astonished at the question.

"Or are they hers to keep?" she asked.

Her mother glanced over her shoulder at her husband, smiling.

"That is not for me to say," said Mirabella's father. "And I doubt if anyone knows."

"Oh. Hm."

• • •

Three days later, as she was playing with a fawn in a garden wood nearby to their home, Mirabella was Scathed. During the following days, scars formed on her back, and her small body was racked with pain, her mind was tortured in a way that a little girl's mind should never be, by memories of blood and strife, and by fears of abandonment. She deliriously clawed her way to her bedroom window to leap out, to fly away into the sky, up beyond care and pain, away from confusion and sorrow. Her father and mother kept her from the window, of course, though she screamed in anger and disappointment while she tried to escape their clutches. She fought her father viciously at first, squirming and kicking and biting. But he held her firmly, though as gently as he could, putting his face against hers, their tears mingling.

After four days, she fell silent. Although Mirabella was now calm, her mother knew, and her father suspected, that the worst of it was only just beginning.

When the outward signs of her torture ended, and the scars of her Scathing were made permanent upon her back and shoulders, the subtle inward torture began. She was changed. As she matured into womanhood, she remembered much, more than her life contained, and her eyes would see more sorrow and strife than she had seen within any of her girlish nightmares. From time to time, she would put her memory upon that day, before she was Scathed, before the troubles of her life began, that bright blue day and those flashing jewels in the sky. Whenever Mirabella relived that day in reflection, and when she remembered the questions she had asked her father, she became uneasy. Even before she learned what those marvelous objects really were, she knew the answer to one of her questions. And when she learned that there were forty-two other objects like the seven that the Queen had held up, she knew the answer to the other. The seven belonging to the Queen were not hers to keep. But she would not give them back, even if she desired to do so, which she most definitely did not. So, like the Bloodcoins of the Queen, her people remained upon the earth, like living symbols of what once was. And her people, the Elifaen, were also like the other objects, the ones the Queen did not possess. Forever lost.

# Part II

# Chapter 12

## Sheila's Inheritance

### Day 30
### 215 Days Remaining

Mirabella rose even earlier than usual, hours before sunrise, and made breakfast. Since the aroma of coffee and bacon did not serve to rouse anyone—all else in the house continued to sleep soundly—she covered the dishes to keep everything warm, took a cup of coffee into the sitting room, and sat. She had intended to take up her knitting for a time, but instead found herself staring at the strongbox across the room and pondering the contents of the ceramic jar locked within it. Almost an hour later, when she heard her husband at last stirring, she shook herself and went to the kitchen to reheat breakfast.

Finally, Mr. Ribbon was able to stay at home for the morning, sleeping a little later than usual. As soon as he awoke, he fixed his mind on taking care of Sheila's business and to put it off no longer. Coming into breakfast, he told his wife of his plans, thinking that he would have to be at the Common House by noon, and that he would like to see Sheila as soon as she was back from a few early errands. Preferring to leave Robby with the store, he finished breakfast, took his coffee to the sitting room, and sat at his desk there, looking over various papers until Sheila arrived.

"Mira says you wanted to see me?" she said from the doorway.

"Oh yes, good mornin'!" Mr. Ribbon beamed. "I figured I'd better take care of yer business this mornin', 'fore too much time goes by an' ye thinks I'm forgetful er lazy."

Sheila chuckled at the idea of Mr. Ribbon ever having either characteristic.

"If you wish. I know you have been very busy."

"Let me just grab a few things, clear off some space, an' so forth," he said, pushing the papers aside. Standing up, he took from a nearby shelf a couple of ledger books, so common around this household, and two rolled-up parchments.

"Why don't ye sit next to me right here," he said, pulling up another chair for her.

She sat beside him facing the desk and put her hands in her lap attentively.

"Well," he began, "as ye know, when yer uncle Steggan died, nobody could find ye. In keepin' with the situation, an' accordin' to law, certain things needed doin', an' this is how they whar done. His remains, by the way, are buried in a field nearby to the property, an' his grave properly marked.

"First, the sheriff posted a watchman to look after yer uncle's place, livin' in a little tent in the yard (the house bein' unfit until it could be cleaned an' aired out, mind ye). An inventory of the house, barns, an' lands was taken by me an' the late mayor, along with witnessin' by Sheriff Fivelpont an' Mr. Bordy, a councilman. The next day, the sheriff posted a notice that if the property went unclaimed by rightful kin, it would be auctioned off. Meanwhile, any person who had claims on yer uncle had to show proof an' register at the Common House. They had a week an' a fortnight to do so. After that, all the claims were tallied up. The way it works is like this:

"After the auction, the county's expense is first taken. Then, if the amount left over is less than the claims, each would get a portion accordin' to the proportion of thar claim amongst all others. If the amount left over after county expense is more than would cover the claims, then all claims are to be paid out an' the excess put into trusteeship for one year. If no rightful kin makes claim within a year an' a day, the amount an' seven-tenths of any growth or earnings tharof go to the common treasury.

"Now, thar warn't much of worth 'cept the land itself an' the house. The acres got broken into parcels accordin' to what lay planted er built on 'em. This right here is the inventory: seven acres fallow, four acres corn, half acre beans (eaten by worms), half acre turnips, six acres barley (much stunted), fourteen acres wood, an' so on an' so forth. The contents of the house an' barn to be sold as individual bits, if fit for sellin' (I'm afraid all of the clothes an' linens had to be burnt, an' thar warn't much in the way of good tools er the like).

"Arkstan's tavern, the Rivertree, had the biggest claim of all (yer uncle bein' a powerful drunkard, as all know), an' me store had the second biggest, then the blacksmith an' sundry others. Now I won't go into all the biddin' 'cept to say that all were allowed to bid who could show coin er specie, includin' claims-people. I stood coin for them what wanted to bid but had naught 'cept trade goods to offer. So the land lots whar done first an', as luck would have it, several of the neighborin' farmers had in mind to increase thar acres an' so the bids went high against each other an' the land went for higher than was expected. Next went the sundries, an' finally the house lot, all of which didn't bring much. Still, all expenses an' debts got covered an' a modest amount was put in trust. Since I applied for an' was named trustee, it falls upon me to be tellin' ye all these things an' explainin' all this."

"I see," said Sheila, nodding as Mr. Ribbon pulled on his spectacles and glanced over them at her.

"Now," he continued, opening a ledger book and running his finger down some lines of orderly writing with amounts and sums at the end of each of the lines. "I managed to buy the house lot, which included the barn an' yards, along with many of the implements. 'Sides that, as trustee, I hold the amount equal to twenty-weight of silver, now increased by my business to twenty-two-weight," Mr. Ribbon turned the ledger book so that Sheila could more easily see, "gained by usin' the amount to buy stock an' resellin' as store goods. Here's the paper on the house," he said pulling over a parchment document, duly signed an' sealed by the Mayor. "An' here's the Trustee Charter."

It was likewise sealed and signed. Sheila looked at the papers and nodded.

"Yes," she said looking back at Mr. Ribbon. There was an awkward silence, and Sheila did not know quite what Mr. Ribbon was getting at.

"Thar yers now," he said gently. "All's we have to do is have the Trusteeship dissolved an', as I'm actin' Mayor now, I can do that an' have it recorded at the Common House. An' I've got a deed all made up for the house right here."

He pulled down another parchment and unrolled it to show her his signature, along with witnesses, under a statement assigning all rights to the property to one Sheila Pradkin of Barley for so long as she may live, and to any of her heirs as she may assign, et cetera, et cetera, and sealed with both the county clerk's seal and the seal of the Mayor of Passdale. As she looked it over, Mr. Ribbon reached to one side and drew out nine bags and counted out one hundred and seventy-six pieces of silver, each one-eighth weight. Sheila stared at the stacks in front of her. Twenty-two weight of silver was not much, yet it was more than Sheila Pradkin had ever seen, much less imagined ever having. In fact, she never had any prospect of owning anything, and had never thought twice about it.

"You must keep the house and the silver," she said at last. "I do not want them."

"But, Sheila—"

"No!" she stammered, her face contorted with conflict. "I want no part of that man!"

"I cannot keep the silver, by law," Mr. Ribbon said. Though he did not expect this reaction, he immediately understood it. "An' the house I only acquired for yer sake."

"For my sake? I do not mean to sound ungrateful, Mr. Ribbon," she answered sharply. "I cannot pay you for the house, even if I wanted it. And the thought of profit coming to me from that man, by any means, makes me sick!"

She clutched at the edge of the desk with her hands, as if to keep herself steady, and Mr. Ribbon smiled painfully and nodded as he put his hand on hers.

"It is not profit, dear lass," he said. "He took from ye more than all the lands an' silver could ever repay. An' it is not as a friend to yer uncle that I pass these things to ye, for he had no friend in this house. Ye must take these coins 'cause thar rightfully yers. A small amount of what he kept from ye all them years. Give it all away, er use 'em as ye wish. If yer uncle whar still alive, these things would do no one any good. But, at least with ye, they might. Now, I never knowed yer folk, never met yer parents, that is. But I went down to see Mick Tatty, the ol' ferryman down at New Green Ferry, 'cause the tavern keep said Mick whar kin to yer uncle somehow. Turns out that ain't so, but Tatty knew somethin' 'bout yer kinfolk, from bein' raised in the same parts way south, in Tracia, an' from some dealin' with yer uncle some years back. Tatty told me he heard yer mum died, an' then yer father took sick, or else got into some kinda trouble. Tatty couldn't remember exactly. Anyhow, he told me that when bad things befell them lands, yer father set up his stepbrother with the farm here in Barley, as a way of gettin' ye away, an' on condition that Steggan take care of ye, protect ye, an' keep ye safe. Tatty's still got kinfolk down that way, but it's a long way off an' he's not even sure of his own folks' situation anymore. An' he couldn't even remember yer father's name, 'cept that Pradkin didn't ring a bell to him. Tatty thought the fever took all yer folk like it did so many of his own down thar an' so many others in them parts. So, the long an' short of it is, I don't think nobody's left to make any claims on yer uncle or on yer own self."

He could see that Sheila knew nothing about any of that. Great, glassy pools formed in her eyes as she stared at Mr. Ribbon, and he sighed as his heart broke for her, and his soft, chocolate eyes stung, too.

"I am so sorry not to have made it me business to learn these things long ago," he said. "It is me own shame an' the shame of all us folk in Barley an' Passdale not to have helped ye. We oughta knowed, at least after a bit, that yer uncle was no good, an' it was right apparent how much he cared 'bout yer keepin'. I guess we minded too much of our own business. Anyhow, yer uncle warn't the only one what didn't treat ye fair, the shame of it on all us other grownups for breakin' our faith to the children an' our oath to the King. So now all this ain't gonna change the past, this here silver an' that run-down house out yonder in Barley, an' no one's to blame ye for cursin' us all an' wishin' us to soak in hell."

The dams holding back the pools in Sheila's eyes broke, and tears fell hard on her lap. Her breathing was short, and she kept swallowing but remained silent, now looking at Mr. Ribbon pleadingly.

"But mebbe," he went on, daring to glance back at her as she put her other hand on top of his and squeezed it between hers, "mebbe it'll help ye do without the likes of weak-willed neighbors such that we are."

"I cannot repay you for the house," she managed to say. "And I can tell you that I will never wish to live there again."

"What ye do with the house, then, can be decided with time," Mr. Ribbon said. "An' I'll be yer helper in any way ye'll let me. Perhaps we'll chat some tomorrow about all this, an' ye've had the time to sink it in, as it were."

• • •

Later that day, Sheila and Robby at last had a real conversation about things that mattered. They worked together rearranging items from the fresh shipment. It was fairly busy in the store, as it always was after new goods arrived, but, between customers and chores, they did speak.

"Your father has done me a great favor," Sheila said to Robby as she handed up some bolts of canvas to put into the high racks. "I mean, how he managed my uncle's property, and how he has passed all of that on to me."

"He has a head for business," Robby nodded, climbing down from the ladder. "And for doing the right thing."

"I suppose so."

"How do you feel about it all? You looked a bit upset for awhile this morning."

"I was. I'm pretty bitter about Steggan. How he treated me. The things he did. I still feel strange about it all. I mean, he is the last man I would ever want to give me anything."

"Even though he, among all men, probably owed you the most?"

"Yes, even though."

Robby pushed the ladder out of the way and rolled a keg of oil out of the narrow aisle and into the space where the cloth had been stacked.

"What am I to do with the place? I hate it! I surely don't want to live there. Those days I spent out at Tulith Attis, with Ashlord, there were times that I felt truly free of my uncle, free of that place. Like I never felt before. If it had not been for Ashlord's instruction to come back here with you, I don't think I ever would have. And if Steggan was still alive, I would have stayed away."

"I can understand that. But, look, he certainly is dead, and I for one am as glad of it as any. I mean, now you really are at last free of Steggan. So, don't you think this is your chance? Didn't you go to Ashlord wanting to make something more of yourself?"

"Yes, I suppose. But—"

"Well, now you have some means to do more. If you want to. To live a little more comfortably, perhaps. As far as the house goes, you can sell it, or rent it, a lot of things. You don't have to live there. And you don't have to decide anything right away. Maybe if Ashlord ever shows up, you can talk to him about it."

"Maybe. Maybe I'll sell it. I'm not sure I want to keep it. I'm grateful to your father, for all that he has done. I shouldn't have acted like such a child this morning. And I'm grateful to you and Mirabella, too, for putting me up here, and, well, for putting up with me."

Robby smiled.

"I can't think of another soul I'd rather put up with."

"You sweet man," she said tenderly. For a moment they shared eyes as they had not for months, drawing closer in heart, if not in body. The spell was broken by the sound of Mirabella's light footsteps on the stairs.

"Robby," she said, as she emerged around a shelf, "don't forget your errands."

"Oh, yes. I had altogether forgotten."

"Errands?" Sheila asked, her face resuming the steady but blank expression she commonly wore these days.

"Yes," Robby said, pulling off his apron. "The store agreed to pick up some pickling cider from Carth's farm. I'll need to go get the wagon from the livery and head on out there. Wanna come?"

"Oh! Well, no. I think I'd better stay. I promised I'd help put away things."

"It can wait," suggested Mirabella.

"No. I'll stay."

"Very well! I'll be back by supper!"

"Be careful!" Mirabella called after him just as several townfolk entered the store to make their purchases.

· · ·

The rest of the afternoon was busy. Between customers, Mirabella showed Sheila how to use the measuring scales and how to count out nails by the pound. Sheila watched carefully how Mirabella waited upon the people who came into the store, making each one feel at home and answering their questions patiently. Around mid-afternoon, Mr. Ribbon popped in for a bite to eat, took care of a few accounts while he ate, and then left again to do more mayoring. Business slowed to a lull, and the two women sat behind the counter watching the occasional carts roll by outside, each to her own thoughts for a long while. In one of the passing carts was Mrs. Greardon and her little boy, riding alongside a worker as they brought more lumber to the mill. Sheila watched her go by, and she could not help but wonder how the widow was coping after the loss of her husband.

"Mira," said Sheila at last, "I don't mean to pry into things that are not my concern, but what would you do if anything ever happened to Mr. Ribbon?"

Mirabella looked at Sheila thoughtfully. "Well, I would miss him terribly. But I would keep all of the memories I have of him."

"Do you think you would ever marry again?"

"Ever is a long time to some of us," Mirabella replied, knowing what Sheila was asking. "Until I met Robigor, I had no mind to ever marry at all. But I wanted to be with him, and when he asked for my hand, he had already won my heart. He knew what it was that he asked, but he asked out of his own heart and cared not for the dowry. He knew I would not age as he, and I knew that I would someday be parted from him just as I have been parted from others that were dear to me. Our lives are together, now, even if our bodies are apart. He is with me now, even as he goes about his work, and I am with him. And so we are bonded."

Sheila turned away, absently watching some workmen ambling along the road, their shovels and other tools over their shoulders, laughing with one another.

"What would become of me?" Mirabella mused aloud. "Would I ever marry again? Hm. I have met those of my own kind who have had many spouses over the years. But I do not know them well enough to know if they..."

Sheila turned back to Mirabella and saw by her creased brow that some profound thought confounded her. The Elifaen lady turned her green eyes searchingly to Sheila.

"I think that maybe love is not everything," she went on. "But maybe, in its many forms, it is what makes everything else bearable. And even the loss of the one you love may somehow be made less of a loss, if one may bear it. My mother died of grief over her sons. And I nearly sank into oblivion. The love of my husband and the love I have for him lifted me away from all that. I hope to honor his love—our love—by never sinking away like that again. I will not know if that strength is within me, shall I? Until faced by that circumstance."

She smiled at Sheila.

"But we are all still young," she said. "There is some bond between you and Robby, too, is there not?"

"Yes," said Sheila awkwardly. "Although I am not sure there ought to be."

"Why do you say that?"

"It is hard for me to explain. He has done so much for me. He taught me to read. You know about that. He taught me about other things by being my friend. With me he is...*gentle*. I don't know how to say it. I know Robby's that way with everyone, but especially so with me. I asked him not to tell anyone about us, but we have been secretly meeting and, well, favoring each other with our attentions for over two years. I made him promise not to tell. And he honored that promise, even though he argued and argued against it. I think he is braver than I am. When it comes to people, that is. But he and I are so different. And the closer we became, and the more I..., I mean, the more we grew to like each other..."

Sheila was now blushing as she struggled to explain. Yet she could not bring herself to say aloud to Robby's mother those things she feared most, that the Wild Girl would always be only that and no more. That Robby was too fine for her, too much of a gentleman for her. She faltered under Mirabella's studied gaze.

"Anyway," she struggled on, "to answer your question, yes, there is a strong bond between us."

"I have suspected something of the sort," Mirabella nodded. "And I suspected even more when Robby became so anxious over your whereabouts this summer. I overheard him questioning Billy about you one day when the boy came to fetch some tinctures for Frizella. I wondered why Frizella needed them since she is always so well-stocked. But Billy said no one had been injured on the farm, as far as he knew. There was your uncle's death, too, which alarmed everyone, even though his demise was a relief to some, I must admit. The day after Robigor and Robby discovered your uncle's body, Frizella came to town. She told Robigor and me about what your uncle did."

"So you knew all along I was with Ashlord?"

"Yes. Frizella cautioned us not to tell anyone, not even to send for you when it came time to dispose of your uncle's property. I hope Robigor managed that to your satisfaction?"

"Yes. He did, of course. But Robby didn't know?"

"We said nothing to him. We didn't try to prevent his looking for you, except to keep him as busy as we could around here. Frizella said it was what you needed. Time away. She said that Robby and you were very fond of each other and that Robby might question us."

"So you knew that he would find me when he came out to Ashlord's."

"Yes, but that couldn't be helped. There was no one else to go. We could not refuse Ullin. We only hoped that by then you wouldn't mind too much. I'm sorry if that was not so. But, as things turned out, I am grateful you were there, when Robby was in need. I only wish we had been more helpful to you when you were in need."

Sheila nodded just as the blacksmith arrived with more nails and hammers to deliver.

"Afternoon, ladies!" he greeted them heartily, dropping the heavy keg on the floor with a thud and putting the box of hammers on top of it. "Thirty pounds of medium nails. An' some fine hammers hot off the anvil, complete with sturdy ash handles."

## Chapter 13

## Robby Takes His Walk

Day 44
201 Days Remaining

For his part, Robby agreed with Mr. Bosk and thought a militia would be a good idea. The memory of how the intruders had fought, unhesitantly taking on more than four times their number, was still keen. And he remembered the Dragonkind, in particular, who had fought in the most ferocious way. A few days after Mr. Bosk's visit, Billy himself, on an errand into town to pick up a few things, came by to see Robby. Billy told Robby how the head of the Dragonkind, still piked over the gate, had become something of an attraction in the area. With typical enthusiasm, Billy related in the most gruesome terms that he could muster how the other heads rotted right away, turning black and pecked to shreds by crows, dripping with maggots, and filled with swarms of flies.

"But old Lizzerd just sits thar turnin' redder 'an scarlet with ever' passin' day," he said. "Not a bird er bug'll touch him, an' his teeth're sharp an' white. Folks come from all over, I tell ye, only to lay eyes on the sight! An' some from as far off as beyond Janhaven. I've been tellin' me ol' man we oughta take a pence for every sightseer, but he'll have nuthin' of it, sayin' it's good advertisement on what happens to bad folk what come marauderin' in our parts."

Billy was soon satisfied that these descriptions filled Robby with a similar morbid fascination as his own, though perhaps Robby was not as enthusiastic as could be hoped, and Billy was delighted to be able to share such disgusting detail with his friend. But, alas, he had to take his leave of Robby, pleading a short leash and saying that his parents hardly ever allowed him out of their sight since the flood.

So the days passed quickly, yet, to Robby, they did not seem to go anywhere, each day seeming very much like the one before. His wounds healed steadily enough, and since returning to Passdale he had not experienced any further fever from the bites. He no longer needed bandages, and he no longer felt any pain, though the scars might always be with him.

Sheila came and went, but mostly stayed nearby, helping Mirabella and sometimes Robby. Though he always looked forward to seeing her, they rarely had a chance to speak. He wondered how much his mother knew, whether Sheila or Frizella had since confided to Mirabella her true condition when she showed up at Bosk Manor that awful night. Robby was careful never to bring up the topic of the lost child with Sheila, for fear that it would just be too upsetting. As for whether and what Sheila shared with Mirabella…well, her business was, after all, her own.

As for himself, he followed his mother's advice and stayed busy, and he told his father no more after the night the strange coins arrived. He continuously pondered everything—Sheila, the Great Bell, the wolves, the stone soldiers, Ashlord—and in his scarce spare time, he mulled over his father's maps more than ever, read and re-read all of the books he could find of tales and histories, borrowing many from Mr. Broadweed.

Along with these activities, he had lately taken up the practice of going on long walks in the evenings after supper and before sunset. While Sheila and Mirabella washed things up, he would check the store one last time for the evening, and then, leaving by the back stairs of the house, he would cross their little backyard, cut along the path through the town wood, and then across the grassy Passdale Green, following the old trail up and into the hills behind Passdale. He usually made it to the top of Knarley Knob, about two miles west of Passdale, nearby to the broad, open ground of Wayford Common where the townfolk had many of their festivals. He would arrive on the heights overlooking the Common just as the sun was setting, or sometimes arriving just after sunset, now that the days were getting shorter. Sometimes he sat and smoked his pipe and watched the stars come out as he tried to think things over. Beyond Wayford Common below, he could just make out through the trees the lights of Passdale as folks lit their evening lamps and even, much beyond, some of the fields of Barley rising away in the distance. Most of the time, he looked west, where the not too distant Thunder Mountains swallowed Sir Sun's cape, turning the thin clouds of his hem first to pink, then rosy to deep purple as it receded, leaving shy Lady Moon, her face only a line of light from behind her fan, to follow her husband, allowing the evening stars to have their dominance over the coming night.

He knew that his mother and father worried about him being out after dark. They said as much, but they realized that Robby needed some freedom away from the store and time on his own. Rather than fuss, they only admonished him to be careful. Robby agreed that there was good reason to stay close to Passdale, after what he had been through. There could well be more unsavory characters about, perhaps the likes of those caught and killed near Boskland. And, too, there was the one that got away. These and many other things Robby thought about, and he wondered if his own behavior was one of denial, defiance, or foolishness. Perhaps, roaming by himself, alone and vulnerable, he was just asking for trouble, or even secretly wishing for it, for anything to break the pensive monotony of these days. Maybe he just felt a little crowded, with so much left unanswered, so much to wonder about. He came to no conclusions, puffed the little pipe that Billy had made for him, and pulled his cloak about himself. Like most nights, his thoughts covered the same ground, came to the same ambivalent conclusions, and circled back through the same questions.

"I'm just unsure of things, unsure of myself," he thought aloud. "Sometimes things seem so false, as if there is ever something more behind the covering, like one of those festival acts, a pretending, yet filled with ironies. Sheila is like a stranger to me, yet I have never before seen her so often or been so near her day after day. Daddy doesn't press me about anything, but I sometimes wish he would. Just too busy right now, I guess. Mother telling me to just be patient and lay low. Sounds a lot like Ashlord. Wonder what ever happened to him?"

He sighed and puffed.

"Never get to see Billy for more than a moment. No telling what he's been hearing."

Suddenly he thought about his cousin, Ullin.

"What would Ullin suggest? What would he say to all of this?"

He realized immediately that he did not know Ullin well enough to guess, yet there was something about the Kingsman that, once he had thought of him, persisted in standing out as some kind of example. Ullin seemed like the sort of man able to handle most anything that came along. He had to, given his line of work.

"He would tell me to prepare myself," Robby realized aloud. "He would tell me to get myself ready should something else happen. Wasn't Ashlord afraid of something else happening? Happening to me? Didn't he tell me to be wary, to be watchful and careful? So Ullin would take that to mean that something else very well might happen. He would tell me to get ready in case something did happen. In case, for instance, whoever Ashlord is worried about finds me out and means me no good."

Suddenly he felt ridiculous, as if having missed the obvious for so long, and he stood up, almost in a panic.

"Yes! I must be prepared to protect myself, if need be. I need to study and learn more about those things Ashlord mentioned. I've put on a stone at least since the flood. All fat, too. I bet I couldn't run home from here without bustin' a gut if my life depended on it. I bet I couldn't pick Sheila up and carry her to safety if need be. And, I know I can't fight. Don't know how. *I need to learn!*"

He tamped out his pipe on the sole of his boot and started off for home. He had gone only a few strides down the steep path when he stopped.

"But how?" he pondered. "How does one go about learning to fight except by being a rogue or by being a soldier or such? I can't exactly go about picking fights, can I? And even if I did, I'm not apt to survive long enough to learn. Up to now my record at winning fights isn't exactly one to brag about. I could ask Billy to help, but I'm not sure he knows much more than I do, though I dare say he's the scrappiest little guy I've ever known."

He took a few more steps in the gathering dim of evening and continued to muse, tentatively deciding to talk to Billy. He descended the hill through the trees, many still green with leaves in spite of the cooler days and nights, and now hovering like thick black clouds under the moonlit sky. At a bend in the path, he caught a glimpse of yellow light below, down on the road, and he immediately slowed his descent. Through the trees he saw another yellow light and realized someone was traveling along the road with lanterns. Easing farther down the path, careful of his step, he halted just behind a large tree at the last bend before the path came out onto the lane. Moving around the tree and crouching low in the brush beside it, he watched the approach of the mysterious lights, which he now saw were held up on poles. His heart began to thump at the sound of hooves and many footfalls in rhythm, and, as they passed beneath him, he saw the lanterns were carried by men on horseback, in gray buttoned jackets and black leather helmets, and that forty or fifty more soldiers followed four abreast, some of them also carrying lanterns. Behind them came a wagon, drawn by two magnificent oxen, pale gray with broadly spaced horns. The wagon itself had four great wheels, was painted yellow and green, and had many windows, though they were curtained. The driver sat on a bench high up on the front, and along beside him was an archer with a notched arrow. On the back of the wagon, two more archers were likewise poised and ready. The vehicle rolled along much more quietly than Robby imagined possible. In fact, the whole procession was most uncanny and quiet for its size. Not a word was spoken, and not a single sound of metal against metal did he hear, though he could see that their armaments, swords and shields, bows and lances, were prodigious.

Following the wagon was another group of soldiers and another wagon, smaller than the first with a curved roof and pulled by a single very large horse. Its pale blue curtains were drawn, lit from within, and Robby heard the gentle tinkling of a harp. As he looked, a hand pulled back the curtain, and a face peered out. It was the face of a lady. The light coming from behind made her yellow hair glow, and he caught the glint of a ring on her finger and another glint off the band around her head that held her hair back. Robby felt as if she was looking straight at him, and though he could not see her eyes, he was certain those eyes were fixed upon the spot where he crouched. A conflict of emotions swept through him, and he did not know whether he should run away or step forward. But neither was possible, as his legs, indeed his whole being, seemed locked by her momentary gaze. The curtain closed, the spell was broken, and he exhaled. The wagon continued on, followed by more soldiers and more riders bearing lanterns. It was not until they were turning the bend on down toward Passdale that Robby stepped out from his hiding place and onto the roadway. He waited until they were out of sight, then he followed, wondering who they were and why they were going to Passdale. He shoved his hands into his pockets and realized that he had dropped his pipe along the way, probably back in the bushes, and, annoyed at himself, he went back to look for it. After feeling around for it for a few minutes, he decided it was hopeless just as he touched something smooth under the leaves.

"Oh there you are!" he said, brushing off the pipe and shoving it back into his pocket where it belonged. As he turned to go, he heard a noise and instinctively froze, peering toward the road. The starlight was bright enough though the overhanging trees to illuminate a few patches of the road, and Robby thought he saw a great shadow moving along it. Straining to see, he heard the soft clop of unshod hooves and his heart beat a great thump when he saw the shadow again. This time he could not mistake the shape of rider and mount moving steadily along, and such a strange shadow it was! The rider was tall and erect in the saddle and completely black, save for white flowing hair, ghostly in the dim light. As he came up even with Robby, and entered another patch of starlit road, he saw the unmistakable hilt of a sword jutting up over the back of the rider's shoulder. Yet the beast that bore the rider was the strangest that Robby had ever seen. Like a huge deer, it was, with antlers fanning out wide and high, with scores of points. Never had Robby imagined that a deer could look so ferocious, and the uncanny sight made him tremble.

Then the rider stopped, just where the lady had opened the curtain, and, like the previous passerby, he looked in Robby's direction. The deer, if that is what it was, snorted. In this light, Robby could see the rider's face, pale and grim, with no sign of beard or whiskers, long thin white hair swirling in the breeze. He drew his sword from over his shoulder and laid it crossways in front of him.

"Come out there!" he called in a strong voice. "Or I will come bring you out!"

Robby slowly moved down out of the trees and onto the edge of the road.

"Closer! You are alone."

It was a statement, but Robby nodded.

"I, um, I dropped my pipe and was looking for it," he said pointing back into the woods.

"You don't have the looks of a spy," the rider said. "And clearly not a highwayman."

"No."

"You saw the train pass by."

"Who could miss it?"

"Aye, none but the blind and deaf."

The rider slid his sword back into its scabbard and lightly dismounted. He was actually not much taller than Robby, and his cloak swirled back as he stepped forward, revealing a glistening coat of mail bound with a jeweled belt. Now that he was closer, Robby could see pale blue eyes and a face that could be twenty or two hundred and twenty, and a small, childlike nose above thin lips and a sharp chin. His bare brow was high over his white eyebrows, and his face had a stern weariness about it.

"Forgive my caution," he said, "but it is my duty to ride behind the train. You are from nearby? I see you have no travel bags."

"I am from Passdale, just ahead of you there, and on my way back home after an evening stroll along the hills."

"Then let us walk on together. I am Thurdun, of the House of Fairlinden. Come, I must not get too far behind the others."

"I am Robigor," Robby held out his hand, and the stranger took it. "But most call me Robby."

"Robby. Aye."

They turned down the road, the strange beast following a few paces behind. Robby noticed there were no reins or bridle.

"I have never seen such an animal as that," Robby said. "Is it a deer? He's as big as a horse."

"I hold with the old ways," said Thurdun. "His name is Celefar. A buckmarl, they are called. They are not often seen in these lands, I expect."

"Then you are one of the Elifaen, one of the Faere People."

"Aye."

"But that train that passed. Were those soldiers your people, too?"

"Aye. Most are Men, but a few of my kind."

"And I saw a lady. At the window of the latter coach. Looking out."

"Aye?" Thurdun looked at Robby. "Then she most likely saw you, too."

"I felt so. Who is she?"

"A great lady from my realm."

"Oh. Where do you come from? And where are you going to?"

"We travel from Vanara on our way to Glareth."

"Glareth by the Sea," said Robby. "And you come from Vanara? I have certainly heard of that place. In the far west? As far as Duinnor?"

"A little more west and south of Duinnor Realm."

"You have come a long way, then."

"Aye. Let us pick up our pace a bit."

"You go to Glareth on business? To visit relatives?"

"You may not be a spy, but you are as inquisitive as one."

"Oh. Sorry."

"Aye, our business is to go a-visiting."

"To the sea?"

"Aye."

"We don't get too many visitors in Passdale. Not from far-off places, anyway," Robby said as they saw again the trailing lights of the train ahead.

"We will not stop in Passdale," Thurdun said bluntly, "nor tarry long on this side of Lake Halgaeth."

"Oh," Robby said. "In that case, my mother will be greatly disappointed, I'm sure. It isn't often that some of her kind pass through."

Thurdun looked askance at Robby.

"You are Elifaen?"

"No. I mean, yes. Well, partly. My mother is."

"Your mother? Then you are, too. Or will be if you do not yet have the scars. Of what House are you?"

"Ribbon."

"No, I mean of what Faere House?"

"I don't know. It is never spoken."

"Never spoken? That is a curse, surely, and a shame. Why might that be?"

"I don't know," Robby shrugged. "I think to fit in better around here. Maybe."

"Hrmph! But I am not too surprised. Our people are mistrusted in many parts."

Robby felt awkward as Thurdun gave him a disappointed glance.

"We know that some of our kind live in the Eastlands. That is why we came this way."

"Oh?"

"Aye. The easier way, the northern river passages through Duinnor are more or less barred to our people."

"I did not know that," Robby said.

"Do you know the place called Tulith Attis?"

Thurdun slowed the pace a little, keeping them a fair distance behind the last soldiers of the train.

"That place is near here," Robby answered.

"Aye."

"Do you go that way?"

"No, I thought we were near there, though the land has changed since the last time I came this way. I confess I have a strange longing to see that place again. And a dread to see the place where Heneil and Lyrium, his wife, lived and fought and died. But we go north, to the lake. Tell me. Have you ever seen it?"

Robby felt a twinge in his side where a wolf-scar ran.

"Tulith Attis? I have been there, yes," he said. "It is much in ruins, though the bridge still stands. Or it did when I was there not long ago."

"Hm. By chance do you know Collandoth, the Watcher, who is said to live near there?"

"The Watcher? Oh, Collandoth! You mean Ashlord."

"Aye, that is what Men call him."

"Yes, I know him. Do you?"

"Aye. It was he who prepared this way for us."

"Did he? You should stop and see him!"

"He is to meet us at the boats at Halgaeth Lake."

"He is?"

"Aye. Does that surprise you?"

"Why, no, not exactly," Robby replied. "Does he meet you in order to guide you to Glareth?"

"I think not. Only to speak with us, I think. Or so his messenger implied."

"His messenger?"

"Aye."

"A little bird, I take it."

"Do you make a joke?" Thurdun asked.

"No, I mean, it was a little owl, I warrant, by the name of Certina."

Thurdun gave Robby what might pass for a smile in better light.

"I believe you know Collandoth better than you let on."

"We're friends."

"Friends?"

"Well, he helped me out of a sort of jam a while back."

"Jam? You fell into a vat?"

"No, not that kind of jam. A problem. He helped me with a problem I had."

"Did he? Well, that is his way. A solver of problems and riddles."

"Sure," Robby said, trying to be nonchalant. "He's not a bad sort, you know. Once you get to know him, I mean."

Thurdun chuckled.

"I don't think anyone will ever truly know Collandoth!"

"Well, he is a private sort of fellow, I'll give you that."

"Aye and aye to that!"

"I wish I could come with you to the lake," Robby burst out impulsively.

"Why?"

"Oh, it's been years since I've been there. I'd love to see the boats. And to see Ashlord, too. It's been nearly six weeks since I last saw him. Oh, and to see the lake now that the wall has fallen."

For the second time, Thurdun stopped dead in his tracks, but this time he shot out his hand and caught Robby by the arm.

"What did you say about the wall? Do you speak of Heneil's Wall?"

"Why, yes," Robby stammered. Thurdun's grip was tight but loosened when Robby put his hand on Thurdun's. Meanwhile, for that brief moment, the look on Thurdun's face was either excitement or terror—Robby could not decide which.

"It has fallen?"

"Yes. The River Saerdulin runs again in its ancient course. The Bentwide is drying up to a little stream."

"When?"

"Since the storms and rains, about six weeks ago."

"Hm. Six weeks ago?" Thurdun turned away, thinking. "Six weeks, upon the full moon?"

"Yes, it was," Robby replied.

"The River Saerdulin." Thurdun shook his head. "Surely Collandoth knew."

"No, I don't think so," Robby said, not quite following the concern of Thurdun. "I mean, I don't think Ashlord knew ahead of time that the floods would come and wash away the wall."

"Don't be silly!" Thurdun shook his head at Robby. "Why do you think he has stayed at Tulith Attis all these years? He is the Watcher of Things, the Knower of Change. He surely knew something of the sort would happen. Maybe he did not know just when, or even precisely what would happen. He is a Watcher, and Watchers know what it is they watch for when it happens. And I tell you this: Heneil built his wall well, just as the bridge and Tulith Attis itself. Nothing built by his hand falls, save by treachery or design. The wall was meant to yield, and the river meant to find its old course. Such things that are unclear to us are studied by Collandoth. Six weeks ago. The night of the great storm in the sky when we were upon the open Plains of Bletharn."

Thurdun walked again and Robby strode alongside, listening.

"We had already made camp for the night. The lady I escort felt, as I did, a great thunder in the ground, and it roused us from our sleep, she in her wagon and I in my tent. All others slept, but we woke with fear and dread upon us. The rain fell hard, and the wind tore at my tent, but when the second great rumble came, I was on my feet with sword in hand and flew out into the night. In the east, I saw a great storm, bruising the horizon with its twisting flashes. Those of our company stirred from sleep, and our mounts were nervous. My lady appeared, frightened as I was, bearing her sword, and at the third rumble, she flew to my side, and we stood together against any enemies that might come. Awakened by the uncanny and loud rumble, our comrades raced to join us, and the alarm went through our camp. My lady and I had our eyes fixed upon the fire-flashing sky in the east, and we felt a terrible urge to run toward the storm and into it! I do not know how I resisted, but I did not answer the call. The rest of our party gathered around us, likewise with swords and lances in hand, with equal alarm. They ran to us and encircled us against whatever may come amidst the noise and blinding crash and wind. As if within a dream, unable to speak, we stood there drenched, watching the eastern heavens burn with lightning, red upon the horizon. For a long while, we trembled, cold and wet, and with fear in our hearts."

Thurdun glanced at Robby.

"Finally, shaking myself, I cried out an alarm and blew my horn, recalling all of the outlying sentries to take up places for our defense. We kept vigil the entire night. But only the wind and the rain entered our camp."

Although Thurdun spoke deliberately and slowly, he walked at a fast pace, with Robby nearly jogging to keep up.

"It rained for the next ten days without relief. But no one in our camp mentioned the sound that my lady and I heard, and we have pondered over it with each other ever since. So it was the falling of Heneil's Wall! What a crash it made!"

"Yes, here the storm was terrible, and some windows of glass were shattered, and homes and fields destroyed, too. Except," Robby shot a nervous look at Thurdun, "it wasn't the wall coming down that you heard."

"What was it, then?"

Robby looked at Thurdun.

"The thing that made the wall come down, and let loose the penned up waters of the lake."

"What thing?" Thurdun asked hesitantly, as if he had some suspicion already.

"Will you swear an oath to me that you are to meet Ashlord? That you are his friend and that you will ask him the questions that you would otherwise put to me if I tell you what it was?"

"I am his friend, if any he has," Thurdun said sternly. "And in his debt by honor, too. I promise you this is the truth, upon my mother's honor."

"And you will ask me no more questions concerning this, until at least you have spoken with Ashlord? And will speak of it to no one but him from now until you meet him? Not even to the people you escort?"

"Aye! Aye! I swear! The mystery of it has made many sleepless nights for me."

"Well, the knowing may not give you sweet dreams, either," Robby said. "But what you heard was the tolling of the Great Bell of Tulith Attis."

Thurdun stopped and looked hard into Robby's face with an expression of disbelief turning to dismay. His mouth opened, but no words came to him for a long moment. Celefar stamped the ground and Thurdun looked down the road where the lights of the train were disappearing around a bend. When at last Thurdun did speak, it was in a foreign dialect, like the one the stone soldiers used, but Robby did not understand his mutterings. He began walking again, somewhat more slowly.

"I will have much to ask Collandoth!" he said in the Common Speech. "I beg thee, allow me to tell one other, the person I escort. She still frets over that terrible night, and has since striven to divine the meaning of what we heard and saw. She would be relieved, in part, to hear this news. At least, I hope."

Robby almost regretted having spoken of the Bell, but the earnestness of Thurdun touched him.

"Very well. But only her."

"Thank you. And I will honor my word and speak nothing of these things to anyone else until I see Collandoth. I think there is much else you could tell me, and why you will not, I will not venture to guess. Dark days are upon us, forsooth! But perhaps some light will come into them, too."

He managed a smile, actually a very light, airy, joyful smile, and he patted Robby on the shoulder, almost laughing.

"Enough of such things! How dour you are, with uncanny words and news. No wonder my lady felt you nearby and peeked from her window!"

"I don't know what you mean!"

"How far is it to Passdale? To the road that leads to the lake?"

"Less than a furlong to the crossroad and to Passdale itself. This is the smithy up here on the left."

"I have a duty to perform," Thurdun said. "I must find the mayor or the chief magistrate of this town and speak with him. I will catch up with my company afterwards."

"Why?" Robby asked, suddenly a little more nervous. "I mean, if you don't mind me asking."

"A formality," Thurdun sighed. "It is the law of this realm that when my people pass through the territory of any town, we must report to the chief magistrate, ruler, or watchman of that town. And to pay a toll."

"Oh. Well, the Mayor might be at home by now, but I can take you to the Common House where meetings are taking place. If he is not still there, then to where he lives. I doubt if there will be any toll."

"I would be thankful if you could show me to him."

"Have you had to pay many tolls?"

"Yes, quite a few. We started out with seven wagons of our goods and have now only one left, and the van."

"You have been traveling very long, I suppose?"

"We left our homeland when the last snow had melted."

"That must have been, what? Six months ago?"

"Nearly. And full of troubles all along the way, one after another. We have been delayed by bandits, feuding warlords, rains, and other business. We have buried six of our company, too."

"Oh, my!"

"We long to be at the end of our journey."

"When will you return to Vanara?"

"I cannot say. We have much to do in Glareth. Among other things, we go to find new homes for our people whose lands are no longer safe. Many Vanarans have given up their lands along our southern borders with the Dragonkind and have left Vanara. Much of their land has been given over by lease to Duinnor who does not care to use or to protect those lands as we would. The Dragonkind to the south of my country take advantage of these weaknesses, and they encroach upon us, ever testing our strength of arms. Duinnor, though it holds a stake in our security, does not help Vanara as it did in the past. Glareth, though far away from our home, remains a friend to Vanara and has welcomed many of our people. Collandoth may tell you more, if you see him. I do not wish to speak further about it just now."

"It is just as well," Robby said, "because there is the Common House, yonder."

He pointed left at a large stone and wood building with a high arched roof and an expansive portico likewise of wood and stone that stretched across the front and sides of the building.

"I did not expect to see such a fine structure in these parts," Thurdun said.

"Yes, I suppose it's something, isn't it?" Robby nodded. "It was built hundreds of years ago, my dad tells me, but it fell into ruin. It was restored some while back, before I was born, and has been our place of government ever since. I see by the lights that the Mayor is still there. The braziers at the end of the steps are only lit when the Mayor is present in the building, day or night. I don't know why. Tradition, I suppose. Seems a waste of good oil to me."

"Traditions are not all bad," Thurdun said, turning toward the walk that led to the steps. "I bid you a good night."

"Would you mind if I came in with you?" Robby asked. "I know most of the people around here, and I am on pretty good terms with the Mayor. I might be helpful to you."

"Very well," Thurdun said. "Celefar! Caes far lo en ian cavad!"

His mount snorted in response and turned to the wood nearby.

"It is probably better for him to hide himself until we finish," Thurdun explained. "No sense in attracting undue attention at this hour."

"I agree," Robby said, pushing open the great oaken door. "Come on in!"

Inside was a fair-sized vestibule, brightly lit with glass lamps that hung from the arched ceilings. There was an old mural on one wall, depicting the labors of the seasons in ancient times, a few portraits hung here and there, and straight before them through a set of open doors was the Common Room. Sagwist, the old man who tended the building and the grounds, who lit the lamps and snuffed them out when it was time to do so, who swept and cleaned and maintained the place, and who had done so since before anyone could remember, was now sitting on a stool just inside the door, half dozing in his present role as doorman. He felt, more than heard, Robby and Thurdun enter and roused himself by lifting his ancient head from his chest where his chin had been resting in the nest-like pillow of his fuzzy white beard that seemed to grow in every direction but downward. At the sight of Robby, he nodded, then, seeing Thurdun, he unfolded his arms and slowly stood, his mouth open in surprise. The old man said nothing, and only stared intently as they passed by and sat on one of the benches near the back. Thurdun pulled his cloak around him, his head down under his hood, while Robby sat up straight and listened to the goings on.

Mr. Bosk was standing and addressing the council, seated behind a long table at the far side of the room. Mr. Ribbon sat at the center of the table, facing Mr. Bosk, listening to him. When he saw Robby, father and son exchanged nods, and Mr. Ribbon lowered his head slightly to look over his spectacles at Robby's companion. Other than a barely perceptible movement of Mr. Ribbon's brow, he gave no expression of interest and turned his eyes back to the speaker.

"An' so it must be decided," Mr. Bosk was saying, "whether to raise a militia. The longer it is put off, the greater the danger. Boskland cannot protect all of Barley an' Passdale, too. We are too few."

"It is not that it ain't a good idea," one of the Passdale men replied. "But at what cost to the treasury? Since the floods, we've spent much on road an' bridge repairs, an' thar's little left."

"You know it is our law," another broke in, "that we purchase one bushel of grain for storage for each family of Passdale, for emergencies and as a guard against famine, and that much of our store had been depleted already. What's more, the flood has destroyed enough of the crops that prices have gone up. Until the Counting, we will have no more in our treasury. How are we to pay for arms?"

"And who will serve?" another chimed in. "All are busy with their own business."

"And who will they serve under? Who will train them? How will they be organized and dispatched?" asked another.

"I'll see to the trainin'," Mr. Bosk broke in. "An' I'll contribute twenty-five men, with all thar equipment, plus another twenty-five as relief. As for the arms, we have two blacksmiths, one here in Passdale an' another at Boskland, who are more than capable of turnin' out most of our arms. More we can get from Furaman as we have the means. An' thar're several around, such as Sheila Pradkin, who can train archers."

"But at what cost? Should we raise the taxes? What of the King's Share? We still have to raise that."

Robby's father remained silent, a concerned look on his face, listening to the others.

"Why not use the King's Share for this?" said a man at the other end of the table. "After all, thar ain't been a King's Company in these parts since last year, an' they was only passing through. What good's a King if he don't offer protection?"

"Maybe he don't think we need protectin'."

"Protecting from what?" said another adamantly. "I still don't see the threat. One lone band of rogues and we're all in an uproar. And that was weeks ago!"

"An' one of 'em's still out thar!"

"Oh, he's long gone off by now!"

"Gentlemen!" Robby's father finally spoke. "It is late an' we're gettin' nowhars. It is a fact that our sheriff is too short-handed to keep a patrol up all over the county. It is also a fact that four riders came unchallenged into our county, killed at least three people, looted an' sacked two farms, an' caused other disturbances before finally bein' stopped. It is also a fact that one of 'em is still unaccounted for, an' we ain't had the folk er resources to search for him."

"Let me remind ye," Mr. Ribbon went on, "that the recent floods left us damaged, true. But not so bad off as folk in the surroundin' lands. Now it stands to reason that we're gonna be seein' some bad conduct on the part of them folk from them parts, an' it's a fair guess that they'll be comin' into Passdale an' Barley as thar own situation worsens durin' the comin' winter. It seems like a good idea to me to raise a militia, askin' for volunteers to trainin'. Furaman, over in Janhaven, surely has some arms to spare in the short while, an' I can see to it we get 'em at a fair price. Meanwhile, I say, let's get our volunteers, an' provide for an allowance for feed an' billetin'. Let's see whar that gets us, I say. If it don't work out, we can come back an' see 'bout the treasury."

"Hear, hear!"

"All that say aye, say aye!"

There were many ayes from the table.

"All that say nay, say nay!"

There were a couple of feeble nays.

"Aye's have said!" Robby's father pronounced. "So let it be written an' signed. When all have signed, we will adjourn."

"Good! I'm ready to go home!"

"Me, too."

"Aye, to that!"

"Very well, Mr. Secretary, please present the adjournment papers."

Mr. Jarn, the secretary, got up from his side table and laid out several large parchments on the council table. The councilmen lined up to sign their names to each sheet upon which was written the various decrees or decisions made that night. When they had done so, Mr. Ribbon stood and went around to the other side of the table and placed a wax seal on each one, adding his own signature.

"We are adjourned!"

As the group left by the nearby side door, talking and discussing the plans for the militia, Mr. Ribbon rolled up the various papers and parchments and sealed them in leather tubes for storage. He gave them to Mr. Jarn who left as well. As Mr. Ribbon gathered other papers from the table, Sagwist walked up the aisle between the benches to the front and stood respectfully behind Mr. Ribbon for a moment before clearing this throat.

"If it pleases yer honor, here's a visitor," he said, bowing slightly as Mr. Ribbon turned around. When Mr. Ribbon saw Robby approaching with the stranger, a look of puzzlement came over his face. Thurdun pulled back his hood and enough of his cloak to walk more comfortably, thus revealing his resplendent mail, covered in part by a blue and green surcoat, with gleaming jeweled buckles on the belts around his waist and the clasps on his shoulders. Robby could see that Thurdun had stiffened his attitude and surmised that he was preparing himself for any amount of haggling about the toll. In the light, he looked as stern as a person could, his fair skin and white hair making him seem somewhat otherworldly. Thurdun stepped forward to greet the Mayor, but Robby cut in front of him.

"I have the honor of presenting to the Mayor of Passdale," he said, trying to be as formal and officious as he could, "Thurdun of the House of Fairlinden, recently of the land of Vanara in the west."

Robby's introduction surprised Mr. Ribbon even more, but no more than it did Thurdun when next Robby turned to him and said, "May I present the Mayor of Passdale, Mr. Robigor Ribbon, my father."

The two men looked at Robby, who could not refrain from grinning as he looked from one to the other.

"Welcome to Passdale!" Mr. Ribbon finally said with a bemused smile, offering his hand. "I see ye've met me son."

"Thank you. Yes, I have," Thurdun glanced at Robby a bit suspiciously, then gave a slight bow and took Mr. Ribbon's hand.

"I hope ye ain't traveled all this way just to see me?"

"I'm afraid not. I am merely passing through, with a party of my kith and kinsmen."

"Ah," Mr. Ribbon nodded, smiling. "I hope me son has not made a pest of himself."

"Oh, no," Thurdun said. "I have been more the pest, for he has delayed his way home to show me to you."

"Oh?" Mr. Ribbon continued smiling, waiting for Thurdun to continue. After an awkward silence, he asked, "Well, is thar anythin' I can do for ye?"

"I am here for you to collect the toll from me for the passing of my people."

Mr. Ribbon looked over his spectacles at Thurdun.

"Pardon me?"

"The toll to be collected of me. We are Elifaen of another realm."

Mr. Ribbon glanced at Robby, who shrugged.

"I'm sorry," Mr. Ribbon said to Thurdun, "but I know of no toll due. We ain't collected tolls for any roads er bridges in these parts since I was a little'un."

"There must be some misunderstanding," Thurdun stated. "Our people are charged with paying a toll to each town and village we pass through, and to each principality, too. So says the writ I bear here."

He reached into a side pouch, removed a small scroll, and handed it to Mr. Ribbon who unrolled it and studied it for a moment.

"It says here, if I can make out this gibbery script, that the Prefect of Duinnor, let's see, 'decrees for the passage of any Elifaen of the Realm of Vanara a toll of the choosin' of each community an' shire.'"

"Aye," Thurdun said. "And to be reported to the King's representative in Glareth Realm upon our arrival by my records of such."

Mr. Ribbon turned and walked back to the table, took up a quill and dipped it. He made a quick scribble with a broad flourish and tossed aside the quill. Turning back and whipping off his spectacles, he reapproached, rolling up the scroll.

"Yer toll is paid in full by the honor of yer visit," he said flatly, handing the scroll to Thurdun. "Though it seems a bit outrageous to me that a feller can't travel the roads without every penny-squeezin' magistrate from here to the settin' sun bein' given the right to rob a feller! Why in heavens would such a decree be made?"

"To keep our people from leaving our lands," Thurdun said. "For the more of us that leave, the fewer there are that can be bound over to service for Duinnor."

"Huh? Ye don't say! Well, I dunno 'bout such things," Mr. Ribbon said. "And I ain't all certain Duinnor knows what's best, sometimes."

Thurdun smiled.

"Then we are free to pass through to Lake Halgaeth?"

"By all means! Though me wife would sorely like to meet ye, I'll warrant," Mr. Ribbon said. "She's Elifaen herself, an' she don't get much chance to see the likes of her own kind."

"Twice invited," Thurdun said, "and, regretfully, twice refused. Your son made the same offer of your hospitality earlier, and I should have known then that we had entered a different kind of land. I am much honored by your treatment of me and will not forget it. But I must away to catch up with my train, so I cannot tarry."

"Not every Man is unkind to the Elf," Mr. Ribbon said. "Even in these parts where much discord twixt Men an' Elifaen came about."

"Yes, forgive my presumptions," Thurdun bowed slightly. "But it has been our rare experience to meet with such understanding outside our own realm. As I said, we will not forget Passdale in Barley!"

It was Mr. Ribbon's turn to bow. "Then it is we who're honored, sir," he said. And then to Robby, "I reckon it's time ye got on off home, Mr. Big Britches."

"Yes, sir. Are you coming, too?"

"It'll be a bit longer 'fore I come, son. A few things to put away an' to see to. Tell yer mum I won't be too long, though."

"I, too, will go," Thurdun said giving Mr. Ribbon his hand. "I may see you again, if fortune favors. Thank you."

"Good journey to ye!"

• • •

Robby walked Thurdun out while his father finished up the paperwork. Thurdun made a clucking sound as they came down the steps into the yard of the Common House, and Celefar immediately emerged from the shadowy trees across the road and approached.

"I wish we could talk more," Robby said. "And that you would tell me about the westlands and your people."

"It would please me greatly to do so," Thurdun smiled, rubbing Celefar's head, "and I am honored by your curiosity. I will tell you this much, at least: We are only the beginning, I fear, of the latest scattering of my people. Our long wars with the Dragonkind and our strife with Duinnor have made us weak and our lands unsafe. Others may follow us, and some may pass this way. When next you see Collandoth, he may tell you more; he knows our ways and our story as well as any and is counted as a friend to us as well as to the race of Men."

"He is not a Man?"

"What do your wits tell you?" Thurdun chuckled. "Have you spent so little time with him that you have not noticed the oddness of his ways?"

"Well, yes," Robby said, "come to mention it. He does have an uncanny way of not sleeping and of moving quietly among timid animals and such. And he seems to know a lot about strange things."

"Perhaps you have never heard of the Melnari? He is one of them, neither Man nor Elf. Few of his kind have ever walked the Earth."

Robby shook his head.

"This troubles you, I can see," Thurdun went on. "Let me assure you that if he is your friend, you could have none better."

Thurdun mounted Celefar and reached his hand down to Robby.

"I am pleased to have met you, Robby Ribbon of Passdale."

Robby shook hands, and said, "Good journey to you, Thurdun. I hope your people find peace."

"Thank you! Celefar! Los es co aff!"

At his command, Celefar turned away from Robby and carried Thurdun down the road. At a word from Thurdun, Celefar turned and halted.

"One more thing about Collandoth," he called back to Robby. "It would be wise to heed his advice, should he give it. As my people have sorely learned, to do otherwise is perilous. Farewell!"

Celefar and Thurdun turned away once more and almost silently bounded away into the shadows of the road until the night's darkness swallowed them completely. Robby watched for moment longer, then turned and walked toward home, the longing to follow Thurdun strong and mysterious in his heart. As he turned down a lane, he heard the blacksmith's anvil chiming mildly across the town. Walking past the weaver's house, the rhythmic knock of a busy loom tapped out from behind yellow-lit windows. Across the way, gruff laughter came from inside the little alehouse, and he thought how mundane it all was to him, how ordinary and safe-seeming, unchanging. It was comforting in a way that he did not want to be comforted. These thoughts filled him with nostalgia, for so much was lost to him now, changed within him. He no longer saw the same sights with the same eyes or heard the familiar sounds with the same ears. The very air he breathed seemed changed, yet it was all the same. He knew the changes were within him; he felt restless to be away, and he did not care very much where he went. A deep melancholy suddenly settled over him, and he thought of the harp playing from the caravan, and the face at the window. His mind wandered to the strange statues deep within Haven Hill, to the stern faces, fair and grim, of the stone soldiers. Suddenly, a phrase came back to him, part of something that Ashlord had said, interrupting Robby's thoughts and jarring him back to more sober contemplations:

*"There is a brooding one...."*

The memory of Ashlord's cryptic warnings brought Robby's thoughts back to where they were earlier, before meeting Thurdun. Turning to take a shortcut through the wood toward Passdale Green near to his house, he wondered again about how he might contrive learning to defend himself in case Ashlord was right and someone did come after him. Just before coming out of the trees, and before coming to any firm conclusion, he was distracted from his thoughts by a movement in the open Green ahead. He stepped cautiously into the shadow of a tree trunk and caught his breath.

A lady walked there, just a few yards away, her head down and her hair glistening in the bright starlight, a braided headband of her own hair flowing down over her shoulders. She wore a dark gown, embroidered with silver that glinted, flowing lightly behind her bare feet in the dewy grass. She hummed a little tune to herself as she reached down and picked some snow-stars, making a posy of them as she went along. She lifted her leg, kicked out into a dance step, and whirled around with her head up to the sky and her arms outstretched, offering her bouquet to the stars. Her body curved gracefully, as only a woman's body can, and she giggled with mirth. Robby, remembering the lady in the window of the caravan, wondered if one of her party had become separated, or if some group of them stayed behind, for he had never seen anything, or anyone, so exotic or beautiful. He could not have been more attracted to her, nor more self-conscious of his attraction, had she been completely nude, yet he was in awe of her beauty and grace as she neared his hiding place. He wanted to make himself known to her, and wanted to know who she was, but dared not move for fear of upsetting this vision before him. Suddenly, she stopped, her expression and composure changed completely as she stood rigidly, looking vainly in Robby's direction. For the third time this night, he had the distinct feeling that he was seen, and now, because of the last two times, he assumed he had been. Just as he made up his mind to step out from behind the tree, she turned and ran away silently across the green and into the trees on the far side, but not before Robby recognized Sheila.

He was stunned. He groaned with longing for her, nearly called out after her, even running a few steps out into the open to catch her. But she was too fast, too sure-footed. He stopped where she had just been dancing and sighed heavily. After a while, he decided to take another way home, so that Sheila would not be followed, and, perhaps his own embarrassment could be kept to himself. So he trudged back the way he had come until he reached the road near the Common House again that led down toward the Bentwide. All the long way around, he thought of nothing else but Sheila, who lived in his own house but was now a stranger to him. How little he knew her, or appreciated her, he felt. The most beautiful girl in all of Barley, he thought to himself, and the saddest. And he felt sad, too. He had witnessed a rare moment of mirth and could not share in it with her. He walked on, feeling, as she must have on so many occasions, like the loneliest creature in the world.

"I might as well be a thousand miles away."

# Chapter 14

# The Party by the Lake

When Robby returned home and went upstairs, he glanced down the hall and saw that Sheila's bedroom door was closed. Then he saw his mother sitting in the room that served both as parlor and study. She had her knitting on her lap and was staring at the strongbox across the room under Mr. Ribbon's desk.

"Mother?"

She turned her head to him, expressionless, her eyes distant.

"I'm home."

"Oh. Robby."

She glanced at the window.

"You have been out very late."

"I just came from the Common House," he said. "Daddy said he'd be home soon."

"I've been worried about you."

"I'm sorry," he said, "but—"

"I don't think it is wise for you to be wandering around so late."

"I know. I would have been home sooner, but I ran into someone passing through town, and he sort of asked the way to the Common House."

"Oh."

He was prepared to explain further, but she did not press him, perhaps not wishing to be overbearing.

"You look tired, Mother."

"I am, after a manner."

"Well, I'll say good-night, then. We'll talk in the morning."

"Good-night, Robby."

• • •

Soon Robby was in bed and tossing in a restless sleep, continuously interrupted by strange dreams of sun-parched landscapes, devoid of trees or life of any kind for as far as one could see.

When Mr. Ribbon returned home, and the store was checked and relocked, he chatted with Mirabella while they prepared for bed. She listened to his account of the meetings and then to his description of the stranger that Robby had brought to the Common House. She regretted not asking Robby more about his evening, and that she did not have the chance to meet the visitor from such a noble House.

"Did you know that the House of Fairlinden rules Vanara?" she asked her husband.

"Do they?" Mr. Ribbon said, yawning.

As they drew up the covers around them, she asked many more questions, but there were very few that Mr. Ribbon could answer. She lay awake for a long time, long after Mr. Ribbon's light snore indicated that further questions should wait until the next day.

• • •

Morning came too early for Mr. Ribbon's comfort, but the persuasive aroma of coffee and the gentle clink of cooking pans from the kitchen got him up in spite of his desire to remain in bed. Soon he was dressed and at the table, and he and Mirabella ate and chatted more about the western stranger and about the day's business to be taken care of. He decided to let Robby sleep, and after his meal, he went downstairs to open the store. Indeed, after a long night of struggle, Robby did sleep late, oblivious to the sounds of others rising in the house, and in spite of the enticing blend of aromas finding their way from the kitchen to his bed. When at last he did rise, Mirabella had breakfast still warm for him. As he sat down, Mirabella told him that Sheila had gone out early to run errands and that Mr. Ribbon was not due at the Common House until after the noon meal and had already opened the store. They talked of Thurdun, Mirabella listening carefully as she cleaned while Robby spoke between bites.

"Do you know anyone of the House of Fairlinden?"

"All Elifaen know of the House of Fairlinden, I should think. For that is the highest of all in Vanara. Surely you remember your lessons. Fairlinden has held the throne since the days of Cupeldain, before even the coming of Men into the world. Lord Thurdun is grandson of Cupeldain, and his sister has sat upon Vanara's throne for this past age or more. I am astonished that you met him. Did he say who it was that he escorted?"

"No, he didn't say."

"Someone very important to the Queen, if she sent her brother as escort on such a long journey. What was he like?"

"Oh, a nice fellow, I guess. Very businesslike, formal, I suppose. A bit weary. Not a big person, about my height, long silver-white hair. He rode a buckmarl and had fine chain mail. I'm afraid I did not recognize his name. I suppose my lessons with Broadweed may have been somewhat lacking. I mean, I do remember that Vanara has a queen, the only one in all the Realms. Your family was from Vanara, were they not?"

"Yes, on my mother's side. I and my brothers were born there."

"Did you ever meet any of Thurdun's people?"

"I have a memory of meeting a lady of that house many years ago. It was shortly before my family moved to the Eastlands, and we visited an estate in Vanara. I do not know the purpose of the visit, and I was left to play while the grownups met with each other. Did Lord Thurdun say how long they would be in these parts?"

"No. That is, they were only passing through."

Mirabella sighed and nodded.

"I would have enjoyed meeting and speaking with him."

"I know. I told him as much, but he wanted to press on."

They talked on, getting off on the subject of buckmarls, until Robby finished eating. He thanked his mother for the meal, helped a little with the dishes, and went downstairs. His father was at the metalwares shelf, putting away new irons that the blacksmith had delivered the day before. Mr. Ribbon was about to bid Robby a good morning when the doorbell jangled. A man and woman, dressed in their best go-to-town clothes, entered. The man was broad-shouldered and sunburned, and his wife was none too dainty, either, carrying a lady's bag that had seen much better days. Robby recognized them as Mr. and Mrs. Gladsten, who owned a farm in Barley not too far from Steggan's old place.

"How d'ye do, Master Robby!" Gladsten grinned. "Been awhiles since yer friends an' ye been fishin' down at Otter's Pond."

"Good morning, Mr. Gladsten," Robby replied, smiling at the memory. "Yes, it has been too long. Been too busy around here, I guess."

"Rightly so, rightly so," Gladsten said, loudly enough for Robby's father to hear from across the room. Mr. Ribbon had turned to face the couple as soon as they walked in, and he was standing with an iron in his hand and a blank look on his face.

"I reckon yer a chip off the block, as they say, for yer father's a mighty worker hisself."

Mrs. Gladsten nodded nervously, grinning with her buck teeth.

"Ah, Mr. Ribbon. Good day, sir," Gladsten said, making as if he had just now seen Mr. Ribbon.

Robby's father gently put the iron on the shelf and turned back to the couple.

"What can I do for ye, today?" he asked. The pleasant smile and enthusiastic tone that normally greeted customers was completely absent.

"I hope yer well as ye look!" Gladsten said coming over to Mr. Ribbon and stretching out his hand.

"An' I hope the Missus is doin' well, too," added his wife.

For the first time in his life, Robby saw his father refuse an outstretched hand. Instead, Mr. Ribbon turned aside to make a slight rearrangement of the spice jars.

"Well, er," Mr. Gladsten glanced at his hand and wiped it on his shirt awkwardly. "I come to see ye 'bout me accounts an' all."

Mr. Ribbon silently seated himself behind his desk and pulled on his spectacles.

"I believe dues were on the fifth," he said, pulling out a ledger book and turning over some pages without looking up. "Why yes, here it is. Yer dues were owed on the fifth."

"Er, well, right ye are. But, ye see, I ain't had the dues to pay ye, what with the storm an' all, an' that's what I mean to discuss with ye."

"Hm," Mr. Ribbon nodded.

Robby had never seen this uncharacteristic coolness in his father. Most of the dues customers owed on accounts were written off for the month, just as for the month before, and Mr. Ribbon was all too glad to do it to save the ruin of his neighbors.

"Well, ye see," Mr. Gladsten went on, "that is, I mean to say—"

"Ye still don't have the dues, eh?" Mr. Ribbon looked over his glasses at Mr. Gladsten.

"No, sir. I ain't got it."

"Well, let's see here," Mr. Ribbon turned back to the ledger. "I see ye've been given thrice a fortnight more on yer account. Added to that, ye've since put on yer account two sacks of grain. A six-weight of nails. A score of candles. Three pints of oil. More lately, ten pounds of salt an' seven yards of sackin' cloth. That's on top of yer previous credits."

"Yes, sir, that sounds 'bout right."

"It is right," Mr. Ribbon removed his glasses and looked at Mr. Gladsten and his wife. "I'm afraid I cannot go without what's due."

"But if ye can only—"

"An' the store cannot lend ye any more credit."

In the silence that followed, Robby felt his face redden and his heart pound. He had never known credit to be denied a customer.

"But, Mr. Ribbon, I ain't got what's due."

"In that case, I reckon Sheriff Fivelpont must perform his duties."

"Now hold on," Mr. Gladsten stiffened. "I know for a fact that ye've given others leeway on thar credit."

"That may be," Mr. Ribbon said calmly.

"Well, it's only fair ye do the same for us!"

"Mr. Gladsten, I happen to know that thar's an offer before ye on yer farm from Sam Winborn. It is a fair offer. I suggest ye take him up on it, an' pay yer debts."

"But that won't leave us with no place to live an' not enough to live on!"

"Then may I suggest to ye that ye find somewhar else to live besides Barley er Passdale."

"Why, Mr. Ribbon!" Mrs. Gladsten finally managed to say.

"Yes, Mrs. Gladsten?"

"Why, I, I..." she stammered, red-faced.

"This ain't right!" Mr. Gladsten pounded his fist on the desk.

"Do not speak to me of right!" Ribbon said through his set jaw, barely holding back his fury. "Yer a bad farmer, Mr. Gladsten. Ye squander yer crops, maltreat yer cattle, an' ye've misused this store. All that might be enough to wish ye away, but what's more, yer a bad neighbor not to be trusted er counted on when thar's a need for help, even when begged an' pleaded of ye. So ye'll go to Sam Winborn this very day. Ye'll make arrangements with him for yer farm. Sam may come to pay yer debts, for ye are not welcome in this store. If by sunset of this day Sam Winborn has not made arrangements with me, an' with all the rest in Passdale that ye owe, I will set the Sheriff on ye. An' I'll see to it ye'll not get half the worth at auction. When all is done, ye will leave this county an' be gone from here by sundown on the morrow. Ye'll do these things, an' ye'll do these things handily, for if the Sheriff's men come for ye, ye'll still go away, but with the mark of hot iron upon yer forehead that none may miss, an' ye'll still get off lucky! This much I'll allow ye, one day for settlin', one day for movin' on. Both for consideration of yer wife, though she is no less a blight on us than ye. Now leave me store, afore I set meself upon ye!"

Mr. Ribbon stepped from around his desk and stood with his arms down and his fists balled and ready. Robby, frozen in disbelief, understood none of what was happening. But Gladsten clearly did, for the man became silent and cowed, and his wife whimpered and sobbed. The two left quickly without another word. Robby watched them go, then stared, stunned and a little frightened at his father who was obviously seething with anger though he never once raised his voice. Mr. Ribbon reached back to the desk and slowly closed the ledger book. Robby watched his deliberate movements as he adjusted the book to the side of the desk before turning to make sure the couple had left. Robby could still feel the palpable fury, held in check, like he had never felt coming from anyone, silent, strong, and hot. When Mr. Ribbon looked at Robby, his eyes flashed for a moment, then his look softened and watered into something almost like embarrassment.

"Business is business, son," he said bluntly. "No matter what the business may be."

Robby said nothing, waiting for more. But there was no more said. Mr. Ribbon mumbled something about getting off to the weaver's to check on some braided ropes and was through the door before Robby could bring himself to speak. Slowly turning, he saw his mother, standing at the stairs unnoticed by any until now, and he understood that she had been there the entire time.

"What was all that about?" Robby asked.

Mirabella stepped down from the stairs and moved over to the window, peering down the road after her husband.

"Your father feels somewhat responsible for Sheila," she said. "He recently learned that the Gladstens turned her away the night she was beaten."

Robby's mother turned back to him as he absorbed this.

"Sheila said nothing to your father about it," she continued. "Frizella found out somehow and sent a note with Billy awhile back."

Robby felt blood rush hot to his face as he realized that if they had taken her in, the baby might have been saved.

"Then good riddance to them!" he said. Mirabella nodded and went back upstairs. Halfway up, she stopped and turned back to Robby.

"Do not question your father about this," she said. "He is upset enough at how Sheila was failed by our community. And he has much on his mind besides."

"I won't," Robby assured her. She smiled sadly and went back upstairs.

After a while, Mr. Ribbon returned but said very little. He ate a light meal, then left to go to the Common House, for this was the day he was to announce the Fall Counting. From all indications, this year's fair was to be rather grand, and Mr. Ribbon had been busy making preparations for the event.

● ● ●

Once every year, during harvest time, when the days waned into autumn, all of the peoples of Passdale and Barley were called to gather and be counted on the census and to renew their pledges to King and community. It was called The Counting, but was actually a festival, a civic affair, with deep, nearly religious overtones. Although the specifics changed somewhat from generation to generation, and from place to place, the tradition of allegiance-pledging had remained relatively the same for hundreds of years. When Duinnor united the Seven Realms, the tradition was made into law, and the ceremonies surrounding them became more formal. In Passdale and Barley, all was done much in the same way as it ever was.

On the day of the autumn equinox, it was the duty of the Mayor of Passdale to issue a proclamation calling for the gathering. He would first call together the combined city and county councils, and they would decide on the days and the place of the gathering. In Passdale and Barley, it was customary to have the event take place on two separate days, one week apart, so that those unable to attend on one day would be able to go to the second appointed day. When the council reached a decision, and had ordered the Mayor to do so, he would leave the council chambers of the Common House and accompany them to the steps outside its entrance. There, where people gathered to await the announcement, he would read the proclamation in a loud voice, which always went something like this:

> "Harken all! And hear ye the King's agent. I, *(name of mayor)*, rightfully appointed as the King's own agent in this the region of Passdale and Barley and nearby lands, am charged by Duinnor to call forth all the inhabitants of these lands to gather at Wayford Common, beginning on the Twenty-Seventh of Tenthmonth. There it will be ordered that each make an oath by his name for the welfare of the lands and in the name of the throne of Duinnor, to give fair account of our faith with our vows,

and to render the tithing due by law. Let it be known by all, and let none be absent!"

The written proclamation would be ceremonially posted on the great door of the Common House, and copies of it would be sent forth throughout the land. Messengers would also be dispatched to every house and farm, carrying the proclamation and reading it to all. It was then that preparations would begin in earnest, for it was customary to fill those days between the two days of reckoning with mirth and merrymaking, feasts and feats of showmanship, of contests and storytelling, and music and all manner of celebration. At Wayford Common, a flat clearing in the hills about a furlong behind Passdale, pavilions were erected and wood gathered for bonfires and kitchens. It was always a great festival for the folks of Barley and Passdale, full of comings and goings, and attracting performers from all over the Eastlands, and sometimes even from more distant realms. One year, a conjurer came from the south and stunned the people with magic that turned flowers into birds and water into dry sand. Another year there came a troupe of acrobats who soared through the air and stood one upon the other ten men high. And yet another year there came a man with all manner of foreign beasts that were both terrible and beautiful to look upon.

So later that day, Robby and his mother closed the shop for a while, walked to the Common House, and waited along with a small crowd for the official announcement they knew would soon be coming.

"This year is bound to exceed all those of the past," Robby heard the blacksmith say to another in the crowd. "I hear tell more 'an two dozen passes have already been given for acts an' innertainers of all sorts."

"I heard tell them Bosklanders'll be puttin' on some militia shows, too, an' Mrs. Bosk is arrangin' the kitchens," replied the other. "Mr. Broadweed's little pupils'll be singin', of course, an thar might even be some Faere Folk coming through with thar songs. Yep, I reckon it'll be a mighty fine time, if folks don't get too drunk, that is."

"A little celebratin' ain't never hurt nobody, I always sez," winked the blacksmith. "An' ye gotta admit it's been a lucky year for most folks around. What with most gettin' in two harvests before the storm an' then not havin' the damage one might expect from the floods. I reckon folks are mighty relieved at havin' their tithe so in hand this year."

"I think so, too!"

As they stood there waiting, Robby turned to his mother.

"Do you know when a new Mayor will be chosen?"

"I suppose it will be sometime in the spring, Robby."

"Oh, I suppose so," he nodded. "That is the usual time."

"I imagine you are wondering when your duties at the store will be lifted somewhat. And whether you'll be able to go off to school in Glareth."

"Well, yes. But to tell you the truth, I'm thinking of taking up another job," Robby said tentatively. "Part time. Sort of."

"Oh?" Mirabella was surprised. "Doing what?"

"That's the thing," Robby said. "I'm not sure, exactly. I'm thinking of joining the militia."

"What's that?" his mother gasped. "Whatever for?"

"I need the training, Mother," Robby said bluntly. "I can't just sit around waiting for the other boot to fall. I've got to be ready, and I'm not."

"This is not the place to talk of such things," Mirabella whispered, looking around.

Robby was silenced by his mother, but she caught a quick glare from him that was most unusual and served to shock her further. Just then, her husband appeared on the portico of the Common House, bearing a scroll and surrounded by the men of the council. He unrolled the scroll and read aloud his pronouncement, making only a few mistakes. When he got to the end and pronounced, "An' let none be absent!" there was a general cheer and clapping from the audience as he bowed and rolled up the scroll. Robby was too young the last time his father had served as Mayor to remember any of these kinds of things, and now he could not help being proud of him. Mr. Ribbon saw his wife and son in the crowd and hurried down the steps to them, receiving pats on the back as he approached.

"So thar!" he said, beaming at his wife.

"Well done, my love!"

"Not bad, Daddy!"

"Thank ye. Thank ye," Mr. Ribbon blushed. "Not bad for a country boy, eh?"

"You are not a country boy anymore," Mirabella teased. "You're too old!"

They all laughed.

"Well, I must be back in to see to the copies an' dispatch the messengers an' all," Mr. Ribbon said. "I'll be home directly afterwards."

Mirabella kissed her husband goodbye, then she and Robby made their way back to the store. They remained silent the whole way, but once they entered the store, Mirabella spoke.

"Now tell me what is on your mind," she demanded.

"I must prepare for what is to come," Robby stated flatly.

"And what do you think that is?"

"Strife," he said. "At least for me. And perhaps to all of this land."

"Why do you say that?"

"You know why, Mother," Robby shot back. "Do not treat me like a boy. You know what has happened to me. The Bell. You know, sooner or later, I'll be found out. And you know about the Dragonkind man and the one who escaped. Now there is word from the west about dangers there."

"There are always dangers in the Westlands," Mirabella interrupted.

"Perhaps, but now they come our way. At any rate, I am ill-prepared to save myself in a fight, and I need training," Robby argued. "It would be less noticeable if I joined the militia and was trained in that way to handle arms than any other way."

"I agree with Robby," came a voice from the doorway. There loomed a tall figure, stooping slightly to step through the doorway, a walking stick in one hand and a saddlebag in the other. He was dressed in a long dark-blue cloak, and when he tossed back the hood, Robby instantly recognized Ashlord.

"Ashlord!" he cried going up to him and shaking his hand. "I have wondered what happened to you."

"I have been busy, my friend," Ashlord said, smiling and nodding. "And I have need of a few things from your store before I depart for Surthquay."

"Surthquay?"

"An old boat landing on the lake."

"Oh, is that where you will meet with Thurdun's party?"

"Yes," Ashlord nodded, "though how you know that worries me."

Ashlord threw a glance at Mirabella, who was eyeing him suspiciously.

"I spoke with Thurdun last night. We met on the road," Robby was saying, noticing some tension between Ashlord and his mother.

"Mrs. Ribbon," Ashlord bowed. "I am honored to make your acquaintance."

"Likewise, Collandoth," she replied. "My husband and I are indebted to you for taking care of Robby."

"Oh, it was nothing." He smiled, then he noticed a certain look in her face. "Ah. I see Robby has told you. And I gather from what I overheard that you do not believe that he is in danger."

"Yes, he has told me," she said. "But not because he wanted to. Only because I caught him in a mistake with his story. As for the danger he is in, well, I am not certain."

"He is in danger," Ashlord bluntly said. "And would now be dead if the raiding party that came for him had not run into the Bosklanders. One of them still escaped and headed straight for Tulith Attis. He almost overpowered me, and there was a stern fight between us. His mission was to discover who rang the Great Bell. I only regret that I could not wrest from him the name of the one that sent him. He died of the wounds I gave him in my defense. I fear there will be others, though."

"Was he a Dragonkind man?" Robby asked.

"No, just a Man. From the West. I do not know the connection between him and the Dragonkind, which is another mystery that disturbs me."

"But it has been nearly two months," Mirabella said. "Surely something would have happened by now."

"As you may know, it takes nearly a fortnight, hard riding, just to get to the borderlands, Mirabella Ribbon," Ashlord pointed out. "If his master was there and no farther, it would be another fortnight, at the least, coming back with another party. Enough time has now passed for the enemy to know that his first effort has failed. They will not give up so easily and will try again. My inclination is to believe that whoever sent the party that Robby ran into must actually be close at hand, or at least his agents must be about. How else could he keep watch? They were obviously ready to move when the Great Bell of Tulith Attis rang, already in waiting for the moment. They had to be nearby. But I doubt they will be as brazen as before. They will wait for a better moment, a better way to discover their prey. If the enemy is anything, he is patient."

"Should I leave Passdale?" Robby asked.

"Perhaps," Ashlord said. "But not right away, I think. There are other things happening in the world that may be a distraction to those who would seek you. However, you would be safer surrounded by armed men that you can trust. So your idea of joining the militia may serve in more ways than one. Only, I did not know there was a militia in Passdale."

"There isn't," Robby said. "Not yet, anyway. But there have been discussions amongst the people. And I think things are leaning that way. I think there will be one pretty soon."

"I see. Lady Mirabella, do you not think your son would be safer if he knew how to defend himself? And kept company with others likewise trained?"

"I don't know," she said, turning away. "Perhaps."

"Until other things come to pass and work themselves out," Ashlord concluded, "I agree with Robby, here. It seems a wise move. Why don't you think about it? Meanwhile, I need a bit of salt and some tea. But I must hurry to fetch my horse from the stable and hie off to the lake."

"Mother," Robby said, "let me go with Ashlord tonight. I can ride with him and be back tomorrow. I want to see Thurdun again, if I can."

Ashlord's eyes flashed with surprise as he looked from Robby to Mirabella and back.

"I'm not sure that's a good idea." She glanced at Ashlord.

"Oh, I will take good care of him," he assured her. "I promise he will not be alone even once. He could hardly be in any safer place than Lord Thurdun's camp. And I think his presence there will be appreciated."

"You will return tomorrow?"

"Yes, Mother."

"We must be off quickly, then," Ashlord put in. "I have much to discuss with Thurdun before he departs this country."

"I'm up to it."

"Very well, if your parents are willing and you have no other duties."

"I'll take care of the store for Robby," Mirabella said as Robby enthusiastically ran upstairs to fetch his shoulder bag. "I'll let his father know as soon as he gets home."

She pulled a bag of tea and offered it for Ashlord to smell, eyeing him as he did so.

"Ah," he said. "That will do nicely."

"How much salt? Will a pound do?"

"Half as much will be more than enough."

Ashlord watched her weigh the salt and then took the small sack she gave him.

"What else may I do for you?" she asked. "Is there anything else that you need?"

"Ah, yes. I was here sometime ago, perhaps more than a year past, and I saw among your things a box of silver-tipped writing pens. I commented to your husband how rare it was to see them in these parts, for they are of a make not usually seen outside of Vanara. Do you know the ones I mean?"

"Yes, I do. Robigor said they came in a consignment from the trader, Furaman. Let's see, I believe they are still here, somewhere."

Mirabella rummaged through a set of drawers near the stationery supplies until she found a small leather-bound case.

"Are these the ones you mean?"

She opened the case and handed it to Ashlord. Inside were four short ink pens, made of carved wood fitted with engraved silver nibs.

"Yes, indeed! Very nice. Quite the thing." Ashlord smiled as he pulled out his purse. "How much for all four?"

"I can't accept your coin," Mirabella stated. "They are yours, along with the other things, with kind thanks for helping Robby."

"Oh, I insist!" he replied. "They are not for me. I mean them to be a gift. Would five-weight in Glareth silver be fair?"

"More than fair, if you do insist," Mirabella nodded, accepting the five coins. "But, to make it fair, at least take something else. A pouch of Westleaf for your pipe?"

"Ah, that would be hard to refuse!"

As she went to the tobacco shelf and prepared a pouch of aromatic smoking leaf, Ashlord gazed about the shop with interest, taking in all the many colors and aromas of the place.

"Ashlord, do you know much about old coins?" Mirabella asked as she tied the pouch.

"Coins?"

"Yes. We came by some unusual coins recently—it's a long story—and I think they may be quite old. I think they may be from Vanara."

"Oh?"

"Yes. I wonder if you might have a look at them sometime and tell me what you think?" she said, handing him the pouch. Ashlord smiled, with a quizzical expression, noting how nervous Mirabella seemed. But he knew that making smalltalk was how some people work through toward whatever was on their mind, and he speculated that she wanted an opportunity to chat more about Robby's situation.

"It's just that we don't know how to value them," she quickly added. "Besides their weight in metal, that is. They are quite exquisitely made, and may have some greater value due to that."

"Well, it is well known that Vanarans were once the finest metalworkers in all the world. I have seen some remarkable examples of their early coinage. Rather like fine jewelry."

"Yes. These are like that. Would you mind looking at them?"

"I would be happy to do so. But truly I must hurry along as soon as Robby is ready to go."

"Of course. It would take a few moments to fetch them, anyway, since they are locked away upstairs," Mirabella said. "Perhaps when you and Robby return."

Hearing a sound at the stairs, they turned to see Robby descending, pulling the strap of his bag over his shoulder.

"I'm ready!" he proclaimed.

"You will be careful, won't you?" Mirabella said, giving Robby a hug.

"Yes, Mother," Robby said, kissing her goodbye. "I'll see you tomorrow!"

"Perhaps we can chat soon," Ashlord said with a slight bow. "Meanwhile, I thank you again, and bid you good day, my lady."

"Goodbye, Ashlord."

Mirabella watched the two depart, and after a long thoughtful pause, she sat behind her husband's desk and fingered the inkwell absently. She thought about the strongbox upstairs and its contents. The key to the strongbox, hanging from a chain under her bodice, suddenly felt very heavy, and she fought the temptation to go upstairs and look at the bejeweled coins once again. The strongbox had not been opened since Sheila put the coins within it, over two weeks earlier. She thought it odd that, with everything else going on around her, those coins kept intruding into her thoughts. At first, she passed it off as worry for their great value, thinking perhaps they were too precious and ancient to be safely held in a store such as theirs. The night she had first seen them, she happened to have a bout of scar pain, like Elifaen sometimes do, but she passed it off as having nothing to do with the coins. But as the busy days passed, they came to mind at the oddest times, such as in the middle of chatting with Robby, or while she walked along the path to the weaver's house, or in the dead of night. And, now, whenever she thought of that terrible night of storm when the Great Bell rang, the night Robby was in such danger, her mind always came back to the mystery of those coins. As she pushed the inkwell aside, she felt again a prickly sensation along her back. It was all very peculiar and inexplicable. Somehow, her worries over Robby seemed conflated by those old coins, and her fears for him strangely mingled with her fear of what those coins might actually be.

The doorbell jangled Mirabella from her musings. But it was only Sheila returning from her errands.

• • •

At the livery stable, Robby saddled a rented horse while Ashlord's was brought out for him.

"Isn't that Ullin's horse, Anerath?" Robby asked Ashlord as they mounted.

"Indeed, this is Anerath! On loan to me, you might say, until Ullin needs him again," Ashlord reined around. "Let us make good time, for the day is getting late."

Robby coaxed his mount, an older mare, to follow along behind Ashlord and Anerath. As if inspired by the stallion ahead, the mare made a better pace than Robby thought she could, and soon they were leaving Passdale, following the river road northward in the direction Thurdun's company had gone. Robby had not been this way in a long time, and had been to New Falls only a few times, the location where the lake had once spilled into what was the Bentwide. The place they made for, Surthquay, was about three leagues north of New Falls.

"I've never been there," Robby said. "I think I've seen it on some maps, though."

"It is where boats will meet Thurdun's company," Ashlord told him, "and convey them north across the lake."

They followed alongside the Bentwide, now a mere brook, leaving Passdale behind, and then entered a wooded and hilly track of road. Here were fewer farms and the ground was rocky. They did pass some apple orchards, and, about two leagues out, they came to Branson's Vineyards, its ancient terraces busy with rows of carefully maintained vines. The workers in the fields tossed friendly waves at them as they passed. Every fall the Bransons provided ample casks of wine for the festival, and they always seemed a merry bunch of folk. This year, in spite of the troubles with the recent flood, the grapes were full and sweet. Robby had recently helped his father arrange for a second shipment of new glass bottles for the Branson's who, under Mr. Ribbon's tutelage, were sending their product far and wide in a variety of containers.

The road turned north sharply, and the old bed of the Bentwide fell off into a ravine. This they followed alongside for a league or two and the farmland fell away for good as the road led them into the shady and cool forest. There they slowed their pace a bit.

"Tell me, what have you been doing with yourself these many weeks?" Ashlord queried. "No incidents of concern, I hope?"

"Oh, no," Robby said. "I've been busy at the store, in my father's absence. That's about all. In the evening I take walks, as I did last night."

"Passdale is lucky to have such a man as your father," Ashlord said. "He has a knack for getting people to cooperate with each other. A very capable man in matters of commerce as well as having a deep sense of civic fairness."

"I'm very proud of him," Robby nodded. "Will you be coming to the Counting?"

"I may. And what of Sheila? I have exchanged a few notes with her, though not enough to well discern how she is."

"I think she is doing fairly well," Robby said. "She dresses differently now, since coming to stay with us. And she helps with the store, too, and with other things around and about. I rarely get to spend any time with her, though, and I haven't talked to her about, well, about those things that happened to her. She is different, now."

"How do you mean?"

"She is less merry than she once was. That is understandable, but," Robby searched for words, "but she also seems more thoughtful, contemplative."

"I'm sure she has a lot to think about."

"Yes, that's true. But she seems to hold me at some distance. It is almost as if she is avoiding me. She comes and goes, lives just across the hall from me, and we often breakfast and sup together, but, well…"

"But she does not act as if she loves you?"

Robby was struck by the boldness of Ashlord's question.

"I guess that's it," he said, a bit embarrassed. "Sometimes she, well, she looks at me as if she still does. I can't explain it. I do think she does love me, but she keeps her distance, in a manner of speaking."

"Ah."

Robby looked at Ashlord who was nodding.

"What?"

"Well," Ashlord said, "I am no matchmaker, and I try to stay out of the affairs of others when it comes to matters of the heart. But I may have some insight here that might be worth considering."

"What is that?"

"When she came to me, she was not trying to escape from you," he told Robby. "She sought to improve herself. It was her plan to come to me long before she was attacked by her uncle. Things did not work out the way Sheila planned, that is obvious. Yet, she came, nonetheless. She sought to gain knowledge and learning to become worthy of you. I think she feared that you would abandon her when enticed by the other girls of the area. Or when you went off to school in Glareth, as she told me you plan to do. And, anyway, as she told me, it is well to learn while one has the opportunity, however late in life, whatever the season or the reason."

"That's what Mrs. Bosk said," Robby agreed. "Or something of the sort. But I tried to assure Sheila on that account."

"Yes, I'm sure you did. But now there is something new, isn't there? Something else that she did not anticipate," Ashlord said. "She now knows that you have a role to play in great affairs. She fears that."

"I don't get it," Robby urged his mount to keep up. "I did what I did out at Tulith Attis, and that's that. There's nothing more to it. I wish I did have something to do with things, at least things beyond Barley and Passdale. I long to see the world, or some other part of it. I can hardly wait to be on my way to Glareth next spring. Some days I just want to go ahead and run away. Especially lately. All this waiting and waiting for something to happen is making me crazy. You say I have a role to play, but I just don't see it. I'm just an ordinary person who is curious about other places. Is that so strange?"

"It is for someone from Passdale!" Ashlord chuckled. "Life there is good, and why anyone would want to leave it is beyond most folks. But I think you are the way you are for a reason. Your longings may only be your own nature speaking to you. Sometimes the heart can piece together that which the mind has not the tools to form."

Ashlord suddenly reined Anerath to a halt and looked at Robby.

"Listen to me, Robby Ribbon," he said. "There are powers at work in this world that are beyond our understanding. They have put their fingers upon you and are working through you, whether you realize it or not. All my divining, and all my intelligence, and all my heart tells me this is so. Why you, and not someone else? Why were you sent to ring the Great Bell and not another person? That is still something of a mystery to me. But it is what it is. These forces are not to be taken lightly, and they have caused the triumph and ruin of many. Sheila knows this, and she fears it. And she knows that to be near you is to have those forces work through her upon you, just as they work through everything on earth. She fears, perhaps, that if she moves one way, she will keep you from your destiny. But if she moves another way, she will drive you into it."

"What fate? What is it that I am to do?" Robby pleaded, shaking his head. "Since I know nothing of these things, and can hardly believe what you say, is there nothing I can do for Sheila?"

"Why, yes there is, Robby," Ashlord said gently. "You can strive to be her friend. Do not hold her conduct against her, and do not allow her to distance herself from you too much. Let your heart encourage you to honor her. Be strong, and let your friendship grow of itself, as if with a new beginning, without the expectations, or hopes, of the past. What will develop will come of its own, and in accord with the nature of things."

Robby nodded thoughtfully, and they proceeded along their way, the sun angling lower behind the trees with a cool breeze rustling down the road in their faces.

"Look there," Ashlord said, pointing to the far bank of the Bentwide. Robby could make out a little waterfall coming down the other side of the old bank.

"That is where Weepingbrook pours into the Bentwide," Ashlord explained. "And there, to the left of that, now revealed since the Bentwide is no more, are the ancient piers that supported the bridge that once stood here."

"Oh yes, I see them."

"Here the old road used to cross the Bentwide and on into Farbarley to become what you call the Line Road, and thence to Tulith Attis and on to Boskland."

Indeed, now the roadway seemed to become wider, and in places paved by ancient stones.

"Why does Duinnor not help Thurdun's people?" Robby asked as he came alongside Ashlord. "He told me that his land is not safe."

"Well, it is a long story and there is no time to tell it all," Ashlord said. "Vanara is the oldest of all the Realms, and the House of Fairlinden the noblest of its people. It is land rich with woodlands and fields, resting against the southern Blue Mountains. On the other side of those mountains are the great deserts of Drakyr, the Dragonkind lands. From there, the Dragonkind have often raided Vanara through passes and secret tunnels in the mountains, and for ages Vanara has borne the brunt of many an assault upon the Realms. Vanara cannot defend against them unaided, but Duinnor insists upon payment. In lieu of that, Vanara must give leases to its lands to Duinnor, which Duinnor does not return without unreasonable payment. In this manner, the treasure of Vanara is depleted. Duinnor insists, too, that its armies be posted within Vanara, and that Vanara must aid Duinnor in its many ill-advised campaigns in the Dragonlands. Slowly, therefore, Duinnor has exerted greater power over Thurdun's people."

"Still," Ashlord went on, "the assaults of the Dragonkind are steady and yet not massive. They raid and harry across the mountains, destroy and burn, and then retreat back into the desert. The Vanarans have built many fortifications along their borders, but still the Dragonkind warriors find ways through. Some think they do so by treacherous intelligence provided to them. At any rate, Duinnor has had its attention elsewhere, and has yielded little useful aid, even though Vanara may be a doorway of assault should war come."

"I thought the Dragon Lands were much farther south and west," Robby questioned.

"They are vast," Ashlord nodded. "And stretch from the southern sea to the northern badlands south of Vanara's border. They have even made war in lands much nearer to us than that, and, as you know, they scoured even this countryside early in this age."

They descended nearer to the riverbed, which was but a trickle of a stream, passing through rocks and boulders. Ashlord pointed on up the riverbed as it rose into a gully some half-mile away.

"That is where New Falls once poured," he said. "It is where the lake once spilled out, forming the Bentwide River."

Robby nodded, remembering what it had looked like many years ago, when his father and mother brought him here for a summer picnic. Then, the river gushed and splashed through the gully, and the surrounding woods were cool and shady. Now it was all quite dry, and somewhat dismal.

"Has anyone ever seen their cities?" Robby asked as the road climbed up and away. "The Dragonkind cities, I mean. Especially the Golden City?"

"Yes," Ashlord said. "I myself have seen Tyrsharat, as the Golden City is properly called. That was long, long ago. I went there in more peaceful times, as an envoy of Duinnor. It is a fabulous city, and it is true that its palaces are roofed in gold and that its courts are tiled in jade and ebony. Yet the Dragonkind people rarely enjoy the wealth of their masters, and there is little but want, poverty, and ignorance surrounding the opulence of the Sun King. His people suffer terrible illnesses born of the desert, with little relief. All serve the masters, and all masters serve the King. No one is permitted any learning or any practice that is not ordered to them, and all, the high and the low, are slaves of their King. The King himself is treated as a god, and when he goes forth, the people praise him as he passes, and they prostrate themselves before him, showering his path with flowers. He is often carried on a magnificent sedan, but sometimes he walks, resplendent in his gold and ebony robes and his jewel-studded jade headpiece. When he does so, many, in their prostrated state, reach out in an effort to touch the hem of his robes, thinking they may be blessed by doing so."

"Have you ever seen him, the Dragonkind King?"

"Only once, from a great distance! My dealings were with a rather low-level adjunct to the Minister of Lands."

"Why were you there?"

"It was my duty to be courier of the border agreements between Duinnor, Vanara, and the Dragonkind, particularly agreements involving trade with one of the northern cities in the desert, a place called Kajarahn. As I said, that was long ago. A different king rules the Dragonlands, now. And such agreements no longer exist, if they ever meant anything in the first place."

They continued to climb upward, and Robby thought about how difficult it must have been for Thurdun's wagons to come this way. He wondered, too, at the forest, its autumn colors more common here than in Passdale, with reds and golds already flashing through the green in the slanting light. They topped the hill and through the trees glistened the waters of Lake Halgaeth in the distance. A moment later, the trees thinned, and Robby could barely see the far eastern shore, even at this point, the narrowest part of the lake. To the right and far off he saw mists rising up from what once was Heneil's Wall. A fury of water now crashed through the gap where the dam once stood, sending the spray high, and for a moment Robby saw a rainbow hovering over the mist.

"Halgaeth quickly resumes its ancient level," Ashlord commented.

They continued on, heading downward off the hill and into the dim evening that had already settled upon the forest. They had not gone another league when two soldiers suddenly stepped out of the shadows and challenged them. They wore gray buttoned jackets and black helmets, and Robby recognized them by their dress as the escorts he had seen the night before.

"Who goes?" one of them called out sternly.

"Collandoth and company," Ashlord answered.

"Ah, Collandoth," the soldier acknowledged as the two riders approached. "You are expected. It is good to see you again."

"And you, Garlan!"

Robby smiled and nodded to the soldiers as he passed them.

"These are not soldiers of Duinnor that go with Thurdun," Robby said to Ashlord a moment later.

"No, they are of the House of Seafar, mostly, and other men of Vanara who are loyal to Fairlinden and whose families have remained loyal to Vanara," Ashlord explained. "There, in Vanara, the bond between Elifaen and Men is the strongest, and no other realm knows its like, surely not Duinnor, and not even Glareth by the Sea."

Robby saw lights flickering ahead, and they soon entered a broad grassy headland, sloping gently downward to the lake. There, near the water, in a clearing surrounded by ancient poplars, tall and massive, was the encampment of Thurdun's party, the wagons and horses drawn up, the campfires and cooking fires lit, and lanterns hung all around. Robby could also see the gray outline of a stone quay jutting out some distance into the lake, at the end of which were two pillars—oddly shaped, bent it seemed—with braziers aflame at their tops. More soldiers waved them through the outer line of the encampment, and, as they dismounted, several men and a lady approached.

"Collandoth! I knew you would be on time!" cried one of the men.

"Aye, and we just made camp this morning," said the other. Robby recognized Thurdun. "Who's this? Robby Ribbon of Passdale? I didn't expect to ever see you again, much less so soon!"

"I talked Ashlord, er, that is, Collandoth into bringing me along," Robby said shaking Thurdun's hand. "I hope you don't mind."

"Not at all! Tonight we have something of a celebration," Thurdun laughed. "We depart in the morning to begin the final leg of our journey, if the boats arrive, that is."

"Oh, they will come," Ashlord assured him.

"This is my good friend, Captain Chanter," Thurdun said, indicating the soldier at his side. "I believe you two have met?"

"Ah, yes," Ashlord nodded, taking the captain's hand. "We first met at Gory Gulch."

"Aye, the same," said Chanter, a tall man with short-cropped brown and gray hair, clean shaven, and with intense blue eyes. "What? Nearly thirty years ago?"

"Yes, thereabouts," Ashlord replied.

"I was but a sniveling squire, then, not even ten years old. And I was terrified the whole while. Yet, was many a lizard we slew that night!"

"Yes, but at too great a cost. And you acquitted yourself in battle as well as any warrior there. The last time we met, though, you were completing your letters at the Queen's Academy. I see you are now one of the Gray Guard. My congratulations to you!"

"Aye, thank you, sir! For the past few years it has been my honor to serve the Queen."

"Here, allow me to introduce my companion, Robby Ribbon, son of Robigor Ribbon, of Passdale."

"Pleased."

"And this is my sister's handmaiden, Gaiyelneth." Thurdun introduced the young lady who stood at the edge of the group. She was about Robby's height, with dark reddish hair like the autumn maple leaf, and white skin. Her eyes were black as coal and her nose small and round over broad lips. She was dressed in a simple costume, bodice, blouse and skirt, with a shawl thrown over her shoulders, and when Ashlord and Robby bowed, she curtseyed.

"We, too, have met, Collandoth," she said. "But I think the last time your shin suffered for it!"

"Oh, no!" Ashlord cried. "It cannot be!"

"Oh, yes," said Thurdun.

"Not the same little rascal that climbed my back, pulled out my hair, stole my walking stick, packed my shoes with honey, and, when caught, dented my shinbones with her kicks?"

"One and the same," she laughed, not a bit ashamed.

"Pray, stay distant from me," Ashlord said with mock seriousness, holding out his hand to push her away. "You are worse than any pixie, and twice as mischievous as an imp!"

"Such is her charm," sighed Chanter. "But, as she is my sister, I warn you not to go too far, or else she'll have me defend her honor. And one of us will have to get cut or bruised or dead, or all three, before she's satisfied. Ah, me! What a burden little sisters can be!"

"I do not envy your fate," Ashlord laughed as Thurdun guided them toward the middle of the camp. "But how does she come to be here?"

"She would not part from Serith Ellyn's side," Thurdun said. "They have been fast for ten years, and will likely be so all their lives."

"Are you a Watcher, like Collandoth?" Gaiyelneth asked, falling in beside Robby.

"Oh, no," he said. "I'm just a shopkeeper."

"I think you keep more than a shop," she said, grinning and looking at him askance. "I think you keep secrets."

"What? What do you mean?"

"I only mean that Collandoth is not known for having shopkeepers in his company."

"He could do worse," retorted Robby.

"Oh, no doubt! And he has done, I'm sure. I only meant that you must be an unusual shopkeeper, or else it is an unusual shop that you keep."

"Hrumph!"

"Now you even sound like Collandoth," she giggled, taking Robby's arm. "Come! Listen to the musicians! They have arrived to see us off and to take our wagons when we depart. Besides, it is always our tradition to celebrate this day, the Autumn Equinox."

Some few yards from the large fire in the middle of the camp stood a half-dozen minstrels, piping and stringing. They were two men and four women, two obviously wives and two obviously daughters, and they were dressed in the colorful attire of wandering entertainers. It was a spirited tune they first played, setting many listeners clapping or stomping with the beat.

"Are they not wonderful!" Gaiyelneth exclaimed, grasping her skirt and whirling around. "They are from the village of Marren, somewhere north of here, I believe. Oh, I have not heard such since we left our homeland! Aren't they the best?"

"Pretty near, I guess," Robby said, a little overcome by her exuberance.

"Let's dance!"

Before Robby could protest, she dragged him by the hand into the open space before the players.

"But, but I don't know how!"

Robby did not know whether he was supposed to lead or follow, and he did a bit of both, quite awkwardly, yet not without some natural ability. He had not danced since last year and had never danced much, though his mother taught him a little when he was a child. Still, he could not help laughing, and there was something mysteriously giddy about the music, or maybe it was the vivacious lass who moved around him. She seemed as light as a feather on her feet, and when she twirled about on one foot as she held his hand, he could have sworn she did not even touch the ground. Suddenly the tune was over and everyone was clapping. Robby, still laughing and clapping, too, felt a little embarrassed when he saw Ashlord among the onlookers, a plate of food in one hand and a tankard in the other.

"Another hidden talent, I see!" Ashlord laughed.

"I am forgetting my manners," Gaiyelneth said. "I am sure you are hungry and thirsty. Come along!"

She led Robby to tables set with all manner of food from baked pies and pots of steaming broth stew, to hams and apples and tomatoes and melons.

"Oh no! Not so much!" Robby cried when he saw that the plate Gaiyelneth filled was intended for him. "Truly, I'm not very hungry."

But he took the plate, and when offered, he chose wine instead of beer. Glancing around for Ashlord, he saw him sitting at a small table between the two wagons, talking with Thurdun. Ashlord was gesturing over his shoulder, and Thurdun looked Robby's way with an expression of amazement. Robby turned away as if he had not noticed, and he looked for a different spot to eat. He went to a bench at a table, put his plate and tankard down, and was about to sit when he heard a lady's voice behind him.

"They are talking about you."

Robby turned and saw Thurdun's sister, Queen Serith Ellyn, standing before him. She was tall and slender with golden hair parted just the way he had seen it the night before. Her gown was black, bound by green and embroidered with gold, and on her head was a circlet of gold. Even in this light, he could see that her eyes were silver-gray, as an unsettled sea in the sunlight, glittering with the same beauty and with deep, ageless ferocity. In her hands, she held the case of pens that Ashlord had purchased earlier. Gaiyelneth stood close behind her. Robby tried to bow, feeling more awkward at that than he had at dancing.

"Queen of Vanara," he managed to utter. "I am honored."

"I dreamed I would meet the Hidden One here by the waters of Halgaeth," she said with an enigmatic smile. She seemed immensely at peace and yet worn. Although she appeared to be only about Robby's age, he sensed that she was far older than anyone he had ever met. "Could that be you, Bellringer?"

"I do not know what you mean, my lady."

"You are the one who rang the Great Bell of Tulith Attis," she said. "And it was you who turned our enemy's attention away from us, though you could not know that. Did you know that you were foretold to me? And not only to me, but to others as well."

Robby shook his head. "I have little understanding of such things," he said. "Why do you call me the Hidden One?"

"I did not call you that. I only asked you if you were the Hidden One."

"Who is it that you mean?"

"He who is sought, but is not found, even by those who most seek him out. He who knows the name of one who is without a name."

Shocked, Robby glanced over his shoulder at Ashlord then at Gaiyelneth for some clue.

"Only the next King can name the name," Robby said bluntly. "I am no king."

"Oh," Serith Ellyn said, smiling. Robby could not tell from her tone and expression if she was mocking him or was sincere.

"Do you seek the Hidden One?"

"No," she answered. "Like Collandoth, I watch. I see the ending of ages and carry their memories, and I see the beginning of ages and carry their hopes. I watch for signs and for tracks in the events of the world. But you cannot watch for the wind, Robby Ribbon, Bellringer. You can only feel it and see its touch upon other things. And hear its coming and its passing. Such is the Hidden One before he is revealed."

Robby felt heavy, as if a weight pressed down from the Queen's eyes. His stomach fluttered and a quiver shot through his knees. A strange nervousness gripped him, as if his body prepared to flee.

"You need not be fearful," she said with a comforting smile. "You are no longer at Tulith Attis. We here are at peace, and greet you in friendship and thankfulness."

"I only did what I had to do to save myself," Robby said. "It was rather an accident. Until Lord Thurdun spoke to me of it last night, I had no knowledge of your danger."

"Such is the way of things," she said. "In the enemy's eagerness to ensnare one prey, his grip loosens on another, so that neither are caught. For though he is contemplative and scrutinizes the happenings of the world, he is sometimes rash and cannot always rightfully interpret things. We now know that on the night the Great Bell of Tulith Attis tolled, the foul legions along our borders were recalled. And those of his agents that lay in wait for us were turned to other directions, and great fear swept the enemy's realm. For such is the power of the Great Bell, so that those who most fear its meaning hear it as loudly as those it was meant to beckon."

"Forgive me, my lady. I do not know about such things," Robby repeated. "But if I have in any way aided you, then I am well rewarded by the honor of it and would that I could do more of the same."

She smiled, and behind her Gaiyelneth grinned.

"You speak well, Bellringer," Serith Ellyn said. "Indeed you are a friend to my heart, though I know you not at all!"

Robby bowed again, saying, "Then I am doubly honored."

"Not everyone would think that such a wonderful thing."

"I cannot help what others may think."

"True," she said. "Now eat and enjoy yourself. We may speak again later."

"Thank you."

Robby watched her glide away toward a tent near the shore, everyone bowing as she passed. She made a mild gesture at Thurdun, who excused himself from Ashlord and went to her.

"I wish to use the Seeing Stone," she said to him.

Thurdun nodded, and glanced around, then turned to the ever-nearby Chanter.

"Post six additional guards around the Queen's tent."

"Yes, Lord Thurdun."

• • •

Gaiyelneth remained behind, eyeing Robby with a mischievous smile. Robby looked at her blankly, realizing that she probably always smiled that way.

"I am mixed up in things well beyond me," he said to her.

"Don't worry," she said sitting at the bench and patting it for him to sit next to her. "At least not now. Enjoy your meal, and let us listen to the music together."

Indeed, Robby was hungrier than he had admitted. He quickly cleaned his plate and had his cup replenished by a passing soldier who served this night as waiter. All while he ate, the minstrels played, Gaiyelneth swaying to the music. As he picked up his fresh cup of wine, one of the young girls began to sing a ballad. It was in a foreign dialect, but Robby sensed that it was a love song, sweet and lonesome. Above them, the stars were out, and the lake was beginning to reflect the light of the low crescent moon. An easy breeze blew down from the hills toward the water and Robby looked at Gaiyelneth. There was some wildness about her, something like the way Sheila once was, and Robby was attracted to her. As he watched her, an expression of weariness crossed her face for a moment.

"Do you miss your home?"

She looked at him, smiling so that he realized what a silly question it was. But her expression softened, and she nodded.

"It is the most beautiful country ever to be seen, I think," she said. "And there is a man there whom I love. But he could not come with us, for he would not forsake his duty, just as I could not forsake my lady."

"Life is not just."

"No, sometimes it is not," she said. "It is my hope to see him again, and in that hope I am not sad."

"Is he in great danger?"

"No more than any of those who stayed behind."

Robby glanced toward Ashlord, who was speaking once again with Thurdun.

"How did Serith Ellyn know they were talking about me?"

Gaiyelneth looked at the two men and back at Robby

"Well, whom else would we all be talking about?"

"Why? What are they, and everyone else, saying?"

"Some are saying you are not truly a Sylphaen, but maybe some other creature with powers unimaginable. You rang the Bell. It has always been said that only a Firstborn could do that. And by doing it when you did, you distracted those who had been chasing us. You probably even saved our lives."

Robby shook his head.

"No one is supposed to know about me and the Bell."

"Few do. Among those here, apart from Ashlord, only Thurdun, the Queen, and I know about you. If that is your secret, then it is probably fairly safe in this region, for the Bell rang louder in the ears of Elifaen, whom it was meant to summon, than in the ears of Men. It was made in such a way."

"Thurdun told me he heard it, yet your party was far away from here," Robby said. "It is hard to believe it carried that far, though it was deafening from where I was."

"It was not just the sound that carried," Gaiyelneth explained. "It was the warning that it was made to carry which traveled so far."

"And who was chasing you?"

"We think they were agents of the King of Ruin."

"I thought he was just a myth."

"He is the Lord of Shades and Shadows."

"You mean Secundur."

"That is his name, though we do not care to speak it."

"But why does he chase you?"

"His agents wish harm to our Queen and ruin to come of our journey. So long as our Queen is alive, no one else may lay rightful claim upon Vanara. She has the ability to divine the answers to things, which makes her a powerful ruler, even when at a far distance from her realm."

"Thurdun told me your lands were no longer safe."

"We go to Glareth by the Sea, our ancient sister city," Gaiyelneth said. "We have kin there and faithful allies to guard the Queen. But we do not flee. Our Queen is fearless. We go to renew bonds with our allies in the east. Also to better understand the plight of those forced by Duinnor to come east from their lands in Vanara. What we have seen and been subjected to has deeply angered us, though we have held our ire in check. The Queen is angry, too. And very much saddened by it all."

"The Queen," Robby repeated, looking at the tent into which Serith Ellyn had gone. He saw Chanter close the flaps and stand between two other guards with his arms crossed, looking back at him.

• • •

Inside her tent, Serith Ellyn opened an iron chest and with both hands removed from it a smaller, heavy box. She carefully placed it on a small table and unlatched it and lifted away the top and sides. There, cradled by large silver prongs, was the Seeing Stone. It looked nothing like how myths and legends describe those fanciful things. Instead, it was merely a large rock, coarse and uneven, appearing in every aspect as never having been carved or shaped since being unearthed ages ago in the distant deserts. Anyone who knows about rocks and stones and such things would immediately recognize it as ordinary amber. It appeared remarkable only in its size and clarity, for it was twice the size of a large apple and of a light, honey-yellow color. The Queen placed a flat sheet of parchment before it and took up one of her new pens. Carefully twisting the top of the amber mass, a hole was revealed into which she dipped her pen.

• • •

"Are you refreshed for another dance?"

Robby shook his head, but could not refuse the lively girl, and he soon found himself being slung this way and that by a crowd of merrymakers. The night wore on, more wine and ale passed around, Gaiyelneth became positively giddy with drink, and Robby, no stranger to the cup, began to stagger.

"I must find my head!" he cried at last, stumbling out of the crowd and onto the ground beside a wagon. No sooner had he propped himself up against one of the wheels, than Gaiyelneth came along and fell down beside him, and, delirious with laughter, she collapsed over onto him. Though Robby did not know what was so funny, her state of joy was so contagious that he laughed, too, until tears ran down his face.

"There there, my child," he kept saying as he laughed, patting her on the back while she buried her head in his shoulder. "It will be all right soon."

After a while, they managed to stop laughing, but the music went on. She kept her head on his shoulder, and he kept his arm around her waist, and they listened. Lady Moon, tiring of the frivolity, was already strolling away below the treetops as the music became soft and sweet, and Robby realized that Gaiyelneth was asleep. As he, too, drifted into sleep, he was contented, almost happy, and oddly protective of her, though he barely knew her. Some while later, he was awakened by the sound of Gaiyelneth quietly crying into the same shoulder where, but a short time before, she had laughed. He put his other arm around her and embraced her tenderly. He became sad, sensing what it must be like to leave home, perhaps never to see it again, and to miss so terribly someone you loved. He thought of Sheila. With her in his thoughts, he soon sank back into slumber.

• • •

The music softened and eventually stopped. The revelers filtered to their tents and wagons, the food was put away, and guards were posted to stand watch at the road and around the encampment. Ashlord and Thurdun still talked, smoking their pipes long into the night. Someone came along and put a blanket over Robby and Gaiyelneth, but they did not stir. Robby dreamt of waterfalls and forest sprites dancing and splashing in the pools. His father was there, asking him to box away the Faere-dust because no one wanted it any more. He saw his mother talking to Queen Serith Ellyn over tea at their kitchen table. Billy danced with Sheila upon the Green while he laughed with Gaiyelneth, and yet he could not take his eyes from Sheila and felt jealous and hurt. When he looked away from the lake and up to where forested hills should have been, he saw instead towering dunes of sand. Distracted by Gaiyelneth's laughter, he looked back at Sheila and Billy. For a moment, he hoped that Sheila would leave Billy and come over to interrupt Gaiyelneth's chatter. However, Sheila seemed not to notice him. He turned his head to look back at the weird dunes and saw a lone figure standing there, black against the bright sky. As he shielded his eyes to look more carefully, the scene dimmed, and he found himself standing in the middle of the camp, an odd light reflecting off the lake and flowing like waves across the wagons and tables. No one was around, and he grew worried as he tried to rub the sleep from his eyes. But there were odd, silvery bubbles sitting all around, on the ground and in the wagons. They were large, much wider than a person was tall, and sometimes two or three of them clumped together. He approached one, still trying to see clearly, and reached out to touch its watery surface. Suddenly an arm shot out of the bubble, and a black, leather-gloved hand grabbed his wrist. Robby woke with a start, tossing off his blanket and struggling onto his knees, his heart pounding.

All was quiet, Gaiyelneth was gone, the fires were smoking embers, and only the braziers at the end of the quay atop the oddly bent columns were lit. Far away, a frog croaked a duet with a distant whippoorwill. Robby stood up, feeling dizzy from the combined effects of sleep, dance, and drink. Hearing voices, he stepped around the wagon and followed the sound until he could hear Ashlord's voice clearly. Stooping down, and looking underneath the wagon, he could see Ashlord's legs, still sitting as before. Another pair, Thurdun's, paced back and forth.

"So if it be he, it is an unexpected turn," Ashlord was saying. "Not at all what many thought would come to pass. For he is ignorant of the world and knows little of what is before him. He has had little in the way of education, and, though he does not know the languages of the West, he speaks from time to time in the First Tongue."

"How can that be? He is Sylphaen, not of the Firstborn. And, anyway, the First Tongue is all but forgotten."

"It is a mystery to me," Ashlord replied, tamping out his pipe. "Sheila is certain it was the First Tongue that he spoke, though she would not say what it was that he said to her. She said she had never heard that language before, yet understood every word he said."

"Then truly he is the Hidden One. For who else may speak the First Tongue who was not here at the making of the world?"

"We cannot yet be sure. And there is another who fits more readily what was expected. Sylphmar though he may be."

"Aye, but he is in service to Duinnor, and is not Elifaen," Thurdun replied. "It hardly seems likely that he would be the one, for he has sworn his loyalty."

"That is true. But he, too, is of the proper lineage, according to prophecy, and so must be considered."

"Has the young one been Scathed?"

"No."

"I see."

Robby knew they were talking about himself and someone else, but it was all riddles, and it irritated him to be treated so. It seemed to him that they could talk all they wanted, and it would not make him any more of anything.

"I am just me," he thought to himself. "All this other stuff is just…stuff!"

He walked away as quietly as he had approached, skirting the center of the encampment and making for the water's edge. Along it he ambled, taking care where he stepped, picking up a stone and skipping it lightly across the placid surface. A sentry posted by the quay saw him and waved. Robby waved back and approached, stepping up onto the stone landing.

"Good morning."

"Good morning, Robby Ribbon of Passdale."

"When will the boats arrive, do you think?"

"I cannot say," replied the sentry, relaxing a little. "But I imagine before day is too far along."

Robby looked eastward and saw the bare hint of dawn.

"Ah." Robby nodded and shoved his hands into his pockets. "I think I'll stroll out there."

The sentry nodded as he passed, and Robby walked along the grassy top of the broad quay. It was wide enough for three wagons abreast, with easy space between, and jutted out about fifty yards into the lake. On either side, at regular intervals, steps led down into the water, and there were iron rings, too, for docking boats. As he neared the end of the quay, he saw that the odd stone columns were actually carved statues of two arms outstretched, as if reaching out from the water, and each hand held a cup from which the flames rolled. They were over twice Robby's height and provided a great deal of light on the end of the quay and upon the surrounding waters. He was nearly at the very end when he noticed a figure, close by the left arm, wrapped in a hooded cloak. Hearing a sound, he stopped and listened more carefully. The person was singing softly. He thought it might be a lullaby, the same, even, as that sung to him as a sick child by the two ladies, the ones he now knew had been Elifaen. Indeed, it was a lullaby, and if Robby had known the language, he would have heard these words:

> *Wide does the sky stretch beyond sight*
> *Long does the river run to the sea*
> *Slow pass the days and slower the night*
> *Soft does the dove sing to me.*
>
> *Gray are the clouds the sun to hide*

*As raindrop turns to snowflake*
*Bare are the trees on the hillside*
*And cold blows the wind on the lake.*

Serith Ellyn stopped singing, gazing out across the water. A puff of wind tossed the flames above, and Robby heard the gentle lapping of the water against stones.

"You are troubled, too," she said without turning. Robby stepped up beside her. "Like me, you are lost in change, not knowing what may come of things."

"Yes."

"You know what you must do, but not what you should do."

"Yes."

"They are the same," she said, turning to him. "When you do what you must, it is as it should be, and leads to the next and the next. This age is coming to an end at last, as all things must, and you are caught between the ending and the beginning of things, born of one but living into another. Why should the Bellringer of Tulith Attis be so different? Does fate ignore the unknown person in favor only of kings and queens and the mighty?"

"I'm not sure I believe in fate," he said, not meaning to be argumentative but realizing too late that it probably sounded that way.

"Fate. Destiny. Chance. Doom. They are but different seasons of the same year," she replied. "Call it what you will. You cannot escape it, no more than you can escape your skin."

"Everyone talks to me and about me, but no one will speak plainly," Robby grumbled.

"We speak as plainly as we can," Serith Ellyn replied sympathetically. "It is for you to hear or not to hear. Listen first from your heart, then let your head guide you."

Robby nodded, but he was not sure that he really understood.

"We Elifaen are afraid of change," she explained. "Perhaps we have seen too much of it. All who live long in this world sense the passing away of things. The forest shrinks before the axe and the plough, and meadows are covered with cobblestone and building-brick. White waters of anxious rivers turn dark and slow and wind more peacefully to the sea. Even the sun seems not so high or so bright as in the days of our youth, and the snow not so fresh or clean, only colder. We attach ourselves to these things, as they to us, and, even as our attachments grow more tenuous with each passing year, we cling the harder to them. Yet so, too, are the works of our hands, as the earth strives to take back what is hers. Proud houses fall into decline and great cities pass into ruin. The stories of those things are lost to forgotten languages and moth-eaten scrolls. Vine and root grapple with the rune carved in stone, and rust carries away, fleck by fleck, the great gates of iron."

The breeze reversed itself, picked up, and blew at them from across the lake, taking the Queen's hood from her head and tossing her hair. She pulled her cloak about her and turned toward the encampment.

"I must prepare to depart," she said, walking away without looking back.

The wind eased, and Robby watched her recede into the darkness of the shore. Looking back out across the water, he resolved to be idle no longer. If there was, in fact, something he was supposed to do, or something important to be involved in, he would not go blindly into it, unprepared and ignorant.

"I've wasted enough time. If there's time left," he said to himself, "I will get ready for whatever may come!"

As he made this pact with himself, he saw, far out on the water, light gray shapes, like several birds hovering strangely just over the lake's surface, motionless between water and air. He realized, with a little thrill, that they were the billowing sails of the distant boats that were coming to take away Queen Serith Ellyn and her people. Looking ashore, he saw that the camp was stirring and fires were being relit for breakfast. Water lapped up against the stone just beneath him, and he sat down, dangling his legs over the side, and fished around in his jacket for his pipe and firesticks. After lighting his leaf, Robby leaned against the right-hand statue and closed his eyes. The tug of the breeze and the lapping of the water almost lulled him back to sleep. Maybe he did doze off for a bit, for when he opened his eyes the night sky was giving over to the coming sun, and purple-pink wisps of thin, high clouds lined the eastern sky. The sails were much closer, now, and Robby could see the darker hulls of the craft although they still seemed motionless. As the first rays of morning swept across the lake, the sails became brilliant pink for a moment, then quickly changed to gold and then bright white. Robby could see eight boats, coming steadily on, each with two triangular sails, one up a mast and another smaller one just before the mast. The closer they came, the faster they seem to move, even though the breeze seemed to lessen. At the bow of the lead boat stood a man with one hand on the forestay and another on his hip, his long brown hair flying about his face. Judging by the man, he estimated that each boat was about ten or twelve yards long and about a fourth as wide. Robby tapped out his cold pipe, put it away, then stood. Several others had come out onto the quay, including Ashlord and Thurdun. The man in the boat waved, and as soon as Robby and the others waved back, he realized who it was.

"Ullin!" he cried. "Is that Ullin?"

"Yes, it is," answered Ashlord. "I thought it would surprise you."

"I'll say! So this is the task he was to carry out?"

"Only one of many," Ashlord said. "He had others, too, but this fit in nicely."

"Do you know Ullin?" Robby asked Thurdun.

"We have never actually met. I know him by his reputation and through his reports to Collandoth. He fought along our southern border against Dragonkind raiders with a contingent from Duinnor some years ago and made a name for himself. When he came to the White Palace, I was not there. For your information, Robby Ribbon, Commander Tallin is of the House of Fairoak, one of the most ancient and honorable of all. It is no wonder that little is spoken of it by your mother, for that House has had misfortune after tragedy. It is too bad that there are not more like Ullin Saheed, though. Ashlord tells me that he is your cousin, by your mother's brother. That makes you of the House of Fairoak, too. Even more so, since Ullin Saheed's mother was not Elifaen, and yours is."

"Hullo!" cried out Ullin at that moment, still a very long stone's throw away. "Is that some kin of mine come to meet me?"

"Hullo, Ullin!" Robby called, waving back. "Oh, I wish he had been here last night!"

"Me, too," Thurdun said.

"Aye," added Ashlord. "But he comes as soon as he is able and would have been here sooner but for some delay, I imagine."

"Whose boats are these?" Robby asked.

"They belong to the Lakemen who serve Prince Danoss, the Earl of Connassa," Thurdun said. "His principality borders the northeastern shores of this lake, and he keeps boats to transfer goods and guests from place to place as well as to patrol the lake. He was kind enough to allow their use for our transport to his castle at Formouth."

"I have heard of him," Robby said. "I thought he was a Sea King."

"You think of his great-grandfather," Ashlord said. "King Thalamir, of the House of Beech, was the last of the Sea Kings, and was the last Sovereign King of Glareth. He was forced to abdicate kingship by Duinnor, but his descendants have been the Ruling Princesses and Princes of Glareth ever since. His grandson, Ruling Prince Carbane, now rules Glareth, and Prince Carbane's son, Prince Danoss, governs the old Eastlands realm from Formouth and the Province of Connassa. Ruling Prince Carbane has granted Queen Serith Ellyn refuge as a welcomed guest and arranges their journey from here through his son. The House of Fairlinden and the House of Beech are distantly related. Though separated by great distance, they have always maintained close ties."

"The House of Beech aided my sister when it was her time to take the throne of Vanara," Thurdun added. "Our Houses and our Realms have been closely allied ever since."

"I see," Robby said, but he did not actually understand at all. The boats were maneuvering past the quay and looping around on the breeze, lowering their foresails and preparing to make their approach to dock. Already, Ullin's boat was luffing its main to slow its approach. Ullin still stood at the bow, now holding a coil of rope. With a graceful sweep of his arm, he tossed it to Robby. It uncurled through the air and Robby grabbed it as it passed his head. Thurdun then gripped the rope behind Robby, for security, as Ullin, with the help of another man, dropped the mainsail and furled it quickly, neatly stowing it and its boom by folding it upright against the mast. At their signal, Robby and Thurdun gave a tug and the boat slid gently toward them. Almost as soon as it came alongside, they had it lined and docked, and Ullin hopped onto the steps and bounded up to Robby.

"Hello, cousin!" he said, giving Robby a handshake and a hug. "This is a happy surprise! I see you've fallen in with Ashlord since I last saw you. I take it the errand you ran for me went well, then?"

"Well," Robby said, glancing at Ashlord. "I guess it turned out well enough. Here, let me introduce you to—"

"Lord Thurdun, of the House of Fairlinden," Ullin said, bowing. "I am Ullin Saheed Tallin, of the House of Fairoak, at your service."

"You do me honor, Commander," Thurdun said shaking Ullin's hand. "And it is I who must be at your service, for all the work you have done on behalf of the Queen and our people."

"I do what it is that I can do," Ullin bowed again. "Collandoth! How are you?"

Robby watched as the two shook hands and hugged and exchanged greetings. From the way they spoke and acted, he saw they were old friends, though Ullin was ever respectful of the other. Yet, Ashlord was most casual and told Ullin how happy he was to see him at last.

"After all these many months of letters and notes," he said, "it is good to see you in person. And well, I hope?"

"Yes, quite well."

"What is the state of the boats?" Thurdun asked.

"They are all fine craft," Ullin said. "Fast and stable. Each can hold ten quite comfortably and many more, if needed. If the wind fails, there are oars stowed, too, though I doubt they will be needed. We have provisions already aboard. Enough for fifty for two and a half days. Each boat is crewed by three, all fine men and boys, experienced and lake-wise. Departure can be as soon as they have eaten and the boats have been loaded."

"Very well, then," Thurdun said. He waved to one of his captains and gave a few orders. Soon there were many soldiers on the quay, lending a hand with the other boats and making the acquaintance of the Connassan Lakemen. Thurdun led Ullin ashore and to the tents and wagons. Standing in front of one of the tents was the Queen, and Robby was surprised to see Ullin kneel and kiss her hand.

"It has been many years, Commander," she said. "Since I last saw you in the Court of Vanara. At that time, I expressed my gratitude to you and your men for your defense of my realm. Now I thank you once more for your aid and your devotion to our friendship."

"I do what it is that I can do, Your Majesty," Ullin repeated, rising. "It is a sorry day that Vanara cannot protect her Queen."

"I do not leave Vanara out of fear for my safety," she returned. "I know that many of my people will never consider leaving when their Queen still resides there. They would stay to the harm of their families. I have not given up my people, nor have I forsaken my pact with them. I lead them away, if they are to be led, to give the enemy less blood and fewer slaves. It is the children of Vanara, mostly, that we fear for, and those unfit to fight. War is coming. Soon it will be too late for them to leave, and I would not have their loyalty to me delay them. If they do choose to leave our home, I would have them find good welcome in Glareth Realm. To make the way for them, should that be necessary, is why I come."

"Yes, Queen," Ullin nodded. "I well understand these things. Perhaps I may assist your return to Vanara someday soon."

"I hope you shall."

Soon they were having breakfast, Ullin and the boatmen, along with all of the company of Vanara as well as the troupe of minstrels who had not yet departed. The narrow tables of the night before were set up in a long line, and Robby sat beside Ullin, who sat beside the Queen, at one end. Across from Ullin on the Queen's other hand sat Ashlord. She seemed quite taken by Ullin and listened as intently as any to the account he gave of his journey from Duinnor through Passdale and thence to Glareth. Standing behind Serith Ellyn, Thurdun had only a cup of hot coffee, which he quickly finished and then excused himself. A little later, when Robby looked around for him, he saw Thurdun organizing the movement of the company's goods onto the quay in preparation for loading.

"Ullin," Ashlord said, "I have already spoken with Thurdun about this, and I wonder if you think you are needed by the Queen or her party from here on."

"It was my intention to see them safely across the lake."

"I know," Ashlord said. "But would you consider returning with me and Robby to Passdale today? There is some urgency to my request."

Ullin looked at Robby then at the Queen.

"I believe you have done all and more than could be asked of you," she said. "Do not feel obliged to continue with us from here."

"Well," he said, "then I suppose, if I am needed elsewhere..."

"You are," Ashlord said. "And I hate to press you on it, but I think we should depart as soon as we may."

It was quickly decided that Ashlord would have one of the horses so the three could ride back to Passdale. Ullin went to the boats to make his farewells to the boatmen, and Robby followed him to the quay, struck by how respectfully they treated Ullin. Most stopped long enough to reach up to shake his hand, or touch his arm, and many hugged him and bade him well, speaking in the odd Glareth accent unfamiliar to Robby.

Meanwhile, the tents were struck and loaded onto the boats, and the wagons were hitched by the minstrels and driven away, singing as they went "Fare thee well, Faere of Dale. Fare thee well, Faere of Hill. Fare thee, fare thee, fare thee well!"

As well, a little barge was prepared for Celefar, and Thurdun led the obedient buckmarl onto it. After a few coaxing words, Celefar knelt down and folded his legs beneath him, as the barge's lines were affixed to the sailboat for towing. Robby watched all this with interest, and followed Ullin as he made his farewells to the remaining few Lakemen he had not already spoken to.

When Ullin and Robby stepped from the quay, they found Ashlord, Thurdun, Gaiyelneth, and Queen Serith Ellyn awaiting them with the horses.

"I wish you to have this, Ullin Saheed," the Queen said, taking from her thumb a ring and offering it to Ullin. It was silver, set with a brilliant sapphire surrounded by crusted rubies in the shape of a small leaf. "It is a token of the friendship between you and your House and the House of Fairlinden of Vanara. It will be a true sign to our allies of your honor and valor in our cause."

"I am very honored, my lady," Ullin bowed deeply as he took the ring and slipped it onto his little finger. "I shall wear it proudly!"

Gaiyelneth handed the Queen a small wooden box. She held it and turned to Robby, opening the box so that he could see into it. Inside was a short coil of rope, reddish-brown in color, much like the barley-snake, about an inch thick, and capped at each end by age-blued steel.

"I have asked Thurdun to give you this," she said, "for it is his heirloom, passed down from father to child from the First Age of this world."

Thurdun took the rope and held it out reverently with both hands.

"It is called Swyncraff," Thurdun said, "and was made by the first smithies of our race from the first tree seeded. It is the last of its kind, and the art of its making is long lost. It is stronger than the iron chains of Gorcastle and will break only when the foundations of the world are torn asunder. No knot tied by its owner may ever be untied except by he. No knife or blade will cut it, and it will never fray. Whatsoever shape is formed by it will stay until released. Behold!"

Thurdun stretched it out straight, extending about five feet long, and it stayed that way when he cast it down, end first, upon a stone. It rang metallically and bounced as if it were solid steel. Snatching it up on the bounce, Thurdun swung it around like a sword, and it whistled lightly through the air. Holding it by one end, he shaped a hook into the other end and it stayed, though he swung it around mightily. He straightened it again and held it out to Robby, who reluctantly took it with both hands. It was as light and as hard as the finest steel, and it was warm to the touch.

"I, Thurdun, of the House of Fairlinden, by the right of my fathers, give to thee Swyncraff to bear and to command, as a token of our gratitude and favor. Take it now, Robby Ribbon, Bellringer. By all rights I relinquish it to thee!"

Immediately, Swyncraff drooped and dangled from Robby's hands as limp and soft as silk.

"You are now its master," Serith Ellyn said. "It will teach you its ways and its secrets, and it will never fail you. And let it be a sign to those who have the eyes to see that you are a great friend of Vanara."

Robby looked at Ashlord, who was nodding back and beaming as proudly as could be. Robby then turned to Serith Ellyn and Thurdun and bowed.

"I promise I will do whatever I may to honor our friendship and this gift."

"We know that you will," Thurdun said.

"Here," Serith Ellyn said. "Allow me to bind Swyncraff about your waist. There! Now go with our blessing and our thanks!"

Robby bowed again, then turned to his horse and took its reins.

"And here," Gaiyelneth said to Robby, stepping up to him as he put one foot in the stirrup. "I have only this to give thee with my own thanks."

She kissed him on the cheek. Surprised, he said nothing as he looked deep into her eyes. For a moment he felt as if he saw all the way to the bottom of her homesick heart, and he was deeply touched. He dipped his head in thanks, then climbed into his saddle.

Soon they were waving farewell and were moving up the road back to Passdale, climbing back into the forest and up the hills. They rode in silence for the most part, each to his own thoughts. When they topped the ridge, Ashlord halted and turned in his saddle, pointing toward a break in the trees behind them where they could see the lake not too distant away. Eight bright sails bent to the wind far out from shore.

"They go quickly," Robby said.

"Yes," Ullin commented, dismounting. "Someone with longer legs has been riding you," he said to Anerath as he adjusted the stirrups.

"He seems glad to have his old traveling partner back with him," Ashlord chuckled. "Though he has been a blessing to me this past month."

"How did Anerath get from you, Ullin, to you, Ashlord?" Robby asked.

"I left him near Colleton, to cross a footbridge that would not bear his weight," Ullin explained, getting back into the saddle. They all set out again as he continued. "An adventure all of itself due to the storms. I knew he could find his way back to Ashlord, perhaps with the guidance of a little bird."

"I knew Ullin would do so," Ashlord took up. "And so Anerath kindly consented to carry me on some errands."

Robby shook his head, looking at Ullin's mount. As if noticing Robby's amazement, Anerath snorted and whinnied gleefully, tossing his mane.

"From the bits and pieces that I've been able to pick up," Ullin said to Robby, "you had some adventure of your own the day we last saw each other."

"I suppose I did."

"Will you tell me about it?"

"If he does not, then I must," said Ashlord, "for that is much in the way of getting to our new business."

"So it was you who rang the Bell?" Ullin said. "I surmised as much from the conversation at the breakfast table earlier and by the words of the Queen and her brother. I did not want to pry too much with others about."

"That was thoughtful of you. And wise. I asked Robby to be quiet about his experience," Ashlord said. "We will tell you what happened."

As Ashlord and Robby described what had happened on the errand, Ullin was much concerned, asking a few pointed questions here and there concerning certain details. He knew of the Great Bell, of course, and about Heneil who made it and the terrible battle that took place at Tulith Attis, and of its fall. So it did not take long for him to grasp the predicament that Robby was in.

"If the traitor of Tulith Attis finds out about this," Ullin said most urgently, "Robby will be in peril. The traitor may think that his secret, his identity, was discovered."

"I know," said Ashlord. "And there's more. A Dragonkind man was killed in Barley, along with other men, on the day Robby returned to Passdale from Tulith Attis. Robby was there when it happened. The Dragonkind and two others were killed as they made their way toward the Hill. The fourth, I was forced to slay in combat later that night."

"Dragonkind? This far east?" Ullin stammered. "Why?"

"That is something that I made every effort to learn," Ashlord said. "They were headed for Tulith Attis, apparently, and the one that confronted me wanted to know about the Bell and who had rung it. I, in turn, wanted to know who sent him. I knew of his coming, by Certina, and laid a trap for him and cornered him within the fortress walls. He was a Westerner, from Duinnor, judging by his accent. He was cunning and wily. We fought a fight such as I have not fought in many years, and we plied each other with steel against steel for three hours along the ramparts of the old fortress. All the while he taunted me with his questions, and I peppered him with my own. In the end, he surmised, I believe, that I was not the one who rang the Bell. I wore him down but learned nothing, except what his retorts implied. Namely, that he was already nearby when the Bell rang. He made haste for Tulith Attis to find some explanation, and, presumably, then to make a report of it to his master. However, I did not learn his master's name, for he then came at me with aimed deathblows, knowing I would not give in to his escape. He would not concede the fight and came at me again and again, until I slew him. I learned nothing else from his clothes, weapons, or his saddlebags."

"Undoubtedly, sent by the traitor of Tulith Attis," Ullin said.

"More likely, he was sent by an agent of the traitor," Ashlord mused.

"So the traitor, or the agent, may not be that far away," Robby suggested.

"I don't know. But I do not think the traitor himself is very close at hand," Ashlord said. "If he was so close, then why did he not come himself to Tulith Attis?"

"So there must be others, an agent, as you say."

"And whoever sent the Dragonkind and the others must know by now that his first attempt to find out who rang the Great Bell has failed," Ullin said. "He will try again."

"Yes, certainly, and by more crafty means, I'm thinking," Ashlord agreed.

"Meanwhile, Robby's role has been kept secret?"

"Besides us, there are only four in Barley and Passdale who know. And all are trustworthy."

They rode along in silence for a mile or so while Ullin thought about all of this.

"Then where do I come in?" he asked.

"I need to find an excuse to have you near Robby," Ashlord said. "At least until we learn more. Idleness makes me nervous, even if it is sometimes required."

"Me, too," Robby said. "And I have an idea about how Ullin can help me."

"Oh?"

"Yes," Robby said enthusiastically. "It is quite simple. A militia is going to be raised. I was there during part of the discussions last night. I think the idea is to have part of it made up of Boskmen who will cover their side of the county and another militia to cover the other side around Passdale. Mr. Bosk will head the Boskmen, as is his place, but we need someone to head up the Passdale militia."

"And who better than an experienced Kingsman?" Ashlord caught on.

"Right! And I would join the militia, to be trained along with the rest," Robby looked eagerly over at Ullin. "I need to learn to defend myself. If someone is going to come looking for me, I'd rather be in with a bunch of armed people that I know and trust than alone."

"I see," Ullin said. "I see."

As Ullin considered the idea, Robby looked at Ashlord who nodded and winked back at him, obviously pleased with the idea.

"We'll need a signal," Ullin said. "To gather the militiamen rapidly from all parts."

"Of course," Ashlord said.

"Yes," agreed Robby. "I suppose that would be needed."

"I have in mind to have the blacksmith fashion a device, say, a bell," Ullin said. "And to designate Robby, here, as Company Bellringer."

"Ha-ha-ha! Splendid cover!" Ashlord laughed. "Then, if accidental references leak out, it may be assumed that they are about one bell and not about the other!"

"Then you'll do it?" Robby asked.

"I will present myself to the authorities for the commission," Ullin said. "But let me warn you: If you serve under my command, I will be no easier on you than anyone else."

"That is only right," said Robby, grinning.

# Chapter 15

## Esildre at Middlemount

Esildre and her two great-nephews traveled north from Duinnor City to Whitefall, then along the river of the same name toward its confluence with the Osterflo. Her intent was to make for Glareth by the Sea, taking boats down river on the Osterflo. But when the trio arrived at Blueshoals, they found no boats capable of taking them and their buckmarls, too, so they continued on, following the river road eastward. As they progressed, Tulleg and Kranneg remained as silent as they always were, and Esildre had little to say. But if her two taciturn escorts noticed that their pace seemed to slow with each passing day, they commented not at all upon it. And by the time they were half way between Blueshoals and the village of Montgate, Esildre seemed even more distracted than ever by her thoughts. On the afternoon of the twenty-fifth day of their trek, she drew her buckmarl to a halt, and so did her escorts. They watched as she looked down the sharp bank to the river where a heavily laden flatboat made its way down stream. She turned her head to the south and gazed for a long time at the rising hills that were the northern rim of Middlemount Plateau. After an hour, she turned her buckmarl in that direction, and her two escorts followed into a sparse wood along a steeply winding path. Near sunset, she halted and dismounted. When they saw her remove her bedroll from her saddle, the two brothers did the same. When night fell, they had eaten, and Esildre sat crosslegged before the fire while Tulleg stretched out nearby and Kranneg lounged beside him smoking his pipe.

"I must thank you two for coming along with me," she said, not taking her eyes from the flames. Tulleg shrugged, and Kranneg tilted his head with interest. "I have taken you away from your studies, and for all I know I am leading you toward danger. My path is paved with uncertainties. I mean to change course. Whereas before I was determined to go to Glareth by the Sea, I now find myself yearning for other parts. I cannot say why. And the region that urges me does not hold pleasant memories for me."

She glanced at them, but their expressions were entirely inscrutable, as if it did not matter one way or the other where they went.

"I mean to go into the Thunder Mountains, to retrace my past somewhat to see what has happened since I was last there. Since you agreed to escort me to Glareth, I release you as my escorts. I am indebted to you for seeing me this far, but I am certain that I will be safe for the remainder of my journey. You have been good companions, wholly suitable to the disposition of my spirit, and I wish you no further inconvenience."

The fire crackled as she paused. She did not expect them to respond, and they did not.

"Indeed, I can think of but one other whom may have served as well as you two have done," she continued. "He served as my escort some while back, and I came to know and to trust him in ways I cannot explain. But that was while I was blind. With my sight restored, I would not trust myself with him because I might wish—"

She stopped herself, glancing again at the silent pair nearby. Through the veil that she wore, she could see their eyes fixed upon her, and the flickering light played upon their expressions in a manner that made Esildre feel as if they were intensely interested in what she had almost let slip out.

Saying no more, she wrapped her blanket around herself and lay down, putting her head on her saddle. She watched the fire burn itself down to embers, then watched the embers slowly dull from yellow to red. When the last dark red coal flicked its last spark and faded to black, she continued to stare. But it was the blackness of her own soul that had her attention, made all the more stark by the memory of Tyrin's kind voice. She absently reached up and touched her cheek, the very spot he had kissed on the day he said goodbye to her. A smile broke across her face.

• • •

The next morning, they saddled their buckmarls and made ready for their departure. Nothing had been said one way or the other about whether Esildre's escorts would turn back, but they were in their saddles first, watching her complete her preparations for the day. She tied the last of her gear onto her saddle, then she mounted, tossing her cloak to drape over her buckmarl behind her. She stood in her stirrups, then sat in her saddle and shifted her weight to settle the cinches. Reining southward, she made off up the steep trail toward the top of Middlemount, and Tulleg and Kranneg followed a short distance behind. Her pace, they noticed, was somewhat faster than it had been for many days.

# Chapter 16

# Ullin's Militia

It was a very busy time for all of Barley and Passdale. Everyone was occupied with harvest, the preparations for the fall festival, or with the forming of the new militias; many with all three. Ullin had been gladly granted a commission by the town leaders to head up the militia based in Passdale, and he quickly worked out the details with Mr. Bosk, who would head up the militia in and around Boskland. The two militias would work together on training and duties, and the Boskland and Passdale units would be commanded by Mr. Bosk and Ullin respectively. Within days, Ullin had sent an order to the blacksmith for certain items and another to Mr. Furaman to supply from his stockade or other sources. Arrangements were made for barracks to be established in the cellar of the Common House, and for a bell tower to be erected in the yard for calling together the militia. The blacksmith, Clingdon, and his helpers worked all of five days, while the tower was being built, enthusiastically smelting, hammering, welding, shaping, and forging the bell, which was somewhat squarish in appearance, made of iron plates welded and riveted together. So diligent was Clingdon, and so masterful of his craft, that within a week it was being proudly hoisted into place on the same day that its tower was completed.

"Best thing I ever made!" Mr. Clingdon said, beaming.

Ullin named Robby his aide and asked that he be relieved of all store duties until further notice. Robby's father and mother agreed to this, a bit reluctantly, but they understood the need for it, in different ways. Mr. Ribbon thought it hardly appropriate to ask for volunteers for the militia if he forbade is own son to join. Mirabella agreed, not sharing her own reasons for supporting the decision.

Word was sent out that any man hearing the bell toll, and who appeared at the Common House within one hour of its sounding, would be considered for the militia. Details of service would be given at that time. Three days later, at dawn, when Ullin was satisfied that the word was well spread, he gave Robby the order to summon the volunteers. Robby pulled the bellrope, swinging a hammer within the bell atop the tower. Several men stood around, with the blacksmith Mr. Clingdon among them, and when the bell clanged out loudly, they all shook hands and nodded, satisfied and proud of their hard work. Soon men and boys began to arrive, some on horseback and others walking or even running so as not to be late. After a few minutes, Ullin asked Robby to stop ringing the bell and to turn his attention to recording the names of the arrivals. Within an hour, he had more than a hundred names of those who had gathered. Ullin stood before them on the front steps of the Common House.

"I am Captain Ullin Saheed Tallin, King's Ranks, First Kingsman, First Army, Third Engineer Battalion, detached to the King's Post as Special Courier. While not serving in an active Kingsman unit, I hold the field rank of commander. I am now commissioned by your people to be commander of the Passdale Militia. You will address me as Commander Tallin, Commander, or Sir. I have appointed Mr. Robby Ribbon to act as my aide and second-in-command until further notice. You will address him as Mr. Ribbon or Sir. Any of you who can follow me this day on foot until I release you may serve in our militia. Any who cannot keep up, or who is not present whenever I take the roll count cannot serve. Those who have horses, hitch them here. Those of you who brought weapons, leave them; this is not a day for weapons, it is one for speed and endurance! Mr. Ribbon, bring the list of names."

Ullin strode down the steps and through the gathering.

"Let us go!" he cried.

"Where are we going?" asked one man.

"Let us go!" was all Ullin replied as he strode out into the road.

So they followed. Robby did not expect this any more than the rest and could only shrug at the questions he was asked. Ullin led them through Passdale, down the road, and across the bridge. He turned them northward, cutting through the woods and fields here and there, then back upon the path. Through streams and over craggy hills he marched until they came to Weepingbrook, and he waded through it to the other side and up the bank. On and on they went, turning now southward across more fields and into a clearing. There, Ullin stopped.

"Answer when your name is called out," he told them. "Mr. Ribbon, call the roll, strike any name not answered, and give me the count of who's left."

This Robby did.

"Forty-two!" he said at the end of his reckoning.

"Forty-two!" Ullin repeated, then he turned to continue on.

All morning he walked them around Barley, until, nearly noon, they came suddenly upon the river road along the banks of the Bentwide.

"Rest!" he called and sat down on a log. After a few moments he stood up. "Call the roll!"

Robby did so once more.

"Thirty-seven!"

Down the banks of the Bentwide, through the shallow water, and up the other side they went. They plunged into the woods and up into the hills. When they reached the top of the ridge of hills, nearly an hour later,

Robby recognized the place where he so often came to meditate. Ullin took another count.

"Thirty-three!"

They went down the path familiar to Robby and along the road and back to the Common House where Robby once again called the roll.

"Thirty-three!" Ullin announced. "You have shown yourselves to be hearty and determined. There is food and refreshment inside. Eat. And we will talk about our militia."

That was how they began. Ullin explained their duties: to patrol the region, to be ready to ward off any hostile intruders, and to be on call to perform any duties fit for the militia. Any who could not abide taking orders or who failed in training would be excluded from the militia, and no man that had any debt could join. Until other arrangements could be made, each was responsible for his own clothes and food and fodder for his own horse, when needed. They would be required to perform hard work, hard training, and to spend time away from their homes, shops, farms, and families. They would earn nothing in return, except perhaps the gratitude of their neighbors.

"My duty is to train you and to lead you. I will teach you the use of weapons, how to fight and kill the enemy, how to avoid being killed, and how to work together. When under my command, you will answer to me, or to other officers I may appoint, and to no one else. Your training will be hard, and, since we are a small force, I will demand much of you. If you cannot be trained, if you cannot take orders and carry them out correctly, or if you do not come when summoned, you will be expelled from the militia and shame will be upon you. Think on all this tonight. If you still desire to be a militiaman, you are to be here tomorrow at dawn to sign your enlistment papers and to take an oath of service."

The next day, all thirty-three showed up. They were sworn before the council to obey their commanders, to defend the region, to act at all times in the best interests of the region, to show no mercy to their enemies, and to be loyal and faithful to one another. With that, the training began in earnest. Ullin introduced them to the battle sword, lance, and shield, and explained to them the purpose of marching in close order and in step. He explained how the bell would signal to them: A slow toll, spaced at about a half-minute between sets of three quick tolls, as the regular call for the militia to gather, and a steady uninterrupted tolling as an emergency call to arms. He ordered that each person should come alone at a certain hour for individual instruction, and they would all be required to report every night two hours before dusk for group training.

Thus, from sun to moon, Ullin's days were spent training each member of the Passdale Militia, more often than not with Robby as an assistant. In this manner, Robby learned quickly, for not only was he himself instructed by Ullin, but he learned from the instruction of others, too. In addition, he learned something of orders, reports, dispatches, and planning from Ullin. As often as possible, Ullin arranged to have meals for his men, too, and as they all ate together, he talked to them of battle and arms, of the right behavior of a faithful soldier, of having honor in battle even when courage fails, and of the times when mercy was right, brave, and noble, and of the times when giving quarter was foolhardy and treacherous.

While the men and boys of Passdale thus trained, Sheila was asked to go to Boskland to instruct those men in the use of the bow, so Robby saw even less of her than before. They had hardly spoken, except for the usual morning and evening greetings, for nearly a month, and now Robby found that he missed even those brief moments. While his heart ached for her, he did not have much time to meditate on it. As well as assisting Ullin with training, the Kingsman also had him running errands, keeping the roll, and even tutoring some members of the militia on their letters, for, as Ullin said, "Instructions may need to be given in written orders, and it would be a poor soldier who could not make them out."

Ullin divided the militia up into squads of about five men each, and each night a squad was to stay at the Common House barracks to keep watch and await orders. Additionally, twice every week, the entire militia stayed the night. In this way, there was always a presence of the militia at the Common House, and there was always a watch on the roof and at the doors.

"This is to be our armoury," Ullin explained. "If the enemy takes this place, he takes all of Passdale."

Two weeks into their training, two new volunteers arrived in the persons of Billy Bosk and Ibin Brinnin. Billy wanted to be a part of the Boskland militia. However, Mr. Bosk, fearing accusations of favoritism, opposed having his son serve in the ranks. So Billy and Ibin came to Passdale to volunteer for service. Everyone knew of Billy's fighting ability, but Ullin was reluctant.

"How will you answer the call in time?" he asked.

"Well," Billy explained, "Ibin an' me'll take up livin' over at the weaver's, who is me uncle on me mum's side, an' who has given us the little cottage out back of his place. It's awful run-down, but close by. For livin', Ibin an' meself have been taken on by Mrs. Greardon to help out at the mill, which also is close by."

"I see," Ullin said. "What skill at arms do you have?"

"I'm a right fair swordsman," Billy said, raising his fists as if to box, "but I specialize in up close handiwork. An' Ibin here, why he's a regular ox, as ye can see, an' can take on four er five ordinary men like swattin' flies."

"We'll see," Ullin said. "I agree only if you can keep up with us on today's march and then match staffs with whosoever I pick to go against you."

Billy and Ibin proved themselves eager and energetic, and it heartened Robby to have them along the march. When they returned to the Common House, Ullin himself tested their skills with staff and sword. He found Billy to be nimble and quick, but somewhat uncoordinated, whereas Ibin was slow but powerful.

"Passing, I would say," he finally admitted. "Particularly since you have had no training to speak of. If you'll take the oath, we will have you. But you will have to work extra hard to get your skills to be the equal of the others."

So, in that manner, Robby was reunited with two of his best friends. The rest of the Passdale men were glad to have them, too, for Billy's tough reputation had at one time or another been proven against most of the noses and chins present, and none of them could gainsay having the sheer mass of Ibin at their side. The two took to the training rather well, learned to obey orders and to understand the bell signals, though Ibin preferred the "little bell" as opposed to the "big bell," the former being the little triangle that was rung as a call to meals.

A few nights later, the whole militia was ordered to stay over at the Common House to take part in a full evening of training and to get an early rise for even more training at dawn. After a long session of instruction lasting well into the night, Ullin showing them over and over again the use of tight formations to resist an attack, the militiamen turned in to their bunks next to the armoury room in the basement. They were full of talk and high spirits, and, though tired from the day's exertions, not so worn out that they could not break out cards and dice, and one fellow lightly strummed a guitar that he had somehow managed to smuggle into the barracks. Billy's presence was a boost, since all appreciated his scrappiness, if not his playful spirit.

"So is it true ye fought with the Dragonkind man?" one of the youngest militiamen asked of him. "An' yer ol' man piked his head to the Bosk Manor gate?"

"Aye! An' a fierce fighter he was!" And off Billy went on a great telling of the epic fight. Most of the group pressed in to hear the tale, many of whom had already heard it once or twice, for at each telling it seemed a mightier battle than before. Just as Billy began, Ullin burst through the door.

"Lights out! Mouths shut! Sleep!" he yelled at them sternly. "Or else you'll wish you had picked another commander to spite!"

That broke up the gathering and soon all were in their bunks. Robby, whose cot was beside Billy's, turned and whispered, "Billy."

"Aye?"

"Have you seen Sheila?"

"Aye."

"How is she? Is she well? "

"She's well. Very busy, though, if me ol' man's got any say."

"I see."

"Ye'll see her again," Billy said.

Robby nodded and closed his eyes. Long after the snores of his comrades ceased to bother him, he was still awake. When sleep at last came, it was deep and dark, and Robby sank to its bottom.

Suddenly the door of the barracks slammed open, and Ullin was banging a sword against a shield.

"Awake and to arms! To arms! Dress and to arms!" he cried. "Intruders in Barley, and we must away! Mr. Ribbon!"

"Yes, sir!?" Robby answered, struggling to get his boots on. "Coming!"

"Have the men armed with swords, shields, and lances. Muster in the parade yard! Double quick! Let's go! Let's go!"

"Yes, sir!"

Soon they were scrambling in earnest for their weapons, Robby handing out a lance to each as they passed through the door. There were lots of questions and shouting and stepping on each other's feet as they went, but they poured out of the Common House and into the side yard to muster in quick order. Ullin had lit several tall braziers in the yard, and the militiamen formed a line facing him, just as they had been taught.

"Mr. Ribbon, if you please," said Ullin.

"Yes, sir," answered Robby stepping up.

"Be so good as to read this to the company," he said, giving Robby a piece of parchment and shining a lamp on it. Robby took the note and cleared his throat.

" 'A party of twenty marauders crossed the bridge at Tulith Attis at midnight," he read. "They make for Passdale on horseback at slow pace, seeking to come upon the town before dawn. If ye proceed to meet them, I will lead me men at their rear, and we will have them trapped between us.' It is signed, 'Bosk.' "

"So men," Ullin immediately took up with a power in his voice of one accustomed to command. "You may not think you are ready for this, but such is our duty, and I know you will rise to it. We march in quick time to the place where the east road toward Weepingbrook leads through the hill near Tully's farm. There, we will await the horsemen, for they cannot turn left or right against the steepness of the banks. And, there, we must stop them every one. For all we know, they are rogues and murderers, come to rape your mothers and sisters and to cut the throats of your fathers and brothers. If we do not stop them, Passdale will be at their mercy. Do you understand?"

"Aye!" the company called back, somewhat unevenly.

"Let no man fail in his duty!" Ullin cried. "Form by twos. No talking, and make no noise to warn of our approach. Let's move!"

Soon they were formed up and quickly marching through Passdale and across the bridge, Ullin and Robby at the lead and then the ranks, with Billy and Ibin near the front.

"Commander, shouldn't someone ring the bell?" Robby asked Ullin. "To raise the alarm?"

"No," Ullin replied. "If the horsemen hear it, they may veer off or scatter at the warning, to regroup and attack Passdale from an unprotected direction. Our best chance is to take them on all together. No more talking."

It was a windy night, and there was a sprinkling of rain as the men and boys of the militia moved nearly at a jog. Their tramp woke a few folk, but any who peered out from their windows must have wondered at the group, shields thrown over their backs, lances in hand, a dark band of shadows moving grimly through the night. Ullin picked up the pace, urging them to stay close and not lose their way on the dark road, and so they trotted the last mile up hill toward Tully's farm. They passed it and continued along until they came to a place where the road, from years of use, had worn a deep trough through the hill. On either side, and for a stretch of nearly forty yards, were twelve-foot banks that rose sharply, slippery with clay and loose gravel. The clouds thinned, and somewhere behind them, Lady Moon peeked from behind her fan and by her low light gave them some notion of their surroundings.

"Halt!" Ullin called back. "Shields at the ready! Form up by squads. First squad front. Second squad left, third squad right, kneeling shield position. Squads four and five, press in behind. Close up your shields, like so! Squads six and seven rearmost standing. Very well!"

They formed a wall across the road from bank to bank, and Ullin inspected their lines, tightening gaps and pushing and pulling men into their proper places.

"If we had archers we could have them from the heights," someone said.

"But we have none," Ullin snapped back.

"Look!" Robby called to Ullin. He was at the front, on one knee behind his shield, and he pointed.

Down the road, a light approached. There was a distant dull thud of hooves and the sound of clinking metal, too. Ullin drew his sword and stood directly behind Robby.

"Lances!"

At his word, the wall of shields bristled with thirty-five steel-tipped lances angled out at the approaching riders. Now they could be seen, coming at full gallop, torches blazing, hooves striking sparks on the rocks as they came.

"Steady!" Ullin said, loud enough only to be heard by his men. "They cannot pass us if we hold firm. Let the butt end of your lances dig the ground. Care not for the horses. They are the servants of the foe. If any pass the lances, draw swords. Mark your enemy and strike not your fellow!"

Now the riders were full into the gully and were charging down at them, the thunder of the hooves resounding dully against the two sides of the embankment.

Robby shook with fear, his mouth was dry, and he kept trying to swallow. He could hear the rasping pant of the horses as they came, could make them out under the torches held by their riders, but could not see the riders themselves. One of his nearby comrades let out a weak whimper, and at last Robby managed to swallow the lump in his throat.

"Do not yield," Ullin said, his voice calm but firm as the thunderous horsemen bore down upon them. "Show no mercy. Rely upon your training. Push into your opponent with your shield and thrust upward or straight with your shortsword. Thrust hard and stab deep, then take on the next."

"Oh, my, oh my!" someone else said.

One youngster in the back rank suddenly broke away to run, but Billy grabbed his collar and jerked him back into line. "Stand fast, cousin!"

Only the roar of the horses outdid the pounding in Robby's chest. He took quick, shallow breaths, tilted his head down, his eyes fixed on the enemy. As all in his company did, he clenched his lance and shield tightly. They braced for impact.

Only thirty feet away, a brilliant white light burst out from the middle of the road between the two opposing groups. Robby and his friends gasped and instinctively flinched at the painful glare. But under the light stood Ashlord, holding the blinding flame aloft on the end of his walking stick. Squinting, Robby saw the horses grind to a halt on the other side of Ashlord, rearing and stamping while their riders cursed and yelled.

"Hold firm!" cried Ullin. "We do not know what this means. Hold firm, I say!"

"Halt!" cried Ashlord. "The test is over!"

Then, from the dimness of the side of the road, another figure joined Ashlord, and Robby immediately recognized his father, who now removed a cover from a lantern and held it up.

"Approach, loyal defenders of Passdale and Barley!" Ashlord called out.

"Wait here," Ullin ordered. "Do not yield unless I signal. Let me pass, Robby."

Robby tilted his shield, and Ullin, sword in hand, stepped through the line between the lances and approached Ashlord, still holding the burning flare. From the ranks of horses another figure dismounted and came forward.

"What the hell's the meanin' of this!" Mr. Bosk bellowed as he neared Ashlord. "Whar 'bouts is them raiders?"

"Thar ain't no raiders," Mr. Ribbon replied. "This here's a test."

"A what?"

"With Ashlord's help," Mr. Ribbon went on, "the council decided on a test to set to ye."

"A test!" Ullin cried in dismay. "Many could have been hurt, maimed, even!"

"Aye! An' the alarm of it!" Mr. Bosk joined the protest.

"That may be so," Robby's father said, "but weakness an' strength must be known by thems that risk the treasury an' thems that give to it."

There was a lot of grumbling by all that heard, Bosklander and Passdale troop alike. But Robby was more relieved than anything else.

"An' what if ye'd not made it here in time?" Mr. Bosk went on, leaning into Mr. Ribbon's face. "Both our sons run down!"

"I doubt that," said Ullin. "Or you've never faced lances!"

"What d'ye mean by that! Boskmen ain't no weaklings!"

"Maybe not," replied Ullin coolly, putting his sword away. "Nor are they a match for a wall of steel, sharp as razors. I dare say another thirty yards would have seen a slaughter of Boskmen."

"Yeah!" Billy's voice burst out at his father from within the Passdale pack that by now crowded up behind Ullin in spite of his order. "Ye'd a caught the sharp end of our business!"

This was loudly seconded by the others of the Passdale Militia.

"Shut-up, ye smart-mouthed brat!" Mr. Bosk cried at his son.

"Into ranks!" Ullin bellowed. "Form up for march!"

His militiamen jumped at his shout, bumbling into each other, but, with much clanging of shields and muttering, they quickly got into marching formation.

"Now, now!" Ashlord cried out, dropping the fizzling flare and stepping on it to put it out. "None are hurt. All are tested. And all have done well this night. Mr. Ribbon and I were already here when we sent the messages to each of you, and we were not going to permit a clash. If you want to defend your homeland, you had better get used to being inconvenienced by the homeland you serve."

"Well, I never!" Mr. Bosk said angrily.

"Ullin, is it not true that Kingsmen of Duinnor are trained an' tested this way?" Mr. Ribbon asked.

"Well, yes," Ullin admitted. "It is true. We never know when we may be called, or whether it is a true alarm or a test by our commanders. As often one as the other."

"Thar ye have it! Now go home all of ye with the pride that ye did yer part well," Mr. Ribbon ordered them. "I report to the council in the morrow evenin'. Have yer reports to me by then for any needs er problems er the like what needs fixin'. The next alarm raised may not end so bloodlessly, so remain alert!"

Soon the Bosklanders were riding back the way they had come, grumbling as they went. Ashlord shook hands with Mr. Ribbon, then turned to Ullin.

"A fine showing, Commander."

"I think so, Collandoth. Will you be coming back to Passdale with us?"

"Oh, no. I have my own business to attend to. Good night!"

Ashlord turned and went the way of the Boskmen, quickly disappearing into the gloom. Soon the Passdale men were marching home as well, with Mr. Ribbon and Ullin leading the way. There was much mumbling and griping, but after a mile or so the talk died down since they were too tired to keep it up. The way was still dark, but the sky overhead continued to lighten as they trudged along. Robby worked his way up to the front, just as they neared the bridge, and listened in as his father and Ullin talked.

"Aye," his father was saying when he came within earshot, "some bowmen on the heights would've been right handy, I'll warrant. 'Cept I'm glad no loose arrows whar flyin' tonight!"

"We have bows and arrows enough," Ullin went on, "though I can't vouch for their sturdiness. I'm handy enough with them and can do some of the training, but I'd like to get Sheila back from Boskland to train our men."

"I imagine it can be arranged. Meanwhile, thar's another thing what's come up."

They passed the midpoint of the bridge, and Ullin looked up at the empty bridge tender's box.

"We need to have a watch on this bridge at all times, Robigor," Ullin commented, interrupting Mr. Ribbon.

"Oh? I suppose yer right. I'll look into it."

"What is it that's come up? That you were about to mention?"

"Oh, well. Thar's this festival comin' up, an' some folk are skittish 'bout leavin' home an' such to come to it. Thing is, we've got to do the Renewin', an' then thar's the Countin' an' so forth. What I'm leadin' up to is like this: I'm thinkin' that it'd be good for us to use the militia to patrol all over the county those days, Bosklanders an' Passdalers workin' together, like. Makin' up an' down the roads on foot an' horse. An' another group at the Wayford Common durin' the festival for keepin' order."

"Sounds good to me," Ullin nodded. "An official assignment would be welcome after all this trickery, er, I mean, training."

"Ha! Ha!" Mr. Ribbon laughed. "Good one! Well said. I'll see to the orders soon as can be. Meantime, I'll write out a request for Sheila to come back to Passdale. I know Mira has sorely missed her, an' others, too, I'm guessin'. Can ye have a dispatch rider by noon?"

"Certainly."

Robby thought for a moment that his father was referring to him. It would be good to see her again, even if it was in an official capacity.

"Mr. Ribbon!" Ullin called back, not knowing that Robby was practically on his heels.

"Yes, sir!"

"Beat on ahead home and get some rest," Ullin ordered. "Then report to me at midmorning. Here, let me have your shield, helmet, and lance. I'll carry them back to the armoury."

"Yes, sir! Daddy?"

"Yes, son?"

"I don't have my keys with me."

"Oh, right. I'll come along, too," he said, handing the lantern to Billy. "Here, this belongs to the Common House."

Robby called his goodbyes to his fellow militiamen as they came off the bridge, then father and son broke from the rest and made their way toward home. The town was quiet and peaceful, with only crickets and the gurgling of the mill brook breaking the silence. Few lights were on, and they strained to watch their steps on the unpaved road. Just as they passed the market they came within sight of the store and their home. A small lamp still burned in the parlor window upstairs—warm and welcoming, it seemed to Robby. Smiling, he looked ahead then shot his arm out at his father's shoulder to stop him.

"What?"

"Shh!" Robby hissed. "Hold up. Look up there ahead. Just in front of the store."

Mr. Ribbon strained his eyes and then saw it, a huge shadow hovering in the road just in front of the store. A horse and rider, no, two horses. Instinctively, they crouched in the middle of the road, and Robby drew his sword slowly so as not to make it ring.

"Look," Mr. Ribbon pointed. Robby saw another shadow move from around the side of the store, peering into the windows. In the dim light, it was difficult to see any details of the figure moving around the store or the one in saddle. Robby could see enough, though, to see that the horses were uneasy, and the one in the saddle twisted back and forth, apparently looking around.

"Burglars?" Robby whispered.

"I doubt it. Whoever heard of burglars standin' thar horses in the middle of the road?"

"Makes sense for a quick getaway."

"Hm. Right ye are, son."

Suddenly, Robby stood up.

"The store is closed!" he shouted, breaking into a run toward them. The horseman reined around to face the shout, as the other shadowy figure ran across the front porch and then out to take his horse. Robby caught a glimpse of a long cloak—reddish, he thought—as the horses wheeled around and were spurred away.

"Halt! Halt!" Robby cried running after them, with his sword raised. As Robby made the front of the store, the air was filled with clods of dirt and the heavy thudding of horses galloping away in the opposite direction, the noise receding long after they had disappeared into the dark. Mr. Ribbon pulled up next to him, puffing. Seeing something light-colored at his feet, Robby picked up a scrap of paper, but could not see what, if anything, was written on it.

"Daddy, open the door!" Robby urged. "We have to see about Mother!"

After a moment of fumbling with the key, Mr. Ribbon finally got it into the lock and had trouble getting the old mechanism to work. Impatient, Robby pushed on the door, the lock sprang open, and they burst into the store, shouting.

"Mira!"

"Mother!"

"Mira!"

She emerged from the bedroom with a candle just as they were about to crash up the stairs.

"My stars! Why all the noise? What's wrong?" she cried, seeing their faces.

"Are you all right?" Robby asked.

"Yes. Why?"

"Have ye had any company?" Mr. Ribbon demanded.

"No. What is wrong?"

"Prowlers. Outside the store," Robby said.

"Are you sure?"

"Yes. We scared 'em when we came along, an' they rode off," Mr. Ribbon explained.

"Well, I'm fine, dear. You nearly frightened me to death roaring in like that!"

"Oh, I'm so sorry, love." Mr. Ribbon took his wife into his arms tenderly. "Forgive me, but I was alarmed an' concerned after ye."

"Of course, sweetness," Mirabella said.

"I'll just go back down and lock up," Robby said.

"It's nearly time to open shop, though," she said.

"I know," Robby called back as he descended the stairs. He lit a lamp and held it high, looking over the familiar tables and shelves for anything missing or out of place. All appeared normal. In a moment, his father came down, lit another lamp and did the same. Together, they circled the room and met at the front door, walking outside to look up and down the road.

"Who do you think they were?" Robby asked. "Thieves?"

"Well," Mr. Ribbon gazed down the road in the direction the riders fled. "I know yer mother's a light sleeper, an' any noise would've woke her right up."

"You think they wanted to steal from the store?"

"I dunno. If they wanted coin, they'd a needed us to show 'em," Mr. Ribbon said. "Maybe they wanted to come on us quiet, like, an' get at us whilst sleepin' all unawares so's we couldn't make an alarm."

"Probably so," Robby nodded.

"I guess the last thing they reckoned on was some crazy lunatic wavin' a sword an' hollerin' at 'em!"

Robby could not help but chuckle with his father.

"I guess not," he said. "Just couldn't help myself. It was pretty dumb, huh?"

"That's fine by me!" Mr. Ribbon said, putting his arm around Robby's shoulders. "Plenty alright! What's on that paper ye picked up?"

"Nothing much," Robby said, giving it to Mr. Ribbon. "Just a list of the names of places. Odd script, though."

"Hm," Mr. Ribbon said, looking at the list of towns and villages throughout the Eastlands.

"I guess it's time we got a dog."

"I guess so. Why don't ye run on off to bed. I'll let Sheriff Fivelpont know 'bout all this first thing in the morning. Mira or I will rouse ye up in time to meet Ullin."

• • •

Mirabella woke Robby late morning and had a big breakfast ready for him. While he ate, his mother informed him that Mr. Ribbon was still out with the Sheriff, attempting to track down the prowlers of the night before.

"I didn't hear a thing!" she said, slipping into a chair across the table from Robby. "Not until I heard you shouting."

"What do you think they were after?" Robby said gulping his coffee. "I mean, I think they must have been after one of three things: Our strongbox, those old coins, or..."

"Or what?"

"Me."

"You? You think they were His men?"

"Maybe. Do they wear red cloaks?"

"I don't know. Why?"

"It was hard to tell in the dark, but I thought their capes or cloaks were reddish in color. Anyway, I wouldn't know His men from anybody else's," Robby shrugged. "Ashlord's concerned for my safety. He helped me talk Ullin into staying, to help with our militia, so that Ullin would be nearby to me."

"I know, Robby. But if they were seriously after something, they would not have been so easily frightened away." Mirabella rose, picking up Robby's plate. "Maybe they were just travelers who needed something from the store. More bacon? Maybe they needed something, but were wary, since it was so late at night."

"No, thanks. If that was the case, they could have answered me instead of riding off as fast as they could go. But what if they were burglars? What if they were after those old coins? Mrs. Starhart probably told plenty of people about them. She seemed quite the talkative lady, if you know what I mean. We ought to get rid of them, the coins, that is. Most folks around here probably know we loan out our money and keep very little around. So maybe we should make a show of getting rid of those coins, just in case."

"Hm. Maybe."

"Maybe I can take them up to Formouth one day. Or even on up to Glareth."

Mirabella, at the sink, looked over her shoulder at Robby.

"You'll be going to Glareth soon enough," she said. "Spring will be here before you know it, and you'll be off with Billy to the Academy. If we still have those coins, your father might ask you to take them along for trade. You aren't thinking of leaving sooner, are you?"

"No. Well, only for the day! I've got to report to Ullin. And I'd better get going, too," Robby laughed, wiping his mouth with his napkin and bringing his plate to the sink. The doorbell rang, and he gave his mother a kiss and thanked her again for the breakfast before she went downstairs to look after the customer. Soon he was ready to go, and, on his way out, he made sure that his mother was comfortable being there alone.

"Oh, I'll be fine. Mrs. Garvin, here, and her nephew are staying awhile, and I'm sure your father will be back soon, anyway. I want you to be careful, though."

"I will be," he nodded as he left.

A few minutes later, he was entering Ullin's room at the Common House and found him at his desk looking over some papers. Ullin rose and shook Robby's hand.

"Good day to you," he said. "I hope you are rested."

"Yes, I am, Commander Tallin."

"Good. I heard about the prowlers last night. I would have gone with your father, but he insisted that I keep to my business here and get my reports ready for him." He picked up a packet. "I'll be going over to your place soon, to look in on Mira. Anyway, here are your orders. Go to Boskland and give Mr. Bosk this request from the Mayor."

Robby read over the parchment, an official request for Sheila to be sent back to Passdale to assist in the training of the Passdale Militia.

"And here is a copy of my report concerning last night's maneuvers that I'll be giving to the council later today; give this to Mr. Bosk, too. Pick up any dispatches that Mr. Bosk might have, and accompany Sheila back with good time. The two of you are to report to me as soon as you get back."

"Yes, sir," Robby nodded, putting the orders into his shoulder bag.

"One more thing before you go." Ullin moved from his desk to a side door that led into the armaments room. Entering, he motioned Robby along, saying, "Your mother and other stitchers and seamstresses, along with the weaver, have prepared surcoats for the Passdale Militia. They dropped them off yesterday, but we didn't have time for fittings."

On a table in the middle of the room was a pile of neatly folded clothes, and Ullin picked up a bundle.

"This is yours," he said unfolding and holding it up so that Robby could look at it. It was of well-spun linen, sky-blue with red trim. On the front and back was sewn an emblem in the likeness of a bridge, also in red. Robby noticed three black chevrons over the emblem that were not on the other surcoats. There was also a trio sewn onto the left breast of the surcoat.

"You will be representing our militia, today," Ullin went on. He handed Robby a leather cuirass and helped him take off his jacket. "Here, it goes like this. Yes. Tighten up here, at the side—not a lot of protection there. Stiff though this may be, it is fair protection against light strokes and long-shot arrows, though not so good as chain. This is a plain one and has no spaulders, upper arm protection. Good. Now, let me help you with these bracers—they go around your wrists, yes, right over your sleeve. And over there are some greaves for your legs. With practice, you'll be able to lace them up yourself."

Ullin helped Robby on with the leather armor, talking as he went. "There are plenty of gaps where an arrow or sword tip can get through—here, tuck the knot just behind the back, right there—it's a start, though, and better than nothing. Furaman sent these down yesterday, not sure where he got them, but they have the looks of Masurthian workmanship. Turn around. Let me tie back your left greave."

"Whoo, kind of stiff, indeed," Robby said after he got the leggings on and straightened up again. "I feel kind of like a tortoise."

"You'll get used to it," Ullin smiled. "We'll all be wearing these as soon as we have enough to go 'round. Hopefully in a few weeks, if Mr. Furaman can find enough. Now, your surcoat over all that, and then your belt, double-wrapped, and your sword belt. I'll get your helmet. You'll be warm enough in all that, I'll warrant. It might seem overly much. But you are a soldier of the Passdale Militia, and, my aide, second-in-command, as these chevrons, here, signify. I'll not have you go to those Bosklanders improperly dressed for your station or for those you represent."

"So I have some rank? Like you?"

"I am a commissioned Commander of the King's First Army. That doesn't really mean much, these days, but I do have authority over anyone up to the rank of captain. We've organized into squads, but I haven't yet made squad leader assignments. However, I need someone who will outrank the others. So I've taken the liberty of making you a sergeant. Don't let it go to your head."

Robby laughed and took the helmet from Ullin with a growing sense of pride and examined it. It was open-faced with hinged side panels that were attached to the chin strap for protecting the side of the wearer's face, and a long back that flared out somewhat at the back of the neck. At the peak of its top, rounded almost to a point, was a small ring.

"That's for tying in some horsehair or other plume," Ullin said. "Tilt your head."

Robby did so and Ullin slipped a padded cap on his head. "That'll help with the helmet."

Robby put the helmet on and tied the chin strap. Ullin stood back and nodded as he sized Robby up, the Kingsman's eyes gleaming as he grinned. "I think you'll do just fine. There's a dispatch pouch beside my table for you to use. And take Anerath. He's out back, saddled and waiting."

• • •

From the saddle, Robby quickly appreciated how fine and how mighty Anerath truly was. The horse had an instinct for direction and needed very little urging from the rider. His gait was smooth and assured, and his turns graceful and sure-footed. Anerath was spirited, almost gleeful, and Robby, riding proud in his new accoutrements, got the notion that Anerath longed to show off a bit. If that was so, then Robby understood the feeling. Finally, after last night, and after all the weeks of training, errands, and roll-keeping, Robby felt something of the soldier's pride. An untried soldier, true. But proud, anyway, with his chin up and jaw set as he rode across the bridge.

"Who goes thar?" cried Mr. Arbuckle, leaning precariously out of his box.

"Robby Ribbon! Of the Passdale Militia!" came Robby's sharp response.

"Ye ought not be ridin' 'cross the bridge!" the old man squeaked out as horse and rider trotted past. "Might get hurt." Robby did not hear him and was long past when the bridge tender shook his head. "Oughta lead him 'cross by the reins, dagummit!"

Once across the bridge, they trotted for a short distance down the road winding along the east bank of the Bentwide. Robby leaned in and gave Anerath a bit of a nudge. The stallion instantly shot to a gallop, and they quickly angled off the road and blazed up the hillside fields and headed across Barley toward Boskland. The sky was clear and the sun warm, but the cool breezes of the waning year kept him from getting hot, and he felt good. He let Anerath gallop at an easy pace for a league or so, sensing that the steed put little effort into it, and Robby was in wonder at the speed Anerath must be capable of if urged. After a while, not wanting to be too quick to end his private joy, he slowed the horse to a walk and enjoyed the day. The clouds and the rain of the previous night had cleared, and the sky overhead was of that particular early autumn blue that is so clear and clean that one almost feels one is breathing the sky itself, color and all, so crisp it is. Certainly, Robby felt that way, lost to his thoughts while crossing country, between fields, up through hilltop copses and down through cool streams. Hardly had he noticed the passage of time and distance before he had gone halfway, and the sun was an afternoon angle. Stopping, he dismounted and led Anerath along most of the final leg, rising upward through the woods until at last he came to the low hilltop overlooking Boskland. He could clearly see Bosk Manor rising on the distant hill on the far side of the valley before him, brown and gold fields neatly arrayed below and between.

"Well, my friend," said Robby as he climbed back into the saddle, "let's go to Boskland."

Not wanting to seem too urgent, he let Anerath set the pace down into the fields. Much of the harvest was already in, but, here and there, gleaners worked and elsewhere teams of plowmen turned over the stubble.

"Hail, soldier!" one fellow called to Robby, "whence come ye? Wherefore bound?"

"From Passdale," he called in return. "To see the master of Bosk Manor."

He saw and passed more workers along the way, and many hailed him. He recognized most of them and knew many of their names. But if any recognized Robby, their faces did not show it, and the satisfaction of that made it difficult for Robby to keep to only a narrow smile. Indeed, he wanted to grin so badly that to hold his face in check actually hurt. Catching a distant note, he turned, looked to the northwest, and saw, on the top of a bald hill, a piper at practice, his tune wavering down the hill and across the breeze to Robby. The somber aire filled his heart with a sudden sternness so that he halted Anerath and listened to the refrain before continuing on.

He remembered the prowlers of the night before and thought again of how his mother had been there all alone. And he thought of the Dragonkind man and the wolves. All desire to smile left him. He tried to stiffen his shoulders and not let them sag with the new weight of these sober thoughts, and, as he neared the gate, he put his left hand on the pommel of his sword. Over the gate were the grisly remains of the severed heads of the raiders. Just as Billy had described, the head of the Dragonkind was deep, rusty red. Two men emerged from behind the gate, wearing Boskland colors, one bearing a pike and the other gird with sword. They stood in Robby's path, gesturing him to halt.

"Who goes?"

"Ribbon of the Passdale Militia," Robby said sternly. "On business to see the Master of Boskland."

"Ribbon, eh?" the one with the sword said, coming alongside the horse and peering up at him. "Might ye be Master Ribbon? The mayor's boy?"

"I am."

"An' yer with the militiamen of Passdale, now?"

"That's right."

"Well, then!" said the other. "Any news of me kinsman, Billy Bosk? He's me cousin, an' I ain't seen him since he went off to join yer townfolk."

"He is well," Robby answered, nudging Anerath on between them.

"Hold on thar! We ain't given ye leave to pass, yet!"

Robby reined Anerath to a stop and twisted around in the saddle to look back at the two awkward fellows.

"Well, I reckon ye can pass on, now," said the one.

"Seein' as how ye done did, anyways," muttered the other.

Robby moved on toward the manor, and all along the way, workmen and charwomen came out to take a look at him, or peered from the windows or doorways of their cottages as he passed. He urged Anerath to a canter and rode jauntily along until at last they came up before the steps of the manor house. An ancient man nimbly hobbled up, elbows flying and knees a-bowed, his feet pointing right and left as he approached.

"I won't be long, Jamie," Robby said, dismounting.

The man took the reins, bending his head as if trying to see past the nose guard on Robby's helmet. A look of recognition began to cross his grizzled face.

"Master Robby?" he asked. "Why, ye be a soldier, now? Ooo, mighty stars! All with yer arms an' great steed!"

"Yes," Robby grinned as he removed his helmet. "I'm with the Passdale Militia."

"Oh, what a fine outfit it must be, what with such fine accoutrements for battle, an' all. Ye got ye helmet, an' ye sard, an' all!"

"Yes, sir. Is Mr. Bosk around?"

Frizella Bosk rounded the side of the house carrying a basket full of fresh herbs, halting when she saw Robby. She burst into a happy jog.

"Robby! Me, oh my! Lord, look at ye!" she cried, putting down the basket and wiping her hands on her apron as she approached. "All growed up into a soldier!"

She stopped herself from giving her customary hug.

"I hope me Billy's half so handsome!"

"I'm sure he is."

"How's he gettin' on? The place just ain't right without his antics an' his gettin' into everthin'. An' ain't nobody near so ready to lend a hand than Ibin. How're me boys doin'?"

"They are both getting on well, and we're lucky to have them."

"Oh, wonderful. Tell 'em they must come home ever once an' awhile, so's I can have a look at 'em."

"I will."

"I takes it yer all mended?"

"Pretty much, thanks."

"Good, good! An' so is it business yer on? Or did ye come to see Sheila? She's missed ye somethin' terrible, I can tell ye, an' sometime's takin' to mopin' about, too. Though she's done her work trainin' our boys well, so I'm told."

"Both, actually. I'm here to see your husband and also to fetch Sheila back to Passdale if he can spare her."

"Oh, I see. Well, Mr. Bosk's over in the southeast fields, seein' to a bridge. An' Sheila's down at the carpenter's place lookin' after some bows bein' made. I'll send for Sheila an' Mr. Bosk, an' ye can talk to him whilst I help Sheila put her things together. Why don't ye come inside to some tea whilst ye wait?"

"Thank you for offering, but I think I'll ride out to see your husband. I know the way well enough. But could you see after Sheila? I'd rather get on back to Passdale as soon as possible."

"Oh, certainly!" Mrs. Bosk said as Robby put on his helmet and climbed back onto Anerath.

Indeed, Robby knew the way from so many stays with Billy. He took Anerath through the gate at a keen gallop and then on up the hill and through the copse that topped it, overlooking the Manor. He circled the crown of the hill then plunged down into the farther fields beyond. Fewer workers were in these fields, as many of the crops had been ruined by the recent floods, but Robby could see swaths where some harvesting had been possible. Less than a league farther along the narrow track, he saw a group of men working along a path that led off from the lane and downward between two fields. A wagon was there, and the men were unloading stones and square-cut timbers. Another group labored nearby, clearing away the remains of a washed-out bridge. This new bridge was to be more substantial than the old one, and it appeared to Robby that it was to be wider, as well.

Seeing the colorful rider and glossy brown horse approaching, the men stopped their work and looked on. Mr. Bosk's head popped up over the pile of stone he was laying on the other side of the ditch, a quizzical look on his face.

"Mr. Bosk!" Robby called out, pulling Anerath up as the laird crawled out of the ditch and wiped his muddy hands on his shirt.

"Aye?"

"I have dispatches from Passdale," Robby said. He eased Anerath down through the ditch, past the gaping workmen up to their shins in mud, and up the other side where Bosk was standing. He dismounted, and pulled the messages from his bag. "And here's a message from the Mayor."

"Aye? Robby Ribbon?" Mr. Bosk asked, taking the packet from him. "I see ye got yer outfits at last."

"Yes, sir," Robby said, handing him the note from his father.

"What d'ye think of last night's goin's on?"

"I think it was a good showing, sir, by Boskland and Passdale alike, and a good test. I wish it had been during the daytime, though."

"Me, too," Mr. Bosk chuckled. "Me, too."

"I am to await your answer on that." Robby gestured to the orders that Mr. Bosk was now reading. The other men stood in a little closer, and Robby felt a bit of tension amongst them.

"Fancy dress don't make no soldier," said one of the men.

"Whar's yer toothpick?" smirked another.

"Bosklanders don't like lances, I take it," Robby replied, smiling.

"It whar a mean trick, to get us all riled an' off on a hunt for shadows in the middle of the night," said another.

"It was not of my making," Robby stated.

"Who d'yer ol' man think he is, orderin' about us Boskmen?"

"Enough of that!" snapped Mr. Bosk. "Robby here was just follerin' orders. No need to blame him. 'Sides, Passdale an' Boskland both showed the stuff well 'nough, if ye ask me. Can't 'spect no enemy to come callin' when it's convenient, like it was for tea or somethin'."

To Robby he said, "Aye, a good test, though I was angry enough 'bout it last night. But I soon seen the light of it. As for this, I figure we can let her go for awhile. She's got us goin', an' now it's up to practice, I reckon, though I'd like her to come back soon an' sort of foller up on us. Bad habits an' flyin' arrows don't mix too well, if ye take me meanin'."

"Yes, sir, I'll pass that along. And I'll go ahead and escort her back to Passdale, by your leave. Do you have any dispatches that I can take back for you?"

"I do. Was gonna send 'em along later. Ask Mrs. Bosk to look on me desk. They're all sealed an' ready."

"Very well," Robby said, remounting Anerath. "Then I'll be on my way. Good day to you all!"

"Good day, Militiaman!"

" 'At's a fine horse ye got thar," called one of the workmen. "Er, or mebbe yer horse has got ye, instead?"

"Ye shore ye can handle him, laddie-boy?" called another one, setting the men laughing in spite of Mr. Bosk's glare.

"Aye," added another. "Mebbe ye should stick to foot soldierin'."

Anerath huffed and kicked the air as Robby, leaning forward, pulled him around. Red-faced, he trotted Anerath off several yards.

"Ho, boy!" he cried, giving Anerath a good prod of the heels. Anerath immediately whirled around, breaking into a gallop right back at the workers in the ditch. Their mirth quickly changed to panic as Anerath bore down on them, hooves pounding sod high into the air behind him. With defiant ease, Anerath and Robby soared over the ditch and continued at a gallop up the hill. At its top, Robby reined Anerath around. As the stallion reared, he saw the workmen picking themselves out of the mud where they had flung themselves atop of each other. Meanwhile, aside and above them leaning over the bank, Mr. Bosk held his side with one hand to keep his laughter from splitting it, while he slapped his knee with the other.

• • •

Sheila was not at the carpenter's, but having finished her work there, she walked up the hill above the shop, picking wildflowers as she went, until she came to a small cairn barely a foot tall. There she knelt, and carefully arranged the flowers around it. She leaned back and studied the arrangement for a long while. Hearing footfalls behind her, she turned and saw Frizella huffing up the hill. Sheila threw another glance at the tiny grave, then stood and walked down to meet Mrs. Bosk halfway.

"Thar's a soldier come from Passdale to fetch ye back," Frizella said.

"Oh?"

"An' it must be for somethin' important, for he's all handsome-dressed, an' armed."

"Oh?"

"That's right," Frizella said, leading Sheila quickly back to the house. "He's gone to see Mr. Bosk over in the fields, but he's sure to be right back. Go get yer things packed, I doubt if ye'll be comin' back real soon. Hurry along. I've got to see to Mr. Bosk's letters to send along with ye. I've already told Jamie to saddle up a horse for ye. Run along."

Somewhat flustered, Sheila did as she was told. It did not take long, for she had little to pack. And when she came back out, indeed, Jamie was bringing a horse around. She thanked him, then slung her packs and bags behind her saddle and tied them down, along with her bow and quiver. Walking around to the other side, she checked the cinches, wondering at the changes that must have taken place in Passdale since her departure. All of the Bosk-folk had been talking that day of last night's stir, of Ashlord's sudden appearance that stopped what would have been a calamity, and of the bright light he showed that nearly blinded them. Mr. Bosk called it a flare, and said they burned most amazingly bright. The men were disgruntled, to say the least, at being roused up and made to charge all over Barley in the middle of the night. And then nearly blundering into what—a few of them at least admitted—would have been certain harm at the lance-ends of "them Passdale boys."

Sheila had gone on about her business of the day, working mainly with the carpenter on the new bows, all the while feeling rather smug at the good showing of the Passdale Militia, even though she was a Barley girl, herself. Now that her gear was all cinched down, she kept eyeing the bend in the road at the top of the hill, a hopeful flutter in her heart. But when she saw the spirited horse with its head up, prancing down the way with the unfamiliar soldier in saddle, she was awed and disappointed at the same time. The rider and horse seemed unreal, like out of a story, so fine they looked. Not tall enough for him to be Ullin, she thought, nor lean enough for Billy, yet not stocky enough for Robby. She was intrigued by the approaching figure. When Robby passed the east gate at last, and she could see his broad unrestrained grin, she recognized him. He saw the look of surprise and unmistakable joy on her face, and he wanted to leap down and take her up in his arms.

Leap down, he did, and she fairly ran up to him.

"Robby!" she cried, laughing and grabbing his hand. "At first, I did not know you! What a fine outfit! Is that your horse?"

"Well, it is me," he said squeezing her hand and then removing his helmet. "Same old me. But a borrowed horse," he added, giving Anerath an affectionate pat. "Finer than I deserve to ride."

"I don't know about that." She smiled with her head tilted. "You look different. Besides the clothes, I mean. Are you taller?"

"Well, maybe all the militia training has moved my weight around some," he nodded, looking down at himself, "and maybe got rid of some. And all this get-up," he tapped the cuirass, "makes me look bigger than I am, I think."

"Your hair is longer, too," she said. "You look fine to me! I'm so glad to see you."

"I've missed you, too. Even though we hardly got a chance to speak, coming and going only, while you were staying with us. That is, those times we did get to chat, and those brief glimpses of you, well, I mean to say, our house seems a bit empty without you."

"Thank you for saying so."

"It's the truth," he said, wanting so much to kiss her, but only taking up her hand again. She looked at him, and he could feel her attraction to him, her eyes alight in a way that put a moth in his chest, and his yearning for her was almost more than he could bear. "Yes, I mean it. So much so that I'm here to fetch you back."

"I've heard. But why?"

"To have you train us, just as you've been training the Bosklanders."

"I reckon ye need to be gettin' right off," said Mrs. Bosk, her approach undetected by either, and, with a bit of embarrassment, they turned to their horses.

"Yes, we ought to be on our way," said Robby, harnessing his helmet to his saddlebag and stuffing the arming cap into it.

"Well, here's a bag of victuals for yer lunches," she said knowingly. "Oh an' I packed the letters an' such off of me husband's desk, as I know he means to have 'em taken to Passdale."

"Yes, thank you. And thank you for the food, too. You shouldn't have."

"Nuthin' of it, Robby." She hung the bag on his saddle hook beside his helmet. She turned to Sheila. "I've been mighty happy to have ye with me, darlin'. I'm gonna sorely miss ye."

"Thank you, as always, for taking such good care of me. And say goodbye to Raenelle and Mr. Bosk for me."

They hugged as Robby mounted up, then Sheila climbed into her saddle. As they reined away, Mrs. Bosk called out after Robby.

"Tell them boys of mine to behave themselves. An' to come see me!"

"Yes, ma'am!"

Soon they had passed through the outer gate, the guards waving them through this time, and only then did they speak again.

"Tell me about your stay," Robby said. "Have you trained the Boskmen?"

"Yes, I think they are well on their way," she said. "But it took some doing, at first, to convince some of them they needed lessons."

"Oh?"

"Yes, a lot of them look at bows and arrows as dishonorable weapons, for killing at a distance. Even some of the hunters amongst them had to be convinced that archery would be good for all to know. There were some, too, that just thought of archery as silly toy-stuff, not able to do much harm. It took putting a few arrows through heavy leather to show them, and a lot of yelling on the part of Mr. Bosk to convince the others. He's good at yelling."

"Yes, he certainly is. I hope our militia won't give you as hard a time!"

"Oh, I've learned a few lessons about giving lessons!" she laughed. "And I daresay there's not a Bosklander who'll want to face archers, now, or be without them."

"I expect we'll take longer to get going along with that, though."

"What do you mean?"

"Well, the Boskmen have a long tradition of arms, at least, and we're just getting started, with little experience and no traditions at all to take inspiration from," Robby tugged at his surcoat. "This rig looks mighty nice, I suppose, but we're a rag-tag bunch, mostly just trying to keep up with Ullin."

"He seemed pretty capable when I saw him."

"Oh, yes, he is! A regular one-man army, Ullin is! We are lucky to have him as our commander. Not just lessons out of a book, either. He's got a lot of experience, though he speaks little of it, from out west. Not unless it has something to do with explaining some lesson or other to us."

"Well, from what I hear, you Passdalers did pretty well last night."

"Oh, yes," Robby agreed. "I think we did, though every single one of us was scared out of his wits, except maybe Ibin and Ullin. I can't tell you how hard it was not to turn and run when I heard those horses thundering down on us."

"But you didn't."

"No. No one panicked. Ullin did a fine job holding us together, I must say. Out of past practice, I suppose. Damn!" Robby jerked Anerath to a sudden halt.

"What is it?" Sheila reined up, alarmed.

"I forgot to tell Mr. Bosk something."

"Do you want to go back?"

Robby turned and looked back the way they had come, but Bosk Manor was now a league or more away.

"No," he said slowly. "I don't know how important it is, and it isn't part of my orders. So I think we should go on. And if I know Ullin, he's probably mentioned it in the dispatches I gave to Mr. Bosk."

They moved along, Sheila looking at Robby's concerned face. Catching her look, he said, "We had an incident of sorts in town last night." And he told her about the prowlers.

"Oh my stars! What do you think they were after?" she asked.

"I don't know. I wonder if they were after the strongbox? That makes the most sense, for they would have had to come up on us while we were asleep and capture us, so to speak, to make us tell them where the strongbox was and how to open it. Only that doesn't make any sense."

"Why not?"

"Because there isn't anything much to take besides store goods. Just a few old coins, you know, the one's Mrs. Starhart traded to us, and a bit of silver. Everyone knows we don't keep much coin. I'm sure Mr. Arkstan keeps more coin down at his tavern than we ever take in. And he does run a moneylending trade on the side."

"Well, what else would they be after?"

"I'm not sure. Mother says they were probably just travelers and rode off when I shouted at them. But, well, do you think someone may have heard about me? I mean, found out?"

"Do you mean Tulith Attis? That you rang the Bell?"

"Yes. Ashlord has been worried. I saw him just a few days ago. He was in town checking on how the militia was coming along. On his way from somewhere to somewhere, as he always is these days. He asked if I'd seen any strangers about. I told him, 'Well, of course I've seen strangers about. People are pouring in from all over for the upcoming festival.' He just shook his head as if I didn't understand his question and said, 'Not those kind of strangers. I mean those who by their dress or manner do not fit in with the others,' he said. And he said for me to be wary of foreigners."

"What did he mean by that?"

"I dunno. He must mean someone who would stand out from the crowd of strangers that are arriving. He hurried off before I could press him on it. And, last night, I didn't get a chance to talk with him at all. Only…"

"Only what?"

"Only, I think I've been seeing Certina about lately."

"That wouldn't surprise me at all," Sheila said sitting back in her saddle. "I'm sure she's keeping an eye on you for Ashlord."

"But how do they talk?"

"I don't know how it works," Sheila said. "I've seen Certina perch on his head and on his shoulder, and, one time I saw her perch on his nose! They do talk, of that I am convinced. Maybe not with words. And, if Ashlord wants to know about something, he's sure to find out. But back to those prowlers. Do you truly think they were sent by the traitor of Tulith Attis? Or by Secundur?"

Robby involuntarily shivered at the name, even though Sheila spoke it only softly, and with a cautious tone. It was not a name to invoke carelessly. He managed a brave, nonchalant shrug.

"No, I guess not. If they were, why would they give up so easily and run away? Not like those men we met on the road back from Tulith Attis that day. It's just that I don't know what the prowlers were after, and I keep going over every possibility. Maybe my mother was right, and they were just travelers. They did drop a scrap of paper in their haste to ride away. It had a list of towns and villages in the Eastlands. Anyway, I should have warned Mr. Bosk to be on the lookout for strange goings on."

They rode silently for a distance, enjoying the afternoon in spite of the unsettling topics. The day had turned cool and breezy, and Sheila pulled a cloak out of her bag and put it on. It was long and dark gray with black trim and a hood, clasped in the front with shiny brass buttons.

"You look very nice in that," Robby commented. "It looks vaguely familiar."

"Thank you, and it should look familiar. Your mother gave it to me just before I left to go to Boskland. She said she hadn't worn it for years and thought I would appreciate it. And I do!"

"I don't remember my mother wearing it, but I can't imagine she looked half so good in it."

Sheila smiled and blushed just a little, saying, "Don't be silly. I'll never be as pretty as Mirabella, or as genteel."

"My mother is striking, I admit. But you have qualities she never has had. Besides, I mistook you for a princess one night, not all that long ago."

"Oh, I'm sure you did!"

"Truly! I was walking home and passed by Passdale Green. I saw you there, but I did not recognize you until you turned to go."

"Passdale Green? Oh! You were there? And you did not make yourself known to me?" Sheila was clearly aghast, and Robby was suddenly nervous and embarrassed.

"I was afraid to," he admitted. "I was only passing by. I did not know it was you. When I realized it was you, I wanted to call out to you. But I was afraid to. I'm sorry."

"Why were you afraid?"

"Because," he muttered. "Because we had not been speaking very much, and you seemed to want it that way. And because, well, I guess I was just embarrassed. The truth is, I had never before seen you dressed so well, and maybe that's why I did not recognize you. I stopped to watch from the shadows of the trees alongside the path. I almost thought I was looking on a dream."

"You were," Sheila said, with no hint of anger in her tone. "I was dressed that way out of curiosity. Those were to be my festival clothes, and I could not wait to try them out. Your mother had them made especially for me. I had never worn anything so fine until that night. I mean, do you know those dresses and clothes I wore around the store? *Those* were the nicest clothes I ever wore until then. Just normal clothes, like everyone has. But I never had any before. With the money your father put aside for me, I bought some clothes for the first time in my life. Brand new clothes, too. And, for the first time ever, I started feeling like a normal girl, a normal woman. That night you saw me, when those special clothes arrived, Mirabella had me try them on, and afterwards I couldn't bring myself to take them off. I sat in front of the mirror in my room, brushing my hair and looking at myself, until I felt so happy that the walls of the room could not keep me any longer. So I ran outside and played in the starlight. I don't think I have ever been so happy in my life! Just to wear something truly fine!" She shrugged, "Then, just a week or so later, I was headed out to Boskland, dressed in man's clothing again, like my old self! So I suppose it was a dream that you were seeing that night. My dream."

Robby heard the wistfulness in her voice, and he regretted not having understood her sooner. He immediately felt he should have known, without having to be told outright, and he was embarrassed and disappointed at his own lack of perception.

"You may dress as a man, in man's clothing, Sheila," Robby said at last. "But you are a woman, no mistake, and a finer one than most who wear skirts or gowns all the time."

"You shower me with compliments, today."

"I guess I have some catching up to do," Robby chuckled, and he was gratified to see her smile back. "Do you remember the last time we rode together, along this way?"

"How could I not remember? Those were eventful days."

"Yes. I suppose we were both in a lot of pain, in more ways than one. You especially. I'm sorry if I seemed thoughtless."

"You have nothing to be sorry about," Sheila responded. "I should have sent you word long before we met at Tulith Attis. I nearly did, too, on several occasions. Ashlord encouraged me to do so, in his odd way. But, as you know, I never did."

"May I ask why not?"

"Well, I told you before, some of the reasons. And I suppose part of me was in shock and part of me was in mourning, too. I was very angry—mostly at myself, I now realize—and I was ashamed, too."

"You have nothing to be ashamed of," Robby said.

They passed over a shallow stream and then back up hill along a shortcut between two terraced fields of grapes.

"Do you still feel the same and as strongly as you did that day?" he asked. "About marrying me?"

"Yes. I do," she answered.

"I see."

"And do you feel the same way as what you said to me that day?" she asked.

"Yes. I do. Perhaps more so."

"I have thought a great deal about what you said that day. And how you said it," Sheila ventured. "Can you recall the words you used?"

"The very words?"

"Yes."

Robby thought for a moment. He remembered what he said, but he had trouble with the words. When he tried to pronounce them, his tongue would not let them pass.

"I remember the words, yes," he said, somewhat flustered, letting Anerath come to a halt, "but I can't seem to make my mouth repeat them just now."

"I was bewildered by them, though I understood each word you said, and I felt in my heart the full passion and honesty of what you spoke, yet..." She shook her head.

"Yet, what?" Robby asked.

"And, yet, I had never heard the language you spoke, not ever in my life."

Robby had heard something like it. Though he could not now say the words in his mind, he did remember a very similar language, that of the two gentlewomen who sang to him when he was ill as a child. And the language that Thurdun muttered the night they met on the road. But those were languages of this world, known and spoken by many. What Sheila heard, and still echoed in Robby's soul was the language of...*where?* The heart? Robby shook his head. It was yet another mystery.

"I was, I admit, very, very stirred up that day. Perhaps your ears heard what they heard only because no one has ever spoken to you truly from the heart as I did."

She thought about that, about how it was often said that love has its own language, and for a moment she wondered seriously if that was it.

"No one ever has, that is true," she said, still thinking. "What I mean, though, is that the very words you spoke were in a tongue foreign to my ears. It was not in the Common Speech, nor was it the Ancient Tongue, some of which Ashlord has taught me. It was a different language, like the tinkling of glass wind chimes, all sharp and smooth at the same time, and like a soft breeze in my mind, or like clear, cool water in the thirsty land of my heart."

Robby thought that what she said made an odd kind of sense. Before he had time to respond, his eye caught something just ahead in the lower branches of a heavy oak.

"What's that?" he asked. As Sheila looked, the large dark shape, almost the color of the tree limb itself, emitted a thin cloud of smoke that drifted toward the riders.

"That's Westleaf if I ever smelled it," said Robby as he noticed the walking stick and small shoulder bag leaning against the broad trunk.

"Hullo!" called the shape in the tree.

"Ashlord!" Sheila cried out in surprise, nudging her horse closer. Robby followed, amused at the gentleman's resting place.

"Do you often roost in trees?" Robby asked, coming up alongside Sheila, nearly eye-level with the reclining Ashlord.

"When it suits," Ashlord smiled, removing his pipe from his mouth. "But only in oaks."

"What are you doing out here?" Sheila asked.

"Waiting for you two to come along," he answered. "I thought you would be passing this way, though I imagined you would be a bit earlier. I saw Mirabella and Ullin this afternoon, and they told me of Robby's errand."

"What is it that you wanted to see us about?" Robby asked. "Or is this a social visit? I hope you have been well?"

"Oh, yes! Well as ever, though busy, going there and here and over yon," Ashlord nodded as he slid off of the limb and lightly dropped to the ground. "You both look as well as can be, and are, I trust? Good. Good. Are you much recovered from last night's outing?"

"Yes, I slept late this morning," Robby said as Ashlord reached for his shoulder bag and his stick at the base of the tree. Robby noticed a movement in the bag before Flitter's head peeked out from under the flap, his large eyes blinking at the two riders before diving back into the bag. "What about that blinding light that you held up? It was incredible!"

"Neat trick, eh?" Ashlord cocked his brow and grinned. "A flare, as they are called in the west. One that I learned from the Flame Masters long ago. Comes in handy, though not as impressive as Mistletoe Fire."

"How was it done?"

"Oh, it involves a highly refined metal of a rare sort—magnium it is called—combined with specially prepared tinctures, along with the ground root of the argov plant, some sulfur, saltpeter, a bit of charcoal, and some wax. All prepared very carefully as a paste, somewhat like firesticks, and wrapped within a small tube of thick parchment. As you saw, very bright, and very hot. Can be quite dangerous."

Robby scratched his head and glanced at Sheila, almost sorry he had asked.

Ashlord's enthusiasm for his explanation faded as he saw that Robby did not follow it. A bit crestfallen, he said, "Some hold it to be magic—"

"Oh!" Robby perked up and smiled. "Magic!"

"—but it is not. Enough of that," Ashlord said, impatiently. "I wanted to speak to you two privately, and that is why I am here. By now, the Enemy must have had word of Tulith Attis. There are many people coming into the county, for the festival, and I believe there may be some of His agents amongst them."

"What makes you think that?" Robby asked.

"How do you know?" asked Sheila.

"Such questions! I am convinced by wind and water, root and rock, and by events near and far, as well as by other sources, nearer to hand. My word to you two is to be cautious of strangers. I know your penchant for striking up conversations with passersby," he said to Robby, apparently referring to Thurdun, "but watch what you say and do. These will not be Dragonkind, and they will not present you with a note saying, 'I am the enemy.' Their master must wonder if his identity has been discovered by he who rang the Great Bell, for the secret of Tulith Attis is linked to his own. And, as I have come to realize, the ringing would have been heard as an omen to many others, a warning that their power will soon be challenged, and their secrets discovered. They, too, besides the traitor of Tulith Attis, may strive to seek you out."

"What do you think they'll do?" Robby asked.

"They will first try to identify you. As bellringer of the Passdale Militia, they will be attracted to you first, if they hear of that. We must hold to our plan and make them think that ringing the militia bell is all that is in your power to do, so that they will dismiss you and look elsewhere. And I don't think they are apt to believe the one they seek is so young."

"What if they do find out it was Robby?" Sheila asked.

Ashlord looked at her sternly and then at Robby, saying to him, "They will kill you, eventually, after they have forced from you the names of all those who are involved with you and who may know or learn the great secret. Then they will do the same to them."

"But I don't know anything! I don't know who betrayed the fortress! I don't know any secrets!"

"And how do you think they will learn the truth of that? You will talk. And you will name names to put a swift end to your torment!"

Sheila stared at Ashlord, open-mouthed at his blunt words.

"Then I should leave!" declared Robby. "No one who knows me is safe!"

"That will not stop them. And leaving conspicuously may only give you away sooner rather than later by raising suspicions about you. The time may yet come for running away, but for now you must stay and do the best that you can. Remain among friends. Be discreet and watchful."

"What about the prowlers? There were prowlers about Robby's place last night."

"Yes, Ullin told me. Alas, I missed your father, who set out early to track them; I should have wanted to go along. However, there may or may not be a connection between the prowlers and those others whom I fear. Ullin said that you thought they wore red cloaks."

"Yes. I think so."

"Well, prowlers aren't likely to be brightly dressed, are they?" Ashlord pulled his hair back into a pony tail and lifted up his shoulder bag. "And those I warn about would not run away as they did. I must be getting back to Tulith Attis. I'll be there for a time, but you will see me again, soon, I hope. Make good time back to Passdale, and do not forget what I have said!"

"Good bye!"

"Good bye!"

Ashlord marched off as Sheila and Robby rode in the opposite direction.

"He never said what he's been doing, exactly," Sheila stated. Robby shrugged and twisted around to look back at Ashlord, his head and shoulders bobbing up and down as he receded along the far side of the hill. Just then, a little bird detached itself from the high branches of the tree and flew away toward Ashlord, darting down past his head and then off away into the sky.

"An odd fellow," Robby said, smiling at Ashlord's familiar, "with odd business, too, I suppose. But let's pick up the pace."

They galloped for a long stretch, and Robby could tell that Anerath was holding back so that Sheila's mount could easily keep up. He drew Anerath down to a quickstep and Sheila came up alongside.

"Let's not wear them too badly," Robby said to her as they further slowed to an easy walk. Anerath puffed out a light snort and tossed his head in agreement. Sheila's mount whinnied in response.

"Good, boy!" Sheila patted her mount's neck. "You were probably out all night last night, huh?"

They did make good time and soon had the top of the Passdale bridge in sight, rising in the distance over the next little ridge.

"I look forward to being back in Passdale, in the Ribbon household," Sheila said. "Frizella taught me how to make a nice ham and potato stew. Maybe Mirabella will let me fix it for supper one night."

"That sounds good!"

"And if I am daring, and if Mirabella is willing to risk having me smoke up her home, I'll make some breakfast stove cakes. Frizella gave me a jar of syrup to give to your mother, too."

"Oh!" Robby grinned. "All that sounds good, too! So you've been spending time in the Bosk kitchen as well?"

"In the evenings, yes. I suppose staying with you gave me a taste of what a real home-life could be like. Anyway, I asked Frizella to show me a few things, and I tried to help her out some. She's been such a good friend to me, probably the nearest thing to a sister I guess I'll ever know. Raenelle and I even managed a few kind words to one another! Between Frizella and your mother, I feel, well, like I've never felt before. I'm very lucky to have the friends that I do."

Robby saw her earnestness, and he nodded back at her.

"I think my mother has missed you, too," he said. "I know I have."

By now they had reached the top of the ridge and had a full view over the sloping fields below to the river Bentwide and Passdale on the other side. Robby had always liked the view from this spot, though it now seemed somewhat bare due to the loss of so many fine old poplars that once lined the banks. On the river road, running along side the far bank of the Bentwide in front of the shops and houses, was a steady line of carts and caravans, gaily painted and with with flags and pennants, and people of all shapes and sizes in colorful costumes, moving like small toys, from south to north and then turning on the westward road.

"Looks like some of the carnival folk are coming in," said Sheila.

"Just as Ashlord said," replied Robby. "Listen!"

Over the sound of the breeze rushing through the dry brush beside the road, they made out the faint noise of people and the distant clanging of carts as well as strains of lively music, all coming up from the troupes and minstrels across the river. Suddenly, overriding all else, came the unmistakable clang of a bell.

"The Militia is being called!" Robby cried, kicking Anerath into an instant gallop. By the time Sheila's somewhat startled mount reacted, and she had him up to a full gallop, Robby and Anerath were already twenty-five yards ahead of them and the gap continued to widen as Anerath effortlessly streaked away. Down the slope they went, and Robby quickly reached the bridge. The arm gate was down on his side and a farmer was crossing toward him just halfway along, prodding a cow with a stick.

Anerath stomped to a halt before the gate and reared, swinging his forelegs in the air and whinnying loudly.

"Raise the gate!" Robby shouted at poor Arbuckle. Having seen Robby and Sheila charging for the bridge, the old man was in a panic about what to do. Clumsily, muttering to himself, he hastily pulled one lever and then another until at last the arm lurched up. Robby galloped onto the bridge with Sheila now coming full speed right behind him.

"Watch out thar!" the Arbuckle shouted. "No riders on the bridge! No riders on…watch the cow!"

"Make way!" Robby yelled at the farmer who tried his best to get his cow aside as Robby and Sheila shot past, sending the poor heifer into a confusion of excitement so that she turned all the way around and trotted quickly after the two riders.

"No! No! No! Ye stupid beast!" shouted the farmer. "Not that way! We just come from over thar!"

The riders ignored the shouting behind them and turned left as they came off the bridge. At the westward road, they plunged right into the convoy of singers, jugglers, and merrymakers that crowded onto the same road. This way passed the Common House and then went up over the hills behind Passdale and on to Wayford Common just beyond, where the fairgrounds were. Sheila and Robby shot around and ahead of the caravan and could soon see some of the militiamen gathering before the Common House steps, some just arriving and others already in their new uniforms. Off in the side yard, at the base of the new bell tower, stood the large, unmistakable form of Ibin, looking ironically fierce in his surcoat and helmet and bearing a great lance. He was watching his best friend Billy pull the bell rope. Sheila and Robby rode up into the yard and dismounted next to Ibin.

"Hello, Robby," he said. "Hello, Sheila. Billy'sringingthe, Billy'sringing-thebell."

"I see," said Sheila.

"What's afoot?" Robby asked.

"Well, it's 'bout dang time ye got here!" Billy responded. "Fine trick traipsin' off while Mr. Commander puts me in charge of bell-clangin'. Me arms're done wore off, almost. Been ringin' this thing for near an hour, now. This here's one job ye can keep!"

"What's happening?" Robby repeated.

"I dunno," said Billy between pulls. "Ask Mr. Commander! He wanted us to, umph!, to gather up!"

"Why do I bother asking Billy anything?" Robby muttered as he trotted off to the side door that led inside to the barracks. He looked around and soon spotted Ullin making his way up the stairs at the far end.

"Ullin!"

"Oh, there you are!" Ullin said, turning to peer under a rafter at him from halfway up the stairs. "Please address me in the proper manner in front of the men. Did you bring Sheila?"

"Yes, Commander Tallin. Pardon me, sir. She's outside with the horses."

"Good. Any dispatches from Bosk? Come along."

Robby followed Ullin upstairs, handing him the packet he brought back from Boskland. Ullin opened the packet and looked through the letters.

"For the Mayor. For the Council. Ah! Here's a note for me," Ullin said as they turned down the hall toward the front of the building. He opened the folded paper and smiled as he looked over it.

"Sir? What's afoot?" Robby asked, keeping up with Ullin's naturally long and quick strides.

Sheila had hitched the horses and was coming up the steps as Ullin and Robby emerged.

"You might as well hear with all the rest," Ullin was saying. "Ah, Sheila! Good to have you back. I'll be with you presently. Mr. Ribbon, have the men fall in and call the roll, if you will."

"Yes, sir," Robby said and then turned to Starton, an older fellow that stood nearby. "Be so good as to ask Billy and Ibin to come along."

"Certainly, sir!"

"Fall in at attention!" Robby ordered.

Robby then made the count while Ullin and Sheila chatted quietly together on the portico at the top of the steps.

"Good, good," Ullin was saying as Robby came up. "We'll talk about it in a bit."

"All present, sir!"

"Very well. Have them at their ease."

"Parade rest!" Robby shouted. The militia men shifted their feet apart. "At ease! Listen up!"

Ullin took a few steps down and stood before his men, pleased that all the drilling was paying off, as evidenced by their stance and obedience.

"Some news and an announcement," Ullin said. "First, the Master of Boskland sends his regards and his warm congratulations to the Passdale Militia for last night's showing." This brought smiles to most of those attending. "I read to you this message, just received: 'A hard test, well met. The new militia in Passdale is already apace with any that Boskland has seen, and will, no doubt, soon be a force not to be reckoned with lightly.' "

"Hear! Hear!" cried several of the men.

"I will add this," Ullin continued. "You made me proud to be your leader last night, and I wish my hearty thanks to your bravery and endurance on such a hard run, facing the dark and the unknown."

Ullin bowed amongst more cheers and several cries of "Ullin Saheed! Ullin Saheed!"

Ullin did not smile, but he held up his hand to restore order. They settled down, and he continued.

"Our training must move forward, and a new task has been set for us. These things will require you to be here for the next fortnight beginning tomorrow morning."

This was met by much murmuring.

"As was pointed out last night," he continued, "though we held a strong position, it would have been stronger if we had placed archers on the heights on either side of the road. But we have no archers. That is why Sheila Pradkin is here. She is known throughout the region for her skill with the bow and arrow. She will share that skill with you, and I will train you on the use of those skills in battle. Now. As you all can plainly see, many people are arriving from all over to participate in the upcoming festival. The Mayor has requested our assistance. So we will help Sheriff Fivelpont keep order and will be on hand if needed. There has never been much in the way of trouble or disorder during the past festivals, so I am told, and none is expected. Still, we will do our best to satisfy whatever need may arise and to provide additional eyes upon any unseemly strangers who may lurk among our visitors."

By now there was again much murmuring and some open opposition. Ullin held up his hand again.

"I know! I know! Many of you are needed in the shops and on the farm, and this is short notice. Such is the militiaman's life. The tests are many, and the rewards are few. Still. Such as this is what we signed on for, and we must do our duty. The Mayor has agreed to provision us, and the Council has agreed to compensate each of you with the token of fourteen silver pieces at the end of service for each man who gives a full fortnight. That is a great sum, and none of us joined with any hope of such compensation. We shall all do our duty regardless of any such reward.

Those of you not yet with uniform, come with me. The rest of you are dismissed until noon tomorrow. Go, now, and put your business in order. That is all!" Ullin turned away from the group, nodding at Robby as he passed through the doors.

"Company! Atten-SHUN!" Robby cried out as taught. The group stiffened with a fair semblance of attention. "Dismissed!"

Robby and Sheila followed Ullin and a few others back into the hall and then down the stairs to the barracks. While Sheila looked over the armoury, and the others tried on their new uniforms, Ullin spoke to Robby.

"How did it go out at Boskland?"

"Oh, fine. Though they are a bit miffed at last night's doings."

"I imagine."

"And I have a feeling we are being looked upon as rivals, in a way."

"That is too bad," Ullin said, sitting down at his desk. "But I suppose it's to be expected. They are a proud bunch, those Bosklanders, and are known far and wide for their pride in tradition and military prowess. I imagine they think us a bunch of motley upstarts."

"Yes, sir. They'll soon learn better, though, won't they?"

Ullin nodded as Sheriff Fivelpont came in, and he stood to shake his hand.

"Commander! Robby! How goes it?"

"We'll be in order and ready to assign the first patrol to you about this time tomorrow," Ullin told him.

"Mighty good! I do appreciate it."

Fivelpont had been Sheriff of Passdale and Barley for nearly twelve years, a capable though aging lawman, fair and careful. He cocked his feathered cap back on his head jauntily, but was fastidious about his appearance, as was evidenced by his habit of keeping his coat of black leather, well-oiled and shiny, along with his black knee boots. Today, he wore a green sash across his large frame to hold his sword and matching green breeches, though much faded. His hair was close-cropped, and his round face had a day or two of gray stubble going from chin to his rosy cheeks.

"Any sign of the prowlers spotted last night at the Ribbon's place?"

" 'Fraid not. The Mayor an' me tracked 'em down the south road, but lost 'em in all the other tracks of folk comin' in. We rode as far as Bentbend, lookin' for horses amongst the comers and for suspicious types. But, lo! What a crowd comin' in! Bunches of folk I never seen afore at any of our rites er festivals. We must've passed by forty wagons an' a hunnerd folk what I wouldn't put past a little bit of sly gamin', if ye take me meanin'. So, no. No luck at all. It'd pay to keep our doors an' winders latched, I warrant."

They talked on about various ways to use the Passdale men, what roads to patrol, what to look for, how many men in a patrol, and a little about the powers of arrest. Robby listened in until they wrapped up their conversation and Fivelpont had departed.

"Where is Sheila?" Ullin asked Robby.

"Just here, sir." Robby motioned to Sheila, and she put down a sword she was examining and re-entered the room.

"Ah, Sheila. What do you think of our little armoury?"

"I'm not a good judge of such things," she shrugged. "But there aren't enough good bows and but a few straight arrows."

"I know. I have the carpenter working on a few things for us and I sent a request by post for more from Furaman. I hope they will arrive by week's end along with more arms. Meanwhile, I can hardly put you up here, unless you want to have a room in the loft under the roof?"

"Oh, no worries there," Robby interrupted. "She'll be staying with us."

"Good, good," Ullin nodded. "I don't think very many of our company have much experience with bow and arrow. I'm a fair archer myself, and I know how to use them in a fight and how to face against them. If you are half so good with arrows as you used to be with dirt clods, you'll make a fine example."

"Dirt clods?"

"Aye," Ullin smiled, "speaking as one on the receiving end, that is. Twelve or so years ago, when I stayed at Passdale for a time with Robby's family, you pelted me all up and down Barley."

Sheila's face reddened as she now remembered Ullin. She had not made the connection, but she now recalled the playful young man from so many years ago. Looking at Ullin for a long moment, she had trouble reconciling the fact that the weary-eyed, somewhat grizzled fellow standing in front of her now was the same person, once so handsome and dashing. She was around eight years old at the time, and she had trailed after him all during his mapmaking business, taunting and aggravating him in any way she could.

"I'm afraid I was quite the little hellion," she managed. "But as I recall, you finally gave back as good as I gave you."

"What's that?" Robby asked.

"He set a trap for me one day," Sheila explained. "He pretended to be napping under a tree, knowing all the while I was sneaking up to clobber him with a stick. Just as I got within five paces of him, he pulled a little string, and before I knew it I was dangling upside down in a snare he'd laid for me."

"You're joking!" Robby said, looking incredulously from Ullin to Sheila. "You all didn't tell me about that! What happened then?"

"Oh, I cut her down and sent her packing," Ullin said, waving his hand to make nothing of it. That was not at all how Sheila remembered it, and she almost said so. But she stopped herself, her thoughts wandering back in time.

## Chapter 17

## The Kingsman and the Imp

"So I've caught me some wild beastie!" Ullin said, standing up and pretending to yawn and stretch. He then walked around the little girl, dangling upside down from his snare, stepping back as she took a swing at him with the stick she still held. The loop of rope held her firmly around both ankles, though, with her head some two feet off the ground. A few pebbles fell from the pockets of her ragged breeches.

"Lemme down!" screamed Sheila, still trying to get at her captor with her stick even from her compromised state. "I'll kick yer kneecaps off, I will, ye basterd! An' poke out yer eyes! Lemme down!"

"Oh my, what a squirmy little thing it is, too! Let me see. Looks too scrawny to eat. Too noisy to keep as a pet. And what language!"

"Lemme down! Lemme down!"

"What's this? Do I see tears? Can it be the creature has feelings? Might it be some woodsprite I've captured? No-o-o, don't think so. Woodsprites are mischievous, but never so dirty. More like some impish thing, as dangerous and full of tricks as they come, I reckon. As vicious as it is dirty."

"I'm not!" Sheila sobbed as her anger turned to fear. "I'm, I'm, I'm only a little girl!"

"I don't believe you!" Ullin crossed his arms and tilted his head. "Yes, I'm convinced you're a gnome, or maybe even a young hobgoblin, come to cast some evil spell on me with your magic stick."

"I'm not! I'm not!" she cried, throwing away the stick.

"Oh, yes. I suppose I'll have to put you in a sack and throw you in the river to break your powers and rid these lands of you. Hm. I don't seem to have a sack big enough."

"Oh, but I'm not. I'm not!"

"Why should I believe you? I bet if I cut you down you'd put a spell on me quicker than I could wink!"

"Oh no, I wouldn't. I can't do spells!"

"Then tell me your rightful name."

"Sheila Pradkin's me name!"

"Do you swear?"

"I do! By me mother's blood, I swear."

"Well! Since you've sworn," Ullin said, lifting her up over his shoulder and drawing his knife, "if you're an gnome, then you'll have no power over me. But what if you're an imp? Imps are most devious liars."

With a quick stroke he cut the rope and held her over his shoulder as he strode quickly toward the river.

"I ain't no imp!" she yelled, kicking and beating Ullin's back with her fists.

"There's a sure test, I hear, for such."

"Lemme go!"

"Not a chance, little beast! Not until I make sure I'm not turning loose some evil fiend upon these hapless lands."

"What're ye doin'? Put me down!"

"Well, fiends hate water, generally, and especially flowing water, they say. And so I'm going to throw you into the river. No sacks needed. If you're a fiend, you'll hate it and try to get out as fast as you can before the water burns you up. That's how I'll know you to be a fiend and will take my dagger and sword to you. But if you stay in the water, I'll know you to be a true little girl."

"What if I can't swim?"

"Oh, it's not deep here."

Ullin waded into the water until it was up to his thighs then dropped her in with a splash. Sheila screamed and then gurgled, splashing frantically with her hands as she went under. Her ankles were still tied, only the tether had been cut, but she quickly got on her feet and stood up in water just above her waist. Infuriated, she jerked her head around. She expected him to be on the bank laughing at her, but there was no sign of him, not in the water and nowhere along the bank. She tried moving toward the shore, but since her feet were tied, she could only hop. After managing a few yards, she finally took a deep breath and crouched down under the water to untie the rope. It came off easily. She stood up and began striding with a mix of pouty triumph and anger to the bank, thinking how she would catch up with that fellow and show him for sure!

Then something caught her eye. Stopping, she saw it was floating just against the bank, a wicker basket, caught by a root on the green ribbon that was tied to its handle. She made her way to it, cautiously looking around before examining it. In the basket was a cake of soap, a washcloth, a small bottle of sweet oil, a lady's comb and brush, and a small looking-glass. On the very bottom was a neatly folded towel. She picked up the looking-glass, which was set into a plate of dark wood with a white ivory handle, and looked at her face for the first time that she could ever remember. For a blink of time, she thought she saw her mother looking back at her from the glass, and she gulped aloud as tears sprang to her eyes. She barely remembered her mother or her father, but had some sense of powerful kindness and caring that still came from the grave whenever she thought of them. She stared for a long time, watching the water drip from her hair to mingle with the silent tears from her eyes.

Soon she was fascinated with the looking-glass, and with it she studied the shape of her nose from many angles and stared close to the glass to examine the color of her amber eyes. At last, she noticed dark smudges on her temple and another just above her right eye. Picking up the bar of soap, she held it to her nose. Nothing ever smelled anything so sweet and wonderful, she thought, inhaling its fragrance with her eyes closed. Almost delicious enough to eat, too. Vague memories stirred, mysterious, long tables draped with linen, with flashing silver and flickering candles.

Suddenly she put the soap and the looking-glass back into the basket and crawled up the bank.

"Whar ye at?" she cried out, looking for Ullin. She saw him in the distance, reclining against the same tree as before, just as asleep as he had been when she had first stalked him. After a moment, she slid back down the bank into the water and unfastened the ribbon from the root. She floated it upstream just a few yards to a little cove sheltered on three sides by thick brambles. Here, a small stream trickled down over the rocks. Crawling out, she took her clothes off and set them out to dry, then slipped back into the water. For the next hour and more, she bathed. With joyous care, she washed every inch of her body, scrubbing her hair and then meticulously combing out the tangles. She used the washcloth sparingly, it being so fine, and when she was done bathing, she climbed out onto the sunny rocks and wrapped herself in the towel. She took out the looking-glass and alternated combing and brushing her hair, learning how each worked and watching her slow transformation with the glass. Sometimes, as she held the looking-glass and combed, she had again the vision of her mother, and she found herself humming, at first, then softly singing a children's song.

"Pluck a posy red and blue, with ivy ribbon tie,
A thimble fill with ivory spoon Lady Luna's dew.
Purple wine in golden cup give to the noonday sun,
Seven suitors soon will come, yer hand an' heart to woo."

She put on her clothes and carefully placed everything back into the basket, hiding it in the bushes. When she was satisfied with that, she made her way out from the brambles and back into the clearing. By now it was late afternoon, yet Ullin still slept under the tree. Walking carefully toward him—for she had no desire to be snared again—she tried to screw up her anger at him. But she knew he had left those lovely things for her to find. Whether intoxicated by her cleanliness, or simply past caring, she could not work up much in the way of ire and passed over several good looking clods of dirt that would have made very suitable missiles. At last she stood right before him, looking at the scrolls and writing stuff scattered about him, and the small book that rested open beside him. He opened his eyes.

"Hello. What is your name?" he asked, yawning. "And where did you come from?"

"I live over yonder a ways off. Me name is Sheila."

"Sheila? Why, I must tell you, there was an imp here just awhile ago that had stolen your name and was doing the most vile and vicious things with it," Ullin said seriously. Before she could answer, he went on. "Only, it looked nothing like you, oh no! Its hair was all matted and tangled, and its face was covered with soot and dirt, and it screamed and screamed when I trapped it. I'm sure it was about to do all manner of bad things when I caught it."

"Oh?" Sheila began to smile.

"Oh, yes. And never could it have a smile as lovely as yours, my dear!"

"Then what happened?" she asked, playing along and putting her hands on her waist and cocking her head.

"Why I threw it into the river!"

"Ye did?"

"Yes, I did. And that made it so mad and furious (you know imps hate water!) that it blew up to the size of a barrel and popped. POOF! Sending its head flying across the river, its arms whirling through the sky, and the rest of it melting away into the river. I ran away from there as fast as my feet could carry me, I can tell you! But it must have thrown a spell at me at the last moment, for no sooner than I made it back here to grab my things than a deep sleep came over me. Say, you are not a princess are you?"

"Me? Naw, I don't think so."

"Well, they say only a princess can break the sleep-charm of an imp, and I just thought you must be one. A princess, that is."

"Yer just makin' all this up!"

"Are you sure that you are not a princess?" Ullin said, eyeing her seriously. "You look like you might be a princess in disguise."

"I'm just me. Right here on the ground, silly!"

Ullin continued to give her a serious look, then his eyebrows rose in an expression of realization.

"Ah-h! I get it. Right! You *are* a princess, but you don't want anyone to know it! Just so!" Ullin nodded knowingly to her and winked and touched his nose with a finger. "I won't tell a soul. I promise. I won't mention to anyone anything about the imp, or how I tossed it into the river, or how it laid a sleep-charm on me just as it exploded, or how I was rescued from the sleep-charm by a beautiful princess who happened to be passing by. I won't say any of that, or anything of the sort."

And, apparently, he never had.

# Chapter 18

## Arrows and Patrols

"...and I'd be interested if you have any notions as to how you might want to begin our training."

Ullin's eyes were deep pools of sunlit green, looking at Sheila expectantly. She was smiling absently, then she shook herself.

"Pardon me? Oh! Yes. I do. And it may be best if I gave a little demonstration first. To the whole group, that is. After that, maybe split up into smaller groups for lessons."

"That sounds good. We gather tomorrow at noon. Can you be ready by then?"

"Yes, if I can come early to prepare."

"As early as you wish!" Ullin stood from his desk and reached out his hand, a gesture not often shared with women. Sheila shook his hand awkwardly as he gave a quick bow. "Then I'll see you and Robby tomorrow!"

"Thank you," she said, meaning more than she could say.

"Thank *you*!" said Ullin.

• • •

On the walk home, Sheila asked Robby about Ullin.

"I guess I don't really know all that much about him," Robby admitted. "I think he and Ashlord have known each other for a long time. He's my mother's nephew. I haven't had a chance to ask Ullin about it, but I don't think he's been home in quite a long while."

"Where's home to him?"

"Well, from what I can piece together, my mother's family came from the West some time back. My mother was only a little girl, and Ullin was not yet born, I expect. She doesn't talk much about it, and until recently she rarely told me anything about her people. They have lands somewhere south of here, where Ullin was born."

"Tallinvale?"

"Yes, that's the place."

"I think I've heard Ashlord mention it."

"Hm. Well, my grandfather is very old, apparently, and by every hint I've gotten he is a very stern man. I gather he's not too happy with his daughter marrying beneath her. In fact, I think she is sort of banished from him. My mother did let it drop once that her father could never be pleased by his two sons. They are dead, now. And Ullin, only child of my mother's youngest brother, is the only male left in that line."

"Yet he is a Kingsman. Of Duinnor."

"Yes, made to serve under the ancient code of the Named Houses. But I think he does so willingly."

"I've met never anyone like him," Sheila uttered, immediately regretting the tone of admiration in her voice. "I mean, he does seem different."

"Oh, he's a handsome fella, if that's what you mean," Robby agreed. "In a rough sort of way."

"Yes, there's that," she nodded. "And something else, too. A kind of sadness, I think."

"Perhaps."

"I think he has changed," she went on. "That is, since I last remember him, years ago."

"Yes, I think so. The scar on his head. His beard is thicker, I think. And, well, the weariness," Robby agreed.

"Is he Elifaen? Like your mother?"

"Oh? No. His mother was not Elifaen."

When they walked into the store, Robby and Sheila were heartily greeted by his parents, who both commented on Robby's outfit and on how well Sheila looked and how they had missed her and were glad for her to be back. She was a bit embarrassed by the attention, but Mirabella soon put her at ease. Robby went immediately upstairs and changed clothes and went back downstairs to help with the store. Mirabella whisked Sheila away, and, for the rest of the afternoon, the two could be heard laughing and chattering on and on about this and that.

Business was steady all the afternoon, with folks coming and going, many strangers entering to look for supplies needed for their wagons or camp kitchens or to make repairs to their equipment before the festival began. Robby heard many different accents, from the coastlands and seaways, from the mountains and foothills, and some, Robby thought, much like that of Thurdun of the far western realm of Vanara. Several times, Robby and his father stopped what they were doing and stood outside on the porch to watch carnival wagons roll by. One of the wagons was pulled by magnificent ponies, and on the flatbed of the wagon was a troupe of acrobats. As the wagon rolled past, they slowly balanced themselves atop one another in various patterns and contorted themselves amazingly while juggling a crazy assortment of knives, dishes, eggs, burning candles, and small animals, and never once dropping a single thing.

Later, after the store closed, they all sat down to a rather jolly meal. Sheila had changed into a dress and was looking happy. While they ate, they talked of the upcoming festival, the new militia and its members, of the prowlers and the changing of the locks on the doors, and the new crossbars that Mr. Ribbon had installed. They laughed when Robby told them about jumping over the ditch with Anerath, and the ladies were impressed, he thought, at his riding prowess. Conversation went from subject to subject, from store to Passdale, and from wine to weather. Robby at last yawned broadly as he helped clear away the dishes.

"Oh! I suppose last night is finally catching up with me."

"Me, too," Mr. Ribbon said, trying to suppress a yawn. "An' I've an early day of it, so I'd better be off to bed."

Robby followed his father's example and said his good nights, and left the ladies to their own soft chatter. Soon he had bathed and was lying in his bed, his hands behind his head on the pillow as he gazed over his feet and out through the window across the room. There, in the strong breeze, the upper boughs of nearby trees swayed in front of the stars.

He considered lighting his lamp and studying more of the books he had borrowed recently. But the movement of the light and shadow, and the coolness of the air through the window, lulled him toward peaceful sleep. He did not fight it, since it had been such a good day, and he was content. After a time, sleep slowly closed his eyes.

Long after all of the lights in the house were out, and all its occupants were fast asleep, after the stars dimmed and night-time began to yield to a coming morning, something stirred at Robby's window. An observer might have thought a leaf had fluttered onto the sill, so small and insignificant a shadow it was. It remained there for a long while, rustling just a little, then sprang into the room, landing on the foot-rail of Robby's bed. It perched there for a moment, turning its head nearly all the way around to examine every aspect of the room, then it flew back to the window sill. Every few minutes it would fly off, only to return shortly, and this it repeated throughout the rest of the night until dawn came and those in the house began to stir, when it flew away and did not return.

• • •

Ullin led the Passdale Militia out along one edge of a large grassy field shortly after noon on the next day. It was a cool day, but they had marched at quick pace from the Common House and so all were warmed up, especially since they carried swords and shields, lances and backpacks, with water and some little food. Indeed, many were sweating in the full sun. Across the long grassy field, over a hundred yards away, stood Sheila, bow in hand and several buckets of arrows on the ground beside her. About twenty yards in front and to her right was a lance stuck into the ground with a long strip of white ribbon flying from it.

"Before you learn how to use the bow, it is well for you to know what a single archer can do. See there across the field, Sheila Pradkin, who will be your instructor," Ullin told them, walking up and down in front of their line. "Strip to your shirts. Cast your arms and surcoats aside, for you will not need them for this exercise. While you do that, I will tell you what we are about. Sheila has one hundred and fifty arrows. They have no tips, only cloth bulbs soaking in buckets of blackberry juice. Your mission is to take down yonder flag and bring it here where we now stand."

"Oo! A game! Ilikegames!" Ibin cried, rubbing his hands together in anticipation.

"Aye. A game," Ullin said. "You may take only your shield and helmet. If you are painted by her arrows on your shield, you may continue. If she strikes you anywhere upon your body or helmet, you must fall down and remain there until I order you to get up. Do you hear me? If you are carrying the flag, and you are struck by an arrow, you must drop it. Do you understand?"

"Yes, sir!" Robby shouted along with many others.

"Very well," Ullin signaled to Sheila. "Then we begin immediately."

Robby picked up his shield and tightened the chin strap of his helmet. "Who goes first, Commander?"

Just then, an arrow struck Ullin on his chest, splattering purple juice all over his shirt.

"Ouch!" he winced. Then he grinned and shook his head. "She's a wonder even at a distance."

"So how do we go about this, sir?"

"That is for you to decide," Ullin told them. "Since you did not protect your leader, he is now dead. So he cannot lead or advise you."

"Aw! That ain't right!"

"Good grief!"

Ullin continued to smile and shrug. At last, the members began to accept the situation.

"Well, why don't we all rush at her. All at once, like?" said someone else. "She can't get us all!"

"Yeah!"

"Why, that don't seem fair! All us goin' at her, an' her bein' a girl an' all."

"Aw, that don't matter none! She's the one with the bow an' arrows, ain't she?"

"I think we oughta go at her in groups, see? She can't aim in more thin one place at a time."

Ullin crossed his arms and let them argue for a bit until at last one said, "Well, Commander, can't ye give us any hints?"

"However seems best to you," he said. "Besides taking orders, sometimes part of soldiering is to figure out things as you come upon them."

"Well, then," said Billy, "I'm off an' goin'!"

"Me, too," said Ibin.

They picked up their shields and strode off confidently into the field.

"Me, too!"

"And me!"

Several paces apart, a group of seven or eight made their way as Robby and the rest watched. They got halfway there before Sheila let fly her first arrow. From where they stood, they saw it soar smoothly up and swiftly downward.

"Owie!" they heard Billy cry out. "That hurt!"

He held his shoulder and sat down on the ground, cursing. In quick succession, the others went down, too, the last flinging away his shield and running flat out toward the flag before he, too, was oozing purple juice from his thigh.

"Use your shields," Ullin muttered softly as the next group departed. They fared no better than the first group, however, and Sheila's aim seemed flawless, for not an arrow was flown that did not find its mark.

"Well, then," said Robby, "that takes care of over half our men. I guess it is time to try something different."

Under Ullin's watchful eye, Robby gathered the rest of the militia together to talk. Sheila watched them huddle, with Ullin standing off to the side with his arms crossed, observing. After a few moments, two shapes began moving toward her, one just a few yards ahead of the other, each made up of two lines of militiamen. The first line of each group held their shields together in front, low to the ground about five men abreast. Behind these came a second line holding their shields above the first and tilted back. Crouching low behind and beneath these covers, the two groups moved slowly like two terribly drunken turtles whose shells kept coming apart and reforming. She smiled at their plan and saw that the closer they came the better they got at holding together.

"Keep low!" Robby cried from his place in the second line of the first group. Just then an arrow struck his shield with a SPLAT!, quickly followed by another and another, bouncing harmlessly away.

"Ouch!" cried out a soldier next to Robby as an arrow made it through the cracks. He fell out and Robby quickly reformed his group. Looking behind, he saw that the following group was still intact, and, farther back, Ullin was grinning broadly at them.

Without expression, Sheila pulled the string, took careful aim, and let loose. The arrow hit the thigh of an exposed leg in the first group and as this man stumbled down, she let loose another into the group as they tried to reform. The fellow next to Robby was hit and as he tried to fall away from the group, he tripped. In an instant, the entire group fell on top of one another in a confusion of clanking shields, kicks, and yells. Quickly, arrow after arrow flew into the pile-up, until Robby alone was unstained, hiding behind two shields that he held before him as he knelt low. Sheila was now openly laughing at them, a bit too gleefully, thought Robby.

"Not so easy as it looks, eh?"

Robby turned and saw Billy lounging with his head propped on one arm and gnawing on a long blade of grass. He, too, was grinning.

"I'm not sure I understand the point of all this," Robby replied as another arrow cracked off of his shield.

"Oh, ye'll get the point ready enough if ye get smeared with that sticky goo flyin' yer way."

"Somebody's eye could get put out!"

"Yep. Oh, an' yer shield's a mess, by the way."

"Thanks very much for letting me know. You're a lot of help."

"Think nuthin' of it."

At that, Robby darted over to the other group that was still making progress toward the flag, but losing a man every five or six steps. Nearby was Ibin, lying on his back. At first Robby thought he was pointing up into the air, but then he realized Ibin was just letting a dragonfly land on his finger. By the time this group had gotten within a few feet of the flag, there were only five of them left, each holding two shields against what seemed a steady stream of arrows.

"Ain't she ever gonna run out of arrows?"

"Robby!" said one of them crouched nearby. "Yer likely the fastest runner of us that are left. Grab that ribbon an' make off the other way whilst we block her aim."

"Right!"

"On three. One. Two. Um, THREE!"

Robby darted to the lance and pulled it up as the others stood and charged straight at Sheila, their shields held high and yelling what they hoped were terrifying war-cries. By the time Sheila had felled them all, Robby was halfway back to Ullin, flinging his shield away and pumping his arms and legs with all his might and speed. Ten yards away from Ullin, he felt a sharp sting in the center of his back.

"Yow! That ain't fair!" he yelled. "In the back?"

Ullin chuckled and gestured for Sheila and everyone else to come.

"Perfectly fair," he said. "Would you hesitate to put an arrow into the back of some foe who was running away with your mother?"

"No, sir."

"Well, then!"

Robby tried to rub his back, sullen with disappointment and a little anger, as Ullin called everyone together.

"You should have slung your shield over your back," Sheila said, walking up. "As it was, it was a lucky shot that got you."

"Oh, I doubt that very much," Robby said, resigned to his failure. "Your skill had more to do with it than luck."

"Very well!" Ullin said loudly. "That was just a taste of what a single archer can do. Now, imagine facing a dozen archers. Or a hundred! We are going to train both sides. How to use arrows and how to defend against them in the face of a determined opponent. That is, not only will you learn to shoot, and shoot well, but you will learn all about how a soldier may try to avoid being hit by arrows. Starting today, one third of us will train. Another third will rest, while the other third will serve with Sheriff Fivelpont. We will draw lots to start off. One group to serve with Fivelpont from noon until midnight and the next group from midnight until noon, then the third group from noon until midnight."

Ullin had to explain the plan several times before they finally drew lots from his helmet and the company was split up. Ullin appointed one militiaman from each group to be in charge of the group, and Robby was one of those he selected.

"There is much that I need you for," Ullin told him, "but I think it wiser to put you in charge of this lot." He nodded toward Billy and Ibin. "Maybe you can keep them out of too much trouble. Fivelpont doesn't care for wisecrackers."

He then sent Robby's group to report to Fivelpont at his office near the Common House and another group off to the barracks to rest. The others remained with Sheila to begin their instruction.

• • •

It was a long and rather boring afternoon and evening, thought Robby as he trudged with his group back to the barracks late that night. Fivelpont had various members of Robby's group tag along with his deputies while the old sheriff led Robby and Billy around to check on the wagons at Wayford Common, to be sure they were properly registered, as it were, and no disorderly conduct was apparent. It all seemed rather nosey to Robby, who knew the carnival-folk were just trying to make a living, and he did not enjoy poking around in their wagons, looking through their belongings for whatever it was they were looking for.

"Just take a look-see that there ain't somethin' amiss," Fivelpont had told him, pointing at a particularly modest caravan. "We want 'em to be comfortable with the notion of us looking 'round, see? In case somethin' happens later on what needs it. Like something goin' missin', ye see?"

So while an old woman holding her grandchild watched, Robby looked around the inside of the wagon, mostly at the little miniature portraits that she specialized in, examples of which were hanging all about the walls.

"Looks all in order to me," Robby said, rather officiously. Feeling embarrassed and ridiculous, he stepped out of the wagon and quickly walked away to where Fivelpont was haggling with another wagon owner over some kind of camping fee. When that was negotiated, and the fee collected, they walked a few miles to Porter's farm, where, as Fivelpont told them, someone was seen poaching fish out of Farmer Porter's pond. Robby and the others waited patiently at the gate, while Fivelpont spoke with Porter. After about an hour of trying to decipher the old farmer's complaint, and with much examination of the pond's edge, Fivelpont finally threw his hands up and waved goodbye.

"Dang raccoons!" said Fivelpont in disgust. "He's been seeing raccoons down at his pond. I know tracks when I sees 'em. An' no wonder they wore masks! Old fool! Well, I ain't no trapper! What a waste of time!"

It was well after dark by the time they got back to Wayford Common, and Fivelpont left Robby and Billy at the gate to the fairgrounds to check any further arrivals until the next shift relieved them. After an hour of shivering in the sudden cool breeze, several other Passdale militiamen came up out of the darkness along with one of Fivelpont's deputies to take over the chore.

"Borin', borin', borin'!" Billy said in disgust as they walked back into town. "I never spent more time doin' nuthin' in all me life! An' I'm well practiced at it!"

"Not exactly what I had in mind, either," Robby agreed. "But I guess it's all part of it."

The next week was more of the same, with the groups shifting around their days and nights. Robby and others had group lessons with Sheila, and he enjoyed how she stood so close to him, with her arms around him to show him the proper way to hold the bow. He tried his best, and with instruction and plenty of practice, Robby became a fair archer, and he better appreciated Sheila's skill. Alas, those lessons were all too brief, it seemed, and were followed by a day of chores at the store and a day of patrol with Fivelpont before again his group gathered with Sheila. Being enthusiastic in more ways than one, Robby was the first one to show up, and the last to leave when her next group of pupils came along.

So all went according to Ullin's plan, the result of which was growing skill on the part of the militiamen, and a growing pride in their duties and their roles. Under his skillful leadership and intense lessons, Ullin's militiamen learned to hold their own against him and each other while sparring with sword or lance. They gained endurance, strength, and quite a few bruises, along the way. They also learned to protect Ullin and themselves from Sheila's rain of arrows, and how to put their own arrows on the mark. And they triumphantly retrieved the ribbon from Sheila's side of the field so consistently (and with hardly any "casualties") that, after a few days, they faced both Sheila and Ullin simultaneously shooting arrows at them. In spite of this added threat, the militiamen proved themselves time and again.

At last, Ullin arranged for all of his militiamen to have an evening off from their duties and training so that they could all meet together at the Common House for supper. As they ate, they celebrated their hard work, their accomplishments, and their good company. When the meal was eaten and the dishes were cleaned away, they assembled into formation out in the Common House yard for a final inspection before being dismissed.

"I want you all to rest and clean your things tonight," he told them. "Tomorrow is the first day of the Counting, and, perhaps more important to most, the first day of the festival. I've arranged a special early ceremony for all of you to make your annual oath. After that, I'll want you to serve as an honor guard for the mayor and council during the opening ceremonies. Most of the wagons have arrived, and Fivelpont's men can handle the few remaining ones. You'll be needed again when the festival is over for a few days. Until then, we go to regular shifts, with half on duty and half off. We rise two hours before dawn and breakfast in the yard. Mayor Ribbon will meet us here at dawn. Afterwards, and for the rest of the week, I want all of you to look your best. Let us take pride in being the defenders of this land and people, and let that pride and honor show in our appearance. Those of you with beards, get them well-trimmed. Haircuts and washings. Polish and shine leather and steel and brass. You will all be closely scrutinized by the townfolk, by the Barley folk, including the Bosklanders, and by our visitors at the fairgrounds. Make them proud of you! Look your best. Good-night!"

# Chapter 19

# The Bellringer

Day 81
164 Days Remaining

The Week of Counting came at last, and the inhabitants of the region came to Wayford Common to open the Fall Festival, to renew their pledges to King and community, and to sign the Census Book. A small dais was set up before the gates of the fairgrounds upon which Mayor Ribbon stood. He was surrounded on either side by the councilmen of Passdale, the heads of the great houses of the area, including Mr. Bosk. Behind the dais stood the Passdale Militiamen all in a line with shields at the ready and lances planted straight and tall. Banners fluttered gaily from tall poles and ribbons decorated the dais. The sky was clear and the air was cool, but by noontime the sun was warm, and the ceremony was begun. A councilman stepped forth and addressed the crowd in a loud voice.

"Hear ye, all gathered here, inhabitants of Passdale, County Barley, and the regions surrounding of the Eastlands Realm! Now attend to the duly appointed master of this day, Mayor of Passdale, Robigor Ribbon."

There was clapping and hurrahs as Mr. Ribbon stepped forward, clearing his throat for the words that had been handed down, practiced, and recited for many, many generations, and now to be delivered once again. Over the eons, the speech was little changed and had remained very much the same from one year to the next, except perhaps with some minor variation if there was anything in particular worth mentioning on a given year.

"My people," he said. "I'm proud an' honored to have been asked to serve in the place of the Honorable Mayor Greardon, recently an' tragically departed. In his name an' for his sake I dedicate these proceedin's. The season is now upon us when the farmers are reapin' the rewards of thar lands, proud of thar good efforts an' hard work. They are a determined lot, an' should rightly be commended for the bounty they provide to us all. All done, I might add, in spite of the great storm what tore up many of our fields an' much of our properties.

"Still! Barley is threshed an' laid by, corn put by, an' beans, an' hams, an' all manner of provision for winter. Times are good, an' our tables'll be heavy with good food all winter long.

"As well, we gain benefit from our workshops an' from folk at thar crafts, makin' the tools an' cloth an' all the things we need for use an' for trade.

"Now, of course thar're some what are poor an' in debt. We also had sickness an' injury among our friends an' kin. Some have passed away, an' our thoughts are sad since we miss 'em so.

"But gen'rally speakin', our people are well off an' fairly prosperous. It's been a year without plague, an' our children an' old folk haven't lacked for care er food. An' with the great storm, we learned again what good neighbors may mean to one another, an' what wealth is stored an' shared by goodness an' by kindness.

"Now I commend ye to yerselves. An' as way of openin' this celebration of the year, an' of each other, I summon all to renew thar pledges, an' to make thar name or thar mark in our census as a record of thar presence an' of thar pledge. In so manner, may we all enjoy the spirit of this bountiful season throughout all the seasons of the year, with thanksgivin' an' goodwill."

Here, Mr. Ribbon motioned to a lady on the podium who moved to stand next to him.

"I ask our Mrs. Greardon to lead us in our pledges."

"Thank you, Mayor Ribbon. And on behalf of my family, I want to thank all of you for your support and for your loving kindness these past months since the great storm."

"Hear-hear for Greardon," someone in the crowd cried out. This was followed by a round of cheers for Mrs. Greardon in honor of her late husband, all of which brought tears to her eyes. For many moments, she was so moved by this outburst that she was unable to continue. Mr. Ribbon put his arm around her, said something to her, and they hugged. Mrs. Greardon faced the hushed gathering and continued. She spoke each line of the pledge, which was then echoed by the crowd.

> I will say the truth.
> I will honor my elders.
> I will protect the young.
> I will obey the law.
> I will respect the property of others.
> I will be a good steward of the land and of the water.
> I will be watchful of strangers.
> I will defend the Realm.
> To these things I give my bond and my oath,
> Upon my blood and upon my life,
> In the name of the King,
> By Duinnor I swear!
> Long live the King!

After this last utterance, there was much applause and cheering, and musicians burst out in a gay tune. Mr. Ribbon motioned all toward the gates, where there was a table. Upon it, a large bound volume was opened, and a cup of quills and a pot of ink set out. As each person passed, they signed their names below the oath that was written upon the page—the one they had just spoken—and then they were admitted into the fairgrounds. Thusly the festival began, much as it had begun year after year, since before the memory of anyone present. Indeed, there was much to be thankful for and much prosperity, in spite of the storm damage, and everyone was in high spirits. Soon children and adults alike were agog with excitement. They were fascinated at the exhibits, amazed by the dancers and tumblers, delighted by the music and food, and by the games and swing-rides.

After the ceremony, Ullin came along to disposition his men. While half were dismissed to rest before their evening watches, Robby, along with several others, including Billy and Ibin, enjoyed the duty of the afternoon and early evening, which mostly involved greeting those that entered. From all over Barley people came, laughing and in high spirits, and none so full of joy and excitement than one large wagon that was crammed full of hay and children and drawn by a team of powerful mules. It was driven by Mr. Broadweed, bringing children along early so that their parents could work until day's end. Though covered with hay and straw, he did not seem to mind and smiled serenely as he guided the wagon along the road toward the entrance. Meanwhile, his young passengers squealed and laughed, thrilled by every bump and jostle, throwing hay into the air and all over each other, leaving a trail of fodder in their wake, jumping up and down, and climbing all over each other and the wagon, too. One boy clung so precariously over the side that Robby felt compelled to run up and shove the precocious lad up and back into the wagon, igniting new howls of mirth. Dusting hay and straw from his head and shoulders, Robby then resumed his station beside his friends at the entrance of the festival ground. Their watch lasted until early evening, when their relief came, just as the last glow of day was overtaken by the colorful lanterns and lamps, and the braziers and torches of the lively fair.

• • •

Many miles away, on the far side of Barley, Ashlord was busy going over the latest dispatches he had received from Glareth. Certina flew in through the open window and circled the room, and Ashlord absently pushed the window closed while still reading a letter. He settled back into a chair at the table, and continued to read, while Certina continued to fly about the room, perturbed beyond containment, fluttering across his table, and upsetting Ashlord's papers for the fourth time in as many minutes.

"What has gotten into you?" Ashlord held his hand out in a useless attempt to get her to perch. She continued to whistle and screech with uncharacteristic impatience, flying around Ashlord's head, sometimes darting so close that his hair blew back from her wings.

"If you would just settle down, perhaps you might show me what disturbs you!" he said in an exasperated tone. He looked around the cottage rafters, glancing at the top of the cupboard and over at the mantel, but Flitter was nowhere to be seen in any of his favorite perches. Now Certina was flying and squawking at the door, going back and forth in front of it as a clear sign for her master to open it. Sighing, he rose from his chair and did so, and she shot out into the darkness of the evening.

"Is that all you wanted?"

But before he could close it, she shot back in, calling even more loudly than before.

"What? What?" he cried.

She flew back outside.

"You mean for me to follow, eh?" Ashlord grabbed his cloak. "Very well! Why didn't you just say so?"

To Tulith Attis she led him, and the closer the two got to the place the more he sensed that something was very wrong. By the time they came within sight of the moonlit fortress, Ashlord was at a long striding run. Through the gate he dashed, Certina circling him, urging him onward. He looked over the interior grounds, then followed, charging up the nearby stairs to the ramparts. Walking swiftly along the south-facing wall and then through the crumbling remains of the western side, he saw nothing amiss with the fortress or beyond the parapets. As he rounded onto the northern side and made his way to the place overlooking the old bridge, he slowed to a careful advance. The river, full and flowing as it had in the old days, could just be heard rushing softly under the bridge, and a fitful breeze rattled the dry leaves still clinging to nearby brush. There was another sound, too, unnatural and muffled, coming from the forest beyond the river. His eyes strained as it came slowly closer, moving vaguely toward the bridge, but the dense brush and trees, dark and gloomy in the low light, were like shadows crowding any view of the source. He heard a distant, dull crack and some slight clink of metal against metal. Cocking his ear and closing his eyes, Ashlord redoubled his efforts and heard the sound of distant voices. Patiently, he waited, listening as the sounds grew ever closer, growing in strength and clarity. An hour passed. By the time his eyes opened again and he saw the first signs of it, he already knew what it was. Instinctively, his legs tensed to run, but still he waited, to be sure of things, watching as the shadowy brush at the far side of the bridge was cleared away by axemen, some bearing torches, the yellow light jabbing through the breaks in the brush and branches. They worked quickly, tossing the brush and saplings over the side of the bridge and pushing fallen logs aside with great effort and strain and grunts. Out of the wood and onto the bridge emerged several riders, their armor glinting dully in the moonlight. More riders came behind them as they poured onto the bridge, and soon soldiers on foot came, too.

"How did I miss this?" Ashlord muttered as he turned to flee.

• • •

The off-duty militia, Robby, Billy, and Ibin amongst them, gladly entered the fairgrounds to enjoy the fun of the evening. Each of them, along with every other militiaman of Passdale, had been given two silver coins by Mayor Ribbon, as tokens of Passdale's appreciation, and they were all eager to partake of the excitement.

As soon as Robby and his fellow militiamen entered, they crowded around a man standing behind a table at a colorful kiosk. He was outfitted in gray and blue, with a large flat-topped hat on his head, and he held a smallish wooden box. A large banner overhead proclaimed, "The Conundrum Box."

"Here is how it works," the man cried. "I place your coin inside the box. I place my coin inside the box. Now I slide this slat of wood through here and this slat of wood through there, and so forth and so on. The box is closed. No locks. No keys. I give you the box, and I turn the sandglass. If you can open the box before the sand runs out, you keep both coins. You cannot break open the box by smashing, banging, or prying. You can only use your hands. If the sand runs out, I keep both coins. Easy as that!"

Behind him stood a large man, his bare arms crossed and bulging with muscles, eyeing the crowd warily, and the man gestured to him.

"This is Trander, my strongman. He will see to any who try to break my Conundrum Box or to any who try to run away with it. Who will play the game? Who will test their wits and their hands against the Conundrum Box? Risk for risk. Coin for coin. No one? Ah, it can be done and there is no magic, only the skill of nimble hands and thoughtful attention. See! Once again it is open! Who will play the game and be a gold piece richer? How about you, young fellow? You look bright enough. What about you, big man? Who will play?"

"I wanna, I wanna, Iwannaplay!" said Ibin, stepping forward, digging into his vest pocket for a coin.

"Ibin, don't be silly. It's rigged," Billy said as he took Ibin by the arm and tried to hold him back. "Ye'll not see yer silver again!"

"ButI, but, butIwanttoplay, Billy."

"Silver for gold! Coin for coin! Who will outwit the Conundrum Box?"

"Go ahead, then!" said Billy as Ibin held up his coin for the man to see. "But don't complain when yer ale money's gone!"

"Here!" cried Ibin, gleefully handing the man his coin.

"A player! Who will be the richer or the poorer at the turn of the sandglass?" said the man to the crowd, taking Ibin's coin. "Here's how it works. I place my gold coin and your silver coin inside for all to see. I slip this wooden slat through here. I slip this wooden slat through there. And so forth and so on. Now! Are you ready? Here's the box, now I turn the sandglass."

Ibin snatched up the wooden box and turned it over and over in his hands as the man continued his verbal routine.

"The sands run and time passes as the moments of our life. Who will be the richer or the poorer when the last grain falls? Soon, now, time will tell!"

Suddenly there was a click and Ibin quickly removed one slat of wood and then another until, before even half of the sand had run out, he held up a coin in each hand, one silver and the other gold.

"My box is outwitted! Alas, I am the poorer and you the richer!"

"Look! Look!" Ibin was almost jumping with joy.

No sooner had he turned from the table to show Billy his winnings than he was being pushed away by all of the others crowding in.

"Let me have at it!" cried Billy.

"Me, too."

"And me!"

"One at a time!" said the man, holding up his hands.

Robby, at the back of the crowd, stayed long enough to watch Billy lose his silver.

"Outwitted by the Conundrum Box!" cried the man. "And I am the richer by a silver coin of Glareth!"

Dejected, Billy was pushed away from the kiosk as others had their turn.

"Just couldn't figure it out," he told Robby as he rejoined him.

"Oh, well! Don't worry about it, Billy. I'll get us a tankard."

"Mighty obliged."

They moved to a nearby table and Robby paid for two ales. They watched others try their luck at the box, some winning, most losing, as they drank their drafts.

"Seems like most of 'em that win are the very one's ye'd figure ain't got a chance," observed Billy. "I wonder how ol' Ibin did it?"

"Don't know," answered Robby, looking at Ibin who was presently approaching with a very large basket. "Maybe he's got the touch."

"Thar's little doubt he's touched. But I still wonder."

Still grinning deliriously, Ibin put his wicker basket down on the table with a heavy thump.

"Billy! Lookatwhat, lookat, lookatwhatIgotforus!"

He started pulling out bottles of wine, legs of mutton, a big wedge of cheese, several baguettes, a sack of roasted nuts, still steaming, and a half dozen sweet rolls, dripping with apple butter.

"AndIstill, I still, andIstillhavemysilverandthensome! Let'seat!"

Billy and Robby shook their heads at each other, laughing, and thanked Ibin as they tore into the feast. The Conundrum Box man kept up a brisk business for a while, but the crowd around his table thinned as people moved off to watch the jugglers or to have their fortunes told by one of the many seers, or to play one of the many tossing games. Music came from the large tent across the way, and there was clapping and cheers mixed with it as the acrobats performed within. Farther down, Robby could see the swing-ride spinning round and round, sending children flying in circles through the air at the end of long ropes. There was also a fire-eating man, drumming up business outside the magic-show tent, and a drama player reciting particular lines from a play that was about to begin in the tent directly across from the fire-eater. Everywhere people laughed and ate and drank and played games and clapped at the wins and losses alike. The air cooled further and the dusky evening sky darkened, but the grounds were lit by hundreds of blue and yellow and green and red and white lanterns hung from lines overhead in web-like profusion from tent to tent and along each lane, crisscrossing this way and that. So gaily they glowed, that it was hard to tell when night-time came, for beneath their globes all was light and levity, merriment and joy. Some on-duty militiamen came by, along with one of Fivelpont's men and several Boskmen, too, all in their finest surcoats with their steel and brass polished and glinting.

"Look over yonder at yer dad, Robby," Billy nudged, gesturing with a half-eaten sweet roll. Robby turned around and saw his father entering the gates of the fair. He was wearing his best breeches and vest, his polished high-boots and a felt jacket, over which he wore the blue Mayor's Sash. Around his shoulders draped a fur-collared long-coat of black wool with silver buttons and cufflinks. On his arms hung two of the most striking women that Passdale had seen in many, many years. On his left was Mirabella, her red hair flowing over a walnut brown cape that hung to her ankles. Underneath she wore a dress of fine satin the color of dark emerald, and above the low cut of the neckline hung a sparkling medallion set in the middle with a blue topaz in a constellation of diamonds. She was tossing her head back, laughing, and bent to look across her husband at her companion, Sheila, who was very finely attired in a long sweeping midnight blue cloak over her blue gown, her light brown hair braided around her forehead and hanging behind her back. Robby saw them as if he had never known them, so struck was he by the beauty of the ladies and the handsomeness of his father. Proudly, Mr. Ribbon approached, and the crowd parted before them as they came, with ladies curtseying and men bowing in honor of the Mayor and his wife. Sheila was radiant with delight, and when she saw Robby and his friends staring at them, she laughed and pointed.

"Ah, Robby, me son!" Mr. Ribbon called, and he guided his entourage toward him. Robby stood up and bowed low before them, honoring the spirit of the moment.

"Good evening, sir and fair ladies," he said. "And what a splendid trio you three make!"

"These ladies outshine the moon, don't ye think?" said his father.

"Most certainly the two most beautiful women in all of Passdale and Barley," Robby agreed, bowing again. "If I did not know you three, I'd say you were from some fabled land, some enchanted city."

"Oh, be quiet!" his mother giggled. Like Robby, they had already imbibed a fair quantity of drink, with all of the incumbent cheer it may bring, and Robby detected a lovely blush on his mother's cheeks.

"It looks as though you three are enjoying quite a feast," Sheila observed.

"Ibin's winnin's," Billy said, rising and bowing. "Won't ye join us?"

"Thank you, and thank Ibin, but we're off to see the acrobats," Mirabella said. "And if I'm not mistaken, one show has just let out, and another line is forming at their pavilion."

"Aye, right ye are, sweet light," Mr. Ribbon said. "Shall we?"

"Yes, let's do!"

"Won't you come along with us?" Sheila asked.

"Thank you, but," Robby motioned to the table, "so much food! I must help out! I'll meet you afterwards, if you are willing. The minstrels of Marren will be playing just over there a bit later. I think you would enjoy them. If you'd care to accompany me, I would be honored."

"I'd be delighted!"

"Then I'll watch for you at the end of the acrobat's performance."

"We must go!" Mr. Ribbon said, pulling the ladies along, "if I am to have my seat of honor. Ye know, as Mayor, an' all." With a wink, he guided them toward the pavilion, and Sheila looked back over her shoulder at Robby, smiling.

Turning back to the table, Robby bumped into Billy, who was staring after them.

"Excuse me! Didn't realize you were standing right there."

"Sorry," Billy said. He shook his head and looked at Robby with a puzzled expression. "Was that truly Sheila Pradkin?"

"Yes."

"Lo! I never seen her so, so, I mean, I never realized how, I mean, she's—"

"Yeah, she is, isn't she?"

"Yeah."

"Sheila'sverybeautiful," Ibin blurted out, louder than he should have, his mouth full of food. He picked up a bottle and pulled the stopper and took a long gulping drink, then wiped his mouth with his sleeve. Slamming down the bottle, he jumped up from the table. "I'm, I'm, I'mgoingtoseethejugglers!"

"But what about all this food?" Billy called after him. He and Robby watched the big fellow hurry off into the crowd.

"Oh well," Billy shrugged, picking up a bottle and uncorking it. "No sense in lettin' it all waste."

Robby resumed his seat and let Billy refill his tankard. All the while, the Conundrum Man barked out his unending verbal advertising, his customers having long since gone to other parts of the festival.

"Perhaps mere coins are not what you desire," the Conundrum Man went on, smoothly shifting his practiced speech. "For some gold, and for others silver. Gold and silver are fine with me and with my box, but see here!" He pulled out a panel on which was displayed many bejeweled rings, bracelets, and other glittering decorations. "I have gathered for your temptation examples of the finest works of the craftsmen of Duinnor, the most exquisite fashions of Glareth. Made with gold from Vanara, rubies from the Tulivana Mountains of Altoria, silver from the mines of Mount Vendril. Look here, at these earrings, studded with diamonds from the fabled lands of Karkarando, so distant within the Dragonlands that no Northman has ever seen the place. Your coin against one of these treasures. What will it be? A gold bangle, the kind worn by the ladies of the desert? Or perhaps an armband is more to your liking? What of this ring, red gold adorned with tiny blue sapphires? Behold, it is the very highest fashion of Duinnor!"

This new tactic brought new prospects to his table, many who had shied away before but were now more tempted to be parted from their silver. Meanwhile, Robby listened to Billy prattle on about how the only girls he could get interested in him were ones he did not particularly want to be interested in him, so desperate for male attention by reason of their general poor looks or other limitations.

"What about Gina Clingdon?" Robby asked, eyeing a dejected loser walking away from the Conundrum table. "I thought you liked her."

"Well, I did," Billy replied glancing across the way at a fair-haired girl wearing a much-too-revealing gown and whispering to a gaggle of her friends. "I mean, to look at her over thar, what's not to like? I spent the better part of two weeks slobberin' over meself just to get a chance alone with her. Well, I finally did get with her, an' things went right nicely, in point of fact. That is, 'til I got her laughin' at some little somethin'. Then I knew I whar in trouble."

"What do you mean?"

Billy leaned in close and said, in a low tone, "She laughs like a horse snortin' for oats."

"What?"

"I ain't jokin'! Nearly turned me to stone!" Billy nodded. "I mean, as soon as she started into laughin', I felt like somebody had run me fingernails along a piece of slate, an' the hair on the back of me neck all stood up, like. Thar's no future in a laugh such as that!"

"Well, putting it that way, I guess not."

"But wait," Billy said, touching Robby's arm. "Thar goes Maggie Shawmill, an' I heard tell she done busted up with that Wintrell feller."

Robby turned and saw a pretty young lady, about a year or two younger than himself, leaving the Magic Tent along with a few young and giddy girls.

"Tell ye what," Billy said, getting up and straightening his tunic and surcoat. "I'm gonna see how she likes a man in uniform!"

"Good luck!"

Robby watched him disappear behind a mob of tumblers leaping and rolling and flipping along the way. Sighing and smiling, he turned his attention back to the Conundrum Box man who was just announcing another loser. Robby's eye kept wandering over to the display of jewelry on the gamester's table. He realized he was fascinated by a particular piece that glittered silver and purple. Taking the last drink from his tankard, he got up and shuffled over just as another player began trying to open the box. The Conundrum Box man called his call, keeping an eye on Robby as he did so. For his part, Robby was bending over the attractive jewelry to get a better view. When the glass ran out of sand, and another loser was announced, the man turned to Robby.

"All those things were made far from these parts, by master craftsmen."

"Is this an amethyst?" Robby asked, pointing at the piece.

"Why, yes, sir. It is, indeed."

"And these little yellow gems? Are they honeytears?"

"Aye, that is what they are called in these parts," the man nodded. "You seem very knowledgeable. For such a young man."

"You mean, 'For someone from these parts,'" Robby corrected.

"Well, I wouldn't presume."

"You may as well, since, in most cases, you'd be right in doing. I only know these jewels from having seen them worn on others, and, from time to time, in the store."

"The store?"

"Ribbon's sundries, here in town."

"Oh, I see. Well, these are of the finest quality, as you can see for yourself. That is a very nice lady's piece, a choker, see?"

The man took the piece up and held it so that the braided silver band could be examined along with the unusual clasp at the back of it.

"The neckband is made of woven silver thread, from Chiroth, near Duinnor, and it is made in such a way that has a little stretch, see, so as not to slip. And the clasp will hold firmly, yet is easy to open and close. And the stones are firmly set, yet are cut so that they cast a fine glimmer."

"Yes. Very nice."

"I am willing to sell any of the things you see, or play you for them, whichever you like."

"How much is this?"

"I'll take two hundred silver pieces for that one."

"Whoa! That's more than I have!"

"Then would you like to play for it?"

"Yes," Robby decided impulsively. "I would! But—"

"What is it?"

"Can we keep it quiet? If I win, I'd like to surprise someone with the necklace."

The Conundrum Box man looked sideways at Robby with a smile.

"Why, certainly," he said. "Would you like to step into my tent, here? It offers more privacy."

Robby looked at the tent and saw another man watching from just within its shadow, leaning against the tent post. Looking around, he saw they were practically alone. He did not trust the man, who was still holding the box and waiting for an answer. After all, it was a trick box or else the man would not be able to make a living with it. Still, a little piece of silver was not much to chance.

"I think playing right here will be fine. Here's my silver."

"And here's my choker. Into the box they go. You've seen this enough tonight to know the routine. This slat goes here, and so forth. There. Are you ready?"

"Yes."

"Very well," the man said, placing the box on the table before Robby. "I turn the glass."

Robby picked up the box and immediately noticed how heavy it was, made of dense, dark wood. He also saw carving upon it, the letters and runes of the ancient script. And, to his surprise, he could make out what they said:

*Star to thumb, finger to moon, what is within will be yours soon.*

"Star to thumb," Robby mumbled, turning the box over until he saw a little crescent moon carved into the other side. Turning it again, he found a little star. Putting his right thumb on the star and his index finger on the moon, he squeezed and pushed and pulled. Nothing happened. The Conundrum Man eyed him warily, seeing that Robby was using the clue written on the box.

"It's a trick," Robby said, flustered and turning red with anger. "The instructions are deceitful."

The Conundrum Man shrugged. Robby glanced at the glass and saw his time would soon be up. Suddenly he remembered something Ashlord said about having a gift for opening things, and he eased up on the box hopefully. He put it down on the table, to the surprise of the Conundrum Man, then simply lifted the lid off of the box, revealing the contents.

"There!" Robby looked triumphantly at the man, who was coldly smiling back.

"I am the poorer by far, young master!" he said, gesturing for Robby to take the contents. "And I beg you not to play my game any more."

"I promise I will not," Robby readily agreed. "Now, if you will excuse me."

Robby turned and walked away from the table, wrapping the gift in a handkerchief as he went. The Conundrum Man picked up his box and examined it carefully. The man within the tent detached himself from the pole, and emerged to look over the shoulder of the Conundrum Box man.

"It must be him," he said.

"This box cannot open this way, yet see?" said the Conundrum Box man, putting the box down and turning to the newcomer. "And he understood the writing."

"Here is your pay," said the stranger, removing a few coins from a purse and handing them over. "You will receive the rest as we agreed when you meet me at my place."

"How did you know? How did you know the one you were looking for would not play for money? And he is so young. Can it possibly be the one we seek?"

"It could be someone else," said the burgundy-cloaked one, picking up the box to examine it for himself. "There may be more than one in these parts who have the gift to open things. Probably are. My bet is that the one who opened this is the one we seek, or else he knows the one we seek. What worries me is that it was too easy. Surely he wouldn't give himself away so lightly."

"Perhaps it is a ploy, to throw us off the scent of the one we are after."

"That is my thinking. He was talking with another one of about his own age for a long time. And he kept looking over this way as they talked."

"You mean the skinny one with red hair? The one they called Billy? He played and lost to the box."

"Which would be a good ruse if he had smoked our intention."

"I see what you mean. He's a sly case, then!"

"Aye."

Suddenly Ibin appeared, grinning at the two men.

"Iwant, I, Iwanttoplayagain," he said.

"We are closed for the evening!" shot back the box-man.

"ButIstill, Istill, butIstillhavesomesilver!"

Then Ullin's strong hand patted Ibin's shoulder.

"Hello, Ibin," Ullin said. "Are you having a good time?"

"OhyessirIam,sir!"

"Good, good. Can you tell me where Billy might be?"

"Doyouwant, doyouwanthimtoring, ringthebigbellagain?"

"Oh, no, I think once is enough for him," Ullin laughed. "I only wanted to see if he knew when his father might be coming back."

"OhIdon'tknow. Butbut, butIthinkBillyisover, overattheringtoss. Attheringtosswithsomegirls."

"Very well, I'll try to find him."

"I'llshowyouwhere!"

Ibin hurried off with Ullin, and the two men at the kiosk looked at each other.

"Did you hear that? Did I not say he was clever?"

"Yes. Yes. There must be many in on it."

"I would say so. Since you are closed for the night, may I borrow your strongman?"

"Certainly, but I don't want to be involved in any mysteries."

"You'll never know a thing. I just need some help with a heavy object, and since Trander is as mute as a horse, he'll not let on to anyone. You know where to find me."

"Trander! Go with Bailorg, and do as he says!"

The big man nodded and turned to the burgundy-cloaked man. Together, they left along the darkness at the edge of the grounds and made their way to the ringtoss.

• • •

Robby saw Sheila and his parents exit the tent, and he walked up just as Sheila was looking around for him.

"Oh, there you are."

"How was the show?"

"It was wonderful! You should have seen how they balanced one atop another and made every kind of shape possible with their bodies."

"I saw them last year," Robby said, taking her hand and leading her away from his nodding mother. "And if they are anything the same now as then, they are indeed wonderful. Shall we listen to some music? Perhaps I'll ask you for a dance."

"Oh," Sheila stopped and pulled the advancing Robby back with a look of terror on her face. "I cannot dance!"

"Don't worry!" Robby laughed. "I can't either. Not really. At any rate, you're bound to have more coordination than I do. If I remember correctly, you kicked a pretty jig on Passdale Green one night."

Sheila's face reddened, and she allowed herself to be towed along to the far end of the fair grounds where a stage of sorts had been set up for the minstrels.

"I've heard these musicians before," Robby told her as they passed the ringtoss where Billy, who was showing off before a pretty girl, took the time to nod and wink at Robby as they passed by. "And I think you'll like them."

They reached the music area just as the group was beginning a lively jig meant to set toes tapping and hands clapping in rhythm. There were benches set about in a semicircle and colored lanterns hanging over a small area in front of the musicians, and several couples were already dancing. Sheila motioned to an empty bench, and they sat down, hand still in hand, to watch and listen. The elder man playing the fiddle recognized Robby and nodded at him with a slight bow. Robby stood up and bowed an acknowledgement as Sheila looked on with some interest.

"Where did you meet them before?" she asked, leaning closer so as not to shout over the music.

"On the shores of Lake Halgaeth," he replied into her ear. Her hair was of the scent of wisteria. "When I saw Queen Serith Ellyn away."

"You never told me about it. I only heard about it from your mother."

"I know. We haven't had much chance to talk about all that's happened. I met her. It was all very pleasant and yet very sad, too."

"Was it not there that you gained your new belt-rope?" she asked, touching Swyncraff.

"Yes. If that is what it is. It was given to me by Lord Thurdun himself."

"Why?"

"I'm not sure," Robby shrugged. "I believe they think more of me than I deserve."

Their conversation was interrupted by intense clapping and hurrahs as the song ended and the exhausted dancers retreated. Before they reached their seats, however, another lively tune sprang from the musicians, one sung by one of the daughters in the Common Speech about a maiden and her love of a faraway seafaring man. Robby and Sheila felt a special enchantment in the music, as the words painted a picture in their minds of the distant sea and windswept shores, as it spun a tapestry of love and longing.

"So what would it take to convince you to dance with me?" Robby asked as the song wound down.

"Oh, I don't know!"

"Are you dead set against trying?"

Sheila looked around and nodded, saying, "Pretty much."

"Would you be open to bribery?"

"What do you mean?"

"Well, for instance, I noticed that you have such a pretty neck, and it is a shame for such a beautiful neck to be unadorned, even though nothing could make it prettier."

Robby unwrapped the choker and put it into Sheila's hand. She sat staring at it, amazed. She looked up at Robby, smiling, her eyes full and glistening with joy.

"It's beautiful!"

"It is for you, with or without a dance," he said, delighted that she obviously liked it.

"Oh, Robby!"

"Shall I help you on with it?"

"Yes, please!"

He took it from her, and she held her hair out of the way so that he could put it around her neck.

"There! I hope it is not too tight?"

"Oh no! It seems lighter than it should be, and it isn't cold, either."

Suddenly she leaned over and gave him a kiss on the lips such as he had not had since they had last kissed those many, many months ago. When she withdrew, he put his hand behind her head and drew her back to him so that, mindless of the others around, he could repay the kiss with the like. The music ended, and there was more applause, and, after the long kiss, Sheila kept her face close to Robby's with a soft look in her shining eyes. A slower tune began, a mellow waltz with a lonesome air, with the fiddle crying softly to the cooing of pipes while the guitars picked an accompanying echo.

"Will you dance with me?" Robby asked again.

"I will try."

And so she did, and did well. Robby held her closer, perhaps, than was customary. But the curve of her waist beneath his hand and the warmth of her hand in his other, the touch of her hand on his shoulder—all this made him as happy as he could ever remember being. He did not care for tomorrow, or for yesterday, and his worries whirled away from him as they spun gracefully around the grass. He reveled in the moment with such feelings of heart that no past problems or new troubles could diminish. Sheila, for her part, felt as if she could be with none other, yet her heart was torn. She desired Robby with her entire body and her whole heart, yet she still felt an impossibility as large as a mountain between her and her desire. The more her desire grew, the more she trembled with conflict. And, as if all her premonitions and all her fears of fallibility and all her sense of caution were summoned into a symbolic form, suddenly that form appeared next to them in the person of Ibin. He had such a look of terror on his face that Robby and Sheila stopped dead and stared at him. Ibin moved his mouth but no words came out. His eyes were wide with despair, and he gestured madly toward some indiscernible direction.

"What is it?" Sheila gasped.

"Ibin, calm down," Robby said, letting go of Sheila and grabbing Ibin by the biceps. "Tell me what is wrong!"

"THEYTOOKBILLY!THEYGOTBILLY!" came his words in a pitiful helpless whine.

"Who? Where?" Robby and Ibin immediately set off, with Sheila trailing close after. They sped up as they went, as Robby tried to get more out of Ibin. "Who? Who took Billy?"

"Thestrongman, thestrongmanandsomeoneelse," Ibin answered. "I-sawthemaskBillytohelpthem! Iwantedtohelp,too, butwhenIgot, whenIgot-thereBillywasfightingthem. Heholleredformetogetyou!"

Robby burst ahead and through the crowd at the ringtoss and on into the shadows.

"There!" Ibin pointed to two men dragging a kicking Billy through the darkness along the outside edge of the line of tents that bordered the fairgrounds. They were making for two horses, and the biggest of the two men was forcing a large burlap bag over Billy. The other man saw Robby and Ibin flying at them as Billy was slung over a horse and tied down.

"Stop them!" he ordered the strongman, who turned to face the oncoming Robby, while he mounted his horse and grabbed the reins of the one bearing Billy.

"Halt!" Robby cried out. So intent he was on Billy's predicament that he did not see the hulk coming at him until a fist hit him in the chest and knocked him sideways against a tent. Ibin barreled right into the huge man, but the strongman deftly tossed him aside. Robby got up, drawing his sword, only to have it immediately knocked out of his hand by the Conundrum Box man who emerged from the tents with a cudgel in one hand and a sword swinging at Robby's head. Robby ducked, pulling Swyncraff from his waist.

"Go get Ullin!" he yelled at Sheila as he straightened Swyncraff and parried the slashing sword. But Robby's opponent countered with his cudgel and struck Robby in the ribs.

"You mind your own business!" the man yelled.

"Out of my way!" Robby furiously swung Swyncraff and shattered the man's sword. Howling in pain, the man backed away, dropping his cudgel and gripping his arm. Robby turned to the strongman who was now being successfully tackled and knocked down by the truly enraged and determined Ibin.

"GoafterBilly! GoafterBilly!" Ibin shouted. Already the two horses were out of the fairgrounds, working up to a gallop onto the road beyond. Robby set off running, leaving his sword where it lay, slinging Swyncraff around his shoulder and letting it tie itself. As Robby reached the far end of the grounds, he saw the hitching area and stopped, panting. He caught his breath just enough to call out, "Anerath!"

Anerath immediately answered from the other side of the hitching area, broke free and bolted through the other horses. Robby sprang into the saddle and off they flew. He did not see Ullin and Sheila running after him, stopping when they realized Robby would not wait for them. The bell of Passdale began ringing frantically in the distance.

"What's that about?" cried Ullin, torn between the direction that Robby went and the opposite direction, toward Passdale. No sooner than he uttered those words than he saw another horseman, tearing up the Passdale road at a desperate gallop. Ullin halted the rider, who was wearing Boskland colors, dirty and soiled from a hard ride.

"I gotta find the Mayor!" the rider cried, dismayed at Ullin for stopping him.

"What is happening?" demanded Ullin.

"See thar!" the man pointed at a red glow on the southeast horizon. "Boskland burns! An army crossed from the Boggy Wood. They took Tulith Attis, set Bosk Manor afire, an' now make their way to Passdale. They could cross the Bentwide afore dawn."

"What army? From where?"

"I dunno! They came out of the Boggy Wood, an' they wear red an' white."

"Redvests! How many?"

"Two, mebbe three thousand? Or more! An' more than two hunnerd horsemen."

"What about Collandoth? Have you seen the one called Ashlord?" Ullin held the reins against the man's desire to ride into the fair.

"Aye, he raised the warnin' to Boskland an' was fightin' alongside me kinsmen. But thar whar too many! We barely got our people away to'ard Passdale. I dunno know what became of him, or of the rest of me people. I outrode 'em. I gotta find the Mayor! Then I gotta get back to Boskland!"

He jerked the horse toward the fairground entrance and rode away. Ullin looked toward the glow in the southeast, then back up the road where Robby had ridden. He turned to Sheila.

"There will be panic at first," he told her, "but we must gather the people and gain our armoury before the invaders reach the bridge. Find Robby's father. Tell him to meet me at the Common House with all the men he can muster. Tell him we are invaded. Then come along quick, spreading word as you come! We will need your bow! We must leave Billy to Robby for now."

"What about the others? The women and children?" Sheila asked as Ullin hurried to the horses and jumped onto the nearest one. Reining around, he started off for Passdale.

"They must flee toward Janhaven! With only what they can carry! We cannot hope to hold the invaders at Passdale for long! Do as I said! Go!"

## Chapter 20

## Pursuit, Rescue, and Capture

Billy Bosk groaned and tried to squirm loose from the ropes that bound him, belly down, across the saddle. He felt his ribs cracking and every shift in the horse's gallop knocked the breath out of him. His head was covered with a sack tied around his neck, and all these things made breathing a great chore.

"Let me go!" he managed to half-yell, half-whimper. The horse he was strapped to was being led along, he realized, probably by the same rogue who oversaw his kidnapping from the festival. He could feel the changes of terrain as they turned, crossed through streams, and moved up or downhill. These course changes gave Billy a little respite, as each one required slowing. But each time that he felt as if he could breathe easier, the horses would speed up again, jolting the air out of him all over again. On top of those difficulties, he was perpetually in fear of sliding off headways under the horse's legs, or falling off halfway, only to be dragged. After a short while, he was in too much misery to care one way or the other, in spite of his fears, as he fell into a kind of swoon of pain and despair within the blackness of the stifling sack.

He hardly noticed when all became still. The sound of crickets that replaced the pounding hooves was slow to filter through to his mind. A hand suddenly grasped the sack on his head and jerked, bending Billy's head backwards painfully.

"Listen to me," a stern voice growled close to his ear. "I will sit you upright into the saddle, now. Do you hear me?"

Billy nodded, and groaned, "Lemme go, ye bastard!"

A hard fist pounded his jaw.

"Shut up! Or I will cut your throat just as easily as I cut these bindings," the voice said. "So do as I say!"

Billy felt a tug on the ropes, and he slid onto his legs. His knees buckled immediately, and he tumbled hard onto the ground. His hands were still tied in front of him, and he felt the tether tied to his wrists pull him up violently.

"Stand up! Climb into the saddle."

After a series of clumsy pushes and shoves, and rather rough handling all around, he was placed into the saddle and his hands were quickly tied to the front saddle ring. He slumped over against the horse's neck as his feet were bound into the stirrups and to each other by a tight tether across the horse's cinches. Before he gained much in the way of rest, they were off again, riding over much rougher ground. Billy sensed from the limbs and brush that struck him, and from how the sound of the hooves were often muffled by leaves and pine straw that they were moving through a dense wood. He tried kicking his mount, to stir some reaction that might help him escape, but his feet were bound too tight for any such movement. Nor could he reach for the reins, so firmly were his hands tied to the saddle-ring. After a while, he could think of nothing else to do, so he tried to strike up a conversation with his abductor.

"So it's a trip, eh?" he said. "I ain't been on a decent trip since, oh, I reckon it's been since me ol' man took me up to Glareth. I hardly remember it, I was so little. Whar might we be headin'?"

"Shut up!"

"Oh, not the talkative kind of feller, eh?" Billy went on. "That's all right by me. Why, me best friend ain't much in the way of the talkative kind, neither. An' most times when he does talk, his words come out all run-together, like."

"I told you to shut up," growled the voice from just ahead. From the sound of it, Billy could tell he was less than a horse-length away and off to one side, probably pulling on the reins.

"Don't see no harm in chattin'."

"You'll be chatting your head off soon enough. Oh, yes! You might as well save it up for then. Meanwhile, if you don't close your mouth, I'll cross you back down on that saddle like before. After I beat you senseless."

Billy remained silent to that threat. Beneath his sack, hot tears of anger and fear burned his eyes, and he licked away the blood that ran down his cracked lips as he pulled on his ropes.

• • •

Robby arrived at a fork in the road, drew Anerath to a halt, and dismounted. He was fairly sure that Billy and his abductor had come this way, but it was too dark to see any tracks. He got down on his hands and knees, hoping to discern something useful. As he moved back from the left fork and onto the rightward fork, his hand touched some loose stones, dirty on one side where they had until recently been embedded in the ground.

"Aha!" he said. Anerath walked along behind him as Robby continued to work the ground with his hands, and the horse stamped impatiently.

"Well, you seem to agree," Robby said as he climbed back into the saddle and patted Anerath on the neck. "Let's go on, then."

It occurred to Robby that this was what Ashlord had warned about. Only, somehow the enemy had mistaken Billy for Robby. Or perhaps it was just a ploy to draw out their real target, to lure him away. He was too preoccupied with keeping on their trail to give much thought about what he would do if he caught up with them. He had Anerath, and his dagger, but very little else. No sword, no food, no water, no way of making a fire, and no idea where he was going, except generally in a westward direction since taking the fork, and along a rougher road rising into the hills. He felt certain that the culprit knew he was being followed, and Robby grew more cautious and worried the farther along he went. Anerath, perhaps sensing Robby's concern, slowed to a canter and then to a walk. The trees leaned over the path, and Robby had to duck under their low branches before he emerged into a small clearing where moonlight shone brightly. He walked Anerath around the clearing, trying to find the right way to proceed, but he could not figure out which was the right way to go. Of several possibilities, he could find no broken limbs or any other sign of recent movement, and he circled and circled within the clearing until he was no longer even certain of the way he had come. So he halted Anerath in the middle of the clearing and sat in the saddle, shoulders hunched, looking around and listening, not knowing what to do. Anerath stamped lightly and turned his head this way and that, waiting patiently for Robby to decide.

But Robby could come to no decision. The air was still and cool, the brush around him glistened with dew, and crickets chirped softly. Something fluttered past his ear, startling him, and he saw a dark shape darting around above him.

"Just a bat!" he said, relieved. Then the creature alighted on top of Anerath's head, facing Robby, and he recognized Certina.

"Hello! Where did you come from?"

Certina gave a soft hoot, hopped into the air, landed again in the same position, and slowly blinked her eyes at Robby. Whether it was the changing moonlight or some other cause, her eyes glowed gold, fixing Robby with a steady stare. He thought her look curious, and even more so when her eyes seemed to brighten, becoming a lighter yellow, then white, and then a bright blue. At the same time, Robby felt some pull, some will in those eyes, commanding his undivided attention. He gazed into them in a trance-like state until nothing else was in his vision, and the sound of the crickets faded into a deep silence. The little owl seemed to grow and grow before Robby, as if coming closer and closer, filling his entire view. Her eyes glowed brighter and brighter until only they were visible. Suddenly Ashlord's face appeared before him.

"Get off the road!" he said. "Follow the follower!"

Certina's eyes dimmed, the crickets sang once more in Robby's ears, and as he shook himself, she flew off. For a moment, he thought he had fallen asleep and had a strange dream, but Certina flew past his ear and into the woods to convince him otherwise.

"Follow the follower," he repeated. Anerath stamped. "Very well, then."

He dismounted and led Anerath into the nearby shadows of the wood.

"We'll wait and see what happens."

Lady Moon continued to play light and shadow with the clouds. A breeze picked up, rattling the leaves in unsteady shudders. As the soft air stirred the trees, Robby strained for any unnatural movement or sound. Standing inside the dark boughs of a fir tree, with Anerath's reins behind him, he watched and listened for only a short while before hearing what sounded like the clinking of metal against metal. He heard it again and stiffened, his heart suddenly beating hard as the sound drew closer from his right. He heard the light plod of hooves and the swish of brush as a horse and rider entered the clearing, crossed through it in front of Robby, and disappeared into the wood to the far side. The light was dim, but Robby easily recognized the form of the Conundrum Box man, with his floppy, flat-topped hat. As soon as the sound was almost too far to hear, he led Anerath by the reins along the same way, going quickly but cautiously, trying to keep the sound ahead of him as they passed through a dark wood. After a short time, he could make out that they followed a narrow path. Trying to be as quiet as possible, they kept on through the wood, sometimes stopping briefly to allow the sound to move farther ahead. After an hour of this, the trees became sparse, and the path grew rocky and sloped downward across the face of a hill. At the bottom they came to a tiny stream. Robby, still hearing the movement ahead, stopped long enough for Anerath and himself to take a few sips of the cold water. Carefully crossing through the stream, they resumed their tracking and climbed a steep, rocky hill to the top of a treeless ridge. Ahead, about fifty yards away, he could see his inadvertent guide ambling along a little faster, now, and then turning westward down off the ridge. Climbing onto Anerath, Robby followed, and when they turned westward he could see the dark, brooding peaks of the Thunder Mountains. Between here and there, the foothills floated up from the thick-gathered mists like islands. Looking behind, he realized that they had come much farther than he had imagined, and he could see nothing familiar in the landscape he had crossed, only the dim glow of twilight on the far eastern horizon.

Moving along the gently descending terrain, keeping the sound of the Conundrum Box man just within earshot, Robby and Anerath soon found themselves in a foggy moor with a damp fennish smell. The mists closed in around them as the ground seemed to level and the sounds of the rider ahead seemed very close. Anerath's hooves were too loud by far, Robby thought, and echoed weirdly. Often he stopped to listen, and once he could hear no sound at all ahead. He waited, wondering if the man had stopped or dismounted, or if he had heard his followers. The sound resumed from farther off than before, and Robby cautiously advanced. In a few moments, the path entered a pine copse, and Robby was momentarily relieved as the sound of Anerath's hooves nearly disappeared altogether on the straw-covered ground. Soon the pines gave way and the path was open and hard again and Robby's caution returned.

This went on for so long that Robby barely noticed that he could see more clearly than before, even though thick banks of mist rolled all around him. Looking up, all he could see was more fog, no stars at all, and he realized that morning had come, though not quite full into this valley. His stomach growled, and he wondered how Billy was faring, hoping his friend was still alive and trusting that he would not think himself abandoned. Robby still did not know what he would do when he caught up with Billy, but he was certain that if he had waited for Ullin or others, Billy would have been lost to some terrible fate. Anger welled up in him, and, with renewed determination, he guided Anerath along, grimly trusting in the message from Certina. He had not seen the little bird since, but she was a sign that Ashlord was somehow aware of the situation.

Robby's surroundings grew less dim, and the mists thinned until at last a blue sky glowed overhead. A few minutes later, yellow beams of sunlight illuminated the tops of the Thunder Mountains, their dark green forests draped in rising wisps of fog. Soon, the sunlight reached the valley, and a light breeze came with it to dry up and sweep away the mists. Robby drew Anerath to a sharp halt behind the thick boughs of one of the few trees in the area. He had caught a glimpse, between the branches, of the Conundrum Box man just ahead, barely fifty yards away. He had stopped and was turned in his saddle, looking toward Robby. Luckily, the pine needles were thick, and Robby had not yet fully rounded the tree, and one of the last remaining wisps of fog rolled silently around him, hiding Robby and Anerath in its thick gray cloak. The man continued to look. Robby held still, and Anerath, sensing the danger, barely even breathed. Perhaps this was just a cautious pause to take advantage of the growing light and the clearing fog. The man turned around at last and nudged his mount onward, leaving Robby and Anerath to breathe again. Robby waited until the man was nearly out of sight before continuing.

As the morning grew brighter, the breeze stiffened into a light wind, and the noise of it swept across the strange landscape in fitful waves, shaking the short scruffy trees and bracken. The land itself was relatively flat, with small rocky hillocks here and there out of which struggled gnarled trees. There were also boggy stretches where many shallow streams wandered as if they had no idea which direction to go, for some ran from left to right across the path and others from right to left. Never was the depth more than an inch or two, and the water moved slowly, pushed as much by the breeze as by its own flow. The dark brown horse and cloak of the Conundrum Box man were in contrast to the wet mossy greens of the bogs and pale tans of the surrounding weeds, making it easy to keep him in sight. Still cautious, Robby let a greater distance grow between them as the one in the lead continued on at a quickened pace. After more than an hour, Robby could see a border of trees far ahead, and, in the distance beyond them, a line of very steep hills. Behind those loomed the closest foot of a brooding mountain, its peak now less than five miles away and suddenly towering over the landscape. Beyond that mountain, and on either side of its shoulders, hovered even higher mountains. Robby did not know the names of each mountain, but knew well why the low forested range was called Thunder Mountains, and it had nothing to do with storms. It was the land of trolls, and it was said that the stomp of their feet gave the mountains their name. Word was, however, that the trolls were all gone. None had been seen for many years, and no one knew where they went, or longed for them to return. Trolls or no trolls, Robby hoped he would catch up to Billy soon, because everyone agreed the mountains were now a place of bandits, renegades, and dangerous rogues of every description. Even the Post Riders went around rather than through these hills whenever they could.

It seemed to Robby, however, that the land tended to descend gradually, rather than rise, as he neared the line of trees into which he was led. As the path became muddy, he saw a lake ahead. The Conundrum Box man splashed straight on, right into the lake, and Robby stopped to remain within the concealment of the trees. Anerath already stood in about a foot of water, and venturing further out into the open lake would certainly give them away. Robby watched the man continue on without turning, and the water reached his horse's belly at the center of the lake. Robby nudged Anerath out a few steps to see around some branches. Only then did he notice the man's apparent destination. On the far side of the lake, rising up out of the water, was an odd structure built against the sheer rock face of the hill behind it. It was like a kind of keep or tiny castle, partially sunken, its single round door yawning like a great mouth with only its upper part out of the water. Two equally dark window-openings above and to each side of the door gave the place the aspect of a giant's head peering blankly across the shallow lake while its mouth swallowed in its water.

"Not sure I like the looks of that place, old boy," Robby said to Anerath.

The Conundrum Box man rode right through the door and disappeared within. Robby saw no guards or any other sign of life about the place, but a well-hidden watch at the top of the keep could easily see all movement on the lake. Since the Conundrum Box man had not given any signal or wave, Robby's feeling was that there was no such guard. Still, if he or Billy's abductor were inside near the window openings, Robby would surely be noticed if he crossed here. He eased Anerath along northward through the trees, keeping the lake within sight while looking for some better approach. They quickly became mired in muddy water up to the stirrups so Robby turned back to go southward past his starting point. This way seemed more manageable, and Robby soon encountered a slight rise in the ground over which the water did not go. Following this, which tended to bend westward, Robby saw that the south side of the lake was dammed by a natural bank that angled into the cliff. He rode carefully atop the bank for a few hundred yards, and came to the place where the lake water spilled away in a shallow stream through an eroded break. Dismounting, he led Anerath down and through the ditch and up the other side where the lake lapped against the base of the cliff. From here, due to a slight bend in the line of the cliff, he could not see the keep, and, more importantly, could not be seen from it. But he saw no way to climb upward and no apparent path along the cliff face.

"Well," Robby sighed, "I guess there's nothing for it but to wade in and swim, if we must."

The water was not as cold as he had feared it might be and was quickly up to his chest as he felt his way along the muddy bottom step by step. Anerath did not protest, and followed along obligingly. Keeping as close to the cliff as he could, he eased along until, rounding an outcrop, Robby saw that the keep, some hundred yards ahead, did not jut out from the cliff as much as he first thought. He estimated that it was only five or six yards from the front to the back, built right into the stone cliff. Its top sloped steeply upward, and he could see there was no level place for anyone to stand watch. There was a single window facing him on this side, level with those in front, but the more Robby looked at the structure the less it seem to him to be any sort of keep or stronghold, though he could not imagine the purpose of the place.

Glancing at the sun, Robby judged it would be another hour or two before it would pass the tops of the cliffs and put him in shadow. Until then, he hoped his light-blue surcoat would blend somewhat with the sunlit water. There was no way for Anerath to hide, but Robby did not want to leave him behind. He could not guess what condition Billy might be in, but he was determined not to leave without him. Anerath was fast and strong, and could easily bear Billy and Robby together, if need be.

"You've been great so far," Robby said to him, scratching around the horse's ear. "I only ask that you bear up a little longer, just as patiently and as quietly as you've been."

Anerath tossed his head, his eyes gleaming, and Robby led him on without incident all the way to the south wall of the keep where the water was only a couple of feet deep. Hugging the wall, he peered around at the door. Except for the nervous wind rippling the water, everything was very still and quiet. Turning back to Anerath, he led him into the corner where the wall of the keep met the wall of the hill.

"I'm going on alone for a little ways," he said to the horse, making ready to tie the reins off on a root that jutted from the rocks.

"No," Robby said, putting the reins back over Anerath's head. "I'll not tie you. For one, I hope you will come if I call, and, for another, if I don't return, I'll not have you yoked to these rocks. I know the water is cold, and you'll soon be in shadow. Please wait for me as long as you can. I hope you won't wander out where you can be seen."

Robby's voice trailed off. In fact, he was more than a little frightened and had been so from the beginning of the chase. Now that he was leaving Anerath, he felt very small. Anerath looked steadily at him, and Robby was somehow reassured by Anerath's gaze. He could feel the horse watching him as he rounded the corner and waded to the doorway. Once there, he saw that it was the entrance to a large cave of sorts, or an underground passage. After the bright sunshine, reflected back up at him from the water, the interior of the place seemed pitch black. He slowly felt his way along the left side of the entranceway while his eyes adjusted, and then he began to make out some details. The walls were thick, and, as he came to the next corner, he could barely discern broad wide steps going up either side to the lookout windows above. The ceiling was made of great stone slabs, carefully laid over heavy lintels and beams, and there were cracks where light stabbed downward in thin rays. Directly in front of him was another opening, and, as Robby approached it, he felt the floor inclining upward. Another few steps forward, and he was no longer standing in water. It was clearly high and wide enough for a rider to pass through. The incline continued gradually until at last Robby could no longer see the lake behind him or much of anything else. Yet there seemed to be a soft yellow glow coming from ahead, and he continued cautiously toward it, dripping a trail as he went. Though he tried to tiptoe, his steps echoed loudly in the silence of the stone passageway, and he was glad he had not brought Anerath. The light continued to grow brighter, and several times he thought he heard a sound ahead and stopped to listen, but it was too faint to discern. As he rounded a bend in the passage, he saw a staircase leading up along the right-hand wall to a landing. There was a doorway up there through which yellow light flickered, and just ahead was another large opening through which the same light came. Easing to it, he got down on his hands and knees and peered around the corner into a cavernous room, nearly a hundred feet to the other side where a fire blazed in a gigantic hearth. Chairs and tables and stools were all around the room, all oversized and crudely made of stone slabs. There were even stone cups, many of them broken, and great rusty iron pots in piles scattered around the place. Thick dust covered everything, and cobwebs draped over every object. Several braziers gave off smoky light. Rough-hewn columns rose into the gloom of the high invisible roof. About halfway across the room, three horses stood tied to a post, and, farther on, in front of the fireplace, stood two figures, the Conundrum Box man and the man who had taken Billy.

Robby could not see Billy until one of the horses moved aside, and he saw him sitting on a great stool, his legs dangling off the floor and his arms tied behind him. He slouched, his head down against his chest. A stone balcony of sorts ran all the way along both sides of the room, and Robby backed away, then hurried back to the stairs in the corridor and quickly climbed them, each step shin high. As he re-entered the great room, easing along the righthand balcony, he heard the men talking. He kept low in shadows well away from the edge and carefully continued to the far end. Suddenly there was a low rumble, and it seemed to Robby that the entire hill shook, and, indeed, dust fell from the ceiling above.

"The creature is restless, Bailorg," said the Conundrum Box man.

"Yes, he must sense we are here," said Bailorg.

"Why you insisted on this place is beyond me. If that thing gets loose!"

Bailorg laughed.

"You worry too much! The chains that hold him will continue to do so. I picked this place for just such reason. People fear to come here, so it has been a good place to watch from. Besides, the only one who could possibly free the old thing sits right here, and he's obviously in no condition to do so."

"Yes, he looks well tied-up."

"And so I have kept him."

"Well, has he given you what you seek from him?"

"Not yet," Bailorg said. "But he soon will. I have allowed him to rest a little, but it will be the last he gets for a long while. See in the fire? My tools are warming up. Soon he will tell me all I need to know."

Robby reached the far end of the room and inched to the edge of the balcony. Now the fireplace chimney was in front of him, where the balcony ended. Billy was almost directly below, apparently unconscious. His shirt was stained with blood. The two men were standing about six feet away from their prisoner, looking at him. The one called Bailorg stood with his arms crossed. He was pale, tall, and his blond hair draped over his shoulders. Underneath his burgundy cloak he wore a fine black velvet jacket buttoned up to the neck of a puffy-collared red blouse. He wore high, close-fitting boots and as he unfolded his arms, one hand came to rest on the hilt of a sword.

"What I don't understand," the Conundrum Box man said, "is if this is the one, then why can't he escape the ropes?"

"I am no fool, Stingorn! My rope, as you call it, is woven of snakewood fibers and will release their knots to none but me."

Hearing this, Robby instinctively passed his hand down to Swyncraff and realized that he was not weaponless after all. But how to free Billy without Bailorg's help?

"Snakewood? I thought those trees were all gone. Stuff of tales."

"The plants are long passed from the earth, but there are a few charmed remains that can be made into such things. Now tell me, are you sure about the box?"

"Oh, I'm sure. This one showed no signs of opening it, but the other opened it right off, and knew the writing, too. And wasn't fooled by it. You saw it. A double test."

"So there are others in the region who possess the power. This one will soon name them, though. And he is the one who rang the Bell, according to his imbecilic friend, so obviously he has the greater cunning."

"Yes. And so this red-headed one must have suspected our ploy, as I said earlier," nodded Stingorn, "and sent the other one to open the box and take the choker."

"I wonder if he told the other one why he wanted him to open the box?" Bailorg mused aloud.

"I don't follow you."

"I'm thinking that if this one knew we were close, he might have been trying to set up another one to take his place."

"Oh, I see. And it nearly worked! If it had not been for that captain fellow coming along when he did, we would never have caught on."

"Yes, yes!" Bailorg said impatiently. "But what I mean is that this one is not so nice to his friends. He might not be so hard to squeeze, after all."

"Oh, well. Er, that may be so. That may be so, indeed. But, well—"

"I suppose you want your pay."

"Well, I really should be getting along now that I'm given away, as it were."

A dark shape suddenly flew into the room, causing Stingorn to flinch and Robby to drop to his belly, recoiling from the edge of the balcony. It was a large black bird, bigger than any Robby had ever seen, and it flapped to the opposite side of the room where it perched atop a broken column in the shadows. It seemed completely black, from its talons, to its crooked beak, and all of its plumage in between. All except its uncanny eyes which, whether from the firelight or from their own accord, glowed dull red as the creature looked down at the gathering.

"Ar! What a fright that thing gave me!" Stingorn put his hand to his chest. "A most unpleasant pet you have. Whew! Now, as I was saying—"

"You'll get your bounty," Bailorg stated, unperturbed by the bird's arrival. He turned to Billy. "And I think it might be good for our guest to see you get paid, so that he knows he is sold away and is entirely in my hands. Wake up!"

Robby inched closer, taking care to make no noise, peering over the edge of his hiding place.

Bailorg gripped Billy by the hair and pulled his head up. Robby saw dried blood caked around Billy's nose and mouth, and he did not miss the blaze of defiance in his friend's eyes as he looked at Bailorg.

"Ah, yer back are ye? Whar did ye go? An' we have company?"

"Yes, are you feeling more talkative, now?"

"Ah, very musch sho. Let'shee, what wash I shayin'? Oh, yeah. I wash tellin' ye 'bout the hill, Haven Hill, Tulith Attish."

"Attis."

" 'Ash what I shaid, Attish. Anywaysh, sho I whar thar, all alone, like. An' nesht thing I know, great big wolvesh whar comin' at me from ever direcshtion. I had nowheresh to go."

"Yes, yes, we've been over all that."

Robby's chest tightened as anger's heat coursed through his body, and his eyes stung at the sound of Billy's slurred voice through his swollen lips. Leaning over the side as far as he dared, Robby saw that it was at least a thirty foot drop to the floor, a little less to a nearby table. His impulse was to jump down anyway and take on the two men, but he would be worse than useless to Billy with a broken neck. Part of his mind raced with his quickened pulse, trying to form some reasonable course of action. Another part was paralyzed, unable to turn away, and he could do nothing but watch the awful thing play out. Below, the conversation continued.

"Ish that the Conundrum Boshx man, over thar? It wush a trick boshx warn't it? Ye let poor Ibin an' the resht think they'd opened it up when allsh along ye jusht whar playin' with 'em."

"I told you he was cunning," said Bailorg to Stingorn. Smiling at Billy, he continued.

"I just wanted you to know that you are all alone here. No one is coming for you, and your friends have all abandoned you. Stingorn, here, is only interested in the pay that I promised him to carry out our little detection work. Now that his work is done, he is only here to collect. Once he is departed, it will be just the two of us and no one else."

"Well, what d'ye want then?"

"I want you to tell me the name of the traitor of Tulith Attis and the names of all those who know it."

"Ah! That'sh what it'sh all about, eh? I shushpected ash musch all along. I wondered how long it'd take ye to get 'round to it."

"Well?"

"Well, I don't think I'll tell ye. Anywaysh, everyone in theshe partsh knowsh all 'bout that. Ye can jusht go ashk some other feller an' lemme go."

"Not until you tell me. You see, I already know the answer."

"You do?" asked Stingorn in obvious surprise. "Then why all this?"

"Shut up!" Bailorg glared at Stingorn. He turned back to Billy. "Yes, I do know. But I want to hear it from you. And I want you to tell me about everyone else who knows. It would spare you a lot of pain."

"But it won't shave me life, I'll warrant."

"No, it won't," Bailorg said, dragging a wooden chopping block closer to Billy and sitting down on it. "But I will tell you what it will do. It will save others from unnecessarily enduring the pain you now suffer, and the pain you will suffer if you continue to be stubborn. Do you want your friends to hurt? Do you want them to die as uselessly as you?"

"Ye whar the one what shent them ridersh into Boshkland, along with that ol' Dragonkind man, warn't ye?"

Bailorg sat upright.

"Yes, I sent them."

"An' it whar ush what killed 'em," Billy said. "Me an' me friendsh. An' shoon yer head will join tharsh over the gatesh of Boshkland!"

Bailorg stood up, smiled wryly, and struck Billy with his fist, sending fresh blood splattering out of his mouth onto the floor.

"Speak only what I wish to hear!" Bailorg hissed at Billy. "Now look!"

Billy raised his head, tears of pain and anger mingling with blood, and watched Bailorg back away toward Stingorn.

"I told you we would be alone," Bailorg said, standing beside the Conundrum Box man. "I will not have him witness what is about to happen here, so I will conduct my business with him first."

Stingorn, who was nervous and obviously had no stomach for the scene, grinned and nodded.

"Yes, I should be on my way, indeed. And so I'll take the purse you agreed would be mine."

"Well, here, take your pay, then," said Bailorg as Stingorn eagerly stepped closer. In a quick, easy, almost casual movement, Bailorg brought out a long, narrow-bladed dagger from his belt and plunged it through Stingorn's throat and as quickly removed it, sudden blood spurting from both sides of the man's neck. Bailorg let the gurgling Stingorn fall and returned to Billy.

"See how quickly death can come?" he said kindly, sitting back down as Stingorn became quiet. He wiped both sides of the blade on Billy's pants, then inspected it. "Just a little nick, and it's all over. All the pain, all the regret, everything. And off to the place of your forefathers you shall go! If you tell me what I want to know, I'll make it quick and easy. But I am patient."

He got up, slipped the dagger back into its sheath, and walked over to the fire, pulling and shifting the many long iron implements that were heating there.

"Do you think your friend, the one you call Ashlord, is the only one who watches? I, too, and my master have watched these lands these many years. From this place, I have often ventured to your little shire, even to the place of Tulith Attis itself, though not so close to give myself away. No, no. My master, from far away, watches, too, in his way." Bailorg threw a smile at the black bird. "But I have had help. Yes, your own Barleymen have helped me, right up until just recently. Though I have never met a lazier, more drunken sort of creature than the Barley farmer. I had the recent misfortune to hire one a while back. Alas, I found that I could not trust him. He was too loose with my money and his tongue, and he was too obsessed with his bratty niece to be of much use. I was forced to, well, to release him from my service, you might say. Since then I have found others willing to help."

Bailorg gestured at Stingorn's body.

"Yes, I am patient when need be, but only as long as being patient is useful. And now that it is just the two of us, I can give you my undivided attention."

He slipped on a thick leather glove and lifted one of the iron bars from the fire, gazed at the glowing hot tip, and then slowly waved the tip a few inches in front of Billy's horrified face.

"You there!" a voice cried out from the doorway. Bailorg turned and saw a Passdale militiaman entering with a confident stride. "Put down that iron and release our man!"

"If you come one step closer, he will die!"

Robby stopped about twenty yards from Bailorg. Billy turned his head and managed a weak smile.

"Heh-heh-heh," he chuckled.

"As you can see," Robby said, trying to muster as much courage as he could, "I am not armed, save for this little knife. The exits to this place are all blocked by my comrades. I convinced them that you would not give up your captive easily. They are prepared to fight and will storm this place very soon unless I emerge with him. If you harm him further, or if you refuse to release him, you will die."

Bailorg hesitated, then smiled.

"You are too few to block all exits, and the north one is guarded by my own men."

"They are captured, and a few of them are dead. The rogues you chose did not serve you well. Ashlord has known of this place for a long while, and his plan to assault your lair was carefully made. The routes of your escape are blocked eastward by the militia and by Boskmen. The west exit is blocked by men of the King's Post Riders along with soldiers recently of Vanara under the service of Thurdun of the House of Fairlinden. The other passages, some of which even you may not know of, are blocked also, both those above and those below," Robby stated bluntly, and, he hoped, convincingly. He also hoped the quiver that he heard in his own voice did not give him away. "You do not have much time, for they have given me only a few moments to bring Billy Bosk back to them."

"Fairlinden? Here? Ashlord, too? I sense that you are bluffing. That you are alone and that you followed my late unfortunate helper, here," retorted Bailorg.

"If you knew anything of my people, you would know that I just this morning renewed my oath. I will speak the truth," Robby shot back angrily. "I suffer your insults only to obtain the release of my friend. Though you may be without honor, I am bound to deliver this message to you. If first you release Billy Bosk, then, within the hour, the west exit will be open to you. You are assured that we will make no effort to take you. So by our honor are we bound."

"I do not trust you," Bailorg said. "If you take him eastward, how will you clear the west passage?"

"I will send a rider."

Robby turned around and walked out of the hall and into the darkness of the passageway. Bailorg strained to see, but could not, and he heard Robby call out.

"Come!"

Soon Bailorg heard hooves pounding closer and closer, but could not tell from which way the sound came. They clatter of hooves slowed to a halt.

"Stay here and await my word. Prepare to ride on to the west exit so that it may be cleared," Robby's said loudly, his voice echoing into the room. Bailorg could also hear the stamping of an impatient horse. Robby re-entered from the gloom and approached.

"Now! Release him!"

Bailorg shoved the iron back into the fire, then removed and threw away his glove angrily. Then, more reluctantly, he moved to Billy and drew his dagger. Robby reached for his and stepped forward.

"Only to cut his bonds," said Bailorg holding up the knife in one hand and his open palm as supplication. Robby nodded. He could not see behind Billy's back, but knew that the action of cutting the rope-that-was-not-a-rope was a ruse. Bailorg stood upright once again with the limp rope in one hand and eased his dagger back into its sheath. Billy struggled to his feet and swerved left and right to Robby who put his arm around him.

"Hold on just a little longer, my friend," Robby said to Billy, taking his eyes from Bailorg only long enough to glance at Billy and see his swollen and blood-caked mouth. "My advice to you, sir," Robby said to Bailorg, trying his best to stifle his anger, "is to flee these lands. Your warrant for safety is only for this day and this night alone. Some of this man's kin have sworn to track you down, but I think they will go no farther than the Thunder Mountains if you can reach them before sunrise on the morrow. Good-bye!"

Robby turned to leave, trying to be gentle with Billy and yet seeking to hurry him at the same time. Bailorg watched them retreat, his face red with a scowl and his fists balled up at his side.

"Pray we never meet again, Barleyman!"

Robby continued on into the gloom of the passage where Anerath waited.

"Listen," he told Billy quietly, helping him up into the saddle. "Take Anerath here and fly to my mother. She will take care of you. Send word to Ullin. Tell him where I am. I will follow you as soon as I can. I want to make sure Bailorg goes west."

"What of the othersh? The one'sh guardin' the waysh out?"

"Shh! There are no others," Robby whispered emphatically. "I lied."

"Lied? Ye *lied*? But, Robby," Billy protested, "I can't leave ye!"

"You must! Go, Anerath!"

Robby slapped Anerath on the flank, and the obedient steed flew down the passageway with Billy. Robby watched them disappear into the gloom, the pound of Anerath's hooves turning into splashes as they exited, then he ran up the stairs to see Bailorg quickly and noisily putting some things into a saddle bag. The villain was unhitching the horses when suddenly the corridor and chamber were filled with the rumble of hooves once more. Bailorg looked up in frightened surprise and dismay, and Robby shrank away as twenty horsemen rode boldly into the chamber. The large bird, passive until now, raised its wings as if to take off, but as the chamber filled, it settled back onto its perch. The men were all dressed in flamboyant garments of velvet, leather and steel, coats and jackets of blue or green or orange, and sporting all manner of caps and feathered hats. They were hard-looking men with beards and long hair, some stout, others thin, old and young together, all with determined looks on their faces. Leading the group was a large man on a black horse. He wore a fancy black coat with silver buttons and polished boots over blue breeches and sported a broad tan hat with a long fluffy blue plume. He dismounted and strode toward Bailorg.

"So where is he? This prize of yers? What's this? What happened to Stingorn? Murdered him, eh?"

Bailorg gaped as he began to realize he had been duped.

"Have you seen any Post Riders?" Bailorg demanded. "Any soldiers?"

"What? No. Why should we?" said the head rogue. "Now what happened?"

"Stingorn was murdered by Passdale men," Bailorg angrily stated. "They made off with my prize but just a few moments ago!"

The head rogue stared at Bailorg for a moment before throwing his head back in laughter.

"What's so funny?" screamed Bailorg.

"Yer a mighty fool to take me for one! Why I'm a mind to part yer head from neck right where ye stand."

"What do you mean?"

"Everbody knows that a Passdaler committin' murder's about as common as the moon takin' a drink with the sun," he said. "Now, this is what I think. I think yer prize got away, an' yer scared yer master might not be too very pleased. At any rate, I guess ye'll not be needin' an escort."

The man turned back to his horse.

"Sorry boys! The job's off! Still," he turned back to Bailorg, "ye did promise a down payment on our services. An' seein' as how through no fault of our own we're now out of a job, the least ye can do is make us a little less, shall we say, upset?"

"What do you mean?"

"I mean, it's obvious that old Stingorn didn't get his pay. An' though he had it comin', I daresay that leaves ye with a coin or two extra. I think we'll pay a pretty penny to ye, if ye'll hand over that purse at yer belt."

"You can go to hell, you scoundrel."

"Who's callin' who names, now? Hand over the purse, or hand over yer head."

The man drew his sword as did Bailorg.

"Hurry it up, would ye, Capt'n? This place stinks!" said one of the men, throwing one leg casually over his saddle to have something to rest his elbow on so that he could put his chin in his hand.

Robby saw the other men get comfortable on their saddles, pleased with just looking on and making no effort to help their leader. Nor did the man indicate he wanted any help. Just as they stepped toward each other, Robby felt a hand grasp him by the collar and hoist him up into the air.

"Lookee here, Capt'n! Lookee what I done found!"

Robby's feet dangled over the edge of the balcony, but, squirming, he could not see who held him.

"Do ye want him?"

"Aye! But bring him down. An' don't drop him!"

## Chapter 21

## The Thunder Mountain Band

Robby was half-carried, half-dragged back down the stairs. He was wise enough not to resist the hulking man's grip, and soon he was released before the captain of the rogues.

"This is one of the Passdalers!" Bailorg cried out lunging at him with his sword. The blade was deftly deflected away from Robby by the captain's, and a sharp kick to Bailorg's ribs sent him sprawling on the floor.

"Hold on just a minute! Where's yer manners?" said the head rogue. And when he was satisfied that Bailorg was well reprimanded, he turned to Robby. "Now what's yer name, son?"

"I am Robby Ribbon, son of Robigor, of Passdale."

"A soldierly-lookin' feller, too, by yer dress, though I think yer missin' a necessary piece of equippin'."

"Yes, my sword. I lost it in a fight."

The men on the horses chuckled, but a glance from their leader tucked their chins.

"Well, that happened to me, a time or two," he said. "I am Martin Makeig, some while back of Tracia, but more recently of the Thunder Mountains, or wherever me horse might lead me. Mad Martin, some calls me, but most here just calls me Captain. I take it ye've run afoul of this feller."

"You could say so."

"Well, ye ain't the first, but I dare say by the sounds of it ye made out better 'an us." He turned back to Bailorg, who had picked himself up and was glowering at them. "I reckon I'll have yer purse, now. Or maybe yer still in the mood to match blades? I'd be glad to do ye the favor of runnin' ye through, an' save yer master the trouble," he grinned, holding out his hand for the purse. "It'd be quicker, too, I'm guessin', than what yer master might do to ye."

Bailorg sheathed his sword and unfastened the purse.

"You'll regret the day we met," he said proudly.

"Oh, I already do, sir!" Makeig said, taking the purse. He hefted it once or twice, then tossed it over his shoulder to be caught by one of the horsemen behind him who wore a pair of fancy gold-rimmed spectacles. He opened the purse and peer into it.

"That there's Lantin Rose," Makeig said to Robby. "Got a head for numbers an' such. Been me purser for many years, now."

"Ain't much here, Capt'n," the man said, looking over his spectacles. "Maybe a week of grog or oats, an' some change."

"Well, go ahead an' pay him out, then."

"Yes, sir."

The accountant jangled through the coins and finally took two out and handed them to Makeig.

"You're giving it back to him?" Robby asked, surprised.

"Oh, we makes the point never to take all," Makeig said. "No exceptions, neither, for when ye make one, ye open yerself up for all kinds of confusion. 'Sides, sort of don't seem fair, it bein' so easy an' all. Here's yer worth," he said to Bailorg, holding out the coins, "an' it's mighty generous we are, givin' ye back more than any two of us together's gettin' from ye."

Bailorg reached for the coins, but just as he was about to take them he slapped his rope around Makeig's wrist and the strange thing transformed with a hiss, binding itself to Makeig as hard as iron. The coins clattered and rang across the floor and before Makeig could react, Bailorg's sword was drawn again, its tip pressed against Makeig's neck before he had gotten his own sword back out with his other hand.

"What the devil!"

"I'll have it all back. And all of you: Off your horses!" he cried. The rope tightened around Makeig's wrist, and he cried out in pain and fell to one knee. All of the men drew their swords in a ringing chorus, but none knew what to do. "Tell them to do as I say!"

"No, don't." cried Robby, stepping closer to Makeig.

"Mind your own business, boy!" Bailorg spat at Robby who was loosening Swyncraff from his waist.

"Don't let's be too hasty, laddie," Makeig painfully groaned as he tried to pry away the coil from his wrist and as Bailorg's swordtip neared Makeig's neck.

Robby swung Swyncraff, curling it around Bailorg's sword and pulling it away. Makeig fell clear as Bailorg lost his hold on the mysterious tether and struggled to pull his sword from the vice-like grip of Swyncraff. Off balance for only a moment, he drew his dagger and suddenly pulled Robby toward him. Robby got his knife out in time to parry, and Bailorg pulled again on his sword to draw Robby in once more. Swyncraff uncurled, sending Bailorg stumbling backward a step, then Swyncraff stiffened and straightened into a long rod, and Robby strode into Bailorg.

"This is for Billy!" Robby cried, clipping Bailorg on the side of the head. Another swing against the wrist sent Bailorg's dagger clattering away, and the next two-handed parry deflected a desperate lunge. Sparks shot from Bailorg's sword as it met with Robby's Swyncraff. The two swung at each other furiously, Robby driving Bailorg back toward the hearth while the men watched, too amazed to act.

"So it was you!" Bailorg cried as he fought. "You are the one!"

"Yes! I am the Bellringer! And it was you who killed Steggan."

"Oh yes, that was me," Bailorg said just before Robby smote him in the ribs.

"And did you also rape his niece?"

"No, no! Ugh!" In spite of the blows he received from Robby, and the blood running from his mouth, he grinned maliciously. "I only watched."

Bailorg fell down onto the hearth, choking for air, but his eyes were crazed, and he began to laugh.

"I let him have his way with her," he wheezed. "You know, didn't want to interfere in a family affair, hee-hee-hee! Oh, oh! I think you've gone and ruptured my windbag."

Bailorg went into a short fit of coughing, then smiled mildly up at Robby as blood and spittle dribbled from his mouth.

"Oh, I know about you two. Yes—*cough-cough! Ugh!* And who doesn't?"

Robby stood over Bailorg, shaking with red rage, glowering at the kidnapper.

"Oh, the dear uncle didn't know I was there, right at first, the drunken fool! *cough-cough!* I only regret that the bitch didn't get the blame for killing him like she should have. But now that I know you to be the One, looking back on it, I must say that I cherish the memory of it! She fought him like a cat! *cough-cough-cough!* And screamed like one, too! But he had his pleasure of her!"

Bailorg leapt up, his sword in one hand and a flaming red-hot iron in the other, swinging both at Robby in a sudden fury. Robby knocked the sword away and before Bailorg could bring the blazing iron around, Robby plunged his dagger hilt-deep upward into his chest. Bailorg gasped and dropped the iron and his sword. His arms fell to his sides, his shoulders raised in an odd frozen shrug. Now nose to nose with Robby, he still managed a little wheezing laugh. Black with anger, Robby twisted his knife, pushing it upward cruelly, and Bailorg's laugh was stifled forever as his body stiffened and his eyes rolled back in his head. He went limp and fell heavily against Robby who then shoved him backwards off of the dagger and into the fire. Robby stood there, panting, dripping with blood up to his elbow, still clutching his dagger as if Bailorg might leap up once more. As he stared, his stomach suddenly churned and heaved violently during a long dizzy moment, and he felt himself sway and stagger uneasily as he watched Bailorg smolder in the flames. The snakewood rope released Makeig and fell away. Robby became vaguely aware of the men gathering around as he absently put his own Swyncraff about his waist again and sheathed his dagger, still unable to take his eyes from Bailorg.

"That shore is some mighty belt," Makeig said. He was rubbing his wrist and looking over Robby's shoulder at the fire. "An' the rope that Bailorg used on me turned to ash an' fell right off into dust."

"Strangest thing I ever saw," said Lantin Rose.

"Some good fightin', though, for a young feller," commented another.

The great black bird suddenly lurched from its place and flapped across the room. The men ducked and dodged, and the horses jumped aside as the bird flew into the corridor and away.

"Whoa!" cried one of the bandits. "What a fright that gave me!"

"Nasty, odorly creature, too!" replied another.

The shock of what he had just done began to overwhelm Robby. He stared at the distorted face of Bailorg, now made even more ghastly by the flames that blackened it. A terrible disgust filled him, and he fought the need to retch. He had seen men killed before, not long ago on the road from Tulith Attis, but he had not taken part in that fight. The sickness he felt then, and that gnawed at him for weeks afterwards, was nothing like this. That first taste of violent death came about almost as if by accident. This time, he realized, it was personal, and, with even greater alarm, he felt a dark satisfaction.

"Come along, son," Makeig said, handing Robby a bit of rag to wipe the blood from his hands. "Let's leave this here place."

"Yes, I must go."

Makeig gently pushed Robby by the shoulder toward the horses where he put the reins of Bailorg's horse in his hands and then led their mounts into the passageway.

"Why did he make me do that?" Robby muttered. "I think I'm gonna be sick."

"What's 'at, son?"

Before Robby could answer, they heard the clopping of a horse approaching from the east passage, and they all became silent, shushing each other and their mounts.

After a moment of listening, Makeig said, "That'll be Winterford comin'. One of our company sent out a few days ago toward Barley."

"How do you know?" Robby asked, wiping his eyes and trying to get his stomach down out of his throat. "It might be one of my friends."

"Listen to them hoof-beats," said Lantin Rose.

"Hear that little ringin' sound?" Makeig added.

Robby listened, then nodded.

"That be our own special way of shoein'. Don't hurt the horse none an' makes a signal-like. Right handy in the dark when ye can't see friend from foe."

From the gloom, a youngish rider approached cautiously.

"It's us, Winterford!" Makeig called out to him.

"An' mighty glad of it, I am!" the rider returned, dismounting and coming up to the group. "Who's this? An' where's Bailorg? Done stood us up?"

"Not 'xactly. Things fell through a bit, ye might say, seein' how's Bailorg's presently roastin' on yonder fire. An' this here's the cook."

Winterford gaped at Robby and craned his neck to see through the doorway and across the hall at the fireplace.

"Ye don't say!"

"I do!"

"Well, good riddance! If ye ask me, that is. I knowed right from the start he'd be trouble!"

"An' right up to the end," one of the men added.

"So what's the story?" Winterford asked.

"That'll wait 'til we're in sunlight again," said Makeig.

"I need to be getting back," Robby said. "Thank you for the horse."

"Gettin' back where to?" Winterford asked.

"Back home. To Passdale."

"Oh, I don't think that'd be a great stroke of an idear."

"Why not?"

Winterford glanced at Makeig, hesitating.

"Well, come on with it," Makeig ordered. "What's the news?"

"The news is that all of Barley's crawlin' with Redvests."

"What's that? No!" Makeig's eyes widened perceptibly. "So they've come at last?"

"Crawling with what?" Robby asked, looking back and forth between the two. "Red whats?"

"Redvests," explained Makeig. "Soldiers out of Tracia, so called because of their bloody surcoats an' tunics."

"Soldiers?"

"Aye," said Winterford. "They come into Barley through the Boggy Wood, up northeast-like, thousands of 'em. They took up at Haven Hill last night an' then more spread out into Boskland. Burned it to the ground. The Bosklanders put up a fierce fight, so I was told, but was overrun. The Redvests moved into Passdale after sunrise this mornin', an' there was lots of fightin' along the riverbank. The Passdalers burned the bridge, but that didn't hardly slow the Redvests, seein' how as the Bentwide's just a little brook, now. Didn't take 'em long 'fore they had the town. Most of the folk got warnin', though, an' are movin' toward Janhaven. Some of the Bosklanders an' what's left of the Passdale Militia are still fightin' rearguard skirmishes, but the Redvests ain't pressin' it too hard right now, it seems. They done took up in the town."

Robby gaped in disbelief at the young man giving the report.

"Lo! Ye don't say," commented one of the rogues.

"Them Boskmen're fighters when it comes to it. Yes, indeed!"

"What're Redvests doin' this far north, I wonder?"

"What about the Mayor? Did you see the Mayor or his wife?" Robby demanded.

"No, no! I was too busy at the bridge most of the time. Knockin' Redvests about beside them Passdaler boys. Sorry, Capt'n, couldn't help joinin' in. Bones to pick, an' all. But I never saw the Mayor, not that I'd know him, anyways, nor any womenfolk in the fray, 'cept one girl with a nasty bow an' arrow."

"Are they burnin' the town?"

"No, Capt'n. They seem content with just takin' over everthin'. They got themselves situated in the Common House, an' in several of the houses, I hear tell."

"I've got to go! I sent Billy back into that! No telling what he'll ride into!"

"You mean that beat-up feller on the fine stallion?"

"Yes!"

"He's with friends, now. I seen 'em on the way. The same girl I mentioned with the bow, along with an odd, skinny feller with long black hair and beard, an' a big lumberin' kind of feller, too, all hurrying this way on foot. Saw the rider an' horse come into them not two miles away. The girl an' the big lug took charge of the hurt feller, then headed off northward. That other feller, the tall one, kept on comin' thisaway. I kept out of sight an' passed around him on the other side of a hill, an' got ahead of him, like. But he's got a long stride. My guess he'll be here in no time."

Robby reached for the reins of the Conundrum Box man's horse.

"Then, by your leave, I'll take this one, too," Robby said to Captain Makeig.

"Wait. Ye say what?"

"That's my friend coming. I must go meet him and get back to my people!"

"Hold on, there!" Makeig ordered flatly, stepping in front of Robby. "I'm thinkin' yer friends must be awful good'uns to risk their lives for one another. But if he's gonna take ye back to Passdale-way, why that's just plain foolish. Ye saved me life back there an', likes it or not, ye got another friend, now. An', anyhow, I'd like to hear what this one comin' might say 'bout these goin's on."

"And who is it that wants to know?"

Robby immediately recognized Ashlord's booming voice, and, realizing he would be careful, Robby covered his eyes with his free hand and looked downward, just in case Ashlord set off one of those blinding lights of his.

"Mad Martin Makeig, it is! Who's that?"

"Release the boy!"

"He's as free as he wishes to be!"

"I'm all right Ashlord," Robby called out. "They are friendly."

"A pack of thieves, is what I think they are," Ashlord said, coming out of the gloom, sword in one hand and his walking stick in the other, held like a cudgel.

"By needs, not by trade, nor by callin'," Makeig shot back. "But our reputation is somewhat sullied by rumor, I warrant."

"So you are the Thunder Mountain Band, I presume."

"That's what some folk call us," Makeig said. "Ye be the Watcher, Collandoth, called Ashlord. I've heard tell of ye."

"Oh? And what have you heard?" Ashlord put his sword away and leaned on his stick.

"More than I care to say. But if I ain't mistaken, 'long 'bout two months ago, right after the big storm, ye dispatched one of the two most surliest, meanest, vilest, contemptiblest, low creatures that ever stood on two legs."

"If you mean one of the four sent to Tulith Attis after the storm passed, yes, I did."

"An' yer friend here," Makeig said, putting his hand on Robby's shoulder, "done got rid of the other one."

"So!" Ashlord looked at Robby's blood covered clothes. "Then the blood I see is that of the kidnapper who took Billy Bosk? Robby, are you hurt?"

"No, no, I'm fine. This is not my blood," Robby said. "Ashlord, I killed a man. It just happened."

Ashlord nodded sympathetically, seeing that Robby was trying to get a grip on his emotions.

"What is done is done," he said. "You are not the first to kill, nor was he the first to die this day."

"What about my mother and my dad? They tell me Barley and Passdale have been attacked by an army. What is happening there? Have you seen my parents? Is Sheila safe?"

Ashlord nodded again, then shook his head and held up his hand.

"Yes, yes, much has happened. Your mother is safe, I know. Sheila is safe, too. Your father I last saw early this morning. He may have been taken, or he may yet be free. I do not know."

"What? Captured? A prisoner?"

"Perhaps."

"I have to get to him!"

"No one can go near Passdale without being taken. I believe the soldiers are rounding up all the men they can find to form work parties. I have to trust that your father, if he did not escape, will be well-treated, or as well as a prisoner may be treated. His interests are in the preservation of the town and county, and I think that suits the purpose of the army, too, for the time being at least. If he is a prisoner, I don't think they will harm him as I trust they will see the value in keeping him well. However, let us hope that he got away to the northeast to warn Glareth."

"But, why? Why are we being attacked? Who are they, these Redvests?"

"Afore ye get into all the explainin'," Makeig interrupted, "I'm thinkin' the two of ye should come to our nearby camp. I'm thinkin' some food an' some cleanin' up for Robby wouldn't go amiss. I'm thinkin', too, I'd like to get out of this stinkin' hole."

Ashlord and Robby looked at each other, and Ashlord nodded.

"The west way is best for us," he said to Robby.

"Good!" Makeig said, mounting up. "Then take a horse apiece an' come along. It ain't far, an' I fancy we'll just make it afore dark."

"Before we do, I should like to take a look at your late adversary," Ashlord said, striding into the room before Makeig could protest.

"Ye'll not find much!" he called after him. "Well, be quick, then!"

Robby handed the reins of his horse to a nearby fellow, and, following with hurried footsteps, caught up with Ashlord. The smell was even more sickening than before, with Bailorg's body smoldering in the fire, adding to the previous stench.

"Do you know his name?" Ashlord asked, looking about as he approached the fireplace.

"He was called Bailorg."

"Bailorg? I have heard of him."

"Look here," Robby said, pointing down to a line of ash-like dust on the floor. "Bailorg had a Swyncraff, almost like mine. He used it to bind Billy and later attacked Captain Makeig with it. When I killed Bailorg, it turned to dust. See?"

Ashlord bent over and picked up some of the dust, rubbing it between his fingers, then held it to his nose to smell.

"It was not like yours," he said, standing up and still smelling the dust. "But very similar, no doubt. This is not the dust of tree, but that of scales and bone, a snake, I think. Swyncraff is made of Shadowbane, I think. A tree not seen for ages. It is said the leaves of that tree glowed so brightly that even in the full sun, it had no shadow."

Ashlord's voice trailed off, then he abruptly turned and walked briskly toward the huge hearth with Robby following.

"What kind of place is this, Ashlord?"

"It is an ancient troll house," he said, bending over Stingorn and turning him over. He went through his pockets, and, finding nothing of interest, Ashlord pulled off Stingorn's coat and shirt and turned the dead man over to examine his back. "Who is this person?"

"One of the festival folk. A huckster. That fellow over there, Bailorg, murdered him. And he would have murdered Billy, too, I'm sure of it. He killed Steggan, Sheila's uncle. He said so. What are you looking for?" asked Robby. Ashlord made no reply as he went over to the fire and leaned as close as he dared. Bailorg's booted feet were splayed out before the fireplace, and the fire had already consumed most of his clothes and was working its way down his leggings. Ashlord saw a nearby bucket of water and suddenly handed Robby his walking stick.

"Hold out your other arm," he said. When Robby did so, Ashlord poured water over Robby's hand and sleeve and rubbed away some of the blood. "That'll have to do until you can wash properly. Now step back."

Ashlord grabbed Bailorg's boots and dragged him out of the fire onto the floor, his burning body sending up plumes of nauseating smoke. Makeig, looking in from the doorway, scrunched up his face.

"Oh, gar!" one of his men said, matching Makeig's expression. Robby held his hand over his mouth and nose. To make matters worse, Ashlord took the bucket of water and dowsed the body, creating even more clouds of steam and smoke. Ashlord bent close to the wretch and examined him in every detail, especially the now-hideous face. He pulled at bits of unburnt clothing, buckles and even examined Bailorg's boots. To Robby's horror, Ashlord then turned Bailorg over, and, with a poker, pulled away the charred bits of cloak and clothing.

"Look here," Ashlord commanded. Robby, still holding his hand over his nose, edged closer until he stood beside Ashlord.

"What?"

"Just there," Ashlord pointed to Bailorg's back, charred and steaming and blistered. Robby saw two thin reddish-black lines, each running down from Bailorg's shoulders and disappearing under his breeches.

"Scars of the Elifaen!" uttered one of Makeig's men who, out of curiosity, had approached and was now backing away. Robby looked at Ashlord who nodded.

"Our enemies are of all races, it seems," he whispered to Robby as he picked up a firebrand. While Robby watched, Ashlord walked around the room, paying careful attention to a table where there were cups, plates, bits of food, and a lamp, which Ashlord now lit, tossing away the brand. He found a leather case and went through its contents, paper parchment, mostly, and other writing tools. This he slung over his shoulder by its strap as the floor rumbled and dust fell from the roof.

Ashlord sniffed, glancing around.

"Was there a bird, here?"

"Yes. Earlier. It flew off. What is this place?" Robby asked again, alarmed.

"It is a troll house," Ashlord repeated, still busy looking over the items around the room. "Have you not noticed the unusual proportions of the tables and chairs? It is told that once a fierce Troll Lord lived here and is still held captive somewhere in deep chambers far below, and that these rumblings are his labors to escape." He glanced at Robby, to see how he took this. Robby was looking around cautiously. "Others say the rumblings are only the ground shifting beneath this ridge. I don't think there is much left for me to see. I'll take these few things and examine them in better light."

Ashlord shuffled through a few of Bailorg's belongings on the table, some books and writing tools. He picked up the purse and opened it, and removed a large silver coin.

"Very old Vanaran coins," Ashlord said, holding up the coin to the light. "From the First Age, I think."

Robby nodded, seeing the small stone set into the middle of the coin.

"What should we do with the bodies?" he asked.

"Leave them. No time to bury them. The wild animals will find them soon enough. Now let us be gone from here!"

• • •

Robby and Ashlord rode in the middle of the group, and when they emerged into the light, they all blinked and squinted until they could see properly. The sun was low over the mountains, bathing the forested hills in bright yellow light. The west side of the ridge was more densely wooded, and the way was sharp with steep climbs and descents, sometimes forcing them to dismount and lead their horses along very rough and rocky paths. Robby managed to keep alongside Ashlord so that they could speak.

"I have so much to ask you about that I hardly know where to begin," Robby said as quietly as possible so that as few of the riders around could hear.

"I think Makeig will have many questions, too," Ashlord said, nodding ahead at the leader. "And I anticipate needing to tell more of the happenings in Barley soon, and you will hear more about that then. But tell me, does anyone here know about your doings at Tulith Attis?"

"I don't think so," Robby said. "I'm not sure. Bailorg seemed only to confide in the Conundrum Box man, Stingorn I think his name was. And he killed him. I saw him do it. I don't think the others here caught on to what Bailorg and I said to each other while we fought. But Bailorg guessed right away that it was me at Tulith Attis."

"It is good that none here knows."

"About that place back there, the troll house, I mean. Why did Bailorg take up there? I heard him tell Billy that he was a Watcher, like you, and that he and his master have also been watching for a long time."

"Yes, I suspected as much, but I had no idea that he was so near," Ashlord acknowledged. "Though many times I sought him out before you and I met. After your return to Passdale, I sought for him even harder. But he was cunning, and I was misled by false signs, I'm afraid."

"So he was a Watcher, like you? A Melnari?"

Ashlord shot a stern look at Robby.

"I wonder how you came to know the name of my kind?" Ashlord said.

"Thurdun told me," Robby said defensively. "Is it wrong to know?"

"No, no, not wrong, just unusual," Ashlord explained. "Bailorg was not of my kind, but an Elifaen of the ancient days. I could tell from his clothes and scars. That and the fact that he had what you called a Swyncraff. You should know that what you have about your waist is named Swyncraff, just as a person has a name. Each is unique and has its own name. They only respond to those to whom they are given. All this tells me that Bailorg was a powerful agent, indeed. With a powerful benefactor. Yes, he was a watcher, of sorts, certainly, but not the same as I. His clues and guidance came from someone else, and Bailorg could only watch for what he was told to find. However, I do not think Bailorg has been here very long, perhaps only for a year or so. And I wonder how much he was told by his master concerning your coming?"

"His master? My coming? What do you mean?"

"What I mean is there were signs that something would happen at Tulith Attis. That is why I took up my abode there. I interpreted the signs one way; the enemy interpreted them another. Watching does not mean seeing, though, and seeing does not mean understanding. I did not expect anyone to ring the Bell, though now I see clearly that I should have expected that. I thought my presence there would flush out the traitor's agents, fearing I would discover his identity. But it was you who stirred Bailorg to action, not I. I and my kind watch for those things that tell us what to watch for, signs and movements. Wind. Water. Rock. Sky and stars. Whisperings and grumblings both of the earth and of the creatures that live upon it, especially Elifaen and Men. But my time of watching seems to be coming to an end."

"What do you mean?"

"I mean, Robby Ribbon, that watching is no longer enough. There are other things that need doing."

"Like what?"

Ashlord looked at Robby with a smile.

"I cannot tell you until I know myself. There are still many questions, many mysteries. I will have some answers very soon, I hope. Tell me, did Bailorg mention anyone? The name of his master?"

"No."

"Too bad. So the traitor's secret is still kept. Forces are moving, it is clear. The attack on Barley is a small consequence of greater designs," he said. "Perhaps we can speak more of this later. Right now we must see that we do not fall behind."

"Greater designs?"

Ashlord nudged his mount on ahead of Robby just as the line of men and horses passed through a narrow gap where a huge rock had split asunder ages ago. The path cut back and forth between these natural columns and then for a long while afterwards they continued up and down and sideways along the ridges as they progressed north and westward. At last the way smoothed somewhat as it also leveled across old stands of pine and fir, and Ashlord was able to ride alongside Makeig.

"As you might guess, I am wondering how you came to fall in with Bailorg," Ashlord ventured.

"Oh, well, Bailorg happened along the first time 'bout a year or so back. Well, back in the late winter, I reckon. We waylaid him on the road down toward Tallinvale way, took a pretty penny an' sent the feller on. Toward early spring, he comes back with four other fellers, bodyguards we reckoned at first, low, dirty-lookin' men with the look of mercenaries about them. Anyhow, they rode brazen among us, right past our posts an' guards—never figured out how, though it caused a big stir I can tell ye. He told us he wanted to hire as many men who'd ride for him, runnin' errands to Barley an' the like. Said he'd have a big job later on, in the way of hirin' safe escort through the mountains, through Damar country, an' on out onto the plains beyond. Bailorg promised sixteen pieces of fine new Duinnor gold for each of twenty men, full weights, too, sayin' there'd be forty times more when the job was done."

The riders negotiated a steep incline downward through a thick copse, and when they'd cleared it, Makeig continued, sometimes speaking over his shoulder at Ashlord.

"Do you know who Bailorg's master is?"

"Oh, no. Though I pressed him on it a few times," answered Makeig. "But I gleaned enough to know that his boss is someone not to be trifled with, someone very powerful out west, in Duinnor Realm, I think. Or, if not in Duinnor, somewheres out west."

"Hm. I see. So Bailorg hired you, you were saying."

"That's right. Anyhow, so we were skeptical of the whole thing. Leastwise, I was, an' so were some of the men, havin' been duped before, if ye take me meanin'. Some of me men figured that if the feller had the gold, we may as well take it, an' they said so, straight to his face. Bailorg only laughed an' said that the gold was to be paid by the purchaser of certain goods we were to deliver in good condition. Wouldn't say what those goods were to be, though now I reckon we all know." Makeig nodded back at Robby. "Course we had no idea it was all for some kidnappin'. Not that we have anything against that line of work, mind ye, 'cept there's a right way an' a wrong way to go about it, an' this feller Bailorg seemed a bit of the kind to lay a loo'ard tack when the shallows are rocky an' lead an' line are stowed."

"I don't follow you."

"I mean to say, he seemed the type to take too many chances. Anyhow, we wound up agreein', I'm ashamed to say, figurin' we'd put that gold in our community chest an' maybe trade it out with Furaman later on. So he went away, an' we didn't see much of him, 'cept once headin' to Janhaven an' another time back from Tallinvale. Suddenly he shows up again sometime shortly after Midsummer wantin' us to raid the Post Station in Janhaven. Said if we'd do the handiwork, all he'd want as his cut was the papers to be had there. Letters an' logbooks an' such. It was an outrageous scheme, an' we fairly laughed him out of town. So he goes away again, with our previous agreement still standin'."

"All he wanted were letters?" Ashlord asked.

"Well, that's what he said. We didn't see him again 'til when the Great Storm came, along with them three great peals of thunder that sure gave these mountains a run for their name. The day the rain let up, he was spotted by one of our scouts, tearin' down the South Road to Tallinvale. 'Bout three or four days later, Bailorg shows up all hot an' aside of hisself, like, wantin' to know what happened to his men, his company of hired men, them four fellers what came with him before. At first he accused us of doin' away with 'em, but we assured him he was haulin' on the wrong line, though we couldn't care one way or the other what became of 'em. Well, it turned out that Bailorg sent 'em on some sort of errand off Barley-way, an' he wanted us to send out after 'em to see where they went, to look around, all private-like."

From his position near to Ashlord, and due to Makeig's husky voice, Robby could follow the tale as they rode along. As he listened, he got a whiff of smoke and as they topped a rise, Makeig waved off a guard that stood out from some rocks. When they rode around the crest, Robby could see smoke filtering up through the trees below and ahead of them.

"Well, as much out of curiosity as for the silver he offered, we sent a few fellers over that way, young Winterford amongst 'em, to see what they could see. 'Course they got wind pretty quick 'bout the so-called raid on Boskland, an' 'bout the fight on the old Line Road, an' the Dragonkind-man, all before they even reached the river near Buckman's Ferry. There Winterford an' the others fell in with some Barley people that work for Furaman an' so they crossed on over with 'em—it was easy since the river's done got so low—an' they rode out to take a look at the gate at Bosk Hall to see for their own selves. Up 'til then, we had no idear one of them fellers was a Dragonkind, so covered up with helmets an' hoods they always were. Anyhow, not long after Winterford an' the others got back from their foray, Bailorg shows up again wantin' to know what was learned. We put to him the question of them fellers pretty sternly, of how he came by them an' all, particularly a Dragonkind, an' what his errands were about. We were pretty mad at hearin' what they'd done over at Boskland, the killin' an' lootin' an' all, an' at what he may have gotten us mixed up in. Last thing we needed was some feud, an' particularly with Bosklanders, who we had some good dealin's with, though they didn't know we was outlaws. Bailorg claimed he was ill-used by them men, who took his coin an' struck off on some fool jaunt of their own with little mind to him or his business. That's our camp up just yonder. So, anyhow, he pleaded with us to lend him some men for runnin' errands an' such since his own had run off an' been killed, deservedly so, he was sure to add, an' he said again the big job was still on. An' that's pretty much how it's been since then. He holed up in that troll cave, an' ever once in a while we'd ride out on some errand or other to Barley or over to Janhaven or such. Awhile back, he took up with one of them travelin' pitchmen who sold jewelry an' the like, but who mostly cheated folk out of their silver. Stingorn was his name, an' never was a cheater like him, what with his confounded Conundrum Box. Anyhow, I reckon he got more than what was comin' to him. Bailorg sent word for us to come meet with him an' that's how we ran into young Robby, there."

They rode into a prepared camp where tents were pitched and supper fires tended under spits of venison and pots of hot broth. There were four small wagons there, the sturdy narrow kind that looked easy to pull through the narrow ways and paths, and from these came all the supplies of the camp. The preparations were being made by several women of various ages, along with a couple of older men, and many others who were armed as well as any soldier. Upon seeing Makeig, they all came swarming over to ask about the "job," as they called it, and Makeig explained as he dismounted that it had all gone south. Lantin consoled them somewhat with the news of the purse as Makeig ushered Ashlord and Robby to a tent. He called out orders about the horses as he went, and more about getting food up, and posting watches. He stopped a girl as she passed by, and then motioned to Robby to come near.

"This here's Robby Ribbon, of Passdale, me sweet," he said to her. "An' this here, Mr. Ribbon, is our dearie, Sally Bodwin."

"Pleased to meet you," Robby said, bowing slightly to the girl. She was about fifteen or sixteen, Robby guessed, and dressed in a country skirt and bodice. Her hair might have been blond, but her head was covered with a kerchief and what little hair showed was sweaty from her toils.

"Happy to know ye," she said with a very graceful curtsey.

"Sally's me adopted daughter, after the death of her folks a while back," Makeig said. "Purty soon she'll be runnin' this outfit. Won't ye, sweetness?"

"What d'ye want, Martin? I've gotta fetch more firewood," she said, shoving Makeig back in embarrassment.

"What I want is for ye to round up a big pot of water, preferably hot, an' some scrubbin' cloth so as Mr. Ribbon can clean up some. An' I want ye to rummage through all the men's things we got, an' see if there's some coat or cloak or shirt or anything he can get into. An', if it can be done, see that his own things get washed out."

"Oh, all that's not necessary," Robby protested. "Just some water to wash my face and hands."

"Nonsense!" said Sally. "Yer a mess! Do ye see any other feller here as dirty?"

Robby looked around. He had to admit they were a fine looking bunch of thieves and rogues, almost unnaturally clean and tidy, and not at all how one would expect desperate men to look.

"I suppose I am a little off," he said.

"I'll say!" Sally wrinkled her nose. "Come along, an' I'll get some soap."

While Robby was cleaning up, Ashlord was invited into Makeig's large tent where there was a cot, a small table, and stools.

"We ain't all savages an' cutthroats, ye know," Makeig said. "An' not without some learnin', either. There's not a soul amongst us over six years of age what can't read an' write in the Common Speech, an' many who speak more languages than I can name. Besides Lantin Rose, who was once a great factor with businesses galore, there's Mrs. Peak over yonder who was a school marm, an' one time taught princes an' kings-to-be. An' back over there, that big oafish-lookin' feller what rode in with us, he's a jeweler by trade, an' though looks as if his big hands would crush anything softer than steel, ye should see the delicate things he makes for the ladies. Here comes Jimmy Dyersly, the old gent with the limp. Ye'd never know he was once a mighty scholar of history an' advisor to lords. That feller comin' along there with them scrolls, he's the son of our cobbler. See the feller over by the horses there, in the gray coat? Once, not too long ago, he was lord an' master over a whole province."

The young one came up and handed the scrolls to Makeig.

"I hope these are the ones ye wanted," he said.

"Looks like it! Thankye kindly, Tommy boy," Makeig replied taking the scrolls.

"If ye don't be needin' me, I'll go tend to the horses."

Makeig nodded as the boy turned away.

"Well, let's see," Makeig said as he tumbled the scrolls onto the table and looked at one then the next until he seemed to find the one he wanted.

"This is it."

He unrolled the parchment, revealing it to be a map of the region.

"I never go anywhere more than a day from home without me charts, if I can help it," Makeig said.

"This is a very keen map, too," Ashlord commented bending over it. "And it looks much like one I've seen in Passdale."

"Well, I bought this off a feller over that way not four years ago," Makeig said. "He copied it from one that he had, one made by a Kingsman a few years earlier. Now, look at that! I thought Robby's name sounded familiar!"

Makeig put his finger on a corner of the map where the copyist had signed it.

" 'Copied in the Year 865 of the Second Age by Robigor Ribbon,' " read Ashlord. "That's Robby's father; they share the same name, and I know the Kingsman who made the original of this map, cousin of young Robby on his mother's side."

Robby, now clean and dressed in a well-fitting dark brown jacket, rejoined them. Together, the three looked at the map while Ashlord related the events of the previous day and night to them.

"They must have worked secretly for months in the Boggy Wood, clearing a path, and taking care to do so without being seen by the hunters who venture there. I now think they must have built up their forces carefully, so as not to alert the men of the lake. It may have been their stirrings from the south that drove the wolves northward. I expect they had planned to cross the Saerdulin farther down, but the rising waters prevented that, forcing them to push farther north. I was at the

fortress when they came streaming across the old bridge there. I barely
made it to Boskland ahead of them. Bosk summoned his men to fight,
and he sent riders to Passdale, but the Redvest horsemen cut most of
them down. Mrs. Bosk got away, as well as most of the women, while
the men fought behind them. Bosk pleaded with me to lead a party
behind their families, to protect their flight, and at last, when I saw we
were overwhelmed, I did so. The last I saw of him, he was on the roof of
Bosk Manor directing his archers at the Redvests. There were only a
dozen or so Boskmen, and the soldiers quickly had the house on fire. I
don't see how any of them could have escaped the blaze and the collapse
of Bosk Manor."

Makeig dragged up another stool and the three sat as he uncorked a
clay jug and poured whiskey into three small tin cups.

"Drink the first one all at once," he suggested aside to Robby. Robby
did so and the stuff burned as it went down, causing him to cough once
or twice. Almost instantly he felt better. "That's right," Makeig nodded,
pouring another portion into each cup. "We'll be eatin' soon. Sip on this
one 'til then."

"We fled," said Ashlord sliding his finger on the map from Boskland to
Passdale. "About thirty or forty of us, and soon we came up on the women
and hurried them along. Somehow the horsemen missed us in the dark
and went on past. I think they were just gathering their forces to march
on Passdale, and maybe expected more resistance in the open fields.
Anyway, the alarm had been raised by the time we got to Passdale.
Ullin—he's the man who made this map, a Kingsman—he was there at the
bridge, ordering defenses and making ready to burn the bridge by placing
kegs of oil about it in preparation. He put men up on the tops of the
bridge pillars to act as lookouts and archers. About a thousand townsmen
and Barleymen, plus a few Bosklanders were there. Many had been at the
festival, otherwise they would have been cut off from Passdale. More men
were pouring in from both sides of the Bentwide. Anyway, the town was
in a panic. Your father was trying to organize wagons, Robby, and did a
fair job, considering, and many folk were fleeing without regard to
neighbor or even possessions. When the sun came up, we could see the
Redvests, lined row upon row across the ridge, their banners and their
pennants flying, their shadows long with the sun at their backs, and their
war drums throbbing. I think there were at least two thousand on the
ridge, with mounted lancers and many more footmen arriving behind
them. Maybe four thousand, all told."

Ashlord took a sip of the whiskey and went on.

"Shortly after dawn, your father, Ullin, and I, rode out to parley, along
with four Passdale Militiamen whom we deemed looked the fiercest,
including your friend Ibin. We told him to frown the whole time and to
not speak a word, and he did as he was told. I think his presence
impressed the general we rode out to meet."

Ashlord spoke without embellishment, gazing back and forth from Robby to Makeig, and his listeners heard not only his words, but also, it seemed, the noise of hoofs in his voice, the desperate ring of iron in his pauses, and the faint cadence of drums coming from his throat. And Robby, who knew better than Makeig the lay of the land and the people concerned, could almost see the encounter with the Redvest general. The general and several officers rode out a few yards from the ranks to await the Passdale delegation. They all remained mounted as they met.

*"I am Collandoth, servant of Duinnor. This is Commander Tallin, Kingsman of the House of Fairoak. And this is Robigor Ribbon, Mayor of Passdale,"* Ashlord said to the general.

*"I am Branthis Vidican, Legion General of Tracia. What is your purpose under truce?"*

*"We bid you leave these lands. They are under the protection of Duinnor, and sovereign under Prince Carbane of Glareth Realm, who is Regent over the Eastlands. The damage and ruin your army has visited upon us is unprovoked and without just cause. Leave these lands."*

*"I have no wish to lay waste and ruin,"* said the general. *"But my orders I will follow, and, if opposed, I will do what is necessary to that end. I entreat you to lay down your arms and give over to the rule of Tracia. You are clearly in no position to gain victory, and your resistance will be paid in blood and sorrow."*

*"Then what terms have ye for the surrender of our town an' lands?"* asked Mr. Ribbon.

*"Lay down your arms, man by man, on the field before us. Make an account of all the goods, grain, fruit, and other harvests, as well as cattle and livestock, including horses, mules, and oxen. Open all stores, shops, and warehouses of textiles, iron goods, leather, and all other sundries. Submit yourselves to the law of my judgment, by right of Tracia. Billet our soldiers as we assign. Deliver all men over the age of twelve into our hands under oath to work and to aid in the delivery of these accounts to Tracia. In exchange, we will not destroy your town, and I will do the utmost to keep my men from your women and to lay aside enough winter store for your people. As well, I have written scripts to exchange for all goods and property taken, so that anyone loyal to Tracia may plead for compensation before the Lord Judge of Tracia. What say you?"*

*"I say we must put this afore our people an' have 'em freely decide,"* replied Mr. Ribbon readily. *"Good day, sir!"*

*"Decide quickly!"* said the general.

"Clearly the Redvest general wanted to save all that he could from destruction," Ashlord continued. "Otherwise his terms would not have been so generous."

"Generous!" cried Robby.

"Not a single man was inclined to give over the products of their hard work and labor," Ashlord said, "and so, foolishly, they made a stand. Your mother, Robby, would not leave, at first, and stayed until early this morning with the last of those who fled. She departed shortly before the battle. Ah, the battle! It was hopeless, of course, and in less than an hour the Redvests were pouring onto the bridge and crossing the Bentwide in various places. It was a great useless slaughter of men on both sides. I don't know the names of many of the Barley and Passdale men who fought. Many were killed, many more were wounded, and several hundred were captured. I never knew the people in this region could fight so fiercely! Many had only farm implements. Sheila stood atop the bridge and laid down twenty men before it was outflanked. Your father set fire to it himself, swearing it would not be used by the despoilers. Ullin fought on the south road and I on the north, but soon it became a rout. Of the men we started with, a few hundred of us made it away, following the women and children toward Janhaven."

"What happened to my father?" Robby asked.

"When it became apparent that we could not hold back the Redvests, he took a horse and rode through the ranks of the attackers. Northward, he went. Toward the lake. They marked him for capture, probably because he knows the land and stores all around and is the Mayor to boot. Anyway, they took care not to harm him. I saw riders break out after your father as he cleared the bend in the north road."

"Where was he going?"

"North, to try to reach Glareth, carrying word of the invasion to Prince Carbane."

"Why couldn't someone else go?"

"There was no one else, Robby," Ashlord said, trying to console him. "He foresaw the outcome and beforehand insisted that Ullin and I stay with the people and organize protection and resistance. He, not being a man of arms to help much with that, knew the way well enough to elude the Redvests and their trackers."

"The Prince'll be furious," Makeig said.

"But what is it all about? What do they want with our land?" Robby asked.

"The rulers of Tracia long ago broke with Duinnor, and, I believe, they are now allied with the Dragonkind. This is the opening move of their plan for conquest. Their plan is not to attack Duinnor directly, but to gather such an army so as to overrun the southern realms first, with Redvests moving from the east and the Dragonkind moving from the west. Between the two are the small weak realms of Altoria and Masurthia. When those are taken, the way across the central plains to Duinnor will be open. This strike, into the Eastlands, is aimed at capturing the harvests and fall accountings, to help supply their main armies that are no doubt already massing in the south. The storm that struck Barley this past summer were nothing compared to that which laid waste to Tracia's farmlands. What we experienced was the mere edge of a great typhoon, but the brunt was borne by the southeast. With little reserves of food and fodder, Tracia's intent is to despoil all of the nearby lands of goods and men for its war against Altoria and Masurthia. I am certain the army now at Passdale plans to winter there and to establish a station for sending goods down river to Kalbrith. From there they will supply the gathering forces that will move westward in the spring. This is as far north as they will go, I think, and they will no doubt be fiercely opposed by Glareth and the Connassan Lakemen, once they learn of the situation. However, the Tracian Redvests need only to hold out until the spoils are on their way southward. I think they will then be removed to join the main forces in battle against the western realms, taking their captives with them as slaves. I imagine they will leave behind only a garrison force in Passdale. Or, if they are cruel, ashes."

"But why? What is the disagreement between Duinnor and Tracia?"

"Ancient wounds, me lad," Makeig said, "long festerin'. How do ye come to know all these things, Ashlord?"

"I have contacts in Tracia and in many far-flung parts. Suffice it to say that my information is reliable. Long have they been irked by the heavy tribute of Duinnor, even before the overthrow of their Prince Lewtrah. And Tracia has disputed its borders with the old Eastlands Realm for many years, and resents Glareth's regency over the Eastlands. Duinnor has always taken the firstborn into service, as elsewhere. But the new rulers of Tracia recalled all those serving Duinnor and forbade any others from going. Since then, Tracia has been cut off from trade with the other realms and has been festering, as Captain Makeig says, for revenge and for greater power. That Tracia has made its move now is a sign that their strength is gathering. Little do they care that they are mere pawns in a bigger game. I have no doubt that their union with the Dragonkind will bode ill for all of the Tracian people. And I fear that great harm will be done in the world before they are undone by their own greed."

"Won't they be opposed?"

"The west is weak, after years of squabbling. Duinnor has squandered the goodwill toward it by alienating the other realms that it rules and by unreasonable treatment of the Elifaen. Vanara, once its closest ally, has been on the brink of collapse these many years. And Duinnor is far away, too. Between here and there, from the slopes of the Thunder Mountains, down into the plains and beyond, many warlords have sprung up, setting up their own rule with little or no allegiance to Duinnor or to any realm. Some places have sunken into the grips of despotic cults ruled by thugs and murderers in the guise of priests. Many other lands are completely without law. All this is due as much to the inattention of Duinnor to its responsibilities as to the machinations of its enemies. The ultimate question is: Will Duinnor stand?"

"Will Duinnor stand? Ye don't think it's that bad, do ye? Surely the King will stir to action, don't ye think?" Makeig asked, stunned.

"The King of Duinnor rules in isolation from his subjects, mysterious and unseen. He is Unknown in more ways than one. How unlike the King of the Dragon People, who stands among his people openly and without fear! The King of Duinnor cannot be touched or even looked on by his people, while the Emperor of the Sun walks freely as his people bow and throw flower petals on his path and sing praises as he passes."

"Yer words're nigh to treasonous, good feller," Makeig stated. "But yer not the only one who's wondered at such. Just such stirrin's an' discontent led to the fall of Tracia into the present band of rascals an' slippery characters."

Makeig was about to tell how he came to be in the mountains when word came that supper was ready. But, just as they sat down at the supper table, he was called away by one of his men. He shoved his plate over to another man at the table.

"Eat this 'fore it gets cold," he said with a sigh. "I forgot I'm to check one of the nearby watches. I'll be back in just a little bit."

Lantin Rose sat down as Makeig jumped on his horse and rode off quickly.

"Nearby watch?" Robby asked.

"Yes, we have many watches posted all around these hills where we station men as we move," said Lantin. "It's the Captain's habit of lookouts."

"I hope there's no alarm," Ashlord said. "Requiring him to leave, that is."

"Oh, no! It is our way to send men to check on the watches from the camp. We've got five such posts nearby. Since we're a bit short-handed, Martin always takes one to check on. The one he rides to ain't far off, only about a furlong, so he'll not be gone long. We always send a man to check each post about halfway through the watch, if we can."

"You seem very well organized," Ashlord commented.

"That's Martin's doings. He don't like movin' so many men away from town without proper precautions. Always been that way. Cautious. But ye won't find one bolder, neither, when it comes to it."

"Town?"

"Oh, yes, we have a town of sorts. It don't have no proper name or nuthin', so we just call it Hill Town. Nuthin' special, but it is defensible, an' we've got a few shops, cottages, an' smithies, an' spinners, like most little towns. So we manage to make it a home. Some of us have learned to hunt, others to farm, but we are not averse to takin' a toll on the roads, an' makin' passin' purses lighter."

"Do you call him 'Captain' because he's your leader?" Robby asked.

"Well, yes an' no. His right name is Martin Makeig, Captain of the Tracian Royal Navy, commissioned by Prince Lantos his own self, brother to the Ruling Prince Lewtrah. It's a long tale, an' the short of it is that there was a takeover, an' the Captain stayed loyal. He lost his lands an' all his family to the rebels while he was at sea. Whilst tryin' to get Prince Lantos an' family away to Glareth, he lost his own ship to the pursuin' Redvests. A mighty sea battle that was, so I hear, and the Golden Swallow, Martin's ship, made the difference. The way his men tell it, Martin saved the Prince, who got clean away. Martin made it off his sinkin' ship with many of his crew, an' they had to scramble an' fight their way through Tracia, losin' a bunch of men along the way. That was about fourteen years ago, I guess. So he an' twenty or so of his men what made it away from Tracia come into the mountains where they fell in with the rest of us. I think they were meanin' to get to Glareth, but got pushed the long way 'round, so to speak. Anyway, when he showed up we were starvin' an' quarrelin' amongst ourselves, an' losin' a man a week to raiders, too. In no time at all, he got us all shipped up, as he puts it, an' most of us soon realized we were better off with him puttin' things together. Some calls him a warlord, but that ain't right. There are a bunch of them warlord-types in the mountains, took up there when the trolls left. Captain Makeig's pretty much held them off our territory, the warlords, I mean, though their raidin' parties are everywhere. He's got a head for fightin' an' battle an' such, an' we ain't lost a soul in nearly a year."

"Where did everyone else come from?" Robby asked

"Most of us came up from Tracia, being mostly Loyalists, but some from Masurthia an' a few from westward parts."

"And what about the warlords? What do you know of them?"

"Well there's 'bout six or seven of 'em now, dependin' on who's killed off who, lately. The most dangerous one's are up northwest an' down southwest of here. Them two's got castles an' keeps an' thousands of soldiers. An' they both claim rights over the other. Luckily for us they're too busy with each other, an' a mite too far off to bother much with us on this side of the range. If they ever join forces, though, we'd be all in a heap!"

"You must be talking about the Galinots and the Damar," Ashlord said. "I've had some dealings with them both."

"That's right, the Galinots up on the northwest parts of the range, the Damar southwest of here."

"My understanding is that the Damar have ties with Tracia." Ashlord added.

"Maybe so. I wouldn't doubt it."

"It's hard to keep it all straight," Robby shook his head.

"Aye, it's a mess," Lantin agreed, chewing on a piece of venison.

"Tell me," Ashlord asked, drawing on his pipe and leaning back. "What are your plans?"

"Plans? About what?"

"About the war?"

"War? I don't rightly know. I guess it is comin', though."

"It is here."

"Maybe. Well, the Capt'n is a deep one for thinkin' on such things, an' not much takes him unawares. He openly longs for a deck under his feet, as do many of his men, an' he often talks of goin' back to sea. 'A fish out of water,' he calls hisself, though ye'd never know it by his skill as a highwayman. Natural-born leader, too. My guess is if he figures a way to hit back at them rebel upstarts what got rid of the Prince, why it'd be the last these mountains saw of Martin Makeig."

"Hm."

"I don't know what the rest of us would do without him, though. We ain't all made of fighting stuff, ye know, an' I ain't just talkin' 'bout the women an' children. Look at me, for one: I can't hardly see without these spectacles. Lotta good I'd do in a battle! But, ol' Martin! Why, when I think on it, I'm kinda surprised he's stayed on this long. Ye done got me worried, now. I imagine he'd leave if he saw a way, particularly if it had to do with puttin' out to sea."

"What're ye goin' on about," said Makeig coming up suddenly and straddling a bench. He put down his second plate of food and a tankard and took his hat off, revealing a receding hairline below his long shaggy black hair and gray locks. "Who's goin' where?"

"Yer the one, if ye could get a ship under ye!" said Lantin.

"Aye," Makeig nodded. "That's sure enough. Only there ain't much chance of that!"

Ashlord puffed a little cloud and said nothing until Makeig asked the mystic how he got caught up in Barley. Ashlord deftly avoided the question by turning the conversation back to Makeig's mountain home. Robby listened, stifling several yawns, slowly slumping lower and lower. At last, Makeig nodded at Robby to Lantin Rose, and the elder man put a hand on Robby's shoulder.

"Why don't ye come with me, an' I'll point out where ye can sleep."

• • •

Clouds raced across an orange sky. Robby shielded his eyes, looking at dunes as far as he could see. A moment later, his arms and legs sank into the hot sand as he struggled up a slippery dune gracefully rippled with rows of small ridges. His hands and feet blistered with heat and his whole body felt afire. The scorching wind stung his face with grit, and he felt as if his mouth would crack and break away if he swallowed another grain, so dry and parched it was. Just as he neared the summit, he saw a lone figure, standing above him at the crest of the dune with a dark robe wrapped around him, flapping in the wind. The sun beat down over the figure's shoulder into Robby's squinting eyes. Burnished copper armor glinted from under his robes and a long, thin sword hung at his side. His helmeted head was wrapped in a black turban crossing his face like a mask. Terror gripped Robby as he realized he was at the feet of a Dragonkind warrior, and as he stared at the copper-sheathed leggings of the creature, he lost his balance and began slipping backwards. Suddenly, a thin hand gripped his wrist, pulling him up to the top. Robby looked up, trying to catch his breath, blinking against the sun, as the warrior stooped and looked down at him. All Robby could make out in the shadow of the black turban were two golden-yellow eyes, and he was drawn into them. Another cloud passed the sun, and the burning day turned to cool night and the sun into moon. The clouds of dust became motionless stars, the golden eyes seemed like mysterious lamps, and Robby realized the creature meant him no harm. And, though a warrior, doubtless fierce and resolute, the realization settled on him that it was a Dragonkind woman who gazed at him.

• • •

"Wake up, Robby!"

Robby stirred and then sat up, suddenly fully alert.

"What is it?" he asked Ashlord, who was bending over him.

"It is an hour after sunrise. We must go."

Robby kicked off the blankets and scrambled to his feet. He was still dressed in the borrowed clothes, but found beside his sleeping place his cleaned surcoat. Looking around, he saw that the camp was broken, the wagons gone, and many of the men already on horseback, apparently waiting for him.

"We let you sleep as long as we could," Ashlord explained, helping him roll up his things and tie them onto a waiting mount. "But we must get moving."

"Of course," Robby said. "You should have gotten me up earlier."

"You needed rest," Ashlord said, getting onto his assigned horse. "No one was against letting you sleep."

"Where are we going?"

"To Janhaven. And we must hurry!"

He packed quickly, and as soon as he had his things stuffed into the saddlebag, they rode, and rode hard. There was little talk, and Robby felt the urgency around him. His anxiety about his family and friends grew with every mile, yet he had no notion of how far they had traveled, or how far that remained to go. He and Ashlord rode at the rear of twenty other riders, all following Captain Makeig along a narrow track; the others of the camp had gone with the women and wagons back to Hill Town. Robby saw how the faces around him now were businesslike and expressionless as they concentrated on guiding their horses through narrow passes and across rocky hillsides. Whenever there was open ground, they urged their mounts into easy gallops, but these were few, and the farther north they went the harder the way became. Soon their path led alongside the steep hills that formed part of the same ridge through which, many miles behind them, tunneled the troll cave where Robby had first met Makeig.

"It just occurred to me to ask where Ibin and Sheila were taking Billy," Robby asked Ashlord during a stretch where they could ride side by side.

"Northward to the west road," Ashlord said. "There to meet with the train of people coming from Passdale to Janhaven."

"And did you get a chance to take a look at Billy?"

"Yes. He will be fine, I think, if well-tended for a few days, and if he goes easy on himself for some while. Two of his ribs were cracked, I think, and he was bruised very badly. I don't think his nose was broken. He had a nasty cut on his left temple, too. All in all, considering the treatment he apparently received, I think it's a wonder he isn't worse off. I think you may have gotten to him just in time."

"I hope so," Robby said thoughtfully. "I regret I wasn't in Passdale."

"I'm sure Billy will regret that, too," Ashlord nodded. "I don't think you two would have made any difference in the end. As it was, you did the right thing going after Billy, and I have no doubt that you saved his life. Quite a brave thing to do. Given the tide of battle at Passdale, it may have saved your life, too."

Robby nodded, "Maybe. Still!"

"I know. But Bailorg had to be stopped. And now with war upon us, it will be more difficult to avoid any future emissaries of Bailorg's master."

"How do you mean?"

"I mean all is in confusion amongst the people, and strangers are mixed with strangers. Who can say which is friend and which is foe? Look about you at these men. Two days ago, could you have imagined that the Thunder Mountain Band would be helping you?"

"I would have thought the idea farfetched."

"Just so." Ashlord reined his horse around a tree and fell in behind Robby as the path narrowed again, saying, "I only wish I knew what we will find in Janhaven. I know that many escaped, but I have no reckoning of how many."

"Where is Certina, by the way?" Robby asked, twisting around on his saddle to face Ashlord. "I got your message, I guess you know."

"Yes, and glad of it. She is off on another errand."

"More messages?"

"In a manner of speaking. And to have a look around."

"I see. And Flitter? What became of him?"

"I wish I knew," Ashlord sighed. "I last saw him at Tulith Attis, scrambling up a tree. He has his own business, I'm sure, and cares little for our troubles. Still, I miss the little fellow. It is true that sometimes it is in the smallest things that one finds the most comfort, and that one misses the most. You know, like a pipe in the evening, or a favorite pair of socks, or even a little squirrel."

Robby smiled. It was odd to hear Ashlord talk this way, and Robby detected a note of weariness in his tone. Glancing back at him, it seemed that Ashlord looked very old, even though at other times he appeared hardly older than Ullin.

The track rose higher and steeper and narrower as they went, winding through stands of pine that cracked tall and straight through the rocky slopes. Abruptly, they emerged onto a wide flat-topped summit above the treetops, and they gathered around on their horses to look about. The north path dropped sharply away to be lost in the trees below, and they could see, here and there, down into the gap before them, the pale line of the West Road far below as it made its way through the forest. To their left, westward, a long line of shapes moved slowly: people on foot, some pulling little carts, others in wagons pulled by oxen, the trailing end of those that were fleeing to Janhaven. Poor and ragged they looked to Robby, and though he strained to see, they were too far away for him to recognize any of the individuals. He estimated there were at least three or four hundred within sight, with doubtless many more on ahead hidden from view.

"That looks to be the tail end of the train," said Makeig.

The road bent around far below and not too far in front of them, was obscured as it passed through a narrow gap, then reappeared to their right leading off east and southeast toward Passdale.

"There!" cried a man to Robby's right, standing in his stirrups and pointing. The others turned, and Makeig eased his horse through next to him. A thin cloud of dust was all Robby could make out at first, then he saw a flash of red. A moment later, red-cloaked horsemen appeared along a portion of the road open to view and then disappeared again into the trees.

"How many, d'ye think?" Makeig asked.

"By their ranks, I'd make about eighty, maybe a hunnerd riders. Movin' purty fast, Capt'n."

"Aye," Makeig nudged his horse back to the precipice and surveyed the refugees who were apparently innocent of the approaching threat. Just over a mile separated the two groups and the distance narrowed with each passing moment.

"There! Look there!" Winterford exclaimed, pointing excitedly down the other way. "Along the Narrows!"

Just ahead of the Redvests by about a half-mile, they could see stirrings along the road. A flash of steel glinted here and there, and Robby could make out men taking up positions on either side of the roadway, along a chokepoint where the gap was most narrow.

"They will not be stopped at the gap," Ashlord muttered as the two forces met. They could see little of the skirmish, and could hear nothing, though their ears imagined now and then the ring of metal and the cry of battle on the air. A moment later, the Redvests reappeared, hardly diminished in numbers, sweeping through the gap.

Makeig craned his head, standing in his stirrups to look the other way at the retreating refugees. Then he took off his hat and clutched it and his reins together, his long hair blowing wildly about his head.

"We just might make it!" he cried. "Let's go, boys!"

With that, he plunged his horse over the side and disappeared. Before Robby knew it, all the others followed, and he found himself clinging desperately to his mount as it, too, lunged fearlessly over the edge. It was a reckless plunge, and the sound of crashing hooves, cracking rocks, breaking branches, and crunching earth echoed from slope to slope. Makeig and his men whooped and yelled as they went, shouting encouragement to their mounts and to each other. Terrified enough by the headlong plummet, and fearful that his horse would stumble and flip hind over head, Robby caught a glimpse of those men around him. The gleam in their eyes and the eagerness in their grins frightened him even more. Down, down they careened, leaning this way and jerking that way around the sudden appearance of tree trunks and boulders. They were no longer in a single file, now spread out in a broad avalanche of sheer madness made of horseflesh, men, and flying debris. Yet, no horse stumbled, no man fell, and Robby managed to hang on, following closely behind Winterford. Winterford suddenly slipped over to hang precariously on his horse's side with a foot in the stirrup and a leg over the saddle. Robby saw the thick low branch that missed Winterford, and he slung himself over just in time to duck it, too. Still they hung on. As Robby clambered to get upright into the saddle, the ground leveled somewhat. Flung on by their momentum, they broke into a gallop one and all through a thinly treed wood, breaking low branches as they went, heedless of the cuts they sustained, dodging tree trunks and spilling down and up shallow gullies. Ahead, through distant gaps in the trees, flashes of red blinked, and, several moments after the Redvests had passed by, the Band burst onto the roadway and turned to follow. Robby now understood the reason for the madness and urged his horse faster and faster, standing in the stirrups and leaning low over the horse's neck, moving through the others until he was near the front of the company. Makeig was several horse-lengths ahead of all, whipping his mount with left and right sweeps of the reins. They rounded a bend, and the Redvests were suddenly before them, unaware of the peril that swept up from behind. To Robby, they looked grand in their red cloaks and in their orderly formations, now eight horses wide on the broadened roadway. Going at an easy pace, the Redvest mounts had come a long way without rest, and the Thunder Mountain Band quickly gained on them. It seemed to Robby that his own mount, seeing those ahead, kicked on with even greater speed and urgency, each man and horse going even faster than before, and it was as if the oblivious Redvests hardly moved at all. At forty paces, Makeig drew his sword, and from his men came the answering refrain of steel-unsheathed. Ashlord passed by, his long black hair flying, making it up alongside Makeig. Robby gripped Swyncraff. It instantly undid itself from his waist and straightened to a long iron-hard staff, one end curling around Robby's wrist and gripping him as tightly as he gripped it.

Twenty-one swords slashed into the rear of the unsuspecting Redvests, and twenty-one heads flew from red-shouldered riders. Robby smashed a soldier cruelly on the back of the neck, unhorsing him, as the middle ranks of the enemy horsemen, reacting to the confusion at their rear, drew their weapons and turned on them. The forward ranks, confident of their rear, charged on, for their quarry was now within sight. Seeing them come, panic ran up the line of refugees ahead.

# Chapter 22

# The Name of the King

Day 83
162 Days Remaining

Mirabella heard the thundering of hooves against the wall of hills and turned from the mule she was trying to move out of the way of an oxcart of children. She knew what the sound meant, and she walked steadily, pushing through the panicked crowds and making her way quickly against their frightened current.

"Move quickly," she urged. "Leave that and go!"

Her face was grim, and none disobeyed her. Most of these people, far behind the main group, were already in debt to her for their lives, and she had managed them well from Passdale, making sure they kept moving and yet did not go so hastily as to cause harm or injury to the young and elderly. For a day and a night without sleep she had been encouraging them, settling arguments, organizing food parties, and tending the hurt and mournful amongst them, imploring them not to camp, but to press on, to keep moving toward Janhaven. For some reason, perhaps in the absence of her husband, they looked to her for leadership, men and women alike, and in her they found it, indeed.

"They are coming," she said loudly as she strode eastward toward the threat. "So they have broken through our fighters. Get off the road! Leave your things! Move up the slopes! Spread out! They cannot follow you far into the trees for they dare not leave their horses. Here! Take this child! Now run!"

At the very rear of the train, a small cart rolled along, driverless, as it had since leaving Passdale. The little donkey pulling it merely followed those ahead in an unhurried way, oblivious to the pressing danger from behind. Mirabella had no idea who owned the cart or the donkey, but she had earlier placed a few things there under some blankets, items from her home, account books from the Common House, a pile of clothes, and the clay jar from the upstairs strongbox. Now, as the Redvests came into sight around the far bend, she drew out from under the blankets a long, slightly curved sword with a fine narrow blade. Without breaking her pace, she continued down the middle of the road to meet the horsemen, the blade held in her left hand, as she undid the ties of her overcloak and let it fall to the ground. She had not taken time to change her clothes, and still had on the fine gown she wore at the festival, now dusty and dirty. The Redvests were less than a furlong away, coming fast and hard. She stopped to wait for them. She looked up at the sky, and it occurred to her what a beautiful day it was, cool and crisp. She gripped her sword before her with both hands, closed her eyes, and inhaled, tasting the autumn air like a deep draught of clean white wine. In the moments left to her, she cleared her thoughts and prayed in her own native tongue, beseeching the gods of her ancestors and the Ruler of All Gods to hear her.

"Great has been thy bounty upon my household and steady thy workings upon my blood. Long has been the peace of thy grace upon my adopted people. Hear me now, in this moment of need. Bring back to me skills long unused. Bring forth the strength of mine ancestors into my blood. Let their hands grip my sword and their spirit beat within my heart! Bring them to me, and let them aid me in this trial for the protection of the children of my people! Hear me, O Lord of Creation, as thou dost all who call upon thee!"

That brief moment stretched out, for, to the Elifaen, time moves more densely than for mortals. When Mirabella opened her eyes, they were dark with calm, like still pools of green water in the shadows of the forest, and all movement seem slower, clearer to her. Even the sound of the horses seemed to struggle to reach her. Her pale face was flushed, and the breeze gently floated her scarlet hair about her head as if she was under water. She felt the spirit of her ancient lineage course through her body, bringing deadly resolve. Her lips swelled with determination as fury welled up within her, forging cold rage, ready for release. Turning her left side to the attackers, she held up her sword above her right shoulder, her hands finding their grip. The sight of her, in the middle of the road, alone and confident, dismayed those in the lead, and their horses revolted in fear of her, kicking and bucking, their riders cursing to control them. But on they came, in greater fear of their masters, foam flying from their muzzles, and their furious riders holding their swords high at the ready.

"Give me strength!" cried Mirabella as she slashed upward taking off a horse's head and halving the rider's torso. Ducking and whirling, she swept aside opposing blades encircling her, removing another rider as he tried to recover. She cared not whether horse or man, she let none that passed within her reach move farther with life still in them, and great chaos she caused in their ranks, with horses stumbling over the newly fallen, and men being trampled and crushed. Yet, many there were that came, and many swept around her terrible butchery, her cold face spattered and her green gown glistening with their warm blood. She never stopped moving, and she hardly noticed the whisper of dozens of arrows flying past her head and into the attackers. Horses and men screamed alike as they went down, crushing others of their kind. But still more, infuriated at the loss of their comrades and having lost their own mounts, now rushed at Mirabella who, showing no sign of mercy or hesitation, met them coming.

• • •

Sheila ran. The effort to keep the horsemen from the retreating people had failed, costing many lives and hardly slowing or reducing the ranks of the enemy. It was a brief intense skirmish, by blade, lance, and arrow, and Ullin hoped to draw off the force to stand and fight there in the Narrows of the gap. But the Redvests knew their business and smashed through with few losses. Sheila could hear the heavy feet of Ibin behind her and Ullin, farther back, urging the others on as he gained on her. But her lungs were pumps of air and Barley folk had no equal to her on foot. In one hand she held her sword and in the other her bow, but they hindered her not. She could feel the heat of the road through the thin soles of her boots and the dust of the Redvests still hung in the air. Glancing back, she saw Ibin with his long bloody lance being passed by Ullin, who had thrown away his bow and empty quiver and now raced with only his sword, jabbing up and down in his hand as his arms beat the pace of his stride. Behind them more men and boys came, all with the same look of desperation on their faces, a mixture of pain, panic, and fury. They ran and they ran, some crying out in the anguish of their failure, others slowing with the loss of blood. But Sheila, Ullin, and Ibin kept on. Sheila heard a crash and the snapping of branches from the wood on her left, and then strangely dressed men on horses erupted onto the road fifty yards ahead. The sight and noise of this grim threat brought her skidding to a sudden halt. Seeing Robby among them, and Ashlord, too, her heart was lifted. With renewed strength and speed, she sprang toward them. Behind her, she heard Ullin give a cry of joy, and Ibin called out Robby's name, but the riders did not see or hear them and were quickly lost to sight. On they ran, now with some new hope, and as Sheila rounded a bend, she dodged the remains of men and horses scattered along the road in a great wreck, some of the horses attempting to stagger to their feet, and one Redvest tottering around in confusion, as if looking for his missing arm.

On she ran, through the grisly remains, hearing the thud of iron behind her as the wounded Redvest was dispatched. She saw a cloud of dust ahead, with shapes moving about within it, some red, some black, some brown, others blue and green, but none with any distinctive form, like a boiling soup churning about, and the bang of iron and steel and the rattling cry of death came to her ears. Ullin was close behind her when they entered the confusion. There she found wild men with colorful clothes fighting ahorse and afoot against the Redvests. As she worked a soldier to his death, she had a glimpse of Robby, swinging a powerful baton with one hand and jabbing his dagger with the other. Ashlord, she saw, lunging with his straight sword, and there was a wild-eyed boy fighting in the most dishonorable way, laying low man after man, and a crazy long-haired man waving a great feathered hat in one hand and a cutlass in the other, singing a bawdy song as he killed. Arrows flitted into the crowd and met their end in red-cloth while horses reared, twisted and fell. Ullin fought with dagger and sword, in a calm and businesslike way that was efficient and final. Ibin crashed into the fray, knocking one Redvest, horse and all, over onto another. Most terrifying of all was Mirabella, her hair the color of the blood that covered her arms and legs, her lithe body kicking one man in the chest as she shattered another's jaw with her sword hilt, in the same graceful and fierce style of fighting that the Dragonkind man had displayed. Suddenly there was a lull as some of the last Redvests fell, while others tried to flee.

"Spare none!" Ullin cried, pointing at one running down the road. Immediately the terrified man's back was filled with a half-dozen arrows. "Let none of them return! If our people are to be safe, the Redvests must fear this road! Let no enemy who comes this way ever be heard of again!"

A cruel order it was, for some of the Redvests were young and handsome, but the anger of the Passdalers and Barleymen could not have spared any, regardless of orders. One young Passdale boy was kneeling over a dead Redvest, stabbing the slain man over and over, tears running down his freckled cheeks, until Ullin stayed his hand.

"He is no more," he told the boy. "Do not dishonor yourself by defiling the dead." The boy looked up at Ullin, then buried his face in his hands, sobbing. Ullin himself was not immune to the carnage, but he controlled himself and turned to the living, sheathing his sword and dagger.

"See to the wounded! Gather the horses and collect the weapons. Robby, it is good to see you!"

Ullin heartily shook Robby's hand and gave him a one-armed hug. Mirabella was right behind him, crying with joy at the sight of her son.

"Mother! Yes, I'm fine. What have you heard of Daddy?" Robby asked, hugging her. Mirabella shook her head, but smiled weakly.

"Nothing," she said. "By all accounts, he got away. And if any man can make it to Formouth and warn Prince Danoss and Ruling Prince Carbane, your father will. But it is too much to hope to see him very soon, even if all goes well."

Then there was Sheila, hanging back and looking on, her face grimy where the dirt of battle mixed with her sweat and her streaming tears. At last, she and Robby found each other's arms, and they held each other for a long time, his own tears now falling on hers.

"It's been awful!" she sobbed. "It's all awful! Oh, I'm so glad you're here!"

"I do not know who you are, sir," said Mirabella to Makeig, "but we are indebted to you."

"I am Martin Makeig, at yer service ma'am," he bowed with a flourish of his hat. "An' at the service of any who may be enemies of the Redvests. I an' me men are Tracians, too, but loyal to Prince Lantos, who is ousted an' exiled an' mayhaps be dead for all we know."

"Without you," Ullin said, pushing through the crowd gathered around Mirabella and Makeig, "this day would have been another dark one for Barley. I am Ullin Saheed, of the House of Fairoak and Tallin. And, by the way, your prince was alive and well when I spoke to him in Glareth only a few months ago."

As Makeig and his men made themselves known, Billy Bosk, his mother, and many boys and women came up, carrying the bows they had used against the Redvests.

"We came as quick as our feet could carry us!" Frizella said to Mirabella. "But the road is still choked with our people. Mr. Furaman himself is tryin' to come along with wagons for the wounded."

"He was plannin' on makin' his deliveries yesterday," Billy said, "but was held up by business. That's lucky. He'd a been taken by the Redvests for sure, 'long with all these weapons meant for the Militia."

" 'Fraid he's got no horses to spare, though," Frizella Bosk added, looking around. "But I reckon we've got some, now."

"You should not be on your feet," Mirabella said to Billy, giving him a grateful hug. "But I'm glad you are."

Billy shrugged, but then saw Robby and broke away to hurry over to him.

"Excuse me!" he said to Sheila, still with her arms around Robby. Robby grinned as Billy took his hand.

"It seems like one of us is ever gettin' beat up," Billy said.

"We have to do something about that," Robby smiled back, nodding. They laughed and hugged, and Billy winced.

"Oof! Now I know what ye felt like after them wolves," he said.

"I think I'd rather have the wolves, myself."

"Well," Billy hesitated, his eyes gleaming. "I thank ye, Robby Ribbon, for me life. An' I'm awful glad to see ye again."

"MetooRobbyI'mgladtoseeyoutoo!"

Robby was lifted off the ground as Ibin hugged him from behind in a completely joyous gesture.

"Easy! Easy, big man!" Billy said, waving at Ibin to put Robby back down. "That ain't no sack of taters!"

"Sorry."

"Good to see you, too, Ibin," Robby said. "Billy, I heard about your father. Is there any chance at all that he made it away?"

"Don't see how, from what I've pieced together. An' I ain't heard nuthin' 'bout yer ol' man, neither."

"And what about Raenelle?"

"She's missin', too, got separated, along with Geever an' some others. But Mum thinks an' we hope she might've made it away to'ard Newstone. Mebbe from thar, she could've made it on to'ard Tallinvale."

"Oh. Well, what of you? You don't look so good, even considering this fight," Robby said, looking at Billy's bruised and cut face, the swollen lip, and the bloody bandage around his head.

"Got a fierce bangin' in me head," Billy said, putting one hand on his head and one on his side, "an' it hurts somethin' terrible to laugh. But I reckon I'll mend."

"And where's Anerath?"

"Oh, Ullin hitched him up to a cart of young'uns yesterday," Billy told him.

"Oo, I bet Anerath didn't like that too much!"

"I reckon not, but was needed, an' ol' Anerath's a fine one for doin' what's needed, ain't he?"

The Redvest dead were dragged together and stripped. Makeig insisted that everything be taken from them beforehand, even their clothes, saying they might be put to some use. Their bodies were put on the side of the road, while those of Barley were laid in a hastily erected barrow in a clearing not far off the road. The surviving horses were rounded up and many, including Ullin and several of Makeig's men, rode back to the Narrows to re-establish their rear protection there. They took with them a small cart of weapons, including strong bows and hundreds of arrows for a weapons cache to be made, along with other weapons and supplies provided by Mr. Furaman. Ullin spent most of the day there, seeing to the construction of strongpoints and places of ambush to be at the ready. Makeig and the rest helped the refugees move on into Janhaven, reaching the town by sunset. Already the place was packed with wagons and makeshift campsites scattered all around the small town. The Post Station was buzzing with people thronging for news that the Post Riders might be bringing from far parts, but few who had routes to the south ever arrived, and the others from the north and west had little to share. The town itself consisted of little more than a blacksmith's, a small tavern, and a few tiny shops, including a butcher's and a carpenter's shop. Around these huddled many small cottages, occupied mostly by the families of the Post Riders and Furaman's workers. On the other side of Janhaven, the road forked, one way continuing westward into the mountains while the other bent south between the mountains and foothills. Along this road, nearly a mile from Janhaven, was Furaman's Stockade, a heavy wooden fortification large enough to contain several storehouses, a bunkhouse for Furaman's men, and another building that served both as the counting house as well as a meeting place. Also within the walls were Furaman's own separate cottage and several barns and stables for their horses and wagon teams. Outside the stockade were additional nearby cottages, and the area was teeming with people, mostly refugees seeking protection and shelter. Furaman's men kept them out of the stockade, fearful of looting, but they shared food and set up large cooking fires outside the stockade walls to feed any that were hungry.

During this time, Robby picked up bits here and there about the events in Passdale. Obviously, the news of Redvests broke up the festival immediately. He learned that his mother had quickly arranged for wagons to move as much of the store's goods as could be loaded. At the request of her husband, she took into another wagon all of schoolmaster Broadweed's books and all of the books, maps and ledgers within the Common House as could be gathered, including the just completed census books. When Passdale fell, Ullin, Ibin, and Sheila formed with a band of men and boys and even a few women to act as rearguard and slowly moved away from Passdale, falling back only enough to let themselves regroup for the next wave of Redvests. At first, the Redvests seemed in no mood to pursue, as if they wanted captives more than victims, and much of their effort seemed directed at consolidating their hold of Passdale. Less than a league from Passdale, the Redvest pursuit ended. The Passdale fighters caught up with the others and hurried them along for the rest of the day and night, through the gaps and passes toward Janhaven. Then word came from scouts that Redvest horsemen were coming, and the men rushed back to the Narrows, which was, as its name implied, the narrowest gap in the hills that the road passed through, bordered on each side by steep banks some twenty feet high. There Ullin and his fighters sought to take positions to stop the Redvests, but it was too late to make adequate preparations.

Robby learned about these things from Sheila and Ibin, between necessary interruptions of pushing broken wagons out of the way and trying to find the families of separated children. Sheila was needed to tend wounded, and Ibin was enlisted to help chop and gather wood for fires. Robby was recruited by his mother who was trying to account for those among their citizens who were missing. They went from group to group, wagon to wagon, and camp to camp all about the roads and fields around Janhaven well into the night, talking to all they met and writing down names of the present and missing. Ashlord spent some of his time with Furaman and Makeig, then he rode back to the Narrows to fetch Ullin to Janhaven. He found the Kingsman and Winterford standing at a campfire in the middle of the road. The two were discussing the idea of making slings made from saplings at the heights above the Narrows.

"Oh, yes, sir. We've used 'em to good effect on several occasions," Winterford was saying. "Capt'n Makeig taught us how. Ye'd be surprised what a little sapling is able to toss."

"It's a good idea. I'd say go ahead and get working on it, since you seem to know what you're doing," Ullin said. Seeing Ashlord, he went to meet him, moving through the men busy building their fortifications. They had already made barricades of logs crisscrossed with sharpened poles that now blocked the road from Passdale, which Ashlord was examining.

"They won't be getting through so easily if they try again," commented Ullin.

Ashlord nodded.

"We need to have a meeting," he said, "and you will be needed there if you can possibly spare yourself and leave your men."

"There is much left to do," Ullin replied, shaking his head.

"It is important that we assess the situation," Ashlord explained. "And make our plans to deal with what needs to be done. I want your ears there, if not also your voice."

"Commander Tallin," Winterford stepped over, hearing their conversation. "I can assure ye that we're in good order here and'll stand fast should anything happen. An' in that case, I'll send word for ye right away. Maybe ye can have some food an' blankets sent back?"

Ullin reluctantly agreed and gathered the men around to speak to them before he left. Ashlord saw why Ullin was so reluctant to leave. They were mostly only boys, and one or two old men. A few wore the tunics of the Passdale Militia and one or two the cloaks of the Bosklanders, but most were farm lads without even decent shoes. Yet they were all armed, and there was grim confidence in their faces as they gathered before the fire and listened to Ullin encourage them.

"…and so I leave Winterford, here, in charge of you. He is young, but cunning and proven in battle. Listen to him and obey him as you would me. I will have food, blankets, and clothing, such as can be found, sent to you before midnight. There are twenty-seven of you here. Those of you who will be on post tonight, do not hesitate to rouse the others at the least suspicion. The rest of you, sleep as well as you can until morning, but sleep with sword in hand."

On the ride back to Janhaven, Ashlord asked about Passdale's militiamen.

"I have seen few Passdale tunics," he said.

"I saw twelve fall in Passdale," Ullin said bitterly. "And two more this afternoon. Several are wounded. I do not know what has happened to many of the others."

"That is very sad."

"Yes, I regret to tell their families, if I can find their families, that is. But this I know: none ran away. Every boy of them, even the smallest, stood and fought like a lion."

The two parted for a time so that Ullin could arrange a wagon to carry supplies to the men he left behind, and to eat and clean himself. Ashlord went to go talk to the Station Master at the Post Station about some business that could not wait.

• • •

Several hours later, far into the night, a council of sorts was gathered at the stockade, in the great room of Mr. Furaman's main warehouse. It was a wide long hall with high heavy rafters and beams, a stone fireplace at one end, and a long table and chairs near the fire. It was brightly lit by oil lamps and a pot of spiced cider warming on the hearth. Martin Makeig was there, and Mr. Furaman and Ullin, who all stood near the fire, chatting as others arrived.

"That Winterford is a good fighter," Ullin said to Makeig. "And a natural leader, too. Especially for his age."

"Aye, he's one to count on at yer back," Makeig nodded.

Robby and his mother arrived, Billy Bosk a little later, and Mr. Bluepipe and Mr. Jarn, two elderly gentlemen and the only surviving councilmen to make it from Passdale. Ashlord entered and went around greeting each person and shaking hands.

"Well," he asked Ullin, "are we all here?"

"I think so," Ullin looked around the room, "such as we are."

"Then I think," Ashlord said, lifting his voice so that the others would hear, "we should first hear about the condition of the people."

"Well," Mirabella began, sitting down at a table before many of the ledgers she and Robby had brought along. "There are about two thousand of us. Mrs. Bosk is still gathering names of the missing and trying to account for them. We may presume many are captives, though some may have escaped in other directions. We have about four hundred wounded or hurt, fifty or so who cannot walk, with many among them who are not expected to live the night. We have suffered the loss of seventy-eight dead today, including women and children. That is how many we know of, besides those that perished in Passdale and Barley during the fighting there. We have about six hundred and fifty from around Passdale that are missing, mostly men, at least according to the Counting Book from the festival. Some of those probably dead, though Frizella told me that a few more people were trickling into Janhaven in small groups."

She let them absorb all that for a moment before proceeding. Mr. Bluepipe sat down heavily in a nearby chair.

"Of those who have made it to Janhaven," she went on, "we have the youngest, the frail, and the wounded housed in various buildings and barns. The rest are sleeping in wagons or on the ground. Mr. Furaman has given out all the blankets he has and much canvas for the making of tents. We will organize tent-making tomorrow. There is ample firewood, but the weather grows colder each night, now, and soon food and the cold will be a problem."

"I have stores of salted beef and ham," said Furaman. "And taters, and onions, and various dry stuffs such as beans and corn. They are yours for distributin' as ye see fit, but it will not last the winter no matter how carefully it is rationed. I suggest slaughtering all stock pretty soon and forming huntin' parties, too."

"Surely we will not be here that long?" said Mr. Jarn.

"We still don't know if we should keep moving," said Mr. Bluepipe.

"For all we know the Redvests could be marching on Janhaven at this very moment!"

"I don't think so," said Ullin.

"You didn't think they would break through your lines, today, either," Mr. Jarn shot back sharply.

"I never said we could hold them!"

"Gentlemen!" cried Ashlord. "Here is how it is. The Tracian Redvests will, for the most part, stay put in Barley for the winter. Their aim is to move all food and supplies they can gather down the Saerdulin to their main supply roads farther south. Already they are building boats and rafts along the Boggy Wood and are gathering wagons. They evidently mean to send their spoils south. They do not have the forces to extend very far and still perform that work, though they will doubtless mount raiding parties. Most of their horsemen were killed today, but I believe their troops will try to infiltrate through the hills to take captives. If they are daring, they may mount a raid on Janhaven. However, I think they lack the reach. They need workers to accomplish their task, for they mean to leave not a stick or twig behind which may be useful to them. They would want to complete the scouring of the country before winter truly sets in, leaving only a garrison force behind. I do not think it likely they will be reinforced before spring, if at all. They move to make war in far parts and will doubtless draw all their forces together in the south."

"How do ye know all this?" Makeig asked.

"I have talked with several late arrivals who worked their way from Barley just tonight," Ashlord replied. "And others who rode in from around Newstone Ferry, making it here by the back ways. And I have other sources, as well. The important thing is that they do not mean to leave Barley any time soon. You should organize your people here for the winter."

"We could hurry them along, perhaps," ventured Ullin, leaning over the fireplace with one hand on the mantel, staring into the embers.

"Oh? What do you have in mind?"

"Assemble our own raiders. Send them to Passdale. Burn the stores and warehouses," Ullin said, turning around to face the aghast looks of the others. Only Makeig was smiling, his thumbs in his belt. "Deny them shelter, food, refuge."

"Those are our stores," said Jarn indignantly. "Our warehouses. You mean to destroy the very things we've worked so hard for?"

"It would mean attacking Barley and Passdale," said Mr. Bluepipe. "Even if it weren't a foolhardy idea, there aren't enough men to do it."

"It could also mean the death of any of our people still in their hands," said Mirabella. "They are sure to take retribution."

"And, besides," added Bluepipe, his voice reaching a shrill, "like Mr. Jarn said, those are our stores and our warehouses yer talkin' about!"

"Not no more," said Makeig bluntly.

"All that is true," nodded Ullin. "And it would require careful planning."

"This is preposterous! Attacking Barley!" said Mr. Jarn moving to the door. "I'm going back to my wagon for some sleep, and I hope you will get some sleep soon, too. I think the day's wears have addled your thinking and maybe in the morning you'll be clearer. Good night!"

"You have to admit," said Mr. Bluepipe, picking up his walking stick and trailing after Mr. Jarn, "it does sound farfetched."

"It does," Ashlord said slyly. "Perhaps that is a good thing, too."

"Tell ye what, I'll work out a plan an' get back with ye," Makeig said headed for the door. "I needs be gettin' back to me own folk tomorrow. I plan on returnin' the day after. An' I'll leave Winterford an' some others behind to lend ye a hand with things."

He opened the door to depart, then turned back and grinned.

"Rest easy on yer south flank," he said. "Ain't no Redvest gonna get at ye through them hills."

They watched the door close and Mr. Furaman threw another log onto the fire.

"Well," he said, dusting his hands. "This building is as good as any for ye to set up some kind of headquarters in." He faced Mirabella and went on. "And I reckon we can move the junk out of the little shed across the way. There's an iron stove in it, and it might be big enough for a school room. There's the warehouse right next door. I'll have my men move out the things from there to the big warehouse, and you can get it set up as a place to take care of the infirm. It'll need lots of cleaning, but it's got windows that can let in some light and can be opened on warmer days. There's plenty of boards for cots and tables and such, and, I've been thinking, the stockade walls are sturdy. It might not be a bad notion to build some shelters against the other side and try and get some of the folk out of the weather. If we set to it hard, we might get it done before it snows."

"You are very generous," said Mirabella, obviously much pleased. "It will be the ruin of you."

"Oh, I don't think so," Mr. Furaman chuckled. "Why half my business is on account of your husband and your people. I've made a good livin' for myself, and seeing how as I ain't got no family 'cept me sister, I reckon I've plenty to spare. I can at least help through the winter. Come next spring, who knows? Meanwhile, it is late, and I'd better make it up early if I'm to get the buildings readied."

They said their good-nights and Mr. Furaman departed.

"We are fortunate to have the likes of Mr. Furaman and Martin Makeig helping us," said Mirabella. "They give the people hope of safety and relief."

Ashlord nodded, "Yes, fortunate, indeed."

There was something about how Ashlord said those words that did not strike Mirabella or the others as hopeful at all.

"What is it, Collandoth?"

"I don't mean to cast a shadow upon hope, for truly today's fortunes have been great compared to what they might have otherwise been. But matters are much worse than you imagine, and I believe getting through the winter is the least of many worries. Indeed, it is the spring that I fear, and the weakness of Duinnor that I fear the most."

Ashlord sat down at the end of the table nearest to the fire and took out his pipe. As he loaded the bowl, he went on. "For many years, Duinnor has wavered in its support of the other Realms. Many feel that it is due to Duinnor's decline into decadence, but I put it more to darker causes, changes in the aims of the highest leadership, perhaps even the King. The western realms have held off the Dragonkind for many generations, but are nigh upon collapse for their efforts. Vanara, the most gallant of these, receives little support from Duinnor, even though Duinnor maintains armies there; indeed, Duinnor bleeds away Vanaran resources. If Vanara falls, the other realms will be open to easy invasion by the Dragonkind. Duinnor seems blind to this threat. But there are other signs. Duinnor has done nothing to put down the many minor warlords and clans that have gained power, and their fights and feuds sap away the strength of the lands they occupy. And Tracia Realm, long jealous of Duinnor's sway, has openly rebelled and is intent on conquest."

He took a straw from a nearby broom, reached into the blaze, and drew the flame to his bowl. A cloud of aromatic smoke was soon wafting away to be sucked into the fire and up the chimney.

"Long has this been foreseen," he continued, "but what no one dared to imagine is that the Redvests would forge an alliance with the Dragon King. That changes everything. The Red Triumvirate of Tracia and the Sun King of Drakyr have between their lands the two weakest and smallest of the Seven Realms, Masurthia and Altoria. No doubt Redvests will march on Masurthia from the east in the spring. If Masurthia falls, and doubtless it will, it matters little if the Dragonkind attack from the west through Altoria; the fall of Masurthia alone opens the way onto the Plains of Bletharn, which stretches from the south all the way to Duinnor at its northwestern edge. There is no force upon the open plain that can oppose such an advance. They will be too far west for Glareth to muster, too far east for weak Vanara to reach, and, unless Duinnor rouses itself, too far south to oppose with any great force before the southern realms fall."

"So the Redvests are aiming for Duinnor?" said Ullin.

"Doubtless. Just as the Dragon King looks to Duinnor as well. I believe their alliance is an uneasy one, and will, in the end, turn into a race with the spoils of Duinnor as the prize."

"So Duinnor faces two enemies, one here in the east and another to the southwest," Ullin stated. "If the alliance between the Redvests and the Dragonkind holds, Duinnor will fall, and Vanara, cut off and surrounded, will then be overwhelmed."

"Yes. And it is a certainty that Tracia and the Dragonkind will then turn on each other. Each wants nothing less than dominion over all others. The Dragon King will win as long as the Houses of Men are divided and those of the Elifaen are in decline. One by one, each realm will fall into bondage, first, perhaps to Tracia, then to the Dragon King. Of course, this all presumes that another darker power in the west does not exert itself."

Ashlord looked around to see who took his meaning. None seemed to understand, but he did not press it.

"And Duinnor knows nothing of this alliance?" Ullin asked.

"I do not know."

"But they'll fight, won't they? When they find out," said Billy. "I mean, surely they'll see what's comin'?"

"Those are two different things, Master Bosk," said Ashlord. "Duinnor is yet the most powerful realm, but not as in previous days. And there are some there who would welcome a potent threat in order to advance their own power and cause. Some will fight, but how many have the will or the means to mount a determined defense?" Ashlord shrugged. "I sent messages of warning before this Redvest invasion. But will those messages fall on deaf ears? I do not know."

Ashlord stopped and stared into the fire, lightly drawing on his pipe in little puffs. The others looked at him and each other.

"I have a feeling," Ullin said, "that you have more to say."

Ashlord nodded.

"This age is coming to an end. The next age will be one of slavery or something else, but whatever it becomes may well be shaped by what we here, in this room, decide this very night."

Everyone stared at Ashlord, bewildered. Finally, Robby stirred.

"You mean the Bell, don't you? The ringing of the Bell at Tulith Attis has something to do with it."

"Yes. It has been foretold that the end of this age would be announced by the ringing of a 'great hammer' and the calling forth of the sentinels of old. It is said that king will fall to king, and the Seven Realms will be split asunder. The old powers will be resurrected, and the forgotten ways will be remembered. There will be a great hope and a great departing, yet none can say whether good or ill will prevail," Ashlord said. "The Great Bell at Tulith Attis was that 'great hammer,' Robby. And the stone guard were the 'sentinels of old.' The Realms are now split and are set upon one another. And there are other signs of the fulfillment of old prophecies, too.

"Evil has a way of unraveling itself, even while it perpetuates itself, spawning ill after ill. Sheila told me that there was a stranger with her uncle, Steggan, on the night Steggan attacked her, the night she fled to Boskland. But it wasn't until Robby told me about Bailorg, and what Bailorg said before he died, that I realized that Steggan and Bailorg were the enemy's agents in these parts."

"Ye mean they spied for them Redvests?" Billy asked.

"Not that enemy. Another, more powerful one, though doubtless Steggan had no idea. Bailorg was foolish to enlist Steggan, and it was Steggan, I am convinced, who went to Janhaven to deliver Bailorg's dispatches. Robby told me some while back about a few old coins that Steggan gave over to the Starharts. On the day the Starharts opened their door to the stranger with the letters and coins, evil tripped over itself. Bailorg and his men were strangers in the region and had to have someone who could move about freely, without suspicion. Steggan fit the bill, though I don't know how they met. I talked to the captain at the Post Station, and when I described Bailorg to him, he remembered the fellow. He said that Bailorg came to the Post Station shortly before Midsummer's asking to retrieve his letters, saying that he failed to add an important note to one of them. The Post captain refused Bailorg, telling him that any letters could not be retrieved once given over to them. The captain also told me that Bailorg was infuriated, and if it had not been for several other armed Post Riders who were there, he was sure Bailorg would have become violent. As Makeig told me, it was around this time that Bailorg tried to convince him to attack and loot the Post Station. Makeig, of course, refused to be a part of any such scheme. But Bailorg's letters had already been taken by Steggan to Janhaven to be dispatched. I just came from the Post Station and learned that Starhart never got around to preparing those letters for dispatch. He was ordered to make his route to New Green Ferry in the south. Knowing it would be a several-day journey, he took the shortest route by way of the old south road that runs behind Passdale. The same road along which you followed Billy and Bailorg, Robby. Somewhere along the way, Bob Starhart ran into Bailorg's men. One of their horses had gone lame, and they took Starhart's. I believe I found the spot where they waylaid him, and I'm sure they murdered him, though I could not find his body."

Ashlord took out Bailorg's purse and showed the old coins within. They were small silver discs, stamped with Vanaran script, and tarnished with age. Some had tiny stones set into the middle of them.

"These old coins I took from Bailorg's things. He must have given Steggan some such as these to pay for the letters that Steggan was to deliver to the Post Station. And so, fearing that Steggan drank away the money without delivering the letters, Bailorg tried to determine if Steggan had actually delivered his letters. Bailorg enlisted some of Makeig's men to ask around for any old coins. I talked to the tavern owner, Arkstan, and, sure enough, Arkstan said Steggan was there drinking on the day, and he said that Steggan did, indeed, pay his tavern bill with old Vanaran coins. The tavern owner told me that another person had asked him the same question the very night after Steggan had last been there, and that the man paid Arkstan twice the face value in silver to retrieve the coins. From the description Arkstan gave me, I am sure that person was Bailorg. But, according to Arkstan, Bailorg was concerned that there were not more of them to be had. Arkstan assured Bailorg, as he assured me, that the ones he gave back to Bailorg were the only ones he had, the ones Steggan used to pay his bill. So it seems apparent that Bailorg thought Steggan had used the money for drink instead of for sending out the dispatches. Bailorg admitted to Robby that he killed Steggan, and it explains why, as I have heard, that Steggan's place was found to be completely ransacked, once Robby and his father discovered Steggan's body. Bailorg was desperate to have his letters back, and perhaps the rest of his money, if any was left over from what he gave Steggan. Of course, Bailorg was completely wrong. Steggan had indeed delivered the dispatches to Starhart, and he had paid for them with some of the old coins that Mrs. Starhart eventually brought to your father."

Mirabella shifted in her seat, shaking her head. She glanced at Robby, and was about to speak. Ashlord looked at her expectantly, but she only shook her head and looked away.

"I imagine Bailorg was further enraged by Steggan's insistence that he had, indeed, seen to the letters," Ashlord went on. "So mistrust, perhaps, led to much confusion and misguided efforts. Bailorg would have been better off had he delivered those letters himself to the Post Station, if he had not enlisted Steggan at all, and if he had simply stuck to his mission here in the Eastlands. But, had Bailorg done so, Steggan would have been spared the torture and death that he had otherwise earned for his other acts."

"I'm not sure I follow you," said Robby. "Or why any of that is important. What mission?"

"I have been a fool, Robby, wrong about so many things, and I am deeply angry at myself for being such a fool," Ashlord said. "I have tried to piece together the frayed threads of many signs and clues, not knowing which were important and which were not. But many things are made clear to me now, and, to make a long apology short, suffice it to say I have come to learn that the greatest threat to you, Robby, does not come from the Dragon People or their leader. Doubtless we are meant to think so, as many are meant to think they are the greatest enemy. I now believe that our immediate threat comes from the courts of Duinnor itself. The King spins his own webs of deceit, biding his time. He knows the age is changing and is exerting all his power to bend it to his will and wish. I know this because I now know that Bailorg communicated not only with agents of the Dragonkind, but with

Duinnor, and with others, perhaps even more powerful. As I said earlier, I just came from the Post Station. Unfortunately, several of the Post Riders were killed today and yesterday in the fighting, and the Post Station is all but abandoned. I easily talked my way past the boy left in charge of the place, and I found the letters from Bailorg, still in Starhart's chest that each Post Rider keeps at the Station. It seems that as soon as Starhart got to the Post Station, he was ordered out on the South Route and never got a chance to prepare the letters. There they have been, in Starhart's chest, all this time since Midsummer's until now. They reveal much, and open new questions."

Ashlord stood and unfolded three parchment paper documents on the table. Ullin looked over Ashlord's shoulder.

"This one is plain enough," he said. "But this one is in Cuwali, judging by the characters. It is a language used in the far southwest by some clans there. But this one," Ullin put his finger on the third, "I cannot make out at all. It looks to be some sort of ancient writing, but whether Elvish or Mannish, I cannot say."

"That one I expected to find," said Ashlord, "and it is written in the First Tongue."

Sheila glanced at Robby, who was leaning forward in his chair to look.

"The First Tongue?" Mirabella asked, leaning as well to see it. "I did not know any still spoke it, much less that it could be written."

"Few can speak it," Ashlord said. "Fewer still know how to write or read it. I will return to that letter in a moment. Let us take these things one at a time. First, the one in plain Common Speech. I shall read it:"

To be delivered to
Misters Norogus & Harmalway,
Number 10 Farbrick Court,
West Noringtown, Duinnor.

Thirteenth Day of Sixthmonth, Year 870, S.A.

Sirs,
I inform you that I am late in my return from the East and hereby instruct you on the disposition of all those properties upon which we have communicated. It is of utmost importance to me that all lands and holdings under my trust in the lands of Vanara be preserved without prejudice in my name. I hereby grant you leave to sell and dispose of all those assets of mine within Duinnor, and every store and holding therein, to secure the rightful deeds of those within Vanara, including the estates late to be abandoned in Thistledown and Graybark. Since our last communication, wherein was stated the terms of our

business, I have been provided with confirmation of the availability of these lands. Whereas previously you received instructions to wait until the spring of 871 before acting, I authorize you to proceed immediately with all haste with our agreed upon plan.

Bailorg Delcorman

"A business deal, obviously," said Robby.

"I know those lands, or know of them, rather," said Mirabella. "They are in Mirse, on the eastern end of the Blue Mountains, in Vanara."

"Yes, they are the lands of the House of Walnut and the House of Juniper," Ullin nodded. "They lay on the passes that open to the deserts of the south."

"Yes," said Ashlord. "Bailorg was seeking to secure those lands, and it is my guess that he holds vast resources in Duinnor that he planned to exchange for those lands."

"But why would they be abandoned?" asked Billy.

"Because of the ongoing strife with the Dragonkind, pushing north through the passes," Ashlord replied. "Those lands have borne the brunt of seventy years of open conflict and have all but been laid waste. Walnut and Juniper stubbornly hold on, with the support of Vanara, but Bailorg seems to have information that those lands will soon fall, or perhaps have already. It is a common practice for those who will abandon their lands to sign deeds to Duinnor for protection. It seems that Bailorg has some means of having those deeds transferred to himself."

"What good would that do him?" Ullin asked. "If they fall to the Dragonkind, no one will profit by them."

"The answer may be in the second letter," said Ashlord. "You were right to think it is in Cuwali. I happen to know that the dialect used here is in particular to a certain area in the southern plains of Bletharn, east of the mountains. I will translate to the best of my skill:"

Most High Lord of Kluker Klag, Keeper of the Southlands, Rightful Giver of Law to the Subjects Thereof to all those living between Grass and Sand:

With the Sun King's blessings I greet thee, and in His Name I bestow upon thee my greetings.

I send thee that my party will depart for thy lands very soon and pray that thou receive us within thy protection and deliver us unto the Hand of Heat without delay. This word I giveth in His Name, that a quantity of gold and other precious metal, including silver, and many likewise precious gems and pearls, will He lavish upon thee for thy faithfulness and for the protection of his servants. To His enemies He sheweth a terrible wrath and none may escape His Mighty Will, yet merciful is He to the Faithful, and kindness and bounty they reap in His service.

Praise be to the King of Day, Lord of Lords, Ruler of Heaven and Earth!

            Braig Bailorg Denuth Delcorman

"Good grief!" cried Billy. "Who's he writin' to?"

"A tribal ruler of the southwest," answered Ashlord. "A proud and fierce warlord who deems himself a mighty leader of his people. Bailorg obviously humors him with grandiose speech in order to play along with his way of thinking. Notice the veiled threat. He refers to the Sun King, the leader of the Dragonkind."

"Why would he be planning to travel that way?" Robby asked.

"I do not believe he was planning to go that way at all," Ashlord replied.

"Then what is the letter about?"

"Bailorg was evidently playing both sides against each other, serving not one but two masters, one in the north and the other in the south. We know that he had a Dragonkind man in his employ. We also know, from the one that attacked me at Tulith Attis, that he had a man of Duinnor in his keeping, too. I think he made bargains to deliver you to the Sun King, or Dragon King as we call him. And I think that he also promised to deliver you to his master in Duinnor. Meanwhile, he must have also been planning to secure in his name lands that may soon fall to the Sun King. Perhaps he wanted to have some claim on them for additional leverage when they are occupied."

"Why? If the traitor of Tulith Attis is in one place, what would the other want with me?" Robby asked.

"That's easy!" said Billy. "The traitor wants to keep secret, right? Well, whoever knows can blackmail him! I'm sure King Lizard needs all the spies he can get. That'd be a handy way of gettin' one. An' a powerful one at that, I reckon."

Ashlord said nothing, merely puffing his pipe while the others took the suggestion in.

"You are much in demand," said Ullin to Robby.

Mirabella and Ashlord gazed at each other, each wondering how much the other actually knew.

"Well, we don't have to worry 'bout none of that, do we?" Billy said. "I mean, Bailorg's dead."

"Ah, well, it isn't so neatly tied up," Ashlord said. "In the first place, we now know there are two powerful forces, enemies of each other, seeking to capture Robby. Since these letters were never delivered, impatience and suspicion will grow. If I had Bailorg in my employ, and if I thought I was being deceived, I'd send someone to find out."

"So you think more will come," said Mirabella.

"I do. Or else some already nearby will be dispatched to find Robby."

"How can I convince them that I don't know who the traitor is?" asked Robby with an all-too-familiar tone of exasperation that came whenever this topic arose.

"In spite of what Billy suggested, I do not think that your enemies in Duinnor and in the Dragonlands care or worry about the traitor's identity. It has remained a secret for hundreds of years, and may remain so. What they are after is the one who has the power to discover that secret, for he may also have the power to discover other secrets as well."

"What other secrets? And what power?" asked Robby. "I mean, I've gone over and over the whole thing in my head a thousand times, and it comes out the same way every single time. I just don't know anything else!"

"I know you think so. However, one can have knowledge and yet hide it from oneself in many ways. And you have a most uncanny ability to unlock things. But too many coincidences have piled upon you. You happened along just when the signs were right that the Great Bell at Tulith Attis would be rung. And you rang it. The wolves that attacked you: Do you think they just happened along? No, they were put upon the scent. As a child, you were Faere Blessed. You wear about your waist more evidence. Do you think anyone may accept a gift from the Faere Folk, much less one of such power? Surely, Thurdun and his sister, the Queen, whose wings were stripped of them, have seen enough to make their judgment keen. Do you think they bestowed anything upon you that you did not already in part possess? The ability to manipulate Swyncraff comes from you, not it."

"No, Collandoth," said Mirabella so softly that no one heard, "I beg of you." But she knew she should not stop him. And probably could not, anyway.

"Yes, my young friend," Ashlord went on, "you have more in you than you are willing to admit. More than you will yet imagine. The mind is a funny thing, Robby. It turns this way and that, seeking answers. Yet it turns just as much to deny the answers it finds. The heart often knows what the head will not admit. Will you tell me you have not felt out of place here? That you have not felt the pull of a mysterious current all your life? Some say to be Faere Blessed is to be Faere Cursed. It is well known that the Elifaen give their blessings upon none who are not already blessed by powers beyond what they themselves possess. I do not know if you are destined, or appointed by powers beyond us, or whether all this simply fell upon you. Yet I think you somehow have the ability to unravel the secret of the traitor of Tulith Attis, and also another completely different secret. A much more powerful secret, the true Name of the King. Perhaps you already have knowledge of the Name but do not realize it. I cannot be certain about that. If you do not already have that knowledge, a way to obtain it will inevitably come to you."

There was silence in the room after Ashlord spoke, except for the crackle of the fire. Sheila looked at her hands in her lap. She knew. Mirabella knew, too, best of any, what Ashlord was saying, though she was shaking her head. Ullin fingered the ring given to him by Queen Serith Ellyn and looked at the reflections of the fire glittering back from it. Only Billy seemed confused as he looked from face to face, trying to find some hint there. At last, he looked back at Ashlord.

"So what yer sayin' is that Robby knows how to smoke out the traitor. An' he's onto the secret of the King's Name. But that ol' Robby don't know that he knows. An' that he, Robby that is, is some kind of, some kind of—"

"King," Ullin stated.

Everyone looked at Ullin then at Robby, then back at Ullin who was now gazing blankly at Robby.

"Ashlord believes that the secret that hides the name of the traitor and the secret that hides the name of the present King of Duinnor can be solved by Robby," Ullin said. "And if Robby knows one, he can learn the other. And if he utters it in the presence of the King, he will become King himself. Or so it is told."

"I don't think it works that way, Ullin," said Ashlord, who was barely heard over Billy's loud exclamation.

"Thar ain't no way!" he cried out, laughing at the idea. "If Robby became King, then we'd all be King 'cause we all know Robby's name. An' whoever calls the Name, becomes King, an' we can't all be King. So thar! So much for yer silly idea 'bout that!"

Billy looked about proudly, nodding his head and getting up to dip hot cider into a cup. "Of all the harebrained," he muttered as he did so. "So what about the other letter? Are ye gonna tell us what it says?"

Ullin did not respond but continued to look at Robby and Ashlord and Mirabella, moving aside so that Billy could get at the pot at the fire. Mirabella remained silent. Robby stared at Ashlord, red-faced and stunned. Sheila, who had been silent during all of this, remained so, sitting upright and stiff, looking back and forth from one to another. Under the table, she put her hand on Robby's and gripped hard.

"It does not work in such a manner as that, Billy." Ashlord shook his head patiently. "Perhaps the content of this final letter might serve to convince you," Ashlord said, holding the parchment close to his face to read. He rubbed his eyes and moved the document back and forth, as if trying to focus upon it. "It seems my eyes are tired, and this light is weak. I wonder if Robby may read it to us?"

"But you said that it's in the First Tongue," Robby said.

Ashlord handed the letter across the table to Robby, keeping his eyes upon Mirabella, who returned his gaze. There was a kind of fire that exchanged between them, though they both smiled, Ashlord with ease and sympathy, but Mirabella with strain and uncertainty. Still under the watch of Ashlord, she blushed and looked down to her hands and then at Robby. Robby took the letter and stood, holding it up to the light, studying it.

"I'm not sure," said Robby. "I think I can make out some of it. A little."

"Just take your time," Ashlord said as he tamped out his pipe and slipped it away. He stood and moved to where his walking stick was leaning against a wooden column. There, he gripped the stick with both hands before him, leaning on it heavily. "Just read and interpret it for us as you go."

Robby looked at the neatly scripted writing.

"This is very different from the other ancient writing I've seen," Robby said.

"Yes, it is different," said Ashlord, bowing his head and closing his eyes as if he had a headache, "but they are related. Go ahead and try."

Robby nodded and looked at the letter again. The shapes of the characters seemed to move, and began squirming around, sliding within the words they formed, and sometimes a rune seemed to detach from the end of one word and move to join another nearby. Suddenly, without his knowing how, they made sense to him. They were supposed to move, or to appear to do so. That was how the script worked. Once he understood that, the words were plain and simple, and he began to read.

It was the voice, Sheila thought, the same voice. Yet this time there was a sharp, cutting, pain-bringing quality to it that struck the listeners about the temples and behind the eyes. The meaning of the words could not be mistaken, and though the sound was strange to their ears, it was an old sound, as old as the trees and rocks, as familiar as the sky. As Robby read to them, the fire died to an ember and warmth fled the room, and the parchment Robby held seemed to glow in his hands. A cold, fearful breath blew down their necks, and, if they had not been so shocked and paralyzed, they would have each fled, except Ashlord, who yet clutched his stick as if holding on against a gale.

> *O, Blindness of the Night,*
> *Thou Lord of the Shadow Legions,*
> *Drinker of Nightmare, Crusher of Bones,*
> *Thy command is nigh upon completion. I am nigh upon he whom thou sent me to discover and soon he will be brought to thee by my hand. Though thy reason for desiring him is yet a mystery to me, I obey, and will protect him from all until he is before thee. Watch for us at the melting of the snows.*
> > *Thy Servant,*
> > *Bailorg.*

"May the stars preserve us!" Billy uttered, sitting down heavily on a bench.

Robby looked up from the paper and saw the aghast faces before him.

"What? What is it?"

"Yer voice, that's what!" Billy exclaimed. "I never heard such a sound!"

"You just read from a letter written in the First Tongue, Robby," Ashlord said. "A message conveying evil intent. That tongue cannot be uttered by any except those who were here from the beginning. But, when uttered, it is understood by all who hear it, with the full intent of the words."

Robby shook his head, confused. Suddenly, the parchment he held began to smoke.

"Throw it away!" cried Ullin stepping forward.

"Whoa!" Robby cried dropping it onto the table as it burst into flame. In a flash of yellow light and black smoke it burned away to nothing, not even ash, leaving the letters that were written on it squirming around in confusion, hiding into cracks in the table and leaping off the side onto the floor. Mirabella and Sheila leapt out of their chairs and backed away with Robby as the letter-creatures disappeared into various cracks in the floorboards like tiny insects scurrying away from sudden light. A scent of sulfur lingered in the air, and all remained still with Robby looking at Ashlord and the others, who returned his confused gaze with confused looks of their own. Sheila slowly nodded her head, as if some unspoken question had been answered for her. Billy had his mouth open, and, when Robby looked at him, he saw surprise and bewilderment in his eyes. Ullin tilted his head, and, though Robby could not read his face, his brow was furrowed with concern. His mother looked at her feet, where the last of the bug-like letters had escaped through a small knothole in the floor. The fireplace crackled loudly and sprang back to life, the lamps seemed to give better light, and a dreamy atmosphere settled upon the room. Ashlord looked at Robby with clear sympathy, a sad smile upon his lips.

"You speak the First Tongue," he said. "A language that few know, not even I, but all understand. Parchment cannot bear the power of being read aloud, the very letters written become as living beings, as you saw. It is a living language, and may only be borrowed. It gives itself only to those who were here first on this earth, and those most closely connected to it."

"You have spoken that tongue to me," Sheila said softly. "We talked about it. Except the sound was different."

"Because the spirit of what Robby had to say was different," nodded Ashlord.

Then Ashlord looked at Mirabella, who was as pale as a living human could be, and, if her expression could be described, it was one part terror and the other part deep sadness. She stared at the coarse grain of the floor, her hair hanging about both sides of her bowed face, shielding it from the view of the others (who were, anyway, still gaping at Robby) so that they could not see the tears falling from her eyes and landing as glittery splotches on the floor about her feet. Ashlord's heart broke for her. He saw that she knew what this meant, what all the signs meant, and though Ashlord needed no further confirmation of his recent suspicions, those tears granted him the final proof of the theory that had slowly formed in his mind over the past months since the Bell was rung.

"What does it all mean?" asked Robby.

"It means you are coming of age, my boy," Ashlord said. "And that, someday, you may be King."

"King?" Billy cried, "We've already been through that—"

"Yes, King," Ashlord said, cutting Billy off. "That is why Bailorg was sent, though he did not know it. His mission was to discover who would ring the Great Bell of Tulith Attis, yes, and to bring to his master the one who threatens to reveal his identity. But it so happens that the Bellringer, the one who may reveal the traitor of Tulith Attis, is also the one who may discover the name of the King, and so become King himself. Do you not know the old rhyme?

> All the world shall know his might,
> Every land in dark and light.
> Faere and Mortal a friend shall find,
> Who looks upon the heart and mind.
> Hope's lost dream he shall defend,
> Arriving at long ages' end,
> To cause all bells on earth to ring,
> The Hidden One who shall name the King."

Mirabella sat back down, her hands flat on the table, her head still bowed.

"But none can name the King whose name is known," Ullin repeated Billy's earlier argument.

"That is true. But we do not know Robby's name, only what he has been called by his parents," Ashlord stated.

"What?" Robby cried out, looking at his mother. She looked up at him and nodded, glistening tracks crossing down her cheeks.

"I am sorry," she said, smiling even though a sob cracked her voice as she reached out for him. Taking his hand, she looked into his confused face as he sat beside her, and she tried to smile again.

"You are my son," she said to him, pushing a curl from his brow as if he was a little boy. "And you are the son of your father. It is true, what Ashlord says. You were named in the Old Way, and not even I know your true name. No one knows from where the next Unknown King may come, but it is said he will be friend to both Men and Elifaen, as in the rhyme. So, accordingly, an offspring of the two races is taken to a dying elder for naming. Your father honored the old ways by allowing this. When my time to bear you neared, we traveled to your father's grandfather who had been ailing for many weeks and who lived in a small cottage near to Boskland. There we stayed, my time growing nearer and your great grandfather growing weaker. You were born there. A few weeks after your birth, as your great grandfather's health rapidly failed, you were taken to him in his deathbed. We asked your great grandfather to name you and to give you your name by saying it thrice to you. Your father and I left you alone with him. Later, when we looked in on the two of you, we found you swaddled in the arms of your great grandfather, who had died. He held, too, a note, written by him, saying, 'It is done.' "

"So your name is known only to the departed," Ashlord said. "You are indeed the Hidden One that Queen Serith Ellyn foresaw. I think she knew it was you, though there was another that some suspected."

Ashlord turned his gaze to Ullin, who had his hand on the mantel and was now looking deep into the fire. Turning to face them, Robby thought him to be a noble figure, far more suited to be a king than himself, who knew nothing of the world and was merely a clerk.

"Truly, I am relieved it is not I," Ullin said. "My true name, too, was given to me by a passing relative, and, like you, Robby, I do not know it. As Mira said, it is the way of my family." Turning to Ashlord he said, "Yet I am not destined to become Elifaen. And I am glad that I am not destined to be king."

"I'm not, either!" Robby stated. "And I have no wish to be a king. I know nothing about such things. I know little enough about this realm, much less those others now at war. My home is Passdale and my land is Barley, and now they are overtaken by the Redvests. It is with them that I have business, not with Duinnor!"

"Well said, my son," Mirabella told him. "But if I understand things rightly, it is with Duinnor that the Redvests ultimately seek to contend. Not only do they seek possession of these realms, but also to have dominion over all the realms." She looked at Ashlord and continued. "Can there be no way from it?"

Ashlord shook his head slowly.

"I'm afraid we must each make our own decisions," he said to Robby. "I can but advise you and help you as I may. You are not safe here. Your identity is safe with us, but the Sun King and the Lord King of Duinnor and the traitor of Tulith Attis all seek you. If the Redvests learn of you, they, too, will place a price on your head. The King sees the end of his days coming, and he will do anything to forestall it. Other attempts have been made on his throne during the long centuries he has reigned, and all before he has thwarted. He knows there is only one way for him to thwart this one. That is to kill the one who might take his place, and all those who may aid the upstart. If he cannot do it himself, he will send his agents. He is not above using those of his enemies, either. And if all fails, he has the armies of many realms sworn to his service." Ashlord glanced at Ullin, who was nodding as if coming to some understanding within himself. "And there is One other whose name is rarely heard but in tales. His aims are dark beyond scrutiny, as is his nature. He is patient. He has waited since before the days of the First Age, and he waits still. He knows Duinnor is weak and wishes it to become weaker. He plays every part against every other part, and desires that no new King come to rekindle the glory of the west. His ways are subtle, yet his agents walk in every land, serving him unwittingly or knowingly, and are with every court and with every people. Whatever Duinnor learns, he will learn. Whatever the Dragonfolk know, he will soon know as well. You must decide what to do."

"You speak of Secundur, the Lord of Shadow," Ullin said softly. "He who brought about the Fall of the Faere."

"Yes, Secundur."

"Then our enemies are dreadful, indeed."

"Aye, and whilst they may be set against one another, they but play at the end of strings they cannot see, tugged to their doom by a shadowed hand."

"So what you are saying is that I may become King, but I don't have to become King. Is that right?" Robby asked.

"I cannot make the decision for you," Ashlord said. "There are many ways you could fail, if you tried to become King. But, yes, you may try to become King, or you may turn away. Either road is fraught with danger, and whether you become King or not, your way will be difficult. Your choice will mean the changing of you. Either way, you will be tried and tested. And you may not survive."

"This is too much!" Billy exclaimed. "A king! Not just any king, neither. THE King. Ruler of the Seven Realms. Lord of Duinnor, the most mightiest an' powerfullest of any! If Robby becomes King of Duinnor, he can send armies to take back Barley. Why, he'd be able to set things straight!"

"Aye, your power to do good will be matched only by your power to do evil," Ullin put forth.

"It is true," Ashlord nodded. "You would be able to do a great many things, according to your desire, whether good or not so good."

Robby thought about this for a moment, then said, "If Tracia succeeds, then Duinnor will fall, and there will be no new King at all and no realm to rule! And Secundur? The very name fills me with dread! What can we do against such powers? Meanwhile, there are our people that need caring for, and many who are prisoners of the Redvests. I must do something to help! If I leave, what can I do?"

"It may be enough for you to just stay alive," Mirabella said. "If staying here puts you in danger, then you must go."

"But whar to?" Billy asked. "Anywhar ye go, them agents Ashlord told of is bound to find out an' foller."

"Glareth by the Sea would be the safest place," Sheila said. "Did you not say that was where Queen Serith Ellyn went? Surely if she is safe there, you will be, too."

"For a time, perhaps," Ashlord said. "But how long can you stay even in Glareth before being found out? Your enemies have vast resources of gold and silver, titles of land, and many other things that may tempt your friends and even members of your own family. And can you live your life in hiding, year after year, thinking each moment could be your last?"

"We'd never betray Robby!" Billy said, indignant at the notion.

"No?" Ashlord said, putting his walking stick back against the column and taking out his pipe. As he loaded it, he spoke. "Then what of your duty and allegiance to your present King? Would you betray one to stand loyal to the other? Some of you here have taken oaths to serve the King without question. Will you break your oath? And if you do, what good would your word be to a New King? Who will you choose to dishonor?"

Ashlord's eyes fell upon Ullin, the Kingsman, who stood now sternly at the fire, his arms crossed over his chest and his head down. When he raised his face to the others, it was filled with determination.

"True enough. I have sworn an oath to protect and serve the throne," he said. "To show no mercy to the enemies of Duinnor. Presently there is a king on that throne, and I serve him. I do not know how I would act if commanded to betray my kinsman, here, but I would sooner die than to see harm come to Robby. This I swear to you all: I pledge my protection, such as it is, over Robby, son of Robigor. If he is to be King, I will then give him any pledge he demands of me. Until then, no one will learn from me who he is."

Billy got up and walked over to Robby and held out his hand.

"I reckon I'm the Master of Boskland, now," Billy said to Robby. "An' I give ye me word upon me ol' man's ashes, I'll stand with ye."

Robby awkwardly shook Billy's hand, then sat down at the far end of the table and did not return the gaze of those around him. He seemed even to ignore them, or at least not to notice that they, like he, looked inward at their own thoughts. Instead, he stared at the table, his hands spread out, intent upon the grain of the wood beneath his fingers.

"It doesn't sound like I have much choice," Robby said, looking up at last. "I am too ignorant of the world and of things in general to be King, yet that way seems the only hope of protecting those I hold truest and most dear to me. I must do something. Can I turn my back on my homeland? Yet what hope do I have, truly, of becoming King? My ignorance is too great!"

"Ignorance has never been a stumbling block to those who seek power," Ashlord stated. "Even so, there are many who are trustworthy and who may teach and counsel you. In this room, you have the beginnings of learning. Sheila and Billy, here, are your friends and through them you have already learned much of what is most important in life. Your father has also taught you much, too, for it is widely known that he values fairness and honesty above silver and gold, and you yourself are a credit to him. Your mother, Ullin, and I may teach you other things that you are needful of, each of us to our own ways of knowledge. All these things are important, and they will serve you well in your dealings with the problems of leadership, whether you become King or not. And there is the rub, for to escape the claws of your enemies, you must use all of your cunning and craft, all of your knowledge and skill, and all of your heart and might and mind. For your enemies will not be restrained from using theirs against you!"

"But there is so little time!" Robby said. "If what you say is true, war will soon tear apart the Seven Realms. Armies are on the march, and Duinnor is too weak to resist. If the Dragonkind take the lands to the west, how will the eastern lands fare? The might of Tracia will be unopposed, and, even if they leave in the spring, they will surely be back."

"Glareth, at least, will surely oppose the Redvests," Ullin said. "Long have they been at odds, at sea and on land. And there are many Tracian exiles who long to free their homeland. There are others, too, who may join with Glareth."

"Still," argued Robby, "if I were to somehow manage to become King today, this very day, how would I know how to unite the Realms? I would just be a bumbling fool!"

Ullin was silent to this retort, and he looked to Ashlord and shrugged.

"There is a way," Ashlord said, with some reluctance. "A way that you could possibly gain the knowledge and skills that you presently lack. It is an ancient way." He looked at Mirabella who was shaking her head at Ashlord.

"No, Collandoth," Mirabella said. "He cannot go there."

"What would you have him do?"

The others said nothing, wondering what they were talking about, sensing the tension in Mirabella's voice.

"I would rather keep my son, than to gain a king."

"If Robby does nothing," Ashlord replied, "you may soon have neither."

"But that way has not been used for years, if not ages," she said. "And it is said the doors of that place are forever closed."

"I do not think so. And you forget," Ashlord replied, "no door, nor any lock, may bar his path."

"Surely you are not talking about Griferis?" asked Ullin.

Robby's back stiffened at the name, Sheila looked at Ullin in horror, and Billy, seeing their reaction, turned his head back and forth from one to another.

"What are ye talkin' 'bout? What place?" he asked the group.

"A place of death, surely," Sheila breathed. "You may have heard it called Bonewalker's Valley."

Billy visibly paled at the name. Disobedient little boys and girls were threatened with the name by cruel parents.

"Griferis lies beyond that place you speak of, which is rightly called Shatuum. It is called by many names, all with some bits of truth in them," Ashlord said. "Yet Griferis is the one place where Robby may acquire the skills to rule and perhaps allies as well."

"The old books say that, some day, one who will pass through that place will be true King of all peoples," Ullin said. "And that no other will rule afterwards forsoever the sun shines on this earth."

"The old writings may be read that way, yes," replied Ashlord. "And many other ways, besides."

"I have heard," said Robby at last, "that it is far from here, ever shrouded in gray mists, and that the men who live in those parts have ice for blood and cannot be touched by fire. They say it is in a wild place where not even the Faere folk go."

"I've heard the seasons thar change from summer to winter in a day," added Billy. "An' one day's as likely to be spring as it is fall the day before, an' so frightful is the land that even the stars fear to shine upon it even though it is always night time."

"Yes, yes, I'm sure there are all manner of tales told about the place," said Ashlord impatiently. "Not all that is said of it, or even written of it, is true. If Robby is to be King, he must be tested and made ready. If he is not to be King, no effort of ours will make him so. Yet, consider the many years that the present Unknown King has ruled. How many fathers have been born and have lived and died since his reign began? For nearly an age he has ruled. Duinnor has prospered, and for the most part the Seven Realms have known peace. But old wounds still fester, and old hatreds have not been quelled. The King grows weak, as does Duinnor under his rule. Tracia breaks away. The Dragonkind reassert their power. Lost are the teachings of the elders, and few now know the lore of old. In many parts, new gods have arisen amongst the people, and blood sacrifice is made. Warlords reign over the greater part of the Thunder Mountains. The rift between Elifaen and Men deepens with every year. Dark powers and insidious forces connive to drive those loyal to Duinnor away. The King himself unwittingly aids his enemies by his treatment of his own subjects and allies. His rule fails. It is time for a New King to rule and to reunite the lands. What more signs will you have? They are everywhere, even in the heavens and woods, in the fields and flocks.

Nowhere may you turn and not see, if you but look with eyes open. This age ends. And there," Ashlord pointed at Robby, "sits the only hope of the age that comes upon us."

"Yet," he went on, "it is not a thing for us to decide."

"You, at least, seem convinced that I am the one," Robby said to Ashlord. "Is there more to know about this place? This Griferis?"

Ashlord sat down at the table and nodded, but it was Ullin who spoke.

"The legends of the west have it named Grigferith Vale, but the elves of Vanara call it by its ancient name, Griferis, and it is also called the Crack Between Worlds. It is said that the kings of old were chosen there, tested and tried. A land of fire and ice and where the living mingle with the dead, and where live the Judges of God. But, so it is said, the way to Griferis has been lost."

"That is not how they do it, now, surely. Not how kings are picked, I mean," Billy put forward.

"No," said Ashlord. "How the present King of Duinnor gained his power is a mystery. Perhaps he went through Griferis. It was he who named the Houses of Men to stand with the Houses of the Elifaen. And it is he who summons children of the Named Houses to serve Duinnor as Kingsmen. Perhaps to keep an eye upon them."

"I don't understand," Sheila spoke up. "Even if Robby wants to be King, and even if we find this place, and even if these judges, whatever they are, still exist, and even if they name him King, how will he actually become King of Duinnor? The present King will surely oppose any who try to take the throne."

"I have few answers, Sheila," Ashlord said. "But it is told that no one who has emerged from Griferis has ever failed to become a ruler, even when opposed by mighty forces, including those of the Dark Lord himself."

"So it boils down to trust," Billy said. "Trust that Robby is to be King. Trust that these here stories are true. Trust that we can find the place. Trust that Robby will pass the test, er trial, er whatever. An' trust that he'll be able to take the throne. It's all crazy."

Billy shook his head, closing his eyes and putting a hand to his bandage that was showing a tiny splotch of red. The fire crackled and a log fell over in the grate. No one spoke or stirred as the weight of what had been discussed drew taut their credulity. Even Ashlord sighed and nodded, but said nothing. Robby bowed his head in thought.

"No, Billy. It's not about trust," Robby said quietly to himself. Looking up, he went on. "It's not about trust at all. It's about hope. What hope do our people have in the face of this disaster? Can they look to the west? Or the north? They pray, but who hears their prayers? If they thought there was some hope, at least, maybe they could hang on for a time. Maybe I don't want to be King. Maybe I don't trust the stories or even myself. But as long as there is hope, I can trust in that, if nothing else. Ashlord, how do I find this place, this Griferis?"

Ashlord looked at Robby, and, seeing his resolve, nodded.

"We must look for it in the west."

End of Volume One

161 Days Remaining

# Afterword

434

# Afterword

Thank you for reading *The Bellringer*! I hope you've enjoyed the tale thusfar. And I cordially invite you to share your thoughts, questions, and comments at

**www.TheYearOfTheRedDoor.com.**

There is much more to come!

Volume 2, *The Nature of a Curse*, picks up where The Bellringer left off, as Robby and his friends begin their quest and set out on a grueling journey, full of unexpected encounters and conflicts. Robby reluctantly learns to assert his will on others. He begins to develop his mysterious abilities, but other powers align to thwart him. As the miles recede behind Robby and his company of friends, the path becomes more difficult, and more treacherous. Soon they will all learn important lessons about the nature of a curse.

Thanks again!

*William Timothy Murray*

# The Door is Open!

# www.TheYearOfTheRedDoor.com

## Maps, Stories, Chronologies, and much more.

Leave a comment or ask a question.

The Author would love to hear from you!

## Sign up for the newsletter.
### *Get perks and exclusives delivered right to your inbox!*

# The Year of the Red Door

Volume 1
The Bellringer

Volume 2
The Nature of a Curse

Volume 3
A Distant Light

Volume 4
The Dreamwalker

Volume 5
To Touch a Dream

# www.TheYearOfTheRedDoor.com